TWO COMPLETE NOVELS

DAVID EDDINGS

TWO COMPLETE NOVELS

DAVID EDDINGS

THE LOSERS
HIGH HUNT

WINGS BOOKS
New York • New Jersey

This 1994 edition is published by Wings Books, distributed by Random House Value Publishing, Inc., 40 Engelhard Avenue, Avenel, New Jersey 07001, by arrangement with Ballantine Books, a Division of Random House.

Random House
New York • Toronto • London • Sydney • Auckland

Printed and bound in the United States of America

Library of Congress Cataloging-in-Publication Data

Eddings, David.
    [Losers]
    Two complete novels / David Eddings.
        p.   cm.
    Contents: The losers—High hunt.
    ISBN 0-517-11908-0
    I. Eddings, David. High hunt.   II. Title.
PS3555.D38A6   1994
813'.54—dc20   94-11789
                                                                CIP

8 7 6 5 4 3 2 1

CONTENTS

THE LOSERS

FORTUNA IMPERATRIX MUNDI

i

Mrs. Muriel Taylor was thirty-eight years old when she found that she was pregnant. Mrs. Taylor was a pale, almost transparent woman of Canadian background, who, until that startling discovery, had lived in a kind of dreamy reverie filled with semiclassical music and the endlessly reworked verses to which she devoted two hours every afternoon and never allowed anyone to read. The pregnancy ran its normal course, although Mrs. Taylor had miscarried twice before. She laid aside her poetry and devoted herself wholly to the life within her, seeming almost to wish at times that she might, like some exotic insect, be consumed from within by it and fall away like a dead husk at the moment of birth.

She labored with the selection of a suitable name for her unborn son (for he would surely be a boy) as she had never before struggled with the surly intransigencies of language, emerging finally with the one name that would lift her still-womb-drowsing infant above the commonplace, beyond that vast, ever-expanding mob of Joeys and Billies and Bobbies and Donnies. She would, she decided, call him Raphael, and having made that decision, she fell back into her drowse.

And in the usual course of time she was delivered of a son, and he was christened Raphael.

Mr. Edgar Taylor, Mrs. Taylor's husband, was a man best described as gray—his hair, the suits he wore to the office, even his face. Mr. Taylor was an accountant, much more at home with columns of figures than with people, and the sudden appearance of an heir, the product of his somewhat tepid passion, seemed to stun him. He gave up all outside activities so that he might hurry home each night to watch his son, not to touch him or speak to him, but simply to watch in a kind of bemused astonishment this prodigy that he and his wife had somehow wrought.

The Taylors lived in Port Angeles, a small, damp city on the extreme northwest coast. The peninsula below it is given over in large part to a national park, roadless and pristine; and the city thus has an insular character, cut off from the sprawling bustle of Seattle, Tacoma, and the

3

other population centers of the state by a deep, island-dotted sound. All significant travel to and from Port Angeles is by ferry. The nearest major city is Victoria in British Columbia, a curiously European metropolis where Mr. Taylor had traveled on business some years earlier and had met and intermittently courted Mrs. Taylor. In due time they had married and he had brought her back across the twenty-six miles of intervening water to the dank clamminess of Port Angeles with its rain and fog and its reek of green hemlock logs lying low in the salt waters of the bay.

From the beginning Raphael was one of those rare children, touched, it seemed, by a singular grace that gave everything he did a kind of special significance. As an infant he seldom cried, and he passed through the normal stages of early childhood with a minimum of fuss. His mother, of course, devoted her entire existence to him. Long after he had matured to the point where her constant attentions were no longer necessary—or even desired—she was forever touching him, her hand moving almost of its own will to lingeringly caress his face or his hair.

Perhaps because of that special grace or perhaps because of some long-fogotten gene in his makeup, Raphael avoided the pitfalls that almost inevitably turn the pampered child into a howling monster. He grew instead into a sturdy, self-reliant little boy, gracious to his playmates and polite to his elders. Even as a child, however, he was adept at keeping his feelings to himself. He was outgoing and friendly on the surface, but seemed to reserve a certain part of himself as a private sanctuary from which he could watch and say nothing. He did well in school and, as he matured, developed into that kind of young man his infancy had promised—tall, slimly muscular, with glowing, almost luminous eyes and pale blond hair that stubbornly curled in spite of all efforts to control it.

Raphael's years at high school were a time of almost unbearable pride for Mr. Taylor as the young man developed into that boy athlete who comes along perhaps once in a generation. Opposing coaches wept on those golden autumn afternoons as Raphael, knees high, the ball carried almost negligently in one hand, ran at will through their best defenses. Important men in the lumber company where Mr. Taylor worked began stopping by his desk to talk about the games.

"Great game, Edgar," they'd say jovially. "Really great."

Mr. Taylor, his gray face actually taking on a certain color, would nod happily.

"Young Rafe really gave it to them," they'd say. "He's a cinch to make all-state this year."

"We think he's got a good chance," Mr. Taylor would say. Mr. Taylor always said "we" when talking about Raphael's accomplishments, as if, were he to say "I," it might seem boastful.

For Mrs. Taylor, however, the whole period was a time of anguish.

There was always the danger of injury, and with morbid fascination she collected gruesome stories of fatalities and lifelong maimings that occurred with hideous regularity on high-school football fields across the nation. And then there was the fact that all the sportswriters and the disgusting man who broadcast the games over the local radio station had immediately shortened her son's name to Rafe—a name that smacked of hillbillies or subhuman degenerates slouching along in the shadows and slobbering over thoughts of unspeakable acts. Each time she heard the name, her soul withered a little within her. Most of all, however, she feared girls. As Raphael's local celebrity increased so did her dread. In her mind Mrs. Muriel Taylor saw hordes of vacant-minded little trollops lusting after her son, their piggish eyes aflame with adolescent desire and their bubble-gum-scented breath hot and panting as they conspired—each in her own grubby little soul—to capture this splendid young man. Mrs. Taylor had, in the dim reaches of her Canadian girlhood, secretly and tragically suffered such pangs for an oafish campus hero, so that she knew in her heart of hearts to what lengths the predatory adolescent female might go, given such a prize as this most perfect of young men, this—and she used the word only to herself in deepest privacy—this angel.

Young Raphael Taylor, however, avoided those girls his mother most feared as adroitly as he avoided opposing tacklers. This is not, of course, to say that he was celibate. It is merely to say that he devoted his attentions to certain local girls who, by reputation and practice, were in no position to make lasting demands on him. For the most part he avoided those girls who might, by the sacrifice of their virtue, have been able to make some kind of viable claim upon him. Once, though, in the summer of his sixteenth year, there was a girl whom he had deeply and desperately loved; but her family had moved away, and he had suffered, but had been safe.

During the fall of Raphael's senior year in high school, Mr. Taylor developed a serious shortness of breath. Despite his wife's urgings, however, he put off visiting the family doctor, maintaining that his condition was just a recurrence of an old bronchial complaint that had plagued him off and on for years.

On a splendid Friday afternoon in late September Port Angeles hosted their traditional rivals from across the sound. As had been the case since his sophomore year, Raphael dominated the game. Although it was obvious from the very beginning that he would carry the ball at least twice during every series of plays, the opposing players were unable to stop him. He scored three touchdowns during the first half, and when the visitors opened the second half with a booming kickoff, he scooped up the ball deep in his own end zone, reversed direction, and feinting, spinning, and dodging with the grace of a dancer, he started upfield. Every opponent on the field, even the kicker, tried to stop him, but he was unstoppable. For the last thirty yards before he crossed the goal line, he was absolutely alone, running in solitary splendor with all tacklers hopelessly far back. .

The home fans, of course, were screaming wildly. And that was the last thing that Mr. Taylor ever heard. He had risen excitedly to his feet to watch his glorious son run the full length of the field, and the sound of the cheers surrounded him. The massive heart attack was like a great blow to his chest, and he toppled forward, dying with those cheers fading like distant thunder in his ears.

The funeral was very sad, as funerals usually are. Mrs. Taylor bore up bravely, leaning on her golden-haired son. After all the ceremonies and condolences, life once again returned to near normal. Mr. Taylor was so close to being a nonentity that he was scarcely missed at the place where he had worked, and even his widow's emotion at his passing might best be described as gentle melancholy rather than overwhelming grief.

Raphael, of course, missed his father, but he nonetheless played in every game that season. "He would have wanted it that way," he explained. He was touched, even moved almost to tears by the moment of silence dedicated to his father just prior to the game the Friday after the funeral. Then he went out onto the field and destroyed the visiting team.

Mr. Taylor's affairs, of course, were in absolute order. Certain wise investments and several insurance policies provided for the security of his family, and his elder brother, Harry, a Port Angeles realtor, had been named executor of his estate. Harry Taylor was a bluff, balding, florid-faced man with a good head for business and a great deal of sound, practical advice for his brother's widow. He took his responsibilities as executor quite seriously and visited often.

That winter, when the question of college arose, Mrs. Taylor faced the issue with dread. Money was not a problem, since her husband had carried a special insurance policy with some very liberal provisions to guarantee his son's education. There were also scholarship offers from as far away as southern California, since Raphael had twice been named to the all-state football team. In the end, however, the question was deferred by the young man's rather surprising decision to attend the local junior college. He had many reasons for the choice, not the least of which was his full realization of what anguish an abrupt separation would cause his mother, coming as it must so soon after her bereavement.

And so it was that Raphael continued to play local football, his uncle Harry basked in reflected celebrity, and his mother enjoyed the reprieve the decision had granted her.

At the end of two years, however, the decision could no longer be put off. Raphael privately considered his options and independently made his choice.

"Reed?" his uncle said, stunned.

"It's a good school, Uncle Harry," Raphael pointed out, "the best school in this part of the country. They say it's one of the top ten colleges in the United States."

"But they don't even have a football team, do they?"

"I don't know," Raphael replied. "I don't think so."

"You could go to Stanford. That's a good school, too."

Raphael nodded thoughtfully. "Yes," he agreed, "but it's too big."

"They've got a good team. You might even get a chance to play in the Rose Bowl."

"Maybe, but I think I'd rather go to Reed. I've had a lot of fun playing football, but I think it's time I moved on to something else, don't you?"

"Where is this college located?" Mrs. Taylor asked faintly.

"Portland," Raphael replied.

"In *Oregon*?" Mrs. Taylor asked even more faintly.

Raphael nodded.

Mrs. Taylor's heart sank.

⟶⟶ **ii**

Portland, the city of the roses, bestrides the banks of the Willamette River near where that stream joins the Columbia. It is a pleasant city, filled with trees and fine old Victorian houses. The campus of Reed College, where Raphael was enrolled, lies somewhat to the east of the river, and has about it a dreamy, timeless quality. The very buildings that rise from the broad lawns identify the place as a college, since such a random collection of Georgian manors, medieval cathedrals, and starkly modern structures of brick and glass could exist for no other reason.

In his car of recent vintage with its backseat filled with the new and expensive luggage his mother had bought and tearfully given him, Raphael Taylor pulled rather wearily into the student parking lot and stopped. The trip had been quite long, and he was unaccustomed to freeway driving. There was, however, an exhilaration about it all. He was on his own for the first time in his life, and that was something.

Thanks to his uncle's careful correspondence with the registrar and the bursar, all arrangements had been made well in advance, and Raphael knew precisely where his dormitory was located. With his jacket under his arm and two suitcases rather self-consciously swinging at his sides, he walked across to the manselike solidity of the dorm, feeling a certain superiority to the small crowd of bewildered-looking freshmen milling uncertainly around in front of the administration building.

His room was on the third floor, and Raphael was puffing slightly as he reached the top of the stairs. The door at the end of the hall was open, and billowing clouds of smoke were rolling out. Raphael's stomach turned cold. Everything had gone too well up until now. He went down the hall and into the smoke.

A young man with olive skin and sleek black hair brushed by him carrying a large vase filled with water. "Don't just stand there, man," he said to Raphael in a rich baritone voice. "Help me put this son of a bitch out." He rushed into the room, bent slightly, and threw the water into a small fireplace that seemed to be the source of all the smoke. The fire hissed spitefully, and clouds of steam boiled out to mingle blindingly with the smoke.

"Damn!" the dark-haired man swore, and started back for more water.

Raphael saw the problem immediately. "Wait," he said. He set down his suitcases, stepped across to the evilly fuming fireplace, and pulled the brass handle sticking out of the bricks just below the mantelpiece. The damper opened with a clank, and the fireplace immediately stopped belching smoke into the room. "It's a good idea to open the chimney before you build a fire," he suggested.

The other man stared at the fireplace for a moment, and then he threw back his head and began to laugh. "There's a certain logic there, I guess," he admitted. He collapsed on the bed near the door, still laughing.

Raphael crossed the room and opened the window. The smoke rushed out past him.

"It's a good thing you came by when you did," the dark-haired man said. "I was well on my way to being smoked like a Virginia ham." He was somewhat shorter than Raphael, and more slender. His olive skin and black hair suggested a Mediterranean background, Italian perhaps or Spanish, but there was no Latin softness in his dark eyes. They were as hard as obsidian and watchful, even wary. His clothing was expensive—tailored, Raphael surmised, definitely tailored—and his wristwatch was not so much a timepiece as it was a statement.

Then the young man looked at Raphael as if seeing him for the first time, and something peculiar happened to his face. His eyes widened, and a strange pallor turned his olive complexion slightly green. His eyes narrowed, seeming almost to glitter. It was as if a shock of recognition had passed through him. "You must be Edwards, right?" His expression seemed tight somehow.

"Sorry," Raphael replied. "The name's Taylor."

"I thought you might be my roomie."

"No. I'm two doors up the hall."

"Oh, well"—the stranger shrugged, making a wry face—"there goes my chance to keep the knowledge of my little blunder a secret. Edwards is bound to smell the smoke when he gets here." He rose to his feet and extended his hand. "J. D. Flood," he said by way of introducing himself.

"Rafe Taylor," Raphael responded. They shook hands. "What were you burning, Flood?"

"Some pieces of a packing crate. I've never had a dormitory room with a fireplace before, so I had to try it. Hell, I was even going out to buy a pipe." He raised one eyebrow. "Rafe—is that short for Raphael?"

"Afraid so. It was a romantic notion of my mother's. You wouldn't believe how many school-yard brawls it started."

Flood's face darkened noticeably. "Unreal," he said. That strange, almost shocked expression that had appeared in his eyes when he had first looked at Raphael returned, and there was a distinct tightening in his face. Once again Raphael felt that momentary warning as if something were telling him to be very careful about this glib young man. In that private place within his mind from which he had always watched and made decisions, he began to erect some cautionary defenses. "And what does the J. D. stand for?" he asked, trying to make it sound casual.

"Jacob Damon Flood, Junior," Flood said with distaste.

"Jake?" Raphael suggested.

"Not hardly."

"J. D. then?"

"That's worse. That's what they call my father."

"How about Damon?"

Flood considered that. "Why not? How about a martini?"

"Is it legal? In the dorm, I mean?"

"Who gives a shit? I'm not going to start paying any attention to the rules at this late date."

Raphael shrugged. "Most of my drinking has been limited to beer, but I'll give it a try."

"That's the spirit," Flood said, opening one of his suitcases and taking out a couple of bottles. "I laid in some ice a bit earlier. I make a mean martini—it's one of the few things I've actually learned." He busied himself with a silver shaker. "Any cretin can swill liquor out of a bottle," he went on with a certain brittle extravagance, "but a gentleman boozes it up with class."

Flood's language seemed to shift back and forth between an easy colloquialism Raphael found comfortable and a kind of stilted eastern usage. There was a forced quality about Flood that made him uncomfortable.

They had a couple of drinks, and Raphael feigned enjoyment, although the sharp taste of nearly raw gin was not particularly to his liking. He was not really accustomed to drinking, and Flood's martinis were strong enough to make his ears hot and the tips of his fingers tingle. "Well," he said finally, setting down his glass, "I guess I'd better go get moved in."

"Taylor," Flood said, an odd note in his voice. "I've got a sort of an idea. Is your roommate up the hall an old friend?"

"Never met the man, actually."

"And I've never met Edwards either—obviously. Why don't you room in here?" There was a kind of intensity about the way Flood said it, as if it were far, far more important than the casual nature of the suggestion called for.

"They don't allow that, do they?" Raphael asked. "Switching rooms, I mean?"

"It's easy to see you've never been in a boarding school before." Flood laughed. "Switching rooms is standard practice. It goes on everywhere. Believe me, I know. I've been kicked out of some of the best schools in the east."

"What if Edwards shows up and wants his bed?"

"We'll give him yours. I'll lie to him—tell him I've got something incurable and that you're here to give me a shot in case I throw a fit."

"Come on." Raphael laughed.

"You can be the one with the fits if you'd rather," Flood offered. "Can you do a convincing grand mal seizure?"

"I don't know. I've never tried."

"The whole point is that we get along fairly well together, and I don't know diddly about Edwards. I *know* that you're white, but I haven't got any idea at all about *what* color he is."

"Is that important?" Raphael said it carefully.

Flood's face suddenly broke into a broad grin. "Gotcha!" he said gleefully. "God, I love to do that to people. Actually, it doesn't mean jack-shit to me one way or another, but it sure as hell does to old J.D. Sooner or later somebody from back home is going to come by, and if word gets back to the old pirate that his son has a nigger roommate— his word, not mine—thee shit will hit thee fan. Old J.D.'s prejudiced against races that have been extinct for thousands of years—like the Hittites—or the Wends."

"It won't work out then, Damon," Raphael told him with a perfectly straight face. "My mother's Canadian."

"That's all right, Raphael. I'm liberal. We'll let you come in through the back door. Have Canadians got rhythm? Do you have overpowering cravings for northern-fried moose?"

Raphael laughed. The young man from the east was outrageous. There was still something slightly out of tune though. Raphael was quite sure that he reminded Flood of someone else. Flood had seemed about to mention it a couple of times, but had apparently decided against it. "All right," he decided. "If you think we can get away with it, we'll try it."

"Good enough. We'll drop the Rafe and Jake bit so we don't sound like a hillbilly band, and we'll use Damon and Raphael—unless you'd like to change your name to Pythias?"

"No, I don't think so. It sounds a little urinary."

Flood laughed. "It does at that, doesn't it? Have you got any more bags? Or do you travel light?"

"I've got a whole backseat full."

"Let's go get them then. Get you settled in."

They clattered downstairs, brought up the rest of Raphael's luggage, and then went to the commons for dinner.

Damon Flood talked almost continuously through the meal, his rich voice compelling, almost hypnotic. He saw nearly everything, and his sardonic wit made it all wryly humorous.

"And this," he said, almost with a sneer as they walked back in the luminous twilight toward their dormitory, "is the 'most intelligent group of undergraduates in the country'?" He quoted from a recent magazine article about the college. "It looks more like a hippie convention—or a soirée in a hobo jungle."

"Appearances can be deceiving."

"Indeed they can, Raphael, Angel of Light"—Flood laughed—"but appearance is the shadow at least of reality, don't you think?"

Raphael shrugged. "We're more casual out here on the coast."

"Granted, but wouldn't you say that the fact that a young lady doesn't wear shoes to dinner says a great deal about her character?"

"Where's your home?" Raphael asked as they started up the stairs.

"Grosse Pointe," Flood said dryly, "the flower on the weed of Detroit."

"What are you doing way out here?" Raphael opened the door to their room.

"Seeking my fortune," Flood said, flinging himself down on his bed. Then he laughed. "Actually, I'm putting as much distance as possible between my father and me. The old bastard can't stand the sight of me. The rest of the family wanted me to go to Princeton, but I preferred to avoid the continuous surveillance of all those cousins. A very large family, the Floods, and I have the distinction of being its major preoccupation. All those dumpy female cousins literally slather at the idea of being able to report my indiscretions back to old J.D. himself."

Raphael began to unpack.

"J.D.'s the family patriarch," Flood went on. "The whole damned bunch genuflects in his direction five times a day—except me, of course. I suppose I've never really forgiven him for tacking that 'Junior' on me, so I set out to be as unlike him as I could. He looks on that as a personal insult, so we don't really get along. He started shipping me off to boarding schools as soon as I lost my baby teeth, though, so we only irritate each other on holidays. I tried a couple years at Pitt, but all that rah-rah bullshit got on my nerves. So I thought I'd saddle up old Paint and strike out for the wide wide west— What do you say to another drink?" He sprang up immediately and began mixing another batch of martinis.

Their conversation became general after that, and they both grew slightly drunk before they went to bed.

After Flood had turned out the light, he continued to talk, a steady flow of random, drowsy commentary on the day's events. In time the pauses between his observations became longer as he hovered on the verge of sleep. Finally he turned over in bed. "Good night, Gabriel," he murmured.

"Wrong archangel," Raphael corrected. "Gabriel's the other one— the trumpet player."

"Did I call you Gabriel?" Flood's voice had a strange, alert tension in it. "Stupid mistake. I must have had one martini too many."

"It's no big thing. Good night, Damon." Once again, however, something in the very back of his mind seemed to be trying to warn Raphael. Flood's inadvertent use of the name Gabriel seemed not to be just a slip of the tongue. There was a significance to it somehow—obscure, but important.

In the darkness, waiting for sleep and listening to Flood's regular breathing from the other bed, Raphael considered his roommate. He had never before met anyone with that moneyed, eastern prep-school background, and so he had no real basis for judgment. The young men he had met before had all come from backgrounds similar to his own, and the open, easy camaraderie of the playing field and the locker room had not prepared him for the complexity of someone like Flood. On the whole, though, he found his roommate intriguing, and the surface sophistication of their first evening exhilarating. Perhaps in time Flood would relax, and they'd really get to know each other, but it was still much too early to know for sure.

━━✦ iii

Raphael's next few weeks were a revelation to him. Always before he had been at best a casual scholar. His mind was quick and retentive, and neither high school nor the community college he had attended had challenged him significantly. He had come to believe that, even as on the football field, what others found difficult would be easy for him. His performance in the classroom, like his performance on the field, had been more a reflection of natural talent than of hard work; everything had been very easy for Raphael. At Reed, however, it was not so. He quickly discovered that a cursory glance at assigned reading did not prepare him adequately for the often brutally cerebral exchanges of the classroom. Unlike his previous classmates, these students were not content merely to paraphrase the text or the remarks of the instructor, but rather applied to the material at hand techniques of reason and analysis Raphael had never encountered before. Amazingly, more often than not, the results of these reasonings were a direct challenge to the authority of the text or of the instructor. And, even more amazingly, these challenges were not viewed as the disruptions of troublemakers, but were actually encouraged. Disturbed and even embarrassed by his newfound inadequacy, Raphael began to apply himself to his studies.

"You're turning into a grind," Flood said one evening.

Raphael pulled his eyes from the page he was reading. "Hmmm?"

"You study too much. I never see you without your face in some damned book."

"That's why we're here, isn't it?"

"Not hardly." Flood threw one leg over the arm of his chair. "A gentleman does *not* get straight A's. It's unseemly. Haven't you ever heard the old formula? 'Three C's and a D and keep your name out of the newspapers'?"

"No. I hadn't heard that one." Raphael's mind was yearning back toward the book. "Besides, how would you know here? They won't let us see our grades." That was one of the peculiarities of what was called the "Reed experience."

"Barbarous," Flood snorted. "How the hell can we be expected to maintain a proper balance if they don't let us see our grades? Do you realize that a man could screw up? Stumble into so many high grades that his reputation's ruined for life?"

"I wouldn't worry too much about that, Damon. I don't think you're in any danger."

"Don't get shitty." Flood got up quickly. "Let's go out and get drunk—see if we can get arrested or something."

"I've got an early class tomorrow." Raphael turned back to his book.

"Talk to me, goddammit!" Flood said irritably, snatching the book from Raphael's hands. "What the hell are you reading, anyway?"

"Kierkegaard." Raphael reached for his book.

"*The Sickness unto Death,*" Flood read. "Now there's a cheery little title. What class is this for?"

Raphael shrugged. "It came up in a discussion. I thought I ought to look into it."

"You mean it's not even *required*?" Flood demanded incredulously, tossing the book back. "That's disgusting, Raphael, disgusting."

"Different strokes," Raphael said, finding his place again and settling back to his reading. Flood sat watching him, his black eyes as hard as agates.

And then there was the problem of the girl. She sat across the room from him in one of his afternoon classes, and Raphael found his eyes frequently drawn to her face. It was not that she was exceptionally beautiful, for she was not. Her face was slightly angular with strong bones, and she was quite tall with a coltish legginess that made her seem somehow very young. Her voice, however, was a deep, rich contralto with a vibrance, a quality, that stirred Raphael immeasurably each time she spoke. But she spoke infrequently. Sometimes a week would pass without a word from her. While others in the class talked endlessly, arguing, discussing, pushing themselves forward, she would sit quietly, taking occasional notes and now and then stirring restlessly as Raphael's gaze became warmly obvious.

He began to try to challenge her—to force her to speak. He frequently said things he did not actually believe, hoping to lever her into discussion. He did not even care *what* she said, but merely yearned for the sound of that voice, that rich, vibrant sound that seemed somehow to plunge directly into the center of his being. She began, in time, to return his glances, but she still seldom spoke, and the infrequency of her speech left him frustrated—even angry with himself for his absurd fascination. Her name, he discovered, was Marilyn Hamilton, and she lived off campus. Beyond that, he was able to find out very little about her.

"You're Taylor, aren't you?" a large, bulky man with a huge black beard asked him one afternoon as he came out of the library.

"Right," Raphael replied.

"Name's Wallace Pierson." The big man held out his hand. "I understand you've played a little football."

"Some." Raphael shifted his books so that he could shake the man's hand.

"We're—uh—trying to put together a team," Pierson said, seeming almost apologetic. "Nothing very formal. Wondered if you might be interested."

"Intramural?"

"No, not exactly." Pierson laughed. "It's just for the hell of it, really. You see, there's a Quaker college across town—George Fox. They have a sort of a team—pretty low-key. They sent us an invitation. We thought it might be sort of interesting." He fell in beside Raphael and they walked across the broad lawn toward the dormitories.

"I haven't got the kind of time it takes for practice," Raphael told him.

"Who has? We're not really planning to make a big thing out of it—just a few afternoons so that we can get familiar with each other—not embarrass ourselves *too* badly."

"That's not the way to win football games."

"*Win?*" Pierson seemed startled. "Hell, Taylor, we weren't planning to win—just play. Good God, man, you could get *expelled* for winning—overemphasis and all that jazz. We just thought it might be kind of interesting to play, that's all."

Raphael laughed. "That's the Reed spirit."

"Sure." Pierson grinned. "If we can hold them to ten touchdowns, it'll be a moral victory, won't it?"

"I'll think it over."

"We'd appreciate it. We're a little thin in the backfield. We thought we'd get together about four or so this afternoon—see if there are enough of us to make a team. Drop on down if you'd like."

"When's the game?"

"Friday."

"Three days? You plan to put a team together in three days?"

Pierson shrugged. "We're not really very serious about it."

"I can see that. I'll think it over."

"Okay," the bearded man said. "Maybe we'll see you at four then."

"Maybe."

But of course he did play. The memory of so many afternoons was still strong, and he had, he finally admitted, missed the excitement, the challenge, the chance to hurl himself wholly into violent physical activity.

Pierson, despite his bulk, played quarterback, and the great black beard protruding from the face mask of his helmet made the whole affair seem ludicrous. On the day of the game their plays were at best rudimentary, and they lost ground quite steadily. The small cluster of students who had gathered to watch the game cheered ironically each time they were thrown for a loss.

"Hand it off to me," Raphael suggested to Pierson in the huddle on their third series of plays when they were trailing 13–0. "If you try that keeper play one more time, that left tackle of theirs is going to scramble your brains for you."

"Gladly," Pierson agreed, puffing.

"Which way are you going?" one of the linemen asked Raphael.

"I haven't decided yet," Raphael said, and broke out of the huddle.

After the snap Pierson handed him the ball, and Raphael angled at the opposing line. He sidestepped a clumsy tackle, found a hole, and broke through. The afternoon sun was very bright, and his cleats dug satisfyingly into the turf. He reversed direction, outran two tacklers, and scored quite easily.

A thin cheer went up from the spectators.

In time his excellence even became embarrassing. He began to permit himself to be tackled simply to prevent the score from getting completely one-sided. More and more of the students drifted down to watch.

On the last play of the game, knowing that it was the last play and knowing that he would probably never play again, Raphael hurled himself up and intercepted an opponent's pass deep in his own end zone. Then, simply for the joy of it, he ran directly into the clot of players massed at the goal line. Dodging, feinting, sidestepping with perfect coordination, he ran through the other team. Once past the line, he deliberately ran at each member of the backfield, giving all in turn a clear shot at him and evading them at the last instant.

The wind burned in his throat, and he felt the soaring exhilaration that came from the perfect functioning of his body. Then, after running the full length of the field and having offered himself to every member of the opposing team, he ran into the end zone, leaped high into the air, and slammed the ball down on the turf so violently that it bounced

twenty feet straight up. When he came down, he fell onto his back, laughing for sheer joy.

iv

On the Saturday morning after the football game Raphael was stiff and sore. His body was out of condition, and his muscles reacted to the exertion and bruising contact of the game. He still felt good, though.

Flood was up early, which was unusual, since he normally slept late on weekends. "Come along, football hero," he said to Raphael, "rise and shine." His eyes glittered brightly.

Raphael groaned and rolled over in bed.

"Quickly, quickly," Flood commanded, snapping his fingers.

"What's got you all bright-eyed and bushy-tailed this morning?" Raphael demanded sourly.

"Today we go a-visiting," Flood said exuberantly. "Today I carry the conquering hero to visit the queen."

"Some other time." Raphael laid one arm across his eyes. "I'm in no condition for queens today."

"I wouldn't touch that line with a ten-foot pole—or a nine-foot Hungarian either. You might as well get up. I'm not going to let you sleep away your day of triumph."

"Shit!" Raphael threw off the covers.

"My God!" Flood recoiled from the sight of the huge bruises and welts on Raphael's body. "You mean to tell me you let yourself get in that condition for *fun?*"

Raphael sat up and glanced at the bruises. "They'll go away. What were you babbling about?"

"We go to visit the fair Isabel," Flood declaimed, "whose hair is like the night, whose skin is like milk, and whose gazongas come way out to here." He gestured exaggeratedly in front of his chest. "She's an old schoolmate of my aunt's, a fallen woman, cast out by her family, living in shame and obscurity by the shores of scenic Lake Oswego some miles to the south. She and I are kindred spirits, since both of us offend our families by our very existence. She's invited us to spend the weekend, so up, my archangel. Put on your wings and halo, and I will deliver you into the hands of the temptress."

"Isn't it a little early for all the bullshit?" Raphael asked, climbing stiffly to his feet and picking up his towel. "I'm going to hit the showers." He padded out of the room and down the hall to the bathroom.

After a hot shower his sore muscles felt better, and he was in a better humor as he dressed. There was no withstanding Flood when he set his mind to something, and finally Raphael gave in. Twenty minutes later they were packed and southbound on the freeway in Flood's small, fast, red Triumph.

"Just exactly who is this lady we're visiting?" Raphael asked.

"I told you," Flood replied.

"This time why don't you clear away all the underbrush and give me something coherent."

"The lady's name is Isabel Drake. She went to school with my aunt, which makes her practically a member of the family."

"I don't quite follow that, but let it pass."

"We have very extended families in Grosse Pointe."

"Okay."

"Helps us avoid contact with the riffraff."

"All right."

"Avoiding contact with the riffraff is a major concern in Grosse Pointe."

"All right, I said."

"Do I digress?"

"Of course you do, but I'm used to that. All right. Miss—Mrs.— Drake is a distant friend of your family's, a lady of middle years who happens to live in the area, and this is by way of a courtesy call, right?"

Flood laughed. "She'll love that," he hooted. "*Mrs.* Drake—definitely *Mrs.*—made, when she was quite young, an excellent marriage and an even better divorce. She's a lady of means now. The aunt I referred to is my father's youngest sister, so Isabel is maybe thirty at most—hardly what you'd call 'of middle years.' And as far as 'courtesy calls' go, you'll soon discover that the term is wildly inappropriate. Isabel Drake is probably who they had in mind when they invented the word 'fascinating.' "

"Why did you call her a fallen woman?"

"That's a tale of dark passion and illicit lust, Raphael, hardly suitable for your tender ears."

"Try me. If there are subjects I shouldn't talk about, I'd like to know in advance."

"Besides which, you're panting to hear the details, right?" Flood smirked.

"Pant, pant," Raphael said dryly. "Get on with it, Damon. You're going to tell me about it anyway; nothing could stop you. I could have your mouth bricked up, and you'd still tell me."

Flood laughed. "All right, Raphael. Shortly after her divorce, Isabel conceived a passion for the husband of one of her cousins, a vapid, colorless girl of no lasting significance. There was a flaming affair which quite rapidly approached the status of a public scandal. The man in question was also of no lasting significance—some semipresentable shithead the cousin's family had bought for her. Anyhow, there were all the usual lurid developments—gossip, people falling over themselves to tell the poor cousin what Isabel was up to. She attempted suicide, of course."

"You're kidding."

"Not a bit of it. Sleeping pills, the tragic suicide note, all of it.

Anyhow, there was a separation, and the poor klutz informed Isabel that he was ready to divorce the cousin and 'make an honest woman' of her. Isabel, who was getting bored with the whole thing at that point, laughed in his face. She was not about to give up that alimony for *anybody*, much less some cretin who couldn't function outside the bedroom. He got huffy about it all and stormed out, but when he tried to go back to the cousin, she told him to buzz off. He took to drinking and made a special point of telling everyone in all the bars about Isabel's bedroom habits—in great detail. In time the rest of the family hinted around that they'd all be a lot happier if she'd take up residence a long, long way from Grosse Pointe, and finally she did."

"Don't the rich have anything better to do?"

"That's the whole point of being rich," Flood replied, turning off the freeway. "It leaves you free to pursue diversions other than money."

"You know, I think you made all that up, Damon. I think you're putting me on."

"Would I put you on?" Flood laughed.

"If you thought I'd swallow it, yes."

The home of Isabel Drake was a chalet-style house set in a grove of fir trees near the shores of the lake. It was about ten-thirty when Flood's small red sports car stopped on the curving gravel drive in front of the house, and morning sun filtered down through the trees with that overripe golden quality that, more than anything, speaks of autumn.

Flood bounced from the car with unusual energy, went up the wooden steps to the wide porch that stretched across the front of the house, and rang the bell. "Come along, Raphael," he said over his shoulder.

Somewhat painfully, his muscles stiffened again from the ride, Raphael climbed from the car and started up the steps to the porch.

The door opened, and a small woman looked out inquiringly. She was short, perhaps just over five feet tall, and she wore jeans and a loose-fitting cambric shirt of the kind Raphael had seen mill workers back home wear. Her hair was quite dark and caught at the back of her neck by a red bandanna. The skin of her face and throat was very white, and her figure under the loose shirt was full. She had a smudge of pale green paint on one cheek. "Junior," she said in an exasperated tone. Her voice was rich and melodious. "You said *noon*."

"Sorry, 'Bel. We got away early." He grinned down at her.

"I'm a mess," she protested, glancing down at the front of her shirt. She was holding two long, pencilike paint-brushes in her right hand. "You always do this to me, Junior."

"This way we get to see the real you, 'Bel." Flood's grin was slightly malicious. "Let me present the Archangel Raphael," he said, turning and beckoning.

Isabel Drake's eyes widened, and she stared directly at Flood as if he had just said something totally unbelievable. Then she turned and looked at Raphael. Very clearly he could see a kind of stunned recognition cross her face. Her eyes seemed to cloud for a moment, and she looked as if she were about to say something. Then she shook her head slightly, and her face became a polite mask.

"Mrs. Drake," Raphael said rather formally, inclining his head in a sort of incipient bow.

"Please," she replied, "just 'Bel.'" She smiled up at him. Her eyes were large, and her lips sensual. "There's no point in being formal, since Junior arranged for you to catch me in my work clothes. Is it really Raphael?"

Raphael made a face. "My mother's idea of a joke. I'll answer to Rafe if it'd make you more comfortable."

"God no," she said. "I love it. Raphael—it's so musical." She switched the paintbrushes and offered her hand. Raphael took it.

"Oh dear," she said. "The paint. I completely forgot."

Raphael looked at his hand and laughed at the smudges on his palm. "It's only watercolor, but I *am* sorry."

"It's nothing."

"Junior," she said sharply, "I positively *hate* you for this."

Flood, who had been watching the two of them intently, laughed sardonically.

"Come and see my little house," she invited them. "Then I'll get cleaned up and change."

The interior of the chalet smelled faintly of the woman's perfume. The walls of the living room were paneled with walnut, and there were dark, open beams at ceiling height, forming a heavy latticework overhead above which open space soared to the peaked roof. The furniture was of dark, waxed wood and leather, very masculine, which somehow seemed to accentuate Mrs. Drake's femininity. The floor was also dark, waxed wood, and fur throw rugs lay here and there, highlighting major points in the room. The morning sun streamed through a window high in the wall above the beams, catching a heavy crystal service on a buffet in the dining area beyond the couch. The gleaming cut glass filled the room with a golden light that seemed somehow artificial, an unreal glow that left Raphael bemused, almost powerless. Here and there on the dark walls muted watercolors added that touch of something indefinable that spoke of class.

"Pretty fancy, 'Bel." Flood looked around approvingly.

"It's comfortable." She shrugged. "The kitchen's through here." She led them into a cheery kitchen with a round table near the broad window that faced a wooden deck that overlooked the sparkling waters of the lake. An easel was set up on the deck with a partially finished watercolor resting on it.

Raphael looked out at the painting and recognized its similarity to the ones hanging in the living room. "You do your own, I see," he said, pointing.

"It passes the time." She said it deprecatingly, but he could see that she was rather proud of her efforts.

"Say," Flood said, stepping out onto the deck, "that's really pretty good, 'Bel. When did you get into this? I thought dance was your thing."

Raphael and Isabel went out onto the deck and stood looking at the watercolor. She laughed, her voice rich. "That was a long time ago, Junior. I found out that I'm really too lazy for all the practice, and I'm getting a little hippy for it. Male dancers are quite small, and it got to be embarrassing the way their eyes bulged during the lifts." She smiled at Raphael. "Good grief, Raphael," she said, her eyes widening, "what on earth did you do to your arm?" She pointed at the large, dark bruise on his upper bicep, a bruise exposed by his short-sleeved shirt.

"The Angel here is our star athlete," Flood told her. "Yesterday afternoon he single-handedly destroyed an opposing football team."

"Really?" She sounded interested.

"He's exaggerating." Raphael was slightly embarrassed. "There were ten other people out there, too. I just got lucky a few times."

"That looks dreadfully sore." She touched the bruise lightly.

"You should see his chest and stomach." Flood shuddered. "He's a major disaster area."

"They'll fade." Raphael tried to shrug it off. "I heal fairly fast." He looked out over the lake.

"Come along now, you two," Isabel ordered. "I'll show you where the bar is, and then I *have* to get cleaned up and change." She led them back through the kitchen into the dining room. She pointed out the small portable bar to Flood and then went upstairs. A few minutes later they heard a shower start running.

"Well," Flood said, busily at work with the shaker, "what do you think of our 'Bel?"

"She's a lady," Raphael said simply.

Flood laughed. "You're naive, Raphael. 'Bel has breeding; she's got class; she's got exquisite manners and taste; but she's *not* a lady—as I'm sure you'll soon discover."

"What's that supposed to mean?" Raphael asked, a little irritated by Flood's flippancy.

"You'll find out." Flood began to rattle the shaker.

"Isn't it a little early for that?" Raphael asked, sitting carefully in one of the large chairs in front of the fireplace in the living room.

"Never too early." Flood's tone was blithe. "It'll anesthetize all your aches and pains. You're gimping around like an arthritic camel." He came into the living room, handed Raphael a glass, and then sprawled on the leather couch.

"Nice house," Raphael noted, looking around, "but isn't it sort of— well—masculine?"

"That's 'Bel for you." Flood laughed. "It's all part of her web. 'Bel's

not like other women—that's why I like her so much. She's very predatory, and she usually gets exactly what she wants."

"You're a snide bastard, Flood."

"Right on." Flood laughed easily. "It's part of my charm."

A half hour later Isabel came back down in a flowered print dress
that was sleeveless and cut quite low in front. Raphael found that he
had difficulty keeping his eyes where they belonged. The woman was
full-figured, and her arms plumply rounded. There was about her a
kind of ripeness, an opulence that the firm-figured but angular girls of
his own age lacked. Her every move seemed somehow suggestive, and
Raphael was troubled by his reactions to her.

They passed the afternoon quietly. They had lunch and a few more
drinks afterward. Isabel and Raphael talked at some length about nothing in particular while Flood sat back watching, his hard, bright eyes
moving from one to the other and an indecipherable expression on his
face.

In Raphael's private place he told himself that he really had no business being there. 'Bel and Flood were aliens to him—bright, beautiful,
and totally meaningless. With a kind of startled perception he saw that
sophisticated people are sophisticated for that very reason. Meaningless people have to be sophisticated, because they have nothing else.

When it grew dark, they changed clothes and went over to a supper
club in Oswego. Raphael rode with Isabel in her sedan, and Flood followed in his Triumph.

At dinner they laughed a great deal, and Raphael could see others in
the restaurant glancing at them with eyebrows raised speculatively.
Isabel was wearing a low-cut black cocktail dress that set off the satiny
white sheen of her skin, and her hair, dark as night, was caught in a
loose roll at the back of her neck. As Raphael continued to order more
drinks he saw that there was about her an air of enormous sophistication that made him feel very proud just to be seen with her.

As the evening wore on and they lingered over cocktails, Raphael
became increasingly convinced that everyone else in the room was
covertly watching them, and he periodically forced his laughter and
assumed an expression of supercilious boredom.

They had a couple more drinks, and then Raphael knocked over a
water glass while he was attempting to light Isabel's cigarette. He was
filled with mortification and apologized profusely, noticing as he did
that his words were beginning to slur. Isabel laughed and laid her white
hand on his sleeve.

Then Flood was gone. Raphael could not remember when he had
left. He forced his eyes to focus on Isabel, seeing the opulent rising
mounds of creamy white flesh pressing out from the top of her dress
and the enigmatic smile on her full lips.

"I'd better catch the check," he slurred, fumbling for his wallet.

"It's already been taken care of," she assured him, still smiling and once again laying her hand lingeringly on his arm. "Shall we go?" She rose to her feet before he could clamber out of his seat to hold her chair.

He offered his arm, and laughing, she took it. They went outside. Once out in the cool night air, Raphael breathed deeply several times. "That's better," he said. "Stuffy in there." He looked around. "Where the hell is Damon?"

"Junior?" She was unlocking her car. "He wanted to take a look around town. He'll be along later."

They climbed into the car and drove in silence back toward Isabel's house. The night seemed very dark outside the car, and Raphael leaned his head back on the seat.

He awoke with a start when they pulled up in the drive.

They got out of the car and went into the house. He stumbled once on the steps, but caught himself in time.

Isabel turned on a dim light in one corner of the living room, then she stood looking at him, the strange smile still on her face. Quite deliberately she reached back and loosened her hair. It tumbled down her back, and she shook her head to free it. She looked at him, still smiling, and her eyes seemed to glow.

She extended her hand to him. "Shall we go up now?" she said.

 V

The autumn proceeded. The leaves turned, the nights grew chill, and Raphael settled into the routine of his studies. The library became his sanctuary, a place to hide from the continuing distraction of Flood's endless conversation.

It was not that he disliked Damon Flood, but rather that he found the lure of that sardonic flow of elaborate and rather stilted speech too great. It was too easy to lay aside his book and to allow himself to be swept along by the unending talk and the sheer force of Flood's personality. And when he was not talking, Flood was singing. It was not the music itself that was so distracting, though Flood had an excellent singing voice. Rather it was the often obscene and always outrageous lyrics he composed, seemingly on the spur of the moment. Flood had a natural gift for parody, and his twisting of the content of the most familiar songs inevitably pulled Raphael's attention from his book and usually prostrated him with helpless laughter. It was, in short, almost impossible to study while his roommate was around.

And so, more often than not, Raphael crossed the dark lawn in the evenings to the soaring cathedral that was the library; and there, in a pool of light from the study lamp, he bent to his books in the vast main hall beneath the high vault of the ceiling.

And sometimes he saw in another pool of light the intent face of the girl whose voice had so stirred him during his first few weeks on campus. They spoke once in a while, usually of material for the class they both attended, but it was all quite casual at first. The vibrant sound of her voice still struck him, but not as much as it had before he had met Isabel Drake.

If his weeks were consumed with study, his weekends were devoted to what he chose to feel was debauchery. Isabel Drake proved to be a woman of infinite variety and insatiable appetite. She seemed to delight in instructing and guiding him in what, a few months earlier, he would have considered perversion. He did not delude himself into believing that it was love. She was charmed by his innocence and took joy in his youthful vigor and stamina. It was so far from being love that sometimes on Sunday nights as he drove back to Portland, physically wrung out and even sore from his exertions, he felt that he had somehow been violated.

For the first few weekends Flood had accompanied him, delivering him, as it were, into Isabel's hands. Then, almost as if he had assured himself that Raphael would continue the visits without him, he stopped going down to the lake. Without Flood's presence, his knowing, sardonic eyes always watching, Isabel's demeanor changed. She became more dominant, more demanding. Raphael sometimes had nightmares about her during the week, vivid, disconnected dreams of being suffocated by the warm, perfumed pillows of her breasts or crushed between the powerful white columns of her thighs. He began to dread the weekends, but the lure of her was too strong, and helplessly he delivered himself each Friday evening to her perfumed lair by the shores of the lake, where she waited—sometimes, he almost felt, lurked—in heavy-lidded anticipation.

"Have you read the Karpinsky book yet?" It was the girl, Marilyn Hamilton, and she spoke to him as they came out of the library one evening after it closed.

"I'm nearly finished with it," he replied.

"I don't know," she said, falling into step beside him, "but it seemed to me that he evades the issue."

"He does seem a little too pat," Raphael agreed.

"Glib. Like someone who talks very fast so you don't have time to spot the holes in his argument."

They had stopped near the center of the broad lawn in front of Eliot Hall.

"Pardee seems to think a lot of him," Raphael said.

"Oh yes," the girl said, laughing slightly. The vibrance of her voice pierced him. "Mr. Pardee studied under Karpinsky at Columbia."

"I didn't know that."

"My sister found out. She took the course a couple years ago. Mr. Pardee won't mention it in class, of course, but it's a good thing to know." She suddenly mimicked their instructor's gruff voice and deliberately antigrammatical usage. "Since he ain't about to accept no disrespect."

Raphael laughed, charmed by her.

She hesitated and then spoke without looking at him. "I saw you play in that game last month," she told him quietly.

"Oh," he said, "that. It wasn't much of a game, really."

"Not the way *you* played, it wasn't. You destroyed them."

"You think I overemphasized?" he asked, grinning.

"I'm trying to pay you a compliment, dammit." Then she grinned back.

"Thank you."

"I'm making a fool of myself, right?"

"No, not really."

"Anyway, I thought it was really spectacular—and I don't like football very much."

"It's only a game." He shrugged. "It's more fun to play than it is to watch."

"Doesn't it hurt when you get tackled like that?"

"The idea is not to get tackled."

"You're a stubborn man, Raphael Taylor," she accused. "It's almost impossible to talk to you."

"Me?"

"And *will* you stop looking at me all the time. Every time I look up, there you are, watching me. You make me feel as if I don't have any clothes on."

"I'm sorry."

"I'll start making faces at you if you don't stop it," she warned. "Then how would you feel?"

"The question is how are you going to feel when people start to think your gears aren't meshing?"

"You're impossible," she said, but her voice was not really angry. "I have to go home and study some more." She turned abruptly and strode away with a curiously leggy gait that seemed at once awkward and almost childishly feminine.

"Marilyn," he called after her.

She stopped and turned. "What?"

"I'll see you tomorrow."

"No, you won't. I'm going to hide under the table." She stuck her tongue out at him, turned, and continued across the lawn.

Raphael laughed.

Their growing friendship did not, of course, go unobserved. By the time it had progressed to the stage of going for coffee together at the Student Union Building, Flood became aware of it. "Raphael's being unfaithful to you, 'Bel," he announced on one of his now-infrequent visits to the lake.

"Get serious," Raphael told him, irritated and a little embarrassed.

"Don't be a snitch, Junior," Isabel said quite calmly. "Nobody likes a snitch."

"I just thought you ought to know, 'Bel." Flood grinned maliciously. "Since I introduced you two, I feel a certain responsibility." His eyes, however, were serious, even calculating.

"Our relationship isn't that kind." She still seemed unperturbed. "I don't have any objections if Raphael has other diversions—any more than he's upset by *my* little flings."

Raphael looked at her quickly, startled and with a sudden sinking feeling in the pit of his stomach.

"Oh, my poor Angel," she said, catching the look and laughing, "did you honestly think I was 'saving myself' for you? I have other friends, too, you know."

Raphael was sick, and at the same time ashamed to realize that he was actually jealous.

In bed that night she brought it up again. She raised up on one elbow, her heavy breast touching his arm. "How is she?" she asked. "The other girl, I mean?"

"It's not that kind of thing," he answered sulkily. "We just talk—have coffee together once in a while, that's all."

"Don't be coy," she said with a wicked little laugh, deliberately rubbing her still-erect nipple on his shoulder. "A young man who looks like you do could have the panties off half the girls in Portland inside a week."

"I don't go around taking people's panties off."

"You take *mine* off," she disagreed archly.

"That's different." He moved his shoulder away.

"Why is it different?"

"She's not that kind of a girl."

"*Every* girl is that kind of a girl." She laughed, leaning forward so that the ripe breast touched him again. "We're all alike. Is she as good as I am?"

"Oh, for God's sake, 'Bel. Why don't we just skip all this? Nothing's going on. Flood's got a dirty mind, that's all."

"Of course he has. Am I embarrassing you, sweet? We shouldn't be embarrassed by anything—not here."

"What about those other men?" he accused, trying to force her away from the subject.

"What about them?"

"I thought—well—" He broke off helplessly, not knowing how to pursue the subject.

"Are you really upset because I sleep with other men once in a while? Are you really jealous, Angel?"

"Well—no," he lied, "not really."

"We never made any promises, did we? Did you think we were

'going steady' or something?" The persistent nipple continued its strok-
ing of his shoulder.

"I just didn't think you were—well—promiscuous is all."

"Of course I'm promiscuous." She laughed, kissing him. "I had you
in bed within twelve hours of the moment I met you. Is that the sort of
thing you'd expect from a nice girl? I'm not exactly a bitch in heat, but
a little variety never hurt anyone, did it?"

He couldn't think of anything to say.

"Don't sulk, Angel," she said almost maternally as she pulled him to
her again. "You've got my full attention at the moment. That's about
the best I can promise you."

His flesh responded to her almost against his will. He'd have liked to
have been stubborn, but she was too skilled, too expert.

"You should try her, Raphael," Isabel said almost conversationally a
couple of minutes later. "A little variety might be good for you, too.
And who knows? Maybe she's better at it than I am." She laughed, and
then the laughed trailed off into a series of little gasps and moans as she
began to move feverishly under him.

 **vi**

The idea had not been there before. In Raphael's rather unsophisti-
cated views on such matters, girls were divided into two distinct categories—those you took to bed and those you took to school dances. It
was not that he was actually naive, it was just that such classification
made his relations with girls simpler, and Raphael's views on such
things *were* simplistic. He had been raised in a small, remote city that
had a strongly puritanical outlook; his Canadian mother had been quite
firm about being "nice," a firmness in part deriving from her lurking
fear that some brainless sixteen-year-old tramp might unexpectedly
present her with a squalling grandchild. Raphael's football coach at
high school, moreover, had taught Sunday school at the Congrega-
tional church, and his locker-room talks almost as frequently dealt with
chastity as they did with the maiming of middle linebackers. Raphael's
entire young life had been filled with one long sermon that concentrated almost exclusively on one of the "thou shalt nots," the only
amendment having been the reluctant addition of "—with nice girls."
Raphael knew, of course, that other young men did not make a distinction between "nice" girls and the other kind, but it seemed somehow unsporting to him to seduce "nice" girls when the other sort was
available—something on the order of poaching a protected species—
and sportmanship had been drilled into him for so long that its sanc-
tions had the force of religious dictum. Isabel's sly insinuations,
however, had planted the idea, and in the weeks that followed he

found himself frequently looking at Marilyn Hamilton in a way he would not have considered before.

His relationship with the girl passed through all the normal stages—coffee dates in the Student Union, a movie or two, the first kiss, and the first tentative gropings in the front seat of a car parked in a secluded spot. They walked together in the rain; they held hands and they talked together endlessly and very seriously about things that were not particularly significant. They studied together in the dim library, and they touched each other often. They also drove frequently to a special spot they had found outside town where they parked, and in the steamy interior of Raphael's car with the radio playing softly and the misted windows curtaining them from the outside, they partially undressed each other and clung and groped and moaned in a frenzy of desire and frustration as they approached but never quite consummated the act that was becoming more and more inevitable.

Flood, of course, watched, one eyebrow cocked quizzically, gauging the progress of the affair by Raphael's increasing irritability and the lateness of his return to their room. "No score yet, I see," he'd observe dryly upon Raphael's return on such nights.

"Why don't you mind your own damned business?" Raphael would snap, and Flood would chuckle, roll over in his bed, and go back to sleep.

In those weeks Isabel became a virtual necessity to Raphael. With her he found a release for the tensions that had built up to an almost unbearable pitch during the course of the week. She gloated over the passion he brought to her, and sent him back to Portland on Sunday nights sufficiently exhausted to keep him short of the point of no return with the girl. The knowledge that Isabel was there served as a kind of safety valve for him, making it possible for him to draw back at that last crucial instant each time.

And so autumn ground drearily on with dripping skies and the now-bare trees glistening wet and black in the rain. Isabel grew increasingly waspish, and finally announced that she was leaving for a few weeks. "I've got to get some sun," she said. "This rain's driving me up the wall."

"Where are you going?" Raphael asked her.

"Phoenix maybe. Vegas—I don't know. I haven't decided yet. I've got to get away from the rain for a while."

There was nothing he could say. He knew he had no real hold on her, and he even welcomed the idea in a way. His visits had become almost a duty, and he had begun to resent her unspoken demands upon him.

After he had seen her off at the airport outside Portland, he walked back to his car almost with the sense of having been liberated.

On his first weekend date with Marilyn he felt vaguely guilty—

almost like an unfaithful husband. The weekends had always belonged to Isabel. He had not been entirely honest with Marilyn about those weekends. It was not that he had lied, exactly; rather, he had let her believe that Isabel was elderly, an old friend of his family, and that his weekly visits were in the nature of an obligation.

After the movie they drove to their special spot in the country and began the customary grappling. Perhaps because the weekends had always been denied to her and this evening was somehow stolen and therefore illicit, Marilyn responded to his caresses with unusual passion, shuddering and writhing under his hands. Finally she pulled free of him for an instant, looked at him, and spoke quite simply. "Let's," she said, her voice thick and vibrant.

And so they did.

It was awkward, since they were both quite tall, and the steering wheel was horribly in the way, but they managed.

And afterward she cried. He comforted her as best he could and later drove her home, feeling more than a little ashamed of himself. There had been some fairly convincing evidence that, until that night, Marilyn had been one of the girls one would normally take to a school dance.

The next time they used the backseat. It was more satisfactory, and this time she did not cry. Raphael, however, was still a bit ashamed and wished they had not done it. Something rather special seemed to have been lost, and he regretted it.

After several weeks Isabel returned, her fair skin slightly tanned and her temper improved.

Flood accompanied Raphael to the lake on the first weekend, his eyes bright and a knowing smile on his face.

Raphael was moody and stalked around the house, stopping now and then to stare out at the rain, and drinking more than was usual for him. It was time, he decided, to break off the affair with Isabel. She was too wise for him, too experienced, and in a way he blamed her for having planted that evil seed that had grown to its full flower that night in the front seat of his car. If it had not been for her insinuating suggestions, his relationship with Marilyn might still be relatively innocent. Beyond that, she repelled him now. Her overripe figure seemed to have taken on a faint tinge of rottenness, and the smooth sophistication that had attracted him at first seemed instead to be depravity now—even degeneracy. He continued to drink, hoping to incapacitate himself and thus avoid that inevitable and now-disgusting conclusion of the evening.

"Our Angel has fallen, I'm afraid," Flood said after dinner when they were all sitting in front of the crackling fireplace.

"Why don't you mind your own business, Damon?" Raphael said, his words slurring.

"Has he been naughty?" Isabel asked, amused.

"Repeatedly. He's been coming in with claw marks on his back from shoulder to hip."

"Why don't you keep your goddamn mouth shut?" Raphael snapped.

"Be nice, dear," Isabel chided him, "and don't try to get muscular. My furniture's too expensive for that sort of foolishness."

"I just want him to keep his mouth shut, that's all." Raphael's words sounded mushy even to him.

"All right then. *You* tell me. Was it that girl?"

He glared sulkily into the fireplace.

"This won't be much of a conversation if you won't talk to me. Did she really scratch you, Angel? Let me see." She came across the room to him and tugged at his shirt.

"Lay off, 'Bel," he warned, pushing her hands away. "I'm not in the mood for any of that."

"Oh"—she laughed—"it's *true* then. I've never liked scratching. It's unladylike."

"How the hell would *you* know?"

Her eyes narrowed slightly, and her voice took on an edge. "All the usual things, I suppose? Parked car, clumsy little gropings in the dark, the steering wheel?"

Raphael's face flamed. She saw the flush and laughed, a deep, throaty sound that made him flush even more. "You *did*!" she exulted. "In a *car seat*! My poor Angel, I thought I'd taught you better. Are motels so expensive now? Or couldn't you wait? Was she a virgin?"

"Why don't we just drop this?"

"I think the boy's in love, Junior," she said to Flood.

"Here's to love." Flood toasted, raising his glass. "And to steering wheels, of course."

"Oh, that's cute, Flood," Raphael said sarcastically. It sounded silly even to him, but he didn't care.

"Don't be nasty, dear." Isabel's tone was motherly. "It doesn't become you."

It was that note in her voice more than anything—that tolerant, amused, superior tone that finally infuriated him. "Don't patronize me, 'Bel," he told her, getting up clumsily. "I won't take that—not from you."

"I don't think I like your tone, Raphael."

"Good. At least I managed to insult you. I wasn't really sure I could."

"I've had about enough of this."

"I had enough a long time ago." He picked up his jacket.

"Where are you going?"

"Someplace where the air's a little cleaner."

"Don't be stupid. You're drunk."

"What if I am?" He started to lurch toward the door.

"Stop him, Junior."

Raphael stopped and turned toward Flood, his jaw thrust forward pugnaciously.

"Not me," Flood said, raising both hands, palms out. "If you want to go, go ahead." His eyes, however, were savage.

"That's exactly what I'm going to do." Raphael turned and stumbled out the door into the rain.

"Raphael!" Isabel called to him from the porch as he fumbled with his car keys. "Don't be ridiculous. Come back into the house."

"No thanks, 'Bel," he replied. "You cost too much for me. I can't afford you anymore." He got the door open and climbed into the car.

"Raphael," she called again.

He started the car and spun away, the rear end fishtailing and wet gravel spraying out behind him.

Because he knew that Flood might try to follow him, he avoided the freeway, sticking instead to the narrow, two-lane country roads that paralleled it. He was still angry and more than a little drunk. He drove too fast on the unfamiliar roads and skidded often—heart-stopping little drifts as he rounded curves, and wrenching, side-to-side slides as he fought to bring the car back under control.

It had all been stupid, of course—overdramatic and even childish. Despite his anger he knew that his outburst had been obiously contrived. Inwardly he almost writhed with embarrassment. It was all too pat and far too easy to attach the worst motives to. Quite bluntly, he had found someone else and had deliberately dumped Isabel. He had been bad-mannered, ungrateful, and even a little bit contemptible. He knew he should go back, but he continued to roar down the wet, winding road, stubbornly resisting even his own best impulses.

He rounded a sharp right-hand curve, and the car went almost completely out of control. In a single, lucid flash he saw directly ahead of him the large white wooden "X" on a pole at the side of the road and the glaring light bearing down on him. As he drove his foot down on the brake, he heard the roaring noise. His tires howled as the car spun and skidded broadside toward the intersection.

The locomotive klaxon bellowed at him as he skidded, tail-first now, onto the tracks in front of the train.

The world was suddenly filled with noise and light and a great stunning shock. He was thrown helplessly around inside the car as it began to tumble, disintegrating, in front of the grinding mass of the locomotive.

He was hurled against a door, felt it give, and he was partially thrown out. Then the remains of the car rolled over on top of him, and he lost consciousness.

vii

At first there was only shattering, mind-destroying pain. Though he feared the unconsciousness as a kind of death, his mind, whimpering, crept back into it gratefully each time he awoke to find the pain still there.

Later—how much later he would never know—there were drugs that stunned him into insensibility. Vacant-eyed and uncaring, he would watch the slow progression of light outside the window of the room. It grew light, and it stayed light for a while, and then it grew dark again. And always, hiding somewhere below the smooth surface, the pain twisted and heaved like some enormous beast reaching up out of the depths to drag him down out of the billowy gray indifference of the drugs and feed upon his shrieking body again. Sometimes, when the drugs were wearing off and their thick, insulating cloud was growing thin, he would cry, knowing that the beast was almost upon him once more, feeling the first feathery touches of its claws. And then they would come and give him more of the drugs, and it would be all right.

There were many bandages. At times it was almost as if the whole bed was one enormous bandage, and there seemed to be a kind of wire cage over his hips. The cage bothered him because it tented the bed-clothes up in front of him, so that he could not see the foot of the bed, but when he tried to move the cage, they came and gave him more drugs and strapped his hands down.

And then his mother was there, accompanied by his uncle Harry. Harry Taylor's usually florid face blanched as he approached the bed, and Raphael vaguely wondered what could be so disturbing. It was, however, his mother's shriek that half roused him. That animal cry of insupportable loss and the look of mindless horror on her face as she entered the room reached down into the gray fog where he hid from the pain and brought him up, partially sitting, staring beyond the tented cage over his hips at the unbelievable vacancy on the left side of the bed.

It was a mistake, of course, some trick of the eye. Quite plainly, he could feel his left leg—toes, foot, ankle, knee, and thigh. He half sat, feeling the leg in exquisite detail while his eyes, sluggish and uncomprehending, told him that it was no longer there.

viii

"Taylor," the blocky, balding man in the wheelchair snapped, "get your weight off your armpits."

"I was just resting, Mr. Quillian." Raphael lifted his body with his hands.

"Don't rest on your armpits. You remember what I told you about crutch paralysis?"

"All right. Don't make a federal case out of it." He went back to his slow, stumping shuffle back and forth across the small, gymlike therapy room. "This is bullshit," he said finally, collapsing into his wheelchair near the door. "I told you people it was too early for this." He sat massaging his aching hands. "They haven't even taken the dressings off yet."

"Taylor," Quillian said coldly, "if you lie around for another two weeks, you won't be strong enough to lift your own dead ass. Try it again."

"Screw it. I'm tired."

"Do you enjoy being an invalid, Taylor?"

"Come on," Raphael objected. "This is hard work."

"Sure it is. You afraid of hard work?"

"Where's the difference? I mean, I've seen people on crutches before—sprained ankles, broken legs—stuff like that. They pick it up right away. What makes it so damned hard for me?"

"Balance, Taylor, balance. A broken leg is still there. You're a one-legged man now. You've lost nearly a fifth of your body weight. Your center of gravity is in your chest instead of your hips. You've got to learn balance all over again."

"Not all at once. I'm tired. I'm going back to my room."

"Quitting, Taylor? I thought you were an athlete. Is this the way you used to win football games?"

"I'm hurting, man. I need a shot."

"Sure you do." Quillian's voice was contemptuous. "But let's not lie to each other. Let's call it by its right name. You need a fix, don't you? You're a junkie, Taylor, and you need a fix."

Raphael spun his chair around angrily and wheeled himself out of the therapy room.

Later, in the hazy euphoria the drug always brought, Raphael lay in his bed and tried to bring his mind to bear on the problem. "Junkie," he said, trying the word out. It sounded funny to him, and he giggled. "Junkie," he said again, and giggled some more.

A day or so later a starched nurse came into his room with a brightly professional smile on her face. "You have a visitor, Mr. Taylor," she said.

Raphael, gritting his teeth at the pain that seemed to have settled in his phantom knee and knowing that it was still hours until they would give him another shot, turned irritably toward her. "Who is it?" he asked harshly.

"A Miss Hamilton."

"No! I don't want to see her. Send her away."

"Oh, come on," she coaxed. "A visit might cheer you up."

"No!" Raphael shouted. "Now get the hell out of here and leave me alone!" He turned his face toward the wall.

After the nurse had left and he was sure that he was alone, he cried.

Her name was Miss Joan Shimp, and Raphael hated her from almost the first moment he laid eyes on her. She was led into the room by the hospital chaplain, who said a few nice things about social workers and then left. Miss Shimp wore a businesslike suit. No starched white uniform for old Shimpsie. Nobody was going to ask *her* to empty a bedpan by mistake. She was a pear-shaped young woman with enormous hips, narrow shoulders, and no noticeable bosom. Her complexion was acne-ravaged, and she had dun-colored hair, an incipient mustache, a nasal voice, and what might best be described as an attitude problem. "Well now," she started briskly, "how are we doing?" The nurses on the floor had all learned rather early not to say "we" to Raphael.

"I don't know about you, lady," Raphael replied in a flat, unfriendly tone, "but *I'm* doing lousy."

"Self-pity, Mr. Taylor? We must avoid self-pity."

"Why? It's a dirty job, but somebody's got to do it."

"This just won't do," she scolded.

"We're not going to get along, lady. Why don't you just go away?"

"We can play this either way, Taylor." Her voice was sharp. "You've been assigned to me, and I *am* going to do my job. There are programs for people like you, and like it or not, you *are* going to participate."

"Really? Don't bet the farm on it."

Things deteriorated rapidly from there.

Shimpsie talked about programs as if programs were holy things that could solve all the world's problems. Raphael ignored her. His half-drugged mind was not particularly retentive, but he soon had a pile of books at his bedside, and every time Shimpsie entered his room, he would select a book at random and use it as a barrier. In one of his more outrageous moments Flood had once described social workers as representatives of a generation of bright young ladies who don't know how to type. Raphael clung to that definition. It seemed to help for some reason.

Shimpsie asked probing questions about his background and family. She liked the phrase "dysfunctional family," and she was desperately interested in his "feelings" and "relationships." Shimpsie, he felt, was queer for feelings and relationships. On one occasion she even screamed at him, "Don't think! Feel!"

"And abandon twenty-five thousand years of human development? Not very likely, Shimpsie."

"*Miss* Shimp!" she snapped.

"Whatever." He said it as insultingly as possible. "Angleworms feel, Shimpsie. So do oysters, I imagine. I don't know about you, but I hope *I've* come further than that."

Just for the sake of variety he would sometimes lie to her, inventing outrageous stories about a background as "dysfunctional" as he could concoct. She lapped it up, her eyes begging for more.

He hated her with a passion, but he began to long for her visits. In a strange sort of way Shimpsie *was* therapeutic.

"That's better, Taylor," Quillian said a week later. "You're starting to get the rhythm now. Don't stump. Make it smooth. *Set* the crutches down, don't jab at the ground with them. Try to keep from jarring your arms and shoulders."

Raphael, sweating profusely, grimly moved back and forth across the therapy room, gritting his teeth at the burning pain in his arms.

"Why are you picking on Miss Shimp?" Quillian said in a half-amused way.

"Shimpsie? I pick on her because she's an asshole."

Quillian laughed. "Never heard a woman called an asshole before."

"Would you prefer asshole-ess?"

"Asshole or not, you'd better at least *try* to get along with her, Taylor."

"Why should I bother?"

"Because you can't get out of here without her okay. She has to sign a release before they'll discharge you. Okay, enough bullshit. Get back to work."

A week or so later Uncle Harry made another trip to Portland, alone this time. "Good to see you again, Rafe," he said, shaking Raphael's hand. He glanced at the crutches leaning in the corner. "I see that you're getting around now."

Raphael looked at him through the haze of the shot he had just been given. "What brings you down here, Uncle Harry?"

"Oh . . ." his uncle replied a bit evasively, "this and that. I thought I'd stop by and see how you were doing."

"I'm coming along."

"Good for you. Have they given you any idea yet about when you'll be getting out of here?"

Raphael shifted in the bed, wincing slightly. "I imagine that it's going to be a while longer."

"You going back to school when you get out?"

"I haven't really thought about it yet."

Uncle Harry gave him a speculative look. "I'm going to give this to you straight, Rafe. I think we know each other well enough for that."

"Okay," Raphael replied, "what is it?"

"It's your mother, Rafe."

"Mom?"

"She's always been a delicate woman, you know, and I'm afraid all of this has been too much for her—your father's death, your accident, all of it. She's a little—well—disoriented. Her doctors say that she'll come out of it eventually, but it's going to take time."

"I'd better go home. I can get around now—a little. I'll see if they'll discharge me."

"Uh—that's going to be a problem, Rafe. You see, what's happened is that your mother has—well, sort of retreated. I mean, she's not catatonic or anything, but it's just that in her mind none of this has really happened. As far as she's concerned, your father's away on a business trip, and you're off at college. She's perfectly happy—talks about you both all the time. The doctors think that it might be best to keep her that way for the time being. If you came back with your—on crutches, that is—she'd have to face things she's just not ready to come to grips with yet."

"I see."

"I hate to have to be the one to tell you, but it's better coming from me than from somebody else. Just give her a little time, that's all. Write to her from time to time—that sort of thing. I'll keep you posted on her progress."

"Thanks for telling me, Uncle Harry."

"That's what family is for. If you're not too tired, there are a couple of other things I need to discuss with you."

"I'm fine," Raphael told him.

"Okay, Rafe." Uncle Harry opened his briefcase. "Financially you're pretty well off."

"Sir?"

"You'll have fairly comfortable income. Edgar—your father—had a number of insurance policies. Edgar was always very interested in insurance."

"He was a careful man."

"That he was, Rafe. That he was. The policies will cover all your medical expenses here and give you an income besides—not very big, actually. Walking-around money is about all. You'll also be receiving Social Security disability benefits."

"I've never had a job, Uncle Harry—not a real one. I'm not eligible for Social Security."

"You worked for four summers at the mill back in Port Angeles."

"That wasn't a real job, Uncle Harry. The owner hired me because of my father—and because I was a football player."

"They withheld Social Security from your check, didn't they?"

"Yes."

"Then you're entitled. Don't rush out and make any down payments on any castles, though. What's really got you set up is the settlement you got from the railroad."

"Settlement? What settlement?"

"I told you about that the last time I was here. I had you sign some papers, remember?"

"To be honest with you, Uncle Harry, there are some big gaps in what I remember. The painkillers sort of erase things."

"I suppose they do at that. Well, to cut it short, the railroad's insurance company got in touch with me not long after your accident. They made an offer."

"What for? It was *my* fault. I was drunk and driving too fast. It wasn't the train's fault."

"You don't necessarily have to make an issue of that, Rafe—not that it really matters now, I guess. The railroad didn't want a messy court case. Jurors in this part of the country are a little unpredictable where railroads are concerned. It's cheaper in the long run for the railroad to make an offer in any case where there are personal injuries. Those ten-million-dollar judgments really bite into company profits. Anyway, you'll be getting a monthly check from them. I still wouldn't get my heart set on any castles, though. If you don't go hog-wild, you'll get by okay. I'll put the money—your settlement, your insurance, and your Social Security check all in the bank back home for you. You remember Anderson, don't you?"

"The banker?"

"Right. He remembers you from the football field, and he'll take care of everything for you. You'll be getting a check every month. I put a few thousand in the hospital safe for you."

"A few *thousand*?"

"You're going to have unusual expenses when you leave the hospital, Raphael. I don't want you to run short. I'm afraid you'll find out just how little it is when you get out on the street. You're set financially, so you can just relax until you get back on your feet again." Harry stopped abruptly and looked away. "I'm sorry, but you know what I mean."

"Sure."

"I'll need your signature on a few things," his uncle went on. "Power of attorney for you and your mother—that kind of thing. That way you can concentrate on getting well and just leave everything else up to me. Okay?"

"Why not?"

"Mr. Quillian," Raphael said to his therapist a few days later while resting on his crutches.

"What is it, Taylor?" the balding man in the wheelchair asked him.

"Did you have any problems with all the drugs they give us?"

"Jesus Christ, Taylor! I've got a broken back. Of course I had a problem with drugs. I fought drugs for five years."

"How did you beat it?"

"Beat it? Beat it, boy?" Quillian exploded. "You *never* beat it. Sometimes—even now—I'd give my soul for one of those shots you get every other hour."

"All right, then. How did you stop?"

"How? You just stop, boy. You just stop. You just don't take any more."

"All right," Raphael said. "I can do that if I have to. Now, when do I get my wooden leg?"

Quillian looked at him. "What?"

"My peg leg? Whatever the hell you call it?"

"Prosthesis, Taylor. The word is prosthesis. Haven't you talked with your doctor yet?"

"He's too busy. Is there something else I'm supposed to know?"

Quillian looked away for a moment, then looked back, his face angry. "Dammit," he swore. "I'm not supposed to get mixed up in this." He spun his wheelchair away and rolled across the room to a file cabinet. "Come over here, Taylor." He jerked open a cabinet drawer and leafed through until he found a large brown envelope.

Raphael crutched across the room, his movements smoother now.

"Over to the viewer," Quillian said harshly, wheeled, and snapped the switch on the fluorescent viewer. He stuck an X-ray picture on the plate.

"What's that?" Raphael asked.

"That's you, Taylor. That's what's left of you. Full front, lower segment. You don't have a left hip socket. The left side of your pelvis is shattered. There's no way that side of you could support your weight. There won't be any prosthesis for you Taylor. You're on crutches for the rest of your life, boy. You might as well get that down in your mind."

Raphael stood on his crutches, looking at the X ray. "All right. I can live with that if I have to."

"You still want to try to get off the dope?"

"Yes." Raphael was still looking at the X ray, a horrible suspicion growing as he looked at the savagely disrupted remains of his pelvis that the shadowy picture revealed. "I think it's time I got my head back together again."

ix

"There really wasn't any alternative, Raphael," the doctor told him. "The damage was so extensive that there just wasn't anything left to salvage. We were lucky to be able to restore normal urinary function."

"That's the reason I've got this tube?" Raphael asked.

"The catheter? Yes. That's to allow the bladder time to heal. We should be able to remove it soon. There'll be some discomfort at first, but that'll pass and the function will be normal."

"Then there was no damage to the—uh—"

"Some, but we were able to repair that—to a degree. That's a pretty tricky area to work with. My guess is that even if we'd been able to save the scrotal area and one or both testes, normal sexual function proba-bly couldn't have been restored."

"Then I'm a eunuch."

"That's a very old-fashioned term, Raphael," the doctor said disap-provingly.

Raphael laughed bitterly. "It's an old-fashioned kind of condition. Will my voice change—all that kind of thing?"

"That's mythology. That kind of thing only happens if the removal takes place before puberty. Your voice won't change, and your beard won't fall out. You can check with an endocrinologist periodically if you like, but it won't really be necessary."

"All right," Raphael said, shifting uncomfortably in his chair. He'd begun to sweat again, and there was an unpleasant little twitching in his left hip.

"Are you all right?" the doctor asked, looking at him with concern.

"I can live with it." Raphael's left foot felt terribly cold.

"Why don't I have them increase your medication for a few days?" the doctor suggested.

"No," Raphael said sharply. He lifted himself up and got his crutches squared away.

"In time it'll begin to be less important, Raphael," the doctor said sympathetically.

"Sure. Thanks for your time. I know you're busy."

"Can you make it back to your room okay?"

"I can manage it." Raphael turned and left the doctor's office.

Without the drugs he found that he slept very little. After nine, when the visitors left, the hospital became quiet, but never wholly silent. When he found his hand twitching, reaching almost of its own volition for the bell that would summon the nurse with the needle, he would get out of bed, take his crutches, and wander around in the halls. The effort and the concentration it required to walk helped to keep his mind off his body and its craving.

His arms and shoulders were stronger now, and Quillian had given him his permanent crutches. They were called Canadian crutches, a term that seemed very funny to Raphael for some reason. They had leather cuffs that fit over his forearms, and they angled slightly at the handgrips. Using them was much less awkward, and he began to develop the smooth, almost stately pace of the one-legged man.

He haunted the halls of the hospital during the long hours of the night, listening to the murmurs and the pain-filled moans of the sick and the dying. Although he realized that it might have been merely coincidence, a series of random occurrences of an event that could happen at any time, Raphael became persuaded that most people die at night. Usually they died quietly, but not always. Sometimes, in the exhaustion with which he sandbagged his craving body to sleep toward the morning of each interminable night, he wondered if it might not somehow be *him*. It seemed almost as if his ghosting passage down the dim halls, like the turbulence in the wake of a passing ship, reached in through the doors and walls to draw out those teetering souls. Sometimes in those last moments before sleep he almost saw himself as the Angel of Death.

Once, during his restless midnight wandering, he heard a man screaming in agony. He angrily crutched his way to the nurses' station. "Why don't you give him a shot?" he demanded.

"It wouldn't do any good," the starched young nurse replied sadly. "He's an alcoholic. His liver's failed. Nothing works with that. He's dying, and there's nothing we can give him to relieve the pain."

"You didn't give him enough," Raphael told her, his voice very quiet, even deadly.

"We've given him the maximum dosage. Any more would kill him."

"So?"

She was still quite young, so her ideals had not yet been eroded away. She stared at Raphael, her face deathly white. And then the tears began to run slowly down her cheeks.

Shimpsie noted from Raphael's chart that he had been refusing the painkilling medication, and she disapproved. "You *must* take your medication, Raphael," she chided.

"Why?"

"Because the doctors know what's best for you."

He made an indelicate sound. "I've got the free run of the hospital, Shimpsie," he told her. "I've been in the doctors' lounge, and I've heard them talking. Don't bullshit me about how much doctors know. They're plumbers and pill pushers. I haven't heard an original thought from one of them since I've been here."

"Why do you go out of your way to be so difficult?"

"It's an attention-getting device, Shimpsie." He smiled at her sweetly. "I want you all to remember me. I quit taking the goddamn dope because I don't want to get hooked. I've got enough problems already."

"There are programs to help you break that habit," she assured him. Her voice was actually earnest.

"You've got a program for everything, haven't you, Shimpsie? You send a couple of orderlies to my room about nine times a week to drag me to meetings—meetings of the lame, the halt, and the blind—where we all sit around spilling our guts for you. If you want to fondle guts, go fondle somebody else's. Mine are just fine the way they are."

"*Why* can't I get through to you? I'm only trying to help."

"I don't need help, Shimpsie. Not yours, anyway."

"You want to do it 'your way'? Every client starts out singing 'My Way.' You'll come around eventually."

"Don't make any bets. As I recall, I warned you that you weren't going to enjoy this. You'd save yourself a lot of grief if you just gave up on me."

"Oh no, Taylor. I *never* give up. You'll come around—because if you don't, you'll stay here until you rot. We'll grow old together, Taylor, because you won't get out of here until *I* sign you off. Think about it." She turned to leave.

He *couldn't* let her get in the last word like that. He absolutely *couldn't*. "Oh, Shimpsie?" he said mildly.

"Yes?"

"You really shouldn't get so close to my bed, you know. I haven't gotten laid for a long time. Besides, you've got a nice big can, and I'm a compulsive fanny-patter."

She fled.

Finally, when the craving for the drugs had almost gone and the last dressings had been removed to reveal the puckered, angry red new scars on his hip and groin, when the Christmas season was upon them, Flood finally came to visit.

Their meeting was awkward, since there was very little they could really talk about. Raphael could sense in Flood that stifling unease all hospital visitors have. They talked desultorily of school, which was out for the Christmas holiday; of the weather, which was foul; and of nearly anything else except those uncomfortable subjects that by unspoken mutual consent they avoided.

"I brought your luggage and books and your other stuff," Flood said. "I decided to get an apartment off campus next semester, and I was pretty sure you wouldn't want the college to store your things. They tend to be a little careless."

"Thanks, Damon."

"Are you going to be coming back to school when you get out of here?" Flood asked, a curiously intent look in his dark eyes.

"I haven't decided yet. I think I'll wait a semester or so—get things together first."

"Probably not a bad idea. Tackle one thing at a time." Flood walked to the window and stood looking out at the rain.

"How's 'Bel?" Raphael asked, crossing that unspoken boundary.

"Fine—as far as I know, anyway. I haven't been going down there much. 'Bel gets a little tiresome after a while, and I've been studying pretty hard."

"You?" Raphael laughed. "I didn't think you knew how."

Flood turned back from the window, grinning. "I'm not much of a scholar," he admitted, "but I didn't think it'd look good to flunk out altogether. Old J.D.'d like nothing better than to find an excuse to cut off my allowance."

"Look," Raphael said uncomfortably, "I really ran my mouth that night at 'Bel's place. If you happen to see her, tell her I apologize, okay?"

"What the hell? You were drunk. Nobody takes offense at anything you say when you're drunk. Besides, you were probably right about her. I told you about that, didn't I?"

"All the same," Raphael insisted, "tell her I apologize."

"Sure"—Flood shrugged—"if I see her. You need anything?"

"No. I'm fine."

"I'd better get going then. I've got a plane to catch."

"Going home for Christmas?"

"It's expected. Scenic Grosse Pointe for the holidays. Hot spit. At least it'll pacify the old man—keep those checks coming." He looked at his watch. "I'm going to have to get cranked up. I'll look you up when I get back, okay?"

"Sure."

"Take care, Gabriel," Flood said softly, and then he left. They did not shake hands, and the inadvertent slip passed almost unnoticed.

The hospital became intolerable now that his body was mending. Raphael wanted out—away—anyplace but in the hospital. He became even more irritable, and the nurses pampered him, mistakenly believing that he was disappointed because he could not go home for Christmas. It was not the holiday, however. He simply wanted out.

Shimpsie was going to be a problem, however. On several occasions she had held her power to withhold her approval for his discharge over his head. Raphael considered it in that private place in his mind and made a decision that cost him a great deal in sacrificed pride. The next day he got "saved." He went through the entire revolting process. Once he even broke down and cried for her. Shimpsie, her eyes filled with compassion and with the thrill of victory, comforted him, taking him in her arms as he feigned racking sobs. Shimpsie's deodorant had failed her sometime earlier that day, and being comforted by her was not a particularly pleasant experience.

She began to talk brightly about "preparation for independent liv-ing." She was so happy about it that Raphael almost began to feel ashamed of himself. Almost.

He was fully ambulatory now, and so one day she drove him to one of those halfway houses. In the world of social workers, *every-thing* had a halfway house. Ex-convicts, ex-junkies, ex-sex offend-ers—all of them had a halfway house—a kind of purgatory midway between hell and freedom. Shimpsie *really* wanted the state of Ore-gon to pick up Raphael's tab, but he firmly overrode that. He was running a scam—a subterfuge—and he wanted to pay for it himself, buying, as it were, his own freedom. He paid the deposit and the first month's rent for a seedy, rather run-down room in an old house on a quiet back street, and Shimpsie drove him back to the hospital. She fervently promised to look in on him as soon as he got settled in. Then, just before she hurried off to one of her meetings, she hugged him, a little misty-eyed.

"It's all right, Joanie," he said consolingly. "We'll be seeing each other again." That had been one of the marks of his rehabilitation. He had stopped calling her "Shimpsie" and used "Joanie" instead. He cringed inwardly each time he did it.

She nodded and went off down the hall, exuding her smug sense of victory.

"So long, Shimpsie," Raphael murmured under his breath. "I'm really going to miss you." The funny thing was that he almost meant it. He turned and crutched his way toward the gym. He wanted to say good-bye to Quillian.

"I see you're leaving," Quillian said, his voice harsh as always.

Raphael nodded. "I stopped by to say thanks."

"It's all part of the job."

"Don't be a shithead. I'm not trying to embarrass you, and I'm not talking about showing me how to use these." He waved one of his crutches.

"All right. Did you finally quit feeling sorry for yourself?"

"No. Did you?"

Quillian laughed suddenly. "No, by God, I never did. You're going to be okay, Taylor. Be honest with yourself, and don't be afraid to laugh at yourself, and you'll be okay. Watch out for booze and drugs when you get out there, though," he added seriously. "It's an easy way out, and a lot of us slip into that. It'd be particularly easy for *you.* All you'd have to do is shamble into any doctor's office in the country and walk out fifteen minutes later with a pocketful of prescriptions. You've got the perfect excuse, and Dr. Feelgood is just waiting for you."

"I'll remember that."

Quillian looked at him for a moment. "Be careful out there, Taylor. The world isn't set up for people like us. Don't fall down—not in front of strangers."

"We all fall down once in a while."

"Sure," Quillian admitted, "but those bastards out there'll just walk around you, and you can't get up again without help."

"I'll remember that, too. Take care, Quillian, and thanks again."

"Get the hell out of here, Taylor. I'm busy. I've got people around here who still need me." They shook hands, and Raphael left the therapy room for the last time.

He stored most of his things at the hospital, taking only two suitcases.

The pasty-faced man from the halfway house was waiting for him outside the main entrance, but Raphael had planned his escape very carefully. He already had his reservation at a good downtown hotel, and he had called a cab, telling the dispatcher very firmly that he wanted to be picked up at the *side* door. As his cab drove him away from the hospital, he began to laugh.

"Something funny?" the driver asked him.

"Very, very funny, old buddy," Raphael said, "but it's one of those inside kind of jokes."

He spent the first few nights in the hotel. It was a good one, and there were bellhops and elevators to make things easier. He began to refer to it in his mind as his own private halfway house. He had his meals sent up to his room, and he bathed fairly often, feeling a certain satisfaction at being able to manage getting in and out of the tub without help. After he had been in the hotel for two days, he bathed again and then lay on the bed to consider the future.

There was no reason to remain in Portland. He was not going back to Reed—not yet certainly—probably never. There were too many painful associations there. He also knew that if he stayed, sooner or later people would begin to come around—to look him up. In his mind he left it at that—"people"—even though what he really meant was Isabel and Marilyn. It was absolutely essential that he have no further contact with either of them.

He called the desk and made arrangements to have the hotel pick up the rest of his belongings from the hospital and ship them to his uncle in Port Angeles. He could send for them later, after he got settled. The sense of resolve, of having made a decision, was quite satisfying; and since it had been a big day, he slept well that night.

The next morning he called Greyhound. A plane would be faster certainly, but airlines keep records, and he could not really be sure just how far Shimpsie might go to track him down. Shimpsie had full access to the resources of the Portland Police Department, if she really wanted to push it, and Shimpsie would probably want to push it as far as it would go. Hell, as they say, hath no fury like a social worker scorned, and Raphael had not merely scorned Shimpsie, he had tricked her, deceived her, and generally made a fool of her. Right now Shimpsie would probably walk through fire to get him so that she could tear his heart out with her bare hands.

It was difficult to explain things over the phone to the man at Greyhound. It was really against policy for an interstate bus to make an unscheduled stop at a downtown street corner. Raphael waved the missing leg at him and finally got around that.

Then there was the question of destination. Raphael quickly calculated the amount of time it would take for a messenger to reach the depot with the money and return with a ticket. He concentrated more on that *time* than upon any given destination. He wanted to be gone from Portland. He wanted to go *anyplace* as long as it wasn't Portland.

Finally the man on the phone, puzzled and more than a little suspicious, ventured the information that there were still seats available on the bus that would leave for Spokane in two hours, and that the bus would actually pass Raphael's hotel. That was a good sign. Raphael had not had any good luck for so long that he had almost forgotten what it felt like. "Good," he said. "Hold one of those seats for me. I'll be outside the front door of the hotel."

"Are you sure you want to go to Spokane?" the man at Greyhound asked dubiously.

"Spokane will do just fine," Raphael said. "Everything I've always wanted is in Spokane."

Fortuna plango vulnera

Stillantibus Ocellis

i

I was snowing when they reached Spokane, a swirling snow-fall of tiny crystalline flakes that glittered in the streetlights and muf-fled the upper floors of the buildings. The traffic on the white-covered streets was sparse, and dark, ill-defined automobiles loomed, bulky and ominous, out of the swirling white with headlights like smeared eyes. The bus pulled under the broad roof that sheltered the loading gates at the terminal and stopped. "Spokane," the driver announced, and opened the door of the bus.

The trip had been exhausting, and toward the end had become a kind of tedious nightmare under a darkening, lead-gray sky that had spat snow at them for the last hundred miles. Raphael waited until the bus emptied before attempting to rise. By the time he had struggled down the steps and reached the safety of the ground, most of the other passengers had already joined family or friends, reclaimed their lug-gage, and left.

The air was crisp, but not bitterly cold, and the Muzak inside the depot came faintly through the doors.

There was another sound as well. At first Raphael thought it might be a radio or a television set left playing too loudly. A man was giving an address of some kind. His words seemed to come in little spurts and snatches as the swirling wind and intermittent traffic first blurred and then disclosed what he said.

"If chance is defined as an outcome of random influence produced by no sequence of causes," he was saying in an oratorical manner, "I am sure that there is no such thing as chance, and I consider that it is but an empty word."

Then Raphael saw the speaker, a tall, skinny man wearing a shabby overcoat of some kind of military origin. He was bald and unshaven, and he stood on the sidewalk at the front of the bus station talking quite loudly to the empty street, ignoring the snow that piled up on his shoulders and melted on his head and face. "For what place can be left for anything to happen at random so long as God controls everything in

45

order? It is a true saying that nothing can come out of nothing." The speaker paused to allow his unseen audience to grasp that point.

"These your bags?" a young man in blue jeans and a heavy jacket who had been unloading suitcases from the bus asked, pointing at Raphael's luggage sitting alone on a baggage cart.

"Right," Raphael said. "What's with the prophet of God there?" He pointed at the skinny man on the sidewalk.

"He's crazy," the young man replied quite calmly. "You see him all over town makin' speeches like that."

"Why don't they pick him up?"

"He's harmless. You want me to put your bags in the station for you?"

"If you would, please. Is there a good hotel fairly close?"

"You might try the Ridpath," the young man suggested, picking up Raphael's suitcases. "It's not too far."

"Can I get a cab?"

"Right out front." The young man shouldered his way into the station and held the door open as Raphael crutched along behind him.

"If anything arises from no causes, it will appear to have arisen out of nothing," the man on the sidewalk continued. "But if this is impossible, then chance also cannot—"

The door swung shut behind Raphael, cutting off the sound of that loud voice. Somehow he wished that it had not. He wished that he might have followed the insane prophet's reasoning to its conclusion. Chance, luck—good or bad—if you will, had been on Raphael's mind a great deal of late, and he really wanted to hear a discussion of the subject from the other side of sanity. His thoughts, centering, as they had, on a long series of "what-if's," were growing tedious.

A few people sat in the bus station, isolated from each other for the most part. Some of them slept, but most stared at the walls with vacant-eyed disinterest.

"I'll set these over by the front door for you," the young man with the suitcases said.

"Thanks."

The Ridpath is one of the best hotels in Spokane, and Raphael stayed there for four days. On the first morning he was there he took a cab to a local bank with branches in all parts of the city and opened a checking account with the cashier's check he had purchased in Portland. He kept a couple hundred dollars for incidentals and then returned to his hotel. He did not venture out after that, since the snowy streets would have been too hazardous. He spent a great deal of time at the window of his room, looking out at the city. While he was there he had all of his pants taken to a tailor to have the left legs removed. The flapping cloth bothered him, and the business of pinning the leg up each time he dressed was a nuisance. It was much better with the leg removed and a neat seam where it had been.

On his third day in Spokane it rained, cutting away the snow and filling the streets with dirty brown slush. It was when he checked his wallet before going to the dining room for supper that a rather cold realization came to him. It was expensive to be disabled. Since the disabled man could do very little for himself, he had to hire other people to do them for him. He skipped supper that night and sat instead with pad and pencil adding a few things up. The very first conclusion he reached was that although the Ridpath was very comfortable, staying there was eating up his funds at an alarming rate. A man of wealth might comfortably take up permanent residence at the Ridpath, but Raphael was far from being a millionaire. The several thousand dollars Uncle Harry had given him in Portland had seemed to be an enormous sum, but now he saw just how small it really was. "Time to pull in the old horns," he said wryly. "I think we'd better make some other arrangements."

He took the phone book and made a list of a half dozen or so nearby hotels and apartment houses. The next morning he put on his coat and went downstairs to the cabstand at the front of the hotel.

The first hotel on his list was the St. Clair. It was totally unsuitable. Then the cab took him up Riverside to the Pedicord, which was even worse. The Pedicord Hotel was very large, and it looked as if it might at one time have had some pretensions about it. It had long since decayed, however. The lobby was filled with stained and broken couches, and each couch was filled. The men were old for the most part, and they smoked and spat and stared vacant-eyed at a flickering television set. There were crutches and metal-frame walkers everywhere. Each time one of the old men rose to go to the bathroom, a querulous squabble broke out among those who stood along the walls over who would get the vacant seat. The smell was unbelievable.

Raphael fled.

"Just what are you lookin' for, man?" the cabdriver asked when Raphael climbed, shaken, back into the cab again.

"A place to live."

"You sure as hell don't wanna move in to *that* dump."

"How can they live that way?" Raphael looked at the front of the Pedicord and shuddered.

"Winos," the driver replied. "All they want is a place that's cheap and gets 'em in outta the cold." He stopped and then turned and looked at Raphael. "Look. I could drive you all over this downtown area—run up a helluva fare—and you're not gonna find anyplace you'd wanna keep a pig in—not if you thought anything about the pig. You're gonna have to get out a ways—outta this sewer. I'm not supposed to do this, but I think I know a place that might be more what you're lookin' for. How much do you wanna pay?"

Raphael had decided what he could afford the previous night. He rather hesitantly named the figure.

"That sounds pretty close to the place I got in mind. You wanna try it?"

"Anything. Just get me away from here."

"Right." The driver started his motor again. They drove on back down Riverside. It was raining again, a misty, winter kind of rain that blurred the outlines of things. The windshield wiper clicked, and the two-way radio in the front seat crackled and hissed.

"You lose the leg in 'Nam?" the driver asked.

"No," Raphael replied. "I had a misunderstanding with a train." He was surprised to find that he could talk about it calmly.

"Ooog!" The driver shuddered. "That's messy. You're lucky you're still around at all. I saw a wreck like that out in the valley once. Took 'em two hours to pick the guy up. He was scattered half a mile down the tracks."

"How far is this place?"

"Not much farther. Lemme handle it when we get there, okay? I know the guy. You want a place where you can cook?"

"No. Not right away."

"That'll make it easier. There's a pretty good little restaurant just down the street. You'll wanna be on the main floor. The place don't have an elevator."

The cab pulled up in front of a brick building on a side street. The sign out front said, THE BARTON. WEEKLY–MONTHLY RATES. An elderly man in a well-pressed suit was coming out the front door.

"Sit tight," the driver said, climbed out of the cab, and went inside.

About ten minutes later he came back. "Okay," he said. "He's got a room. It's in the back, so there's no view at all, unless you like lookin' at alleys and garbage cans. He's askin' 'bout thirty-five a month more than what you wanted to pay, but the place is quiet, pretty clean, and like I said, there's that restaurant just down the street where they ain't gonna charge you no ten bucks for a hamburger. You wanna look at it?"

"All right," Raphael said, and got out of the cab.

The room was not large, but it had a good bed and an armchair and a sturdy oak table with a few magazines on it. There was a sink and a mirror, and the bathroom was right next door. The walls were green—every rented room in the world is painted green—and the carpet was old but not too badly worn.

"Looks good," Raphael decided. "I'll take it." He paid the landlord a month's rent and then went back to the Ridpath to get his luggage and check out. When they returned to the Barton, the driver carried his bags into the room and set them down.

"I owe you," Raphael said.

"Just what's on the meter, man. I might need a hand myself someday, right?"

"All right. Thanks."

"Anytime," the driver said, and left. Raphael realized that he hadn't even gotten his name.

The weather stayed wet for several weeks, and Raphael walked a little farther each day. Quillian had told him that it would be months before his arms and shoulders would develop sufficient strength to make any extensive walking possible, but Raphael made a special point of extending himself a little more every day, and he was soon able to cover a mile or so without exhausting himself too much.

By the end of the month he could, if he rested periodically, cover most of the downtown area. He considered sending for the rest of his things, but decided against it. The room was too small.

Spokane is not a particularly pretty city, especially in the winter. Its setting is attractive—a kind of basin on the banks of the Spokane River, which plunges down a twisted basalt chute in the center of town. The violence of the falls is spectacular, and an effort was made following the World's Fair in 1974 to convert the fairgrounds into a vast municipal park. The buildings of the downtown area, however, are for the most part very old and very shabby. Because the city is small, the worst elements lie side by side with the best.

Raphael became accustomed to the sight of drunken old men stumbling through the downtown streets and of sodden Indians, their eyes a poached yellow, swaying in bleary confusion on street corners. The taverns were crowded and noisy, and a sour reek exhaled from them each time their doors opened. In the evenings hard-faced girls in tight sweaters loitered on street corners, and loud cars filled with raucous adolescents toured an endless circuit of the downtown area, their windows open and the mindless noise of rock music blasting from them at full volume. There were fights in front of the taverns sometimes and unconscious winos curled up in doorways. There were adult bookstores on shabby streets and an X-rated movie house on Riverside.

And then it snowed again, and Raphael was confined, going out only to get his meals. He had three or four books with him, and he read them several times. Then he played endless games of solitaire with a greasy deck of cards he'd found in the drawer of the table. By the end of the week he was nearly ready to scream with boredom.

Finally the weather broke again, and he was able to go out. His very first stop was at a bookstore. He was determined that another sudden change in the weather was *not* going to catch him without something to read. Solitaire, he decided, was the pastime of the mentally deficient. He came out of the bookstore with his coat pockets and the front of his shirt stuffed with paperback books and crutched his way on down the street. The exercise was exhilarating, and he walked farther than he ever had before. Toward the end of the day he was nearly exhausted, and he went into a small, gloomy pawnshop, more to rest and to get in out of the chill rain than for any other reason. The place was filled with the usual pawnshop junk, and Raphael browsed without much interest.

It was the tiny, winking red lights that caught his eye first. "What's that thing?" he asked the pawnbroker, pointing.

"Police scanner," the unshaven man replied, looking up from his newspaper. "It picks up all the police channels—fire department, ambulances, stuff like that."

"How does it work?"

"It scans—moves up and down the dial. Keeps hittin' each one of the channels until somebody starts talkin'. Then it locks in on 'em. When they stop, it starts to scan again. Here, I'll turn it up." The unshaven man reached over and turned up the volume.

"District One," the scanner said, "juvenile fifty-four at the Crescent security office."

"What's a fifty-four?" Raphael asked.

"It's a code," the man behind the counter explained. "I got a sheet around here someplace." He rummaged through a drawer and came up with a smudged and tattered mimeographed sheet. "Yeah, this is it. A fifty-four's a shoplifter." He handed Raphael the sheet.

"Three-Eighteen," the scanner said. The row of little red lights stopped winking when someone spoke, and only the single light over the channel in use stayed on.

"This is Three-Eighteen," another voice responded.

"We have a man down in the alley behind the Pedicord Hotel. Possible DOA. Complainant reports that he's been there all day."

"I'll drift over that way."

"DOA?" Raphael asked.

"Dead on arrival."

"Oh."

The lights went on winking.

"This is Three-Eighteen," the scanner said after a few minutes. "It's Wilmerding. He's in pretty bad shape. Better send the wagon—get him out to detox."

Raphael listened for a half an hour to the pulse that had existed beneath the surface without his knowing it, and then he bought the scanner. Even though it was secondhand, it was expensive, but the fascination of the winking flow of lights and the laconic voices was too great. He had to have it.

He took a cab back to his hotel, hurried to his room, dumped his books on the bed, and plugged the scanner in. Then, not even bothering to turn on the lights, he sat and listened to the city.

"District Four."

"Four."

"Report of a fifty at the Maxwell House Tavern. Refuses to leave."

"Spokane Ambulance running code to Monroe and Francis. Possible heart."

"Stand by for a fire. We have a house on fire at the corner of Boone and Chestnut. Time out eighteen-forty-seven."

Raphael did not sleep that night. The scanner twinkled at him and spoke, bringing into his room all the misery and folly of the city. People had automobile accidents; they went to hospitals; they fought with each other; they held up gas stations and all-night grocery stores. Women were raped in secluded places, and purses were snatched. Men collapsed and died in the street, and other men were beaten and robbed.

The scanner became almost an addiction in the days that followed. Raphael found that he had to tear himself from the room in order to eat. He wolfed down his food in the small restaurant nearby and hurried back to the winking red lights and the secret world that seethed below the gloomy surface of the city.

Had it lasted much longer, that fascination might have so drugged him that he would no longer have had the will to break the pattern. Late one evening, however, a crippled old man was robbed in a downtown alley. When he attempted to resist, his assailants knifed him repeatedly and then fled. He died on the way to the hospital, and Raphael suddenly felt the cold constriction of fear in his stomach as he listened.

He had believed that his infirmity somehow exempted him from the senseless violence of the streets, that having endured and survived, he was beyond the reach of even the most vicious. He had assumed that his one-leggedness would be a kind of badge, a safe-conduct, as it were, that would permit him to pass safely where others might be open to attack. The sportsmanship that had so dominated his own youth had made it inconceivable to him that there might be any significant danger to anyone as maimed as he. Now, however, he perceived that far from being a guarantee of relative safety, his condition was virtually an open invitation to the jackals who hid in alleys and avoided the light. He didn't really carry that much cash on him, but he was not sure how much money would be considered "a lot." The crippled old man in the alley had probably not been carrying more than a few dollars.

Raphael was unused to fear, and it made him sick and angry. In the days that followed he became wary. He had to go out; hunger alone drove him from the safety of his room. He took care, however, always to go in the daylight and at times when the streets were most crowded.

In time it became intolerable. He realized that even his room was not an absolute sanctuary. It was, after all, on the ground floor and in the back. The front door of the building was not that secure, and his window faced on an unlighted alley. The night was filled with noises—small sounds he had not heard before and that now seemed unspeakably menacing. He slept fitfully and dreamed of the feel of the knives going in. It was not pain that he feared, since for Raphael pain was no longer relevant. It was the indignity of being defenseless, of being forced to submit to violation simply because he would not be able to protect himself that he feared.

It could not go on. He could not continue to let this fear so dominate him that it became the overriding consideration of his life. And so he decided to move, to take himself out of the battle zone, to flee even as Christian had fled from the City of Dreadful Night. And ultimately it was for much the same reason—to save his soul.

There were apartments to be had; the want ads were full of them. He bought a city map and rode the buses, seeking a location, a neighborhood that could offer both convenience and greater security. The newer apartment houses were all too expensive. The insurance settlement and his disability income from Social Security and the policy his father had carried for him provided him with enough to live on if he was careful with his money, but there was not really enough for extravagance. He began to concentrate his search on the north side, beyond the churning turbulence of the river, as if that barrier might somehow hold off the predators who roamed the downtown streets.

It was luck, really, when he found it. The apartment was not listed in the paper, but there was a discreet sign in a downstairs window. The bus he customarily rode had passed it a half-dozen times before he realized that the sign was there. He got off at the next stop and went back, his paces long and measured, and his crutches creaking with each stride.

The building had been a store at one time, wooden-framed, and with living quarters for the owner upstairs. There was a large screened porch across the front of the second floor and five mailboxes beside the bayed-in downstairs door that had at one time been the entrance to the business. The entire structure was somewhat bigger than a large house, and it sat on a corner facing two quiet streets with older houses and bare trees poking up stiffly at the gray winter sky. The roof was flat, and there was a small building up there, windowed on three sides.

"I saw your sign," Raphael said to the T-shirted man who came in answer to his ring. "Do you suppose I could look at the apartment?"

The man scratched his chin doubtfully, looking at the crutches and the single leg. "I don't know, buddy. It's that place up on the roof. Those stairs might give you a problem."

"One way to find out," Raphael said to him.

"You working?" the man asked, and then went on quickly: "Don't get me wrong. I'm not trying to be a shithead, but if you got behind in your rent, I'd look like a real son of a bitch if I tried to kick you out. I had a woman on welfare in here last year who stopped paying her rent. Took me six months to get her out. I had social workers all over me like a rug—called me every dirty name in the book."

"I've got an income," Raphael replied patiently. "Social Security and disability from an insurance policy. They bring in enough to get me

by. Could I look at it?'' He had decided not to mention the railroad
settlement to strangers.

The man shrugged. ''I'll get the key. The stairway's around on the
side.''

The stairway was covered, a kind of long, slanting hallway attached
to the side of the house. There was a solid handrail, and Raphael went
up easily.

''You get around pretty good,'' the man in the T-shirt commented as
he came up and unlocked the door at the top of the stairs.

''Practice.'' Raphael shrugged.

''It's not much of an apartment,'' the man apologized, leading the
way across the roof to a structure that looked much like a small, square
cottage. ''There sure as hell ain't room in there for more than one guy.''

''That much less to take care of.''

It was small and musty, and the dust lay thick everywhere. There
was a moderate-sized living-room/dining-room combination and a
Pullman kitchen in the back with a sink, small stove, and tiny refrigerator. Beside the door sat a table with two chairs. A long sofa sat
against the front wall, and an armchair angled back against one of the
side walls. There were the usual end table and lamps, and solid-looking
but somewhat rough bookcases under the windows.

''The bedroom and bath are through there,'' the man in the T-shirt
said, pointing at a door beside the kitchen.

Raphael crutched to the door and looked in. There was a three-
quarter-size bed, a chair, and a freestanding wardrobe in the bedroom.
The bathroom was small but fairly clean.

''Hotter'n a bitch up here in the summer,'' the man warned him.

''Do all these windows open?'' Raphael asked.

''You might have to take a screwdriver to some of them, but they're
all supposed to open. It's got baseboard electric heat—you pay your
own utilities.'' He quoted a number that was actually twenty-five dollars a month less than what Raphael had been paying at the Barton.
''You'll roast your ass off up here in July, though.''

Raphael, however, was looking out the window at the top of the
stairs. The slanting enclosure that protected the stairs had a solid-
looking door at the top. ''Is there a key to that door?'' he asked.

''Sure.'' The man seemed to have some second thoughts. ''This
won't work for you,'' he declared. ''You got those stairs, and what the
hell are you gonna do when it snows and you gotta wade your way to
the top of the stairway?''

''I'll manage,'' Raphael said, looking around at the dusty furniture
and the dirty curtains over the windows. ''This is what I've been looking for. It'll do just fine. I'll write you a check.''

ii

The landlord's name was Ferguson, and Raphael made arrangements with him to have someone come in and clean the apartment and wash the dusty windows. He also asked Ferguson to get in touch with the phone company for him. Telephones are absolute necessities for the disabled. Back at his hotel he sat down and drew up a careful list of the things he would need—sheets, blankets, towels, dishes, silverware. He estimated the cost and checked the balance in his checkbook. There was enough to carry him through until the first of the month when his checks would begin to arrive from home. Then he went to the pay phone down the hall, called his uncle in Port Angeles to ask him to ship his things to his new address.

"You doing all right, Rafe?" Harry Taylor asked him.

"Fine," Raphael replied, trying to sound convincing. "This downtown area's a little grubby and depressing, but the new place is in a lot nicer neighborhood. How's Mom?"

"About the same."

"Look, Uncle Harry, I've got to run. I've got a lot of things to take care of before I move. You know how that goes."

"Lord yes." Harry Taylor laughed. "I'd rather take a beating than move. Take care of yourself, Rafe."

"You too, Uncle Harry."

The last few nights in the hotel were not so bad. At least he was getting away. The scanner did not seem as menacing now. There was a kind of excitement about it all, and he felt a sense of genuine anticipation for the first time in months.

He moved on a Friday and stopped only briefly at the apartment to have the cabdriver carry up his bags and turn on the heat. Then he had the cab take him to the shopping center at Shadle Park, where there were a number of stores, a branch of his bank, and a supermarket.

The shopping was tiring, but he went at it methodically, leaving packages with his name on them at each store. His last stop was at the supermarket, where he bought such food as he thought he would need to last him out the month. The prices shocked him a bit, but he reasoned that in the long run it would be cheaper than eating in restaurants.

At last, when the afternoon was graying over into evening, he called another cab and waited impatiently in the backseat as the driver picked up each of his purchases.

After the patient cabdriver had carried up the last of the packages and come back down, Raphael climbed to the top of the stairs, stepped out onto the roof, and locked the door behind him with an immense feeling of relief.

"There, you little bastards," he said softly to the city in general, "try to get me now." And then, because the night air was chilly, he hurried inside to the warm brightness that was home. He locked the apartment door and closed all the drapes.

He put a few things away and made the bed. He fixed himself some supper and was pleased to discover that he wasn't that bad a cook, although working in the tiny kitchen was awkward with the crutches. After dinner he unpacked his suitcases and hung his clothes carefully in the wardrobe. It was important to get that done right away. It was all right to live out of a suitcase in a hotel, but this was his home now. Then he bathed and sat finally at his ease in his small living room, secure and warm and very pleased with himself, listening to the scanner murmuring endlessly about the terrors from which he was now safe.

For the first few days there was an enormous satisfaction with being truly independent for the first time in his life. At home and at college there had always been someone else in charge, someone to prepare his meals and to look after him. The hospital, and to a lesser degree the hotels where he had stayed, had been staffed. Now he was alone for the first time and able to make his own decisions and to care for himself.

He puttered a great deal, setting things first here, then there, arranging and rearranging his cupboards and his refrigerator. When his belongings finally arrived from Port Angeles, he dived into them with enthusiasm. He hung up the rest of his clothes and spent hours meticulously sorting and placing his books and the cassettes for his small but quite good tape player in the low bookcases. He rather lovingly ran his fingers over his cassettes—the usual Bach, Beethoven, and Brahms and the later Romantics, as well as a few twentieth-century compositions. He worked to music after that. He kept very busy, and the days seemed hardly long enough for everything he wanted to accomplish. The apartment was small enough so that he could move around quite easily in it, and he felt very comfortable knowing that the door at the top of the stairs was locked and that he had the only key.

And then, after a week, it was done. Everything was arranged to his satisfaction, and he was quite content.

He stood in the center of the room and looked around. "Okay, baby," he said quietly to himself, "what now?" His independence was all very fine, but he finally realized that he didn't have the faintest idea what he was going to do with it. His life suddenly loomed ahead of him in arid and unending emptiness.

To be doing something—anything—he crutched outside onto the roof, although the air was biting and the leaden skies were threatening. It was only midafternoon, but the day seemed already to be fading into a gloom that matched his mood.

A light in the upstairs of the house next door caught his eye, and he glanced at the window. The man in the room was talking animatedly, gesturing with his hands. Several cats sat about the room watching him. He did not appear to be talking to the cats. Something about the man's face seemed strange. Curious, Raphael watched him.

The man turned toward the window, and Raphael looked away quickly, not wanting to be caught watching. He feigned interest in something down over the railing that encircled the roof. The man in the lighted window turned back to the room and continued to talk. Raphael watched him.

After several minutes the iron-cold air began to make him shiver and he went back inside. When he had been about nine, he had developed an interest in birds, and his mother had bought him a pair of binoculars. The interest had waned after a summer, and the seldom-used binoculars had become merely an adjunct, a possession to be moved from place to place. He went into the bedroom and took them down from the top shelf of the wardrobe. He turned out the lights so that he would not be obvious, sat by the window, and focused the glasses on the face of the man next door.

It was a curious face. The mouth was a ruin of missing teeth, and the nose and chin jutted forward as if protecting that puckered vacancy. The eyes were wary, fearful, and moved constantly. It was the hair, however, that began to provide some clue. The man was not bald, at least not entirely. Rather, his head was shaved, but not neatly. There were razor nicks here and there among the short bristles. Two unevenly placed patches of sparse, pale whiskers covered his cheeks. They were not sideburns or any recognizable beard style, but were simply unshaven places.

The strange man suddenly froze, his eyes cast upward, listening. He nodded several times and tried once to speak, but the voice that only he could hear seemed to override him. He nodded again, reached up with both hands, and ran searching fingers over his scalp and face.

"Crazy," Raphael said with almost startled realization. "This whole goddamn town is filled with crazies."

The man in the house next door got out a shaving mug and brush and began stirring up a lather, his face intent. Then he started to slap the lather on his head and face, stopping now and then to listen raptly to instructions or urgings from that private voice. Then he picked up a razor and began to scrape at his head and face. He did not use a mirror, nor did he rinse his razor. He simply shook the scraped-off lather and stubble onto the floor and walls. The cats avoided those flying white globs with expressions of distaste. Lather ran down the man's neck to soak his shirt collar, but he ignored that and kept on scraping. Little rivulets of blood ran from cuts on his scalp and face, but he smiled beatifically and continued.

Raphael watched until his eyes began to burn from the strain of the binoculars. The name "Crazy Charlie" leaped unbidden into his mind, and he watched each new antic with delight. He sat in the dark with the scanner twinkling at him and watched the strange, involved rituals by which Crazy Charlie ordered his life.

Later that night when Charlie had gone to his bed, leaving the lights on, Raphael sat in the dark on his couch listening to the scanner and musing, trying to probe out the reason for each of those ritual acts he had just witnessed. The despair that had fallen over him that afternoon had vanished, and he felt good—even buoyant—though he could not have explained exactly why.

━━◥◤━ iii

And then there were two weeks of snow again, and Raphael was housebound once more. He listened to the scanner, played his music, and read. As Quillian had told him he would, he had reached a certain competence with his crutches and then had leveled off. He could get around, but he was still awkward. Fixing a meal was a major effort, and cleaning his tiny apartment was a two-day project.

"That's when you need to get your ass back to a therapist," Quillian had said. "If you don't, you'll stay right at that point. You'll be a cripple all your life, instead of a guy who happens to have only one leg."

"There's a difference?" Raphael had asked.

"You bet your sweet ass there is, Taylor."

He considered it now. He could put it into the future since there was no way he could go out and wade around in knee-deep snow. It seemed that it would be a great deal of trouble, and he got around well enough to get by. But in his mind he could hear Quillian's contemptuous verdict, "Cripple," and he set his jaw. He was damned if he'd accept that. He decided that he would look up a therapist and start work again—as soon as the snow was gone.

Most of the time he sat and watched Crazy Charlie next door. He had no desire to know the man's real name or background. His imagination had provided, along with the nickname, a background, a personal history, far richer than mundane reality could ever have been. Crazy Charlie had obviously once been a somebody—nobody could have gotten *that* crazy without a certain amount of inspiration. Raphael tried to imagine the kind of pressures that might drive a man to take refuge in the demon-haunted jungles of insanity, and he continued to struggle with the problem of the rituals. There was a haunting kind of justification for each of them, the shaving of the head and face, the avoidance of a certain spot on the floor, the peculiar eating habits, and all the rest. Raphael felt that if he could just make his mind passive enough and merely watch as Charlie expended his days in those ritual acts, sooner or later it would all click together and he would be able to see the logic that linked them all together and, behind that logic, the single thing that had driven poor Charlie mad.

It was enough during those snowy days to sit where it was warm and secure, to listen to music and the scanner with an open book in front of him on the table, and to watch Crazy Charlie. It kept his mind occupied enough to prevent a sudden upsurge of memories. It was very important not to have memories, but simply to live in endless now. Memories were the little knives that could cut him to pieces and the little axes that could chop his orderly existence into rubble and engulf him in a howling, grieving, despairing madness that would make the antics of Crazy Charlie appear to be profoundest sanity by comparison.

In time the snow disappeared. It did not, as it all too frequently does, linger in sodden, stubborn, dirty-white patches in yards and on sidewalks, but rather was cut away in a single night by a warm, wet chinook wind.

There were physical therapists listed in Raphael's phone book, but most of them accepted patients by medical referral only, so he called and made an appointment with an orthopedic surgeon.

It was raw and windy on the day of his appointment, and Raphael turned up the collar of his coat as he waited for the bus. A burly old man strode past, his face grimly determined. He walked very fast, as if he had an important engagement somewhere. Raphael wondered what could be of such significance to a man of that age.

The receptionist at the doctor's office was a motherly sort of lady, and she asked the usual questions, took the name of Raphael's insurance company, and finally raised a point Raphael had not considered. "You're a resident of this state, aren't you, Mr. Taylor?" she asked him. She had beautiful silver-white hair and a down-to-earth sort of face.

"I *think* so," Raphael replied. "I was born in Port Angeles. I was going to college in Oregon when the accident happened, though."

"I'm sure that doesn't change your residency. Most people who come to see the doctor are on one of the social programs. As a matter of fact I think there are all kinds of programs you're eligible for. I know a few of the people at various agencies. Would you like to have me call around for you?"

"I hadn't even thought about that," he admitted.

"You're a taxpayer, Mr. Taylor. You're entitled."

He laughed. "The state didn't make all that much in taxes from me."

"It did from your parents, though. I'll call around and see what I can find out. I can give you a call later, if you'd like."

"I'd appreciate that. Thank you." He signed the forms she handed him and sat down to wait for the doctor. It was good to get out. He had not realized how circumscribed his life had been for the past several weeks.

The doctor examined him and made the usual encouraging remarks about how well he was coming along. Then he made arrangements to enroll him in a program of physical therapy.

Because he still felt good, and because it was still early when he came out of the doctor's office, Raphael rode buses for the rest of the day, looking at the city. Toward late afternoon, miles from where he had first seen him, he saw the burly old man again. The old man's face still had that grimly determined expression, and his pace had not slowed.

In the days that followed, because the scanner and the books and Crazy Charlie were no longer quite enough, Raphael rode buses. For the most part it was simply to be riding—to be doing something, going somewhere. For that reason rather than out of any sense of real need, he called the helpful receptionist.

"I was meaning to get in touch with you, Mr. Taylor," she said. "The people at social services are *very* interested in you."

"Oh?"

"You're eligible for all sorts of things, did you know that? Food stamps, vocational guidance—they'll even pay for your schooling to train you in a new trade."

"I was a student," he told her dryly. "Are they going to make a teacher out of me instead?"

"It's possible—if you want to get a degree in education." Her voice took on a slightly confidential note. "Do you want to know the *real* reason they're so interested in you?" she asked.

"Why's that?"

"Your particular case is complicated enough to provide full-time work for three social workers. I don't really care for those people. Wouldn't it make more sense to just give the money to the people who need it rather than have some girl who's making thousands and thousands of dollars a year dole it out to them in nickels and dimes?"

"A lot more sense, but the girl can't type, so she can't get an honest job."

"I don't quite follow that," she admitted.

"A friend of mine once described a social worker as a girl who can't type."

She laughed. "Would you like to have me give you a few names and phone numbers?"

"I think we might as well drop it," he decided. "It's a little awkward for me to get around."

"Raphael," she said quite firmly, asserting her most motherly authority, "*we* don't go to *them. They* come to *us.*"

"We?"

"You probably didn't notice because I was sitting down when you came in. I'm profoundly arthritic. I've got so many bone spurs that my X rays look like pictures of a cactus. You just call these people, and they'll fall all over themselves to come to your house—at *your* convenience."

"They make house calls?" He laughed.

"They almost have to, Raphael. They can't type, remember?"

"I think I'm in love with you," he joked.

"We might want to talk about that sometime."

Raphael made some calls, being careful not to commit himself. He remembered Shimpsie and wondered if she had somehow put out the social-worker equivalent of an all-points bulletin on him. He was fairly sure that escaping from a social worker was not an extraditable offense, however.

He was certain that the various social agencies could have saved a great deal of time and expense had they sent one caseworker with plenipotentiary powers to deal with one Taylor, Raphael—cripple. He even suggested it a couple of times, but they ignored him. Each agency, it appeared, wanted to hook him and reel him in all on its own.

He began to have a great deal of fun. Social workers are always very careful to conceal the fact, but as a group they have a very low opinion of the intelligence of those whom they call "clients," and no one in this world is easier to deceive and mislead than someone who thinks that he, or in this case, she, is smarter than you are.

They were all young—social workers who get sent out of the office to make initial contacts are usually fairly far down on the seniority scale. They did not, however, appear to have all attended the same school, and each of them appeared to reflect the orientation of her teachers. A couple of them were very keen on "support groups," gatherings of people with similar problems. One very earnest young lady who insisted that he call her Norma even went so far as to pick him up one evening in her own car and take him to a meeting of recent amputees. The amputees spent most of the evening telling horror stories about greater or lesser degrees of addiction to prescription drugs. Raphael felt a chill, remembering Quillian's warning about Dr. Feelgood.

"Well?" Norma said, after the meeting was over and she was driving him home.

"I don't know, Norma," Raphael said with a feigned dubiousness. "I just couldn't seem to relate to those people." (He was already picking up the jargon.) "I don't seem to have that much in common with a guy who got drunk and whacked off his own arm with a chain saw. Now, if you could find a dozen or so one-legged eunuchs—"

Norma refused to speak to him the rest of the way home, and he never saw her again.

Once, just to see how far he could push it, he collected a number of empty wine bottles from the garbage can of two old drunks who lived across the street. He scattered the bottles around on the floor of his apartment for the edification of a new caseworker. *That* particular ploy earned him a week of closely supervised trips to Alcoholics Anonymous meetings.

It stopped being fun at that point. He remembered the club Shimpsie had held over his head at the hospital, and realized just how much danger his innocent-seeming pastime placed him in. Because they had nearly total power over something the client wanted or needed, the caseworkers had equally total power over the client's life. They could—and usually did—use that power to twist and mold and hammer the client into a slot that fit their theories—no matter how half-baked or unrealistic. The client who wanted—needed—the thing the social worker controlled usually went along, in effect becoming a trained ape who could use the jargon to manipulate the caseworker even as she manipulated him. It was all a game, and Raphael decided that he didn't want to play. He didn't really need their benefits, and that effectively placed him beyond their power. He made himself unavailable to them after that.

One, however, was persistent. She was young enough to refuse to accept defeat. She could not be philosophical enough to conclude that some few clients would inevitably escape her. She lurked at odd times on the street where Raphael lived and accosted him when he came home. Her name was Frankie—probably short for Frances—and she was a cute little button. She was short, petite, and her dark hair was becomingly bobbed. She had large, dark eyes and a soft, vulnerable mouth that quivered slightly when someone went counter to her wishes.

"We can't go on meeting this way, Frankie," Raphael said to her one afternoon when he was returning from physical therapy. "The neighbors are beginning to talk."

"Why are you picking on me, Raphael?" she asked, her lip trembling.

"I'm not picking on *you*, Frankie. Actually, I rather like you. It's your profession I despise."

"We're only trying to help."

"I don't need help. Isn't independence one of the big goals? Okay, I've got it. You've succeeded. Would you like to have me paste a gold star on your fanny?"

"Stop that. I'm your caseworker, not some brainless girl you picked up in a bar."

"I don't need a caseworker, Frankie."

"Everybody needs a caseworker."

"Have you got one?"

"But I'm not—" She faltered at that point.

"Neither am I." He had maneuvered her around until her back was against the wall and had unobtrusively shifted his crutches so that they had her blocked more or less in place. It was outrageous and grossly chauvinistic, but Frankie really had it coming. He bent forward slightly and kissed her on top of the head.

Her face flamed, and she fled.

"Always nice talking to you, Frankie," he called after her. "Write if you get honest work."

His therapy consisted largely of physical exercises designed to improve his balance and agility, and swimming to improve his muscle tone. The sessions were tiring, but he persisted. They were conducted in an office building on the near north side of Spokane, and he did his swimming at the YMCA. Both buildings had heavy doors that opened outward and swung shut when they were released. Usually someone was either going in or coming out, and the door would be held open for him. Sometimes, however, he was forced to try to deal with them himself. He learned to swing the door open while shuffling awkwardly backward and then to stop the seemingly malicious closing with the tip of his crutch. Then he would hop through the doorway and try to wrench the crutch free.

Once the crutch was so tightly wedged that he could not free it, and, overbalanced, he fell.

He did not go out again for several days.

He called the grim-faced old man "Willie the Walker," and he saw him in all parts of the city. The walking seemed to be an obsession with Willie. It was what he did to fill his days. He moved very fast and seldom spoke to anyone. Raphael rather liked him.

Then, one day in late March, the letter from Marilyn came. It had been forwarded to him by his uncle Harry. It was quite short, as such letters usually are.

Dear Raphael,

There isn't any easy way to say this, and I'm sorry for that. After your accident I tried to visit you several times, but you wouldn't see me. I wanted to tell you that what had happened to you didn't make any difference to me, but you wouldn't even give me the chance. Then you left town, and I hadn't even had the chance to talk to you at all.

The only thing I could think was that I wasn't very important to you anymore—maybe I never really was. I'm not very smart about such things, and maybe all you really wanted from me was what happened those few times. No matter what, though, it can't go on this way anymore. I can't tie myself to the hope that someday you'll come back.

What it all gets down to, dear Raphael, is that I've met someone else. He's not really very much like you—but then, who could be? He's just a nice, ordinary person, and I think I love him. I hope you can find it in your heart to forgive me and wish me happiness—as I do you.

I'll always remember you—and love you—but I just can't go on hoping anymore.

Please don't forget me,
Marilyn

When he finished the letter, he sat waiting for the pain to begin, for the memories with their little knives to begin on him; but they did not. It was past now. Not even this had any power to hurt him.

His apartment, however, was intolerable suddenly, and although it was raining hard outside, he pulled on his coat and prepared to go down to the bus stop.

For only a moment, just before he went out, there was a racking sense of unspeakable loss, but it passed quickly as he stepped out onto the rain-swept rooftop.

Willie the Walker, grimly determined, strode past the bus stop, the beaded rain glistening on his coat and dripping from the brim of his hat. Raphael smiled as he went by.

Across the street there was another walker, a tall, thin-faced young Indian moving slowly but with no less purpose. The Indian's gait was measured, almost fluidly graceful, and in perhaps a vague gesture toward ethnic pride, he wore moccasins, silent on the pavement. His dark face was somber, even savagely melancholy. His long black hair gleamed wetly in the rain, and he wore a black patch over his left eye.

Raphael watched him pass. The Indian moved on down to the end of the block, turned the corner, and was gone.

It kept on raining.

 iv

By mid-April, the weather had broken. It was still chilly at night and occasionally there was frost; but the afternoons were warm, and the winter-browned grass began to show patches of green. There was a tree in the yard of the house where Crazy Charlie lived, and Raphael watched the leaf buds swell and then, like tight little green fists, slowly uncurl.

He began walking again—largely at the insistence of his therapist. His shirts were growing tight across the chest and shoulders as the muscles developed from the exercises at his therapy sessions and the continuing effort of walking. His stamina improved along with his strength and agility, and he soon found that he was able to walk what before would have seemed incredible distances. While he was out he would often see Willie the Walker and less frequently the patch-eyed Indian. He might have welcomed conversation with either of them, but Willie walked too fast, and Patch, the Indian, was too elusive.

On a sunny afternoon when the air was cool and the trees had almost all leafed out, he was returning home and passed the cluttered yard of a house just up the block from his apartment building. A stout, florid-faced man wheeled up on a bicycle and into the yard. "Hey," he called to someone in the house, "come and get this stuff."

A worn-looking woman came out of the house and stood looking at him without much interest.

"I got some pretty good stuff," the stout man said with a bubbling enthusiasm. "Buncha cheese at half price—it's only a little moldy—and all these dented cans of soup at ten cents each. Here." He handed the woman the bag from the carrier on the bicycle. "I gotta hurry," he said. "They put out the markdown stuff at the Safeway today, an' I wanna get there first before it's all picked over." He turned the bicycle around and rode off. The woman looked after him, her expression unchanged.

Raphael moved on. His own supply of food was low, he knew that, and there was a Safeway store only a few blocks away. He crutched along in the direction the man on the bicycle had gone.

The store was not very large, but it was handy, and the people seemed friendly. The stout man's bicycle was parked out front when Raphael got there.

It was not particularly busy inside as Raphael had feared that it might be, and so he got a shopping cart and, nudging it along the aisles ahead of him with his crutches, he began picking up the items he knew he needed.

Back near the bread department the stout man was pawing through a large basket filled with dented cans and taped-up boxes of cereal. His florid face was intent, and his eyes brightened each time he picked up something that seemed particularly good to him. A couple of old ladies were shamefacedly loitering nearby, waiting for him to finish so that they might have their turns.

Raphael finished his shopping and got into line behind the stout man with his cartful of damaged merchandise. The man paid for his purchases with food stamps and triumphantly carried them out to his bicycle.

"Does he come in often?" Raphael asked the clerk at the cash register.

"Bennie the Bicycler?" the clerk said with an amused look. "All the time. He makes the rounds of every store in this part of town every day. If he'd spend half as much time looking for work as he does looking for bargains, his family could have gotten off welfare years ago." The clerk was a tall man in his mid-thirties with a constantly amused expression on his face.

"Why do you call him that?" Raphael asked, almost startled by the similarity to the little name tags he himself used to describe the people on his block.

The clerk shrugged. "It's a personal quirk," he said, starting to ring up Raphael's groceries. "There's a bunch of regulars who come in here. I don't know their names, so I just call them whatever pops into my mind." He looked around, noting that no one else was in line or standing nearby. "This place is a zoo," he said to Raphael in a confidential tone. "All the weirdos come creeping out of Welfare City over there." He gestured vaguely off in the direction of the large area of run-down housing that lay to the west of the store. "We get 'em all—all the screwballs in town. I've been trying to get a transfer out of this rattrap for two years."

"I imagine it gets depressing after a while."

"That just begins to describe it," the clerk replied, rolling his eyes comically. "Need anything else?"

"No," Raphael replied, paying for his groceries. "Is there someplace where I can call a cab?"

"I'll have the girl do it for you." The clerk turned and called down to the express lane. "Joanie, you want to call a cab?"

"Thanks," Raphael said.

"No biggie. It'll be here in a couple of minutes. Have a good one, okay?"

Raphael nudged his cart over near the door and waited. It felt good to be able to talk with people again. When he had first come out of the hospital, his entire attention had been riveted upon the missing leg, and he had naturally assumed that everyone who saw him was concentrating on the same thing. He began to realize now that after the initial reaction, people were not really that obsessed by it. The clerk had taken no particular notice of it, and the two of them had talked like normal people.

A cab pulled up, and the driver got out, wincing in obvious pain. He limped around the cab as Raphael pushed his cart out of the store. The driver's left foot was in a slipper, and there was an elastic bandage around his grotesquely swollen ankle.

"Oh, man," the driver said, looking at Raphael in obvious dismay. "I *told* that half-wit at dispatch that I couldn't handle any grocery-store calls today."

"What's the problem?"

"I sprained my damn ankle. I can drive okay, but there's no way I could carry your stuff in for you when we get you home. Lemme get on the radio and have 'em send another cab." He hobbled back around the cab again and picked up his microphone. After a couple minutes he came back. "What a screwed-up outfit. Everybody else is tied up. Be at least three quarters of an hour before anybody else could get here. You got stairs to climb?"

"Third floor."

"Figures. Would you believe I did this on a goddamn *skateboard*?" Would you *believe* that shit? My kid was showin' me how to ride the damn thing." He shook his head and then looked across the parking lot at a group of children passing on the sidewalk. "Tell you what. School just let out. I'll knock a buck off the fare, and we'll give the buck to a kid to haul your stuff up for you."

"I could wait," Raphael offered, starting to feel ashamed of his helplessness.

"Naw, you don't wanna stand around for three quarters of an hour. Let's go see if we can find a kid."

They put Raphael's two bags of groceries in the cab and then both got in.

"You know," the driver said, wheeling out of the lot, "if I'd been smart, I'd have called in sick this morning, but I can't afford to lose the time. I wish to hell the bastard who invented skateboards had one shoved up his ass."

Raphael laughed. He still felt good.

They pulled up in front of the apartment house, and the driver looked around. "There's one," he said, looking in the rearview mirror.

The boy was about fourteen, and he wore a ragged denim vest gaudy with embroidery and metal studs. He had long, greasy hair and a smart-sullen sneer on his face. They waited until he had swaggered along the sidewalk to where the cab sat.

"Hey, kid," the driver called to him.

"What?" the boy asked insolently.

"You wanna make a buck?"

"Doin' what?"

"Haul a couple sacks of groceries upstairs."

"Maybe I'm busy."

"Sure you are. Skip it then. There's another kid just up the street."

The boy looked quickly over his shoulder and saw another boy on a bicycle. "Okay. Gimme the dollar."

"*After* the groceries are upstairs."

The boy glowered at him.

Raphael paid the driver and got out of the cab. The boy got the groceries. "These are *heavy*, man," he complained.

"It's just up those stairs." Raphael pointed.

The cab drove off, and the boy looked at Raphael, his eyes narrowing.

"I'll go up first," Raphael told him. "I'll have to unlock the door at the top."

"Let's go, man. I ain't got all day."

Raphael went to the stairs and started up. Halfway to the top, he realized that the boy was not behind him. He turned and went back down as quickly as he could.

The boy was already across the street, walking fast, with the two bags of groceries hugged in his arms.

"Hey!" Raphael shouted at him.

The boy looked back and cackled a high-pitched laugh.

"Come back here!" Raphael shouted, suddenly consumed with an overwhelming fury as he realized how completely helpless he was.

The boy laughed again and kept on going.

"You dirty little son of a bitch!" a harsh voice rasped from the porch of the house directly across the street from Raphael's apartment. A small, wizened man stumbled down the steps from the porch and staggered out to the sidewalk. "You come back here or I'll kick the shit outta ya!"

The boy began to run.

"Goddamn little bastard!" the small man roared in a huge voice. He started to run after the boy, but after a couple dozen steps he staggered again and fell down. Raphael stood grinding his teeth in frustrated anger as he watched the boy disappear around the corner.

The small man lay helplessly on the sidewalk, bellowing drunken obscenities in his huge rasping voice.

 **V**

After several minutes the wizened little man regained his feet and staggered over to where Raphael stood. "I'm sorry, old buddy," he said in his foghorn voice. "I'da caught the little bastard for ya, but I'm just too goddamn drunk."

"It's all right," Raphael said, still trying to control the helpless fury he felt.

"I seen the little sumbitch around here before," the small man said, weaving back and forth. "He's always creepin' up an' down the alleys, lookin' to steal stuff. I'll lay fer 'im—catch 'im one day an' stomp the piss outta the little shit." The small man's face was brown and wrinkled, and there was dirt ingrained in the wrinkles. He had a large, purplish wen on one cheek and a sparse, straggly mustache, pale red— although his short-cropped hair was brown. His eyes had long since gone beyond bloodshot, and his entire body exuded an almost overpoweringly acrid reek of stale wine. His clothes were filthy, and his fly was unzipped. In many ways he resembled a very dirty, very drunk banty rooster.

"Them was your groceries, wasn't they?" the small man demanded.

Raphael drew in a deep breath and let it out slowly. He realized that he was trembling, and that angered him even more. "It doesn't matter," he said, even though it did.

"Was that the last of your money?"

"No."

"I got a idea. I'll go get my truck, an' we'll go look fer that little bastard."

Raphael shook his head. "I think it's too late. We'd never catch him now."

The little man swore.

"I'll have to go back to the store, I guess."

"I'll take you in my truck, an' me'n Sam'll take your groceries upstairs for ya."

"You don't have to do that."

"I know I don't hafta." The little man's voice was almost pugnacious. "I *wanna* do it. You come along with me." He grabbed at

Raphael's arm, almost jerking him off balance. "We're neighbors, god-dammit, an' neighbors oughta help each other out."

At that moment Raphael would have preferred to have been alone. He felt soiled—even ashamed—as a result of the theft, but there was no withstanding the drunken little man's belligerent hospitality. Almost helplessly he allowed himself to be drawn into the ramshackle house across the street.

"My name's Tobe Benson," the small man said as they went up on the creaking porch.

"Rafe Taylor."

They went inside and were met by a furnace blast of heat. The inside of the house was unbelievably filthy. Battered furniture sat in the small, linoleum-floored living room, and the stale wine reek was overwhelming. They went on through to the dining room, which seemed to be the central living area of the house. An old iron heating stove shimmered off heat that seemed nearly solid. The floor was sticky with spilled wine and food, and a yellow dog lay under the table, gnawing on a raw bone. Other bones lay in the corners of the room, the meat clinging to them black with age.

A large gray-haired man sat at the table with a bottle of wine in front of him. He wore dirty bib overalls and a stupefied expression. He looked up, smiling vaguely through his smudged glasses.

"That there's Sam," Tobe said in his foghorn voice. "Sam, this here's Rafe. Lives across the street. Some little punk bastard just stole all his groceries. It's a goddamn shame when a poor crippled fella like Rafe here ain't safe from all the goddamn little thieves in this town."

The man in the overalls smiled stupidly at Raphael, his eyes unfocused. "Hi, buddy," he said, his voice tiny and squeaking.

"Sit down, Rafe," Tobe said, and lurched across to a rumpled bed that sat against the wall opposite the table. He collapsed on the bed, picked up the wine bottle sitting on the floor near it, and took a long pull at it. "You want a drink?" he asked, offering the bottle.

"No. Thanks all the same." Raphael was trying to think of a way to leave without aggravating the little man.

"Hi, buddy," Sam said again, still smiling.

"Hi, Sam," Raphael replied.

Tobe fished around in a water glass he used as an ashtray and found a partially burned cigarette. He straightened it out between his knobby fingers and lit it. Then he looked around the room. "Ain't much of a place," he half apologized, "but we're just a couple ol' bachelors, an' we live the way we want." He slapped the bed he half lay on. "We put this here for when we get too drunk to make it up the stairs to go to bed."

Raphael nodded.

"Hi, buddy," Sam said.

"Don't pay no mind t' ol' Sam there," Tobe said. "He's been on a toot fer three weeks. I'm gonna have t' sober 'im up pretty quick. He's been sittin' right there fer four days now."

Sam smiled owlishly at Raphael. "I'm drunk, buddy," he said.

"He can see that, Sam," Tobe snorted. "Anybody can see that you're drunk." He turned back to Raphael. "We do okay. We both got our pensions, an' we ain't got no bills." He took another drink from his bottle. "Soon's it gets dark, I'll get my truck, an' we'll go on back over to the Safeway so's you can buy more groceries. They took my license away from me eight years ago, so I gotta be kinda careful when I drive."

They sat in the stinking room for an hour or more while Tobe talked on endlessly in his raucous voice. Raphael was able to piece together a few facts about them. They were both retired from the military and had worked for the railroad when they'd gotten out. At one time, perhaps, they had been men like other men, with dreams and ambitions— meaningful men—but now they were old and drunk and very dirty. Their days slid by in an endless stream, blurred by cheap wine. The ambition had long since burned out, and they slid at night not into sleep but into that unconsciousness in which there are no dreams. When they spoke, it was of the past rather than of the future, but they had each other. They were not alone, so it was all right.

After it grew dark, Tobe went out to the garage in back and got out his battered truck. Then he erratically drove Raphael to the supermarket. Raphael did his shopping again, and Tobe bought more wine. Then the little man drove slowly back to their street and, with wobbly steps, carried Raphael's groceries up the stairs.

Raphael thanked him.

"Aw, don't think nothin' about it," Tobe said. "A man ain't no damn good at all if he don't help his neighbors. Anytime you wanna use my truck, ol' buddy, you just lemme know. Anytime at all." Then, stumbling, half falling, he clumped back down the stairs.

Raphael stood on the rooftop, looking over the railing as Tobe weavingly drove his clattering truck around to the alley behind the house across the street to hide it in the garage again.

Alone, with the cool air of the night washing the stench of the two old men from his nostrils, Raphael was suddenly struck with an almost crushing loneliness. The light was on in the upstairs of the house next door, but he did not want to watch Crazy Charlie anymore.

On the street below, alone under the streetlight, Patch, the one-eyed Indian, walked by, his feet making no sound on the sidewalk. Raphael stood on his rooftop and watched him pass, wishing that he might be able to call out to the solitary figure below, but that, of course, was impossible, and so he only watched until the silent Indian was gone.

vi

Sadie the Sitter was an enormously fat woman who lived diagonally across the intersection from Raphael's apartment house. He had seen her a few times during the winter months, but as the weather turned warmer she emerged from her house to survey her domain.

Sadie was a professional sitter; she also sat by inclination. Her throne was a large porch swing suspended from two heavy chains bolted to the ceiling. Each morning, quite early, she waddled onto the porch and plunked her vast bulk into the creaking swing. And there she sat, her piggish little eyes taking in everything that happened on the street, her beet-red face sullen and discontented.

The young parents who were her customers were polite, even deferential, as they delivered their children into her custody each morning. Sadie's power was awesome; and like all power it was economic. If offended, she could simply refuse to accept the child, thus quite effectively eliminating the offending mother's wages for the day. It was a power Sadie used often, sometimes capriciously—just for the sake of using it.

Her hair was a bright, artificial red and quite frizzy, since it was of a texture that accepted neither the dye nor the permanent very well. Her voice was loud and assertive, and could be heard clearly all over the neighborhood. She had, it seemed, no neck, and her head swiveled with difficulty atop her massive shoulders. She ate continually with both hands, stuffing the food into her mouth.

Sadie's husband was a barber, a thin man with a gray face and a shuffling, painful gait. The feelings that existed between them had long since passed silent loathing and verged now on open hostility. Their arguments were long and savage and were usually conducted at full volume. Their single child, a scrawny girl of about twelve, was severely retarded, physically as well as mentally, and she was kept in a child's playpen on the porch, where she drooled and twitched and made wounded-animal noises in a bull-like voice.

Sadie's mother lived several houses up the street from her, and in good weather she waddled each morning about ten down the sidewalk in slapping bedroom slippers and a tent-like housecoat to visit. Sadie's mother was also a gross woman, and she lived entirely for her grandchildren, a raucous mob of bad-mannered youngsters who gathered in her front yard each afternoon when school let out to engage in interminable games of football or tag or hide-and-seek with no regard for flower beds or hedges while Granny sat on her rocker in bloated contentment like a mother spider, ready to pounce ferociously upon any neighbor with the temerity to protest the rampant destruction of his property.

At first Raphael found the entire group wholly repugnant, then gradually, almost against his will, he began to develop a certain fascination. The greed, the gluttony, and the naked, spiteful envy of Sadie and her mother were so undisguised that they seemed not so much to be human, but were rather vast, primal forces—embodiments of those qualities—allegorical distillations of all that is meanest in others.

"She thinks she's so much," Sadie sneered to her mother. "She has all them delivery trucks come to her house like that on purpose—just to spite her neighbors. I could buy new furniture, too, if I wanted, but I got better things to do with my money."

"Are you Granny's little love?" Sadie's mother cooed at the idiot. The child drooled and bellowed at her hoarsely.

"Don't get her started, for God's sake," Sadie said irritably. "It takes all day to quiet her down again." She glanced quickly at her mother with a sly look of malice. "She's gettin' too hard to handle. I think it's time we put her in a home."

"Oh no," her mother protested, her face suddenly assuming a helplessly hurt look, "not Granny's little darling. You couldn't *really* do that."

"She'd be better off," Sadie said smugly, satisfied that she had injured her mother's most vulnerable spot once again. The threat appeared to be a standard ploy, since it came up nearly every time they visited together.

"How's *he* doing?" Sadie's mother asked quickly, changing the subject in the hope of diverting her daughter's mind from the horrid notion of committing the idiot to custodial care. As always, the "he" referred to Sadie's husband. They never used his name.

"His veins are breakin' down," Sadie replied, gloating. "His feet and hands are cold all the time, and sometimes he has trouble gettin' his breath."

"It's a pity." Her mother sighed.

Sadie snorted a savage laugh, reaching for another fistful of potato chips. "Don't worry," she said. "I keep his insurance premiums all paid up. I'll be a rich woman one of these days real soon."

"I imagine it's a terrible strain on him—standing all the time like that."

Sadie nodded, contentedly munching. "All his arteries are clogged almost shut," she said smugly. "His doctor says that it's just a question of time until one of them blows out or a clot of that gunk breaks loose and stops his heart. He could go at any time."

"Poor man," her mother said sadly.

"Soon as it happens, I'm gonna buy *me* a whole buncha new furniture." Sadie's tone was dreamy. "An' I'm gonna have all them delivery trucks pullin' up in fronta *my* house. *Then* watch them people down the street just wither up an' blow away. Sometimes I just can't hardly wait."

*   *   *

Raphael turned and went back into his little apartment. Walking was not so bad, but simply standing grew tiring after a while, and the phantom ache in the knee and foot that were no longer there began to gnaw at him.

He sat on the couch and turned on the scanner, more to cover the penetrating sound of Sadie's voice than out of any real interest in morning police calls. A little bit of Sadie went a long way.

It was a problem. As the summer progressed the interior of the apartment was likely to become intolerably hot. He knew that. He would be driven out onto the roof for relief. The standing would simply bring on the pain, and the pain would drive him back into the apartment again. He needed something to sit on, a bench, or a chair or something like Sadie's swing.

He checked his phone book, made some calls, and then went down to catch a bus.

The Goodwill store was a large building with the usual musty-smelling clothes hanging on pipe racks and the usual battered furniture, stained mattresses, and scarred appliances. It had about it that unmistakable odor of poverty that all such places have.

"You've come about the job," a pale girl with one dwarfed arm said as he crutched across toward the furniture.

"No," he replied. "Actually, I came to buy a chair."

"I'm sorry. I just assumed—" She glanced at his crutches and blushed furiously.

"What kind of a job is it?" he asked, more to help her out of her embarrassment than out of any real curiosity.

"Shoe repair. Our regular man is moving away."

"I wouldn't be much good at that."

"You never know until you try." She smiled shyly at him. Her face seemed somehow radiant when she smiled. "If you're really looking for something to do, it might not hurt to talk with Mrs. Kiernan."

"I don't really need a job. I've got insurance and Social Security." It was easy to talk with her. He hadn't really talked with one of his own kind since the last time he'd spoken with Quillian.

"Most of us *do* have some kind of coverage," she said with a certain amount of spirit. "Working here makes us at least semiuseful. It's a matter of dignity—not money."

Because he liked her, and because her unspoken criticism stung a little, he let her lead him back to the small office where a harassed-looking woman interviewed him.

"We don't pay very much," she apologized, "and we can't guarantee you any set number of hours a week or anything like that."

"That's all right," Raphael told her. "I just need something to do, that's all."

She nodded and had him fill out some forms. "I'll have to get it cleared," she said, "but I don't think there'll be any problem. Suppose I call you in about a week."

He thanked her and went back out into the barnlike salesroom. The girl with the dwarfed arm was waiting for him. "Well?" she asked.

"She's going to call me," Raphael told her.

"Did she have you fill out any forms?"

He nodded.

"You're in then," she said with a great deal of satisfaction.

"Do you suppose I could look at some chairs now?" Raphael asked, smiling.

 **vii**

His world quite suddenly expanded enormously. The advent of the chair enabled him to see the entire neighborhood in a way he had not been able to see it before. Because standing had been awkward and painful, he had not watched before, but the chair made it easier—made it almost simpler to watch than not to watch. It was a most serviceable chair—an old office chair of gray metal mounted on a squat, four-footed pedestal with casters on the bottom. It had sturdy arms and a solid back, and there were heavy springs under the seat that enabled him to rock back to alter his position often enough to remain comfortable. The addition of a pillow provided the padding necessary to protect the still-sensitive remains of his left hip. The great thing about it was that it rolled. With his crutches and his right leg, he could easily propel himself to any spot on the roof and could watch the wonderful world expanding on the streets below.

Always before they had seemed to be quiet streets of somewhat run-down houses only in need of a nail here, a board there, some paint and a general squaring away. Now that winter had passed, however, and the first warm days of spring had come, the people who lived on the two streets that intersected at the corner of the house where he lived opened their doors and began to bring their lives outside where he could watch them.

Winter is a particularly difficult time for the poor. Heat is expensive, but more than that, the bitter cold drives them inside, although their natural habitat is outside. Given the opportunity, the poor will conduct most of the business of their lives out-of-doors, and with the arrival of spring they come out almost with gusto.

"Fuckin" bastard." It was an Indian girl who might have been twenty-three but already looked closer to forty. Her face was a ruin, and her arms and shoulders were covered with crudely done tattoos. She cursed loudly but without inflection, without even much interest, as if she already knew what the outcome of the meeting was going to be. There was a kind of resignation about her swearing. She stood swaying drunkenly on the porch of the large house two doors up from Tobe and Sam's place, speaking to the big, tense-looking man on the sidewalk.

"That's fine," the tense man said. "You just be out of here by tomorrow morning, that's all."

"Fuckin' bastard," she said again.

"I'll be back with the sheriff. He'll by God *put* you out. I've had it with you, Doreen. You haven't paid your rent in three months. That's it. Get out."

"Fuckin' bastard."

A tall, thin Negro pushed out of the house and stood behind the girl. He wore pants and a T-shirt, but no shoes. "Look here, man," he blustered. "You can't just kick somebody out in the street without no place to go."

"Watch me. You got till tomorrow morning. You better sober her up and get her ass out of here." He turned and started back toward his car.

"You're in trouble, man," the Negro threatened. "I got some real mean friends."

"Whoopee," the tense man said flatly. He got into the car.

The Indian girl glowered at him, straining to find some insult sufficient for the occasion. Finally she gave up.

"Fuckin' bastard," she said.

"Oh, my God!" the fat woman trundling down the sidewalk exclaimed. "Oh, my God!" She was very fair-skinned and was nearly as big as Sadie the Sitter. Her hair was blond and had been stirred into some kind of scrambled arrangement at the back of her head. The hair and her clothes were covered with flecks of lint, making her look as if she had slept in a chicken coop.

She clutched a tabloid paper in her hand and had an expression of unspeakable horror on her face. "Oh, my God!" she said again to no one in particular. "Did you see this?" she demanded of Sadie the Sitter, waving the paper.

"What is it?" Sadie asked without much interest.

"Oh, my God!" the woman Raphael had immediately tagged "Chicken Coop Annie" said. "It's just awful! Poor Farrah's losin' her hair!"

"Really?" Sadie said with a faint glint of malicious interest. Sadie was able to bear the misfortunes of others with great fortitude.

"It says so right here," Chicken Coop Annie said, waving the paper again. "I ain't had time to read it yet, but it says right here in the headline that she's losin' her hair. I just hadda bring it out to show to everybody. Poor Farrah! Oh, poor, poor Farrah!"

"I seen it already," Sadie told her.

"Oh." Annie's face fell. She stood on the sidewalk, sweating with disappointment. "Me 'n her got the same color hair, you know," she ventured, putting one pudgy hand to her tangled hairdo.

"That so?" Sadie sounded unconvinced.

"I gotta go tell Violet."

"Sure." Sadie looked away.

Annie started off down the street.

"Oh, my God!" she said.

Their cars broke down continually, and there were always a half dozen or so grimy young men tinkering with stubbornly exhausted iron brutes at the curbs or in the alleys. And when the cars did finally run, it was at best haltingly with a great deal of noise and smoke, and they left telltale blood trails of oil and transmission fluid on the streets behind them.

They lost their money or their food stamps, and most of the men were in trouble of one kind or another. Each time a police car cruised through the neighborhood, back doors slammed all up and down the street, and furtive young men dashed from the houses to run down the alleys or jump fences and flee through littered backyards.

Raphael watched, and gradually he began to understand them. At first it was not even a theory, but rather a kind of intuition. He found that he could look at any one of them and almost smell the impending crisis. That was the key word—crisis. At first it seemed too dramatic a term to apply to situations resulting from their bumbling mismanagement of their lives or deliberate wrongheaded stupidity, but they themselves reacted as if these situations were in fact crises. If, for example, a live-in boyfriend packed up and moved out while the girl in question was off at the grocery store, it provided her with an irresistible opportunity to play the role of the tragic heroine. Like a Greek chorus, her friends would dutifully gather around her, expressing shock and dismay. The young men would swagger and bluster and leap into their cars to go importantly off in search of the runaway, forming up like a posse and shouting instructions to each other over the clatter of their sick engines. The women would gather about the bereaved one, commiserating with her, supporting her, and admiring her performance. After a suitable display of grand emotion—cries, shrieks, uncontrollable sobbing, or whatever she considered her most dramatic response—the heroine would lapse into a stoic silence, her head nobly lifted, and her face ravaged by the unspeakable agony she was suffering. Her friends would caution each other wisely that several of them at least would have to stay with her until all danger of suicide was past. Such situations usually provided several days of entertainment for all concerned.

Tobe was roaring drunk again. He staggered out into the yard bellowing curses and waving his wine bottle. Sam came out of the house and stood blearily on the porch wringing his hands and pleading with the little man to come back inside.

Tobe turned and cursed him savagely, then collapsed face-down in the unmowed grass and began to snore.

Sam stumbled down off the porch, and with an almost maternal tenderness, he picked up the sleeping little man and bore him back into the house.

Mousy Mary lived in the house on the corner directly opposite Raphael's apartment and right beside Tobe and Sam's house. She was a slight girl with runny eyes and a red nose and a timid, almost furtive walk. She had two children, a girl of twelve or so and a boy about ten. Quite frequently she would lock herself and her children in the house and not come out for several days. Her telephone would ring unanswered, sometimes for hours.

And then a woman Raphael assumed was her mother would show up. Mousy Mary's mother was a small, dumpy woman with a squinting, suspicious face. She would creep around Mary's house trying all the doors and windows. Then she would return to her car and drive slowly up and down the streets and alleys, stopping to jot down the license numbers of all the cars in the neighborhood. Once she had accomplished that, she would find a suitable spot and stake out the house, sometimes for as long as a day and a night. The blinds in Mousy Mary's house would move furtively from time to time, but other than that there would be no sign that anyone was inside. When it grew dark, no lights would come on, and Raphael could imagine Mary crouching in the dark with her children, hiding from her mother.

"I wonder if I might use your telephone," Mousy Mary's mother said to Sadie one afternoon.

"What's the problem?" Sadie asked.

"I have to call the police," the old woman said in a calm voice that seemed to indicate that she had to call the police quite frequently. "Somebody's holding my daughter and her children hostage in her house there."

"How do you know?" Sadie sounded interested.

"I've checked all the evidence," Mousy Mary's mother said in a professional tone. "There's some tiny little scratch marks around the keyhole of the back door. It's obvious that the lock's been picked."

"That so?"

"Happens all the time. They'll probably have to call out the SWAT team." Mousy Mary's mother's voice was dry, unemotional.

In time the police arrived, and after they talked with Mousy Mary's mother for a few minutes, one of them went up on the front porch and knocked. Mousy Mary answered the door immediately and let them in, but she closed the door quite firmly in her mother's face. In a fury the dumpy little woman scurried around the house, trying to look in the windows.

After a while the police came out and drove away. Mousy Mary's mother stomped up onto the front porch and began pounding on the door, but Mary refused to open it.

Eventually, the dumpy woman returned to her car and continued her surveillance.

"Couldn't you at least look into it, Raphael—for me?" Frankie's lower lip trembled.

Raphael, sitting in his chair on the roof where they were talking, rather thought he might like to nibble on that lip for a while. He pushed that thought away. "I was a student, Frankie," he said. "I can still do that. I don't need both legs to study."

"Our records show that you were a worker in a lumber mill."

"That was a summer job back home when I was in high school and junior college. It wasn't a lifelong career."

"I'm really going to get yelled at if I don't get you into vocational rehabilitation," she told him. "And there are support groups—people to see and to talk to."

"I've got a whole street full of people to see, Frankie." He waved his hand at the intersection. "And if I want to talk with somebody, I can talk with Tobe and Sam."

"But they're just a couple of old alcoholics. We gave up on them years ago."

"I'll bet they appreciated that."

"Couldn't you at least *consider* vocational rehab, Raphael?"

"Tell you what, Frankie." He smiled at her. "Go back to the office and tell them that I've already chosen a new career and that I'm already working at it."

Her eyes brightened. "What kind of career are we talking about here, Raphael?"

"I'm going to be a philosopher. The pay isn't too good, but it's a very stimulating line of work."

"Oh, *you*," she said, and then she laughed. "You're impossible." She looked out over the seedy street. "It's nice up here." She sighed. "You've got a nice breeze."

"I sort of like it."

"Wouldn't you consider the possibility of shoe repair?" she asked him.

That was startling. He remembered the Goodwill store and the girl with the dwarfed arm. Coincidence, perhaps? Some twist of chance? But the prophet on the downtown street had said that there was no such thing as chance. But what had made the words "shoe repair" cross Frankie's trembling lips? It was something to ponder.

*   *   *

It was not that they were really afraid of him. It was merely that there was something so lost, so melancholy about his dark face as he walked with measured pace and slow down the shabby streets that all sound ceased as he passed. They did not mention it to each other or remark about it, but each time Patch, the one-eyed Indian, walked by, there was an eerie hush on the street. They watched him and said nothing. Even the children were still, suspended, as it were, by the silent, moccasin-footed passage of the dark, long-haired man with the black patch over one eye.

Raphael watched also, and was also silent.

And then in a troop, a large, rowdy group of more or less young men and, with a couple of exceptions, younger women moved into the big old house from which the tattooed Indian girl and her black boyfriend had been evicted.

They were nearly a week moving in, and their furniture seemed to consist largely of mattresses and bedding. They arrived in battered cars from several different directions, unloaded, and then drove off for more. They were all, for the most part, careful to be away when the large, tense-appearing man who owned the house stopped by. Only the oldest woman and her five children—ranging in age from nine or ten up to the oldest boy who was perhaps twenty—remained.

After the landlord left, however, they would return and continue moving in. When they were settled, the motorcycles arrived. In the lead was a huge man with a great, shaggy beard who wore a purple-painted German helmet. The front wheel of his bike was angled radically out forward, and his handlebars were so high that he had to reach up to hold them. Two other motorcycles followed him, one similarly constructed and ridden by a skinny, dark-haired man in a leather vest, and the other a three-wheeled affair with a wide leather bench for a seat and ridden by another thin fellow, this one with frizzy blond hair and wearing incredibly filthy denims. None of the motorcycles appeared to be equipped with anything re-motely resembling a muffler, and so the noise of their passage was deafening.

After they dismounted, they swaggered around in front of the house for a while, glowering at the neighborhood as if daring any comment or objection, then they all went inside. One of the young men was sent out in his clattering car and came back with beer. Then they settled down to party.

Their motorcycles, Raphael observed in the next several days, were as unreliable as were most of the cars on the block. They bled oil onto the lawn of the big old house, and at least one of them was usually partially or wholly dismantled.

With the exception of the big, bearded man in the German helmet, whom they respectfully called Heintz, the bikers for the most part appeared to be a scrawny bunch, more bluster than real meanness. In his mental catalog Raphael dubbed the group "Heck's Angels."

At his ease, sitting in his chair on the roof, Raphael watched them. From watching he learned of the emotions and turmoil that produced the dry, laconic descriptions that came over the police radio. He learned that a family fight was not merely some mild domestic squabble, but involved actual physical violence. He learned that a drunk was not simply a slightly tipsy gentleman, but someone who had either lapsed into a coma or who was so totally disoriented that he was a danger to himself or to others. He learned that a fight was not just a couple of people exchanging a few quick punches, but usually involved clubs, chains, knives, and not infrequently axes.

As his understanding, his intuition, broadened and deepened—as he grew to know them better—he realized that they were losers, habitual and chronic.

Their problems were not the result of temporary setbacks or some mild personality defect, but seemed rather to derive from some syndrome—a kind of social grand mal with which they were afflicted and which led them periodically to smash up their lives in a kind of ecstatic seizure of deliberate self-destruction.

And then they were taken over by the professional caretakers society hires to pick up the pieces of such shattered lives. Inevitably, the first to arrive were the police. It seemed that the police were charged with the responsibility for making on-the-spot decisions about which agency was then to take charge—social services, mental health, the detoxification center, child protective services, the courts, or on occasion the coroner. Society was quite efficient in dealing with its losers. It was all very cut and dried, and everyone seemed quite comfortable with the system. Only occasionally did one of the losers object, and then it was at best a weak and futile protest—a last feeble attempt at self-assertion before he relaxed and permitted himself to be taken in hand.

Raphael was quite pleased with his theory. It provided him with a convenient handle with which to grasp what would have otherwise been a seething and incomprehensible chaos on the streets below.

And then Patch went by again, followed by that strange hush that seemed always to fall over the neighborhood with his passage, and Raphael was not so sure of the theory. Into which category did Patch fit? He was totally unlike the others—an enigma whose dark, melancholy presence seemed somehow to disturb the losers as much as it did Raphael. Sometimes, after he had passed, Raphael felt that if he could only talk with the man—however briefly—it might all fit together, the whole thing might somehow fall into place. But Patch never stopped, never looked up, and was always gone before Raphael could call to him or do anything more than note his silent passage.

Omnia Sol temperat puris et subtilis

i

In the end Raphael took the job at Goodwill Industries more because he could find no reason not to than out of any real desire to work. The sour hunchback who was moving to Seattle to live with his sister taught him the rudiments of shoe repair and then, without a word, got up and left. "Don't worry about Freddie," the pale girl with the dwarfed right arm said to him. "He's been like that ever since his family ganged up on him and made him agree to move to Seattle."

The girl seemed always to be hovering near the bench where Raphael worked, and her concern for him seemed at times almost motherly. She was a very fair young woman with long, ash-blond hair and a face that was almost, but not quite, pretty. Her name was Denise, and Raphael forced himself to think of her as Denise to avoid attaching a tag name to her as he had to all the sad losers on his block. A nickname for Denise would be too obvious and too cruel. Denise was a real person with real dignity, and she was not a loser. She deserved to be recognized as a person, not oversimplified into a grotesque by being called "Flipper," even in the hidden silences of his mind.

The dwarfed arm bothered him at first, but he soon came to accept it. Although it was somewhat misshapen and awkward, and the tiny knuckles and fingers seemed always chapped and raw as if it had been brutally windburned, it was not a totally useless appendage. Denise wrote with it and was able to hold things with it, although she could not carry much weight on that side.

There were others who worked at Goodwill also, assorted defectives, the maimed, the halt, the marginally sighted, dwarves, and some who seemed quite normal until you spoke with them and realized that anything more than the simplest tasks was beyond their capabilities. They were not, however, losers. Common among them was that stubborn resolve to be independent and useful. Raphael admired them for that, and wished at times that he could be more like them. His own work record, he realized, was spotty. There were days when he had to go to therapy, of course, but there were other days as well, bad days when the phantom ache in thigh and knee and foot made work impossible, and other days when he deliberately malingered simply to avoid the tedium of the long bus ride to work.

On one such day, a fine, bright day in late April when the trees were dusting the streets with pale green pollen and the air was inconceivably bright and clear, he called in with his lame apologies and then crutched out to his chair and his roof to watch the teeming losers on the streets below.

"Try the son of a bitch again," Jimmy, one of the scruffier of Heck's Angels, called from under the hood of a battered Chevy convertible parked on the lawn of the house up the street.

The car's starter ground spitefully, but the engine refused to turn over.

"Ain't no use, man," Marvin, the frizzy-haired blond one sitting in the car, said. "The bastard ain't gonna start."

"Just a minute." Jimmy crawled a little farther into the engine compartment. "Okay, now try it."

The starter ground again, sounding weaker.

Big Heintz came out on the porch holding a can of beer. "You're just runnin' down the battery," he told them. "Give it up. The fucker's gutted."

Jimmy came out from under the hood, his face desperate. "It's *gotta* run, man. I *gotta* have wheels. A guy ain't shit if he ain't got no fuckin' wheels."

"The fucker's gutted," Heintz said again with a note of finality.

"What am I gonna *do*, man?" Jimmy's voice was anguished. "I *gotta* have wheels."

"Start savin' your nickels," Heintz suggested, and laughed.

"Dirty useless son of a bitch!" Jimmy yelled at his car in helpless fury. He kicked savagely at one of the tires, winced, and then began to pound on one of the front fenders with a wrench. "Bastard! Bastard! Bastard!" he raged.

Marvin went up and joined Heintz on the porch, and the two of them stood watching Jimmy pound on his car with the wrench. Finally he gave up and threw the wrench down. There were tears on his face when he turned toward the two men on the porch. "What am I gonna *do*, man?" he demanded. "I *gotta* have wheels. Maybe Leon can fix it."

Big Heintz shook his head and belched. "Forget it, man. Nobody can fix that pig. The fucker's gutted."

Jimmy's shoulders slumped in defeat. "I *gotta* have wheels. I just *gotta.*"

The idea had not really occurred to Raphael before. His injury had seemed too final, too total, and he had resigned himself to using public transportation, but now he began to consider the possibility. Driving, after all, was *not* really impossible. You only needed one leg to drive. The memory of the crash was still there, of course, but it was not something insurmountable. The more he thought about it, the more possible it all seemed.

He went back into his apartment and methodically began to draw up a list. The amount he would spend on buses and taxi fare in the course of a year surprised him, and when he added to that the wages he would lose on those days when the decision to go to work or not was weighted by his distaste for the bus ride, the number began to approach a figure he might reasonably expect to pay for reliable transportation.

He decided to think about it some more, but that evening he bought a newspaper and checked the used-car section of the want ads.

More than anything, what he wanted was a sense of independence. He had not particularly missed it before because he had not even considered the possibility of driving again, but now it became a matter of urgent necessity. "I *gotta* have wheels," he said to himself in a wry imitation of Jimmy's anguished voice. "I just *gotta*."

The car was adequate—not fancy, certainly—but it had been well maintained, and the price was right. He was startled to discover how nervous he was when he test-drove it. By the time he had gone three blocks, he was sweating, and his hands were shaking. He had not thought that he would be so afraid. He set his teeth together and forced himself to continue driving.

After he had paid for it and brought it home, he went out onto his roof quite often to look down at it. He did not drive it to work or to his therapy sessions yet, but concentrated on growing accustomed to it and to driving in traffic again. The fear was still there, but he drove a little farther every day and inserted himself carefully into heavier and heavier traffic. His accident had made a cautious driver of him, but he managed to get around, and he finally worked up enough nerve to drive it to work.

Because Denise lived on the same bus route as he, they had usually ridden together when they got off work. On that first night, however, realizing that he was showing off his new toy, he gave her a lift home.

"Why don't you come up?" she suggested hesitantly when he pulled up in front of her apartment house. "I'll make a pot of coffee." She blushed and turned her face away.

"Could I take a raincheck on it? I have to go grocery shopping tonight, and it takes me hours."

"Oh," she said quickly, "sure. Maybe next time."

"You can count on it."

She got out of the car. "See you in the morning, then. Thanks for the ride." She closed the door and hurried across the sidewalk to her apartment building.

The shopping had been a lie, of course, but Raphael had not wanted to become involved in anything just yet. The implication of the invitation might have been wholly imaginary, but it was the kind of thing that he had to avoid at all costs. Still, he was just a bit ashamed of himself as he drove home.

Flood was waiting for him when he got there. "Where the hell have you been?" he demanded, leaning against the rear fender of his little red sports car with his arms crossed, "and what the hell are you doing in Spokane, for God's sake?" His tone was matter-of-fact, as if they had seen each other only the week before.

Raphael crutched toward him, feeling a sudden surge of elation. He had not realized until that moment how desperately lonely he had been. "Damon! What are you doing here?"

Flood shrugged, his eyes strangely hard and his smile ambiguous. "The world is wide, my Angel," he said, "but there are only a few places in it where my face is welcome." The rich baritone voice, so well remembered, with all its power to sway him, to persuade, to manipulate him, had lost none of its force. Raphael immediately felt its pull upon him.

One of Heck's Angels roared by, his motorcycle sputtering and coughing. "Come on upstairs." Raphael was suddenly aware of the curious eyes of the people on the street, and he did not want to share Flood with any of them. He led the way to the stairs at the side of the house, and they went up.

"A penthouse, no less," Flood noted when they reached the roof.

"Hardly that." Raphael laughed. "More like a pigeon loft." They went on inside. "Sit down," Raphael told him. "I'll make some coffee." He needed something to do to cover his confusion, to get him past that first stiff awkwardness that was always there when he met someone again after a long time. He was quite suddenly painfully aware of his one-leggedness and particularly anxious that Flood should not think of him as a cripple, so he made a special show of his competence, even though he was aware at the time that it was childish to do so.

Flood had not changed much. His skin was a bit sallower, and there were circles under his eyes that had not been there before. His grin was still sardonic, and his eyes still had that same hard glitter, but he seemed less sure of himself, almost ill at ease, as if he had somehow lost control of his life or something important had gotten away from him.

"Why aren't you in school?" Raphael asked, filling his coffeepot at the sink.

"I dropped out at midterm," Flood replied, sitting on the couch. "The Reed experience got to be a bit overpowering. Scholarship was never one of my strong points."

"How did your father take that?"

"He was moderately unenthusiastic—until I assured him that I wasn't coming home to dear old Grosse Pointe. We struck a bargain. The old pirate will keep those checks coming as long as I stay west of the Mississippi. It's a pretty good working arrangement."

Raphael put the pot on and then crutched over to the armchair. "How did you find me?"

Flood shrugged. "It wasn't that hard. I stopped by the hospital after Christmas vacation, but you'd already left. I talked with some of the nurses and that bald guy in the wheelchair."

"Quillian?"

Flood nodded. "There's a man with all the charm of a nesting rattlesnake."

"He's rough," Raphael agreed, suddenly remembering all the sweating hours in therapy under the lash of Quillian's contemptuous voice, "but he's damn good at his job. You might not want to walk when he starts on you, but you're damn well walking when he gets done."

"If only to get away from him. Anyway, I finally wound up in the administration office. I seduced the name of your uncle in Port Angeles out of one of the file clerks—blew in her ear, that sort of thing. You really don't want all the sordid details, do you?"

"Spare me."

"Sure. Anyhow, I filed Port Angeles away for future reference, and then after I hung it up at Reed, I drifted on up to Seattle. There was a girl who got fed up with the Reed experience about the same time I did. We got along—for a while, anyway. I was thinking about San Francisco, but she convinced me that we'd have a ball in Boeing City. We went on up and set up housekeeping for a month or so. It didn't work out, so I pulled the plug on her."

"You're still all heart, Damon."

"I improved her life. I taught her that there are more important things in the world than rock concerts and political theory. Now she's got a deep and tragic affair in her past. It'll make her more interesting for the next guy. God knows she bored the hell out of me." Flood had been speaking in a dry, almost monotonous tone with few of the flashes of that flowery extravagance Raphael remembered from the days when they had roomed together. The feeling was still there that something had gone out of him somehow, or that he had suffered some obscure and hidden injury that still gnawed at him. "I knocked around Seattle for a while," he went on, "and then I decided to take a quick run up to Port Angeles to see how you were doing."

"What made you think I'd be there?"

Flood shrugged. "It just seemed reasonable. That's your home. I just had it in my mind that you were there. It seemed quite logical at the time."

"You should have called first."

"You know, your uncle Harry told me exactly the same thing. Anyway, after I found out that I was wrong and got your address here from him, I took a quick turn around Port Angeles and then bombed on over. Once I set out to do something, I by God do it. I'd have followed you all the way to hell, my friend."

"What did you think of Port Angeles?"

"Would you accept picturesque?"

"You were unimpressed."

"Moderately. I don't want to offend you, but that is one of the gloomiest places I've ever had the misfortune to visit."

"It was raining, I take it."

"It was, and you can. I get the impression that it rains there about ninety percent of the time."

Raphael got up and poured two cups of coffee. Flood came over to him and took one. "I don't imagine you've got anything to drink?" he asked.

"Water."

"I'm thirsty, Raphael, not dirty. I'll go pick something up in a bit." He went back to the couch. "So much for the expedition of J. D. Flood, Junior. How are *you* doing? And what the hell are you doing in Spokane, of all places?"

"I'm adjusting. I suppose that answers both questions, really. I had to get away from Portland, so I took the first bus to anyplace. I wound up here. It's as good as anyplace for what I have to do at the present time."

"This is just temporary then?" Flood was looking intently at Raphael.

"Everything's temporary, Damon. Nothing's permanent."

"Have you been reading Kierkegaard again?"

Raphael grinned at him. "Sorry about that. Quillian told me that I had a choice between being a cripple or a man who happened to only have one leg. I decided not to be a cripple. I'm in physical therapy right now, but it takes a while to get it all put together. Spokane's a good place to do that. There aren't many distractions."

"You can say that again. From what I've seen this is the *least* distracting place in the whole damned world."

"What's got you so down, Damon?" Raphael asked bluntly, trying to get past that seeming reserve.

"I don't know, Raphael." Flood leaned back and looked at the ceiling. "I'm at sixes and sevens, I guess. I haven't really decided what to do with myself. I think I need a diversion of some kind."

"Have you thought of work?"

"Don't be insulting."

"How long are you planning to be in town?"

"Who knows? Who knows?" Flood spread his hands. "I've got a motel room downtown—if I can ever find it again. I'm paid up for a week. I don't have to make any decisions until then." He got up quickly. "Goddammit, I need a drink. I'm going to go find a boozeria. You'll be here?"

"Until the end of the month at least. My rent's paid up, too."

"Don't be snide. I'll be back in a little bit." He crossed the small room and went out.

It was strange—even unreal. Even with the sound of Flood's

footsteps going down the stairs, it seemed almost as if he had not really been there. Something had happened to Flood since they had last talked. Something had somehow shaken that enormous self-confidence of his. Even his presence here had seemed in some way tentative, as if he were not really sure that he would be welcome. And why had he come at all? His motives were unclear.

Raphael crutched out onto the roof and to the railing at the front of the house. Flood's little red car was pulling away from the curb, its engine snarling, and across the street Patch stood watching with a strange expression on his somber face.

━━━ **ii**

By the end of the week Raphael had become accustomed to Flood's presence again, and Flood's moody abstraction seemed to be letting up a bit. There was no pattern to his visits. He simply appeared without warning, stayed for a time and talked, and then left. From his conversation Raphael gathered that he was out exploring the city and the surrounding countryside.

On Friday, the day when Flood's rent ran out at his downtown motel, he did not show up, and Raphael began to think that he had checked out and left town without even saying good-bye. He knew it was foolish, but he was hurt by it, and was suddenly plunged into a loneliness so deep that it seemed almost palpable.

He called Flood's motel.

"I'm sorry," the woman at the motel said, "but Mr. Flood checked out just before ten this morning."

"I see," Raphael said. "Thank you." He hung up slowly.

"Well," he told himself, "that's that, then." The loneliness fell on him like a great weight, and the small room seemed suddenly very silent, very empty.

To be doing something, to fill up that silence, he made out a meticulous grocery list and went shopping.

When he returned, it was just growing dusk. He parked in front of the house and started to get out of his car. Across the street Patch walked by on silent feet, crossed over, and went on up past the houses of Sadie the Sitter and Spider Granny, her mother. On an impulse Raphael took out his crutches, closed the car door, and followed the melancholy Indian.

At the corner he had to wait while a couple of cars passed. He looked at the cars with impatience, and when he looked back up the street, Patch was gone. Raphael knew that he had not looked away for more than a second or so, and yet the silent man he had intended to follow had vanished.

He crutched on up past Sadie's house and then past Spider Granny's.

Maybe Patch had gone down an alley. But there was no alley, and the yards in the part of the street where he had last seen Patch were all fenced.

Troubled, Raphael went slowly back down the street toward his apartment in the gathering darkness.

Flood had just pulled up behind Raphael's car and was getting out. "Training for the Olympics?" he asked sardonically as Raphael came up.

"Damon," Raphael said with a sudden sense of enormous relief, "where have you been all day? I tried to call you, but they said you'd checked out."

"I've been moving," Flood explained. "I found a place so grossly misnamed that I *had* to live there for a while."

"What place is that?"

"Peaceful Valley," Flood said, drawing the words out. "Isn't that a marvelous name?"

"Sounds moderately bucolic. Where is it?"

"Down at the bottom of the river gorge. Actually, it's almost in the middle of town, but it might as well be a thousand miles away. There's only one street that goes down there. The banks of the gorge are too steep to build on, so they've just let them go to scrub brush and brambles. There's a flat area along the sides of the river, and that's Peaceful Valley. The whole place is a rabbit warren of broken-down housing, tarpaper shacks, and dirt streets that don't go anyplace. The only sounds are the river and the traffic on the Maple Street Bridge about fifty feet overhead. It's absolutely isolated—sort of like a leper colony. Out at the end of the street there's an area called People's Park. I guess all the hippies and junk freaks camped there during the World's Fair. It's still a sort of loitering place for undesirables."

"Are you sure you want to live in a place like that?" Raphael asked doubtfully. "There are new apartment houses all over town."

"It's perfect. Peaceful Valley's a waste disposal for human beings—a sort of unsanitary landfill."

"All right." Raphael was a little irritated. "It's picturesque, but what are *you* doing down there? I know you can afford better."

"I've never lived in a place like that," Flood explained. "I've never seen the lower depths before. I suppose I'm curious."

"That kind of superior attitude can get a jack handle wrapped around your head. These people are touchy, and they've got short fuses. Give me a hand with the groceries in the car, and I'll fix us some supper."

"Do you cook?" Flood asked, almost surprised.

"I've found that it improves the flavor. You can have yours raw if you'd like."

"Smart-ass."

They went upstairs, and Flood nosed around while Raphael stood in the kitchen preparing their supper.

"What's this thing?" he demanded.

"Scanner," Raphael replied. "If you want to know what Spokane is *really* like, turn it on."

"I've heard about them. Never saw one before, though." He snapped it on. "Is that all it does? Twinkle at you?"

"District Four," the dispatcher said.

"Four."

"We have a forty-two at the intersection of Boone and Maple."

"Okay. Do you have an ambulance on the way?"

"What's a forty-two?" Flood demanded.

"Auto accident," Raphael told him, "with injuries."

"Terrific." Flood's tone was sarcastic. "They talk in numbers—'I've got a seventeen and a ninety-three on my hundred and two. I think they're going to twelve all over the eighty-seven.' I don't get much out of all that."

"It's not quite that complicated. There's a sheet right there on top of the bookcase. It's got the numbers on it."

Flood grunted, picked up the sheet, and sat on the couch with it.

"Attention all units," another dispatcher said. "We have an armed robbery at the Fas-Gas station at Wellesley and Division. Suspect described as a white male, approximately five-foot-seven. One hundred and forty pounds, wearing blue jeans and an olive-green jacket—possibly an army field jacket. Suspect wore a red ski mask and displayed a small-caliber handgun. Last seen running south on Division."

"Well now." Flood's eyes brightened. "That's a bit more interesting."

"Sticking up gas stations is a cottage industry in Spokane," Raphael explained.

While they ate they listened to the pursuit of the suspect in the ski mask. When he was finally cornered in an alley, the anticlimactic "suspect is in custody" call went out, and the city returned to normal.

"That's all you get?" Flood objected. "Don't they report or something? How did they catch him?"

"Either they ran him down and tackled him or flushed him out of somebody's garage."

Flood shook his head. "You never get any of the details," he protested.

"It's not a radio program, Damon. Once he's in custody, that's the end of it. They take him back for identification and then haul him downtown."

"Will it be in the paper tomorrow?"

"I doubt it. If it is, it'll be four or five lines on page thirty-five or something. Nobody got hurt; it was probably only about fifty or sixty dollars; and they caught him within a half hour. He's not important enough to make headlines."

"Shit," Flood swore, flinging himself down on the couch. "That's frustrating as hell."

"Truth and justice have prevailed," Raphael said, piling their dishes into the sink. "The world is safe for gas stations again. Isn't it enough for you to know that all the little gas stations can come home from school without being afraid anymore?"

"You know, you're growing up to be a real smartmouth."

Raphael went back to his armchair. "So you've decided to stay in Spokane for a while."

"Obviously. The town intrigues me."

"Good God, why? The place is a vacuum."

"Why are *you* staying here then?"

"I told you. I need some time to get it all together again. This is a good place for it."

"All right." Flood's eyes were suddenly intent. "I can accept that. But what about afterward—after you get it together? You're not going to stay here, are you? Are you going back to school?"

"I don't know."

"You'll feel better about it later. Sure, it's going to take a while to get squared away, but you ought to make some plans—set some goals. If you don't, you're just going to drift. The longer you stay here, the harder it's going to be to pull yourself away."

"Damon." Raphael laughed. "You sound like you just dug out your freshman psychology text and did some brushing up."

"Well, dammit, it's true," Flood said hotly, getting to his feet. "If you stay here, you're going to get so comfortable that nobody's going to be able to blast you loose."

"We'll see."

"Promise you'll think about it."

"Sure, Damon."

"I'm serious." For some reason it seemed terribly important to him.

"All right. I'll think about it."

They looked at each other for a moment, and then let it drop.

Flood leaned down and looked out the window. "What the hell?" he said, startled. "What in God's name is he doing?" He pointed.

Raphael glanced out the window. "Oh, that's just Crazy Charlie. He's shaving his head again."

"What does he do that for?"

"Hard to say. I think God tells him to—or maybe one of his cats."

"Is he really crazy?"

"What do you think? He hears voices, he shaves his head like that once a week or so, and he's got a whole set of rituals he lives by. Doesn't that sound sort of schizophrenic?"

"Is that his real name—Charlie?"

"I don't know what his real name is. That's just what I call him."

"What's he doing now?"

Raphael glanced out the window again. "That's where he keeps his towel. He always wipes his head down with the same towel after he shaves. He has to lean way over like that because he's not allowed to step on that spot in front of the cupboard—either there's a big hole that goes straight down to hell or there's a dragon sleeping there, I haven't quite figured out which yet.''

''Why don't they haul him off to the place with the rubber rooms?''

''He's harmless. I don't see any reason to discriminate against somebody just because he's crazy. He's just one of the losers, that's all.''

''The losers?'' Flood turned and looked at him.

''You're not very observant, Damon. This whole street is filled with losers.''

''The whole town's a loser, baby.'' Flood went back to the couch and sprawled on it. ''Wall-to-wall zilch.''

''Not exactly. It's a little provincial—sort of a cultural backwater—but there are people here who make it all right. The real hard-core loser is something altogether different. Sometimes I think it's a disease.''

Flood continued to look at him thoughtfully. ''Let's define our terms,'' he suggested.

''There's the real Reed approach.''

''Maybe that's a disease, too,'' Flood agreed ruefully. ''Okay, exactly what do you mean when you say 'loser'?''

''I don't think I can really define it yet.'' Raphael frowned. ''It's a kind of syndrome. After you watch them for a while, it's almost as if they had big signs on their foreheads—'loser.' You can spot them a mile off.''

''Give me some examples.''

''Sure, Winnie the Wino, Sadie the Sitter, Chicken Coop Annie, Freddie the Fruit, Heck's Angels—''

''Hold it,'' Flood said, raising both his hands. ''Crazy Charlie I understand. Who are all these others?''

''Winnie the Wino lives on the floor beneath Crazy Charlie. She puts away a couple gallons of cheap wine a day. She's bombed out all the time. Sadie the Sitter lives on the other street there. She baby-sits. She plops her big, fat can in a swing on her porch and watches the neighborhood while she stuffs her face—with both hands. She's consumed by greed and envy. Chicken Coop Annie is a blonde—big as a house, dirty as a pig, and congenitally lazy. She makes a career of sponging. She knows the ins and outs of every charity in Spokane. She's convinced that her hair's the same color as Farrah's, and every so often she tries to duplicate the hairdo—the results are usually grotesque. Freddie the Fruit is a flaming queen. He lives with a very tough girl who won't let him go near any boys. He has to do what she tells him to because her name's the one on the welfare checks. Heck's Angels are a third-rate motorcycle gang. There are eight or ten of them, and they've got three motorcycles that are broken-down most of the time. They swagger a lot and try to look tough, but basically they're only vicious and stupid. They've lumped together the welfare checks of their wives and girlfriends and rented the house up the street. They peddle dope for walking-around money, and they sneak around at night siphoning gas to keep their cars and motorcycles running."

"And you can see all this from your rooftop?"

Raphael nodded. "For some reason they don't look up. All you have to do is sit still and watch and listen. You can see them in full flower every day. Their lives are hopelessly screwed up. For the most part they're already in the hands of one or two social agencies. They're the raw material of the whole social-service industry. Without a hard-core population of losers, you could lay off half the police force, ninety percent of the social workers, most of the custodians of the insane, and probably a third of the hospital staffs and coroners' assistants."

"They're violent?" Flood asked, startled.

"Of course. They're at the bottom. They've missed out on all the goodies of life. The goodies are all around, but they can't have them. They live in filth and squalor and continual noise. Their normal conversational tone is a scream—they shriek for emphasis. Their cars are all junkers that break down if you even look at them. Their TV sets don't work, and they steal from each other as a matter of habit. Their kids all have juvenile records and are failing in school. They live in continual frustration and on the borderline of rage all the time. A chance remark can trigger homicidal fury. Five blocks from here last month a woman beat her husband's brains out with a crowbar after an argument about what program they were going to watch on TV."

"No, *shit*?" Flood sat looking at Raphael, his dark eyes suddenly burning. "What are you doing in this sewer, Raphael?"

Raphael shrugged. "Let's call it research. I think there's one single common symptom that they all have that makes them losers. I'm trying to isolate it."

"How much consideration have you given to sheer stupidity?"

"That contributes, probably," Raphael admitted, "but stupid people *do* occasionally succeed in life. I think it's something else."

"And when you do isolate it, what then? Are you going to cure the world?"

Raphael laughed. "God, no. I'm just curious, that's all. In the meantime there's enormous entertainment in watching them. They're all alike, but each one is infinitely unique. Let's just say that they're a hobby."

The expression on Flood's face was strange as he listened to Raphael talk, and his eyes seemed to burn in the faint red glow of the winking scanner. It might have been Raphael's imagination or a trick of the light, but it was as if a great weight had suddenly been lifted from the dark-faced young man's shoulders—that a problem that had been plaguing him for months had just been solved.

iii

Raphael worked only a half day on Wednesday, since he was just about to the bottom of the pile of repairable shoes that lay to one side of his worktable.

About eleven-thirty Denise brought him a cup of coffee, and they talked. "You've changed in the last week or so, Rafe."

"What do you mean, 'changed'?"

"I don't know, you just seem different, that's all."

"It's probably Flood. He's enough to alter anybody."

"Who?"

"Damon Flood. He was my roommate at college. His family has money, and he's developed a strange personality over the years. He came to Spokane a couple weeks ago—I'm not really sure why."

"I don't think I like him."

"Come on, Denise." Raphael laughed. "You've never met him."

"I just don't like him," she repeated stubbornly, pushing a stray lock of hair out of her face. "I don't like what he's doing to you."

"He hasn't done anything to me."

"Oh yes, he has. You're not the same. You're flippant. You say things that are meant to be funny, but aren't. The humor around here needs to be very gentle. We're all terribly vulnerable. We can't be flip or smart aleck or sarcastic with each other. Don't put us down, Rafe. Don't be condescending. We can smell that on people the way you can smell wine on a drunk. If this Damon Flood of yours makes you feel that way about us, you'd better stay away from here, because nobody'll have anything to do with you."

Raphael looked at her for a moment, and she blushed furiously. "Has it seemed that way?" he asked her finally. "Have I really seemed that bad?"

"I don't know," she wailed. "I don't know anything anymore. All I know is that I'm not going to let anyone hurt any of my friends here."

"Neither am I, Denise," Raphael said softly. "Neither am I. Flood makes me defensive, that's all."

"You don't have to be defensive with *us*." She made a little move toward him, almost as if she were going to embrace him impulsively, but she caught herself and blushed again.

"Okay, Denise. I'll hang it on the hook before I come to work, okay?"

"You're mad at me, aren't you?"

"No. I wasn't paying attention to how I was treating people. Somebody needed to tell me. That's what friends are for, right?"

It troubled him, though. After he left work, he drove around for a while, thinking about what she had said. There was no question that Flood could influence people—manipulate them. Raphael had seen it too many times to have any doubts. He had, however, thought that *he* was immune to that kind of thing. He had somehow believed that Flood would not try his skills on him, but apparently Flood could not resist manipulation, and it was so very subtle that it was not even evident to someone who knew Flood as well as he did.

When he pulled up in front of his apartment, Sadie the Sitter and Spider Granny were in full voice. "Just wait," Sadie boomed. "As soon as I collect his insurance, I'll show her a thing or two. I'll be able to spend money on fancy clothes, too—*and* a new car—*and* new furniture."

It was evident by now that Sadie regarded the insurance money on her husband as already hers. The fact that he was still alive was merely an inconvenience. She counted the money over and over in her mind, her piggish little eyes aflame and her pudgy, hairy-knuckled hands twitching. When her husband came home at night, walking slowly on feet that obviously hurt him, she would glare at him as if his continued existence were somehow a deliberate affront.

Spider Granny, of course, cared only about the bellowing-idiot grandchild, and hurriedly agreed to anything Sadie said simply to prevent the horrid subject of commitment from arising again.

Raphael shook his head and checked his mailbox. There was some junk mail and an envelope from his uncle Harry. Harry Taylor forwarded Raphael's mail, but he never followed the simple expedient of scribbling a forwarding address on the original envelope.

Raphael went on upstairs. He dumped the junk mail in the wastebasket without even looking at it and opened Uncle Harry's envelope.

There was a letter from Isabel Drake inside. The envelope was slightly perfumed. Raphael stood at the table holding the envelope for a long time, looking out the window without really seeing anything. Once he almost turned to pitch the unopened letter into the wastebasket. Then he turned instead and took it to the bookcase and slipped it between the pages of his copy of the collected works of Shakespeare, where Marilyn's letter was. Then he went out onto the roof. He made a special point of not thinking about the two letters.

Flood arrived five minutes later. He was in high good humor and at his sardonic best. "What a wonderful little town this is," he said ebulliently after he had bounded up the stairs and come over to where Raphael sat in the sun beside the railing. "Do you realize that you managed to find perhaps the one place in the whole country that's an absolute intellectual vacuum?"

"What's got you so wound up?" Raphael asked, amused in spite of himself. When Flood was in good spirits, he was virtually overpowering, and Raphael needed that at the moment.

"I've been out examining this pigsty," Flood told him. "Were you aware that the engineering marvel of the entire city—the thing they're proudest of—is a sewage-treatment plant?"

Raphael laughed. "No, I didn't know that."

"Absolutely. They all invite you to go out and have a look at it. They all talk about it. It's terribly important to them. I suppose it's only natural, though."

"Oh? Why's that?"

"Old people, Raphael, old, old, old, *old* people. Spokane has more hospitals and doctors per square inch than cities five times its size because it's full of old people, and old people get sick a lot. Spokane is positively overwhelmed by its sewage-treatment plant because old people are obsessed with the functioning of their bowels. They gloat over their latest defecation the way young people gloat over their most recent sexual conquest. This place is the prune-juice and toilet-paper capital of America. It's got more old people than any place this side of Miami Beach. And the whole town has a sort of geriatric artsy-craftsy air about it. They do macramé and ceramics and little plaster figurines they pop out of ready-made rubber molds so they can call themselves sculptors. They crank out menopausal religious verse by the ream and print it up in self-congratulatory little mimeographed booklets and then sit around smugly convinced that they're poets."

"Come on." Raphael laughed.

"And the biggest thing on their educational TV station is the annual fund-raising drive. There's an enormous perverted logic there. They hustle money to keep the station on the air so that it can broadcast pictures of them hustling money to keep the station on the air. It's sort of self-perpetuating."

"There are some colleges here," Raphael objected. "The place isn't a total void."

Flood snorted with laughter. "Sure, baby. I've looked into them—a couple of junior colleges where the big majors are sheet metal, auto mechanics, and bedpan repair, and a big Catholic university where they pee their pants over basketball and theology. I love Catholic towns, don't you? Wall-to-wall mongoloids. That's what comes of having a celibate priesthood making sure that their parishioners are punished for enjoying sex. A good Catholic woman can have six mongoloids in a row before it begins to dawn on her that something might be wrong with her reproductive system."

"You're positively dazzling today, Damon. You must be in a good humor."

"I am, babes, I am. I'm always delighted to discover elementals—things that seem to be a distillation of an ideal. I think I'm a Platonist—I like to contemplate concepts in their pure state, and Spokane is the perfect place to contemplate such concepts as mongolism, senility, perversion, and bad breath in all their naked, blinding glory."

"Bad breath?"

"It must be something in the water. Everybody in town has breath that could peel paint at forty yards. I could stand that, though, if they weren't all about three quarters 'round the bend."

"It's not quite *that* bad."

"Really? The biggest growth industry in the area is the loony bin out at Medical Lake. The whole town is crawling with maniacs. I saw a man on the sidewalk giving a speech to a fifty-seven Chevy this morning."

"Tall?" Raphael asked. "Skinny? Bald and with a big, booming voice?"

"You've seen him?"

"He was in front of the bus station when I first got into town. Is he still talking about the nonexistence of chance?"

"No. The old bastard was lecturing on Hegel as close as I could tell—thesis, antithesis, synthesis, all that shit."

"Did it make any sense?"

"Not to *me* it didn't, but that doesn't mean anything. Even the original didn't make sense to me."

"It's nice to know that he's still around." Raphael smiled. "It gives the place a sort of continuity."

Flood looked at him, one eyebrow raised. "*That's* the sort of continuity you like? You sure you don't want me to reserve you one of those rubber rooms out at Medical Lake?"

"Not just yet. What else have you been up to? I haven't seen much of you in the last few days."

Flood leaned out over the railing, looking down into the streets.

"Careful," Raphael warned.

"It's solid enough," Flood said negligently. "I've been playing your game, Angel."

"What game is that?"

"Watching people—examining loserhood in all its elemental purity. You picked the wrong place, Raphael. Come on down to Peaceful Valley. *That's* the natural and native habitat of the archetypal loser. Did you know that people throw things off the Maple Street Bridge down onto the roofs of the houses down there? It's the only place in the world where it rains beer cans. A couple years back a drunken old woman got her head caved in when somebody chucked a potted plant over the side up there. Can you imagine being *geraniumed* into eternity? Now that's a real, honest-to-God loser for you."

"You're not serious."

"May the great and eternal flyswatter of God squash me flat right here if I'm not. Who's that?" He pointed down at the street.

Raphael glanced over the rail. "That's Patch."

"Another one of your losers?"

"No, I don't think so. He doesn't look like a loser, and he doesn't act like one. I haven't figured him out yet."

"Gloomy-looking bastard, isn't he? He's got a face that could curdle milk." Flood walked away from the railing as if the sight of Patch were some kind of personal affront. "Anyway," he went on quickly as if trying to recapture his mood, "I've started collecting losers, too. We got a whole 'nother class down in Peaceful Valley. Take Bob the Buggerer, for example. He's been busted four or five times for molesting little boys. One more time and he goes off to the slammer for the rest of his natural life plus about seventy-five years. Every time a kid goes by on a bicycle, he gets that same desperately longing look on his face you see on the old geeks downtown when a wine truck passes. It's just a matter of time until it'll get to be too much for him. And then there's Paul the Pusher. He's got stashes of dope all over the valley down there. The cops shake him down every time they go through—just to keep in practice—so he's afraid to keep the stuff in his house. He buries it in tin cans under logs and behind trees up on the hillside. He's worried that somebody's going to find it, so he's always digging it up to make sure it's still there. Every night you can see him scurrying out of his house with a shovel and a panic-stricken look on his face. Freddie the Flasher creeps around exposing himself to little girls. Polly the Punchboard is a raging nymphomaniac. She frequents some of the raunchier taverns and brings home horny drunks by the busload.''

Flood's tone was harsh, contemptuous, and his descriptions were a kind of savage parody of Raphael's earlier observations. It was almost as if the silent passage of Patch had somehow set him off, somehow made him so angry that he went beyond the bounds of what he might normally have said. Raphael watched him and listened closely, trying to detect the note of personal ridicule he knew must be there, but Flood was too smooth, too glib, even in his anger, and the flow of his description moved too fast to be able to pin him down.

It had been private before, a kind of passive observing that hadn't harmed anyone, but he had made the mistake of telling Flood. He should have known that the dark young man with the obsidian eyes would twist it, pervert it for his own amusement. Raphael began to wish that he had kept his mouth shut.

iv

Raphael had been swimming, and he had spent an hour in the weight room at the YMCA. The car made getting around much easier, but it had definitely disrupted his exercise routine. Since Flood had arrived in Spokane, Raphael's life had suddenly become so full that he no longer had time for everything. All in all, though, he preferred it that way. He thought back to those long, empty hours he had spent when he had first arrived in Spokane, and shuddered.

Frankie was waiting for him again when he got home. She stood on the sidewalk wearing a sleeveless blouse. It had been warm for the past week, and Frankie had started to work on her tan. Her arms and shoulders were golden. Her eyes, however, were flashing, and her lips were no longer tremulous. Her raven's-wing eyebrows were drawn down, and she looked very much like a small volcano about to erupt.

Raphael crossed the sidewalk. "Hi, babe." He leered at her. "You wanna go upstairs and fool around?" He had begun to use innuendo and off-color remarks to keep her off balance.

Frankie, however, was not off balance this time. "*'Sfacim!*'" she almost spat at him.

He blinked. He had a sort of an idea what the word meant, and it was not the sort of word he expected from Frankie. Then she said a few other things as well.

"I didn't know you spoke Italian," he said mildly.

"Bastard!"

"Frankie!"

"Get up those goddamn stairs!" She pointed dramatically. This was *not* the Frankie he knew.

He went around to the side of the building and started up the stairs. He could hear her coming up behind him, bubbling curses like a small, angry teapot.

"What's got you so wound up?" he asked her when they reached the roof.

"You got me in trouble, you son of a bitch!"

"Come on, Frankie, calm down. We're not going to get anywhere if all you're going to do is swear at me." He went over and sat down in his chair.

"Why didn't you *tell* me that you'd gone to work?"

"I didn't think it was particularly important. It's not much of a job."

"You're supposed to report *any* kind of a job. You've got a hole in your progress chart you could drive a truck through. You didn't even go to vocational rehab. What were you *thinking* of?"

"You didn't tell me the rules. How was I supposed to know?"

"You stupid, inconsiderate bastard!"

"If you feel like swearing, Frankie, you can probably handle it without having me around."

"Cabrone!"

"Spanish, too? You *are* gifted."

"We had Spick neighbors when I was a kid." She drew in a long, shuddering breath and seemed to get control of herself. "We have to fill out reports, Raphael," she told him, her dark eyes still flashing. "Am I going too fast for you?"

"Be nice."

She made a somewhat elaborate obscene gesture that involved both hands. "There's a procedure, Raphael. First we discuss various occupations and decide what sort of job's compatible with your disability. Then you go to vocational rehab to get the training you need to qualify you for the job. Then *we* set up the interviews for you. You didn't do any of that. Now I'm going to have to fake all kinds of reports. My supervisor thinks I'm incompetent."

"I'm sorry, Frankie. Why didn't you tell me?"

"Because you were too busy trying to talk dirty to me to see if you could embarrass me." She laughed derisively. "Fat chance. I'm what's known as a tough little broad. You couldn't embarrass me no matter *what* you said."

"What was all that puppy-dog stuff about then?"

"You use what you've got, Raphael. It makes other people feel superior, and then they go out of their way to help you. It makes my job easier. I thought I had you all tied up with a neat little bow, and then you turn around and stab me in the back. Now we've got to fix it."

"Why don't you start at the beginning, Frankie?"

"All right. You've been assigned a number."

"Who's idea was that?" His voice was cold.

"My supervisor's. She's queer for numbers. She even assigns numbers to the pencils on her desk. You can be sure it wasn't *me*. I know how you feel about us, so I thought I'd handle you sort of informally. Then Goodwill sent in their quarterly report, and guess who's name was right at the top of the list of new hires. My supervisor got all over my case for not reporting your progress. I told her that I hadn't had time to fill out all the reports."

"You lied," he accused.

"Of course I lied. I had to cover my ass."

"You're gonna burn in hell, Frankie."

"Whatever. How did you learn to repair shoes without any training?"

He shrugged. "Something I picked up."

"It takes *weeks*."

"Not if you don't spend the first twelve sessions having somebody explain to you how a sewing machine works. I ruined a few pair of shoes when I started, but what the hell? They were throwaways to begin with anyway. I'm getting better at it now. Would you like a leather brassiere? I'll make you one if you'll model it for me."

Her hands went to the neck of her blouse. "Do you want to check the size? My left boob's a little bigger than the right one."

He almost choked on that. This was *definitely* not the Frankie he'd known.

"Do you still want to play?" she said. "Or should we get down to business?"

"Sorry, Frankie."

"Let's get to work then. I'm going to need to put down dates and names for the progress reports—all the usual dog doo-doo. Nobody's ever going to read the reports anyway, but we have to have them in your file."

"You're a fraud, Frankie."

"Of course I am, but I'm a very good fraud." She started asking questions and taking notes. "If anybody ever asks, tell them that I sort of guided you through all this. I'll put in enough comments about your initiative to keep our asses out of the soup, but you're going to have to cooperate."

"It'll cost you."

"Anytime, Raphael, but you might just be biting off more than you can chew." Frankie knew about his condition, of course, but for some reason she chose not to let that knowledge modify her comments. Raphael rather ruefully admitted to himself that *he* had been the one who had started it, and this new Frankie he had just discovered beneath the disarming, little-girl exterior would not back away from *anything*.

She sighed. "Why do you have to be so different, Raphael? Why do you insist on not fitting into any of the compartments?"

"It's a gift."

"It's a pain in the ass. And *why* do you have to be so damn good-looking? Those cute remarks you've been making came very close to getting you in all kinds of trouble."

He thought of something he'd been meaning to ask. "Frankie—is that short for Frances?"

"Sort of." She said it evasively.

"Sort of?"

"All right, smart-ass, it's Francesca. Francesca Dellamara. Happy now?"

"That's gorgeous, Frankie. Why don't you tell people?"

"I don't want them to know I'm a wop."

"You ashamed of bein' a wop?"

"Blow it out your ass."

When she had finished taking notes, she looked around, her soft lower lip pushed out in a kind of thoughtful pout. Her dark eyes, however, were twinkling mischievously. "This is a very nice roof you've got up here," she said. "A girl could get an all-over tan up here if she wanted one. I could tan places that don't usually get tanned, and I wouldn't even get arrested for it." She looked at him archly. "You could watch, if you'd like," she offered.

Raphael suddenly blushed. He couldn't help it.

"*Gotcha!*" she squealed delightedly.

"You're a naughty girl, Frankie."

"Do you want to spank me?" She opened her eyes very wide with a little-girl eagerness.

"Stop that." Somehow she'd shifted the whole thing around, and now *he* was on the receiving end.

Then Flood arrived. Raphael made the introductions, and Frankie told them that she had to go back to work and left.

"She looks good enough to eat." Flood smirked.

"Don't pick on my caseworker," Raphael told him.

"Your *what*?"

"My caseworker. I made a mistake when I got here, and now I'm in the toils of the Department of Human Resources. Frankie comes by now and then to make sure that I don't cheat—sprout a new leg while they're not looking or something."

"You actually let those leeches get their hands on you?" Flood seemed amazed.

"Frankie's not hard to manage. She's young and pliable. I'm molding her character—making a closet dissident out of her." In the light of what he had just discovered, that might not have been entirely true.

"Why in hell did you ever go near those people?"

"I was playing games with them, and the games got out of hand. Social workers are notoriously devoid of any kind of sense of humor— except for Frankie. There might be some hope for that one."

"Don't ever bet on that," Flood said darkly. "Social science was my first major. You knew that, didn't you?"

"You don't seem the type."

"You've got *that* right, baby. The smell drove me off."

"The smell?"

"Haven't you ever noticed? Social workers all smell like rotting flesh—the same way vultures do, and probably for the same reason. Do you know what their ultimate goal is, Raphael?"

"To tend the wounds of the casualties of life—or so they say."

"Bullshit! Their goal is to take over—to take over everything and everybody—to make us live *their* way, and to make us pay for it, of course. It's all money and power, Raphael, the same as everything else. Once a social worker gets her hooks into you, you never get well, because you're a renewable resource. Anytime they need more money, they screw around with you until you have to go back into some kind of therapy—at so much an hour. They never let you get free, because someday they might want to squeeze some more money out of you or out of your insurance company. And power? What greater power can you have than to be able to make somebody not only *do* what you tell him to but *think* what you tell him to as well?"

"Aren't you exaggerating a bit?"

"Grow up, Raphael. Their magic word is 'programs.' They've got programs for everything, and every program is based on thought control. They've already taken over the schools. Every teacher in the public schools has a de facto degree in social work. I doubt if you could find a real English teacher or a real history teacher anywhere in America. Johnny can't read because his teachers are too worried about his 'relationships,' and their major tool is 'the group.' Modern Americans are sheep. They herd up by instinct. You won't find no Lone Rangers out there no more, Kimo Sabee. Peer pressure, baybee, peer pressure. That's the club they use. Americans would sooner die than do anything that runs counter to the wishes of the peer group. Before I finally threw the whole thing over, I spent *hours* taking notes in those group meetings. If I ever hear anybody say the words 'y'know' again, I'll throw up right on the spot."

Raphael remembered the endless, monotonous repetition of the 'y'knows' during his enforced attendance at AA meetings when he'd tried playing games with a new caseworker. "They *are* sort of fond of that, aren't they?"

"It's the Ave Maria and Paternoster of the groupie. It's a part of the recognition system, the badge of membership in the cult."

"Cult?"

"God, yes. They're all cults, Raphael. They're based on the mind-destroying success of AA. You can cure somebody of *anything* if you put him in a cult and grind off all his individuality and alienate him from such distractions as friends, families, wives—little things like that. Be glad you're not married, my friend, because the very first thing your cute little caseworker would have done would have been to poison your wife because your marriage hadn't been approved by the group—whatever group it is she's hustling for." Flood's expression was strange, intent, and he seemed almost to have his teeth clenched together. "Have you ever noticed how much they all want you to 'talk about it'?"

"Of course. That's what they do—talk."

"Do you want to know why? Social workers are almost all women, and women *talk* about problems. They don't *do* things about them. If John and Marsha's house catches on fire, John wants to put the fire out. Marsha wants to sit down and discuss it—to find out why the fire feels hostility toward them."

"Get serious."

"I am. Most social workers are women, and they know that they can control women by talking to them. It doesn't work that well with men, so the first thing a social worker does to a man is castrate him."

Raphael stiffened. How much did Flood know?

Flood, however, didn't seem to notice. "Social workers have to castrate their male clients so that they can turn them into women so that they'll be willing to sit around and *talk* about their problems rather than *do* something about them. If somebody actually *does* something about his problems, he doesn't need a social worker anymore. That's the *real* purpose of all the programs. They want to keep the poor sucker from really addressing his problem. If he does that, he'll probably solve it, and then he gets away. They won't have the chance to leech off his bank account or his emotions anymore. The bitches are vampires, Raphael. Stay away from them. The content of any social-science course is about fifty-percent vocabulary list—the jargon—and about fifty-percent B. F. Skinner behavior-modification shit. And as I said, the whole idea is to get everybody in the whole goddamn world into a program. They've probably even got a program for normal people—a support group for people who don't need a support group—a group to screw up their minds enough to make them eligible for the really *interesting* programs. Give those bastards a few years, and ninety percent of the people in the United States will be social workers. They'll have to start branching out then—spread the joy to other species. Guide dogs and cats through the trauma of divorce. Death counseling for beef cattle—so that we can all get happy hamburgers at the supermarket. Eventually they'll probably have to start exhuming the dead just to have enough customers to keep them all working. How about 'Aftercare for the Afterlife'? Ten social workers to dig up your uncle Norton to find out how he's doing? 'How's it going, Nort?' ' 'Bout the same—still dead.' 'Would you like to talk about it?' ''

"Aren't you reaching just a bit, Damon?"

"Of course I am. I'm doing this off the top of my head. You didn't give me any time to prepare. I'd still like to tumble your little caseworker, though."

"Tumble?"

"It's an old-fashioned term. It means—"

"I know what it means. You keep your hands off Frankie. I'm raising her as a pet." That was not really true anymore, but he decided that it might be better for all concerned if he kept what he'd just found out to himself.

"*Sure* you are, baby. Next time she comes around though, check real close to find out which one of you is wearing the dog collar."

V

In mid-May the weather turned foul. Denise told Raphael that this was normal for Spokane. "April and the first half of May are beautiful. Then it starts raining and keeps it up until the end of June. Then it gets hot."

"You mean it's going to do this for six weeks?"

"Off and on. It makes the lilacs bloom."

"Why does everybody in Spokane pronounce that word ly-*lock*?" he demanded irritably. "The word is ly-*lack*."

"Don't get grumpy with *me*, Blue Eyes," she told him tartly. "It's not *my* fault it's raining."

"Oh, go sell a refrigerator or something." He faked a scowl to let her know that he was not angry with her so much as with the weather.

"Why don't you go back to your little bench," she suggested, "and take that nice stout little machine of yours and sew all your fingers together? That way you'll have something to worry about besides the weather or how I pronounce the word 'lilac.' ''

"You did it again. You said ly-*lock*."

"So beat me."

He made a threatening move toward her, and she scampered away, laughing.

That afternoon he sat in his apartment drinking coffee and staring dispiritedly out at the dirty gray clouds scudding by overhead. He had the scanner on—more for company than out of any interest.

"District Four," the scanner said.

"Four."

"Nineteen-nineteen West Dalton," the dispatcher said. Raphael looked quickly at the scanner. The address was on his block.

"Check on the welfare of the Berry children. Complainant is the children's grandmother—states that the children may be abused or neglected. Child Protective Services is dispatching a caseworker."

"You want me to check it out or just back up the caseworker?" District Four asked.

"See what the situation requires first. We've had calls from this complainant before. There might be some kind of custody dispute involved."

"Okay," District Four said.

Raphael realized that it was Mousy Mary that they were descending upon. The dumpy woman with the pinched-in face had finally figured out a way to get into Mary's house.

He reached for his crutches and went out on the roof. The rain had stopped, at least for the moment, and the gusty wind blew ripples across the surface of a puddle of water standing in a low spot on the roof. Raphael crutched over to the front railing and stood looking down at the soggy street.

The police car, followed closely by a gray car from the state motor pool, drove up slowly and stopped. The policeman got out and put on his cap. A very nervous young woman got out of the gray car and hurried over to him, carrying her briefcase self-consciously. They spoke together briefly and then went up onto Mousy Mary's porch.

Across the street, in front of Sadie the Sitter's house, Mousy Mary's mother stood watching, her face gripped with an expression of unspeakable triumph.

The policeman and the nervous young caseworker went inside, and the dumpy little woman scurried across the street to stand directly in front of the house.

After a few moments the screaming started. Raphael could hear the anguish and the outrage in Mary's shrieks, but not the words. Then they all came out onto the porch, the caseworker holding protectively on to the arms of Mary's two confused-looking children, and the policeman interposing himself between her and the now-hysterical Mary.

"It's *her*!" Mary shrieked, leveling a shaking finger at her mother. "Why don't you make her leave me alone?"

The caseworker said something to her in a low voice, but Mary continued to scream at her smug-faced mother.

The policeman removed the small portable radio unit from his belt. "This is District Four." The voice came from the scanner inside Raphael's apartment. "You'd better respond Mental Health to this nineteen-nineteen West Dalton address. There's a female subject here who's pretty hysterical."

The caseworker led the two wide-eyed, crying children down to the sidewalk.

"I'll take them," Mousy Mary's mother declared in an authoritative voice. "I'm a personal friend of Sergeant Green's, and he said that I'd get custody."

"I'm very sorry," the young social worker told her firmly, her voice louder now, "but custody is a matter for the courts to decide."

"Don't let her take them," Mary screamed. "She'll never let me see them again. She's been trying to take them away from me for five years now. Don't let the old bitch have them."

"Don't you *dare* call me that in front of the babies!" her mother scolded. Then she turned back to the caseworker. "I'm *taking* those children," she announced.

"Officer," the caseworker called.

"All right, ma'am," the policeman said to Mary's mother, "you're going to have to stand aside."

"But I have custody," Mary's mother insisted.

"At the moment Child Protective Services has custody," the caseworker said, leading the children around the old woman toward her car.

"You come back here!" the dumpy woman screamed. "Sergeant Green said I could have custody."

"Go ahead and take off, miss," the officer on the porch said.

"What are you talking about? She can't take those children. I have custody."

The social worker got into her car with Mary's children and pulled away from the curb.

"You come back here! You come back here!" Mary's mother shrieked.

Then the car was gone, and she spun to confront the officer who had come down off the porch. "What's your badge number?" she demanded. "You're in a great deal of trouble, young man. Sergeant Green will take care of you."

"Just calm down, ma'am," the policeman said to her. "We'll get this all sorted out, but we're not going to get anywhere if we all stand around yelling at each other."

Then Mary said something, and the two women began screaming again.

Raphael turned and went back inside. The wind was brisk, and he had begun to feel chilled.

An hour later, after the affair across the street had quieted down, Flood arrived with a pizza. He had been drinking and was in high spirits. "Bob the Buggerer got busted today," he announced gleefully. "The temptation of budding boyish buttocks finally got to him, I guess."

"What's with the alliteration?" Raphael asked. He was not really in the mood for Flood. The weather and the incident across the street had soured him.

"Purely unintentional." Flood grinned. "To alliterate or not to alliterate—that's the question," he declaimed. "Whether 'tis fancier to consonantize constantly or to rhyme in time."

"Consonantize?"

"Poetic license—number forty-seven eighteen. Anyhow, poor old bumbling Bob nailed a paperboy on his morning route this A.M., and then he made his getaway—or at least he thought so. But the fuzz showed the rapee a bunch of mug shots, and the kid fingered Bob. About two this afternoon three squad cars came roaring down the hill into Peaceful Valley. Hey, baybee, that's like throwing a brick into a hornet's nest. You absolutely wouldn't *believe* what happens in Peaceful Valley when the pigs come down there in force. It looked like an impromptu track meet. There were people running every which way. Two guys came running out of Polly the Punchboard's house stark-ass naked and bailed into the river. Last I saw of them they were being swept around the bend. Guys I'd never even *seen* before came out of some of those houses. It looked like a convention of jackrabbits there for a while. Poor old Bob tried to run, too, but he's a little too old and a little too fat, so the cops caught up with him about fifty yards up the side hill. He tried to fight, and they literally kicked the shit out of him—I mean, they flat stomped a mud puddle in his ass right there on the spot. You've got some real unfriendly cops in this town."

"Was he hurt?" Raphael asked, not knowing whether to believe Flood or not. In his present mood Flood could expand and embellish a simple incident into an extended narrative that would be related to the truth only by implication.

"Hard to say. He looked pretty comfortable—lying there."

"Damon," Raphael said irritably, "I don't think I believe one single word of all this."

"Would I lie to you?"

"Yes, I think you would—just to see if I'd swallow all this crap."

"May the motor scooter of the Almighty run over my bare toes if it didn't happen just the way I described it."

"I think you're missing the whole point, Damon. I'm just not *too* entertained by this unsympathetic attitude of yours."

"Unsympathetic? *Me?* What about you, Raphael? What's your excuse for *your* attitude?"

"What about my attitude?"

"You're playing God. You sit in splendid isolation on top of your grubby little Mount Zion here, using your injury as an excuse not to come down among the real people. You've created a little fantasy world instead and peopled it with these losers of yours—'and whatsoever the God Raphael called them, so were they named.' But let me tell you something, Archangel, old buddy. You can sit brooding on your lonely mountaintop here with those seraphic wings outspread to shade these rickety streets, but your cute little fantasy names have no relationship whatsoever to these people and who they *really* are. Those are *real* people down there with real emotions and real problems, and you did *not* create them.''

''I've never said I did.'' Raphael was startled by the sudden intensity of Flood's words.

Flood stood up and began pacing in the small apartment, his eyes burning. ''Okay, so you had a little accident—you've got a certain disability. Big goddamn deal! What if it had been your *eyes*, baby? Think about that.''

Raphael flinched, the sudden horrid picture of a world of total darkness coming over him so palpably that he could almost feel the anguish of it.

''You've created this little dreamworld of yours so you can hide.'' Flood jabbed at him. ''You want to sit up here where it's safe, wallowing in self-pity and dreaming away the rest of your life. Well, I've got a flash for you, Rafe, baby. Jake Flood is here, and he's goddamned if he's going to let you just vegetate your life away like this—doped out on melancholy musings, drunk on mournful little fantasies. If you're so damned interested in these shitty little people, get *involved*, for Chrissake. Go out and meet them. Find out who they *really* are.''

''Why don't you mind your own business, Flood?'' Raphael was getting angry. ''Why don't we just forget all this. Just go away and leave me alone. Go back to Portland—go back to Grosse Pointe—go to hell for all I care. Just get off my back.''

Flood stopped, turned sharply, and stared at Raphael. Then he grinned broadly. *''Gotcha!''* he said exultantly. ''By God, you're alive after all! For a while there I was starting to have some doubts. You're going to make it after all, baby. It may be in spite of yourself, but you're going to make it. If you can get mad, at least it proves you're not dead.''

''Oh, go to hell!''

''Anyplace, baby, anyplace.'' Flood laughed. ''I finally got a rise out of you. Have you got any idea how I've been busting my ass to do just that?''

''Flood,'' Raphael said, feeling suddenly sheepish, ''don't play games with me. Exactly what are you up to now?''

''What's necessary, Raphael, what's necessary. I'll set fire to your crutches if I have to, but I'll be a son of a bitch if I'm going to sit back and let you lie down and play dead.''

It sounded very convincing, but the look in Flood's eyes was too familiar. Raphael remembered it, and it stirred doubts. It was all very complicated. Flood almost never did things for the apparent or obvious

reason; his motives were usually obscure. It would be easy—even flat-
tering—to accept this protestation of hardheaded friendship at face
value, but the agatelike eyes and that faintest shadow of a sardonic
smile that flickered at the corners of his mouth made Raphael cautious,
uncertain. As always with Flood, he decided, it might be better to wait
and see.

vi

The next day when he was coming home from his therapist's office,
Raphael stopped by the grocery store to pick up a few things, and as he
usually did, he stopped to talk with the blond clerk. The man had a dry
wit Raphael liked and an open, friendly manner that was a relief from
the deviousness of Flood or the tart touchiness he sometimes encountered in the people with whom he worked.

"Hey, Rafe," the clerk said, looking up from the milk case he was
filling, "what's shakin', baby?"

"Just passin' through, Darrel."

"That friend of yours was in a while ago."

"Damon?"

"Is that his name?" the clerk asked, straightening. "I thought it was
Jake."

"It is. The other is a name he used to use at school."

"Whatever turns him on, I guess," Darrel said. "I don't want to hurt
your feelings or anything, Rafe, but I'm not *too* partial to that young
man. I think a lesson or two in manners wouldn't hurt him all that
much."

"His family's got money. Sometimes he lets that go to his head a
little."

"You might suggest to him that he's using up his welcome in here
pretty fast. If he bad-mouths one of the girls about one more time, he
and I are going to tangle assholes—definitively."

"Was he offensive?"

"That gets pretty close to it. He had one of the girls in tears before he
left."

"I'm sorry, Darrel. I'll have a talk with him about it."

"I'd appreciate it, Rafe." The clerk started to return to the milk case,
but stopped and turned back suddenly. "Hey, you live over there on
the same street with Tobe and Sam, don't you?"

"Yeah, right across the street. Why?"

"Have you seen them lately?"

"I haven't really paid that much attention."

"They're usually in here two or three times a day to buy wine, but I
haven't seen them all week."

"Maybe I'd better stop by and see if they're okay."

"Might not hurt. They're a couple of likable old bastards. They don't *smell* too good sometimes, but they're good-natured old farts. I'd hate to see anything happen to them."

"I'll look in on them," Raphael promised, starting off down one of the aisles. "Later, Darrel."

"I'll be here," the clerk said wryly, "unless I can figure out a way to get fired."

Raphael laughed perfunctorily and finished his shopping.

It was curious, he thought, sitting in his car at the stoplight on Boone Avenue. This store was a long way from Peaceful Valley. The only reason Flood would be over here would be to visit him, but he hadn't seen him that morning. "What the hell is he up to?" Raphael was puzzled.

The light turned green, and he drove on home. Several weeks before, he had picked up a canvas bag of the type used by newspaper boys. It provided an excellent means for carrying groceries up to his apartment since it left both of his hands free for the business of loco-motion. At the moment, however, it was neatly rolled and tucked in the cupboard under the sink.

"Damn," he swore, and got out of the car.

He was halfway across the sidewalk when, on an impulse, he turned and went back, crossed the street, and climbed up onto the sagging porch of Tobe and Sam's house.

He knocked, but there was no answer. He knocked again and lis-tened. There was no sound from inside.

"Hey, Tobe?" he called, his face close to the door.

There was still no sound.

He tried the door. It was unlocked, and he opened it an inch or two. Their yellow dog started to bark.

"Tobe?" he called again. "Sam? Are you guys okay?"

The dog kept on barking, and the sour stink of the house exhaled out through the partially open door.

"Tobe? It's Rafe. You guys all right in there?" He did not want to go into their house uninvited.

"Hi, buddy," Sam's wheezy little voice said weakly from inside. "Come on in an' have a drink."

The dog kept on barking.

Raphael steeled himself and shoved the door open.

The yellow dog stood and barked at him, his tail wagging.

"Shut up, Rudy," Raphael told the dog.

The dog barked a couple more times dispiritedly, came over to sniff Raphael's leg, and then padded on into the dining room, his nails click-ing on the linoleum.

Sam sat at the table, a half-full bottle of wine in front of him. He looked up, smiling blearily. "Hi, buddy," he said in his wispy voice.

Tobe lay on the floor, his wiry little body twisted grotesquely. His mouth was agape, and his eyes, half-open, were glazed. A piece of grayish lint was stuck to one of his eyeballs, and he did not move. He had fouled himself, and a filthy brown puddle had oozed through his pants and dried on the floor under his scrawny haunches. The stink was overpowering.

"All right, Sam," Raphael said disgustedly. "What happened?"

"Hi, buddy," Sam said happily.

"Never mind the 'hi, buddy' crap. What's the matter with Tobe?"

Sam slowly moved his head to look at the man lying on the floor. He took a long drink.

"Come on, Sam," Raphael insisted. "What happened to Tobe?"

"Poor old Tobe," Sam said, shaking his head. "He had the fits. You wanna drink, buddy?" He offered the bottle.

"No, I don't want a goddamned drink. How long has he been like this?"

"Two—maybe three days. I dunno. I forget."

"Jesus Christ! You said he had fits. What kind of fits?"

"He took to jerkin' an' twitchin'. Then he fell down an' started bangin' his head on the floor. Then he kinda stiffened up a little, an' then he went all limp, kinda. That's when he shit his pants like that. You sure you don't want a drink, buddy?" He held up the bottle and squinted at it. "I could get you a glass, if you like."

Raphael took a deep breath. "No thanks, Sam," he said in a gentler tone. "Not right now." He braced himself, reached out, and touched Tobe gently with the tip of his crutch. The body seemed soft, yielding.

He pushed a little harder, and Tobe moved loosely on the floor.

The yellow dog growled at him from under the table.

"Have you got a telephone, Sam?" Raphael asked.

"Why would we want a phone, buddy? Ain't nobody gonna call us."

"Just sit tight," Raphael said, and then realized how stupid a thing that was to say. He turned and crutched on out.

Flood's car was parked behind his own, and Flood was coming back down the outside stairway, his face puzzled.

"Damon," Raphael called, "I need some help."

"What's up?" Flood came quickly across to the shabby little house.

"I think there's a dead man in here."

"No shit? Who is he?" Flood's eyes narrowed, and his face grew wary.

"Tobe Benson," Raphael told him. "He lives here."

"Maybe we shouldn't get involved."

"Flood, this isn't a dead dog we're talking about."

Flood looked at him. "All right, Raphael," he said finally. "It's going to be a pain in the ass, but if it's that damned important, let's see what we can do." He came on into the house. "Jesus! What the hell is that stink?"

"They drink. Old men who drink don't smell very good." Raphael stumped on into the dining room, and the yellow dog started to bark again.

"Rudy," Raphael snapped, "will you shut your goddamn mouth and lay down?"

The dog glowered at him and slunk back under the table.

"Hi, buddy," Sam said.

Flood looked quickly at Raphael.

"He's bombed," Raphael explained. "Ignore him." He pointed at Tobe with his crutch. "What do you think? Is he dead?"

"Christ, how the hell should I know?"

"See if he's breathing. I couldn't get down there to find out."

Flood's face was a pale green. "I wouldn't do this for just anybody." He knelt beside Tobe and put a hesitant hand on the little man's chest. "He's still warm, and I think I'm getting a beat. It looks like he's still alive—if you want to call it that. What the hell zonked him out like this?"

"Booze. They drink a lot."

"Hi, buddy," Sam said to Flood. "You wanna drink?"

"How long's he been down like this?" Flood asked.

"Two or three days, I guess. It's a little hard to get specifics out of Sam there. He doesn't know Tuesday from Saturday."

"Really," Flood agreed. "What do you think?"

"Here's my keys." Raphael dug them out of his pocket. "They don't have a phone. Why don't you go over to my place and get hold of the police?"

"Shouldn't we call an ambulance?"

"Let the police handle that. It'll save time in the long run."

"I'll be right back."

Five minutes later the house was filled with the official stomping of two policemen. "What made you think there might be a problem here, Mr. Taylor?" the one who had come to Mousy Mary's house the day before asked Raphael.

"I was at the grocery store over on Boone," Raphael replied. "One of the clerks there—Darrel—said that he hadn't seen them in several days. I came by to see if they were okay."

"Not many people would have taken the trouble."

"Mr. Taylor has a unique concern for his fellow man," Flood said dryly from the rickety chair across from Sam. "Will the old man live?"

The policeman shrugged. "Hard to say. He's not in very good shape—neither one of them is, really. We're going to send them both to the hospital and then out to the detoxification center—see if they can't dry them out a little."

"You don't sound very optimistic."

"They're both in their sixties, Mr. Flood, and they've been drunk for ten or fifteen years now. Their brains are pickled, and their livers are shot. I don't see too much to hope for, do you? Is there somebody who can take care of the dog?"

"The backyard's fenced," Raphael told him. "Put him out there. I'll see to it that he gets fed."

"I don't think there's any need for you gentlemen to hang around," the officer decided. "We know these two. We know what has to be done."

"It's happened before?" Flood asked.

"They haven't been any problem since we took the gun away from them."

"The gun?" Raphael was startled.

The policeman laughed shortly. "They got all boozed up one night here four, maybe five years back. The fat one there shot the little one in the belly with a twenty-two."

"*Sam?*" Raphael exclaimed. "Sam wouldn't hurt anybody—least of all Tobe. He loves the little old guy."

"He had a pretty good head of steam that night."

"What happened?"

"The little one wouldn't press charges. Claimed it was an accident. All we could do was take the gun away." He looked at Raphael. "I'm glad you came when you did, Mr. Taylor. It's messy if somebody dies in a situation like this. There are always questions and not too many answers. Thanks."

Later, on the roof, as they watched the ambulance carry off the two old men, Flood started laughing.

"What's so funny now?" Raphael demanded.

"It just goes to prove what I said last night, Gabriel. Your two old drunks had a big shoot-out. God only knows what else is happening on this block."

As always when Flood made that strange slip, Raphael felt a peculiar chill in the pit of his stomach. He knew that Flood was not even aware of the fact that he had used that name. He also knew that the name had a much deeper significance. He somehow felt that if he could only find out exactly who this mysterious Gabriel was, he would have the key to Flood's entire personality.

"Reality, Angel, reality," Flood went on. "Reality is infinitely more interesting than fantasy. Look at the real world. Look at the real people. Come down from Zion. Fold your wings and walk among us. I'll show you a world your wildest imaginings could never approach." And he threw back his head and laughed. But the laugh sounded hollow somehow and savagely mocking.

In taberna quando sumus

~~ i

Toward the end of May the weather broke, and there were five or six days of sunshine. Raphael moved outside to luxuriate in the warmth, coming in off his rooftop only to eat and sleep or go to work. Quite early one morning he saw Crazy Charlie coming furtively out of the house next door. Charlie always tried to attend to those things that required him to leave the safety of his apartment early in the day when there were few people on the streets and in the stores. He avoided contact with people as much as possible, even crossing the street when he saw someone coming up the sidewalk toward him in order to make chance meetings or the possibility of conversation impossible.

This morning, however, Flood was waiting for him. The small red car came down the street a moment or so after Charlie emerged, pulled into its usual parking place behind Raphael's car, and Flood bounded out. Without any preliminary word, he came around the back of his car and placed himself on the sidewalk directly in front of Crazy Charlie.

" 'Morning, friend," he said with a breezy cheerfulness.

Charlie mumbled something, his head down, and tried to cringe back off the sidewalk onto the grass.

"I wonder if you could give me some information," Flood pressed. "I seem to be lost. Could you tell me how to get back to Interstate 90?"

Charlie pointed south mutely.

"I go *that* way?" Flood assumed an expression of enormous perplexity. "Man, I'm completely turned around. I could have sworn that I had to go *that* way." He pointed north.

Charlie shook his head and gave more specific directions in a nasal, almost trembling voice.

"Man," Flood said with an ingenuousness so obviously faked that Raphael, watching from his rooftop, cringed. "I sure do want to thank you." Without warning, he reached out, grabbed Charlie's hand, and shook it vigorously.

Charlie looked as if he were ready to faint. Having someone talk to him was bad enough, but to have someone actually *touch* him—

"Beautiful morning, isn't it?" Flood went on in the same breezy tone, releasing Charlie's hand.

Charlie looked around, confused. In all probability he had not paid any attention to the weather for several years now. "Yes," he said in the same hesitant voice, "it seems pretty . . . nice."

"All that rain was starting to destroy me."

Charlie had begun sidling away, moving up the sidewalk away from Flood's car, but Flood kept talking, walking along beside him.

Raphael watched the two of them move slowly up toward the end of the block, Flood talking animatedly and Charlie appearing to grow less apprehensive as they went. By the time they reached the corner they were talking and laughing together like old friends.

They stood on the corner for almost ten minutes in the slanting, golden light of the early-morning sun, and when they parted, they shook hands again. Charlie seemed almost wistful as he looked at Flood's retreating back, then his shoulders slumped again into their usual slouch, and he crossed the street to pursue his early-morning errand.

Flood was buoyant when he came up the stairs and onto the roof. "How 'bout that?" he crowed. "Were you watching?"

"Of course. Wasn't I supposed to be?"

Flood ignored that. "I've been laying for that silly bastard for four days now. I knew he'd have to come out sooner or later."

"Why don't you just leave him alone?"

"Don't be ungrateful. Look at all the sleep I've missed for your benefit."

"Mine?"

"Of course. *You're* the one who's so damned interested in him. His name's Henry, not Charlie, and he gets a disability pension because he's nervous—that's the way he put it—'I get nervous.' He's supposed to be in therapy of some kind, but he doesn't go. He has seven cats—he told me their names, but I forget what they are—and he used to have a little dog named Rags, but Rags ran away. Sometimes, late at night when everybody's asleep, he goes out and looks for Rags. He calls him—very softly so that he won't wake anybody up—but Rags never comes. Henry misses him terribly. He didn't tell me the name of the dragon who sleeps on the floor in front of that cupboard—as a matter of fact, we didn't get into the question of the dragon at all."

"Jesus," Raphael said, feeling a sudden wrenching pity for Crazy Charlie and the abysmal emptiness of his life.

"Sad as hell, isn't it?" Flood agreed. "A couple times there I almost broke down and cried while he was talking."

"You?"

"Come on," Flood protested, "I'm not *totally* insensitive, you know."

"You could have fooled me."

Later, when they had gone inside to have coffee, Charlie returned to his apartment. He put down his packages and began to talk animatedly.

Flood watched him intently through Raphael's binoculars. "I think he's going through the whole conversation again, word for word."

"Why don't you leave him alone?" Raphael said disgustedly, realizing that he had said it before.

"I didn't hurt him." Flood was still watching through the binoculars. "For all I know, I might have done him some good. God knows how long it's been since he actually talked to somebody."

"That's not the point. You're *using* him—that's the point."

"Everybody uses people, Raphael." Flood still had the binoculars to his eyes. "That's what we're here for. You used him for months and never even talked to him—didn't even take the trouble to find out his real name. At least when I used him, he got something out of it. Here." He shoved the binoculars at Raphael. "Go on and take a look at him. He's genuinely happy. When did you ever do anything like that for him?"

Helplessly, feeling somehow furtive, Raphael took the binoculars and looked across the intervening space at Crazy Charlie's broadly smiling face. He knew that what Flood had done was wrong, but he could not put his finger on exactly what it was that had made it wrong. And so he watched, and for the first time he began to feel ashamed.

Chicken Coop Annie had waddled out of her house to yell at her kids. Flood came down the street and stopped to talk with her.

On his rooftop Raphael knew that the meeting was once again deliberate and that it had been carefully staged for his benefit. He had even seen the brief flicker of Flood's eyes as he had thrown a quick glance up to be sure that he was sitting there.

Chicken Coop Annie was wearing a tentlike wrapper that somehow accentuated rather than concealed the enormous nudity that lay beneath it. She giggled often as she spoke with Flood, her pudgy hands going nervously to the tangled wrack of her hair.

Flood eyed her boldly as they spoke, an insinuating smile playing about his lips, and Annie glowed, her eyes sly and her expression and gestures grossly coquettish.

They talked for quite a long while as Raphael watched helplessly from his rooftop. As Flood left, Annie raised her arms, ran all ten fat fingers through her hair, and shook her head with a movement that was somehow enormously sensual. When she walked back toward her house, her waddle seemed to become almost a conscious strut.

"Her name's Opal," Flood announced when he reached the rooftop.

"Really?"

"She has urges," Flood said, leaning against the railing.

"I noticed. Are you two going steady?"

"Interesting idea. Maybe if she was a little cleaner . . ."

"Why let that bother you? If you're going to wallow, why not go all the way?"

"Don't be crude." Flood suddenly laughed. "My God, she's a big woman! You don't realize it until you get up close to her. She's like a monument. A woman like that could scare a whole generation of young men into monasteries."

"Aren't you getting tired of this game?"

"No, not just yet. The street still has enormous possibilities."

And again, in bright and vivid morning air, Flood strode step for step with grim-faced Willie the Walker, deep in conversation, their words chopped and measured by the steady rhythm of their feet upon the sidewalk.

Sitting, Raphael watched them pass and turned away in disgust.

"Name's George," Flood informed Raphael later. "He had a heart attack ten years ago. His doctor advised him to get more exercise—suggested walking. That might have been the wrong thing to say to George."

"How much longer are you going to keep this up?"

"The old boy covers fifteen miles a day," Flood said, ignoring the question. "His doctor dropped dead three years ago, but old George keeps on walking. The only trouble with it is that it's the only thing he's got to talk about. He's a walking city map. He talked at me for a solid half hour, reciting the street names from the river to the North Division Y." He stopped and winced, shaking one foot. "Goddamn, my feet hurt."

"Good."

And again as Mousy Mary struggled down the street with two huge sacks of groceries, the ever-present Flood came to her aid with overwhelming gallantry. Suspicious at first and even apprehensive, she finally permitted him to carry one, then both. By the time they reached her porch, they were chatting together as if they had been neighbors for years. Her runny eyes brightened, and her slack mouth trembled now and then into a fleeting and tenuous smile. They talked together for almost half an hour before Flood came back across the street and up the stairs to the roof.

"Would you believe that her name really *is* Mary?" he told Raphael.

"Whoopee."

"They're going to give her kids back this weekend. Somebody finally got smart enough to really sit down and *listen* to that mother of hers. I guess the old bag's genuinely certifiable. They ought to fit her for a straitjacket."

"I could have told you that. So, what are you proving by all of this?"

"Just verifying your theory. You know—scientific method, empirical data, independent observer, all that shit. A theory isn't worth much if it isn't subject to verification, right?"

"I think there's also some question about the presence of the observer as a factor in the validity of the tests, isn't there?"

"Shit!" Flood said disgustedly. "Next you'll be talking about the noise in the woods."

"Why not? It'd be a damn sight more useful than all these fun and games."

"Oh no, Raphael. You're not going to put me off the track *that* easy. I'm going to turn down each and every one of your losers before I'm through. We're going to have a good hard look at the face of reality— warts, pimples, and all—and nothing less than getting run down by a garbage truck is going to stop me."

"That's an interesting thought."

"Be nice."

And again, in conversation with Freddie the Fruit under the hard and watchful eye of Freddie's girlfriend. Freddie, almost girlish, wriggled under the full impact of Flood's charm. Even the girl thawed a bit, though her expression was still suspicious.

"Harold and Wanda," Flood told Raphael. "He's Harold, she's Wanda."

"Obviously."

"Not entirely. A very tough broad, that one. She had a boyfriend named Douglas once. She's got his name tattooed on her shoulder— D-U-G. Can you imagine carrying an illiteracy to your grave like that? Anyway, they've completely reversed the traditional male-to-female roles, and they're really quite happy. He flirts with men to make her jealous, but he's probably not very serious about it. It's all part of a very elaborate game they play. Your original theory was an oversimplification this time. That's a very subtle and complex relationship."

"So?"

"I just thought you'd like to know, is all. After all, they're your losers, not mine." And Flood grinned, his dark eyes glittering in the sunlight.

And again on the porch with Sadie the Sitter, both of them lounging at their ease. "He drinks, of course," Sadie told Flood.

"I didn't know that."

"Oh, sure. He has for years now. Sometimes when he comes home, it's all he can do to make it into the house, he's so drunk."

"Then why does *she* act as if they were so special?" Flood asked, playing the straight man.

Sadie smiled knowingly. "Her family had money. They're the ones who set him up in business—and she never lets him forget it, let me tell you. That's why he drinks, naturally."

"Naturally."

"And the one next to her," Sadie went on, pointing. "*She's* always bustin' a gut tryin' to keep up. They spend all their time tryin' to out-uppity each other. It makes me sick."

"I don't know why people have to be like that."

"That's all right. *I'll* be comin' into some money pretty soon. *Then* we'll see who's gonna outfancy who."

"Good for you," Flood approved.

Sadie nodded smugly and stuffed another handful of potato chips into her mouth. "Get the hell away from that rosebush, you little bastard!" she bellowed at one of the children she was watching.

"That woman is an abomination," Flood told Raphael later. "I'm moderately immoral myself, but she's not even human. She hates *everything*. Talking to her is like crawling into a sewer."

"It was your idea," Raphael pointed out. "Had enough yet?"

"What keeps her *alive*?" Flood exclaimed. "What keeps her from exploding from all that sheer, overwhelming envy? Oh, by the way, her name's Rita. They call her husband Bob the Barber."

"So?"

Flood shrugged. "I just thought you'd be interested."

"What made you think I'd be interested? I could see what she is from here. I didn't have to sit on her porch and let her spew on me to find out everything I needed to know about her."

"I don't see how she fits into your theory, though."

"She's a loser. You can smell it from here. There's a catastrophe just around the corner—something crouching, waiting to pounce on her."

"That'd be one helluva pounce." Flood laughed. "Maybe it's Jamesean—'Beast in the Jungle' and all that crap. Maybe her catastrophe is going to be the fact that no catastrophe ever happens to her."

"Aren't we getting a little afar afield? How much longer are you planning to play this little game?"

"Only as long as necessary, Angel," Flood said with an infuriating blandness. "Only as long as necessary."

Jimmy and Marvin were on the lawn of the house up the street laboring with Jimmy's new car—a battered Ford in only slightly better shape than his old one. They had brought speakers out of the house and connected them to the car's radio and had turned the volume all the way up. The mindless bawling they called music bounced and echoed off the front of the houses and shook windows from one end of the block to the other. As they worked they had to scream at each other to be heard over the noise, but that was not as important as the fact that the music attracted attention—that everyone knew that they were out there doing something important.

And then, inevitably, Flood came sauntering down the street, hands in his pockets and a cigarette dangling from one corner of his mouth though Flood rarely smoked. "Hey, man," he said to Jimmy, who had just come out from under the gaping hood of the Ford to stare at him truculently, "what's happening?"

Jimmy answered shortly, his face still suspicious, but his words were lost in a fresh blare of noise from the radio. Flood walked a few steps toward him, his face questioning, and Jimmy nervously backed up a step or two. Raphael had noticed that Jimmy's mouth often got him into more trouble than he could handle.

"What'd you say, man?" Flood asked pleasantly. "I didn't quite catch it." He spoke quite loudly.

Jimmy mumbled something, his eyes down.

"I'm sorry," Flood said over the music. "I still can't hear you." He went closer to Jimmy, who backed up a little farther.

"What's the matter with it, man?" Flood asked Marvin, who was struggling under the hood with the stubborn guts of the sick car.

Marvin answered shortly and then began to swear as his wrench slipped and his knuckles smashed against the solidity of the engine block.

"Ouch," Flood said, "I'll bet that hurts like a son of a bitch. Did you check the coil?" He pointed at something under the hood and murmured some instructions.

"Jimmy," Marvin shouted exasperatedly, "will you turn that fuckin' radio *down*?"

"What for?" Jimmy's tone was still belligerent.

"Because I can't hear myself think, for Chrissake."

Jimmy glowered at him.

Flood reached into the engine compartment and carefully disconnected a wire. The music stopped abruptly in mid-squawl. The sudden silence was stunning.

"Sorry," Flood said. "Wrong wire."

"What the hell you think you're *doin,*' man?" Jimmy screamed at him. He went to the side of the car and started to bang on one of the speakers.

Flood reattached the wire, and naked noise erupted into Jimmy's face. The pasty-faced young man flinched visibly and stepped back a few paces. "Jesus!"

The music stopped again.

"Hang on," Flood said. "I'll get it."

Jimmy approached the car again, and once again the full volume blasted into his face. "Aw, for Chrissake!" He climbed into the car and turned the radio off. "Hey, man," he said to Flood, "quit fuckin' around with my car, huh?"

"Shut up, Jimmy," Marvin told him, still leaning into the engine compartment.

"What the fuck you talkin' about?" Jimmy demanded. "It's my goddamn car, ain't it?"

"Okay." Marvin straightened up. "*You* fix the bastard then." He threw down his wrench.

"Come on, Marv," Jimmy pleaded, "you know more about this than I do."

"What's the problem with it?" Flood asked.

"Son of a bitch runs like a thrashin' machine," Marvin replied. "Half the time it won't start at all; and when it does, it sounds like it's tryin'' to shake itself to pieces."

"Timing," Flood diagnosed. "You got a timing strobe?"

Marvin shook his head.

"Leon's got one," Jimmy offered hopefully. "You think you could fix it, man?" He looked at Flood with an almost sick yearning on his face.

"Shouldn't be too tough. I'll need that strobe, though."

"Lemme use your car, Marv," Jimmy said. "I'll go get it."

"Why not?" Marvin gave Jimmy his keys and then turned back to Flood. "Hey, man, what's your name?"

"Jake."

"I'm Marvin. This is Jimmy. Let's have a beer while we're waitin' for him to get back."

"Don't drink up all the beer, man," Jimmy protested.

"Get some more. Pick up the strobe and go over to the store an' get some more."

"I ain't got no money."

"Here." Flood took out his wallet and pulled out a bill. "Why don't you pick up a case?"

"Hey, Darla," Marvin yelled at the house, "bring out a couple beers, huh?"

Jimmy went to the curb and climbed into Marvin's car. Flood and Marvin went up on the porch and sat down as he pulled away. One of the girls, a blonde with stringy hair, brought out some beer, and they sat around on the porch, talking.

On the roof Raphael watched. He wished that Flood would get away from them. He felt strangely angered by the easy way Flood had insinuated himself into the rowdy, clannish group up the street. He was startled to suddenly realize that he was actually jealous. In disgust he pushed his chair away from that side of the house, rolled himself across the roof, and sat staring moodily into the alley at the back of the house.

He could still hear their voices, however, laughing and talking. Then they turned the radio on again, and some bawling half-wit began to sing at the top of his lungs about true love in a voice quavering with technically augmented emotion.

Raphael got up and stumped into his apartment. In part it was anger with Flood, but it was more than that, really. Raphael had never been particularly attracted to rock music. In the first place it was normally played at a volume about two decibels below the pain level, and in the second place he found the lyrics and the actual musical quality of the stuff absurdly juvenile—even simpleminded. He was quite convinced that most adolescents listened to it not so much out of preference, but rather so that other adolescents could *see* them listening to it. It was a kind of badge, a signal to other members of the tribe. There was something beyond that, however. Since his accident Raphael had rather carefully kept himself in an emotional vacuum. The extent of his injury had made that necessary. There were thoughts and feelings that he simply could not permit if he were to retain his sanity.

Even inside, however, the blaring music penetrated, and Raphael grew angrier. "The hell with that." He crutched to the bookcase and ran a finger across the backs of his tape cassettes. It was childish, but he was too irritated to care. "Let's see how they like *this*." He pulled out a cassette and clicked it into the player. Then he turned the volume up and opened the doors and windows.

The tape he played was a pyrotechnic work by Orff, an obscure German composer of the early twentieth century. It was quite satisfyingly loud, and the choral lyrics, in Low German and corrupt Latin, were suitably cynical and of course quite beyond the comprehension of the cretins up the street.

Raphael waited in the maze of naked sound.

After several minutes the phone rang.

"Yes?" he answered it.

"Don't you think that's a little loud?" Flood asked acidly.

"Not particularly. Sounds just about right to me. It pretty well covers certain undesirable noises in the community."

"Don't get shitty. Other people don't want to listen to that crap."

"What's the matter, baby? All your taste in your mouth?"

"Grow up. Turn the goddamn thing down."

"Just as soon as you persuade your new friends down there to turn down that garbage they're listening to."

"We aren't hurting anybody."

"Neither am I."

"Just turn it down."

"Stuff it." Raphael hung up.

The tape played through, and Raphael turned it off and went back outside.

Flood and Marvin were leaning under the hood of the car while Jimmy hovered anxiously behind them. The speakers were gone, and the neighborhood was silent.

"I think that's got it," Flood announced, straightening. "Give it a try."

Jimmy got into the car and started it. "Hey, wow!" he exulted. "Listen to that baby purr!"

There was a racking snarl up the street, and two of the motorcycles came down to the house, bumped up over the curb, and stopped on the lawn. Big Heintz and the skinny one Raphael had named Little Hitler dismounted and swaggered over to the car.

"You still fuckin' around with that pig?" Heintz demanded.

"Hey, Heintz," Jimmy said proudly, "listen to her now." He revved his engine.

Heintz cocked one ear toward the car. "Not bad," he admitted. "What was wrong with it?"

"Timing," Marvin told him. "Jake here spotted it right off."

"Jake?" Heintz looked suspiciously at Flood as if the inclusion of someone new into the group without his express permission was a violation of some obscure ethic.

"This is Jake," Marvin introduced him. "We got Leon's timing light, and he fixed the bitch in no time at all."

Jimmy backed his car into the street and roared off, tires squealing.

"You a mechanic?" Heintz asked Flood.

"I tinker a little now and then." Flood shrugged, wiping his scarcely dirty hands on a rag.

"Know anything about bikes?"

Flood shook his head. "I'm not into bikes."

"Where you from?"

"Detroit."

"Never been there."

"I wouldn't make a special trip just to see it."

"Let's have a beer," Heintz suggested, his manner relaxing a bit.

"You bet, Heintz," Marvin said quickly. "We got a whole case. Jake bought it." He hurried up onto the porch and yelled into the house. "Hey, Darla, bring out some beer, huh?"

Heintz draped a meaty arm over Flood's shoulders as they went up onto the porch. "What brings you way out here, Jake?" he asked in a friendlier tone.

"I'm on the run." Flood laughed shortly.

Heintz game him a startled look.

"I don't get along with my family," Flood explained. "We all decided it'd be better if I kept about a thousand miles distance between us."

Heintz laughed harshly. "I *know* that feeling."

They gathered on the porch, and the women came out of the house. The sun was just going down, and they all sat around talking and drinking beer.

Jimmy roared up and down the street several times, showing off, then parked at the curb in front of the house.

The talk grew louder, more boisterous, and more people arrived or came out of the house. Raphael had never been able to determine exactly how many people actually lived in the big house, since the population seemed to fluctuate from week to week. Their relationships were casual, and it was difficult to determine at any one time just who was sleeping with whom. Sourly he sat on his rooftop and watched Flood insinuate himself into the clan. By the time it had grown dark, he had been totally accepted, and his voice was as rowdy and boisterous as any.

The party continued, growing louder and more raucous, until about eleven-thirty when two police cars arrived and the officers got out to break it up.

Flood came down the street, got into his car, and drove away. He did not even glance up at the rooftop where Raphael sat watching.

ii

The first of June fell on a Wednesday, and Raphael went in to work early. Normally he waited until about ten in order to avoid the rush of traffic, but the first of the month was different.

Heavy traffic still made him jumpy, and he was in a bad humor when he reached the store. Denise was inside, and she unlocked the door to let him in. "You're early."

"Mother's Day," Raphael replied shortly, crutching into the barn-like building. "I have to get home early to guard the mailbox."

"I don't follow that." She locked the door again.

"The welfare checks come today. It's also the day when I get a check from my bank in Port Angeles. The kids over there in Welfare City find unwatched mailboxes enormously fascinating on Mother's Day."

"Why don't you move out of that place?"

He shrugged. "It's not that big a thing. You just have to be careful is all."

"You want some coffee?"

"I thought you'd never ask."

They went back through the dimly lighted store to the cluttered workroom in the rear. It was very quiet in the big building, and shadows filled the corners and crouched behind the endless racks of secondhand clothes that reeked of mothballs and disinfectant.

"Is your friend still in town?" Denise asked as she poured coffee.

"Flood?" Raphael lowered himself into a chair. "Oh yes. The pride of Grosse Pointe still lurks in Fun City."

"Now that's exactly what I mean," she said angrily, bending slightly to bang down his coffee cup with her dwarfed arm.

"That's what you mean about what? Come on, Denise, it's too early in the morning to be cryptic. I'm not even awake yet."

"All those cute little remarks. You never used to talk that way before he came. When is he going to go away and leave us alone?"

"Us?"

"You know what I mean."

Raphael smiled briefly. "Sorry. I'm grumpy today. It's always a hassle on the day when the checks come. I'm not looking forward to it, that's all."

"Why don't you just have your bank in Port Angeles transfer the money directly to your bank here?" she asked him, sitting on the edge of the table. "That way you wouldn't have to worry about it."

Raphael looked up, startled. "I never thought of that."

"I think you need a keeper, Rafe. You're a hopeless incompetent when it comes to anything practical. What's he up to now?"

"Who? Oh, Flood? I'm not sure. He's playing games. He's going around introducing himself to all my neighbors. It's all very obscure and not particularly attractive. He says he's doing it to 'bring me out of my shell,' but I'm sure there's something else behind it as well. Jake Flood is a very devious young man."

"I hate him." She said it flatly.

"You've never met him."

"I never met Hitler, either—or Attila the Hun."

"You're a very opinionated person, Denise." He smiled at her.

"He's going to hurt you, Rafe. I can see it coming, and I hate him for it."

"No. He's not going to hurt me. Flood likes to manipulate people, that's all. I know him, and I know what he's up to. I can take care of myself."

"*Sure* you can."

"Little mother of the world," Raphael said fondly, reaching out and taking her misshapen little hand, "you're going to rub raw spots on your soul if you don't stop worrying about all of us."

"Well, I *care*, dammit!" She did not pull her hand away.

"You're cold," he noted, feeling the tiny, gnarled bones in the dwarfed hand.

"It's always cold. The other one's fine, see?" She reached out to put her other hand briefly on his wrist.

"Well." Raphael released her and reached for his crutches. "I guess I'd better get to work."

She sighed. "Me too, I suppose."

Raphael rose and crutched smoothly through the dim light to his bench and the pile of battered and broken shoes that awaited him.

He went home about eleven, and Flood was waiting for him. The top was down on the little red sports car, and Flood half lay in the front seat, his feet propped on the opposite door.

"Loitering, Damon?" Raphael asked, coming up beside the car.

"Just watching your people. They're all out today, aren't they?"

"Mother's Day. They're waiting for the mailman."

"Mother's Day?"

"The day the welfare checks arrive. Big party night tonight. Let's go upstairs."

"Right." Flood climbed out of the car. "Is that why all the kids are out of school?"

"Sure. It's sort of like Christmas—very exciting. Lots of money and goodies and stuff."

"Nigger rich," Flood said as they climbed the stairs.

"That's one way to put it."

Later they sat by the railing, watching the street.

"Who's that kid belong to?" Flood asked, pointing at a long-haired fourteen-year-old with a permanent sneer on his face lounging against the light pole on the corner. "I don't think I've seen him before."

"He's a thief. He's probably looking for the chance to steal somebody's welfare check."

"You've seen him before?"

"I sure have. He stole my groceries once."

"He did *what*?" Flood was outraged.

Raphael told him about the incident with the cabdriver and the two bags of groceries.

"Slimy little bastard," Flood growled.

"That he is."

"Can I use your phone for a minute?" Flood asked, his eyes narrowing.

"You know where it is."

Flood went inside and then came back in a few minutes, a malicious smile on his dark face. He sat down again and watched the street.

"What are you up to now?" Raphael asked him.

"That'd spoil it. Just keep your eyes open."

Up the street at the house of Heck's Angels, Jimmy and Marvin came out and began tossing a Frisbee back and forth, casually walking down toward the corner where the kid stood.

Raphael suddenly had a horrid suspicion. "Look out, kid!" he shouted.

But it was too late. Jimmy and Marvin pounced on the kid and held him, laughingly avoiding his desperate kicks.

"What do you guys want?" the kid yelled at them. "Lemme go."

Marvin held the kid's skinny arms, and Jimmy squared off in front of him.

"Help!" the kid screamed. "Somebody help me!"

Jimmy hit him in the mouth.

"Help!" the kid cried.

Jimmy hit him again.

They pounded him for several minutes, and after he fell to the sidewalk, they kicked him in the stomach and face for a while. Then they sauntered across the street and glanced up at the rooftop.

"Good job!" Flood called down to them. "Thanks."

"Anytime, Jake," Marvin called back up, grinning. They went on back up the street, talking and laughing.

On the corner the kid pulled himself up, using the light pole. His mouth and nose streamed blood, and his eyes were swollen nearly shut. "Dirty bastards!" he sobbed at the backs of the two who had just beaten him.

They turned and started back, and the kid ran, half crouched over, holding his stomach with both hands.

"Quite satisfying, wasn't it?" Flood said to Raphael, his eyes burning.

"It was disgusting. Sickening."

"Of course it was, but satisfying all the same. Right? I liked that little touch—the warning you gave him—just a moment too late. Nicely done, Raphael. Perfect timing. You get all the satisfaction out of watching the little bastard get the shit stomped out of him with no guilt attached to it at all, because you *did* try to warn him."

"You're contemptible."

"Of course I am." Flood laughed. "We're *all* contemptible. We all have these base, vile, disgusting little urges—revenge, hate, spite, malice. Each man's soul is a seething sewer. I just bring it out into the open, that's all. I take a certain pride in my disinterestedness, though."

"In your *what*?"

"That was for you, Raphael. I didn't give a shit about that kid one way or the other. You're the one who had a hard-on for him. Look upon me as an instrument of a vengeful God. The Archangel proposes, and Jake Flood disposes. Just be careful about the things you wish for while I'm around, though, because you'll probably get exactly what you want." His eyes were very bright now. "Admit it. Deep down in that part of your mind nobody likes to look into, you really enjoyed that, didn't you?"

Raphael started to say something, but suddenly could not, because it was true. He *had* enjoyed it.

Flood saw his hesitation and laughed, a long, almost bell-like peal of pure mirth.

And then the mailman came, and the streets below exploded with people. Impatiently, they waited on the sidewalk for him and literally grabbed the checks out of his hands as he approached. As soon as they had the checks, they dashed to their cars and raced away in a frenzy, as if the world might suddenly run out of money before they could convert the checks into spendable cash. "Get in the car! Get in the car!" mothers screamed urgently at their children, and their men hovered closely, even anxiously, over the women who held, each in her own two tightly clenched hands, that ultimate reality in their lives—the welfare check. For those brief, ecstatic hours between the time when the checks arrived and the time when they all watched in anguish as the seemingly vast wealth dwindled down to the last few paltry dollars that were surplus, the women were supreme. The boyfriends who had beaten them and sworn at them, ridiculed and cheated on them, were suddenly docile, even fawning, in the presence of the awful power represented by the checks. As the day wore on and so much went for rent, so much for the light bill, and so much for payments on this or this or that, the faces of the men became more desperate. Mentally, each man watched that huge stack of tens and twenties melt away like frost in the sun, and since he knew that he could only wheedle a third or even a quarter of what was left, his eyes grew wide with near panic.

But first there was the orgy of shopping, of filling the house with food. An hour or two after the checks arrived, the cars began to return, clattering and smoking as always, but filled with boxes and sacks of groceries. The children screamed and squabbled and ran up and down the sidewalks almost hysterical with excitement. They gorged themselves on candy and potato chips and swilled soda pop as fast as they could drink it, knowing that what they could not eat or drink today would be lost forever.

And then, when the food was in and the money orders for the bills were all bought and safely in the mail, the men took their women inside and, each in his own fashion, cajoled a share of the loot. It was only then that the parties started.

"My God!" Flood said, watching. "It's a circus down there. Does this happen every month?"

"Every month," Raphael told him. "It's Christmas and New Year's Eve and Fourth of July all rolled into one—and it happens on the first of every month."

The all-powerful women emerged from their houses, contented and enormously satisfied that they had once again provided bountifully for their dependents. The scrimping and borrowing and hunger of the last week were forgotten in an orgy of generosity and openhanded benevolence. For the moment at least, they were all rich.

"Let's cruise around a bit," Flood suggested.

"What for?"

"Because you're taking root in that chair. It's unhealthy to sit in one spot for so long. Let's away, my Angel, and behold the wonders of Welfare City on payday. Call it research if you like—an observation of the loser at play."

As he almost always did, Raphael succumbed in the end to Flood's badgering. It was not so much that he accepted his friend's feeble excuses, but rather that he, too, felt the contagious excitement from the streets below. The thought of remaining stationary while so much was going on became unbearable under Flood's prodding.

And so they cruised in Flood's small red car, drifting slowly up and down the streets of shabby houses with junked cars sitting up on blocks in the yards and broken-down appliances and boxes of junk piled on the porches. The streets were alive with people, and they sat on porches and lawns drinking and laughing. Music blasted from a dozen radios and record players, and packs of kids on bicycles rode wildly up and down the streets.

"A good old-fashioned truant officer could have a ball today," Flood observed.

"They don't seem to pay that much attention in Spokane."

"Sure. After all, how much education do you need to be able to sign a welfare check?"

They pulled up in front of a tavern on Broadway.

"Now what?" Raphael asked.

"Let's have a beer and take a look at party time in the poor man's social club."

"Why not?" Raphael dug his crutches out from behind the seat and they went in.

The first thing that struck them was the noise. The place seethed with people, most of them already drunk and all of them shouting.

Flood found a small table near the corner, got Raphael seated, and then went to the bar for beer. "Loud, huh?" he said when he came back.

"You noticed."

"What time do the fights start?"

Raphael looked around. "Hard to say."

An Indian shambled by their table with his mouth gaping open and a sappy look of bludgeoned drunkenness on his face.

"The old-timers were right," Flood observed. "They can't hold their liquor, can they?"

"He doesn't seem much drunker than anybody else."

"Really? I'd give him another five minutes before he passes out."

"He could surprise you."

"Let's get up a pool on which way he falls. I'd bet on north—that's the side of the tree the moss grows on."

"What's that got to do with it?"

"You know—child of nature, all that crap."

"Why not south then—the way the geese fly? Or east to west—with the rotation of the earth? Or west to east—with the prevailing winds?"

"Interesting problem. There he goes."

Raphael turned in his seat. The Indian had reeled against a wall and was sliding slowly to the floor, his eyes glazed.

"No bet," Flood said. "The son of a bitch passed out vertically."

An argument broke out at the pool table, and two drunken young men threatened each other with pool cues until they were separated.

Everyone was a big shot today, and loud arguments erupted about who was going to pay for the next round. The noise was stunning, and Raphael began to get a headache. "Had about enough?" he asked Flood.

"Let's have one more." Flood got up quickly and went back to the bar. As he turned, a glass in each hand, a tall black man with graying hair lurched into him, knocking one of the glasses to the floor.

"Hey, man," the black man apologized quickly, "I'm sorry."

Flood's eyes were flat and his expression cold.

"Let me buy you another."

"Forget it."

"No, man—I mean, it was me that spilled it."

"I said to forget it." Flood deliberately turned his back on the man to return to the bar.

The black man's eyes froze, and his face went stiff. He drew himself up as if about to say something, then looked around as if suddenly realizing how many whites were in the bar and where their sympathies would lie in the event of an argument. "Shit," he muttered, and cautiously made his way to the door, his face still carrying that stiff, defensive expression.

Flood returned to the table and put down the two beers.

"You could have let him buy," Raphael said.

"I don't like niggers. I don't like the way they look; I don't like the way they smell; and I don't like the way they're trying to niggerize the whole country."

"The man was only trying to be polite. You didn't have to shit on him."

"That's what they're *for,* Gabriel. The only reason they exist is to be shit on."

Once again Raphael felt that strange shock that always came when Flood let the other name slip.

"Look around out there," Flood went on, obviously unaware that he had called Raphael by the wrong name. "You've got a whole generation of white kids trying to wear Afros and speak in fluent ghetto. Something's radically wrong when white kids knock themselves out trying to look and sound like niggers."

"Ship 'em all back to Africa, huh?"

Flood grinned at him. *"Gotcha!"*

"Damon," Raphael said in exasperation, "quit that."

Flood laughed. "You're still as innocent as ever, Raphael. You still believe everything anybody says to you. You ought to know me better than that by now."

"May all your toenails fall out. Let's get out of this rattrap. I'm starting to get a headache."

"Right on." Flood drained his glass.

They got up and made their way through the seething crowd of half-drunk people between them and the door.

Outside, the sun had gone down and the streetlights were just coming on. They got into Flood's car and sat for a few moments, letting the silence wash over them.

"Great group," Flood said.

"Letting off steam. They build up a lot of pressure during the course of a month."

"Doing what?"

"Living, Damon. Just living—and waiting for the next check."

Flood started his car, and they wound slowly through the streets. "Haven't you had about enough of this sewer?" he asked finally.

"What's that supposed to mean?"

"Let's find some other town. Let's pack up and go on down to San Francisco—or Denver, maybe."

"What brought all that on?"

"The place is starting to irritate me, that's all." Flood's voice was harsh, almost angry. "You can only take so much of a place like Spokane. It's called Spokanitis. That's when you get sick of Spokane."

"I'm settled. I don't feel like moving just yet."

"Okay, Raphael." Flood's voice was strangely light. "It was just a thought."

"Look, Damon," Raphael said seriously. "I appreciate your coming here and all. You've pulled me through some pretty rough times; but if the town bothers you all that much, maybe you ought to cut out. We can keep in touch. Maybe by the end of the summer I'll want to try something new, but right now I'm just not ready to take on that much change. You can understand that."

"Sure," Flood said, his voice still light. "Forget I said anything."

"When do you think you'll be leaving?"

"Oh no." Flood laughed. "I can stand it as long as you can."

They pulled up in front of Raphael's apartment.

Across the street the light was on in Tobe and Sam's place, and Flood looked speculatively at the house. "Let's go see how the old boys are doing," he suggested, and bounded out of the car before Raphael could answer.

Uncertain of what he was up to, Raphael crutched along behind him toward the shabby little house.

The two old men had made some effort to clean the place, and they themselves were clean for the first time since Raphael had known them. There was still caked dirt in the corners, but the floors had been mopped and the woodwork wiped down.

They had been playing cribbage at the table in the dining room, and their cups held coffee. They were a little embarrassed by company and stood around, not knowing exactly what to say. Finally Tobe ordered coffee.

"Wait one," Flood said quickly, and dashed out of the house again. He came back a moment later with a brown-bagged bottle of whiskey and set it down on the table. "Why don't we have a drink instead?" he suggested, his eyes very bright.

Tobe and Sam sat at the table, looking at the bottle with a terrible longing on their faces.

"What do you think, Sam?" Tobe asked hesitantly.

"I don't know," Sam said, still looking at the bottle. "Maybe one won't hurt."

"I'll get some glasses." Tobe got up quickly.

In a fury, almost sick with rage, Raphael stood up, took his crutches, and stumped out of the house. Blindly, he went down the steps, jabbing down hard with the tips of his crutches. For a moment he actually hated Flood.

On the corner, in the pale glow of the streetlight, Patch stood watching him as he came out of the house. Then, after a moment when they had looked wordlessly at each other, he turned and went on silent feet out of the light and into the darkness, and then he was gone.

 **iii**

Flood was in a foul humor when he came by a few days later, and he'd only been at Raphael's apartment for a few minutes before they were snapping at each other.

"Maybe!" Flood said. "Don't be so goddamn wishy-washy. Give me a date—some kind of approximation."

"I don't *know.* I told you before I'm just not ready for that kind of change yet. If this place bothers you so much, go ahead and take off."

"How can you stand this town? There's absolutely nothing to do here."

"All right." Raphael said it flatly. "I'm going to explain this once more. Maybe you'll listen this time. I've got some pretty damned big adjustments to make, and this is a good place to make them. The fact that there's nothing to do makes it all the better."

"Come *on.* You're fine. You're not going to adjust by just sitting still."

"I'm not sitting still. I'm in therapy. I'm still learning how to walk, and you want to drag me off to a town that's wall-to-wall hills. Have you got any idea how far I'd bounce if I happened to fall down in San Francisco?" It was the first time either of them had directly mentioned Raphael's injury, and it made him uncomfortable. It also made him angry that it was finally necessary. It was because of the anger that he went on. "That's the one thing you can't understand, Damon—falling down. If *you* trip or stumble, you can catch yourself. I can't. And even if you *do* happen to fall, you can get up again. I can't. Once I'm down, I'm *down,* baby—until somebody comes along and helps me get back up again. I can't even bend over to pick up my crutches. I have nightmares about it. I fall down in the street, and people just keep on walking around me. Have you got the faintest idea how degrading it is to have to ask somebody to help you get up? I have to lie there and *beg* strangers for help."

Flood's face was sober. "I didn't realize. I'm sorry, Raphael. I guess I wasn't thinking. You *have,* I suppose?"

"Have what?"

"Fallen."

"What the hell do you think I've been talking about? Christ, yes, I've fallen—a dozen times. I've fallen in the street, I've fallen in hallways, I've fallen down stairs. Once I fell down in a men's room and had to lie there for a half hour before some guy came in and helped me up. Don't beat me over the head about moving until I get to the point where I can get back on my feet without help. *Then* we'll talk about it. Until then I'm going to stay right where I am, and no amount of badgering is going to move me. Now, can we talk about something else?"

"Sure. Sorry I brought it up."

They talked for a while longer, but Raphael's mood had turned as sour as Flood's, and both of them were unnecessarily curt with each other.

"I'll catch you later," Flood said finally, standing up. "All we're going to do is snipe at each other today."

"All right." Raphael also got up and crutched out onto the roof behind Flood.

At the railing he looked down into the street and watched Flood come out at the bottom of the stairs.

Next door Crazy Charlie was furtively putting out his garbage. His face brightened when he saw Flood. "Hi, Jake," he offered timidly.

Flood turned, changing direction in midstride without changing his pace. He bore down on Crazy Charlie and stopped only a few inches from the nervously quailing man. "Henry," he said, his voice harsh. "I've been meaning to talk to you—for your own good."

Charlie's head swiveled this way and that, his eyes darting, looking for a way to escape.

"How come you shave your head like that, Henry?" Flood demanded. "It looks silly as hell, you know. And you missed a place—just over your left ear."

Horror-stricken, Charlie reached up and felt his head.

"And why don't you take a bath? You stink like cat piss all the time. If you can't keep the cats from pissing on your clothes, get rid of the goddamn things. And just who the hell are you talking to all the time? I've seen you talk for hours when there's nobody there. Do you know what they call you around here? Crazy Charlie, that's what they call you. They watch you through the windows and laugh at you because you're so crazy. You'd better straighten up, Henry, or they're going to come after you with the butterfly net and lock you up in the crazy house." Flood's voice was ruthless, and he kept advancing on the helpless man in front of him.

Quite suddenly Charlie broke and ran, stumbling up the stairs, almost falling.

"Nice talking to you, Henry," Flood called after him, and then he laughed mockingly.

Charlie's door slammed, and Flood, still laughing, went to his car.

Upstairs, Raphael caught one quick glimpse of Crazy Charlie's haunted face before the shades came down.

They did not go up again.

iv

Several afternoons later they were in the tavern again. Some need drove Flood to such places occasionally. They hadn't spoken of the incident with Crazy Charlie, nor had Flood raised again the issue of leaving Spokane.

The tavern was quieter this time and less crowded. The orgy of drunken conviviality that always accompanied Mother's Day had passed when the money ran out, and the losers had settled down to the grim business of grinding out the days until the next check came. The ones in the tavern spaced their drinks, making them last.

The only exception was the large table where Heck's Angels sat in full regalia—creaking leather and greasy denim. They drank boisterously with much raucous laughter and bellowed obscene jests. They all tried, with varying degrees of success, to look burly and dangerous.

Big Heintz, his purple helmet pulled low over his eyes, bulked large and surly at the head of the table like some medieval warlord surrounded by his soldiers, and drank and glowered around the tavern, looking for some real or imagined slight—some excuse to start a brawl. The others—Marvin, Jimmy, Little Hitler, and two or three more Raphael had seen but never bothered to put names to—glanced quickly at him after each joke or remark, looking for some hint of a laugh or expression of approval, but Big Heintz remained morose and pugnacious.

"Hey Jake," Marvin said to Flood, "why don't you two join us?"

Flood raised his glass in mock salute, but made no move to shift around from the table at which he and Raphael sat.

"Maybe he don't want to," Big Heintz rumbled, staring hard at Flood. Suddenly he turned irritably on Little Hitler, who had just punched the same song on the jukebox that he had already played three times in succession. "For Chrissake, Lonnie, ain't there no other fuckin' songs on that sumbitch?"

"I like it," Little Hitler said defensively.

The song was a maudlin lament by some half-witted cracker over his recently deceased girlfriend. Little Hitler sat misty-eyed, his thin, pimply face mournful as the lugubrious caterwauling continued.

"Shit!" Heintz snorted contemptuously when the song ended.

"I think he left out the last verse," Flood said, grinning.

"I never heard no other verses." Little Hitler sounded a bit truculent.

"I thought everybody knew the last verse. It's the point of the whole song."

"Well, I never heard it. How does it go?"

Flood looked up at the ceiling. "Let's see if I can remember it." And then he started to sing in his rich voice. The impromptu verse he added was cynical and grossly obscene. There was an almost shocked silence when he finished.

"Hey, *man!*" Little Hitler said in the almost strangled tone of someone mortally offended.

Suddenly Heintz burst out with a roar of laughter, pounding on the table with glee.

The other Angels, always quick to follow, also began to laugh.

Big Heintz's laughter was gargantuan. He kept pounding on the table and stomping his feet, his beefy face red and contorted. "You slay me, Jake," he finally gasped, wiping at his eyes. "You absolutely fuckin' slay me." And he roared off into another peal of laughter.

Flood's impromptu parody changed the tone of the afternoon. Big Heintz was suddenly in better spirits, and the Angels quickly became gleeful and sunny-tempered. Raphael had almost forgotten Flood's gift for parody, which had so amused him when they were in school. The Angels still swaggered back and forth to the bar for more beer or to the men's room to relieve themselves with their cycle chains and chukka sticks dangling from their belts and their eyes flat and menacing, but their mood was no longer one of incipient riot.

Flood pulled their table closer to that of the Angels and introduced Raphael as Rafe, casting one apologetic glance at him as he did.

Big Heintz watched Raphael hitch his chair around to the newly positioned table.

"Hey, Rafe," he said good-humoredly, "how'd you lose the pin?"

"Hit a train." Raphael shrugged.

"Hurt it much?" Big Heintz asked, grinning.

"Scared it pretty bad."

This sent Heintz off into another gale of table-pounding, foot-stomping laughter. "You guys absolutely fuckin' *slay* me. Fuckin' absolutely *waste* my ass."

The party went on for another half hour or so. Raphael watched and listened, but didn't say anything more. Finally he turned to Flood. "I think I'll cut out."

"Stick around," Flood urged. "We'll go in a little bit."

"That's okay. It's not too far, and I need some exercise anyway."

"Don't be stupid."

"I'm serious. I really want to walk for a bit. I've been riding so much lately that I'm starting to get out of practice."

Flood looked at him for a moment. "Suit yourself. I'll stop by later."

"Sure." Raphael pushed himself up. Carefully, avoiding the tables and chairs, he crutched out of the tavern into the pale, late-afternoon sunlight.

It had rained that morning, and the streets all had that just-washed look. The air was clean, and it was just cool enough to make the exertion of walking pleasant.

The houses were all turn-of-the-century style, and many of them had a kind of balcony or sitting porch on the second floor. Raphael thought that those porches might have been used quite frequently when the houses were new, but he had not seen anyone on one of them since he had come to Spokane.

Bennie the Bicycler rode past on his way to the grocery store.

Raphael kept walking, consciously trying to make his pace as smooth as possible. It was important to measure the stride. Too short and he stumped; too long and he had to heave with his shoulders. The idea was to kind of flow along.

It was farther back to his apartment than he had thought, and about halfway there he stopped to rest. He had not walked much since he'd bought the car, and he was surprised to discover that his arms and shoulders were tired.

The snarling roar of the motorcycles was several blocks away when he first heard it. He leaned against a tree and waited.

The three bikes, with Big Heintz in the lead, came charging down the street, popping and smoking as always. Oddly, or perhaps not, Flood was mounted on one of the bikes, and he didn't seem to be having much difficulty with it. Big Heintz had a vicious grin on his face as they roared by. Trailing behind the bikes were two of the Angels' clattering cars, and behind them Marvin was driving Flood's little red sports car. They toured the neighborhood slowly, letting themselves be seen.

Bennie the Bicycler came peddling back with two sacks of groceries balanced in the basket on his handlebars. The Angels came sputtering back and spotted him.

The original intention, if it had even fully formulated itself in Heintz's thick skull, was probably simply to buzz Bennie once and then go on, but Flood was aboard one of the bikes, and that was not enough for him. As he passed Bennie he suddenly cramped his front wheel over hard and drove in a tight circle around the man on the bicycle. Bennie wobbled, trying to avoid the snarling motorcycle. Big Heintz and Little Hitler, already halfway up the block, turned, came back, and followed Flood in the circling of the wobbling bicycle. Bennie's eyes grew wide, and his course grew more erratic as he tried to maintain control of his bicycle. The noise was deafening, and Bennie began to panic. With a despairing lunge he drove his bicycle toward the comparative safety of the sidewalk, but in his haste he misjudged it and smashed headlong into the rear of a parked car. With a clatter he pitched over the handlebars of his bicycle onto the car's trunk and then rolled off.

The front wheel of his bicycle was twisted into a rubber-tired pretzel, and the bags fell to the street and broke. Dented cans rolled out, and a gallon container of milk gushed white into the gutter.

With jackal-like laughter the Angels roared away, leaving Bennie sprawled in the street in the midst of his bargains. As he passed, Flood flickered one quick glance at Raphael, but his expression did not change.

Slowly, painfully, Bennie got up. Grunting, he began to gather the dented cans and moldy cheese and wilted produce. Then he saw the bicycle. With a low cry he dropped his groceries again and picked up the bike. He took hold of the wheel and tried to straighten it with his hands, but it was obviously hopeless.

Raphael wished that he might do something, but there was nothing he could do. Slowly he crutched on past the spot where Bennie stood in the midst of the garbage that had been his whole reason for existence, staring at the ruin of his bicycle. His lip was cut and oozed blood down onto his chin, and his eyes were filled with tears.

Raphael went by and said nothing.

When he got home, he went up the stairs and locked the door at the top.

Up the street the Angels were partying again, their voices loud and raucous. Flood was with them, and his red car was parked at the curb among theirs. Raphael went inside and pulled his curtains.

The party up the street ground on, growing louder and louder until about midnight, when somebody on the block called the police.

 **V**

Toward the end of June the rainy weather finally broke, and it turned warm. The stunning heat of July had not yet arrived, and it was perhaps the most pleasant part of the year in Spokane.

Raphael found that the mornings were particularly fine. He began to arise earlier, often getting up with the first steely light long before the sun rose. The streets below were quiet then, and he could sit on his rooftop undisturbed and watch the delicate shadings of colors in the morning sky as the sun came up. By seven the slanting light was golden as it came down through the trees and lay gently on the streets almost like a benediction.

Flood came by infrequently now, although he often visited with Heck's Angels just up the street until the early hours of the morning. A kind of unspoken constraint had come between Raphael and Flood. It was as if some unacknowledged affront had taken place that neither of them could exactly remember but that both responded to. They were studiously correct with each other, but no more than that.

Raphael considered this on one splendid morning as he sat with his third cup of coffee, looking down over the railing into the sunlit street. He had placed his scanner in an open window, but it merely winked and twinkled at him as the city lay silent in sleep, with yesterday's passion and violence and stupidity finished and today's not yet begun. He felt strange about Flood now. Weeks before he had even experienced a sharp pang of jealousy when Flood had first begun to hang around with the Angels, but now he was indifferent. He noticed Flood's comings and goings at the crowded house up the street without much interest.

A movement caught his eye, and he turned slightly to watch.

Spider Granny, housecoat-wrapped and slapping-slipper shod, trundled down the other street on her morning pilgrimage to the porch where Sadie was already enthroned in ponderous splendor.

Ruthie, the retarded child, recognized her and bellowed a bull-like greeting from the playpen where she spent her days.

"There's Granny's little darling," Sadie's mother cooed. She bustled up onto the porch and fussed over the drooling idiot in the pen.

Sadie said nothing, but sat stolidly, her head sunk in the rolls of fat around her neck, and her face set in its usual expression of petulant discontent.

"She seems more alert today," Spider Granny observed hopefully. "She recognized me right off—didn't you, love?"

The idiot bellowed at her.

Sadie still said nothing.

"Are you all right, Rita?" Sadie's mother asked her. "You sure are quiet this morning. I'll fix us some coffee, and you can tell Mother all about it." She patted the idiot's head fondly and bustled on into the house. A few minutes later she came out with two steaming cups and offered one to her daughter.

Sadie did not move, and her face did not change expression.

"Will you take this?" her mother demanded irritably, bending over with the coffee.

Sadie sat, mountainlike in her gross immobility.

"Rita," Spider Granny said sharply. "Snap out of it." She set the coffee cups down on the porch railing and turned back to her daughter. "Aren't you feeling well, dear?" She reached out and touched the sitting woman.

The scream was enormous, a sound at once so vast and so shocking that it seemed to lie palpably in the street. Even the birds were stunned into silence by it.

Spider Granny backed away, her hands to the sides of her face, and screamed again, another window-shaking shriek.

The idiot in the playpen began to bellow a deep-throated bass accompaniment to her grandmother's screams.

Doors began to bang open up and down the street, and the losers all came flooding out in response to the primal call of Granny's screams. Mostly they stood watching, but a few went down to Sadie's house.

Sadie, sitting in vast and splendid silence, neither moved nor spoke, and her expression remained imperially aloof.

"District Four," the scanner said.

"Four."

"Fourteen-hundred block of North Birch. We have a report of a possible DOA on a front porch."

"Have you got an exact address?" District Four asked.

"The complainant stated that there were several people there already," the dispatcher said. "Didn't know the exact house number."

"Okay," Four said.

Spider Granny had finally stopped screaming and now stood in vacant-eyed horror, staring at the solid immensity of her daughter. The idiot in the playpen, however, continued to bellow and drool.

More of the neighbors came down to stand on the lawn. The children came running to gape in silent awe. Chicken Coop Annie waddled down, and Mousy Mary scurried across the street.

Queenlike Sadie, sat to death, received in silence this final tribute.

Then the police arrived, and shortly thereafter the ambulance.

Bob the Barber drove up and pushed his way through the crowd on his front lawn. He spoke with the policemen and the ambulance drivers on the porch, but he did not touch his wife or even seem to look at her.

They struggled with Sadie's vast bulk, and it took two policemen as well as the two attendants to carry the perilously bending stretcher to the back of the ambulance.

The crowd on the front lawn lingered after the ambulance drove off, murmuring among themselves as if reluctant to leave. Two of the women led Spider Granny, weeping now, back up the street to her house, and the rest of the crowd slowly, reluctantly broke up. The children hung around longer, hoping to see something else, but it was over.

Bob the Barber sank into Sadie's vacant swing and sat, his gray face seemingly impassive, but Raphael could quite clearly see the tears that ran slowly down his cheeks.

The idiot in the playpen drooled and bellowed, but otherwise the street was quiet again.

From up the street, his black hair glistening in the sun, Patch came. Somber-faced, he passed the house where the idiot bellowed and the thin, gray-faced man mourned. He crossed the street and walked on past Mousy Mary's house. He glanced up at Raphael once. There seemed for an instant a kind of brief flicker of recognition, but his face did not really change, and as silently as always he passed on up the street and was gone.

AVE FORMOSISSIMA, GEMMA PRETIOSA, AVE DECUS VIRGINUM, VIRGO GLORIOSA

THEY BROKE FOR LUNCH AT NOON as they usually did, and Raphael and Denise sought out a quiet place in the storeroom to eat. "You seem to be down lately," she said. "Is something bothering you?"
"Not really. A woman died on my block last week. That's always sort of depressing."
"A friend of yours?" she asked, her voice neutral.
"Not hardly. She was a monster."
"Why the concern then?"
"Her husband took it pretty hard. I didn't think he would."
"What did she die from?"
"She sat herself to death."
"She *what*?"
Raphael told her about Sadie the Sitter, and Denise sat listening. It was easy to talk to Denise. There was about her a kind of calmness, a tranquility that seemed to promise acceptance of whatever he said. She was sitting in a patch of sunlight that streamed through a dusty window. He noticed for the first time as he spoke with her that her skin was not pale so much as it was translucent, and her sunlit hair was not really limp and dun-colored but was really quite thick and shaded through all the hues of blond from palest gold to deep ash. In response, as it was now, her face was Madonna-like.
She looked up and caught him watching her. "Please don't stare at me, Rafe," she said, blushing slightly. Her tone, however, was matter-of-fact. "We don't do that to each other. We don't *avoid* looking at each other, but we don't stare. I thought you knew that." She turned slightly so that the dwarfed arm was hidden from him.
"I wasn't staring at that. Did you know that your hair isn't all the same color?"
"Thanks a lot. Now I've got something else to worry about."
"Don't be silly. Everybody's hair has different colors in places. Mine's darker at the neck and sides than it is on top, but you're seventeen different shades of blond."

"I'll get it all cut off," she threatened, "and start wearing a wig—bright red, maybe."

"Bite your tongue."

"Is what's-his-name still around?"

"Who? Flood? Yes, he's still here. I haven't seen much of him lately, though. He's found other diversions."

"Good. Let's hope it's a sign that he's getting bored and won't stay much longer."

"Be nice."

"No. I don't want to. I want to be spiteful and bitchy about him. I'd like to spit in his eye."

"Sweet child." He shifted around in his chair.

"There's something else, isn't there, Rafe?"

He grunted. "My caseworker's been on my case lately." It was an outrageous pun, but he rather liked it.

"I didn't know you had one."

"It's sort of semiofficial. I pick on her a lot, but she keeps coming back for more."

"You have to be very careful with those people, Rafe."

"If I could handle Shimpsie, I can sure as hell deal with Frankie."

"Who's Shimpsie?"

"She was the social worker in the hospital where they modified me." He told her the story of Shimpsie and of his daring escape from her clutches. "Frankie's definitely not in Shimpsie's league," he added.

"That's where you're making your mistake, Rafe. You won once. You got away from this Shimpsie person, and now you've got a caseworker who seems to be no more than a cute little bubblehead. You're overconfident, and they'll eat you alive."

"Frankie's hardly dangerous."

"Don't kid yourself." Her pale face was deadly serious. "They're *all* dangerous."

"Only if you want something from them. I'm more or less independent, so I don't have any handles on me. It makes Frankie crazy."

"Their power goes a lot further than that, Rafe. The whole system is on their side. They have the police, the courts—everything—on their side. They can *make* you do what they tell you to do. They can put you in jail, they can tear your family apart, they can have you committed to an asylum. There's almost nothing they can't do to you. Isn't it a comfort to know that some little froth-head who spent her college years on her back and graduated with a solid C-minus average has absolute power over your life?"

"Frankie's not like that. She's more like a puppy."

"Puppies have very sharp teeth, Rafe."

"You've had bad experiences, I take it."

"We've *all* had bad experiences. Caseworkers are our natural enemies. They're the cats and we're the mice. You want another cup of coffee?''

"That'd be nice," he said, smiling at her.

She got up and started to squeeze past him. There was a warm, almost sweet fragrance about her. When she was behind him, she touched his hair. "It *is* darker in places, isn't it?" Her hand lingered on his head.

"Careful. It takes a week to untangle it."

"I'd give my soul for curly hair like that."

"It's vastly overrated."

"Why don't you let it grow a little longer?"

"I prefer not to look like a dust mop."

"You're impossible." She laughingly mussed his hair and scampered away.

"Rat!" he called after her.

He felt good. For the first time in weeks he actually felt good. After work he ran a couple of errands and drove on home, still feeling in good spirits. The sun was warm, and the sky was bright. Ever since his accident he had become accustomed to a kind of dormancy, settling for the most part for a simple absence of pain, but now he began to perceive that somewhere—maybe a long way down the road yet, but someday certainly and inevitably—he would actually be happy again. It was a good feeling to know that.

A young woman he did not recognizing was standing at the row of mailboxes at the front of the apartment. For an instant his chest seemed to constrict almost with fear. From a particular angle she almost exactly resembled Marilyn Hamilton. Then she turned, and it was all right. The similarity was not that great.

He got out of his car in order to give her time to get her mail and go back inside, but she did not move. Instead, she stood looking somewhat distracted, one hand to her stomach, and her face turning suddenly very pale.

"Are you all right?" he asked.

She looked sharply at him with quick, hard suspicion. Then she saw the crutches and relaxed. "I think I'm going to faint," she announced quite calmly.

"Around here," Raphael said, loping toward her with his long one-legged stride. "Hang on to the building." He led her around the corner to the stairs that went up to his rooftop. "Sit down. Put your head between your knees."

Gratefully, she sank down onto the bottom step and put her head down.

"Breathe deeply," he instructed.

"I know."

"Are you sick? I mean, do you want me to take you to a hospital or anything?"

"No. I'm just pregnant," she said wryly, lifting her head. "There's no cure for that except time—or a quick trip to a non-Catholic doctor."

"Is it—" He faltered. "I mean, it's not time or anything, is it?"

She grinned at him suddenly, her face still pale. "Either you aren't very observant, or you haven't been around very many pregnant women. You swell up like a balloon before you get to the point of the trip to the hospital. I'm getting a little hippy, but my tummy hasn't started to pooch out that much yet. I've still got months of this to look forward to."

"Are you feeling better now?"

"I'll be all right. It's a family trait. My mother used to faint all the time when she was carrying Brian—that's my kid brother." She got up slowly.

"Maybe you ought to sit still for a little longer."

"It's all passed now. Thanks for the help."

"You sure you're going to be all right?"

"I'll be fine. Do you live here?"

"Up there." He nodded his head at the steps.

"The penthouse? I wondered who lived there. Isn't it a little . . ." She glanced at the crutches.

"It's no particular problem."

"Well, I guess I'd better get back to cleaning my apartment. I think that whoever lived there before kept goats or something." She smiled at him. "See you." She went back around to the front of the building again.

Later, on his rooftop, Raphael thought about the girl. In some ways she seemed to be much like Marilyn, but there were differences. Her voice was lighter, and the expressions were different. And this girl seemed wiser, less vulnerable than Marilyn had been.

It surprised him that he could think about Marilyn now without pain or even the fear of pain that had locked away that part of his memory for so long. He found that he could even remember Isabel without discomfort. He experimented with the memories—trying consciously to stir some of the old responses, wondering almost clinically if there might be some vestigial remnants of virility left. But there were not, of course. Finally, disgusted with himself, he thought about other things.

Flood drove by late that afternoon and came up to the rooftop instead of stopping at the house where Heck's Angels lounged belligerently on the lawn, daring the neighbors to complain. Raphael resisted the temptation to make some clever remark about Flood's new friends. Things were uncomfortable enough between them already.

Flood leaned negligently against the railing as always. His face seemed strained, and his complexion was more sallow. There was something tense about him, almost as if somehow, in some obscure fashion, things were going wrong, and he was losing control—not only of the situation, but of himself as well. He smoked almost continually now, flipping the butts out to arc down into the street below and almost immediately lighting another. "I *hate* this goddamned town," he said finally with more passion than he'd probably intended.

"You don't have to stay."

Flood grunted and stared moodily down at the street. "It doesn't *mean* anything. This is the most pointless place in the whole damned universe. What the hell is it doing here, for Chrissake? What possessed them to build a town here in the first place?"

"Who knows? The railroad, probably."

"And the people are just as pointless as the town," Flood went on. "Empty, empty, empty—like the residents of a graveyard. They have no meaning, no significance. I'm not just talking about your losers— I'm talking about all of them. Good God, the vacancy of the place! How the hell can you stand it?"

"I grew up in a pretty vacant place, remember?"

"You're wrong. I saw Port Angeles. At the end of his life a man there can say, 'I cut down some trees and made some lumber. They took the lumber and built some houses with it.' That's *something*, for God's sake! What the hell can a man say about his life here? 'I buried my grandpa in 1958, my mother in seventy-two, and my old man in eighty-five; I contributed about eight tons of shit to the sewage-treatment plant; and they're going to bury me right over there in that dandy little graveyard on the other side of the river.' Fertilizer—that's all they're good for, fertilizer." He turned to Raphael suddenly. "Well, by God, I decline to be a fertilizer factory for the greater glory of the shit capital of America. I've had it with this place."

"When do you think you'll be leaving?" Raphael asked, his voice neutral.

Flood grinned at him suddenly. "Gotcha again," he said.

"Damon," Raphael said in annoyance, "quit playing games."

"Oh, no, Raphael," Flood declaimed. "You won't escape me so easily. I will hound you; I will dog your footsteps; I will harry you out of this vacuum and deliver your soul to the Prince of Darkness, who sits expectant in steamy hell. Double-dipped in vilest corruption shall I send you to the eternal fire and the loathsome embrace of the Emperor of the Inferno."

"Oh, that's good," Raphael said admiringly. "I thought you'd lost your touch for a while there. That was particularly fine."

"I rather liked it," Flood admitted modestly, and then he laughed, the mocking laughter that Raphael remembered so well, and his eyes glittered in the ruddy glow of the dying sun.

And then in mid-July it turned suddenly hot. With no apparent transition from pleasant to unbearable, the temperature soared to the one-hundred-degree mark and stuck there. The streets shimmered like the tops of stoves, and lawns that were not constantly watered wilted and browned under the blasting weight of the swollen sun.

Sleep was impossible, of course. Even long past midnight the interiors of the houses on Raphael's block were like ovens. The losers sat on their porches or their lawns in the dark, and the children ran in screaming packs up and down the streets. Fights broke out with monotonous regularity. Since they lived in continual frustration anyway, always on the verge of rage, the added aggravation of the stunning heat made the smallest irritation a *casus belli*.

Raphael's tiny apartment on the roof was unprotected from the sun for the largest part of the day, and the interior heated up like a blast furnace. The rooftop was unbearable under the direct weight of the sun. He lingered at work, finding refuge in the dim coolness of the barnlike store, and he helped Denise with the volumes of paperwork that were a part of her job.

The heat added a new dimension to his discomfort. Perspiration irritated the relatively new scar tissue on his hip, and he sometimes writhed from the phantom pain of the missing leg. The swimming that was a part of his therapy helped, but ten minutes after he had pulled himself out of the pool, he was sweltering again.

Only at night when there was sometimes a slight breeze, could he find any kind of comfort. He would sit on his rooftop stupefied by lack of sleep and watch the streets below.

"Hello? Are you up there?" It was the girl from downstairs. She stood one midnight on the sidewalk in front of the house, looking up at the roof.

"Yes," Raphael said, looking over the railing.

"Would it be all right if I came up? I'm suffocating in there."

"Sure. The stairs are on the side."

"I'll be right up." She disappeared around the corner of the house. He heard her light step on the stairs, and then she came out onto the roof. "It's like a stove in my apartment," she said, coming over to where he sat.

"I know. Mine's the same way."

"I've got a fan, but all it does is move the hot air around. If I take off any more clothes, I'll get arrested for indecent exposure." She wore a light housecoat and kept her arms crossed tightly in front of her body.

"It's brutal," Raphael agreed, "and it's probably not going to get any better for a while."

Up the street one of Heck's Angels was fighting with his girlfriend. They stood on the lawn, screaming obscenities at each other.

"Does that go on all the time?" the girl asked.

"More or less."

"Aren't there an awful lot of them living in that house?"

"Fifteen or twenty. It varies from week to week."

The young man up the street got into his car, slammed the door, and roared away. The girl on the lawn screamed at him until he turned the corner. Then it was quiet again.

The girl from downstairs sank down onto the small bench Flood had brought up to the roof a few weeks ago and laid her arm on the railing. "This is a fun neighborhood," she said dryly.

"That it is." Raphael thought briefly of telling her about the losers—simply to pass the long hours until things cooled down enough to allow two or three hours of sleep just before dawn—but he decided not to. He didn't know her that well, and he didn't want to take the chance of offending her.

They sat in the silent darkness on the roof, watching the children loitering on corners or creeping furtively around the houses.

"Is your husband out of town?" Raphael asked finally.

"I'm not married."

"I'm sorry. I just assumed—" He stopped, embarrassed.

"Because I'm pregnant? You don't have to be married to get pregnant. It happens in the best of families these days."

"I'm not being nosy. It's none of my business."

She laughed. "In a few months it'll be *everybody's* business. It's a condition that's pretty hard to conceal."

"Things'll work out."

"*Sure* they will. Nothing like a little unwed pregnancy to add spice to a girl's life."

A police car cruised by, and there was the usual scramble out the back doors of the neighborhood.

The night wound on, still hot and close, and, as the losers began to seek their beds for a few hours of restless sleep, the crickets and tree frogs began to sing the raspy song of summer.

Lulled by their song, Raphael caught himself half dozing in his chair a few times.

The girl talked about many things—mostly about the little town near the Canadian border where she had grown up. Her voice was soft, almost dreamy, and in his weariness Raphael listened not so much to her words as to the soft murmur of her voice.

"It's all so trite, she said. "It's almost like a bad soap opera. Poor little girl from Metalline Falls comes to the big city to go to college. Girl meets boy. Boys seduces girl. Girl gets pregnant. Boy runs away. I feel like the heroine in one of those gloomy nineteenth-century novels we used to have to read in high school. I guess I'm supposed to drown myself or something."

"I don't particularly recommend it. That river over there's got a fierce current to it. You could get yourself pretty thoroughly beaten up by all the rocks in the process."

"You've got a point there." She laughed. "Drowning yourself in the Spokane River could be a pretty hectic experience. I checked out a couple of those homes they have, but I don't think I'd like that. The girls all looked kind of pale and morning-sicky, and the nuns were very kind and maternal, but you can see that they disapprove. I just don't feel like being disapproved of right now."

"Do you plan to keep the baby?"

"Of course. I'm not going to go through all of this and then not have anything to show for it." She fell silent again.

Quite clearly, almost like the obvious plot of a piece of bad fiction, Raphael could see the girl's life stretched out in front of her. The baby would come at its appointed time; and because there was no alternative and a baby must be clothed and fed and suitably housed, the girl would turn to those social agencies that even now lurked on the horizon waiting for her. The agencies were very kind, very understanding, but they demanded of their clients a certain attitude. First of all there must be no pride, no dignity. The girl would have to learn to grovel. Groveling is one of the most important qualifications for welfare recipients. Once she had been taught to grovel in front of the desks of superior young ladies with minimal degrees in social science, she would almost be ready to join the ranks of the losers. With her pride and self-respect gone, she would be ready to accept the attentions of one of the horde of indolent young men who can smell a welfare check the way a shark smells blood. Her situation would quickly become hopeless, and her humor and intelligence would erode. She would begin to court crisis out of sheer boredom, and any chance for meaning or improvement would be blown away like dry leaves in the first blast of winter.

"Not *this* one," Raphael murmured more to himself than to any blind impish gods of mischance.

"What?" the girl asked.

"Nothing. Do you have to stay here—in Spokane, I mean?"

She shrugged, and Raphael almost ground his teeth at the futility of the gesture. Indifference was the first symptom of that all-prevalent disease that infested the streets below. If she was to be salvaged, that would have to be attacked first.

"The hospitals are good," she said, "and I'm going to need a hospital before the year's out."

"There are hospitals everyplace, and it's not like you were going to be going in for brain surgery, you know."

She shrugged again. "Spokane's as good as any place—certainly better than Metalline Falls. I couldn't go back there."

"Why not?"

"I just couldn't. You don't know small towns."

"I know big ones," he said grimly.

The night was still warm, and the hot reek of dust still rose from the sun-blased street below, and the crickets and tree frogs sang endlessly of summer as Raphael for the first time began carefully to attack the disease that until now he had only observed.

iii

One night, several evenings later, Flood came by with some beer, and he sat on the rooftop with Raphael, talking dispiritedly.

"I thought you were a martini man," Raphael observed.

"I've fallen in with evil companions. Most of these cretins don't know a martini from a manhattan. Besides, it's too hot. Unless you swill it right down, a martini turns lukewarm on you in this kind of weather."

"Nothing like a belt of warm gin to fix you right up."

Flood shuddered.

Down at the corner a motorcycle snarled and popped as Big Heintz made his appearance. He pulled up onto the lawn of the house up the street and stepped off his bike. "The Dragons are in town," he announced to the Angels and their women, who lounged in wilted discomfort on the porch.

"Dragons?" Raphael murmured. "What's that big clown been smoking?"

"It's a rival gang," Flood told him, his voice tensing slightly. "They're from Seattle. They come over here every so often, and there's always a big fight."

"Whoopee," Raphael said flatly.

On the lawn Heck's Angels gathered around Big Heintz, all talking excitedly. "Who seen 'em?" Jimmy demanded.

"Leon was at the Savage House." Heintz flexed his beefy shoulders. "He seen a couple of 'em come in flyin' their colors. The Mongol was one of 'em."

"Wow!" Jimmy said. "They mean business, then. The Mongol is one bad motherfucker. I seen 'im a couple years ago. He absolutely *creamed* Otto."

"I ain't afraid of that fuckin' Mongol," Heintz declared belligerently.

"Anybody know where they're hangin' out?" Little Hitler asked.

"We'll find 'em." Heintz said it grimly.

Jimmy ran into the house and came back out with a length of heavy chain. He swung it whistling around his head.

"This is it," Big Heintz announced solemnly. "This is really it—the last and final war. Them fuckers been comin' over here every summer. They find one or two of our guys and stomp 'em, and then they all run back to Seattle. This time it's gonna be different. This is gonna be the last and final war." He strode up and down in front of the Angels, his beard bristling and his helmet pulled low over his eyes. "I sent out the word," he went on. "Everybody's comin', and I mean *everybody*. This time them fuckers ain't gonna find just one or two of us. They're gonna find *all* of us, and it's gonna be a *war*!"

They were all talking at once now, their voices shrill and excited. Several of the others ran into the house for chains and lengths of pipe and nail-studded baseball bats.

"You gonna take the Mongol, Heintz?" Jimmy asked breathlessly.

Heintz struck a dangerous pose. "Yeah. I'm gonna take that fuckin' Mongol. I'm gonna *waste* that motherfucker. Somebody get my gear." He tucked his thumbs into his belt and puffed out his chest. "Anybody that ain't got the guts for real war better split now, 'cause there's gonna be blood, man, *blood*!"

Flood was breathing rapidly. Suddenly he stood up.

"Where are *you* going?" Raphael demanded.

"I thought I—" Flood broke off.

"What in God's name is the matter with you, Damon? You don't really *care*, do you? All they're going to do is ride around looking tough, and then they'll all get drunk and spend the rest of the night telling each other how mean they would have been. Don't be childish."

Flood stared at him, hard-faced, and then he suddenly laughed. "Shit," he said, sitting back down. "This goddamn place is turning me into a ding-a-ling. You know? I was actually going down there. We've got to get out of this town, Raphael. It's starting to percolate our god-damn brains."

Two of the women came out of the house carrying Heintz's imple-ments of combat. He stood very straight while they solemnly put his nail-studded leather vest on him. Then they wrapped his thick waist several times around with a long length of heavy, tinkling chain. One of the women knelt reverently and tucked a long, sheathed knife into his right boot while the other attached a heavy length of taped pipe to the chain around his waist.

"I want you to take the kids inside and bolt all the doors," Heintz instructed. "Put stuff in front of the windows and don't turn on no lights. Them bastards might try to come here an' mess you up while we're gone."

With mute, almost worshipful respect Jimmy handed Big Heintz a can of beer. The big man tipped back his head, drained the can, and then threw it away.

"All right!" he roared. "Let's *go*!"

With a clatter of chains and clubs the Angels piled into their battered cars or aboard their motorcycles. Their engines roared to life, and with smoking exhausts and screeching tires they blasted off, grim-faced, to that last and final war their leader had promised them. Their women, equally grim-faced, gathered the shouting children and retreated to the house, slamming the door behind them.

Big Heintz, his meaty arms proudly crossed, stood in splendid solitude on the now-deserted front lawn. Then slowly, majestically, girt in steel and leather, he strode to his bike, mounted, and tromped savagely down on the starter crank.

Nothing happened.

He tromped again—and again—and yet again. The big Harley wheezed.

"Come on, you bastard," Big Heintz rasped hoarsely. "Come on, *start*!"

For ten minutes Big Heintz tromped, and for ten minutes the big Harley stubbornly refused to start. "Son of a bitch!" Heintz gasped, sweat pouring down his face. "Come on, *please* start!"

Finally, in desperation, he grasped the handlebars and pushed the heavy machine into the street. Running alongside, he pushed the balky bike along the empty street in the long-vanished wake of his departed warriors. At the end of the block he pushed it around the corner and was gone.

The street was silent again except for the strangled sound of Flood's muffled laughter drifting down from the rooftop.

 **iv**

"I'm not the least bit sorry for her," Denise said. "It's her own fault."

"Come on, Denise," Raphael objected.

"Come on, my foot. There's a little pill, remember? If a girl gets pregnant these days, it's because she *wants* to get pregnant. It's just a cheap ticket to an early wedding. I'm glad it didn't work. Next time she'll know better."

"She isn't that kind of girl."

"Really? Then how come she's got a big belly?"

"Don't be coarse."

"Oh, grow up, Rafe," she said angrily, slapping her dwarfed hand down on the table in irritation. "If she's such a nice girl, why didn't she keep her legs crossed? Why are *you* so concerned about what happens to some dim-witted trollop?"

"She's not a trollop. That kind of thing can happen. Young men can be very persuasive sometimes. Don't be so Victorian."

"You haven't answered my question." Her pale face was flushed. "Why are you so interested in her?"

Raphael took a deep breath. "All right," he said finally. "There's a disease on my street. It's a combination of poverty, indifference, stupidity, and an erosion of the will. You could call it the welfare syndrome, I suppose. The people are cared for—they get a welfare check and food stamps. After a while that welfare check is the only important thing to them. They live lives of aimless futility, without dignity. Society feeds them and puts them in minimal housing, and then it quite studiously tries to ignore the fact that they exist. But people are more than cattle. They need more than a bale of hay and a warm stall in some barn. The people on my street turn to violence—to crisis—in an effort to say to the world, 'Look at me. I'm here. I exist.' I'd like to salvage just one of them, that's all. I'd like to beat the system just once. I'd like to keep one of them—just one—out of the soft claws of those bright young ladies you warned me about—the ones who smother lives with welfare checks like you'd smother unwanted kittens with a wet pillow. *That's* what my interest is."

"You're trying to save the world," she said with heavy sarcasm.

"No. Not the world—just one life. If I can't salvage just one life, I don't see much hope for any of us. The social workers will get us all. That's what they want, of course—to get us all—to bury us all with that one universal welfare check—to turn us into cattle."

"And she's pretty, of course," Denise said acidly.

"I hadn't really paid that much attention." That was not entirely true. "She's a human being. Frankly, I wouldn't give a damn if she looked like Frankenstein."

"But she *doesn't* look like Frankenstein, does she?" Denise bored in.

"I didn't notice any bolts sticking out of her neck." Raphael was starting to get tired of it.

"Why don't you *marry* her then?" she suggested. "That'd solve everything, wouldn't it?"

"Don't be silly."

"It's a perfect solution. You can marry her, and you can save her from the goblin social workers. You legitimize her bastard, and then you can spend the rest of your life looking for bolts. I wouldn't worry too much about that—" She pointed at his missing leg. "After all, a girl in her situation can't afford to be *too* choosy, can she?"

"Why don't we just drop this?"

"Why don't we just drop the whole damned thing?" she said hotly. "Why don't you get back to work? We're not paying you to sit around and drink coffee and philosophize about saving the world; we're paying you to fix shoes."

His face tightened, and he got up without saying anything. He grabbed his crutches and stumped back toward his workbench.

"Rafe!" Her voice was stricken. He heard her feet, quick and light on the floor behind him, and then she had her arms around him and her face buried in his chest. He fought to keep his balance. "I'm sorry," she wailed. The tiny hand, twisted and misshapen, clutched the fabric of his shirt at the shoulder, kneading, grasping, trying to hold on. He was surprised at how strong it was.

Denise cried into his chest for a few moments, and then she turned and fled, her face covered with her normal hand.

Raphael stood, still shifting his weight to regain his balance, and stared at her, his face troubled and a hollow feeling in his stomach.

He was still profoundly troubled when he got home that afternoon. He sat for several minutes in his car, staring vacantly out the window.

Hesitantly, old Tobe came out of the house across the street and walked over to Raphael's car. For once he did not seem particularly drunk. "Hello, Rafe," he said, his foghorn voice subdued.

"Tobe."

"You think you could come over to the place for a minute, Rafe?" Tobe asked, his tone almost pleading. "Old Sam's took sick, an' I'm awful worried about him. I don't know what the hell to do."

"How do you mean sick?" Raphael asked, getting out of his car.

"He's just layin' on that couch in the dinin' room there," Tobe said. "He can't get up, an' he talks funny—like he can't quite get the words put together right."

"Let's go." Raphael started across the street.

"I don't think it's nothin' very serious," Tobe said hopefully. "Old Sam's as strong as a horse. He just needs some medicine or somethin' to get him back on his feet."

"You guys drinking again?" Raphael asked, carefully going up the steps onto the porch.

"Not like before. We cut way back. We don't even really get drunk no more."

The little house was almost as filthy as it had been the first time Raphael had seen it. The yellow dog stood in the center of the living room and barked as Raphael entered.

"Shut up, Rudy," Raphael said.

"Go lay down," Tobe ordered the dog.

Rudy gave one last disinterested bark and went back into the dining room.

Sam lay on the rumpled daybed in the dining room partially covered by a filthy quilt. He recognized Raphael and tried to smile. "Hi, buddy," he said weakly in his wheezy voice. His left eye was half-closed, and the left corner of his mouth hung down slackly.

"Hi there, Sam." Raphael steeled himself against the smell and went to the side of the bed. "How you feeling?"

"Funny, kinda." Sam's words were slurred.

Raphael reached down and took hold of the old man's left hand. "Squeeze my hand, Sam."

"Sure, buddy."

The hand in Raphael's grasp did not move or even tremble.

"How's that?" Sam asked.

"That's fine, Sam." Raphael gently laid the hand back down.

"All right?" Sam slurred. " 'M I gonna be all right?"

"Sure, Sam." Raphael turned and crutched toward the living room, motioning with his head for Tobe to follow.

"You come back—real soon now, buddy," Sam said haltingly, and his head fell back on the pillow.

"Can you figure what's wrong with 'im?" Tobe asked anxiously in a low voice.

"We'd better call in an ambulance."

"No!" Tobe shook his head. "He don't want no more hospitals. He told me that when we come outta that detox place after I got sick that time."

"This is different."

"No," Tobe said stubbornly. "He said no more hospitals."

"Tobe, I think he's had a stroke. He could *die* in there if we don't get him to a hospital. His whole left side's paralyzed."

Tobe stared at him for a moment. "Oh, God," he said. "I was afraid that's what it was. Poor old Sam. What are we gonna do, Rafe?"

"We're going to call an ambulance. Sam's got to see a doctor right away."

"All right, Rafe." Tobe's narrow shoulders slumped. "Anything you say. You think he's gonna die?"

"I don't know Tobe. I'm not a doctor. I'll go call an ambulance."

"Okay, Rafe." Tobe's voice was broken. Tears had begun to fill his eyes and spilled over, plowing dirty furrows down his cheeks.

Raphael went out quickly and crutched across the street to call the ambulance.

 **V**

It was early, very early, even before the first faint hint of dawn. Raphael had endured the heat until about two in the morning when the breeze had finally turned cool, and then he had gone to bed. It seemed that he had only slept for a few minutes when he heard the faint, muffled banging on the locked door at the top of the stairs. Groggily, almost sick with the heat and the lack of sleep, he fumbled his way into his pants and reached for his crutches. The leather cuffs that fit around his forearms seemed cold, even clammy, and he shivered slightly at their touch.

"Who's there?" he asked when he reached the locked door.

"It's me." Flood's voice came from the other side. "Unlock the goddamn door." His words seemed mushy, thick.

"Damn!" Raphael muttered, slipping the latch. "Come on, Damon," he said, opening the door, "I'm tired, and I've got to get some sleep."

Flood was bent slightly, and his hands were pressed against his ribs. Raphael could not see his face in the dark stairwell. "Let me in, dammit." He moved into the light, and Raphael could see the blood on his face.

"What happened, Damon?"

"I got hit with a chain," Flood said thickly, "and kicked in the ribs for good measure. Can I sit down?"

"Come on in." Raphael stepped back awkwardly. "Let me have a look at that cut."

Flood lurched across the roof to the apartment, went in, and sank carefully on the couch. There was a long, bruised cut on one side of his forehead, just above the eye, and his lip was cut and swollen. The blood had run down the side of his face and dried there. His olive skin was greenish, and little beads of perspiration stood out on his face. His breathing was shallow, and he kept his hands pressed to his ribs on the right side.

"Let me get some things and clean you up," Raphael said. He turned and went into the bathroom. He got a washcloth and a small bottle of antiseptic. He juggled them around until he could hold them between his fingers and then crutched out to the kitchen. "What happened?" he asked from the sink where he ran cold water on the cloth.

"We went out to visit scenic Hillyard—a very unfriendly part of town. We found the Dragon, and Big Heintz got his last and final war. Jimmy and Marvin are in the hospital, and Heintzie's bleeding out of his ears. A most unsavory group, the Dragons." He laughed slightly and winced. "I think I've got a couple of cracked ribs."

"Why are you running with that bunch anyway?" Raphael demanded, going to the couch and beginning to carefully wash away the caked blood on Flood's face.

"For laughs. All that bully-boy bravado is sort of amusing." Flood's voice was muted and quavered with shock.

"How much fun are you having right now?"

"Not much." Flood winced and stifled a groan.

"This is going to hurt." Raphael carefully started to clean the cut.

"You're right." Flood said it through his clenched teeth.

"That's going to need some stitches," Raphael said, looking at the cut. "You want me to take you to the hospital?"

"You're going to have to, Raphael," Flood said shakily. "I damn near passed out a couple times on my way down here. I dropped Heintzie off up the street, and this was as far as I could make it. The big clown bled all over my front seat. They got him down and kicked him in the head a time or twelve. Jesus!" Flood doubled over, holding his side. "That hurts like hell."

"Don't move around too much. If those ribs are broken, you could puncture a lung."

"You're a little bundle of good news, aren't you?"

"Let me throw on a shirt and a shoe." Raphael went into the bedroom.

"I need a gun," Flood said through the door. "The bastards wouldn't have gotten me if I'd had a gun."

"That's a real sensible approach you've got there." Raphael was lacing up his shoe. "You shoot somebody, and they'll lock you up for-ever. Why don't you just stay away from those half-wits instead?"

"Nobody's going to run Jake Flood off. I'll go where I damn well please and with whoever I damn well please, and the next time some greasy punk comes at me with a chain, I'll make him eat the damned thing."

"You're getting as bad as they are." Raphael came out into the living room again.

"Nobody's going to run me off. I'll get a gun and then I'll make it my personal business to obliterate every one of those bastards."

"Damon," Raphael said firmly, "knock off this bullshit about guns. You don't know anything about them in the first place—and do you actually think you could deliberately pull the trigger on a man? I had to shoot a sick cat once, and I couldn't even do *that*."

"You're different from me, Raphael."

"Not *that* different. It takes a special kind of sickness to shoot a fellow human being, and you're not that sick."

Flood coughed and then he groaned slightly. "I'm pretty sick right now." He was holding his ribs tightly. "All I'll need is a little practice—a bit of plinking."

"Plinking beer cans and shooting people are altogether different, Damon."

"I wasn't thinking of beer cans." Flood's eyes were flat.

It was useless to talk with him. Raphael could see that. Maybe later, when he had calmed down, there might be some hope of getting through to him, but right now he was too angry, too hurt, too affronted and outraged by the beating even to be rational.

"Can you make it downstairs?" Raphael asked. "There's no way I can help you."

"I'll make it." Flood got up from the couch carefully and went back out, still half bent over.

Raphael followed him. "Get into my car," he said when they reached the street. "You aren't going to do those ribs any good trying to fold yourself into that sports car, and I can't work the clutch anyway."

"All right." Flood slowly got into Raphael's car.

Raphael went around to the other side, got in, and started the motor.

Flood was still holding his ribs, and he had his head laid back on the seat. "I've got to get a gun," he said.

 **vi**

After work on Thursday, Raphael gave Denise a lift home as he usually did when he worked late. Things had been a bit strained between them since her outburst the week before, even though they both tried to behave as if the incident had not happened.

"Would you like to come up for coffee?" she asked routinely when he pulled up in front of her apartment house. She did not look at him, and her tone indicated that she did not expect him to accept the invitation.

But because he genuinely liked her and wanted to bury the uneasiness between them, he did not, as usual, start looking for some excuse to beg off. "Sure. For once I don't have a thing to do when I get home."

She looked at him quickly, almost surprised. "Let's go then, before you have time to change your mind."

Her apartment was on the second floor in the back. The building was clean, although the carpeting in the hallway was slightly worn. Denise seemed nervous as she unlocked her door. "The place is a mess," she apologized as they went in. "I haven't had time to clean this week."

It was cool and dim inside, the drapes drawn against the blast of the summer sun. The air was faintly scented with the light fragrance she wore—a virginal, almost little-girl perfume that he noticed only when he was very close to her. The apartment was small and very clean. Probably every woman alive has declared that "the place is a mess" before escorting someone into her living quarters for the first time. Denise had a surprising number of books, Raphael saw, and they ranged from light fiction to philosophy with a far smattering of poetry thrown in. She also had a small record player, and he saw a record jacket. Rather strangely, Denise seemed to have a taste for opera— Puccini in this case.

She led the way into the small kitchen, turned on the light, and pulled a chair out from the table for him. "Sit down. I'll put the pot on."

Raphael eased himself down into the chair and set his crutches against the wall behind him.

At the sink Denise was nervously rinsing out her coffee-pot, holding it in her left hand and leaning far forward to reach the faucet handle with the dwarfed hand. She dropped the pot with a clatter and stepped back quickly to avoid the splash. "Damn. Please don't watch me. I'm not very good at this. I don't get much company."

He looked away, smiling.

She put the pot on the stove, came over, and sat down at the table across from him. She carefully turned so that her right arm was hidden. "I'm going to say something. Don't try to stop me, because this is hard enough to say without being interrupted."

"Okay," he said, still smiling at her.

"I want to apologize for last week. I was being bitchy and there wasn't any excuse for it."

"Forget it. Everybody's cranky right now. It's the heat."

"The heat didn't have anything to do with it. I was jealous—it was just that simple."

"Jealous?"

"Are you blind, Rafe? Of course I was jealous. As soon as you started talking about that girl, I turned bright green all over—I know, there's never been any reason—I mean, there's nothing—no hint or anything that gives me any excuse to feel that way, but I did. I can't help it. It's the way I am."

"Denise—" he started.

"Don't patronize me, Raphael. In spite of everything I'm a woman. I'm not experienced at it or anything, but I *am* a woman, and I *do* get jealous."

"There's no reason to feel that way. There's nothing like that involved. There couldn't be, of course."

"Don't be stupid. Do you think that"—she gestured vaguely at his crutches—"really makes any difference at all? You're intelligent; you're gentle; and you're the most beautiful person I've ever seen." She stopped quickly. "I'm making a fool of myself again, aren't I?"

On the stove the coffeepot started to percolate.

Raphael took a deep breath. It had been bound to happen, of course—someday. It was one of the risks he had taken when he had decided to try to live as normally as possible. Sooner or later it had been bound to happen. "Denise." He tried to keep his voice as neutral as possible.

"Don't try to smooth it over. It's your life, after all. I was stupid even to build up any hopes or anything. Look at me. I'm a freak." Her tone was harsh. She was punishing herself. She turned and laid the tiny hand on the table in plain sight. "Like I say, it's your life. If that girl's attractive to you, go ahead. It's none of my business. I just hope we can still be friends after all my stupidity."

"Denise, there's no real point to all of this. In the first place you're not a freak, and I don't want to hear any more of that kind of crap. In the second place I'll be your friend no matter what. You're stuck with me. You're one of the few people in the world I care anything about. If it hadn't been for you, I'd still be hiding from the world in that apartment of mine. Before I met you, I'd managed to cut myself off from everybody. I was pretty well down the road toward becoming one of those bitter, reclusive cripples you see once in a while. At least I've managed to get past that part of it."

"All right, that's something, I suppose. Now that you realize that a leg or more or less doesn't have anything to do with what you really are, you ought to be able to pick up your life where you left off before the accident. Why don't you go back to school? I'm sure you don't plan to spend the rest of your life fixing shoes. You'll be able to have a career, a wife, a family—the whole bit."

"Denise—"

"No. Let me finish. I knew from the start that you'd get over it—adjust to it—and I knew that when you did, you'd go back to being normal again. I just let myself get carried away, that's all. I had you all to myself. A girl like me can't really compete with normal girls—I know that. I've never even tried. Do you know that I've never had a date?—not once in my whole life? No one has ever taken me to the movies or out to dinner or any of it. Anyhow, I began to think that because we were both—well, special—that somehow, when you got over it all, you'd look around and there I'd be. It was foolish of me, of course. If you really like this girl you met, *do* something about it. Just please don't stop being my friend is all."

"Denise, I don't think you understand. I'm not going to go back to being what you call 'normal' again. There was never any question about that part of it. I lost more than just a leg in that accident, so all the things you've been talking about just aren't really relevant. I'm interested in that girl for exactly the reasons I said I was—I want to salvage one human life. I don't want her to become a loser. And I'll always be your friend—but that's all. Maybe I should have told you earlier, but it's not exactly the sort of thing you go around bragging about."

She was staring at him, her face stricken and pale. Suddenly she was out of her chair and was cradling his head in her arms, pressing him tightly against her body. "Oh, my poor Angel," she sobbed.

Why was it always "Angel"? Why was that always the first word that came to people's lips? Why that and not something else?

She held him for a long time, crying, and then she turned and fled into her bedroom, slamming the door behind her. He could hear her still crying in there.

After a few minutes he took his crutches, got up, and went to the closed door. "Denise?"

"Go away. Just go away, Rafe."

He went back into the kitchen, turned off the coffeepot, and then quietly left her apartment.

When he got home, old Tobe was sitting on the porch of the shabby little house across the street. A half-full wine bottle sat beside him, but he did not seem to be all that drunk. More than anything right now Raphael did not want to be alone. He went across to the little man. "How's Sam?" he asked.

"He's dyin', Rafe. Ol' Sam's dyin.' They found out he's got the lung cancer, too."

"Aw, no. I'm sorry, Tobe."

"They got 'im in a nursin' home out in the valley," Tobe went on quietly. "I went out there an' seen 'im today. He told me he don't want me comin' to see 'im no more. We been together for damn near twenty years now, an' now he says he don't wanna see me no more." The little man shook his head.

"I'm really sorry, Tobe."

Tobe looked up, his eyes filled with tears. "How come he done that, Rafe? How come he done that, Rafe? How come ol' Sam said a thing like that to me After all these years?"

"I don't know, Tobe."

And then Tobe bowed his face into his gnarled hands and began to cry.

Raphael gently laid his hand on the little man's shaking shoulder, and then, because there was nothing else he could do, he turned and started toward the street.

Patch stood at the corner in the twilight watching him, his dark face set in that impenetrable expression of stony melancholy.

Raphael looked at the solitary figure for a moment and then crutched slowly across the street to his apartment house.

By the time he reached the roof, Patch was gone.

vii

Frankie's tan was progressing nicely, and she seemed quite proud of it.

"You're beginning to look like an old saddle," Raphael told her as she came out on the roof.

"Thinking about taking a ride?" she asked archly.

"Knock it off, Frankie. That sort of remark makes you sound like a hooker."

"You're the one who started all the cute stuff. I can be just as tough As you can, Raphael. I know all sorts of dirty words in Italian."

"I'll bet. Am I in trouble again?"

"Not that I know of. Have you been naughty lately?"

"That's why you usually come by—to chew me out for something."

"That's not altogether true, Raphael." She sat on the little bench. "Sometimes I come by just to visit—and to get away from all those losers I have to deal with day in and day out."

Her use of the word startled him. As closely as he could remember, he had never discussed his theory with her.

"You're one of my few successes," she went on moodily. "And you did it all by yourself. You didn't enroll in any programs, you didn't go to vocational rehab, you don't have a support group, and you haven't once cried on my shoulder. You cheated, Raphael. You're a dirty rotten cheater. According to all the statistics, you should be a basket case by now. Do you have any idea how many hours I spent studying statistics in school? I *hated* that course. I passed it, though. You have to if you want your degree."

"Anomalies, Frankie. Your course didn't teach you about anomalies—probably because they shoot statistical theory in the butt."

"Explain."

"An anomaly is an unpredictable event."

"I know what it means."

"Groovy—or is that gravy? We're way ahead then. Statistics are used to predict things. Your profession is almost totally dependent on an ability to predict what's going to happen to people, isn't it?''

''Well—sort of.''

''I'm not a basket case because I'm an anomaly. I beat the odds.''

''But the question is *how*. If I could find out how you did it, maybe I could use it to help other people.''

''How does sheer, pigheaded stubbornness grab you?''

''That depends on what you're being stubborn about. I like a certain amount of persistence.'' She rolled her eyes wickedly.

''Never mind that. It's too hot right now.'' He thought of something then. He hadn't really intended to tell anybody about it—not Flood certainly—but Frankie was a professional, and professionally she was one of the enemy. He liked her, though, and he felt that she deserved a sporting chance. It wouldn't really be sportsmanlike to potshoot Frankie off a fence rail when she wasn't looking. ''I met a girl,'' he told her.

''Are you being unfaithful to me, Raphael?''

''No. You more than satisfy my lust, twinkle butt.''

''*Twinkle-butt?*'' she objected.

''You've got an adorable fanny.''

She stood up, thrust out her bottom, and looked back over her shoulder at it. ''Do you really like it? She asked, actually sounding pleased.

''It's dandy. Anyhow, there's this girl—''

''A *relationship*?''

''That's bullshit, Frankie. Say what you mean. Don't babble about people having a 'relationship.' Use the right term. They're shacking up.''

''That's crude.''

''Isn't that what they're really doing?''

''Well—yes, I suppose so, but it's still a crude way to put it.''

''So beat me.''

''You want me to? Really?''

''Quit. I met a girl and she's pregnant—without benefit of clergy. She's right on the verge of going down to your office to apply for welfare.''

Frankie took out her notebook. ''What's her name?'' She was suddenly all business.

''Jane Doe.''

She almost started to write it down. ''Raphael, this is serious. Don't kid around.''

''I'm not kidding, Frankie. I'm dead serious about it. I won't tell you her name, and I won't tell you where she lives.''

''Why?''

''Because I'm not going to let you ruin her life.''

''She needs us, Raphael.''

''Statistically? I'm going to make another anomaly out of her,

Frankie. I'm going to train her to make it on her own—without you.''

She threw her notebook across the roof, jumped to her feet, and began yelling at him in snarling, spitting Italian, waving her arms and shaking her fingers in his face. It was fairly obvious that she was not talking about the weather.

He sat grinning impudently at her.

''You dirty, rotten, miserable son of a bitch!''

''Why, *Francesca*,'' he said. ''I'm shocked at you. Don't you love me anymore?''

She stormed across the roof, picked up her notebook, and bolted down the stairs, slamming the door behind her.

He didn't even think. The fact that his crutches were leaning against the railing fifteen feet away did not even cross his mind. He had meant to irritate Frankie—to make her think. He had not meant to hurt her.

It was the most natural thing in the world to do. He stood up, intending to follow her, to call her back.

And of course he fell.

His stomach suddenly constricted in a moment of icy terror. He was completely alone on this roof. It might be days before anyone came up those stairs.

''Frankie! Help me!'' His voice had that shrill note of panic in it that more than anything else strikes at the ears of others.

He heard her running back up the stairs. ''Raphael!'' She was there then, kneeling beside him, turning him over. She was surprisingly strong. 'As you all right?''

''A little scared is all. I have nightmares about this.''

''You idiot! What the hell were you thinking?'' She cradled his head in her arms, pulled his face tightly against her breast, and rocked back and forth with him. If there had ever been any doubts, they vanished. Frankie was definitely a girl. She exuded an almost overpowering girlness.

Raphael began to feel very uncomfortable, ''I'm all right, Frankie,'' he assured her, his words muffled by her body. ''I just panicked, that's all. I could have managed—crawled inside to the phone or something.''

''What the hell were you *doing?* You *know* you can't get around without your crutches.''

''Maybe I was hoping for a miracle—spontaneous regeneration or something.'' He wished that she would let him take his face away from her body. He laughed a muffled little laugh. ''I just didn't think, Frankie,'' he admitted. ''Would you believe that I actually forgot that I don't have a left leg anymore? What a dumb thing.''

''What did you think you were going to do?''

''I was going after you. I got cute and hurt your feelings. I had to try to fix that.''

She pulled him tighter and nestled her cheek in his hair. Then he felt the quiver of a strange little laugh run through her.

"What's so funny?"

"I've *really* got you now, Raphael." Her voice was strangely vibrant. "You're completely helpless, do you know that? I can do anything to you I want to do—and you've got no idea of the kinds of things I'd like to do to you."

"Quit kidding around, Frankie."

"Who's kidding?" Then she sighed and let him come up for air. "I'm sorry, Raphael," she apologized. "That was a rotten thing to say, wasn't it? Here." She pulled his chair closer and helped him into it. Then she went after his crutches. "Are you all right now?" she asked him.

"Yes. Thanks, Frankie."

"Good." Then her eyes narrowed. "I'm still pissed off at you, Raphael. Don't start thinking that you're off the hook just because my hormones got the best of me there for a minute." She stormed back to the door and opened it. Then she slammed it shut. Then she slammed it again. And again. "I get a kick out of doing that," she said in an almost clinical tone. Then she gave him an impish little grin. "See ya," she said, went through the door, and slammed it behind her.

 # viii

And then, early one evening, there was a crashing, gutter-flooding thunderstorm, and the heat wave was broken. For several days the storm fronts that had stacked up in the western Pacific crossed in successive waves. The sky glowered and dripped, and the burned grass began to turn green again.

Flood came by one afternoon, still moving stiffly from the tape on his ribs and with his forehead still bandaged. Raphael had not seen him since the night of the brawl in Hillyard. "What are you up to?" he asked, coming into Raphael's apartment.

"Nothing much," Raphael replied. "Reading."

"You ought to get yourself a TV set." Flood sprawled on the couch.

"What for? So I can watch soap operas?"

"The great American pastime. How do you expect the economy to expand if you don't give all those hucksters out there in TV land a chance at your bank account?"

"You're in an odd mood today."

"Edgy. I'm bored—God, I'm bored. This is a singularly unattractive town when it rains. I wandered around downtown for a while this morning. What a dump!"

"I could have told you that."

"When are we going to get out of here? Haven't you had about enough? Tell you what. Why don't we throw a few clothes in a bag and run down and see 'Bel? Get out of here for a couple days."

Raphael shook his head. "No. 'Bel and I didn't exactly part friends last time. I don't think it'd be a good idea to stir all that up again." He had not told Flood about the letter from Isabel. He had almost forgotten that he had it in fact, and for the first time he wondered what she had said in it.

"Oh hell," Flood scoffed. " 'Bel doesn't hold grudges. Forget it then. It was just a thought."

"Why don't you go ahead?" Raphael suggested. "Maybe if you get away for a while, it'll clear your head. You're starting to vegetate, Damon. This place is all right for me, but it's not doing you much good."

"I can stand it as long as you can. Oh, hey, I saw your friend again this morning."

"Which friend is that?"

"The public speaker. He was standing on a corner downtown delivering a sermon."

"It's nice to know he's still around. What was he talking about?"

"It was a sermon. He preaches rather well, actually—a bit hellfire and brimstone for my tastes, but impressive. You could hear him for a block and a half."

Raphael laughed. "I'll bet he scares hell out of the tourists."

"Really," Flood agreed. He looked out the window with distaste. "It's going to rain again."

"Probably."

"Well, now that we exhausted *that* particular topic of conversation, what'll we do? Shall we go out and get drunk?"

"I'll pass."

"Goddammit, *do* something!" Flood exploded in sudden exasperation. "All you ever want to do is sit. Let's go pick up some girls—get laid or something."

"I don't know that I'm ready for that yet," Raphael said carefully. He had never discussed that particular issue with Flood.

"You're a regular ball of fire. I think I'll go down and see how Heintzie's doing."

"Didn't you get enough last time? It looks to me as if Heintzie's parties usually wind up filling the emergency rooms at the hospitals."

"Oh, Heintzie's not so bad. He isn't very bright, but he's good to his friends."

"Why don't you tell that to Jimmy and Marvin? Look, Damon, you're getting in over your head with that bunch. Why don't you stay away from them?"

"They amuse me."

"It's contagious, you know."

"What's contagious?"

"Being a loser. If you hang around with them long enough, it's going to rub off."

"Bullshit! You're getting all hung up on that theory of yours. There's no such thing as a class of losers. It's not a disease, and it's not a syn-drome. It's simply a matter of economics and intelligence. People get *off* welfare, too, you know. They smarten up a little, get a job, and boom! End of theory."

"I don't think so. There's more to it than economics. It's the whole business of crisis, disaster, turmoil. Right now you're just itching to go out and get into trouble."

"I'm *bored*, for Chrissake!"

"Sure. That's part of it too."

"Bullshit! Anything at all is a symptom the way you look at it. I've got a hangnail. How does that fit in, Herr Professor?"

"Don't be silly."

"Shit!" Flood snorted. "I'll come back when you've got your head together. Right now you're just babbling. He got up and stamped out of the apartment.

Raphael watched out through the window as Flood crossed the roof-top to the door at the top of the stairs and disappeared.

 ix

After a few days of rain the sun came out again, but the temperatures were no longer as extreme as they had been in July. Raphael noticed that the sun came up later and that evening came earlier as the summer wound down into those last dusty, overripe days of mid-August. It was an unusual period for him. For the first time since his childhood, late summer was not accompanied by the anticipation of a return to school. There was a certain pang involved in the fact that the turn of the sea-sons would not be matched by that ritual return from vacation. The stately, ordered progress of the year seemed somehow disrupted. It was as if he had been cast into some timeless world of endless now with nothing to distinguish August from November except the weather. He even considered enrolling for a few classes in one of the local colleges simply to maintain some kind of continuity with the past, but he dropped that idea. He was not quite ready for that yet.

Very early one morning, almost before the sun came up, Flood came by. His eyes were very bright, and he seemed enormously keyed up.

"What are you doing out of bed so early?" Raphael asked him a bit sourly. The mornings were his, and he rather resented Flood's intru-sion.

"I haven't been to bed yet," Flood replied. He had obviously been drinking, but his excitement seemed to have nothing to do with that. Without asking, he went over and turned on the scanner.

"There's not much doing in the morning," Raphael told him. "The assorted perpetrators tend to sleep late."

"That's all right." Flood grinned broadly. "You never know what daylight might turn up." He lit a cigarette, and Raphael was startled to see that his hands were actually shaking.

"You want some breakfast?" he asked.

"God, no. You know I never eat breakfast."

"Coffee then?"

"Why not?"

Raphael went toward the tiny kitchen.

"District One," the scanner said.

"One," came the curt reply.

"We have a report of a man down in the alley behind the Pedicord. Possible DOA."

"I'll check it out."

"You'll have to come and get this," Raphael said after he had poured Flood a cup of coffee.

"Yeah," Flood replied tensely. "In a minute." He was staring intently at the scanner.

Raphael shrugged and went to the small refrigerator for a couple of eggs. "You sure you don't want any breakfast?"

"What? No, none for me, thanks." Flood was still concentrating on the scanner.

"This is District One," the tinny voice came from the small speaker. "You'd better have the coroner come down here to the alley behind the Pedicord. We've got a DOA here. Gunshot wound to the head—at close range."

"Any ID on the subject?"

"I don't want to disturb the scene until the detectives get here, but the subject's pockets are all turned inside out, and he doesn't have any shoes."

Flood suddenly laughed. "Picked clean. Vultures couldn't have done it any better."

"You're in a charming frame of mind this morning." Raphael put a frying pan on the stove and turned back to the refrigerator for bacon.

"God's in his heaven, and all's right with the world," Flood said expansively. "Where's that coffee?"

"Sitting on the counter there."

Flood came to the kitchen, picked up the coffee cup, and returned to the scanner. Raphael continued to make his breakfast as his friend listened to the progress of the investigation. Predictably, there was no immediate identification of the dead man in the alley behind the Pedicord.

"Funny that nobody heard the shot," Raphael said, sitting down to eat.

"A gun doesn't make that much noise when you hold it right up against something before you pull the trigger," Flood told him. "Just a little pop, that's all."

"How did you find that out?"

"Read it someplace." Flood shrugged.

Raphael frowned. "A wino like that couldn't have had more than a few dollars on him. Doesn't seem like much of a reason to shoot him."

"Not to you, maybe—or to me either, for that matter, but there are strange passions out there in the garbage dump, Raphael. There could be all kinds of reasons for putting the muzzle of a gun against a sleeping wino's head and sending him on to his reward."

"How do you know he was asleep when it happened?"

"Deduction, Raphael, pure deduction. Put a gun to a man's head, and he's going to shy away—it's instinctive."

"How do you know he didn't?"

"No report of a shot, remember? Somebody just walked through the alley, saw him sleeping in a doorway, and blew him away—just for the hell of it." He laughed again and stuck out his finger, imitating the shape of a pistol. "*Plink.* Just like that, and there's one less sodden derelict stumbling through the downtown streets. No reason. No motive. Nothing. Somebody just plinked him like a beer can."

"That's a shitty attitude."

"Does anybody really care about what happens to a drunken bum? Basically, what happened to him was nothing more than a form of street cleaning. If the street cleaner hadn't gotten him, cirrhosis of the liver would have in another year or two."

"He was still a human being."

"Bullshit. He was garbage."

"That's no reason to blow his brains out."

"It's as good a reason as any." Flood stood up. "I'm going to split. Thanks for the coffee." And without saying anything more, he left.

 **X**

Although the worst of the heat had broken, the girl from downstairs still came up to the rooftop occasionally. They would sit and talk through the long, idle hours of evening, watching people in the streets below. Often, for no reason other than the simple need to talk, they sat until long after midnight, their conversations drowsy and their voices blurring on the edge of sleep. Perhaps it was chance, perhaps not, but not once during any of her visits did Flood appear. Raphael was apprehensive about that. For some reason it was quite important to keep Flood and the girl apart.

"Have you thought any more about going back home?" he asked her late one evening when the tree frogs and crickets sang monotonously from nearby lawns and the cars had thinned out in the streets.

"Not really. I'm settled in now. I don't feel like going through the hassle of moving—facing family and friends and all that."

"And it's easier to sit?" He probed at her, trying to test her will.

"Bodies at rest tend to remain at rest." She said it glibly. "As time goes on and I get progressively bigger, I suspect I'll tend to remain at rest more and more."

"You hardly even show yet, and that's all the more reason to do something now—before you get cemented in."

"I show," she disagreed wryly. "My clothes are starting to get just a teensy bit snug. Besides, what's all this to you? Are you secretly working for the Metalline Falls tourist bureau?"

"Have you looked around you lately—at the people on this street?"

"It's just a street, and they're just people."

"Not exactly. This is Welfare City, kid. These people make a career out of what my father used to call 'being on the dole.' That's a corrosive kind of thing. It eats away at the ambition, the will. After a while it becomes a kind of disease."

"They're just down on their luck. It's only temporary."

"Eighteen years? That's your idea of temporary?"

"Eighteen years? Where did you get that number?"

"That's how long you're eligible for welfare—Aid to Families with Dependent Children. What the hell do you do when you're thirty-eight years old and the check stops coming? You don't have any skills, any trade or profession, and you've been a welfairy for eighteen years—just sitting. What happens then?"

She frowned.

"Most of the girls down there have come up with a fairly simple answer to the problem," Raphael went on. "Another baby, and you're back in business again. With luck you could stretch it out until you're in your early sixties, but what then? What have you done with your life? You've sat for forty or forty-five years collecting a welfare check every month. You've lived in these run-down hovels scrounging around at the end of the month for enough pennies or pop bottles you can cash in so you can buy a loaf of bread or a package of cigarettes. And at the end of it all you have nothing, and you are nothing. You've existed, and that's all."

"It doesn't *have* to be that way."

"But it is. Like you say, bodies at rest tend to remain at rest. That's a physical law, isn't it?"

"That's about objects—things, not people."

"Maybe that's the point. At what point do people stop being people and start being things—objects."

"It's not the same."

"Are you sure? Are you willing to bet your life on it? You said you didn't feel like going through the hassle of moving. Are you going to feel any more like it after the baby comes?"

"I'll think about it." Her voice was troubled.

"Do that."

"It's late." She stood up. "I guess I'll go to bed. See you." Her tone was abrupt, but that was all right. At least he had gotten through to her.

After she was gone and he was alone, Raphael sat for a long time in the silent darkness on the rooftop. Maybe it was time to give some consideration to *his* situation as well. Flood was probably right. Perhaps it was time to give some serious thought to moving on. It was too easy to sit, and the longer he remained, the more difficult it would be to uproot himself. His own arguments came back to gnaw at him.

"All right," he promised himself. "Just as soon as I get the girl squared away. *Then* I'll think about it."

The sense of having made a decision was somehow satisfying, and so he went to bed and slept very soundly.

Estuans interius ira vehementi in amaritudine loquor me menti

i

By late August the worst of the summer heat was past, and there was a faint haze in the air in Spokane. The evenings were cooler now, and sometimes Raphael even wore a light jacket when he sat up late.

Flood visited seldom now. His time seemed mostly taken up by his growing attachment to Heck's Angels. Raphael could not exactly put his finger on what caused the attraction. The Angels were stupid, vicious, and not very clean. None of those qualities would normally attract Flood. Although they blustered a great deal, they were not really very brave. Their idea of a good fight appeared to be when three or preferably four of them could assault one lone opponent. They talked about fighting much of the time, and each of them attempted to exude menace, but with the possible exception of Big Heintz, they were hardly frightening.

Flood's status among them was also puzzling. At no time did he assume the clothing or the manner of the Angels. He did not wear leather, and he did not swagger. His speech was sprinkled with "man" and "What's happening?" and other identification words, but it was not larded with the casual obscenity that characterized the everyday conversation of the Angels and their women.

But Heintz clearly respected Flood's intelligence and laughed uproariously at his jokes and his parodies of popular songs. But although Flood was not a full-fledged member, neither was he a court jester or simple hanger-on.

One evening they sat on the porch of their big house up the street, drinking beer and talking. Raphael, sitting on his rooftop, could hear them quite clearly.

"They ain't left town yet," Big Heintz was saying. "You can fuckin' take that to the bank."

"Nobody's seen any of 'em,' Jimmy ventured.

"The Dragons are still around," Heintz insisted. "You can fuckin' take that to the bank. They know fuckin' well that this ain't over yet. Me 'n that fuckin' Mongol still got somethin' to settle between us, and he ain't gonna leave this fuckin' town till we do." He belched author-itatively and opened another can of beer.

"Unless you can come up with more attractive odds, I think I'll pass next time," Flood said wryly. "I didn't get *too* much entertainment out of having two of them hold me down while another one kicked me in the ribs."

"Shit, man." Marvin laughed. "At least they was only kickin' you in the *ribs*. They was kickin' me 'n Jimmy and Heintz in the fuckin' *head*, man. I still hear bells ringing' sometimes."

"Them was just games." Heintz dismissed it. "Just playin'—sorta to let us know they was in town. Next time it won't be no fuckin' games—it's gonna be fuckin' war, man. I mean fuckin' *war*!"

They continued to drink and talk about the impending battle, work-ing themselves up gradually until their need for action of some kind sent them into the secret hiding places in the house where they kept their weapons. In half-drunken frenzy each of them in unself-conscious display moved to a separate quarter of the lawn and began to swing his favorite implement of war.

Chains whistled in the air and thudded solidly against the ground, churning up the grass. Spike-studded clubs sang savagely. Knives were brandished and flourished. The air resounded with hoarse grunts and snarls as Heck's Angels bravely assaulted the phantom Dragons they had conjured up with beer and bravado to meekly accept the mayhem inflicted upon their airy and insubstantial bodies.

"District Four," the scanner said.

"Four."

"We have a report of a seventy-six at 1914 West Dalton. Several bikers threatening each other with knives and chains."

Raphael smiled. A seventy-six was a riot, and the police usually at-tended such affairs in groups.

"District One," the scanner said.

"One."

"Backup Four at 1914 West Dalton. Report of a seventy-six."

"Right," District One said.

"Three-Eighteen," the scanner said.

"Three-Eighteen," the car responded.

Raphael waited.

On the lawn Heck's Angels continued their war with their unseen enemies until five carloads of police converged upon them. The police spoke with the Angels at some length and then methodically and quite systematically confiscated all their toys.

A couple days later, after supper, Raphael went out onto the roof to watch the sunset. He felt strangely contented. His life, though it was circumscribed, was interesting enough. The vague ambitions he'd had before seemed unrealistic now. Probably they always had been. He idly wondered what his life might have been like if it all hadn't happened. It seemed somehow as if what had happened to him had been the result of sheer, blind chance—rotten bad luck. That was very easy to believe, and like most easy things, it was wrong. There had been a definite cause-and-effect sequence operating that night. He had been drunk, for one thing, and he had been drinking hard to incapacitate himself—to keep himself out of Isabel Drake's clutches, and he had done that because it had been Isabel's suggestions that had led to the events in the front seat of his car, and on, and on. It had *not* been sheer blind chance. Of course the appearance of the train had not been all that predictable, but considering the way he had been driving when he had fled from Isabel's house, if it hadn't been the train, it would have been another car or even a tree. Trees are very unforgiving when automobiles run into them. The train had maimed him; a tree most probably would have killed him outright. He sat for quite a white, thinking about it.

"Hey up there, can I come up?"

Raphael leaned over the railing and looked down. It was the girl from downstairs. She stood on the sidewalk below in the early-evening dusk, her face turned up toward him. "Come ahead," he told her.

A minute or two later she came out on the roof. "Oh my," she said, pointing.

Raphael turned. The last touches of color from the sunset lingered along the western horizon, and the contrail from a passing jet formed a bright pink line high overhead where the sun was still shining.

The girl came over and sat on the bench near his chair. "You've got the best view in town up here."

"If you like sunsets. Otherwise it's not too much. On a clear day you can almost see to the sewage-treatment plant."

She laughed and then crossed her arms on the railing, leaned her chin on them, and looked down into the street below. "You were right, you know?"

"About what?"

"That street—those people. I've been watching them since we talked that time. All they do is exist. They don't really live at all, do they?"

"Not noticeably."

"You scared me, do you know that? I saw myself at forty—a welfairy—screaming like a fishwife and with a whole tribe of grubby little kids hanging on to me. You really scared me."

"I was trying hard enough."

"What for? Why did you bother? And why me?" She looked straight at him.

"Let's just say it's a bet I've got with myself."

"You want to run that past me again? You can be infuriatingly obscure at times."

He looked at her for a moment. In the faint light on the rooftop she seemed somehow very much like Marilyn. "It's not really that complicated. I've lived here for six or seven months now, and I've been watching these poor, sorry misfits living out their garbage-can lives for all that time. I just wondered about the possibility of beating the system. I thought that maybe—just maybe—if I could reach somebody before the habits had set in, I might be able to turn things around. Let's call it a private war between me and that street down there."

"Then it isn't anything personal?"

"Not really."

"I just happened along?"

"It's not exactly that. I like you well enough to care what happens to you. It's not just a random experiment, if that's what you mean."

"Thanks for that anyway." She laughed. "For a minute there I was starting to feel like a white rat."

"No danger."

"You don't even know my name."

"Of course I do. You're the girl on the roof."

"That's a hell of a thing to call somebody."

"It keeps things anonymous—impersonal." He smiled. "That way I can beat that thing down there with no strings attached. It can't come back and say I was out to get something for myself."

"Okay, I think it's a little nuts, but I won't tell you my name. You can keep on calling me the girl on the roof. I know your name though. You're Raphael Taylor—it's on your mailbox. That doesn't spoil it, does it?"

"No. No problem."

"All right, Raphael Taylor, you can chalk up one for our side. The girl on the roof is going back to Metalline Falls."

"Well, good *enough*!"

"I don't know if I'd go *that* far. When the girl on the roof shows up back home with a big tummy, tongues are going to wag all over town. My father might send me back out into the snow—and let me tell *you*, Raphael Taylor, we get a *lot* of snow in Metalline Falls—whole bunches of snow."

"You'll be all right. It might be a little rough, but at least the street didn't get you."

"It almost did, you know. I was ashamed. Girls from small towns are like that. You're ashamed to go home because everybody knows you, and you know they'll all be talking about you. It's easier to hide on some street like this—to pull it around you and hide. I'll just bet that if you went down there and asked them, you'd find out that most of those poor welfairy girls down there come from small towns, and that they first came here just to hide."

"It's possible," he admitted.

"And now what about you, Raphael Taylor? Since you've saved me from a fate worse than death, the least I can do is return the favor. Nobody's going to accuse the girl on the roof of being ungrateful."

"I'm fine."

"*Sure* you are," she said sarcastically. "Are you sure that street hasn't got its hooks into *you*?"

"I don't think there's much danger of that."

"Can you be sure?" she persisted. "I mean *really* sure? Except for that first day I've never seen you anyplace but up here. Are you really sure you're not just settling in? You made me think about it; now I'm going to make you think about it, too. I'd hate to remember you just sitting up here, growing old, watching that lousy street down there."

"I won't grow old up here," he told her. "I had some things to sort out, and I needed a quiet place to do that in."

"You'll be leaving then?"

"Before long."

"Before the snow flies?"

"All right."

"Promise?"

"Before the snow flies," he said.

They sat quietly then. The streetlights came on, and the crickets began their drowsy drone.

"This is the only part of it that I'll miss," she said finally. "I only wish we'd met each other before—before a lot of things." She stood up suddenly, her movements abrupt as always. "I have to pack. I'm going to be leaving first thing in the morning."

"Good luck."

"We make our own luck, Raphael Taylor." She said it firmly. "Or somebody else makes it for us—the way you did for me. How did you know exactly what to say to me to keep the street from getting me?"

He shrugged. "Experience," he suggested. "Intuition maybe. How does divine intervention grab you?"

"God's not all that interested in me. He's too busy watching sparrows fall." She paused. "It's not really the same because the word usually means something so totally different, but I want you to know that the girl on the roof loves you, Raphael Taylor. I wanted to say that before I left." And then she came over, kissed him lightly, and was gone.

For a long time after that Raphael sat alone in the darkness. Then about midnight it turned chilly, and he went inside to bed.

iii

Two days later when Raphael came home from work, old Tobe was standing in the middle of the street. He was roaring drunk and a wine bottle hung loosely in his hand.

"Tobe!" Raphael called to him as he parked. "For Christ's sake get out of the street! You're going to get yourself killed!"

"Who says so?" Tobe demanded belligerently in his foghorn voice, swaying, and squinting at Raphael.

"*I* say so." Raphael got out of his car and pulled his crutches out of the backseat

"Oh." Tobe squinted and tottered toward Raphael's car. "It's you, ol' buddy. I didn't reconnize ya. How's it goin'?"

"What the hell are you doing out in the middle of the street, Tobe?"

"I was goin' someplace." Tobe swayed back and forth. "I forget now just where."

"The way some of these kids drive around here, that's a real bad place to stand. If one of them came ripping around that corner, you'd be inlaid right into his grille before he could stop."

"Maybe it'd be better that way."

"Don't be stupid."

"Sam's dyin'. He's got the lung cancer. Y'know that?"

"You told me. Let's get you off the street, okay?"

"I'm going someplace."

"Where?"

Tobe thought about it. "I forget." His face was almost purple, and his eyes were yellowish and puffed nearly shut. The stale wine reek of his breath was so sharp and acrid that it was close to being overpowering.

"Why don't we go over there and talk?" Raphael suggested, pointing at Tobe's lawn.

"Sure, ol' buddy."

They crossed the street.

"They got ol' Sam so doped up he don't even know what he's sayin' no more," Tobe said. "You know, he even tol' me he didn't want me comin' out to see 'im no more. Can you imagine that?"

"Those drugs can do funny things to you." A sudden cold, sharp memory of the endless, foggy days in the hospital came back to Raphael as if it had been only yesterday.

"That wasn't ol' Sam talkin'." Tobe stumbled over the curb. "That was all that dope he's got in 'im. Ol' Sam, he wouldn't say nothin' like that to *me*, would he?"

"Of course not."

"Poor ol' Sam. Helluva damn thing, him dyin' on me like this. We been together twenty years now, I ever tell you that?"

"Once, I think."

"I'd rather lose a wife than lose my ol' buddy like this."

"I've got to run. I've got a lot to do this afternoon. You think you can remember to stay out of the street?"

"What the hell difference does it make?"

"If the cops come by and catch you, they'll call the wagon and haul you out to detox again."

"Can they do that?" Tobe looked frightened.

"You bet your ass they can."

"That's a terrible place out there." Tobe shuddered.

"Stay out of the street then, okay?"

"Sure, buddy. Hey, if you wanna use my truck anytime, you just lemme know, okay?"

"Sure, Tobe." Raphael turned.

Across the street Patch moved silently by, his face dark and mournful. At the corner he stopped and looked back at Raphael and Tobe.

"Who is he?" Raphael asked.

"Who?"

"That fellow on the corner there."

Tobe squinted, swaying back and forth. "I don't see nobody."

Raphael turned back quickly.

The Indian was gone.

"Anytime you wanna use my truck, you jus' lemme know, ol' buddy," Tobe said. "Anytime at all. Night or day, don't make no difference to me. You jus' lemme know."

"Okay, Tobe. I'll do that." He crutched on across the street.

"Anytime at all," Tobe called after him.

iv

"Very well, Mr. Taylor," Frankie said briskly. "This is just a periodic report. We need to know what kind of progress you're making." She was very businesslike, even abrupt.

"Getting by," he replied laconically, leaning his chair back and looking down at the street.

"You know better than that, Raphael. I can't just put 'getting by' in an official report."

"I'm getting better at repairing shoes, Francesca. It only takes me about fifteen minutes a pair now. Of course they pay me by the hour, so it doesn't really make any difference. Put down 'job satisfaction.' That makes them pee their pants. The defective is so resigned to his lot that he even enjoys it. I see you're still pissed off at me—about Jane Doe, I mean."

"You're a stubborn, inconsiderate asshole, Raphael." She waved her hands at him. It was a cliché, but Frankie couldn't talk without waving her hands. "Your poor Jane Doe is going through a pregnancy without any prenatal care. Does that make you happy?"

"You're wrong, Francesca."

"Don't call me that."

"I think I will. I like it. It's a beautiful name. You're still wrong, though. Jane Doe went back home. Her family's taking care of her now—prenatal care, support, love—all the goodies, and no strings attached. I guess that means that I won, Francesca. I beat your system—again. I saved her from you. You'll never be able to assign her a number, you'll never be able to control her life, and you'll never get your hands on her baby. She got away. It's not much of a victory, but a man in my position has to take what he can get. I'm sort of proud of it, actually."

She stared at him, her huge soft eyes very wide and her lower lip trembling. Then with a wail she turned and fled.

━━◀ V

On the first of September Raphael went in to work early again. His mailbox was still vulnerable, and although he had the best of intentions, he forgot each month to request the banks involved to make the transfer of funds automatic.

It was very early. The streets of Spokane were quiet, and the morning sunlight was bright in the clear air. Later, of course when the exhaust fumes began to collect, it would begin to grow murky.

Denise let him in, speaking only briefly. Since that terrible evening they had, as if by mutual consent, limited their conversations to business or the weather or other totally neutral subjects. Frequently they passed each other in the store without even speaking. The other employees, those who had watched their growing friendship that summer, were convinced that they had had some kind of fight—a lovers' quarrel. At first, of course, neither had spoken to the other because of the lacerating embarrassment over the things they'd had to reveal to each other. Then, as time went on and their taciturnity had become habitual, they became embarrassed at the thought of breaking the pattern, of intruding upon each other. And so they were silent, each wishing that the other would speak first, and each afraid to say anything to break the long silence.

Raphael went to his bench, switched on the light, and sat down. He turned on his machine and began to repair shoes. Always before he had rather liked coming to work. Now the job seemed suddenly tedious and boring. After a while of bending over the machine, his hip and back began to ache, and faint flickers of phantom pain began skittering like spiders up and down the thigh and knee of the leg that was no longer there.

He kept at it doggedly. There were not that many shoes in the bin, and he wanted to finish them all before he left. They piled up quickly, since shoes are the kind of thing that everyone throws away, and to leave even one pair would mean that he would start his next day's work in the hole. He began to take shortcuts, and some of the work was not entirely the sort that he took any pride in, but he managed to finish by nine.

He signed out, nodded briefly to Denise, and left.

As soon as he reached the street the depression that had settled on him and the vague ache that had begun in the missing leg vanished, and he felt good again. It was still early, and he drove to a small restaurant he knew and treated himself to breakfast. He was still puzzled by Frankie's reaction when he had told her of the escape of the girl on the roof. Irritation or anger or another outburst of lyric Italian swearing he could have understood. Frankie was sometimes a bit volcanic, but *tears*? That was not at all like Frankie. He wondered how the girl on the roof was doing back in Metalline Falls. Then he sighed, got his crutches together, and left the restaurant.

It was almost eleven by the time he got home, and his arrival only moments before the mailman came down the street earned him a savage scowl from a greasy-haired adolescent loitering on the corner.

It was quite warm by the time he reached the roof, and so he sat in his chair on the roof watching the frenzy of Mother's Day in the streets below. A car pulled up in front of the house where Heck's Angels lived, and a man got out. He seemed tense, as if he had been working himself up to do something unpleasant. The man seemed familiar, and Raphael tried to remember where he had seen him before. Flood was sitting on the front porch with Marvin and Little Hitler as the man came up the walk. "I'd like to speak with Mrs. Collins."

"She ain't here," Marvin said flatly.

"When do you expect her back?"

"Beats me."

"Look, friend," the tense man said, "I don't have time for the kind of games you people like to play. I told her last week that today was the deadline. Now, either she comes up with the back rent by midnight tonight, or you're going to have to move out—all of you."

Little Hitler stood up and swaggered down the steps. "And what if we don't?" he demanded.

"Then I'll put you out." The tense man's voice tightened even more.

"Now *that* I'd like to see," Little Hitler said. "Hey, Marv, did you hear that? This shithead says he's gonna put us out. You, me, Jimmy, Heintz, Jake—all of us. All by himself he's gonna fuckin' *put* us out."

"Maybe he'd like to start right now," Marvin said, also coming down the stairs. "Maybe he'd like to try to put you and me out."

"I won't be the one who'll be moving you out," the man on the walk told them. "That's what the sheriff gets paid for."

"Too chickenshit to do it yourself, huh?" Little Hitler sneered. "Gotta run to the fuckin' pigs."

"Friend, I'm too buy to be bothered with all this happy horseshit. You tell Mrs. Collins to get that money to me by tonight, or I'll go to the sheriff tomorrow. That's it."

Flood ambled to the front of the porch and stood leaning against one of the pillars. "I don't think you can do that without due process, sport," he said pleasantly.

"Watch me, sport. I've been in this business for fifteen years, and I've bounced a hundred of you welfare bums out of one house or another. Believe me, I know exactly how it's done—who to see and which papers to have signed. If I say you're going to move, you might as well start packing, because you *are* going to move."

"Who you callin' a bum," Little Hitler demanded hotly.

The man on the walk looked him up and down. "Are you working, boy?"

"None of your fuckin' business."

"That's what I figured. I won't apologize then. You just tell Mrs. Collins what I said."

"And what if we don't?"

"You're making me tired, boy. You can tell her or not—it doesn't make diddly-squat to me—but if I don't get that money by tonight, I go to the sheriff tomorrow, and you'll be in the street by the end of the week." He turned and went back to his car.

"Chickenshit bastard," Little Hitler called after him.

The man at the car looked at him for a moment, then got in and drove off.

"Why didn't you take 'im?" Marvin asked Little Hitler.

"Shit!" Little Hitler stomped back up onto the porch. "The fucker had a piece."

"Oh?" Flood said. "I didn't see it."

"You can take my word for it. All them fuckers carry a piece when they come down here. You seen 'im, didn't you Jake? I mean, he stood right up to us. There was three of us, an' he didn't back down an inch. Take my word for it, the fucker had a piece."

Big Heintz roared up, his motorcycle popping and sputtering. "Where's the girls?" he demanded. "I need some bread. This hog's gotta go into the shop."

"They're out buyin' groceries," Marvin replied, "an' we got a problem. Powell was just here, an' he says we gotta pay 'im the back rent or he's gonna call the sheriff—have us evicted."

"Fuck 'im. My bike's gotta go in the shop."

"He means it," Little Hitler warned. "We ain't gonna be able to put 'im off no more."

"Fuck 'im. There was three of you. Why didn't you take 'im?"

"The fucker had a piece," Little Hitler said without much conviction. "You can take my word for it, the fucker had a piece."

Heintz grunted. "How much does he want? He went up onto the porch.

"All of it, man," Marvin replied. "Every fuckin' nickel."

"Bullshit! That'd flat wipe us out for the whole month, an' my bike's gotta go in the shop. The bastard's gonna have to wait. We'll give 'im a few bucks and put 'im off till next month."

Flood looked at the big man. "I don't think it'll work, Heintzie. I think the man's made up his mind. If you don't settle up with him, he'll call in the pigs and you'll be picking deputy sheriffs out of your hair for a solid week."

"Fuck 'im," Heintz burst out with a worried frown on his face. "My bike's *gotta* go in the shop."

"Christ, man," Marvin said. "We sure as shit don't want no cops pokin' around in the house there. We got coke in there, man. We could lose our whole goddamn stash."

Jimmy's battered car came squealing around the corner, made a sharp right, and drove up onto the lawn. "I seen 'em," he said breathlessly, getting out. "I seen the motherfuckers."

"Who?" Heintz demanded.

"The fuckin' Dragons. They're camped out down in People's Park. Must be thirty or forty of the bastards down there. Bikes all over the fuckin' place."

"I *knew* the bastards hadn't left," Heintz exulted.

"What are we gonna do?" Marvin asked, his voice also excited.

"We're gonna pass the word. Get hold of Leon. All the guys stop by that gas station of his, an' he can get the word out. Tell 'em we'll all get together tomorrow night in that big field out toward Newport where we had the party last month. We'll put this thing together, and then we'll fuckin' move, man. We'll *waste* them fuckin' Dragons once and for all, man—I mean once and for fuckin' all."

"You want just our guys, Heintz?" Jimmy demanded breathlessly.

"Yeah. No, wait a minute. Have 'im pass the word to Occult, too. Them guys got a hard-on for the Dragons same as us. With us and Occult, we oughta be able to raise sixty, seventy guys. We'll flat *waste* them fuckin' Dragons. They won't *never* come back to fuckin' Spokane after we get done with 'em."

"What about Powell?" Marvin asked him.

"Fuck Powell! We ain't got no time to mess with that shithead now. We got a fuckin' *war* on our hands. Crank up your ass, Jimmy. Get to Leon an' pass the word."

"Yeah!" Jimmy dived back into his car.

Like some general marshaling his troops, Big Heintz began barking orders. Marvin and Little Hitler scurried away on errands, and Heintz stood spread-legged on the porch, his chest expanded and his beefy arms crossed. "War, Jake," he said, savoring the word. "It's gonna be a fuckin' war. We're gonna cream them fuckin' Dragons once and for fuckin' all.

" 'Seek out the enemy and destroy him,' " Flood quoted.

"What?"

"Von Clausewitz on war," Flood explained. "That's what it's all about."

"Yeah," Big Heintz growled enthusiastically. "Seek and destroy. Seek and fuckin' destroy. I like that kinda shit, don't you?"

"It's got a nice ring to it." Flood grinned tightly.

"You comin' tomorrow night?"

"I might tag along. I think the Dragons still owe me for a few broken ribs, and I always collect what people owe me."

"That's the stuff." Heintz slapped Flood's shoulder.

"I'll see you tomorrow then." Flood walked down onto the street in the bright glare of noon. His shoulders were braced, and there was a slight swagger to his walk.

A couple of minutes later he came up onto Raphael's rooftop.

"Well, well," Raphael said dryly, "if it isn't the newest recruit in Big Heintz's limp-brained little army."

"You were listening," Flood accused.

"Obviously. You're not seriously going to participate in this shindig, are you?"

"Only as an observer, Angel." Flood laughed. "You're the physical one in this little group. I *do* anticipate a certain satisfaction out of watching the punks who kicked in my ribs get theirs, however."

"That's stupid. Either you're going to get yourself arrested, or you're going to get the crap stomped out of you again."

Flood leaned over the rail to look down at the street. "Not this time, Angel," he said in a quiet voice.

Raphael looked at him sharply. Almost casually Flood raised the back of his jacket to let his friend see the polished black butt of an automatic pistol protruding from his waistband at the back.

"Have you completely lost your mind? If you get picked up with that thing, they'll put you away forever."

"I'm not going to get picked up with it, Raphael. I've been carrying it for several weeks now, and nobody even notices that it's there."

"You wouldn't actually *use* it."

"Oh?" Flood replied in that same calm voice. "It holds fifteen, Raphael. That gives me plenty of time to make up my mind, wouldn't you say?"

"You're starting to sound just like those morons up the block. Get rid of that goddamn thing."

"I don't think so." Flood's eyes were flat.

Raphael stared at him and suddenly realized that he had not really been looking at Flood lately, but rather at some remembered image. Certain subtle changes had taken place sometime in the last month or so—a tightening around the lips, a kind of agate-hard compulsion to violence in the eyes, an expression that seemed to imply that Flood had somehow been pushed into a corner and would explode at the next nudge—no matter what the consequences. It was, Raphael realized, the look of the loser.

It was a certainty now. Flood was gone. The street had claimed him.

 **vi**

After Flood left, Raphael sat staring sourly down into the teeming street. The Mother's Day hysteria was upon the losers. The children ran shrieking up and down the sidewalks, and the men who lived off the women and their welfare checks brushed up on their technique for wheedling just a few extra dollars.

Raphael had always been able to watch this monthly outburst objectively before, even with a certain amusement, but today he found it all enormously irritating. He realized quite suddenly that he was totally alone now—even more alone than he had been before Flood's arrival last spring.

"District One," the scanner said.

"One. Go ahead."

"We have a report of a possible suicide attempt on the east side of the Monroe Street Bridge."

"Is the subject still there?"

"The witness advised us that the subject has already jumped."

"I'll check it out."

Raphael shook his head. The Monroe Street Bridge was the most surely lethal place in town. It was not that it was so high, for it was not. A leap into the water from that height would prove fatal only if the jumper suffered from extremely bad luck. The bridge, however, overlooked the foot of the falls of the Spokane River. The riverbed broke there, and the waste hurtled savagely down a polished basalt chute. It was not a straight drop where the force of the water is broken by the impact at the bottom, but rather was a steeply angled and twisting descent where the water picked up terrific speed and built up seething, tearing currents that swirled with ripping force around the jumble of house-sized boulders in the pool at the bottom of the falls. To jump there quite frequently meant not only death, but total obliteration as well. Bodies often were not found for a year or more, and sometimes not at all.

"District One," the scanner said.

"One."

"Are you at the scene?"

"Right. There are several citizens here who state that the subject definitely did go over the side."

"Any possibility of an ID?"

"There was a jacket draped over the rail. One of the citizen states that the subject took it off before he jumped. Wait one. I'll look through it." There was a silence while the red lights of the scanner tracked endlessly, searching for a voice. "This is District One. There's a card in this jacket—identifies the subject as Henry P. Kingsford, 1926 West Dalton. He appears to be an outpatient from Eastern State Hospital."

Numbly, Raphael got up and went over to the scanner. He switched it off, then went slowly to the railing and looked across at the tightly drawn shades in Crazy Charlie's apartment—the shades that had been drawn ever since that day when Flood had so savagely turned on the strange little man. Raphael turned and went into his apartment, feeling a pang of something almost akin to personal grief. Of all the losers, he had been watching Crazy Charlie the longest, and his apparent suicide left a sudden gaping vacancy in Raphael's conception of the street upon which he lived.

Finally, after several minutes, he picked up the phone and dialed the number of the police.

"Crime Check," the voice came back.

"I live on the 1900 block of West Dalton," Raphael said. "I've got a police scanner."

"Yes, sir?" The voice was neutral.

"I just heard a report that one of my neighbors, Mr. Henry Kingsford, has committed suicide."

"We're not really allowed to discuss things like that over the phone, sir."

"I'm not asking you to discuss it," Raphael said. "All I wanted to do was to tell you that Mr. Kingsford was a recluse and that he's got six or eight cats in his apartment."

"Yes, sir?"

"Don't you think it might be a good idea to notify the Humane Society?" Raphael said, trying to control his temper.

"I'm not sure we're authorized to do that, sir. Maybe a neighbor—or a friend—"

"The man's a recluse—a crazy. He doesn't have any friends, and none of the neighbors here even know he exists."

"How about you, sir? Maybe you could—"

"I'm a cripple," Raphael said bluntly. "It's all I can do to take care of myself. Tell you what—either you can get hold of the Humane Society in the next day or so, or you can wait for a couple of weeks and then get hold of the health department. It doesn't really matter to me which." He slammed down the phone.

The apartment was suddenly stifling, and the thought of looking at the street anymore was unbearable. He felt an insistent nagging compulsion to do *something*. To simply sit passively listening to the scanner was no longer possible. Although he had used the word "cripple" in describing himself to the officer he'd just talked with, he realized that it was probably no longer true. Somehow, somewhere during the last summer, he had without realizing it crossed that line Quillian had told him about. He was no longer a cripple, but rather was simply a man who happened to have only one leg. "All right," he said, facing it squarely. "That takes care of that then. Now what?"

A dozen ideas occurred to him at once, but the most important was to get out, to go someplace, do something. He pulled on a light jacket because the evenings were cool and he was not sure just how long he would be out. Then he crutched smoothly out of the apartment and across the rooftop, conscious of the grace and flow of his long, one-legged stride. The stairs had become simplicity itself, and even the once-awkward shuffle into the front seat of his car was a smooth, continuous motion now.

He drove then, aimlessly, with no goal or purpose in mind, simply looking at the city in which he had lived for more than half a year but had never considered home.

The Spokane River passes east to west through the center of town and then swings north on its way to meet the Columbia. The gorge of Spokane on its northward course ends the city in that quarter. The streets do not dwindle or the houses grow farther apart. Everything is very paved and neat, landscaped and mowed right to the edge of that single, abrupt gash that cuts off the city like the stroke of a surgeon's knife. Raphael had never seen a place where the transition from city to woods was so instantaneous.

The rock face of the gorge on the far side of the river was a brownish black, curiously crumbled looking because of the square fracture lines of the volcanic basalt that formed the elemental foundation of the entire region.

And then, of course, he looked at the river, and that was a mistake, really. It seemed more like a mountain stream than some docile, slow-moving urban river. The water thundered and ripped at its twisted rock bed. Somewhere down there Crazy Charlie, broken and dead, turned and rolled in the tearing current, his shaved head white—almost luminous—in the dark water. The dragon on his floor would no longer threaten him, and the voices were now forever silent.

Raphael turned away from the river and drove back through the sunny early-autumn afternoon toward town.

Sadie the Sitter was dead, old Sam was dying, and now Crazy Charlie had killed himself. Bennie the Bicycler rode no more, and Willie the Walker had not strode by since early summer. Chicken Coop Annie and Freddie the Fruit had moved away, playing that game of musical houses that seemed part of the endless life of Welfare City, where moving from shabby rented house to shabby rented house was the normal thing to do. Everything was temporary; everything was transitory; nothing about their lives had any permanence. They were almost all gone now, and his street had been depopulated as if a plague had run through it. There were others living in some of those houses now, probably also losers, but they were strangers, and he did not want to know them.

Raphael suddenly realized even more sharply that he was absolutely alone. There was no one to whom he could talk. There were not even familiar faces around him. The victory that he had only just realized had been won sometime during the summer was meaningless. The fact that he was no longer a cripple but rather was a one-legged man was a fact that interested not one single living soul in the entire town.

It was at that point that he found himself parked in front of the apartment house where Denise lived. He could not be sure how deep the break between them was, but she was the only one in the whole sorry town who might possibly still be his friend. He got out of his car, went up the steps to the front of the building, and rang the bell over her mailbox.

"Who's there?" Her voice sounded tinny coming out of the small speaker.

"It's me—Rafe. I have to talk with you."

There was a momentary pause, and Raphael felt himself shrivel inside as he considered the possibility of refusal—some easy, offhand excuse. But she said, "All right," and the latch on the door clicked.

She was waiting warily at the door to her apartment. Mutely, she stood to one side and let him in.

"I think it's time we got this squared away," he said as soon as he was inside, knowing that if they started with vague pleasantries, the whole issue would slide away and they would never really come to grips with it.

"There's no problem, really." Her voice had that injured brightness about it with which people attempt to conceal a deep hurt.

"Yes, there is. We know each other too well to start lying to each other at this point."

"Really, Rafe—" she started, but then she glanced up and saw that he was looking very intently at her, and she faltered. "All right," she said then, "let's go into the kitchen, and I'll make some coffee."

They went in, she put the pot on, and they sat down.

"I made a fool of myself that night," she told him, "and I'm sorry. I was stupid and thoughtless. My silly little jealousy forced you to tell me something no man ought to be forced to admit."

"Have you got that out of your system, now?"

She looked at him sharply.

"Why do you continually beat yourself over the head? There's no need for it. We had a misunderstanding—that's all. It's no big thing. We were both embarrassed by it, but nobody dies from embarrassment, and it's not important enough to make the two of us spend the rest of our lives not talking to each other, is it?"

"I wanted to speak," she objected, "but you wouldn't even look at me."

"Okay. I'm looking at you right now—right straight at you. Speak, Denise, speak."

"Woof-woof," she said flatly. And then she smiled, and everything was suddenly all right.

And then the words that had been dammed up in those weeks of silence came pouring out. They talked until very late, their hands frequently touching across the table.

About eleven she reached across the table and took his hand. "Stay with me tonight," she said simply.

"All right." He didn't even hesitate.

And so they got up and turned out the lights and went to bed.

Raphael woke early the next morning, coming from sleep into wakefulness without moving. Denise lay quietly beside him, her arm across his chest and her face burrowed into her pillow. Her skin was pale and very soft, and she smelled faintly of wildflowers.

In the close and friendly darkness of the night before, they had lain very close together and had talked drowsily until long after midnight. There had been no hint of sexuality in their contact, merely comfort and the sense of being together. They had said things to each other in the darkness that would have been impossible to say in the light, and Raphael was content.

In the steely, dim light of dawn filtering through the curtains, he was surprised to discover how content he really was. The closeness, the simple thing of holding each other, the affection, had produced in him an aftermath of feeling not significantly unlike that which he remembered from times before his accident when the other had been involved also. Idly, he wondered how much of the afterglow of sex was related to sex itself and how much was merely this warm euphoria of closeness—and naturally, in all honesty, he realized he was to some degree rationalizing away his incapacity; but he felt much too good to worry about it all that much.

She stirred in her sleep and nestled closer to him. Then, startled, she awoke. "Oh, my goodness," she said, blushing furiously and covering herself quickly with the blanket.

" 'Oh, my goodness'?"

"Don't look at me." She blushed even more.

"What?"

"Don't look at me."

He laughed and lay looking at the ceiling.

"Rafe," she said finally, "you don't think I'm terrible or cheap or anything because of this, do you?"

"Of course not. Are you sorry?"

In answer she reached out and pulled him to her, making small, contented noises into his shoulder. Her tiny, misshapen hand gently caressed his back. "Oh dear," she said after a moment.

"What?"

"We have a problem."

"What's that?"

"Do you realize that we're both stark naked?"

"So?"

"So who gets up first?"

He laughed.

"It's not funny."

"It's like a cold shower. After the initial jolt it's not so bad."

"Oh, no. You're not going to catch *me* parading around in the altogether. My whole body would go into shock. I'd absolutely *die*. I'd blush myself to death right on the spot."

"I think you're exaggerating."

"Come on, Rafe, she pleaded. "We have to get up. I have to be at work."

"All right," he relented. "I'll turn over and cover my head with a pillow. Would that be okay?"

"You won't peek?"

"Would I do that?"

"How should I know what you'd do? If you peek, I'll die."

"You won't die, but I won't peek."

"Promise?"

"Promise."

He rolled over and pulled the pillow over his head. He felt the bed quiver as she slipped out and then heard the quick scurrying as she gathered up her clothes and dashed into the bathroom.

Later, over breakfast, she would not look at him.

"Hey," he said finally.

"What?" She still did not look at him.

"I'm here."

"I know that."

He reached across the table and lifted her chin with his hand. "If you don't look at me, I'll tell everybody at work that we slept together last night."

"You *wouldn't!*"

"Oh yes, I would." And then he laughed.

"You're not a nice person," she accused, and then she also laughed, and everything was all right again.

Before they left for work, he kissed her, and she sighed deeply. "I love you, Rafe," she said. "It's stupid and useless and probably a little grotesque, but I love you anyway."

"And I love you, Denise, and that's even stupider and probably a whole lot more grotesque, but that's the way it is."

"We'll work it out." She squeezed his hand. "What we feel about each other is *our* business, right?"

"Right," he agreed, kissing her again. And then they opened the door and went out together into the hallway and down the stairs and on out into the bright morning sunlight.

                              *   *   *

Raphael finished work about noon, turned off his machine, and went over to the desk where Denise was intent on some papers. "Hey you."

"What, hey?" She looked up at him. Her eyes seemed to sparkle, and her face glowed. He was startled to realize how pretty she was, and wondered why he had never seen it before.

"I'm going to take off now. I'll give you a call when you get off work."

"Do" She smiled at him.

"Maybe we can go to dinner or something."

"Are you asking?"

"All right, I'm asking."

"Let me check my appointment schedule—see if I can fit you in."

"Funny."

Billy, a retarded boy, was standing nearby, concentrating very hard on some clothing he was unfolding and putting on hangers. He looked up at them. "Rafe," he said, his thick tongue slurring the word.

"Yes, Billy?"

"You an' Denise ain't mad at each other no more, huh?"

"No, Billy," Raphael said gently. "We're not mad at each other anymore."

"I'm real glad. I didn't like it when you was mad at each other. It made me real sad."

"It made us sad, too, Billy. That's why we decided not to be mad anymore."

"I'm real glad," Billy said again. "Please don't be mad at each other no more."

"We won't, Billy," Raphael promised.

Denise reached out and squeezed his hand.

Raphael went outside, crossed the street to the graveled parking lot, and opened his car doors to let the blast-furnace heat out. After a few minutes he climbed in, opened the front windows, and started the car.

He drove down to Sprague, went west to Lincoln, and then over to Main. He followed Main along behind the Chamber of Commerce and the Masonic Temple and then down the hill into Peaceful Valley. If he could catch Flood before he went over to the house on Dalton, before, by his arrival and his presence, he committed himself to another of Heintzie's "last and final wars," he might be able to talk him out of the ultimate idiocy.

But Flood was gone. The shabby house where he had a second-floor apartment sagged on its patch of sun-destroyed grass, its paint peeling and its cracked windows patched with cardboard and masking tape, and Flood's red sports car was nowhere in sight.

The little red car was not parked in front of the house where Heck's Angels lived either, and Raphael wondered if perhaps Flood had perceived on his own how truly stupid the whole affair was and had found other diversions to fill his day.

Raphael parked his car and went up to his apartment. He bathed and shaved and put on clean clothes. He set the scanner in the window and went out onto the rooftop.

"District One," the scanner said.

"One."

"We have a report of a subject sleeping in a Dumpster in the alley behind the Saint Cloud Hotel."

"I'll drop by and wake him up."

Raphael looked down at his street. It seemed somehow alien now. The familiar faces were all gone, and he realized that there was no longer any reason to stay. For the first time since he had come here, he began to think about moving.

"This is District One," the scanner said. "This subject in the Dumpster is DOA. Gunshot wound to the head."

Raphael felt suddenly very cold. He had heard about it. Everyone hears stories about gangsters and the like. The Mafia is as much a preoccupation of Americans as are cowboys and Indians. Someone had once told him that young men of Sicilian background who aspire to membership in the family test their nerve in this precise manner. Nobody really investigates the death of a wino in an alley. It is a safe way for a young hoodlum to get his first killing behind him so that his nerve won't falter when the *real* shooting starts. Almost without realizing what he was doing, he went over to the window and turned off the scanner. He did not want to hear any more, and he did not want to think about it. He returned to his chair and sat in silence, looking down at the shabby street.

Up the block Big Heintz sat alone on the porch, his booted feet up on the rail and his purple helmet pulled down low over his eyes.

Marvin drove up in his car, closely followed by Little Hitler on his motorcycle. They stopped in front of the house and pulled several bags and blanket-wrapped objects from the backseat of Marvin's car. They went up onto the porch. "We got 'em," Marvin said, "lotsa good stuff—chains, baseball bats, stuff like that."

"Baseball bats?" Heintz scoffed.

"We took 'em over an' had Leon drill 'em out for us," Little Hitler explained. "Then he poured lead in 'em."

"*Now* you're talkin'." Heintz grinned. "Where's that fuckin' Jimmy?"

"He's over talkin' to Occult," Marvin replied, "seein' if they wanna go with us when we go to have it out with the Dragons."

"Goddamn that little shithead!" Heintz exploded. "He's gonna screw it up. Occult ain't gonna take a scrawny little bastard like Jimmy serious. They're gonna just think he's runnin' his fuckin' mouth. That's the kinda thing *I* oughta handle myself—*me*—or maybe Jake. Fuckin' Jimmy ain't got no sense."

"Have you seen Jake?" Little Hitler asked.

"He'll be here," Heintz assured them. "Ain't *nothin'* gonna keep ol' Jake away from what's goin' down."

Marvin had pulled one of the baseball bats out of a blanket and was tapping it solidly on the porch railing.

"Don't be wavin' that fuckin' thing around," Heintz ordered. "Like Jake says, we gotta cool it. One of the neighbors sees it, and they'll call the pigs on us again. We don't want no hassles with the fuckin' pigs today."

"Sorry." Marvin quickly wrapped the bat again.

"Better lug all that shit inside," Heintz told him. "Get it outta sight. Like I say, we don't want no hassles with the fuckin' pigs today."

Marvin and Little Hitler took their bundles into the house, and Big Heintz sat in menacing splendor on the porch, glowering at the street.

About four o'clock Jimmy arrived, breathless as always. "They're in!" he announced excitedly as he got out of his car.

"Who's in?" Heintz demanded.

"Occult. I talked to the Hog, an' he says to count 'em in."

"Jesus Christ! You ain't got no fuckin' sense at all, Jimmy."

"What's the matter?"

"It ain't *done* like that, you dumb little fucker. You don't just go runnin' off to somebody like the Hog and spillin' your guts like that. This ain't no fuckin' tea party we're talkin' about—it's a fuckin' war."

"I don't see what the difference is," Jimmy objected.

"If you're too dumb to understand, I sure as shit ain't gonna try to explain it to you. It's *courtesy*, you dumb shit. You ain't got no fuckin' manners, Jimmy. *Me*." Heintz stabbed himself in the chest with his thumb. "Me—*I'm* the one that shoulda talked with the Hog. That way he's got my word it ain't no setup—that we ain't gonna be waitin' out there to jump *them*. But you ain't smart enough to see that, are you?"

"Sorry," Jimmy said sullenly.

"Sorry don't cut it, shithead. Now I'm gonna have to apologize to the fuckin' Hog. This is *serious*, man—serious. *You* don't invite fuckin' Occult to a war, *I* do. That's somethin' that's gotta be settled between the *leaders*—me an' the Hog. From now on you keep your fuckin' nose outta stuff like this. You just do what I tell you to, an' don't get fuckin' *creative* on me. You got it?"

Jimmy sulked into the house, once again leaving Heintz sitting in sour imperial solitude on the front porch.

At five Flood showed up, and Raphael felt suddenly sick.

"Hey, Jake," Heintz called in a relieved tone. He got up and swaggered down off the porch. "Where you been all day?"

"Here and there," Flood said with a shrug. "I drifted down to People's Park to get the lay of the land."

"Shit, man!" Heintz stared at him. "That's dangerous. Were the Dragons there?"

"Some of them."

"They mighta jumped you."

"Why would they do that? Look at me, Heintzie. Do I look like a biker?"

"Well . . ." Heintz still looked dubious.

"I look like a tourist. They didn't even pay any attention to me."

"You got balls, Jake—real balls."

Flood shrugged. "I wanted to see the ground, that's all. Now I know the way in and the way out. There won't be any surprises—not for me, anyway. The Dragons might be in for a shock or two, though."

Heintz gurgled with laughter. "You slay me, Jake. You absolutely fuckin' slay me."

"Are we all set for tonight?" Flood asked.

"All set. Fuckin' Jimmy even went and talked to Occult. The Hog musta been drunk or stoned outta his mind to take the little fucker serious, but Occult's in."

"Good enough."

Raphael was stunned. The plan had obviously changed. He had thought that he would have more time. Tonight was supposed to be the council-of-war-cum-beer-bust out on the Newport highway, but those festivities had appeared to have been scratched. Talking to Flood had been something fairly serious before, but now it was a matter of urgency.

Raphael swore and went back inside to the telephone to call Denise.

"Where have you been?" she demanded. "I've been waiting for your call."

"I've got a problem," he told her.

"What?"

"It's Flood. He's been running with a motorcycle gang, and they're getting geared up for a war with a rival gang. I'm going to have to see if I can't get him off to one side and try to talk him into staying out of it."

"Why?" She said it flatly.

"Come on, Denise. The man's a friend of mine."

"Some friend." There was a long pause. "It's not Flood at all," she accused him. "It's that girl again, isn't it?"

"What are you talking about?"

"That girl—the one with the big belly. It's *her* you want to be with, isn't it?"

He was stunned. He'd never expected *this*. "Denise." He said it very calmly.

"What?"

"Stop and think for a minute. Think about me and then about what you just said."

There was another long pause and then a slightly embarrassed laugh. "I've never been jealous of anyone before," she admitted. "I'm not very good at it, huh?"

"Would you accept incompetent?"

"All right. I'm sorry. What's her name?"

"She's the girl on the roof."

"That's all? You don't even know her name?"

"Why would I want to know her name? She's not here anymore anyway. She went home to Metalline Falls. I persuaded her to make a run for it before the social workers got her. My caseworker broke down and cried when I told her that the girl on the roof made a getaway."

"The puppy?"

"That's the one. She probably went home and chewed up a pair of slippers after I told her about it. The problem really *is* Flood, Denise. Look, why don't you come over here? Why don't I come and get you? I could fix dinner for us here."

"No thanks, Rafe. That might not be a good idea. I've never met this wonderful friend of yours, and I'd like to keep it that way."

"Look. Let me see if I can get him squared away, and then I'll call you back."

There was a long, slightly sulky silence. "I'm sorry, Rafe," she said finally, her voice contrite. "I was being selfish. I'm just disappointed, that's all. I've never been stood up before. You do what you have to and call me back, okay?"

"Thanks, dear."

"Dear?"

"Would you prefer 'sweetie'?"

"You ever call me sweetie, I'll steal your crutches."

"Love you," he said.

"Me too."

━━ vii

It was all very well to speak of talking Flood out of the evening's insanity, but the question was how to go about it. He knew that the woman who rented the house was named Collins, and that the phone would be in her name, but would a phone call pull Flood away from the tense excitement that was erasing his brain at the moment? Perhaps some false emergency would do it—some personal appeal for help. At this point, however, Raphael was not sure that Flood would even respond to that. Perhaps the answer was simply to drive slowly by, stop, and call Flood over to the car. The problem with that, of course, was that Flood would be directly under the jealous gaze of Big Heintz, and there would be no way that he could get out of his commitment to the Angels, even if Raphael could talk some sense into him.

From up the street there came a roar of engines, and Raphael hurried out onto the roof. It was too late. He had been sure that they would not leave until after dark, but the tension apparently had built up to such a pitch that they were not able to sit anymore, or perhaps the gathering of the clans was going to involve a great deal of driving around looking tough. The motorcycles pulled slowly into the street, with Big Heintz in the lead and Little Hitler and Marvin flanking him. Flood's sports car was behind them, and the battered, smoking cars of the rest of the Angels were strung out to the rear.

They pulled down in front of Raphael's apartment house, grim-faced and girt for war. Flood glanced up once as they passed and waved at Raphael with a cryptic smile on his face. The street had claimed him. The thing that Raphael had feared had happened. There would be no reasoning with him now. Somehow, in spite of everything, Flood had become a loser.

Raphael watched helplessly from his rooftop. The caravan rounded the corner and was gone, leaving the late-afternoon street filled with silence and the stench of exhaust fumes.

Raphael went back into his apartment and switched on the scanner. Then he went to the telephone.

"Crime Check."

"I'm not sure exactly how to put this," Raphael apologized, "but would you be interested in something I heard about a gang fight in the making?"

"Could I have your name, sir?" It was the same officer Raphael had spoken with about Crazy Charlie's cats.

"I don't think that's important. I overheard a conversation. There's a motorcycle gang camped out down in People's Park. I heard some members of another gang talking about them. The plan is to go down there in force for a confrontation. From what I gather they aren't planning to make it just a fistfight. There was quite a bit of talking about knives, clubs, and chains." He hesitated, then decided to mention it. A week or two in jail would be far better for Flood than twenty years to life for second-degree murder. "I think one of them has a gun," he added.

The other end of the line seemed to crackle with a sudden alertness. The word "gun" seems to do that to policemen. "Were you able to get any kind of notion about when this is supposed to happen, sir?" the officer asked.

"Sometime tonight, I think. Bikers tend to be a little vague about things like time. This group was pretty well fired up about it, though, and they looked very determined when they took off."

"We'll check it out, sir."

Raphael slipped the receiver back into its cradle. He had just violated a fairly elemental rule; he had snitched. Under the circumstances, however, he felt no particular guilt about it. He watched the winking red lights of the scanner and listened intently.

It was fully twenty minutes before the call went out. "Three-

Eighteen," the dispatcher said. Three-Eighteen was one of the down-town units, the one who usually got the messy calls. Raphael knew that Three-Eighteen was a *very* tough cop.

"Three-Eighteen." The man even sounded bored.

"We have a citizen's report that wasn't really very specific. The citizen told us that there's the possibility of a fight between two rival motorcycle gangs down in People's Park sometime this evening. Do you want to take a swing down there and have a look around?"

"I'll check it out."

Raphael waited.

"This is Three-Eighteen."

"Go ahead."

"I'm down here in People's Park. There are some people camped down here, all right. They *could* be bikers, I suppose. It's mostly the women, though. I didn't see any bikes around. Maybe the fight's been called off. There's nothing going on now. I'll keep an eye on the place."

Raphael almost howled in frustration. The Dragons had obviously made a beer-and-burger run. They'd be back, and Heintzie would get his war. "Dumb cops!" Raphael almost shouted.

The sun went down lingeringly, staining the sky off to the west.

Raphael listened to the scanner and waited. By nine o'clock his nerves were wound up like springs. He felt himself actually start at each new voice on the scanner. He called Denise and told her what was happening. Her tone was still disappointed, but they talked for a while and smoothed that over.

Raphael fixed himself a sandwich and continued to listen.

"All downtown units," the dispatcher said, "we have a report of a disturbance in People's Park. Complainant states that several dozen bikers are involved."

Raphael's stomach tightened. He waited, almost holding his breath as the scanner winked its tiny red lights, reaching out in search of a voice.

"This is Three-Eighteen," a tense voice came through after several minutes. "This thing down here in People's Park is completely out of hand. There are nearly a hundred of them—knives, clubs, and chains. We're going to need a lot of help."

"All units," the dispatcher said, his normally calm voice edging up a notch, "we have a seventy-six in People's Park." Rapidly he began diverting cars and reassigning areas to provide minimal coverage of the rest of the city while releasing every possible car to the trouble area.

"This is Three-Eleven," a new voice, crackling with authority, came on. "Advise all units that I want a lot of lights and sirens down here. I want these people to know we're here."

"Yes, sir," the dispatcher said.

"Also, contact Spokane County Sheriff's Department and Washington State Patrol. We're going to need every unit they can spare."

"Yes, sir."

"Come *on*, people!" Raphael said. "Come *on!*"

"All units responding to the seventy-six situation in the People's Park area," the dispatcher said, "be advised that the situation is *not—repeat not*—under control. Approach with caution. Three-Eleven requests the use of lights and sirens. All other units go to channel two. Channel one is restricted to emergency traffic unit until further notice."

"This is Three-Eleven."

"Yes, sir?"

"Alert the hospitals and respond ambulances to this location. We have numerous injured subjects. Also respond the fire department. Ask the battalion chief if he can get a pumper truck down here. We might have to use fire hoses to break this up." In the background behind his voice Raphael could hear shouts and curses.

"Spokane PD," another voice came in.

"Unit calling?" the dispatcher said.

"WSP. Advise Three-Eleven that we have four cars responding to his location. ETA approximately two minutes. Find out where he wants us."

"Stand by. Three-Eleven?"

"Go ahead."

"Washington State Patrol is responding four cars to your location. They should be there in approximately two minutes. Where do you want them deployed?"

"Have them move to the extreme left end of the line of cars. I want to—" A faint popping sound came over the shouts in the background.

"We have shots fired!" Three-Eleven said sharply.

"Shots fired!" the dispatcher repeated. "All units responding to the People's Park area, be advised that shots have been fired!"

Raphael stared helplessly at the blinking scanner.

For the next few minutes the transmissions were a garbled mishmash of confused and contradictory calls. Then Three-Eleven's voice cut in sharply. "Has anyone got a positive on the subject with the gun?"

"This is District Four. The subject crossed to the other side of this creek that runs into the river here. He had a car over there."

"Can he get out through that way?"

"He can go out through the cemetery, Lieutenant," another voice cut in. "Once he hits Government Way, he can go just about anyplace."

"Did we get a make on the car?"

"A red Triumph," District Four said. "Out-of-state plates. I couldn't make them out."

Raphael felt suddenly hollow. There was no question now. It was Flood. The voices of the policemen coming over the air were very excited, and there was still shouting in the background. Raphael found himself quite suddenly on the other side of the law. It was probably very natural, but it seemed strange to be rooting *against* the police. It was still possible that Flood might escape entirely. Without a license-plate number to identify the red Triumph, the police had very little to go on; and despite their other faults Heintz and his cohorts would absolutely refuse to reveal Flood's name. It all depended on his getting his car out of sight.

"Three-Eleven," the dispatcher said.

"Go ahead."

"We've had a report by a citizen that a red Triumph has been seen westbound on Driscoll Boulevard at a high rate of speed."

Raphael quickly opened his city map.

"It must be a different car," Three-Eleven said. "There's no way to get across the river between here and there, is there?"

But Raphael saw a way, and so did the dispatcher. "Yes, sir, there is. He could have gone down through the junior-college campus and across the Fort Wright Bridge."

"Do we have any cars up there?"

"This is District Nine," another voice came in. "I'm at Francis and Maple. I'll try to intercept."

Raphael looked at the map intently. The Triumph was very fast, and Flood was clever—assuming the fight and the shooting had not completely scrambled his brains. To the north of Driscoll there was a rabbit warren of winding streets where he might drop out of sight. But if he stuck with Driscoll after it turned into Nine Mile Road, he would be out of the city with no side streets to dodge into. After that the only alternative would be flight—full-out, pedal-to-the-floorboards flight.

"District Nine, what's your location?" the dispatcher said after several minutes.

"This is Nine. I have a late-model red Triumph with Michigan plates northbound at a high rate of speed on Nine Mile Road. Am in pursuit." The voice that came back was excited, and the siren wailed in the background.

"What is your location, District Nine?"

"Just passing Seven Mile. Subject vehicle is going in excess of one hundred miles an hour."

"All units," the dispatcher said, "be advised that District Nine is in pursuit of a late-model red Triumph with Michigan license plates northbound on Nine Mile Road. Subject vehicle possibly involved in a shooting incident at People's Park within the past few minutes."

"See if Stevens County sheriff can get a unit down there to block him off," Three-Eleven said.

"Yes, sir."

Raphael sat tensely, his map clutched in his hands. "Come *on*, Flood! Get off that goddamn highway!"

The scanner tracked in silence, the tiny flickering red lights reaching out, looking for voices.

"He lost it!" District Nine said. "He missed the S-curve at Nine Mile!"

"Is he in the river?" Three-Eleven demanded.

"No, sir. He hit the rock face on the right-hand side and then bounced across and hit a tree. You'd better respond an ambulance out here—and a fire-department unit. It looks like we're going to have to cut him out of that car."

The tiny red lights continued to wink, fingering the air, searching the night for misery and violence and despair, and Raphael sat listening alone.

 # viii

He sat tensely in a chair in the waiting room, a loungelike place just off the emergency admitting area at Sacred Heart Hospital. The night was long and filled with confusion. Much of the human wreckage of the city passed through the wide doors of Sacred Heart emergency, and their cries and moans made the night hellish. The families and beloved of the wounded and the slain hunched in gray-faced shock in the waiting room, wearing mismatched clothes thrown on in moments of crisis.

Raphael did not know Flood's father, and the family telephone number in Grosse Pointe was unlisted. In desperation he finally tried to call Isabel Drake. Her phone rang three times, and then the recording came on. "I'm not at home just now," her voice told him. "Please leave a message at the tone."

He was not really ready when the insistent beep came over the wire. "Uh—'Bel—this is Raphael. Damon Flood—Junior—has been in an accident. He's at Sacred Heart Medical Center in Spokane. I'm here, too. You'd better call me."

After he had hung up the telephone, he realized that he hadn't given her a phone number or much of anything else. He thought of calling back to add more detail, but could not bring himself to talk to a machine again.

And then he waited, and because he was tired and emotionally wrung, he dozed fitfully in his chair. At four in the morning a crisply starched nurse came into the waiting room and woke him. "Mr. Taylor, you have a phone call—long distance." There was no hesitation in her voice. She knew who he was. He was marked as one of their own—deserving that special kind of courtesy the medical profession gives to those who have survived its most radical ministrations.

"Of course," he said, shaking off the sleep instantly. He rose and followed the nurse through the now-quiet admissions area.

It was Isabel. "Raphael," she said, "I just got in and found your message on my answering machine. What happened?" it was strange to hear her voice again.

"It was an automobile accident," he told her. "He's in critical condition. I tried to get hold of his family, but I can't get through."

"I'll call his father. How bad is it?"

"They're not talking about it. I think you'd better hurry."

"Have you seen him?"

"No. I understand that he isn't conscious. Please hurry, 'Bel. I know quite a bit about hospitals, and the signs aren't too good."

"Oh, dear God! I'll call his father right now."

Raphael held the phone in his hand for a long time after 'Bel hung up, then, on an impulse, he called Denise.

"Hello?" Her voice was warm and sleepy.

"It's me." He felt a bit foolish for having awakened her for no reason.

"Did he . . .?" She left it hanging.

"No. I just wanted to hear your voice. Hospitals scare me a little. I'm sorry I woke you up."

"Don't worry about it." Her voice was almost contented. "I've never had anybody wake me up in the middle of the night before. It's kind of nice."

"Nice?"

"You know what I mean."

They talked for a while, and then Raphael went back to the waiting room.

At ten in the morning 'Bel arrived. She was dressed in a dark suit and carried a small overnight case. She stopped hesitantly just inside the wide glass doors to emergency, and Raphael went out to meet her.

"How—" she started, and then broke off.

"No change," Raphael replied.

In a single glance she took in the crutches and the vacant space where his left leg should have been. She half reached out to touch him, but let her hand drop. "Is there someplace where we can get some coffee?" she asked to cover the moment.

"The hospital cafeteria."

"Can we leave word here?"

"I'll take care of it." He turned and went smoothly to the desk. He spoke briefly with the nurse and then led 'Bel to the elevators.

"J.D.'s on his way," she told him in the elevator. It was a moment before he realized that she meant Flood's father.

"I'm a little surprised," Raphael said. "From the way Damon talked—talks—I get the impression that he and his father are barely on speaking terms."

"That's nonsense. You should never believe anything Junior says."

"I've noticed."

They had coffee and looked out through the huge windows in the cafeteria at Spokane, spread out in the valley below them in the morning sun.

"Pretty little town," she said.

"Looks can be deceiving."

"Don't be cryptic, Raphael. That can develop into a very annoying habit."

He smiled then. The tone was so familiar that it seemed as if the time that had intervened since their last meeting had simply dropped away. He was surprised to discover that he was not uncomfortable with her. He smiled at her familiarly then, knowing all the lush, creamy opulence that lay beneath her trimly tailored suit.

"You've matured, Raphael," she said, catching the look and arching one eyebrow at him.

Later, back in the waiting room again, because his reserve was worn down by exhaustion, because he needed to talk with someone, and because 'Bel of all people would understand, Raphael began to talk—randomly at first, and then more and more to the point. "I suppose it's my fault, really," he admitted finally. "Damon asked me a dozen times to leave here. If I'd gone—if we'd gone to San Francisco or Denver or Seattle the way he wanted to in the middle of the summer, none of this would have happened."

"Don't beat yourself over the head with it, Raphael," she told him. "You can't go back and change things, and this—or something like it—has been waiting for Junior all his life. You could almost smell it on him."

A sudden thought occurred to him. "Bel, who is Gabriel?"

She gave him a startled look. "He actually mentioned Gabriel to you?"

Raphael shook his head. "He lets it slip from time to time. I don't think he was even aware that he said it, but several times he's called me Gabriel. For some reason I get the feeling that if I can find out just exactly who this Gabriel is, I'll be able to understand Damon a lot better."

"Didn't you get my letter?"

"Yes, but I didn't open it. It came at one of those times when—" He let that drop. "I've still got it, though. I've been meaning to read it."

"You should have," she told him quite firmly. "Last spring I had to go back to Grosse Pointe to attend a family funeral. I found out some things about Junior—things I didn't really want to know—but I heard enough to realize that it was something *you* really ought to know about. In some ways I suppose I'm not very admirable, but I do feel a loyalty to my friends." She laid her hand affectionately on his. "I spent a week or so asking questions, and I had the whole story when I came back. I called the college to get your address and found out that Junior had dropped out and left a Seattle forwarding address. I knew that your home was in this state, and I thought he might be following you. That's why I wrote you the letter. I wanted to warn you." She looked around. "Is there someplace where we can talk?"

"The hospital chapel's usually deserted."

She threw back her head and laughed. "How perfectly appropriate. All right, Raphael, let's go melt down a few plaster saints."

Raphael told the duty nurse where they were going and got directions.

The chapel was dimly lighted and quite religious. Sacred Heart *is* a Catholic hospital, after all. They seated themselves, and Isabel began. "You shouldn't feel any guilt about what's happened to Junior, Raphael," she said quite firmly. She gestured at the inside of the chapel. "You're in the right place. You should fall down on your knees—" She broke off. "I'm so sorry, Raphael. I didn't mean—"

"It's only an expression, 'Bel. It doesn't mean anything."

"All right. You should thank God that it was Junior and not you."

"Me?"

"That's why he really came here—to destroy you—maybe even to kill you, for all I know."

"*Kill?*" He was startled at that.

"You'll understand more as we go along. I saw a little bit of this myself, but I got most of it when I went back to Grosse Point."

"All right, who's Gabriel?"

"Junior's cousin," she answered. "Did Junior ever tell you very much about his family?"

"Not really. Bits and pieces mostly. I gather that there's money and that he and his father don't get along too well. You know Damon—he exaggerates a great deal."

"That's a clever way to put it. There *is* money—a great deal of money. Old J.D.—everybody calls him that—hit upon a very simple idea when they were developing one of the newer components in all cars. It's the simplest thing in the world—or so I'm told—but a car won't work without it, and J.D. has the patent."

"No kidding? Damon never said a word about that."

She nodded. "Maybe he considers it beneath him. It's hard to know about Junior. Did he ever tell you about his cousins?"

"I think he mentioned them once—something about a large number of girls."

"There are plenty of girls, all right. The Floods are prolific, but they seem to have trouble producing male children. There's only one other aside from Junior—Gabriel. They grew up together, and Junior hates Gabriel to the point of insanity."

"Hate? Damon?"

"Oh, my dear Raphael, yes. Hate may even be too timid a term. You see, Junior's mother died when he was about four, and J. D. buried himself in the business. It happens sometimes, I guess. Anyway, Junior was raised by servants, and he grew up to be a sullen, spiteful child, delighting in tormenting cats and puppies and his legion of female cousins.

"At any rate, the shining light of the entire family was Gabriel.

Because he and Junior were the only two boys, comparisons were inevitable. Gabriel was everything that Junior wasn't—blond, sunny, outgoing, athletic, polite—the kind of little boy people just naturally love. Junior, on the other hand, was the kind of little boy that you send away to military school. I gather that for a great number of years, about the only thing old J.D. ever said to Junior was, 'Why can't you be more like Gabriel?'' I understand that it all came to a head when the boys were about nine—at Christmastime. Junior had been tormenting one of the girls—as usual—and Gabriel came to her rescue. Old J.D. caught them fighting and made them put on boxing gloves. Then, in front of the entire family, Gabriel gave Junior a very thorough beating, and old J.D. rooted for him all the way.''

"You're not serious.''

"Oh yes. The Floods are a vicious family. After that there was no hope of reconciliation. J.D. told them to shake hands when it was over, and Junior spat in Gabriel's face. From then on he not only hated Gabriel, but his father as well. It was about then that he started being sent away to school.''

Raphael thought about that. "What kind of person is Gabriel?''

"He's an insufferable prig. He's been trained since babyhood to butter up old J.D.—the rest of the Floods know where the money is. He graduated with honors last year from Dartmouth—J.D.'s old school—and he's now busily backstabbing his way up the ladder in the family company.''

"Good group. I can see now why Damon wanted to get away from there. But what's all this got to do with what happened here in Spokane?''

"I'm coming to that. This is all a little bit complicated, and you have to understand it all before it makes any sense.''

"Okay. Go ahead.''

"Anyhow,'' she continued, "at school Junior continued his charming ways, spending most of his time trying to bully smaller boys and usually getting soundly beaten up for it by older ones. Since the schools he attended are little WASP sanctuaries, more often than not the boys who thrashed him were blond, Nordic types—replicas of dear Cousin Gabriel. So, by the time Junior was fifteen or so, he'd developed a pretty serious kind of attitude.

"The turning point, I suppose, came at prep school when Junior set out quite deliberately to 'get' the school's star athlete—a blond, curly-headed half-wit who was almost a carbon copy of Gabriel. Junior charmed the young man into accepting him as his best friend—Junior can be *very* charming—and then he planted some cocaine in the boy's room. An anonymous tip to the school authorities, and the boy was expelled.''

"Flood?'' Raphael said incredulously.

She nodded firmly. "Junior Flood. After the first time he did it again—and again—not always with drugs, naturally. He turned a promising young halfback into a sodden alcoholic. He introduced another boy to the joys of heroin. A brilliant young mathematician now has the cloud of possible homosexuality hanging over him. One boy went to jail. Another killed himself. Junior's been a very busy young man. He's made a lifelong career of destroying young men who look like his cousin Gabriel. I suppose that in time he might even have worked up the nerve to go after Gabriel himself."

"And I . . .?"

"Exactly, Raphael. You look more like Gabriel than Gabriel himself—and of course there's your name. The coincidence was just too much for Junior. He *had* to try to get you. I suppose that's where I came in. I was part of whatever he had in mind, but probably not all of it. Whatever it was going to be, it was undoubtedly fairly exotic. Junior was—is—quite creative, you know."

"It doesn't hold water, 'Bel. Why did he bother to come to Spokane, then? Wasn't this enough for him?" He passed his hand through the vacancy where his left leg had been.

She turned her head away. "Please don't do that, Raphael," she said, her tone almost faint. "It's too grotesque."

"You haven't answered me."

"I don't know," she said helplessly. "Who knows what's enough for someone like Junior? Maybe it was because it was an accident and he didn't make it happen; maybe he wanted to gloat; maybe a hundred things. And then I suppose there's always the possibility that he genuinely likes you. Maybe after the accident you no longer threatened him, and he found that you could really be friends. I really don't know, Raphael. I have enough trouble sorting out my own motives—and God knows *they're* elemental enough."

A nurse came into the chapel, her starched uniform rustling crisply. "Mr. Taylor?"

"Yes?" Raphael answered tensely.

"Mr. Flood has regained consciousness. He's been asking for you."

Raphael got up quickly and reached for his crutches.

" 'Bel?" he said.

"No. You go ahead. I don't think I'm really up to it."

Raphael nodded and followed the nurse out of the chapel and down the long hallway. "How's he doing?" he asked her.

"He'll be fine."

"Lady," he said, stopping, "I've spent too much time in hospitals to buy that."

She turned and looked at him. "Yes. I guess you have."

"It won't go any further, but I need to know."

She nodded. "His condition is critical, and they can't take him to surgery until they get can get him stabilized."

"He's not going to make it, is he?"

She looked at him without answering.

"Okay, I guess that answers that question. Lead the way."

ix

Even though Raphael was used to hospitals and was familiar with the stainless-steel and plastic devices used to maintain life, he was unprepared for Flood's appearance. The dark-faced young man was swathed in bandages, and tubes ran into him from various bottles and containers suspended over his bed. Flood's face, what Raphael could see of it, was greenish pale, and his eyes were dull with pain and drugs.

A youngish man wearing a business suit sat in a chair a little way from the bed. He was obviously not a doctor, but seemed to have some official status. He looked at Raphael, but he did not say anything. Raphael crutched to the side of the bed and sat down in the chair that was there. "Damon," he said. "Damon."

"Raphael." Flood's voice was thick and very weak, and his eyes had difficulty finding Raphael's face.

"How are you doing?" Raphael asked, knowing it was a silly thing to say.

"Excellent," Flood said dryly with a spark of his old wit. "How do I look?"

"Awful."

"You ought to see it from in here."

" 'Bel's here," Raphael told him, "and your father's on his way. He should arrive anytime now."

"Terrific," Flood replied sardonically. "That'll be a touching reunion." His eyes closed, and Raphael thought he had drifted off. Then the eyes opened again, filled with pain.

They were silent for several minutes. The machines that were attached to Flood shirred and whooshed softly.

"Why did you come to Spokane, Damon?"

"It wasn't finished yet," Flood said, his voice almost a whisper. Raphael recognized the tone. Flood had almost been stunned into insensibility by the drugs.

"Couldn't you have just let it go?"

Flood's eyes took on some of their old glitter. "Oh, no. You don't get away from me that easily, Gabriel." He seemed a little stronger.

"Damon." Raphael ignored the slip. "I didn't even try."

"Of course not. They never do." Flood caught his breath and twisted slightly on the bed.

"I'll call the nurse." Raphael reached for the buzzer at the head of the bed.

"Get your goddamn hand away from that thing. You always have to be helpful, don't you? Saint Raphael, friend of man."

"Hasn't this gone about far enough?"

"It's *never* enough." Flood's eyes were flashing, and his breath was coming in short, bubbling little gasps. He half raised his head, and then he slumped back on the bed, his eyes closed.

Raphael reached quickly for the buzzer.

"Why does it always have to be Gabriel?" Flood mumbled, his voice barely a whisper. "Why can't it be me—just once?"

"Take it easy, Damon."

Flood's eyes opened then. "You didn't even feel it. What kind of man are you, anyway? You didn't feel any of it, damn you. Haven't you got any feelings at all?"

"I felt it."

"I *hate* you, Angel."

"I know. Is that why you did this?"

"That's why I do *everything.*"

"But why?" Raphael pressed. "I'm not Gabriel. None of them were ever Gabriel. What have you really accomplished?"

A startled look came into Flood's eyes. Then he laughed—a faint, wheezing sound. "Very good, Angel," he said. "You always were the best. It's a damn shame you have to look like that. We could have been friends."

"We are friends, Damon. You might not believe it or understand it, but we're friends."

"Don't be stupid. Don't disappoint me at this stage of the game."

"The game's all played out."

"I got you, though, didn't I? I finally got you."

"All right, Damon. You win."

Flood smiled briefly then and lapsed into unconsciousness again.

It was sometime later when he opened his eyes once more. "I'm afraid, Angel," he whispered weakly.

Without thinking, Raphael reached out and took his hand. He sat for a long time holding Flood's hand, even for quite some time after Flood had died. Then, gently, he laid the hand back on the bed, got up, and slowly crutched his way out of the room.

 X

It happened because he was tired and sick and in a hurry. All Raphael wanted to do was get upstairs, call Denise, and then bathe the hospital stink off and fall into bed. When he came around the front of his car, the tip of one crutch caught the curb, and he fell heavily to the sidewalk.

Because he had not had time to catch himself, the fall knocked the wind out of him, and he lay for several minutes gasping, his cheek resting on the gritty cement. At first there was anger—at himself, at the curb, at the crutch that had so unexpectedly betrayed him—then there was the cold certainty that on this street of all the streets in the city, no one would help him.

He heard a light step behind him.

"Could you give me hand, please," he asked, hating the necessity for asking, not even turning his head, ashamed of his helplessness and half-afraid that whoever stood there would simply step around him and, indifferent, walk away.

And then a pair of strong hands slid under his arms and lifted, and he was up, leaning against the front fender of his car.

It was Patch.

At close range his face seemed even more darkly somber than at a distance. There was a kind of universal melancholy in that face, a sadness that went beyond any personal bereavement or loss or seemed somehow to reflect the sum of human sorrow.

The Indian bent, picked up the crutches, and handed them to Raphael. "Are you all right now?" he asked, his voice very soft, and his single dark eye searching Raphael's face.

"Yes," Raphael said. "Thanks."

"Are you sure?"

Raphael drew in a deep breath. "Yes. I think everything's fine now. I just got careless, that's all. I should know better."

"Everybody falls now and then," Patch said in his soft voice. "It's not just you. The important thing is not to let it throw you, make you afraid."

"I know. It took me a long time to figure that out, but I think I've got it now."

"Good. You'll be okay then." The brown hand touched his shoulder briefly, and then Patch turned and silently went on down the street.

Raphael stood leaning against his car watching that solitary passage until the dark-faced man was out of sight and the street was empty again.

O Fortuna, velut Luna statu
VARIABILIS

IF THE SUBPOENA HAD COME a week or two later, they might have been gone. The leaves had turned, and Raphael wanted to be away before the first snow. Denise was unhappy about his being summoned to testify, and they came as close to having a fight about it as they did about anything now. "It's absurd," she said the morning of the hearing. "I don't see why you want to bother with it."

"I have to go. If I don't show up, they'll send a couple of eight-foot-tall policemen to get me."

"Don't be ridiculous! All you have to do is pick up the telephone. We can get out of things like this anytime we want to. That's one of our fringe benefits. We don't owe anything to their grubby little system. We're exempt."

"No. I won't do that. That's the kind of thing a cripple would do, but I'm not a cripple anymore. Besides, I want to get it all cleared up. Just for once I want to explain who Flood really was."

"Who cares? The judges don't care; the lawyers don't care; the police don't care—nobody cares. They've all got their neat little categories. All they're going to do is stuff him into one of their pigeonholes and then forget about it. That's the way they do things. Nobody cares about the truth, and if you tell them something that doesn't fit their theories, all you'll do is make them mad at you."

"People have been mad at me before."

"You're impossible."

"Will you come along with me?"

"No," she said tartly. "I've got packing to do. If we're ever going to get out of this town, *one* of us has to be practical."

"You'll be here then?" he asked her, looking around at the clutter of boxes in her apartment.

"Where else would I be? What a dumb question."

"It's just that I get jumpy when I don't know where you are."

She smiled suddenly and then kissed him.

The courthouse in Spokane is a very large, sprawling building with a high, imitation-Renaissance tower looming above it. It makes some pretense at reflecting civic pride while ignoring the human misery that normally fills it. As luck had it on the morning of the hearing, Raphael found a parking spot directly across the street from the main entrance on Broadway. He hated parking lots. They were always filled with obstacles that seemed sometimes deliberate. That luck made him feel better right at the start. There was that word again, however—luck. More and more he had come to know that it was a meaningless word. There was a perfectly rational explanation for why the parking place was there. He didn't know what it *was*, but it was certainly rational.

He went up to the intersection, waited for the light, and then crossed. The courthouse lawn was broad and well cared for and was raised above the level of the sidewalk with a stone retaining wall. There was about the whole thing a kind of self-important aloofness that Raphael secretly found amusing. Slowly, step by step, he went up the stairs and into the building.

Frankie was waiting for him just inside the door. Her face was determined, and her dark eyes were flashing. "It's about time you got here," she snapped, looking up at him.

"The hearing isn't for another half hour, Frankie."

"Where the hell have you been? I've been trying to call you all morning."

"I'm shacked up with a girl."

She actually blushed. "That's *really* crude, you know."

"Sorry."

"I have to talk to you, Raphael. It's important." She led him to a room a few doors away.

"Are we allowed to go in there?" he asked dubiously as she opened the door.

"It's one of the places we have here in the building. They have to give us rooms to conduct our business in, because most of the time we're more important in the courtroom than the lawyers. Give us a few more years, and we'll be able to eliminate the lawyers altogether."

They went into the room, and she closed the door. "We're laying for you, Raphael," she warned him. "We've got a couple of crack troops in that courtroom. We've got a lot of time invested in that motorcycle gang. If those hairballs go to prison, three caseworkers and a supervisor are going to be out of work, so watch what you say in there. I know how you feel about us, but watch your mouth when you get on the stand. Those two girls have all the compassion of a pair of meat grinders. They'll hang you out to dry if you screw up things for us. They've been literally sleeping with the defense attorney—who's also a girl, which makes for a *very* interesting situation."

"You've got a dirty mind, Frankie."

"What else is new? Anyway, the defense is going to try to lay all this on your friend. He was the one with the gun, after all. Did you know that he killed two people that night?"

"I'd heard."

"The defense is going to try to picture him as a Detroit hoodlum who led these poor, innocent young local boys astray. If you say anything that damages their case, my colleagues will cream you."

"Why are you telling me, this Frankie?"

"Because I gave notice yesterday morning. I'm quitting. I'm changing sides."

"Hell, babes, don't do that. You're one of the *good* ones."

"Not anymore. You peeled my soul raw when you told me about how Jane Doe got away from us. I didn't realize how much the people we're trying to help really hate us. I can't live with that, Raphael. I cried for three days. I hope you're proud of yourself."

"Aw, Frankie." He half reached for her.

"None of that. If you start groping me now, you'll get us both arrested."

He stared at her, not comprehending. "You lost me on that one, kid."

"I've got a letch for you, you dumb klutz. If you put your hands on me, I'll peel you like a banana right here on the spot, and I don't have a key, so I can't lock the door."

He had to put a stop to that. "Francesca," he said firmly, "don't even talk about things like that. You know it's out of the question."

"I have enormous self-confidence, Raphael."

He suddenly realized that she was about half-serious.

She sighed. "You've saved three of us, do you know that? You saved yourself, you saved Jane doe, and you saved me. You got the three of us out of the goddamn system. That may be the only victory for our side in this whole freaking century. That's why you have to be very careful in that courtroom. Don't let them rattle you enough to make you get mad and start running your mouth. Keep it all strictly business, because if you start ranting and raving, and if the wrong judge is sitting on the case, those two girls will have you committed before you ever get out of the courtroom. You watch your ass, Raphael Taylor. Jane Doe and I won't be able to have much of a victory celebration if our glorious leader's in the loony bin."

"They can't do that to me, Frankie," he scoffed.

"Like hell they can't. If you get the least bit excited, they'll have you out at Medical Lake before the sun goes down."

"Maybe I should call in sick." She actually had him a little worried.

"That's what I wanted to *tell* you, but you wouldn't answer your goddamn telephone! It's too late now. If you don't show up at this stage, they'll put out a bench warrant for you. Just go in there, keep a smile on your face, and keep your big mouth shut." She glared up at him, her lower lip very active. "At least I was able to cover your ass a little bit."

"What?"

"I purged your file. There aren't any reports in it but mine."

"Why?" That really baffled him.

"Because you were playing games when you first got here. What the hell were you doing with all those empty bottles? You're listed as an alcoholic, did you know that?"

"I'm *what*?"

"There was a report in your file. It said that there were wine bottles all over that pigeon coop you live in. What were you thinking of?"

He laughed ruefully. "I was trying to be cute, I guess. They gave me a caseworker I didn't like. I thought I'd give her something to worry about.

"Dumb! How can you *be* so goddamn dumb? Don't you know that when you talk to one of us, you're talking to *all* of us? That's what those files are *for*, dummy. You owe me at least one roll in the hay, Raphael Taylor, because *I'm* the one who punched the erase button and covered your ass. And I did it with *this* finger." The finger she held up was *not* her index finger.

He grinned at her. "You're a buddy, Frankie." He was genuinely grateful.

"They don't have a single goddamn thing on you," she continued. "I even cleaned up some of my own reports. There's nothing in your file that says that you can't walk on water or raise the dead. What are you going to say in there?"

"I'm going to tell them the truth."

She said a dirty word in Italian. "They'll eat you alive if you do that, Raphael. Just let it slide. Nobody gives a damn about the truth."

"I do."

"That's because you're a weirdo. Just say what they want you to say and get out of there before they get their hooks into you. Your friend is dead. Nothing can hurt him now."

"I want to set the record straight."

"The record's *never* straight, you idiot! Haven't you ever read *1984*? They rewrite the record anytime it doesn't suit them. You're spinning your wheels and exposing your bare fanny for nothing." She looked up at him and then threw her hands in the air. "All right. Do it your way—you will anyway—but *please* be careful. Now come here." She grasped the front of his jacket and pulled him slightly off balance. Then she kissed him very savagely.

"*Mar*-rone!" she breathed. "Why do you have to be—" She stepped back and wiped at her eyes with the back of her hand. "I've wanted to do that since the moment I laid eyes on you. You're lucky you're out of action, Raphael Taylor. I'd have destroyed you. I'd have devoured you. If you've never had an Italian girl jump your bones, you don't know what you've missed."

"I love you, too, Frankie." He really meant it.

"I'm not talking about love, Taylor. That might have come later, but there would have been much, much more important things to take care of first. Be careful in there, my Angel. Be very, very careful." She wiped her eyes again. "Now get out of here."

He smiled at her fondly and half turned.

"Raphael?" She said it in an almost little-girl voice.

"Yes?"

"I love you, too, dammit."

The assistant prosecutor was the young man who had been sitting in Floyd's hospital room the day he had died, and he was waiting nervously near the elevators when Raphael came up.

"I've been trying to get hold of you all week, Mr. Taylor," he said, coming up to Raphael. "I wanted to go over your testimony with you."

Raphael immediately disliked the man. "Why?"

"No lawyer likes surprises in the courtroom."

"Life is full of surprises. Is this likely to take long? I have a lot of things to do today."

The prosecutor looked at him, a bit startled by his tone. "I'll speak with the judge. I think he'll agree to letting you testify first—because of your disability. To be perfectly honest with you, Mr. Taylor, I didn't really understand what you and Flood were talking about the night he died. Are you going to be getting into that? I mean, is it relevant?"

Raphael drew in a deep breath. There wasn't really any way to avoid it. It all had to come out. "Ask me the kind of questions that'll give me some leeway, okay? It's sort of long and complicated, but I don't think anybody's really going to understand what Flood was doing unless I tell the whole story."

"I could have the judge delay the proceedings to give us time to go over it if you'd like."

Raphael shook his head. "I don't have more than one recitation of this in me. It's going to be hard enough to say it once. Shall we get on with it?"

They went into the courtroom.

In due time the judge, a balding man with thick glasses and a slightly wrinkled robe, marched in while everyone stood, and the hearing began.

The preliminaries dragged on for a half hour or so with the nervous young prosecutor and an equally nervous young woman from the public defender's office both behaving with an exaggerated formality that spoke volumes about their amount of experience.

Raphael glanced idly over at Heck's Angels. Big Heintz was there with one side of his face bandaged. Jimmy's nose was broken, and both of his eyes were swollen nearly shut. Marvin's arm was in a cast, and Little Hitler was holding a pair of crutches. There were a dozen or so others—strangers—with various bruises and bandages.

Since some of the defendants were quite young, there was a great deal of polite bickering between the two lawyers about whether or not the juveniles should be separated from the adults. Two hard-eyed

young women in professional-looking suits sat protectively near the
younger members of the gang, furiously scribbling notes and passing
them across the railing to the defense counsel. These were the two
Frankie had warned him about.

The judge finally ruled that the problem of jurisdiction could be
sorted out later, since this was simply a preliminary hearing. The young
woman from the public defender's office hotly took exception, which
the judge wearily noted.

"All right then," the judge said finally, "I guess you may proceed,
Mr. Wilson."

"Thank you, Your Honor," the prosecutor said. "This is one of three
hearings to be held in this matter. At the request of the police department and in the interests of maintaining order, it was deemed wise to
keep the members of the three gangs strictly segregated."

"Objection, Your Honor," the defense counsel said, leaping to her
feet. "The word 'gangs' is pejorative."

"Sustained," the judge decided. "Select another word, Mr. Wilson."

"Would counsel accept 'groups'?" the prosecutor asked.

" 'Groups' is all right," she replied.

The prosecutor turned back to the judge. "If it please the court, I
have one witness who is severely disabled. His testimony may be out of
sequence, but he has asked that he be allowed to testify early in the
proceedings since he experiences a great deal of discomfort when required to sit for extended periods."

"Of course, Mr. Wilson."

The prosecutor called Raphael's name, and Raphael rose, went to
the witness stand, and sat. He drew in a deep breath and pulled an icy,
detached calm about himself. Frankie's warnings were very much on
his mind, and he knew that he could not allow anything to rattle him.
He was sworn in, and then they began.

"Mr. Taylor," the prosecutor said, "are you acquainted with this
group of young men?" He indicated the assembled Angels.

"I've met some of them—briefly. They live a few doors up the street
from me."

"But you were, I take it, much better acquainted with a Mr. Jacob D.
Flood, Junior—now deceased."

"Yes."

"Would you please elaborate on that acquaintance?"

"We were roommates at college," Raphael replied. "He came to Spokane last spring when he found out that I was here."

"You were friends then?"

"I thought so."

"Mr. Flood was educated?"

"Yes."

"He came from a wealthy family?"

"Yes."

"Did he ever explain to you the nature of his association with the group of individuals here in this courtroom? I mean, they do not appear to be the sort of people with whom someone of education and wealth would normally associate."

"They amused him. He had other reasons, but basically it was because they amused him."

"Objection, Your Honor," the defense attorney said, coming to her feet. "Purely speculative."

"I think we can allow a certain latitude, Miss Berensen," the judge told her patiently. "These proceedings are preliminary after all, and whether or not Mr. Flood was amused by the defendants hardly seems to be a major issue."

"Your Honor!" she protested.

"Overruled, Miss Berensen." The judge sighed.

Quite suddenly, perhaps because of the hard chair or his nervousness or the aggravation of the defense attorney's objection, Raphael's left thigh and leg and foot began to ache intolerably. He grimaced and shifted his position.

"Are you in pain, Mr. Taylor?" the judge asked, a note of concern in his voice.

"No more than usual, sir."

The judged frowned slightly and looked down at his notes for a moment. "Mr. Wilson," he said looking up, "what is the proposed thrust of your examination of Mr. Taylor?"

"Uh"—the prosecutor faltered—"background, primarily, Your Honor. Mr. Taylor appears to be the only person in Spokane who really knew Mr. Flood, and since Mr. Flood and his role in this matter are likely to play a major part in any trials resulting from these proceedings, I felt that Mr. Taylor's testimony would help us all to understand that rather strange young man."

"Then Mr. Taylor is here not so much as a witness for the prosecution as he is in the capacity of a friend of the court?"

"Uh—I suppose that's true, Your Honor."

"Miss Berensen." The judge turned to the defense. "Would *you* take exception to designating Mr. Taylor a friend of the court?"

"Most strenuously, Your Honor. The man Flood was the instigator of this whole affair. The defense could never accept testimony from his close friend with an *amicus curiae* label attached to it."

"Your exception will be noted, Miss Berensen. It does not become any of us, however, to inflict needless suffering upon the witness. What I propose is to permit Mr. Taylor to present narrative testimony concerning the man Flood—his background and so forth—in order to allow the testimony to be completed as quickly as possible. Would you accept narrative testimony from the witness based upon *humanitarian* considerations, Miss Berensen?"

The defense attorney seemed about to protest further, but thought better of it. "Very well, Your Honor." She was almost sullen about it.

Behind her the two young women scribbled furiously.

"All right then, Mr. Taylor," the judge said, "why don't you just give us a brief outline of Mr. Flood's background—insofar as you know of it?"

"Yes, Your Honor." Raphael thought for a moment, looking at the patch of golden morning sunlight slanting in through the window at the back of the courtroom, and then he started. "Damon Flood's dead now, so nothing I can say will matter to him. It's taken me a long time to piece his story together, so I hope you'll be patient with me. Flood himself isn't on trial, but his motives in this business may be important." He looked inquiringly at the judge, silently seeking permission to continue.

"I think we can all accept that, Mr. Taylor. Please go on."

"Thank you, Your Honor. Jacob Damon Flood, Junior was born in Grosse Pointe, Michigan. His family is well-to-do. Mr. Flood's mother died when he was four, and his father was totally immersed in the family business. Flood was not particularly lovable as a child, and he was in continual competition with a cousin who appears to have been everyone's favorite—even his own father's. I suppose it finally came to a head during one of those confrontations between Flood and his cousin. Whatever the reason, they fought, and Flood received a very public and humiliating beating while his own father looked on approvingly. As closely as I can reconstruct it, that was the point where something slipped or went off center. He knew who he was. He knew that it was *his* father who was the head of the company that was the source of all family wealth. I guess that all his relatives kowtowed to his father, and he expected the same kind of respect. When he didn't get it, it unsettled him. He became obsessed with the idea of getting revenge—on the cousin certainly and probably on his own father as well. Of course a child can't attack an adult—or a physically superior child—directly, so Flood transferred his rage and hatred to others—to people who resembled the cousin and whose destruction or disgrace would most severely hurt some older authority figure, who represented his father, I suppose. Does that make any sense at all? I've thought about it for a long time, and it's the only explanation I can come up with."

"It's not inconsistent with things we encounter occasionally, Mr. Taylor," the judge said approvingly. "Please continue."

Raphael took a deep breath and looked down into the courtroom. The two young women Frankie had warned him about had stopped writing and were staring at him with open hostility. "In time Flood was sent to a number of those exclusive and very expensive private boarding schools in the east where the wealthy dump their children. He developed a game—a very personal and vicious kind of game. He made a point of seeking out boys who resembled his cousin. He would befriend them—and then he would destroy them. Sometimes he planted evidence of crimes or expellable violations of the rules among their belongings—those were his earliest and crudest efforts. Later he grew more sophisticated, and his plots—if that's not too melodramatic a term—grew more complicated. I'm told that this happened several times in various prep schools and during his first two years at college. It was at that point that I met him. We both transferred to Reed College in Portland from other schools, and we roomed together there. I've been told that I closely resemble Flood's cousin, so I suppose his reaction to me was inevitable."

The judge looked startled. "Mr. Taylor," he interrupted, "are you implying that this man was responsible for your injury?"

"No, Your Honor. The accident was simply that—an accident. Flood really had nothing to do with it. I can't be sure exactly *what* it was that he originally had planned for me. By this time he had refined his schemes to the point where they were so exotic and involved that I don't think anyone could have unraveled them. I honestly believe that my accident threw him completely off. It was blind chance—simple stupid bad luck—and he couldn't accept that.

"Anyway, after the accident, when I had recovered enough to be at least marginally ambulatory, I left Portland and came here to Spokane. I didn't tell anyone where I was going, and it took Flood five months to find me. He wasn't going to let me get away from him, but my condition baffled him. How can you possibly hurt someone who's already been sawed in two?"

"Your Honor," the defense counsel protested. "I don't see the pertinence of all this."

"Miss Berensen, please sit down."

The young woman flushed and sank back into her seat.

"Go on, Mr. Taylor."

"When I first came to Spokane, I entered therapy. Learning to walk again is very tedious, and I needed a diversion, so I started collecting losers."

"Losers?" I'm not sure I understand, Mr. Taylor."

"In our society—probably in every society—there are people who simply can't make it," Raphael explained. "They're not skilled enough, not smart enough, not competitive enough, and they become the human debris of the system. Because our society is compassionate, we take care of them, but in the process they become human ciphers—numbers in the system, welfare cases or whatever.

"I was in an ideal spot to watch them. I live in an area where they congregate, and my apartment is on a rooftop. I was in a situation where I could virtually see everything that went on in the neighborhood."

"Your Honor," the prosecutor said, "I don't want to interrupt Mr. Taylor, but isn't this getting a bit far afield?"

"Is this really relevant, Mr. Taylor?" the judge asked.

"Yes, Your Honor, I believe so. It's the point of the whole thing. If you don't know about the losers, nothing that Flood did will make any sense at all."

"Very well, Mr. Taylor."

"It's easy to dismiss the losers—to ignore them. After all, they don't sit in front of the churches to beg anymore. We've created an entire industry—social workers—to feed them and keep them out of sight so that we never have to come face-to-face with them. We've trained whole generations of bright young girls who don't want to be waitresses or secretaries to take care of our losers. In the process we've created a new leisure class. We give them enough to get by on—not luxury, regardless of what some people believe—but they know they won't be allowed to starve. Our new leisure class doesn't have enough money for hobbies or enough education for art, so they sit. I suppose it's great for a month or two to know that you will never have to work again, but what do you do then? What do you do when you finally come face-to-face with the reality of all those empty years stretching out in front of you?

"For most of the losers crisis is the answer. Crisis is a way of being important—of giving their lives meaning. They can't write books or sell cars or cure warts. The state feeds them and pays their rent, but they have a nagging sense of being worthless. They precipitate crisis—catastrophe—as a way of saying, 'Look at me. I'm alive. I'm a human being.' For the loser it's the only way to gain any kind of recognition. If they take a shot at somebody or OD on pills, at least the police will come. They won't be ignored."

"Mr. Taylor," the judge said with some perplexity, "your observations are very interesting, but—"

"Yes, Your Honor, I'm coming to the connection. It was about the time that I finally began to understand all of this that Flood showed up here in Spokane. One day I happened to mention the losers. He didn't follow what I was talking about, so I explained the whole idea to him. For some reason I didn't understand at the time, the theory of all the sad misfits on the block became very important to him. Of course with Flood you could never be entirely sure how much was genuine interest and how much was put on.

"Anyway, as time went on, Flood started to seek out my collection of losers. He got to know them—well enough to know their weaknesses anyway—and then he began to destroy them one by one. Oh, sure, some of them fell by natural attrition—losers smash up their lives pretty regularly without any outside help—but he did manage to destroy several people in some grand scheme that had *me* as its focus."

"I'm afraid I don't follow that, Mr. Taylor," the judge said.

"As I said, sir, I collect losers," Raphael explained. "I care about them. For all their deliberate, wrongheaded stupidity I care about them and recognize their need for some kind of dignity. Social workers simply process them. It's just a job to all those bright young girls, but I cared—even if it was only passively.

"Flood saw that, and it solved his problem. He'd been looking for a way to hurt someone who'd already been hurt as badly as he was likely to ever be hurt, and this was it. He began to systematically depopulate my block—nothing illegal, of course, just a nudge here, a word there. It was extraordinarily simple, really. Losers are pathologically self-destructive anyway, and he'd had a lifetime of practice."

"Your Honor," Miss Berensen protested, "this is sheer nonsense. It has no relation to any recognized social theory. I think Mr. Taylor's affliction has made him . . ." She faltered.

"Go ahead and say it," Raphael said to her before the judge could speak. "That's a common assumption—that a physical impairment necessarily implies a mental one as well. I'm used to it by now. I'm not even offended at being patronized by the intellectually disadvantaged anymore."

"That'll do, Mr. Taylor," the judge said firmly.

"Sorry, Your Honor. Anyway, whether the theory is valid or not is beside the point. The point is that *I* believe it—and more importantly Flood believed it as well. In that context then, it *is* true.

"In time Flood insinuated himself into this group of bikers up the street. The gang posed special problems for him. He'd been able to handle all the others on the street one-on-one, but there's a kind of cumulative effect in a gang—even one as feebleminded as this one."

Big Heintz came half to his feet. "You watch your mouth, Taylor!" he threatened loudly.

The judge pounded his gavel. "That will be all of that!"

Big Heintz glowered and sank back into his chair.

The judge turned to Raphael then. "Mr. Taylor, we've given you a great deal of latitude here, but please confine your remarks to the business at hand."

"Yes, Your Honor. Once he became involved with the gang, I think Flood began to lose control. Crisis is exciting; it's high drama, and Flood was pulled along by it all. He could handle the gang members on a one-to-one basis quite easily, but when he immersed himself in the entire gang, it all simply overpowered him. Being a loser is somehow contagious, and when a man starts to associate with them in groups, he's almost certain to catch it. I tried to warn him about that, but he didn't seem to understand." Raphael paused. "Now that I stop and think about it, though, maybe he did at that. He kept after me—begging me almost—to move away from Spokane. Maybe in some obscure way those pleas that we get out of this town were cries for help. Maybe he realized that he was losing control." He sighed. "Perhaps we should have gone. Then this might not have happened—at least not here in Spokane. Anyway, when I saw the gun, I knew that he'd slipped over the line. It was too late at that point."

"Then you knew he had a gun?" the judge asked.

"Yes, Your Honor. There'd been a skirmish between the two gangs, and Flood had been beaten pretty severely. I suppose that's what finally pushed him over the edge. In a sense it was like the beating he'd received from his cousin in his childhood, and Flood could never let something like that just slide. He *had* to get even, and he had to arm himself to make sure that it didn't happen to him again. I think that toward the end he even forgot why he'd gotten mixed up with the gang in the first place. Anyway, when Heintzie's grand and final war came, Flood was caught up in it—hooked on crisis, hyped on his own adrenaline, not even thinking anymore—a loser. I suppose it's sort of ironic. He set out to destroy the gang, but in the end they destroyed him. And what's even more ironic is that all Flood really wanted to do when he started out was to try to find a way to hurt *me*. He knew that I cared about my losers, so he thought he could hurt me by destroying them. In the end, though, he became a loser himself and wound up destroying himself. I suppose that his plan really succeeded, because when he destroyed himself, it hurt me more than anything else he could have done. It's strange, but he finally won after all." Raphael looked up at the ceiling. He'd never really thought of it before, and it rather surprised him. "I guess that's about it, Your Honor," he told the judge. "That's about all I really know about Damon Flood." He sat quietly then. It had not really done any good; he realized that now. Denise and Frankie had been right. The categories and pigeonholes were too convenient, and using them as a means of sorting people was too much a part of the official mentality. But he had tried. He had performed that last service that a man can perform for a friend—he had told the truth about him. In spite of everything, he realized that he still thought of Flood as a friend.

"Mr. Wilson?" the judge asked.

The prosecutor rose and walked toward Raphael. "Mr. Taylor, from your observation then, would you say that Mr. Flood was definitely *not* the leader of this—ah—group?"

"No, sir. It was Heintzie's gang, and it was Heintzie's war. The gun was Flood's, though. I think it's what they call escalation. About all Heintze wanted to do was put a few people in the hospital. Killing people was Flood's idea. In the end, though, he was just another member of the gang—a loser."

"Uh—" The prosecutor looked down at his notes. It was obvious that he had not expected the kind of testimony Raphael had just given them. "I—uh—I guess I have no further questions, Your Honor."

"Miss Berensen?" the judge said.

"Your Honor, I wouldn't dignify any of this by even questioning it. My only suggestion would be that Mr. Taylor might consider seeking professional help."

"That's enough of that, Miss Berensen!" The judge sat for a long time looking at the bandaged and sullenly glowering young men seated behind the defense table. Finally he shook his head. "Losers," he murmured so softly that only Raphael could hear him. Then he turned. "Mr. Taylor, you're an intelligent and articulate young man—too intelligent and articulate to just sit on the sidelines the way you're doing. You seem to have some very special talents—profound insight and extraordinary compassion. I think I'd like to know what you plan to do with the rest of your life."

"I'm leaving Spokane, Your Honor. I came here to get some personal things taken care of. Now that all that's done, there's no reason for me to stay anymore. I'll find another town—maybe I'll find another rooftop and another street full of losers. Somebody has to care for them after all. All my options are open, so I suppose I'll just have to wait and see what happens tomorrow—trust to luck, if you want to put it that way."

The judge sighed. "Thank you, Mr. Taylor. You may step down."

Raphael got his crutches squared away, stood up, and went carefully down the single step from the witness stand. Then he walked smoothly up the center aisle with the stately, flowing pace of a one-legged man who has mastered his crutches and is no longer a cripple. He hesitated a moment at the door. There was still the matter of the two derelicts who had been found shot to death in downtown alleys. He realized, however, that he really had no proof that it had been Flood who had so casually shot them as a means of proving to himself that he did in fact have the nerve to shoot another human being. Raphael also realized that he would prefer to leave it simply at that. A suspicion was not a certainty, and for some reason he did not want that final nail driven in. If it *had* been Flood, it would not happen again; and in any case, it would probably delay the escape from Spokane with Denise that had become absolutely necessary. The bailiff standing at the back opened the door for him, and Raphael went on out.

The two young women who had been in the courtroom were waiting for him in the hall. "Mr. Taylor," the blond one said, "we're from the department of—"

"I know who you are." Raphael looked directly into the face of the enemy.

"We'd like to talk to you for a moment, if you're not too busy," she went on, undeterred by his blunt answer.

"I am, but I don't imagine that'll make much difference, will it?"

"Really, Mr. Taylor," the brunette one protested, "you seem extremely hostile."

"You've noticed."

"Mr. Taylor," the blonde said, "you really should leave social theory to the experts, you know. This notion of yours—it just isn't consistent with what we know about human behavior."

"Really? Maybe you'd better go back and take another look then."

"Why are you so hostile, Mr. Taylor?" the brunette asked. She kept coming back to that.

"I'm bad-tempered. Didn't you study that in school? All of us freaks have days when we're bad-tempered. You're supposed to know how to deal with that."

He could see their anger, the frustration in their eyes under the carefully assumed professional masks. His testimony had rather neatly torpedoed their entire case, and they were furious with him. He'd done the one thing Frankie had warned him not to do.

"I'd really like to discuss this theory of yours," the blond one said with a contrived look of interest on her face.

"Oh really?" Raphael was very alert now. He knew that he was on dangerous ground.

"And you really ought to try to control your hostilities," the brunette added.

"Why? Nobody else does. Could it be that you think I should control my hostility because I'm a defective and defectives aren't permitted to dislike people?"

"We'd really like to talk to you, Mr. Taylor," the blonde said. "Could we make an appointment for you at our office—say next Tuesday?"

"No. Now, if you don't mind, I have things to do."

"We really think we could help you, Mr. Taylor," the brunette said, her eyes hardening.

"I don't need any help," Raphael told her. "There's not one single thing I need you for."

"*Everybody* needs help, Mr. Taylor," the blonde said.

"I don't. Now, you'll have to excuse me." He set the points of his crutches down firmly and began to walk down the hallway toward a waiting elevator.

"We'll always be there," the blonde called after him. "Don't hesitate to call—anytime at all."

She sounded almost like old Tobe. That made Raphael feel better somehow. He was almost safe now—close enough to safety at any rate to take the risk. "If you girls really want to help, you ought to learn how to type," he threw back over his shoulder. Flood would have liked that.

"What's that supposed to mean?" the blonde demanded.

"It's sort of an inside joke," he replied. "It'd take much too long to explain." He stepped into the elevator.

"You'll call," the brunette yelled after him in a shrill voice. "Someday you'll call. Someday you'll need our help. Your kind always does."

He might have answered that, but the elevator door closed just then.

It was good to have it all over. In a very personal way he had put Flood finally to rest, and now it was over.

It was just before noon when he came out of the courthouse, and the autumn sun was bright and warm. He went down the several steps to the sidewalk and started up toward the intersection, moving along beside the low retaining wall.

At the corner the bald, skinny philosopher was delivering one of his speeches to the indifferent street. Although Flood had reported seeing him in various parts of town, Raphael had not really been certain in his own mind that the crazy orator who had greeted him on that first snowy night in Spokane was still roaming the streets, or if he had ever really existed at all.

"Whenever anything is done with one intention," the orator boomed, "but something else, other than what was intended, results from certain causes, this is called chance. We may therefore define chance as an unexpected result from the coincidence of certain causes in matters where there was another purpose."

Raphael stopped and leaned back, half sitting on the low retaining wall to listen. He leaned his crutches against the wall on either side of his single leg and crossed his arms.

"The order of the universe," the bald man went on, "advancing with its inevitable sequences, brings about this coincidence of causes. This order itself emanates from its source, which is Providence, and disposes all things in their proper time and place."

Raphael found himself smiling suddenly. Without knowing exactly why, he uncrossed his arms and began to applaud, the sound of his clapping hands quite loud in the momentarily quiet street.

Startled, the crazy man jerked his head around to regard his audience of one. And then he grinned. There was in that grin all the rueful acknowledgement of human failure, of lives futile and wasted, and at the same time a sly, almost puckish delight in all the joy that even the most useless life contained. It was a cosmic kind of grin, and Raphael found its sly, mischievous twinkle somehow contagious.

Still applauding, he grinned back.

And then, that impish smile still on his face, the crazy man extended one arm to the side with exaggerated formality, placed his other hand on his chest, and took a florid, theatrical bow. His face was a sly mask when he came erect again, and he looked directly at Raphael and gave him a knowing wink before he turned back to continue his oration to the swiftly moving traffic.

HIGH HUNT

For JUFELEE

The more things change
The more they remain the same.

PROLOGUE

WHEN we were boys, before we lost him and before my brother and I turned away from each other, my father once told us a story about our grandfather and a dog. We were living in Tacoma then, in one of the battered, sagging, rented houses that stretch back in my memory and mark the outlines of a childhood spent unknowingly on the bare upper edge of poverty. Jack and I knew that we weren't rich, but it didn't really bother us all that much. Dad worked in a lumber mill and just couldn't seem to get ahead of the bills. And, of course, Mom being the way she was didn't help much either.

It had been a raw, blustery Saturday, and Jack and I had spent the day outside. Mom was off someplace as usual, and Dad was supposed to be watching us. About all he'd done had been to feed us and tell us to stay the hell out of trouble or he'd bite off our ears. He always said stuff like that, but we were pretty sure he didn't really mean it.

The yard around our house was cluttered with a lot of old junk abandoned by previous tenants—rusty car bodies and discarded appliances and the like—but it was a good place to play. Jack and I were involved in one of the unending, structureless games of his invention that filled the days of our boyhood. My brother—even then thin, dark, quick, and nervous—was a natural ringleader who settled for directing my activities when he couldn't round up a gang of neighborhood kids. I went along with him most of the time—to some extent because he was older, but even more, I suppose, because even then I really didn't much give a damn, and I knew that he did.

After supper it was too dark to go back outside, and the radio was on the blink, so we started tearing around the house. We got to playing tag in the living room, ducking back and forth around the big old wood-burning heating stove, giggling and yelling, our feet clattering on the worn linoleum. The Old Man was trying to read the paper, squinting through the dime-store glasses that didn't seem to help much and made him look like a total stranger—to me at least.

He'd glance up at us from time to time, scowling in irritation. "Keep it down, you two," he finally said. We looked quickly at him to see if he really meant it. Then we went on back out to the kitchen.

"Hey, Dan, I betcha I can hold my breath longer'n you can," Jack challenged me. So we tried that a while, but we both got dizzy, and pretty soon we were running and yelling again. The Old Man hollered at us a couple times and finally came out to the kitchen and gave us both a few whacks on the fanny to show us that he meant business. Jack wouldn't cry—he was ten. I was only eight, so I did. Then the Old Man made us go into the living room and sit on the couch. I kept sniffling loudly to make him feel sorry for me, but it didn't work.

"Use your handkerchief" was all he said.

I sat and counted the flowers on the stained wallpaper. There were twelve rows on the left side of the brown water-splotch that dribbled down the wall and seventeen on the right side.

Then I decided to try another tactic on the Old Man. "Dad, I have to go."

"You know where it is."

When I came back, I went over and leaned my head against his shoulder and looked at the newspaper with him to let him know I didn't hold any grudges. Jack fidgeted on the couch. Any kind of enforced nonactivity was sheer torture to Jack. He'd take ten spankings in preference to fifteen minutes of sitting in a corner. School was hell for Jack. The hours of sitting still were almost more than he could stand.

Finally, he couldn't take anymore. "Tell us a story, Dad."

The Old Man looked at him for a moment over the top of his newspaper. I don't think the Old Man really understood my brother and his desperate need for diversion. Jack lived with his veins, like Mom did. Dad just kind of did what he had to and let it go at that. He was pretty easygoing—I guess he had to be, married to Mom and all like he was. I never really figured out where I fit in. Maybe I didn't, even then.

"What kind of a story?" he finally asked.

"Cowboys?" I said hopefully.

"Naw," Jack vetoed, "that's kid stuff. Tell us about deer hunting or something."

"Couldn't you maybe put a couple cowboys in it?" I insisted, still not willing to give up.

Dad laid his newspaper aside and took off his glasses. "So you want me to tell you a story, huh?"

"With cowboys," I said again. "Be sure you don't forget the cowboys."

"I don't know that you two been good enough today to rate a story." It was a kind of ritual.

"We'll be extra good tomorrow, won't we, Dan?" Jack promised quickly. Jack was always good at promising things. He probably meant them, too, at the time anyway.

"Yeah, Dad," I agreed, "extra, extra, special good."

"That'll be the day," the Old Man grunted.

"Come on, Dad," I coaxed. "You can tell stories better'n anybody." I climbed up into his lap. I was taking a chance, since I was still supposed to be sitting on the couch, but I figured it was worth the risk.

Dad smiled. It was the first time that day. He never smiled much, but I didn't find out why until later. He shifted me in his lap, leaned back in the battered old armchair, and put his feet upon the coffee table. The wind gusted and roared in the chimney and pushed against the windows while the Old Man thought a few minutes. I watched his weather-beaten face closely, noticing for the first time that he was getting gray hair around his ears. I felt a sudden clutch of panic. My Dad was getting old!

"I ever tell you about the time your granddad had to hunt enough meat to last the family all winter?" he asked us.

"Are there cowboys in it?"

"Shut up, Dan, for cripes' sakes!" Jack told me impatiently.

"I just want to be sure."

"You want to hear the story or not?" the Old Man threatened.

"Yeah," Jack said. "Shut up and listen, for cripes' sakes."

"It was back in the winter of 1893, I think it was," Dad started. "It was several years after the family came out from Missouri, and they were trying to make a go of it on a wheat ranch down in Adams County."

"Did Grandpa live on a real ranch?" I asked. "With cowboys and everything?"

The Old Man ignored the interruption. "Things were pretty skimpy the first few years. They tried to raise a few beef-cows, but it didn't work out too well, so when the winter came that year, they were clean out of meat. Things were so tough that my uncles, Art and Dolph, had to get jobs in town and stay at a boardinghouse. Uncle Beale was married and out on his own by then, and Uncle Tod had gone over to Seattle to work in the lumber mills. That meant that there weren't any men on the place except my dad and my granddad."

"He was our great-granddad," Jack told me importantly.

"I know that," I said. "I ain't that dumb." I leaned my head back against Dad's chest so I could hear the rumble of his voice inside my head again.

"Great-Granddad was in the Civil War," Jack said. "You told us that one time."

"You want to tell this or you want me to?" the Old Man asked him.

"Yeah," I said, not lifting my head, "shut up, Jack, for cripes' sakes."

"Anyhow," the Old Man went on, "Granddad had to stay and tend the place, so *he* couldn't go out and hunt. Dad was only seventeen, but there wasn't anybody else to go. Well, the nearest big deer herd was over around Coeur d'Alene Lake, up in the timber country in Idaho. There weren't any game laws back then—at least nobody paid any attention to them if there were—so a man could take as much as he needed."

The wind gusted against the house again, and the wood shifted in the heating stove, sounding very loud. The Old Man got up, lifting me easily in his big hands, and plumped me on the couch beside Jack. Then he went over and put more wood in the stove from the big linoleum-covered woodbox against the wall that Jack and I were supposed to keep full. He slammed the door shut with an iron bang, dusted off his hands, and sat back down.

"It turned cold and started snowing early that year," he continued. "Granddad had this old .45-70 single-shot he'd carried in the war, but they only had twenty-six cartridge cases for it. He and Dad loaded up all those cases the night before Dad left. They'd pulled the wheels off the wagon and put the runners on as soon as the snow really set in good, so it was all ready to go. After they'd finished loading the cartridges, Granddad gave my dad an old pipe. Way he looked at it, if Dad was old enough to be counted on to do a man's work, he was old enough to have his own pipe. Dad hadn't ever smoked before—except a couple times down in back of the schoolhouse and once out behind the barn when he was a kid.

"Early the next morning, before daylight, they hitched up the team—Old Dolly and Ned. They pitched the wagon-bed, and they loaded up Dad's bedding and other gear. Then Dad called his dogs and got them in the wagon-bed, shook hands with Granddad, and started out."

"I'll betcha he was scared," I said.

"Grown men don't get scared," Jack said scornfully.

"That's where you're wrong, Jack," the Old Man told him. "Dad was plenty scared. That old road from the house wound around quite a bit before it dropped down on the other side of the hill, and Dad always said he didn't dare look back even once. He said that if he had, he'd have turned right around and gone back home. There's something wrong with a man who doesn't get scared now and then. It's how you handle it that counts."

I know that bothered Jack. He was always telling everybody that he wasn't scared—even when I knew he was lying about it. I think he believed that growing up just meant being afraid of fewer and fewer things. I was always sure that there was more to it than that. We used to argue about it a lot.

"You ain't scared of anything, are you, Dad?" Jack asked, an edge of concern in his voice. It was almost like an accusation.

Dad looked at him a long time without saying anything. "You want to hear the story, or do you want to ask a bunch of questions?" It hung in the air between them. I guess it was always there after that. I saw it getting bigger and bigger in the next few years. Jack was always too stubborn to change his mind, and the Old Man was always too bluntly honest to lie to him or even to let him believe a lie. And I was in the middle—like always. I went over and climbed back up in my father's lap.

The Old Man went on with the story as if nothing had happened. "So there's Dad in this wagon-bed sled—seventeen years old, all alone except for the horses and those two black and tan hounds of his."

"Why can't we have a dog?" I asked, without bothering to raise my head from his chest. I averaged about once a week on that question. I already knew the answer.

"Your mother won't go for it." They always called each other "your mother" and "your father." I can't think of more than two or three times while we were growing up that I heard either one of them use the other's name. Of course most of the time they were fighting or not speaking anyway.

"Well, Uncle Dolph had loaned Dad an old two-dollar mail-order pistol, a .32 short. Dad said it broke open at the top like a kid's cap gun and wouldn't shoot worth a damn, but it was kinda comfortable to have it along. Uncle Dolph shot a Swede in the belly with it a couple years later—put him in the hospital for about six months."

"Wow!" I said. "What'd he shoot him for?"

"They were drinking in a saloon in Spokane and got into a fight over something or other. The Swede pulled a knife and Uncle Dolph had to shoot him."

"Gee!" This was a pretty good story after all.

"It took Dad all of three days to get up into the timber country around the lake. Old Dolly and Ned pulled that sled at a pretty steady trot, but it was a long ways. First they went on up out of the wheat country and then into the foothills. It was pretty lonely out there. He only passed two or three farms along the way, pretty broken-down and sad-looking. But most of the time there wasn't anything but the two shallow ruts of the wagon road with the yellow grass sticking up through the snow here and there on each side and now and then tracks where a wolf or a coyote had chased a rabbit across the road. The sky was all kind of gray most of the time, with the clouds kind of low and empty-looking. Once in a while there'd be a few flakes of snow skittering in the wind. Most generally it'd clear off about sundown, just in time to get icy cold at night.

"Come sundown he'd camp in the wagon, all rolled up in his blankets with a dog on each side. He'd listen to the wolves howling off in the distance and stare up at the stars and think about how faraway they were." The Old Man's voice kind of drifted off and his eyes got a kind of faraway look in them.

The wood in the stove popped, and I jumped a little.

"Well, it had gotten real cold early that year, and when he got to the lake, it was frozen over—ice so thick you coulda driven the team and wagon right out on it, and about an inch of snow on top of the ice. He scouted around until he found a place that had a lot of deer-sign and he made camp there.''

''What's deer-sign, Dad?'' I asked.

''Tracks, mostly. Droppings. Places where they've chewed off twigs and bark. Anyhow, he pulled up into this grove, you see—big, first-growth timber. Some of those trees were probably two hundred feet tall and fifteen feet at the butt, and there wasn't any of the underbrush you see in the woods around here. The only snow that got in under them was what had got blown in from out in the clearings and such, so the ground was pretty dry.''

From where I sat with my head leaned against the Old Man's chest, I could see into the dark kitchen. I could just begin to build a dark pine grove lying beyond the doorway with my eyes. I dusted the linoleum-turned-pine-needle floor with a powder-sugar of snow made of the dim edge of a streetlight on the corner that shone in through the kitchen window. It looked about right, I decided, about the way Dad described it.

''He got the wagon set where he wanted it, unhitched the horses, and started to make camp.''

''Did he build a fire?'' I asked.

''One of the first things he did,'' the Old Man said.

That was easy. The glow of the pilot light on the stove reflected a small, flickering point on the refrigerator door. It was coming along just fine.

''Well, he boiled up some coffee in an old cast-iron pan, fried up some bacon, and set some of the biscuits Grandma'd packed for him on a rock near the fire to warm. He said that about that time he'd have given the pipe and being grown-up and all of it just to be back home, sitting down to supper in the big, warm, old kitchen, with the friendly light of the coal-oil lamps and Grandma's cooking, and the night coming down around the barn, and the shadows filling up the lines of footprints in the snow leading from the house to the outbuildings.'' Dad's voice got faraway again.

''But he ate his supper and called the dogs up close and checked his pistol when he heard the wolves start to howl off in the distance. There probably wasn't anybody within fifty miles. Nothing but trees and hills and snow all around.

''Well, after he'd finished up with all the things you have to do to get a camp in shape, he sat down on a log by the fire and tried not to think about how lonesome he was.''

''He had those old dogs with him, didn't he, Dad?'' I asked, ''and the horses and all? That's not the same as being *all* alone, is it?'' I had a thing about loneliness when I was kid.

Dad thought it over for a minute. I could see Jack grinding his teeth in irritation out of the corner of my eye, but I didn't really look over at him. I had the deep-woods camp I'd built out in the kitchen just right, and I didn't want to lose it. "I don't know, Dan," the Old Man said finally, "maybe the dogs and the horses just weren't enough. It can get awful lonesome out there in the timber by yourself like that—awful lonesome."

I imagine some of the questions I used to ask when I was a kid must have driven him right up the wall, but he'd always try to answer them. Mom was usually too busy talking about herself or about the people who were picking on her, and Jack was too busy trying to act like a grown-up or getting people to pay attention to him to have much time for my questions. But Dad always took them seriously. I guess he figured that if they were important enough for me to ask, they were important enough for him to answer. He was like that, my Old Man.

The wood popped in the stove again, but I didn't jump this time. I just slipped the sound on around to the campfire in the kitchen.

"Well, he sat up by his fire all night, so he wouldn't sleep too late the next morning. He watched the moon shine down on the ice out on the lake and the shadows from his fire flickering on the big tree trunks around his camp. He was pretty tired, and he'd catch himself dozing off every now and then, but he'd just fill up that stubby old pipe and light it with a coal from the fire and think about how it would be when he got home with a wagon-load of deer meat. Maybe then his older brothers would stop treating him like a wet-behind-the-ears kid. Maybe they'd listen to what he had to say now and then. And he'd catch himself drifting off into the dream and slipping down into sleep, and he'd get up and walk around the camp, stamping his feet on the frosty ground. And he'd have another cup of coffee and sit back down between his dogs and dream some more. After a long, long time, it started to get just a little bit light way off along one edge of the sky."

The faint, pale edge of daylight was tricky, but I finally managed it.

"Now these two hounds Dad had with him were trained to hunt a certain way. They were Pete and Old Buell. Pete was a young dog with not too much sense, but he'd hunt all day and half the night, too, if you wanted him to. Buell was an old dog, and he was as smart as they come, but he was getting to the point where he'd a whole lot rather lay by the fire and have somebody bring him his supper than go out and work for it. The idea behind deer hunting in those days was to have your dogs circle around behind the deer and then start chasing them toward you. Then when the deer ran by you, you were supposed to just sort of bushwhack the ones you wanted. It's not really very sporting, but in those days you hunted for the meat, not for the fun.

"Well, as soon as it started to get light, Dad sent them out. Pete took right off, but Old Buell hung back. Dad finally had to kick him in the tail to make him get away from the fire."

"That's mean," I objected. I had the shadowy shapes of *my* two dogs near my reflected-pilot-light fire, and I sure didn't want anybody mistreating *my* old dogs, not even my own grandfather.

"Dog had to do his share, too, in those days, Dan. People didn't keep dogs for pets back then. They kept them to work. Anyway, pretty soon Dad could hear the dogs baying, way back in the timber, and he took the old rifle and the twenty-six bullets and went down to the edge of the lake."

"He took his pistol, too, I'll bet," I said. Out in *my* camp in the forests of the kitchen, *I* took *my* pistol.

"I expect he did, Dan, I expect he did. Anyway, after a little bit, he caught a flicker of movement back up at camp, out of the corner of his eye. He looked back up the hill, and there was Old Buell slinking back to the fire with his tail between his legs. Dad looked real hard at him, but he didn't dare move or make any noise for fear of scaring off the deer. Old Buell just looked right straight back at him and kept on slinking toward the fire, one step at a time. He knew Dad couldn't do a thing about it. A dog can do that sometimes, if he's smart enough.

"Well, it seems that Old Pete was able to get the job done by himself, because pretty soon the deer started to come out on the ice. Well, Dad just held off, waiting for more of them, you see, and pretty soon there's near onto a hundred of them out there, all bunched up. You see, a deer can't run very good on ice, and he sure don't like being out in the open, so when they found themselves out there, they just kind of huddled up to see what's gonna happen."

I could see Jack leaning forward now, his eyes bright with excitement and his lips drawn back from his teeth a little. Of course, I couldn't look straight at him. I had to keep everything in place out on the other side of the doorway.

"So Dad just lays that long old rifle out across the log and touches her off. Then he started loading and firing as fast as he could so's he could get as many as possible before they got their sense back. Well, those old black-power cartridges put out an awful cloud of smoke, and about half the time he was shooting blind, but he managed to knock down seventeen of them before the rest got themselves organized enough to run out of range."

"Wow! That's a lot of deer, huh, Dad?" I said.

"As soon as Old Pete heard the shooting, he knew his part of the job was over, so he went out to do a little hunting for himself. The dogs hadn't had anything to eat since the day before, so he was plenty hungry, but then, a dog hunts better if he's hungry—so does a man.

"Anyway, Dad got the team and skidded the deer on in to shore and commenced to gutting and skinning. Took him most of the rest of the day to finish up."

Jack started to fidget again. He'd gone for almost a half hour without saying hardly anything, and that was always about his limit.

"Is a deer very hard to skin, Dad?" he asked.

"Not if you know what you're doing."

"But how come he did it right away like that?" Jack demanded.

"Eddie Selvridge's old man said you gotta leave the hide on a deer for at least a week or the meat'll spoil."

"I heard him say that, too, Dad," I agreed.

"Funny they don't leave the hide on a cow then when they butcher it, isn't it?" the Old Man asked. "At the slaughterhouse they always skin 'em right away, don't they?"

"I never thought of that," I admitted.

Jack scowled silently. He hated not being right. I think he hated that more than anything else in the world.

"Along about noon or so," Dad continued, "here comes Pete back into camp with a full belly and blood on his muzzle. Old Buell went up to him and sniffed at him and then started casting back and forth until he picked up Pete's trail. Then he lined out backtracking Pete to his kill."

Jack howled with sudden laughter. "That sure was one smart old dog, huh, Dad?" he said. "Why work if you can get somebody else to do it for you?"

Dad ignored him. "Old Pete had probably killed a fawn and had eaten his fill. Anyway, my dad kinda watched the dogs for a few minutes and then went back to work skinning. After he got them all skinned out, he salted down the hides and rolled them in a bundle—sold the hides in town for enough to buy his own rifle that winter, and enough left over to get his mother some yard goods she'd wanted. Then he drug the carcasses back to camp through the snow and hung them all up to cool out.

"He cleaned up, washing his hands with snow, fed the team, and then boiled up another pan of coffee. He fried himself a big mess of deer liver and onions and heated up some more of the biscuits. After he ate, he sat on a log and lit his pipe."

"I'll bet he was tired," Jack said, just to be saying something. "Not being in bed all the night before and all that."

"He still had something left to tend to," Dad said. "It was almost dark when he spotted Old Buell slinking back toward camp. He was out on the open, coming back along the trail Pete had broken through the snow. His belly looked full, and his muzzle and ears were all bloody the same way Pete's had been."

"He found the other dog's deer, I'll betcha." Jack laughed. "You *said* he was a smart old dog."

Beyond the kitchen doorway, one of my shadowy dogs crept slowly toward the warmth of the pilot-light campfire, his eyes sad and friendly, like the eyes of the hound some kid up the block owned.

"Well, Dad watched him for a minute or two, and then he took his rifle, pulled back the hammer, and shot Old Buell right between the eyes."

The world beyond the doorway shattered like a broken mirror and fell apart back into the kitchen again. I jerked up and looked straight into my father's face. It was very grim, and his eyes were very intent on

Jack, as if he were telling my brother something awfully important.

He went on without seeming to notice my startled jump. "Old Buell went end over end when that bullet hit him. Then he kicked a couple times and didn't move anymore. Dad didn't even go over to look at him. He just reloaded the rifle and set it where it was handy, and then he and Old Pete climbed up into the wagon and went to bed.

"The next morning, he hitched up the team, loaded up the deer carcasses, and started back home. It took him three days again to get back to the wheat ranch, and Granddad and Grandma were sure glad to see him." My father lifted me off his lap, leaned back and lit a cigarette.

"It took them a good two days to cut up the deer and put them down in pickling crocks. After they finished it all up and Dad and Granddad were sitting in the kitchen, smoking their pipes with their sock feet up on the open oven door, Granddad turned to my Dad and said, 'Sam, whatever happened to Old Buell, anyway? Did he run off?'

"Well, Dad took a deep breath. He knew Granddad had been awful fond of that old hound. 'Had to shoot him,' he said. 'Wouldn't hunt—wouldn't even hunt his own food. Caught him feeding on Pete's kill.'

"Well, I guess Granddad thought about that for a while. Then he finally said, 'Only thing you could do, Sam, I guess. Kind of a shame, though. Old Buell was a good dog when he was younger. Had him a long time.' "

The wind in the chimney suddenly sounded very loud and cold and lonesome.

"But why'd he shoot him?" I finally protested.

"He just wasn't any good anymore," Dad said, "and when a dog wasn't any good in those days, they didn't want him around. Same way with people. If they're no good, why keep them around?" He looked straight at Jack when he said it.

"Well, I sure wouldn't shoot my own dog," I objected.

Dad shrugged. "It was different then. Maybe if things were still the way they were back then, the world would be a lot easier to live in."

That night when we were in bed in the cold bedroom upstairs, listening to Mom and the Old Man yelling at each other down in the living room, I said it again to Jack. "I sure wouldn't shoot my own dog."

"Aw, you're just a kid," he said. "That was just a story. Grandpa didn't *really* shoot any dog. Dad just said that."

"Dad doesn't tell lies," I said. "If you say that again, I'm gonna hit you."

Jack snorted with contempt.

"Or maybe I'll shoot you," I said extravagantly. "Maybe some day I'll just decide that *you're* no good, and I'll take my gun and shoot *you*. Bang! Just like that, and you'll be dead, and I'll betcha you wouldn't like that at all."

Jack snorted again and rolled over to go to sleep, or to wrestle with the problem of being grown-up and still being afraid, which was to worry at him for the rest of his life. But I lay awake for a long time staring into the darkness. And when I drifted into sleep, the forest in the kitchen echoed with the hollow roar of that old rifle, and my shadowy old dog with the sad, friendly eyes tumbled over and over in the snow.

In the years since that night I've had that same dream again and again—not every night, sometimes only once or twice a year—but it's the only thing I can think of that hasn't changed since I was a boy.

The Gathering

1

I GUESS that if it hadn't been for that poker game, I'd have never really gotten to know my brother. That puts the whole thing into the realm of pure chance right at the outset.

I'd been drafted into the Army after college. I sort of resented the whole thing but not enough to run off to Canada or to go to jail. Some of my buddies got kind of excited and made a lot of noise about "principle" and what-not, but I was the one staring down the mouth of that double-barrelled shotgun called either/or. When I asked them what the hell the difference was between the Establishment types who stood on the sidelines telling me to go to Nam and the Antiestablishment types who stood on the sidelines telling me to go to a federal penitentiary, they got decidedly huffy about the whole thing.

Sue, my girlfriend, who felt she had to call and check in with her mother if we were going to be five minutes late getting home from a movie, told me on the eve, as they used to say, of my departure that she'd run off to Canada with me if I *really* wanted her to. Since I didn't figure any job in Canada would earn me enough to pay the phone bill she'd run up calling Momma every time she had to go to the biffy, I nobly turned her down. She seemed awfully relieved.

I suppose that ultimately I went in without any fuss because it didn't really mean anything to me one way or the other. None of it did.

As it all turned out, I went to Germany instead of the Far East. So I soaked up *Kultur* and German beer and played nursemaid to an eight-inch howitzer for about eighteen months, holding off the red threat. I finished up my hitch in late July and came back on a troopship. That's where I got into the poker game.

Naturally, it was Benson who roped me into it. Benson and I had been inducted together in Seattle and had been in the same outfit in Germany. He was a nice enough kid, but he couldn't walk past a deck of cards or a pair of dice if his life depended on it. He'd been at me a couple times and I'd brushed him off, but on the third day out from Bremerhaven he caught me in the chow line that wandered up and

235

down the gray-painted corridors of the ship. He knew I had about twenty dollars I hadn't managed to spend before we were shipped out.

"Come on, Alders. What the hell? It's only for small change." His eyes were already red-rimmed from lack of sleep, but his fatigue pockets jingled a lot. He must have been winning for a change.

"Oh, horseshit, Benson," I told him. "I just don't get that much kick out of playing poker."

"What the fuck else is there to do?"

He had a point there. I'd gotten tired of looking at the North Atlantic after about twenty minutes. It's possibly the dullest stretch of ocean in the world—if you're lucky. Anyway, I know he'd be at me until I sat in for a while, and it really didn't make that much difference to me. Maybe that's why I started winning.

"All right, *Arsch-loch*." I gave in. "I'll take your goddamn money. It doesn't make a shit to me." So, after chow, I went and played poker.

The game was in the forward cargo hold. They'd restacked the five hundred or so duffle bags until there was a cleared-out place in the middle of the room. Then they'd rigged a table out of a dozen or so bags, a slab of cardboard, and a GI blanket. The light wasn't too good, and the place smelled of the bilges, and after you've sat on some guy's extra pair of boots inside his duffle bag for about six hours, your ass feels like he's been walking on it, but we stuck it out. Like Benson said, what else was there to do?

The game was seven-card stud, seven players. No spit-in-the-ocean, or no-peek, or three-card-lowball. There were seven players—not always the same seven guys, but there were always seven players.

The first day I sat in the game most of the play was in coins. Even so, I came out about forty dollars ahead. I quit for the day about midnight and gave my seat to the Spec-4 who'd been drooling down my back for three hours. He was still there when I drifted back the next morning.

"I guess you want your seat back, huh?"

"No, go ahead and play, man."

"Naw, I'd better knock off and get some sleep. Besides, I ain't held a decent hand for the last two hours."

He got up and I sat back down and started winning again.

The second day the paper money started to show. The pots got bigger, and I kept winning. I wondered how much longer my streak could go on. All the laws of probability were stacked against me by now. Nobody could keep winning forever. When I quit that night, I was better than two hundred ahead. I stood up and stretched. The cargo hold was full of guys, all sitting and watching, very quietly. Word gets around fast on a troopship.

On the morning of the third day, Benson finally went broke. He'd been giving up his place at the table for maybe two-hour stretches, and he'd grab quick catnaps back in one of the corners. He looked like the wrath of God, his blond, blankly young face stubbled and grimy-looking. The cards had gone sour for him late the night before—not completely sour, just sour enough so that he was pretty consistently holding the second-best hand at the table. That can get awfully damned expensive.

It was on the sixth card of a game that he tossed in his last three one-dollar bills. He had three cards to an ace-high straight showing. A fat guy at the end of the table was dealing, and he flipped out the down-cards to Benson, the Spec-4, and himself. The rest of us had folded. I could tell from Benson's face that he'd filled the straight. He might as well have had a billboard on the front of his head.

The Spec-4 folded.

"You're high," the fat dealer said, pointing at Benson's ace.

"I ain't got no money to bet," Benson answered.

"Tough titty."

"Come on, man. I got it, but I can't bet it."

"Bet, check, or fold, fella," the dealer said with a fat smirk.

Benson looked around desperately. There was a sort of house rule against borrowing at the table. "Wait a minute," he said. "How about this watch?" He held out his arm.

"I got a watch," the dealer said, but he looked interested.

"Come on, man. I got that watch when I graduated from high school. My folks give a hundred and a half for it. It'll sure as hell cover any bet in this chickenshit little poker game."

The fat guy held out his hand. Benson gave him the watch.

"Give you five bucks."

"Bull*shit*! That watch is worth a hundred and a half, I told you."

"Not to me, it ain't. Five bucks."

"Fuck you, Buster. You ain't gittin' *my* watch for no lousy five bucks."

"I guess you better throw in your hand then, huh?"

"Christ, man, gimme a break."

"Come on, fella," the fat guy said, "you're holdin' up the game. Five bucks. Take it or leave it."

I could see the agony of indecision in Benson's face. Five dollars was the current bet limit. "All right," he said finally.

He bet two. The dealer raised him three. Benson called and rolled over his hole cards. He had his straight. His face was jubilant. He looked more like a kid than ever.

The fat guy had a flush.

Benson watched numbly, rubbing his bare left wrist, as the chortling fat man raked in the money. Finally he got up and went quickly out of the cargo hold.

"Hey, man," the fat dealer called after him. "I'll give you a buck apiece for your boots." He howled with laughter.

Another player took Benson's place.

"That was kinda hard," a master sergeant named Riker drawled mildly from the other end of the table.

"That's how we play the game where I come from, Sarge," the fat man said.

It took me two days to get him, but I finally nailed him right to the wall. The pots were occasionally getting up to forty or fifty dollars by then, and the fat man was on a losing streak.

He had two low pair showing, and he was betting hard, hoping to get even. It was pretty obvious that he had a full house, sevens and threes. I had two queens, a nine and the joker showing. My hand looked like a pat straight, but I had two aces in the hole. My aces and queens would stomp hell out of his sevens and threes.

Except that on the last round I picked up another ace.

He bet ten dollars. I raised him twenty-five.

"I ain't got that much," he said.

"Tough titty."

"I got you beat."

"You better call the bet then."

"You can't just *buy* the fuckin' pot!"

"Call or fold, friend." I was enjoying it.

"Come *on*, man. You can't just *buy* the fuckin' pot!"

"You already said that. How much you got?"

"I got twelve bucks." He thought I was going to reduce my bet so he could call me. His face relaxed a little.

"You got a watch?" I asked him quietly.

He caught on then. "You bastard!" He glared at me. He sure wanted to keep Benson's watch. "You ain't gettin' this watch *that* way, fella."

I shrugged and reached for the pot.

"What the hell you doin'?" he squawked.

"If you're not gonna call—"

"All right, all right, you bastard!" He peeled off Benson's watch and threw it in the pot. "There, you're called."

"That makes seventeen," I said. "You're still eight bucks light."

"Fuck you, fella! That goddamn watch is worth a hundred and fifty bucks!"

"I saw you buy it, friend. The price was five. That's what you paid for it, so I guess that's what it's worth. You got another watch?"

"You ain't gettin' *my* watch."

I reached for the pot again.

"Wait a minute! Wait a minute!" He pulled off his own watch.

"That's twenty-two," I said. "You're still light."

"Come on, man. My watch is worth more than five bucks."

"A Timex? Don't be stupid. I'm giving you a break letting you have five on it." I reached for the pot again.

"I ain't got nothin else."

"Tell you what, sport. I'll give you a buck apiece for your boots."

"What the fuck you want my fuckin' boots for?"

"You gonna call?"

"All right. My fuckin' boots are in."

"Put 'em on the table, sport."

He scowled at me and started unlacing his boots. "There," he snapped, plunking them down on the table, "you're called."

"You're still a buck light." I knew I was being a prick about it, but I didn't give a damn. I get that way sometimes.

He stared at me, not saying anything.

I waited, letting him sweat. Then I dropped in on him very quietly. "Your pants ought to cover it." Some guy laughed.

"My *pants*!" he almost screamed.

"On the table," I said, pointing, "or I take the pot."

"Fuck ya!"

I reached for the pot again.

"Wait a minute! Wait a minute!" His voice was desperate. He stood up, emptied his pockets, and yanked off his pants. He wasn't wearing any shorts and his nudity was grossly obscene. He threw the pants at me, but I deflected them into the center of the table. "All right, you son of a bitch!" he said, not sitting down. "Let's see your pissy little straight beat a full-fuckin' house!" He rolled over his third seven.

"I haven't got a straight, friend."

"Then I win, huh?"

I shook my head. "You lose." I pulled the joker away from the queens and the nine and slowly started turning up my buried aces. "One. Two. Three. And four. Is that enough, friend?" I asked him.

"Je-sus Christ!" some guy said reverently.

The fat man stood looking at the aces for a long time. Then he stumbled away from the table and almost ran out of the cargo hold, his fat behind jiggling with every step.

"I *still* say it's a mighty hard way to play poker," Sergeant Riker said softly as I hauled in the merchandise.

"I figured he had it coming," I said shortly.

"Maybe so, son, maybe so, but that still don't make it right, does it?"

And that finished my winning streak. Riker proceeded to give me a series of very expensive poker lessons. By the time I quit that night, I was back down to four hundred dollars. I sent the fat guy's watch, boots, and pants back to him with one of his buddies, and went up on deck to get some air. The engine pounded in the steel deck plates, and the wake was streaming out behind us, white against the black water.

"Smoke, son?" It was Riker. He leaned against the rail beside me and held out his pack.

"Thanks," I said. "I ran out about an hour ago."

"Nice night, ain't it?" His voice was soft and pleasant. I couldn't really pin down his drawl. It was sort of Southern.

I looked up at the stars. "Yeah," I said. "I've been down at that poker table for so long I'd almost forgotten what the stars looked like."

The ship took a larger wave at a diagonal and rolled with an odd, lurching kind of motion.

"You still ahead of the game, son?" he asked me, his voice serious.

"A little bit," I said cautiously.

"If it was me," he said, "I wouldn't go back no more. You've won yourself a little money, and you got your buddy's watch back for him. If it was me, I'd just call 'er quits."

"I was doing pretty well there for a while," I objected. "I think I was about fifteen hundred dollars to the good before I started losing. I'll win that back in just a few hours, the way the pots have been running."

"You broke your string, son," Riker said softly, looking out over the water. "You been losin' 'cause you was ashamed of yourself for what you done to that heavyset boy."

"I still think he had it coming to him," I insisted.

"I ain't arguin' that," Riker said. "Like as not he did. What I'm sayin', son, is that you're ashamed of yourself for bein' the one that come down on him like you done. I been watchin' you, and you ain't set easy since that hand. Funny thing about luck—it won't never come to a man who don't think he's got it comin'. Do yourself a favor and stay out of the game. You're only gonna lose from here on out."

I was going to argue with him, but I had the sudden cold certainty that he was right. I looked out at the dark ocean. "I guess maybe the bit about the pants *was* going a little too far," I admitted.

"Yeah," he said, "your buddy's watch woulda been plenty."

"Maybe I will stay out of the game," I said. "I'm about all pokered out anyway."

"Yeah," he said, "we'll be gettin' home pretty quick anyway."

"Couple, three days, I guess."

"Well," he said, "I'm gonna turn in. Been nice talkin' to you, son." He turned and walked off down the deck.

"Good night, Sergeant Riker," I called after him.

He waved his hand without looking back.

So I quit playing poker. I guess I've always been a sucker for fatherly advice. Somehow I knew that Riker was right though. Whatever the reason, I'd lost the feeling I'd had that the cards were going to fall my way no matter what anybody tried to do to stop them. If I'd have gone back the next day, they'd have cleaned me out. So the next day I watched the ocean, or read, and I didn't think about poker.

Two days later we slid into New York Harbor. It was early morning and foggy. We passed the Statue and then stacked up out in the bay, waiting for a tug to drag us the rest of the way in. We all stood out on deck watching the sun stumble up out of the thick banks of smoke to blearily light up the buildings on Manhattan Island.

It's a funny feeling, coming home when you don't really have anything to come home to. I leaned back against a bulkhead, watching all the other guys leaning over the rail. I think I hated every last one of them right then.

Two grubby tugboats finally came and nudged us across the bay to a pier over in Brooklyn. Early as it was, there must have been a thousand people waiting. There was a lot of waving and shouting back and forth, and then they all settled down to wait. The Army's good at that kind of thing.

Benson dragged his duffle bag up to where I was and plunked it down on the deck. I still hadn't told him I had his watch. I didn't want him selling it again so he could get back in the game.

"Hey, Alders," he puffed. "I been lookin' for you all over this fuckin' tub."

"I've been right here, kid."

"Feels good, gettin' home, huh?" he said.

"It's still a long way to Seattle," I told him. His enthusiasm irritated the hell out of me.

"You know what I mean."

"Sure."

"You think maybe they might fly us out to the West Coast?"

"I doubt it," I said. "I expect a nice long train ride."

"Shit!" He sounded disgusted. "You're probably right though. The way my luck's been goin' lately, they'll probably make *me* walk."

"You're just feeling picked on."

Eventually, they started unloading us. Those of us bound for West-Coast and Midwest separation centers were loaded on buses and then we sat there.

I watched the mass family reunion taking place in the dim gloom under the high roof of the pier. There was a lot of crying and hugging and so forth, but we weren't involved in any of that. I wished to hell we could get going.

After about a half hour the buses started and we pulled away from the festivities. I slouched low in the seat and watched the city slide by. Several of the guys were pretty boisterous, and the bus driver had to tell them to quiet down several times.

"Look," Benson said, nudging me in the ribs. *"Eine amerikanische Fräulein."*

"Quit showing off," I said, not bothering to look.

"What the hell's buggin' you?" he demanded.

"I'm tired, Benson."

"You been tired all your life. Wake up, man. You're home."

"Big goddamn deal."

He looked hurt, but he quit pestering me.

After they'd wandered around for a while, the guys who were driving the buses finally found a train station. There was a sergeant there, and he called roll, got us on the train, and then hung around to make sure none of us bugged out. That's Army logic for you. You couldn't have gotten most of those guys off that train with a machine gun.

After they got permission from the White House or someplace, the train started to move. I gave the sergeant standing on the platform the finger by way of farewell. I was in a foul humor.

First there was more city, and then we were out in the country.

"We in Pennsylvania yet?" Benson asked.

"I think so.

"How many states we gonna go through before we get back to Washington?"

"Ten or twelve. I'm not sure."

"Shit! That'll take *weeks*."

"It'll just seem like it," I told him.

"I'm dyin' for a drink."

"You're too young to drink."

"Oh, bullshit. Trouble is, I'm broke."

"Don't worry about it, Kid. I'll buy you a drink when they open the club car."

"Thanks," he said. "That game cleaned me out."

"I know."

We watched Pennsylvania slide by outside.

"Different, huh?" Benson said.

"Yeah," I agreed. "More than just a little bit."

"But it's home, man. It's all part of the same country."

"Sure, Kid," I said flatly.

"You don't give a shit about anything, do you, Alders?" Sometimes Benson could be pretty sharp. "Being in Germany, winning all that money in the game, coming home—none of it really means anything to you, does it?"

"Don't worry about it, Kid." I looked back out the window.

He was right though. At first I'd thought I was just cool—that I'd finally achieved a level of indifference to the material world that's supposed to be the prelude to peace of mind or whatever the hell you call it. The last day or so, though, I'd begun to suspect that it was more just plain, old-fashioned alienation than anything else—and *that's* a prelude to a vacation at the funny-farm. So I looked out at the farmland and the grubby backsides of little towns and really tried to feel something. It didn't work.

A couple guys came by with a deck of cards, trying to get up a game. They had me figured for a big winner from the boat, and they wanted a shot at my ass. I was used up on poker though. I'd thought about what Riker had told me, and I decided that I wasn't really a gambler. I was a bad winner. At least I could have let that poor bastard keep his pants, for Christ's sake. The two guys with the cards got a little snotty about the whole thing, but I ignored them and they finally went away.

"You oughta get in," Benson said, his eyes lighting up.

"I've *had* poker," I told him.

"I don't suppose you'd want to loan me a few dollars?" he asked wistfully.

"Not to gamble with," I told him.

"I didn't think so."

"Come on, Kid. I'll buy you a drink."

"Sure," he said.

The two of us walked on down the swaying aisles to the club car. I got myself about half in the basket, and I felt better.

In Chicago there was another mob of relatives waiting, and there was a general repetition of the scene on the dock back in New York. Once we changed trains though, we highballed right on through.

I spent a lot of time in the club car with my heels hooked over the rung of a bar stool, telling lies and war stories to a slightly cross-eyed Wave with an unlimited capacity for Budweiser and a pair of tightly crossed legs. At odd moments, when I got sick of listening to her high-pitched giggle and raucous voice, I'd ease back up the train to my seat and sit staring at North Dakota and Montana sliding by outside. The prairie country was burned yellow-brown and looked like the ass-end of no place. After a while we climbed up into the mountains and the timber. I felt better then.

I had a few wild daydreams about maybe looking up the guy Sue had told me about in her last letter and kicking out a few of his teeth, but I finally decided it wouldn't be worth the effort. He was probably some poor creep her mother had picked out for her. Then I thought about blousing her mother's eye, and that was a lot more satisfying. It's hard to hate somebody you've never met, but I could work up a pretty good head of steam about Susan's mother.

I generally wound up back at the club car. I'd peel my cock-eyed Wave of whomever she'd promoted to beer-buyer first class and go back to pouring Budweiser into her and trying to convince her that we were both adults with adult needs.

Anyhow, they dropped us off in Tacoma about five thirty in the morning on the fourth day after we'd landed in New York. My uniform was rumpled, my head was throbbing, and my stomach felt like it had a blowtorch inside. The familiar OD trucks from Fort Lewis were waiting, and it only took about an hour to deliver us back to the drab, two-story yellow barracks and bare drill fields I'd seen on a half dozen posts from Fort Ord to Camp Kilmer.

They fed us, issued us bedding, assigned us space in the transient barracks, and then fell us out into a formation in the company street. While they were telling us about all the silly-ass games we were going to play, my eyes drifted on out across the parade ground to the inevitable, blue-white mound of Mount Ranier, looming up out of the hazy foothills. I was dirty, rumpled, hung over, and generally sick of the whole damned world. The mountain was still the same corny, picture-postcard thing it had always been—a ready-made tourist attraction, needing only a beer sign on the summit to make it complete. I'd made bad jokes about its ostentatious vulgarity all the way through college, but that morning after having been away for so damned long, I swear I got a lump in my throat just looking at it. It was the first time I'd really felt anything for a long time.

Maybe I was human after all.

2

They weren't ready to start processing us yet, so they filled in the rest of the day with the usual Mickey-Mouse crap that the Army always comes up with to occupy a man's spare time. At four-thirty, after frequent warnings that we were still in the Army and subject to court-martial, they gave us passes and told us to keep our noses clean. They really didn't sound too hopeful about it.

I walked on past the mob-scene in the parking lot—parents, wives, girlfriends, and the like, crying and hugging and shaking hands and backslapping—and headed toward the bus stop. I'd had enough of all that stuff.

"Hey, Alders," someone yelled. "You want a lift into town?" It was Benson naturally. He'd been embarrassingly grateful when I'd given him back the watch, and I guess he wanted to do something for me. His folks were with him, a tall, sunburned man and a little woman in a flowered dress who was hanging onto Benson's arm like grim death. I could see that they weren't really wild about having a stranger along on their reunion.

"No thanks," I said, waving him off. "See you tomorrow." I hurried on so he wouldn't have time to insist. Benson was a nice enough kid, but he could be an awful pain in the ass sometimes.

The bus crawled slowly toward Tacoma, through a sea of traffic. By the time I got downtown, I'd worked up a real thirst. I hit one of the Pacific Avenue bars and poured down three beers, one after another. After German beer, the stuff still tasted just a wee bit like stud horsepiss with the foam blown off even with the acclimating I'd done on the train. I sat in the bar for about an hour until the place started to fill up. They kept turning the jukebox up until it got to the pain level. That's when I left.

The sun was just going down when I came back out on the street. The sides of all the buildings were washed with a coppery kind of light, and everybody's face was bright red in the reflected glow.

I loitered on down the sidewalk for a while, trying to think of something to do and watching the assorted GI's, Airmen, and swab jockeys drifting up and down the Avenue in twos and threes. They seemed to be trying very hard to convince each other that they were having a good time. I walked slowly up one side of the street, stopping to look in the pawnshop windows with their clutter of overpriced junk and ignoring repeated invitations of sweaty little men to "come on in and look around, Soljer."

I stuck my nose into a couple of the penny arcades. I watched a pinball addict carry on his misdirected love affair with a seductively blinking nickle-grabber. I even poked a few dimes into a peep-show machine and watched without much interest while a rather unpretty girl on scratchy film took off her clothes.

Up the street a couple girls from one of the local colleges were handing out "literature." They both had straight hair and baggy-looking clothes, and it appeared that they were doing their level best to look as ugly as possible, even though they were both not really that bad. I knew the type. Most of the GI's were ignoring them, and the two kids looked a little desperate.

"Here, soldier," the short one said, mistaking my look of sympathy for interest. She thrust a leaflet into my hand. I glanced at it. It informed me that I was engaged in an immoral war and that decent people looked upon me as a swaggering bully with bloody hands. Further, it told me that if I wanted to desert, there were people who were willing to help me get out of the country.

"Interesting," I said, handing it back to her.

"What's the matter?" she sneered. "Afraid an MP might catch you with it?"

"Not particularly," I said.

"Forget him Clydine," the other one said. That stopped me.

"Is that *really* your name?" I asked the little one.

"So what?"

"I've just never met anybody named Clydine before."

"Is anything wrong with it?" she demanded. She was very short, and she glared up at me belligerently. "I'm not here for a pickup, fella."

"Neither am I, girlie," I told her. I dislike being called "fella." I always have.

"Then you *approve* of what the government's doing in Vietnam?" She got right to the point, old Clydine. No sidetracks for her.

"They didn't ask me."

"Why don't you desert then?"

Her chum pitched in, too. "Don't you *want* to get out of the country?"

"I've just *been* out of the country," I objected.

"We're just wasting our time on this one, Joan," Clydine said. "He isn't even politically aware."

"It's been real," I told them. "I'll always remember you both fondly."

They turned their backs on me and went on handing out pamphlets.

Farther up the street another young lady stopped me, but she wasn't offering politics. She was surprisingly direct about what she *was* offering.

Next a dirty-looking little guy wanted to give me a "real artistic" tattoo. I turned him down, too.

Farther along, a GI with wasted-looking eyeballs tried to sell me a lid of grass.

I went into another bar—a fairly quiet one—and mulled it around over a beer. I decided that I must have had the look of somebody who wanted something. I couldn't really make up my mind why.

I went back on down the street. It was a sad, grubby street with sad, grubby people on it, all hysterically afraid that some GI with money on him might get past them.

That thought stopped me. The four hundred I'd won was in my blouse pocket, and I sure didn't want to get rolled. It was close enough after payday to make a lone GI a pretty good target, so I decided that I'd better get off Pacific Avenue.

But what the hell does a guy do with himself on his first night back in the States? I ticked off the possibilities. I could get drunk, get laid, get rolled, or go to a movie. None of those sounded very interesting. I could walk around, but my feet hurt. I could pick a fight with somebody and get thrown in jail—that one didn't sound like much fun at all. Maybe I could get a hamburger-to-go and jump off a bridge.

Most of the guys I'd come back with were hip-deep in family by now, but I hadn't even bothered to let my Old Lady know I was coming back. The less I saw of her, the better we'd both feel. That left Jack. I finally got around to him. Probably it was inevitable. I suppose it had been in the back of my mind all along.

I knew that Jack was probably still in Tacoma someplace. He always came back here. It was his home base. He and I hadn't been particularly close since we'd been kids, and I'd only seen him about three times since the Old Man died. But this was family night, and he was it. Ordinarily, I wouldn't have driven a mile out of my way to see him.

"Piss on it," I said and went into a drugstore to use the phone.

"Hello?" His voice sounded the same as I remembered.

"Jack? This is Dan."

"Dan? Dan who?"

Now there's a great start for you. Gives you a real warm glow right in the gut. I almost hung up.

"Your brother. Remember?" I said dryly.

"Dan? Really? I thought you were in the Army—in England or someplace."

"Germany," I said. "I just got back today."

"You stationed out here at the Fort now?"

"Yeah, I'm at the separation center."

"You finishing up already? Oh, that's right, you were only in for two years, weren't you?"

"Yeah, only two," I said.

"It's my brother," he said to someone, "the one that's been in the Army. How the hell should I know?—Dan, where are you? Out at the Fort?"

"No, I'm downtown."

"Pitchin' yourself a liberty, huh?"

"Not really," I said. "I've only got three more days till I get out, and I think I'll keep my nose clean."

"Good idea—hey, you got anything on for tonight? I mean any chickie or anything?"

"No," I said, "just kicking around. I thought I'd just give you a call and let you know I was still alive, is all."

"Why don't you grab a bus and bag on out? I'd come and pick you up, but Margaret's workin' tonight, and she's got the car."

"Your wife?"

"Yeah—and I've got to watch the kids. I've got some beer in the fridge. We can pop open a few and talk old times."

"All right," I said. "How do I find the place?"

"I'm out on South Tacoma Way. You know which bus to take?"

"I think I can remember."

"Get off at Seventy-eighth Street and come down the right hand side. It's the Green Lodge Trailer Court. I'm in number seventeen—a blue and white Kenwood."

"OK," I told him. "I'll be out in a half hour or so."

"I'll be lookin' for you."

I slowly hung up. This was going to be a mistake. Jack and I hadn't had anything in common for years now. I pictured an evening with the both of us desperately trying to think of something to say.

"Might as well get it over with," I muttered. I stopped by a liquor store and picked up a pint of bourbon. Maybe with enough anesthetic, neither one of us would suffer *too* much.

I sat on the bus reading the ads pasted above the windows and watching people get off and on. They were mostly old ladies. There's something about old ladies on buses—have you ever noticed? I've never been able to put my finger on it, but whatever it is, it makes me want to vomit. How's that for an inscription on a tombstone? "Here Lies Daniel Alders—Old Ladies on Buses Made Him Want to Puke."

Then I sat watching the streets and houses go by. I still couldn't really accept any of it as actuality. It all had an almost dreamlike quality—like coming in in the middle of a movie. Everybody else is all wrapped up in the story, but *you* can't even tell the good guys from the bad guys. Maybe that's the best way to put it.

The bus dropped me off at Seventy-eighth, and I saw the sickly green neon GREEN LODGE TRAILER COURT sign flickering down the block. I popped the seal on the pint and took a good belt. Then I walked on down to the entrance.

It was one of those "just-twenty-minutes-from-Fort Lewis" kind of places, with graveled streets sprinkled with chuckholes. Each trailer had its tired little patch of lawn surrounded by a chicken-wire fence to keep the kids out of the streets. Assorted broken-down old cars moldered on flat tires here and there. What few trees there were looked pretty discouraged.

It took me a while to find number seventeen. I stood outside for a few minutes, watching. I could see my brother putzing around inside— thin, dark, moving jerkily. Jack had always been like that—nervous, fast with his hands. He'd always had a quick grin that he'd turn on when he wanted something. His success with women was phenomenal. He moved from job to job, always landing on his feet, always trying to work a deal, never quite making it. If he hadn't been my brother, I'd have called him a small-time hustler.

I stood outside long enough to get used to his face again. I wanted to get past that strangeness stage when you say all kinds of silly-ass things because most of your attention is concentrated on the other person's physical appearance. I think that's why reunions of any sort go sour—people are so busy looking at each other that they can't think of anything to say.

Finally I went up and knocked.

"Dan," he called, "is that you? Come on in."

I opened the screen door and stepped inside.

"Hey there, little brother, you're lookin' pretty good," he said, grinning broadly at me. He was wearing a T-shirt, and I could see the tattoos on his arms. They had always bothered me, and I always tried not to look at them.

"Hello, Jack," I said, shaking his hand. I tried to come on real cool.

"God damn," he said, still grinning and hanging onto my hand. "I haven't seen you in three or four years now. Last time was when I came back from California that time, wasn't it? I think you were still in college, weren't you?"

"Yeah, I think so," I said.

"You've put on some beef since then, huh?" He playfully punched me in the shoulder. "What are you now? About a hundred and ninety?"

"One-eighty," I said. "A lot of it's German beer." I slapped my belly.

"You're lookin' better. You were pretty scrawny last time I seen you. Sit down, sit down, for Chrissake. Here gimme your jacket. It's too fuckin' hot for that thing anyway. Don't you guys get summer uniforms?"

"Mine are all rolled up in the bottom of my duffle bag," I told him, pulling off the jacket. I saw him briefly glance at the pint I had tucked in my belt. I wasn't trying to hide it.

He hung my blouse over a kitchen chair. "How about a beer?"

"Sure." I put the brown-sacked pint on the coffee table and sat down on the slightly battered couch. He was fumbling around in the refrigerator. I think he was a little nervous. I got a kick out of that for some reason.

I looked around. The trailer was like any other—factory-made, filled with the usual cheap furniture that was guaranteed to look real plush for about six weeks. It had the peculiar smell trailers always have and that odd sense of transience. Somehow it suited Jack. I think he'd been gravitating toward a trailer all his life. At least he fit in someplace. I wondered what I was gravitating toward.

"Here we go," he said, coming back in with a couple of caps of beer. "I just put the kids to bed, so we've got the place to ourselves." He gave me one of the cans and sat in the armchair.

"How many kids have you got?" I asked him.

"Two—Marlene and Patsy. Marlene's two and a half, and Patsy's one."

"Good deal," I said. What the hell else can you say? I pushed the pint over to him. "Here, have a belt of bourbon."

"Drinkin' whiskey," he said approvingly.

We both had a belt and sat looking at each other.

"Well," I said inanely, "what are you up to?" I fished out a cigarette to give myself something to do.

"Oh, not a helluva lot really, Dan. I've been workin' down the block at the trailer sales place and helping Sloane at his pawnshop now and then. You remember him, don't you? It's a real good deal for me because I can take what he owes me out in merchandise, and it don't show up on my income tax. Margaret's workin' in a dime store, and the trailer's paid for, so we're in pretty good shape."

"How's the Old Lady? You heard from her lately?" It had to get around to her sooner or later. I figured I'd get it out of the way.

"Mom? She's in Portland. I hear from her once in a while. She's back on the sauce again, you know."

"Oh, boy," I said with disgust. That was really the last damned straw. My mother had written me this long, tearjerker letter while I was in Germany about how she had seen the light and was going to give up drinking. I hadn't answered the damned thing because I really didn't give a shit one way or the other, but I'd kind of hoped she could make it. I hadn't seen her completely sober since I was about twelve, and I thought it might be kind of a switch.

"You and her had a beef, didn't you?" Jack asked, lighting a cigarette.

"Not really a beef," I said. "It just all kind of built up. You weren't around after Dad died."

"Naw. I saw things goin' sour long before that. Man, I was in Navy boot camp three days after my seventeenth birthday. I barely made it back for the funeral." He jittered the cigarette around in his hands.

"Yeah, I remember. After you left, she just got worse and worse. The Old Man hung on, but it finally just wore him down. His insurance kind of set us up for a while, but it only took her a year or so to piss that away. She was sure Mrs. High Society for a while though. And then, of course, all the boyfriends started to show up—like about a week after the funeral. Slimy bastards, every one of them. I tried to tell her they were just after the insurance money, but you never could talk to her. She knew it all."

"She hasn't got too much upstairs," Jack agreed, "even when she's sober."

"Anyway, about every month, one of her barroom Romeos would break it off in her for a couple of hundred and split out on her. She'd cry and blubber and threaten to turn on the gas or some damned thing. Then after a day or so she'd get all gussied up in one of those whorehouse dresses she's partial to and go out and find true love again."

"Sounds like a real bad scene."

"A bummer. A two-year bummer. I cut out right after high school— knocked around for a year or so and then wound up in college. It's a good place to hide out."

"You seen her since you split?"

"Couple times," I said. "Once I had to bail her out of jail, and once she came to where I was staying to mooch some money for booze. Gave me that 'After all, I *am* your mother' routine. I told her to stick it in her ear. I think that kind of withered things."

"She hardly ever mentions you when I see her," Jack said.

"Maybe if I'm lucky she'll forget me altogether," I said. "I need her about like I need leprosy."

"You know something, little brother?" Jack said, grinning at me, "you can be an awful cold-blooded bastard when you want to be."

"Comes from my gentle upbringing," I told him. "Have another belt." I waved at the whiskey bottle.

"I don't want to drink up *all* your booze," Jack said, taking the pint. "Remember, I *know* how much a GI makes."

"Go ahead, man," I said. "Take a goddamn drink. I hit it big in a stud-poker game on the troopship. I'm in fat city." I knew that would impress him.

"Won yourself a bundle, huh?"

"Shit. I was fifteen hundred ahead for a while, but there was this old master sergeant in the game—Riker his name was—and he gave me poker lessons till who laid the last chunk."

"How much you come out with?"

"Couple hundred," I said cautiously. I didn't want to encourage the idea that I was rich.

"Walkin' around money anyway," he said, taking a drink from the pint. He passed it back to me, and I noticed that his hands weren't really clean. Jack had always wanted a job where his hands wouldn't get dirty, but I saw that he hadn't made it yet. I suddenly felt sorry for him. He was smart and worked hard and tried his damnedest to make it, but things always turned to shit on him. I could see him twenty years from now, still hustling, still scurrying around trying to hit just the right deal.

"You got a girl?" he asked.

"Had one," I said. "She sent me one of those letters about six months ago."

"Rough."

I shrugged. "It wouldn't have worked out anyway." I got a little twinge when I said it. I thought I'd pretty well drowned that particular cat, but it still managed to get a claw in my guts now and then. I'd catch myself remembering things or wondering what she was doing. I took a quick blast of bourbon.

"Lotsa women," Jack said, emptying his beer. "Just like streetcars."

"Sure," I said. I looked around. The furniture was a bit kid-scarred, and the TV set was small and fluttered a lot, but it was someplace. I hadn't had any place for so long that I'd forgotten how it felt. From where I was sitting, I could see a mirror hanging at a slant on the wall of the little passage leading back to the bedrooms. The angle was just right, and I could see the rumpled, unmade bed where I assumed he and his wife slept. I thought of telling him that he might be making a public spectacle of his love life, but I decided that was his business.

"What'd you take in college anyway?" Jack demanded. "I never could get the straight of it out of the Old Lady."

"English, mostly," I said. "Literature."

"English, for Chrissake! Nouns and verbs and all that shit?"

"Literature, Stud," I corrected him. "Shakespeare and Hemingway, and all *that* shit." I figured this would be the issue that would blow the whole reunion bit. As soon as he gave me the "What the hell good is that shit?" routine, he and I would part company, fast. I'd about had a gutful of that reaction in the Army.

He surprised me. "Oh," he said, "that's different. You always did read a lot—even when you were a kid."

"It gives me a substitute for my own slightly screwed-up life."

"You gonna teach?"

"Not right away. I'm going back to school first."

"I thought the Old Lady told me you graduated."

"Yeah," I said, "but I'm going on to graduate school."

"No shit?" He looked impressed. "I hear that's pretty rough."

"I think I can hack it."

"You always were the smart one in the connection."

"How's your beer holding out?" I asked him, shaking my empty can. I was starting to relax. We'd gotten past all the touchy issues. I lit another cigarette.

"No sweat," he said, getting up to get two more. "If I run out, the gal next door has a case stashed away. We'll have to replace it before her old man gets home, but Marg ought to be here before long, and then I'll have wheels."

"Hey," I called after him. "I meant to ask you about that. I thought your wife's name was Bonnie."

"Bonnie? Hell, I dumped her three years ago."

"Didn't you have a little girl there, too?"

"Yeah. Joanne." He came back with the beer. I noticed that the trailer swayed a little when anyone walked round. "But Bonnie married some goof over at the Navy Yard, and he adopted Joanne. They moved down to L.A.''

"And before that it was—"

"Bernice. She was just a kid, and she got homesick for Mommie."

"You use up wives at a helluva rate, old buddy."

"Just want to spread all that happiness around as much as I can." He laughed.

I decided that I liked my brother. That's a helluva thing to discover all of a sudden.

3

A car pulled up outside, and Jack turned his head to listen. "I think that's the Mamma Cat," he said. "Sounds like my old bucket." He got up and looked out the window. "Yeah, it's her." He scooped up the empty beer cans from the coffee table and dumped them in the garbage sack under the sink. Then he hustled outside.

They came in a minute or so later, Jack rather ostentatiously carrying two bags of groceries. I got the impression that if I hadn't been there, he wouldn't have bothered. My current sister-in-law was a girl of average height with pale brown hair and a slightly sullen look on her face. I imagine all Jack's women got that look sooner or later. At any rate Margaret didn't seem just exactly wild about having a strange GI brother-in-law turn up.

"Well, sweetie," Jack said with an overdone joviality, "what do you think of him?"

I stood up. "Hello, Margaret," I said, smiling at her as winningly as I could.

"I'm very happy to meet you, Dan," she said, a brief, automatic smile flickering over her face. She was sizing me up carefully. I don't imagine the pint and the half-full beer can on the coffee table made very many points. "Are you stationed out here at the Fort now?" I could tell that she had visions of my moving in on them as a semipermanent houseguest.

"Well," I said, "not really what you'd call stationed here. I'm being discharged here is all. As soon as they cut me loose, I'll be moving back up to Seattle." I wanted to reassure her without being too obvious.

She got the message. "Well, let me get this stuff put away and then we can talk." She pulled off the light coat she was wearing and draped it over one of the kitchen chairs.

I blinked. She had the largest pair of breasts I've ever seen. I knew Jack liked his women that way, but Margaret was simply unbelievable.

"Isn't she something?" Jack said, leering at me as he wrapped a proprietary arm about her shoulders. The remark sounded innocent enough, but all three of us knew what he meant.

"Come on, Jack," she said, pushing him off. "I want to get all this put away so I can sit down." She began bustling around the kitchen, opening cupboards and drawers. The kitchen area was separated from the living room by a waist-high divider, so we could talk without yelling.

"Dan just got back today," Jack said, coming back and plunking himself on the couch. "He's been in Germany for a couple of years."

"Oh?" she said. "I'll bet that was interesting, wasn't it, Dan?"

"It's got Southeast Asia beat all to heck," I said.

"Did they let you travel around any—I mean visit any of the other countries over there?"

"Oh, yeah. I visited a few places."

"Did you get to London at all? I'd sure like to go there." Her voice sounded a little wistful.

"I was there for about ten days on leave," I told her.

"I never made it up there," Jack said. "When I was with the Sixth Fleet, we stayed pretty much in the Mediterranean."

"Did you get to see any of the groups while you were in London?" Margaret persisted. She really wanted to know; she wasn't just asking to have something to say.

"No," I said. I didn't want to tell her that groups weren't particularly my thing. She might think I was trying to put her down.

"My wife's a group-nut," Jack said tolerantly. "That one cabinet there is stacked full of albums. Must be twenty of the damn things in there."

"I dig them," she said without apologizing. "Oh, Jack, did you get the kids to bed OK?"

"All fed, bathed, and tucked in," he told her. "You know you can trust me to take care of things."

"Patsy's been getting a little stubborn about going to bed," she said. "She's at that age, I guess."

"I didn't have no problems," Jack said.

"Are you guys hungry?" she asked suddenly. Woman's eternal answer to any social situation—feed 'em. It's in the blood, I guess.

"I could eat," Jack said. "How about you, Dan?"

"Well—"

"Sure you can," he insisted. "Why don't you whip up a pizza, Mamma Cat? One of those big ones."

"It'll take a while," she said, opening herself a beer. She turned on the overhead light in the kitchen. She looked tired.

"That's OK," he said. "Well, Dan, what are you going to do with yourself now that you're out?" He said it as if he expected me to say something important, something that would impress hell out of Margaret.

"I'll be starting in at the U in October," I told him. "I got all the papers processed and got accepted and all by mail. I'd have rather gone someplace else, but they were going to bring me back here for separation anyway, so what the hell?"

"Boy, you sure run rampant on this college stuff, don't you?" He still tried to use words he didn't know.

"Keeps me off the streets at night." I shrugged.

"Dan," Margaret said. "Do you like sausage or cheese?" She was rummaging around among the pots and pans.

"Either one, Margaret," I said. "Whichever you folks like."

"Make the sausage, sweetie," Jack said. He turned to me. "We get this frozen sausage pizza down at the market. It's the best yet, and only eighty-nine cents."

"Sounds fine," I said.

"You ever get pizza in Germany?" Margaret asked.

"No, not in Germany," I said. "I had a few in Italy though. I went down there on leave once."

"Did you get to Naples?" Jack asked. "We hauled in there once when I was with the Sixth Fleet."

"Just for a day," I said. "I was running a little low on cash, and I didn't have time to really see much of it."

"We really pitched a liberty in Naples," he said. "I got absolutely *crazed* with alcohol." We drifted off into reminiscing about how we'd won various wars and assorted small skirmishes. We finished the pint and had a few more beers with the leathery pizza. Margaret relaxed a little more, and I began to feel comfortable with them.

"Look, Dan," Jack said, "you've got a month and a half or so before you start back to school, right? Why don't you bunk in here till you get squared away? We can move the two curtain-climbers into one room. This trailer has three bedrooms, and you'd be real comfortable."

"Hell, Jack," I said, "I couldn't do that. I'd be underfoot and all."

"No trouble at all," he said. "Right, Marg?"

"It wouldn't really be any trouble," she said a little uncertainly. She was considerably less than enthusiastic.

"No," I said. "It just wouldn't work out. I'd be keeping odd hours and—"

"I get it." Jack laughed knowingly. "You've got some tomato lined up, huh? You want privacy." I don't know if I'd ever heard anyone say "tomato" for real before. It sounded odd. "Well, that's no sweat. We can—"

"Jack, how about that little trailer down the street at number twenty-nine?" Margaret suggested. "Doesn't Clem want to rent that one out?"

He snapped his fingers. "Just the thing," he said. "It's a little forty-foot eight-wide—kind of a junker really—but it's a place to flop. He wants fifty a month for it, but seeing as you're my brother, I'll be able to beat him down some. It'll be just the thing for you." He seemed really excited about it.

"Well—" I said doubtfully. I wasn't really sure I wanted to be that close to my brother.

"It'll give you a base of operations and you'll be right here close. We'll be able to get together for some elbow-bendin' now and then."

"OK," I said, laughing. "Who do I talk to?" It was easier than arguing with him. I hadn't really made any plans anyway. It was almost as if we were kids again, Jack making the arrangements and me going along with him because I really didn't care one way or the other. It felt kind of good.

"You just leave everything to me," Jack said importantly. He'd always liked to take over—to manage things for people—and he'd always make a big deal out of everything. He hadn't really changed at all. "I'll check it over from stem to stern and make old Clem give you some decent furniture from the lot—He owns the place where I work as well as this court. We've got a whole warehouse full of furniture. We'll put in a good bed and a halfway decent couch—we might even be able to scrounge up a TV set from someplace."

"Look, Jack," I said, "it's only going to be a month or so. Don't go to any special trouble." I didn't want to owe him too much. Owing people is a bum trip.

"Trouble? Hell, it's no special trouble. After all, you're my brother, ain't you. No brother of *mine* is going to live in some broken-down junker. Besides, if you've got some tomato lined up, you'll want to make a favorable impression. That counts for a lot, doesn't it, Marg?"

"You really will want some new stuff in there," she agreed. "Nelsons lived in there before, and Eileen wasn't the neatest person in the world." Now that I wasn't going to move in with them Margaret seemed to think better of me. I could see her point though.

"Neat?" Jack snorted, lighting a cigarette. "She was a slob. Not only was she a boozer, she was the court punchboard besides. Old Nels used to slap her around every night just on general principles—he figured she probably laid three guys a day just to keep in practice, and usually he was guessin' on the low side."

"How would you know about that, *Mister* Alders?" Margaret demanded.

"Just hearsay, sweetie, just hearsay. You know me."

"That's just it," she said, "I *do* know you."

"Now, sweetie—"

There was a heavy pounding on the side of the trailer. I jumped. "OK, in there," a voice bellowed from outside, "this is a raid."

"Hey," Jack said, "that's Sloane." He raised his voice. "You'll never take us alive, Copper!" It sounded like a game that had been going on for a long time.

A huge, balding man of about forty came in, laughing in a high-pitched giggle. His face was red, and he wore a slightly rumpled suit. He looked heavy, but it wasn't really fat. He seemed to fill up the whole trailer. His grin sprawled all over his face and he seemed to be just a little drunk. He had a half-case of beer under one arm.

"Hi, Margaret, honey," he said, putting down the beer and folding her in a bear hug. "How's my girlfriend?"

"Sloane, you drunken son of a bitch," Jack said, grinning, "quit pawin' my wife and shake hands with my brother Dan. Dan, Cal Sloane."

"Dan?" Sloane asked, turning to me. "Aren't you Alders' college-man brother?"

"He went in the Army after he got out of college," Jack said. "He's out at the separation center now."

"You on leave?" Sloane asked, shaking my hand.

"I told you, Cal," Jack said, "he's at the *separation center*. He's gettin' out. Why don't you listen, you dumb shit?" The insults had the ring of an established ritual, so I didn't butt in.

"Hey, that's a reason for a party, isn't it?" Sloane said.

"Isn't everything reason enough for you?" Jack demanded, still grinning.

"Not *everything*. I didn't drink more than a case or two at my Old Lady's funeral."

"Dan here's been drinkin' German beer," Jack boasted. "He can put you under the table without even settlin' the dust in his throat."

"Didn't we meet a couple times a few years back?" Sloane asked me, pulling off his coat and settling down in a chair.

"I think so," I said.

"Sure we did. It was when Alders here was still married to Bonnie." He loosened his tie.

"Yeah," I said, "I believe it was."

We talked for about an hour, kidding back and forth. At first Sloane seemed a little simple—that giggle and all—but after a while I realized that he was really pretty sharp. I began to be very glad that I'd called Jack and come on out here to his place. It began to look like I had some family to come home to after all.

About eleven or so we ran out of beer, and Sloane suggested that we slip out for a couple glasses of draft. Margaret pouted a little, but Jack took her back into the hallway and talked with her for a few minutes, and when they came back she seemed convinced. Jack pulled on a sport shirt and a jacket, and Sloane and I got ourselves squared away. We went outside.

"I'll be seeing you, Margaret," I said to her as she stood in the door-way to watch us leave.

"Now you know the way," she said in a sort of offhand invitation.

"Be back in an hour or so, sweetie," Jack told her.

She went back inside without answering.

We took Jack's car, a slightly battered Plymouth with a lot of miles on it.

"I won't ride with Sloane when he's been drinking," Jack said, explaining why we'd left Sloane's Cadillac. "The son of a bitch has totalled five cars in the last two years."

"I have a helluva time gettin' insurance." Sloane giggled.

We swung on out of the trailer court and started off down South Tacoma Way, past the car lots and parts houses.

"Go on out to the Hideout Tavern," Sloane said. He was sprawled in the back seat, his hat pushed down over his nose.

"Right," Jack said.

"I hear that a man can do some pretty serious drinking in Germany," Sloane said to me.

"Calvin, you got a beer bottle for a brain," Jack told him, turning a corner.

"Just interested, that's all. That's the way to find out things—ask somebody who knows."

"A man can stay pretty drunk if he wants to," I said. "Lots of strange booze over there."

"Like what?" Sloane asked. He seemed really interested.

"Well, there's this one—Steinhäger, it's called—tastes kind of like a cross between gin and kerosene."

"Oh, God"—Jack gagged—"it sounds awful."

"Yeah," I admitted, "it's moderately awful, all right. They put it up in stone bottles—probably because it would eat its way out of glass. Screws your head up something fierce."

We wheeled into the parking lot of a beer joint and went inside, still talking. We ordered pitchers of draft and sat in a booth drinking and talking about liquor and women and the service. The tavern was one of those usual kind of places with lighted beer signs all along the top of the mirror behind the bar. It had the usual jukebox and the usual pinball machine. It had the uneven dance floor that the bartender had to walk across to deliver pitchers of beer to the guys sitting in the booths along the far wall. There were the solitary drinkers hunched at the bar, staring into their own reflections in the mirror or down into the foam on their beer; and there was the usual group of dice players at the bar, rolling for drinks. I've been in a hundred joints like it up and down the coast.

I realized that I was enjoying myself. Sloane seemed to be honestly having a good time; and Jack, in spite of the fact that he was trying his damnedest to impress me, seemed to really get a kick out of seeing me again. That unholy dead feeling I'd been fighting for the last months or so was gone.

"We got to get Dan some civilian clothes," Cal was saying. "He can't run around in a uniform. That's the kiss of death as far as women are concerned."

"I've got some civvies coming in," I said. "I shipped them here a month ago—parcel post. They're probably at the General Delivery window downtown right now."

"I've got to run downtown tomorrow," Jack said. "I'll stop by and pick them up for you."

"Don't I have to get them myself?" I asked. "I mean, don't they ask for ID or anything?"

"Hell, no," Jack scoffed. "You can get anybody's mail you want at the General Delivery window."

"Kinda shakes a guy's faith in the Hew Hess Government," I said. "I mean, if you can't trust the goddamn Post Office Department—say, maybe we ought to take our business to somebody else."

"Who you got in mind?" Sloane asked.

"I don't know, maybe we could advertise—'Deliver mail for fun and profit'—something like that."

"I'm almost sure they'd find some way to send you to Leavenworth for it," Jack said.

"Probably," I agreed. "They're awfully touchy about some things. I'd sure appreciate it if you could pick those things up for me though. If you can, dump them off at a cleaner's someplace. I imagine they're pretty wrinkled by now." I emptied my beer.

"Another round, Charlie," Sloane called to the barman. "Put your money away," he told me as I reached for my wallet. "This is my party."

About a half hour later, a kind of hard-faced brunette came in. She hurried across to the booth and sat down beside Cal. She glanced back at the door several times and seemed to be a little nervous. "Hi, Daddy," she said. She made it sound dirty.

"Hello there, baby," he said. "This is Alders' brother, Dan. Dan, this is Helen."

"Hi," she said, nodding briefly at me. "Hi, Jack."

I looked carefully at her. She had makeup plastered on about an inch thick. It was hard to see any expression under all that gunk. Maybe she didn't have any expression.

She turned back to Sloane with an urgent note in her voice. "Baby's got a problem, Daddy." It still sounded dirty. I decided that I didn't like her.

"Well, tell Daddy." Sloane giggled self-consciously.

She leaned over and whispered in his ear for a moment. His face turned a little grim.

"OK," he said shortly, "wait in the car—drive it around in back."

She got up and went out quickly.

"Dumb bitch!" Sloane muttered. "She's been gettin' careless and her Old Man's suspicious. I'd better get her a room someplace until he cools off."

"Is he pretty steamed?" Jack asked. "You've got to watch yourself with that husband of hers, Cal. I hear he's a real *mean* mother."

"He just wants to clout her around a little," Sloane said. "See if he can shake a few answers out of her. I'd better get her out of sight. I'll have her swing me by your trailer lot, and I'll pick up my car. Then we'll ditch hers on a back street. I know a place where she can hole up." He stood up and put a five-dollar bill on the table. "Hate to be a party-poop but—" He shrugged. "I'll probably see you guys tomorrow. Drink this up on me, OK?" He hurried across the dance floor and on out, his hat pulled down low like a gangster in a third-rate movie.

"That dumb bastard's gonna get himself all shot up one of these days," Jack said grimly.

"He cat around a lot?"

"All the time. He's got a deal with his wife. He brings in the money and doesn't pester her in bed, and she doesn't ask him where he goes nights."

"Home cookin' and outside lovin'?" I said. "Sounds great."

Jack shrugged. "It costs him a fortune. Of course, he's got it, I guess. He's got the pawnshop, and a used car lot, and he owns a piece of two or three taverns. He's got a big chunk of this joint, you know."

"No kidding?"

Jack nodded. "You wouldn't think so to look at him, but he can buy and sell most of the guys up and down the Avenue just out of his front pockets. You ought to see the house he lives in. Real plush."

"Nice to have rich friends," I said.

"And don't let that dumb face fool you," Jack told me. "Don't ever do business with Cal unless I'm there to keep an eye on him for you. He'll gyp you out of your fillings—friend or no friend."

"Sure wouldn't guess it to look at him."

"Lots of guys think that. Just be sure to count your fingers after you shake hands with him."

"What's the deal with this—baby—whatever her name is?"

"Helen? She's married to some Air Force guy out at McChord Field— Johnson, his name is. He's away a lot and she likes her nookie. Sloane's had her on the string for a couple of months now. I tried her and then passed her on. Her Old Man's a real mean bastard. He kicked the livin' shit out of one guy he caught messin' with her. Put the boots to him and broke both his arms. She's real wild in the sack, but she's got a foul mouth and she likes it dirty—you know. Also, she's a shade on the stupid side. I just didn't like the smell of it, so I dumped her in Sloane's lap."

"You're a real friend," I said.

"Sloane can handle it," Jack said. He looked warily around the bar and then at the door several times. "Hey, let's cut out. That Johnson guy might come in here, and I'd rather not be out in plain sight in case he's one or two guys behind in his information. I think I could handle him, but the stupid bastard might have a gun on him. I heard that he's that kind."

"I ought to be getting back out to the Fort, anyway."

"I'll buzz you on out," Jack said, pocketing Sloane's five.

We walked on out to the parking lot and climbed into Jack's Plymouth. We were mostly quiet on the way out to the Fort. I was a little high, and it was kind of pleasant just to sit back and watch the lights go past. But I was a little less sure about the arrangement than I had been earlier in the evening. There was an awful lot going on that I didn't know about. There was no way I could back out gracefully now though. Like it or not, I was going to get reacquainted with my brother. I almost began to wish I'd skipped the whole thing.

4

The following Saturday I got out of the Army. Naturally, they had to have a little ceremony. Institutions always feel they have to have a little ceremony. I've never been able to figure out why really. I'm sure nobody really gives a rat's ass about all that nonsense. In this case, we walked in a line through a room; and a little warrant officer, who must have screwed up horribly somewhere to get stuck with the detail, handed each of us a little brown envelope with a piece of paper in it. Then he shook hands with us. I took the envelope, briefly fondled his sweaty hand, walked out, and it was all over.

"You sure you got my address, Alders?" Benson asked as we fished around in the pile for our duffle bags.

"Yeah, kid, I got it," I told him.

"Les-ter," a woman's voice yodeled from the parking lot.

"That's my mom," Benson said. "I gotta go now."

"Take care, kid," I told him, shaking his hand.

"Be sure and write me, huh? I mean it. Let's keep in touch."

"Les-ter! Over here."

"I gotta run. So long, Dan." It was the only time in two years he'd ever used my first name.

"Bye, Les," I said.

He took off, weighted way off-balance by his duffle bag. I watched him go.

I stood looking at the parking lot until I located Jack's Plymouth. I slung the duffle bag by the strap from my left shoulder and headed toward my brother's car. It's funny, but I almost felt a little sad. I even saluted a passing captain, just to see if it felt any different. It did.

Jack was leaning against the side of his car. "Hey, man, you sure throw a sharp highball." He grinned as I came up. "Why didn't you just thumb your nose at the bastard?"

I shrugged. "He's still in and I'm out. Why should I bug him?"

"You all ready? I mean have you got any more bullshit to go through?"

"All finished," I said. "I just done been civilianized. I got my divorce papers right here." I waved the envelope at him.

"Let's cut out, then. I've got your civvies in the back seat."

I looked around once. The early afternoon sun blasted down on the parking lot, and the yellow barracks shimmered in the heat. It looked strange already. "Let's go," I said and climbed into the back seat.

There was a guy sitting in the front seat. I didn't know him.

"Oh," Jack said, "this is Lou McKlearey, a buddy of mine. Works for Sloane."

McKlearey was lean and sort of blond. I'd have guessed him at about thirty. His eyes were a very cold blue and had a funny look to them. He stuck out his hand, and when we shook hands, he seemed to be trying to squeeze the juice out of my fingers.

"Hi, Dogface," he said in a raspy voice. He gave me a funny feeling— almost like being in the vicinity of a fused bomb. Some guys are like that.

"Ignore him," Jack said. "Lou's an ex-Marine gunnery sergeant. He just ain't had time to get civilized yet."

"Let's get out of here, huh?" Suddenly I couldn't stand being on Army ground anymore.

Jack fired up the car and wheeled out of the lot. We barreled on down to the gate and eased out into the real world.

"Man," I said "it's like getting out of jail."

"Anyhow, Jackie," McKlearey said, apparently continuing what he'd been talking about before I got to the car, "we unloaded that crippled Caddy on a Nigger sergeant from McChord Field for a flat grand. You know them fuckin' Niggers; you can paint 'Cadillac' on a baby buggy, and they'll buy it."

"Couldn't he tell that the block was cracked?" Jack asked him.

"Shit! That dumb spade barely knew where the gas pedal was. So we upped the price on the Buick to four hundred over book, backed the speedometer to forty-seven thousand, put in new floor mats, and dumped it on a red-neck corporal from Georgia. He traded us a '57 Chevy stick that was all gutted out. We gave him two hundred trade-in. Found out later that the crooked son of a bitch had packed sawdust in the transmission—oldest stunt in the book. You just can't trust a reb. They're so goddamn stupid that they'll try stuff you think nobody's dumb enough to try anymore, so you don't even bother to check it out.

"Well, we flushed out the fuckin' sawdust and packed the box with heavy grease and then sold that pig for two and a quarter to some smart-ass high school kid who thought he knew all about cars. Shit! I could sell a three-wheel '57 Chevy to the smartest fuckin' kid in the world. They're all hung up on that dog—Niggers and Caddies; kids and '57 Chevies—it's all the same.

"So, by the end of the week, we'd moved around eight cars, made a flat fifteen hundred clear profit, and didn't have a damn thing left on the lot that hadn't been there on Monday morning."

"Christ"—Jack laughed—"no wonder Sloane throws money around like a drunken sailor."

"That lot of his is a fuckin' gold mine," McKlearey said. "It's like havin' a license to steal. Of course, the fact that he's so crooked he has to screw himself out of bed in the morning doesn't hurt either."

"Man, that's the goddamn truth," Jack agreed. "How you doin' back there, Dan?"

"I'm still with you," I said.

"Here," he said. He fumbled under the seat and came out with a brown-bagged bottle. He poked it back at me. "Celebrate your new-found freedom."

"Amen, old buddy," I said fervently. I unscrewed the top and took a long pull at the bottle, fumbling with my necktie at the same time.

"You want me to haul into a gas station so you can change?" he asked me.

"I can manage back here, I think," I told him. "Two hundred guys got out this morning. Every gas station for thirty miles has got a line outside the men's room by now."

"You're probably right," Jack agreed. "Just don't get us arrested for indecent exposure."

It took me a mile or two to change clothes. I desperately wanted to get out of that uniform. After I changed though, I rolled my GI clothes very carefully and tucked them away in my duffle bag. I didn't ever want to wear them again—or even look at them—but I didn't want them wrinkled up.

"Well," I said when I'd finished. "I may not be too neat, but I'm a civilian again. Have a drink." I passed the bottle on up to the front seat.

Jack took a belt and handed the jug to McKlearey. He took a drink and passed the bottle back to me. "Have another rip," he said.

"Let's stop and have a couple beers," I suggested. I suddenly wanted to go into a bar—a place where there were other people. I think I wanted to see if I would fit in. I wasn't a GI anymore. I wanted to really see if I was a civilian.

"Mama Cat's got some chow waitin'," Jack said, "but I guess we've got time for a couple."

"Any place'll do," I said.

"I know just how he feels, Jackie," Lou said. "After a hitch, a man needs to unwind a bit. When I got out the last time in Dago, I hit this joint right outside the gate and didn't leave for a week. Haul in at the Patio—it's just up the street."

"Yeah," Jack agreed, "seems to me I got all juiced up when I got out of the Navy, too. Hey, ain't that funny? Army, Navy, Marines—all of us in here at once." It was the kind of thing Jack would notice.

"Maybe we can find a fly-boy someplace and have a summit conference," I said.

Jack turned off into the dusty, graveled parking lot of a somewhat overly modern beer joint.

"I'm buying," I said.

"OK, little brother," Jack said. "Let's go suck up some suds." We piled out of the car and walked in the bright sunlight toward the tavern.

"This is a new one, isn't it?" I asked.

"Not really," Jack told me, "it's been here for about a year now."

We went inside. It was cool and dim, and the lighted beer signs behind the bar ran to the type that sprinkled the walls with endlessly varying patterns of different colored lights. Tasteful beer signs, for Chrissake! I laid a twenty on the polished bar and ordered three beers.

The beer was good and cold, and it felt fine just to sit and hold the chilled glass. Jack started telling the bartender that I'd just got out, and that I was his brother. Somehow, whenever Jack told anybody anything, it was always in relation to himself. If he'd been telling someone about a flood, it would be in terms of how wet *he'd* gotten. I guess I hadn't remembered that about him.

Lou sat with us for a while and then bought a roll of nickels and went over to the pinball machine. Like every jarhead I've ever known, he walked at a stiff brace, shoulders pulled way back and his gut sucked in. Marine basic must be a real bitch-kitty. He started feeding nickels into the machine, still standing at attention. I emptied my beer and ordered another round.

"Easy man," Jack said. "You've got a helluva lot of drinkin' to do before the day's over, and I'd hate to see you get all kicked out of shape about halfway through. We've got a party on for tonight, and you're the guest of honor."

"You shouldn't have done that, Jack," I said. What I'd really meant to say was that I wished to hell he hadn't.

"Look," he said, "my brother doesn't get out of the Army every day, and it's worth a blowout." I knew there was no point arguing with him.

"Is Marg really waiting?" I asked.

"Sure," he said. "She's got steak and all the trimmings on. I'm supposed to call her and let her know we're on the way."

"Well," I said, "we shouldn't keep her waiting. Hey, Jack, who's this McKlearey guy anyway?" I thumbed over my shoulder at Lou.

"He works at Sloane's used car lot. I knew him when I was in the Navy. We met in Yokosuka one time and pitched a liberty together. He's got ten years in the Corps—went in at seventeen, you know the type—washed out on a medical—malaria, I think. Probably picked it up in Nam."

"Bad scene," I said. "He seems a little—tight—keyed-up or something."

"Oh, Lou's OK, but kind of watch him. He's a ruthless son of a bitch. And for God's sake don't lend him any money—you'll never see it again. And don't cross him if you can help it—I mean *really* cross him. He's a real combat Marine—you know, natural-born killer and all that shit. He was a guard in a Navy brig one time, and some poor bastard made a break for the fence. McKlearey waited until the guy was up against the wire so he couldn't fall down and then blasted him seven times between the shoulder blades with a .45. I knew a guy who was in there, and he said that McKlearey unloaded so fast it sounded like a machine gun. Walked 'em right up the middle of the guy's back."

"Kill him?"

"Blew him all to pieces. They had to pick him up in a sack."

"Little extreme," I said.

"That's a Gyrene for you. Sometimes they get kill-happy."

I finished my beer. "Well," I said, "if you're done with that beer, I think I'm ready to face the world again. Besides, I'm coming down with a bad case of the hungries."

"Right," he said, draining his glass. "Hey, Lou, let's go."

"Sure thing," McKlearey said, concentrating on the machine. "Just a minute—goddamn it!" The machine lit TILT, and all the other lights went out. "I just barely touched the bastard," he complained.

"We got to go, anyway," Jack said. "You guys go on ahead, and I'll give Marg a quick buzz."

Lou and I went back on out in the sunlight to Jack's Plymouth and had another belt from the bottle.

"I'd just hit the rollover," Lou said, "and I had a real good chance at two in the blue." His eyes had the unfocused look of a man who's just been in the presence of the object of his obsession.

"That pay pretty good?" I asked.

"Hundred and sixty games," he said. "Eight bucks. Goddamn machines get real touchy when you've got half a chance to win something."

"I prefer slots," I said. "There was this one over in Germany I could hit three times out of four. It was all in how you pulled the handle."

He grunted. Slots weren't his thing. He wasn't interested.

"She's puttin' the steaks on right now," Jack said as he came across the parking lot. He climbed in behind the wheel. "They'll be almost ready by the time we get there." He spun us out of the nearly empty lot and pointed the nose of the car back down the highway.

We pulled in beside his trailer about ten minutes later and went on in. Margaret came over and gave me a quick kiss on the cheek. She seemed a little self-conscious about it. I got the feeling that the "cousinly" kiss or whatever wasn't just exactly natural to her. "Hi, Civilian," she said.

"That's the nicest thing anybody ever said to me," I told her, trying to keep my eyes off the front of her blouse.

We all had another drink—whiskey and water this time—while Marg finished fixing dinner. Then we sat down to the steaks. I was hungry and the food was good. Once in a while I'd catch myself looking at McKlearey. I still didn't have him figured out, and I wasn't really sure I liked him. To me, he looked like a whole pile of bad trouble, just looking for someplace to happen. Some guys are like that. Anyway, just being around him made me feel uncomfortable. Jack and Margaret seemed to like him though, so I thought maybe I was just having a touch of the "first day out of the Army squirrelies."

After dinner Marg got the kids up from their naps, and I played with them a little. They were both pretty young, and most of the playing consisted of tickling and giggles, but it was kind of fun. Maybe it was the booze, but I don't think so. The kids weren't really talking yet, and you don't have to put anything on with a kid that age. All they care about is if you like them and pay attention to them. That hour or so straightened me out more than anything that happened the rest of the day. We flopped around on the floor, grabbing at each other and laughing.

"Hey, Civilian," Jack said. "Let's dump your gear over at your trailer. I want you to see how we got it fixed up."

"Sure," I said. "Uncle Dan's gotta go now, kids," I told the girls. Marlene, the oldest—about two—gave me a big, wet kiss, and Patsy, the baby, pouted and began to cry. I held her until she quit and then handed her to Marg. I went to the door where Jack was waiting.

"You guys go ahead," Lou said. "I got my shoes off. Besides, I want to watch the ballgame."

I glanced at the flickering TV set. A smeary-looking baseball game was going on, but I'd swear he hadn't been watching it. I caught a quick glance between him and Margaret, but I didn't pay much attention.

"You guys going to be down there long?" Margaret asked.

"We ought to unpack him and all," Jack said. "Why?"

"Why don't you put the girls out in the play yard then—so I can get the place cleaned up?"

"Sure," Jack said. "Dust McKlearey, too—since he's a permanent part of that couch now."

Lou laughed and settled in a little deeper.

"We'll take the jug," Jack said.

"Sure," Lou answered. "I want to rest up for tonight anyway."

Jack and I put the little girls out in the little fenced-in yard and drove his Plymouth down the street to the trailer I'd rented. We hauled my duffle bag out of the back seat and went in.

It was hot and stuffy inside, and we opened all the windows. The trailer was small and dingy, with big waterstains on the wood paneling and cracked linoleum on the floor. Jack had been able to scrounge up a nearly new couch and a good bed, as well as a few other odds and ends of furniture, a small TV set, dishes, and bedding. It was kind of a trap, but like he said, it was a place to flop. What the hell?

"Pretty good, huh?" he said proudly. "A real bachelor pad." He showed me around with a proprietary attitude.

"It's great," I said as convincingly as I could. "I sure do appreciate all you've done in here, Jack."

"Oh, hell, it's nothing," he said, but I could see that he was pleased.

"No, I mean it—cleaning up the place and all."

"Margaret did that," he said. "All I did was put the arm on Clem for the furniture and stuff."

"Let's have a drink," I said. "Christen the place."

"Right." He poured some whiskey in the bottom of·two mismatched glasses and we drank. My ears were getting a little hot, and I knew I'd have to ease up a bit or I'd be smashed before the sun went down. It had been a real strange day. It had started at six that morning in a mothball-smelling barracks, and now I'd left all of that for good. Soon I'd be going back to the musty book-smell and the interminable discussions of art and reality and the meaning of truth. This was a kind of never-never land in between. Maybe it was a necessary transition, something real between two unrealities—always assuming, of course, that this was real.

We hauled my duffle bag and my civvies back to the tiny little bedroom and began hanging things up in the little two-by-four closet and stashing them in the battered dresser.

"You gonna buy a set of wheels?" he asked.

"I guess I'd better. Nothing fancy, just good and dependable."

"Let's see what we can finagle out of Sloane tonight."

"Look, Jack," I said, "I don't want to cash in on—"

"He can afford it," Jack interrupted. "You go to one of these two-by-four lots on the Avenue, and they'll screw you right into the wall. Me and Lou and Sloane will put you into something dependable for under two hundred. It may not look too pure, but it'll go. I'll see to it that they don't fuck over you."

I shrugged. Why fight a guy when he's trying to do you a favor? "OK," I said, "but for a straight deal—I want to pay for what I get."

"Don't worry," Jack said.

"Where's the big blowout tonight?" I asked him.

"Over at Sloane's place. Man, wait'll you see his house. It's a goddamn mansion."

"McKlearey going to be there?"

"Oh, sure. Lou'll show up anywhere there's free booze."

"He's an odd one."

"Lou's OK. You just gotta get used to him is all."

"Well," I said, depositing my folded duffle bag in the bottom of the closet, "I think that's about got it."

"Pretty good little pad, huh?" he said again.

"It'll work out just fine," I said. "Hey, you want to run me to a store for a minute? I'd better pick up some supplies. I guess I can't just run down to the friendly neighborhood mess hall anymore."

"Not hardly." He laughed. "But, hell, you could eat over at my place tomorrow."

"Oh, no. I'm not fit to live with until about noon. Marg and I get along fairly well, and I sure don't want to mildew the sheets right off the bat."

"What all you gonna need?"

"Just staples—coffee, beer, aspirin—you know."

"Get-well stuff." He laughed again.

We went out and climbed into his car.

"Hadn't you better let Marg know where we're going?" I asked him as he backed out into the street.

"Man, it's sure easy to see *you've* never been married. That's the first and worst mistake a guy usually makes. You start checkin' in with the wife, and pretty soon she starts expectin' you to check in every five minutes. Man, you just go when you want to. It doesn't take her long to get the point. Then she starts expecin' you when she sees you."

The grocery store was large and crowded. It took me quite a while to get everything. I wasn't familiar with the layout, and it was kind of nice just to mingle with the crowd. Actually, I wound up getting a lot more than I'd intended to. Jack kept coming across things he thought I really ought to have on hand.

"Now you'll be able to survive for a few days," he told me as we piled the sacks in the back seat of his car.

We drove back to my trailer, unloaded the groceries, and put the stuff that needed to be kept cold in the noisy little refrig beside the stove. Jack picked up the whiskey bottle, and we drove his car back up to his trailer. We got out and went up to the door. The screen was latched.

"Hey," Jack yelled, rattling the door, "open the gate."

Lou got up from the couch, looking a little drowsy and mussed. "Keep your pants on," he said, unlocking the door.

"Why in hell'd you lock it?" Jack asked him.

"I didn't lock it," Lou answered. "I dropped off to sleep."

"Where's Marg?"

"I think I just heard her in the can."

"Marg," Jack yelled, "what the hell'd you lock the front door for?"

"Was it locked?" Her voice was muffled.

"No, hell, it wasn't locked. I'm just askin' because I like the sound of my own voice."

"I don't know," her voice came back. "Maybe it's getting loose and slipped down by itself."

He snapped the latch up and down several times. It seemed quite stiff. "It couldn't have," he yelled back at her, "it's tighter'n hell."

"Well, I don't know. Maybe I latched it myself from force of habit." The toilet flushed, and she came out. "So why don't you beat me?"

"I just wanted to know why the door was latched, that's all."

"Lou and I were having a mad, passionate affair," she snapped, "and we didn't want to be interrupted. Satisfied?"

"Oh," Jack said, "that's different. How was it, Lou?"

"Just dandy," Lou said, laughing uneasily.

"Let's see now," Jack said, "am I supposed to shoot you, or her, or both of you?"

"Why not shoot yourself?" Margaret suggested. "That would be the best bet—you *have* got your insurance all paid up, haven't you?"

Jack laughed and Margaret seemed to relax.

"Where'd you guys take off to in the car?" she asked me.

"We made a grocery run," Jack said. "Had to lay in a few essentials for him—you know, beer, aspirin, Alka-Seltzer—staples."

"We saw you take off," she said. "We kinda wondered what you were up to."

"Hey, Alders," Lou said, "what time are we supposed to be at Sloane's?"

"Jesus," Jack said, "you're right. We better get cranked up. We've got to pick up Carter."

"Who's he?" I asked.

"Another guy. Works for the city. You'll like him."

"We'll have to stop by a liquor store, too, won't we?" I said.

"What for? Sloane's buying."

"Sloane always *buys*," McKlearey said, putting on his shoes. "He'd be insulted if anybody showed up at one of his parties with their own liquor."

"Sure, Dan," Jack said. "It's one of the ways he gets his kicks. When you got as much money as old Calvin's got, you've already bought everything you want for yourself so about the only kick you get out of it is spendin' it where other guys can watch you."

"Conspicuous consumption," I said.

"Sloane's conspicuous enough, all right," Jack agreed.

"And he can consume about twice as much as any three other guys in town." Lou laughed.

"We'll probably be late," Jack told Margaret.

"No kidding," she said dryly.

"Come on, you guys," Jack said, ignoring her. We went out of the trailer into the slanting late-afternoon sun.

"I'll take my own car," McKlearey said. "Why don't you guys pick up Carter? I've got to swing by the car lot for a minute."

"OK, Lou," Jack said. "See you at Sloane's place." He and I piled into his Plymouth and followed McKlearey on out to the street. I knew that my brother wasn't stupid. He *had* to know what was going on with Margaret. Maybe he just didn't care. I began not to like the feel of the whole situation. I began to wish I'd stayed the hell out of that damned poker game.

5

Mike Carter and Betty, his wife, lived in a development out by Spanaway Lake, and it took Jack and me about three-quarters of an hour to get there.

We pulled into the driveway of one of those square, boxy houses that looked like every other one on the block. A heavyset guy with black, curly hair came out into the little square block of concrete that served as a front porch.

"Where in hell have you bastards been?" he called as Jack cut the motor.

"Don't get all worked up," Jack yelled back as we got out of the car. "This is my brother, Dan." He turned his face toward me. "That lard-ass up there is Carter—Tacoma's answer to King Kong."

Mike glanced around quickly to make sure no one was watching and then gave Jack the finger, *"Wie geht's?"* he said to me grinning.

"Es geht mir gut," I answered, almost without thinking. Then I threw some more at him to see if he really knew any German. *"Und wie geht's Ihnen heute?"*

"Mit dieses und jenes," he said, pointing at his legs and repeating that weary joke that all Germans seem to think is so hysterically funny.

"Es freut mich," I said dryly.

"How long were you in Germany?" he asked, coming down the steps.

"Eighteen months."

"Where were you stationed?"

"Kitzingen. Then later in Wertheim."

"Ach so? Ich war zwei Jahren in München."

"Die Haupstadt von die Welt? Ganz glücklich!"

Jack chortled gleefully. "See, Mike, I told you he'd be able to *sprechen* that shit as well as you."

"He's been at me all week to talk German to you when he brought you over," Mike said.

"Man"—Jack laughed—"you two sounded like a couple of real Krauts. Too bad you don't know any Japanese like I do. Then we could *all* talk that foreign shit. Bug hell out of Sloane." Very slowly, mouthing the words with exaggerated care, he spoke a sentence or two in Japanese. "Know what that means?"

"One-two-three-four-five?" Mike asked.

"Come on, man. I said, 'How are you? Isn't this a fine day?' " He repeated it in Japanese again.

"Couldn't prove it by me," I said, letting him have his small triumph.

He grinned at both of us, obviously very proud of himself. "Hey,

Mike, how's that boat comin'?" he asked. "Is it gonna be ready by duck season?"

"Shit!" Mike snorted. "Come on out back and look at the damn thing."

We trooped on around to the back of the house. He had a fourteen-foot boat overturned on a pair of sawhorses out by the garage. It was surrounded by a litter of paint-scrapings which powdered the burned-out grass.

"Look at that son of a bitch," Mike said. "I've counted twelve coats of paint already, and I'm still not down to bare wood. It feels pretty spongy in a couple places, too—probably rotten underneath. I'm afraid to take off any more paint—probably all that's holding it together."

Jack laughed. "That's what you get for doin' busines with Thorwaldsen. He slipped you the Royal Swedish Weenie. I could have told you that."

"That sure won't do me much good right now," Mike said gloomily.

We went into the house long enough for me to meet Betty. She was a big, pleasant girl with a sweet face. I liked her, too. Then the three of us went out and piled into Jack's car. Betty stood on the little porch and waved as we pulled out of the driveway.

Jack drove on out to the highway, and we headed back toward town through the blood-colored light of the sunset.

"You have yourself a steady *Schatzie* in Germany?" Mike asked me.

"Last few months I did," I told him. "Up until then I was being faithful to my 'One and Only' back here in the States. Of course 'One and Only' had a different outlook on life."

"Got yourself one of those letters, huh?"

"Eight pages long," I said. "By the end of the fourth page, it was all my fault. At the end of the last page, I was eighteen kinds of an unreasonable son of a bitch—you know the type."

"Oh, *gosh*, yes." Mike laughed. "We used to tack ours up on a bulletin board. So then you found yourself a *Schatzie*?"

I nodded. "Girl named Heidi. Pretty good kid, really."

"I got myself tied up with a nympho in a town just outside Munich," Mike said. "She even had her own *house*, for God's sake. Her folks were loaded. I spent every weekend and all my leave-time over at her place. Exhausting!" He rolled his eyes back in his head. "I was absolutely *used* when I came back to the States."

I laughed. "She had it pretty well made then. At least you probably didn't get that 'Marry me Chee-Eye, und take me to der land uf der big P-X' routine."

"No chance. I said good-bye over the telephone five minutes before the train left."

"That's the smart way. I figured I knew this girl of mine pretty well—hell, I'd done everything but hit her over the head to make her realize that we weren't a permament thing. I guess none of it sunk in. She must have had visions of a vine-covered cottage in Pismo Beach or some damned thing. Anyway, when I told her I had my orders and it was *Auf Wiedersehen,* she just flat flipped out. Started to scream bloody murder and then tried to carve out my liver and lights with a butcher knife.''

They both laughed.

"You guys think it's funny?" I said indignantly. "You ever try to take an eighteen-inch butcher knife away from a hysterical woman without hurting her or getting castrated in the process?"

They howled with laughter.

I quite suddenly felt very shitty. Heidi had been a sweet, trusting kid. In spite of everything I'd told her, she'd gone on dreaming. Everybody's entitled to dream once in a while. And if it hadn't been for her, God knows how I'd have gotten through the first few months after that letter. Now I was treating her like she was a dirty joke. What makes a guy do that anyway?

"I had a little Jap girl try to knife me in Tokyo once," Jack said, stopping for a traffic light. "I just kicked her in the stomach. Didn't get a scratch. I think she was on some kinda dope—most of them gooks are. Anyway she just went wild for no reason and started wavin' this harakari knife and screamin' at me in Japanese. Both of us bare-assed naked, too."

The light changed and we moved on.

"How'd you get the knife away from the German girl?" Mike asked.

I didn't really want to talk about it anymore. "Got hold of her wrist," I said shortly. "Twisted her arm a little. After she dropped it, I kicked it under the bed and ran like hell. One of the neighbor women beaned me with a pot on my way downstairs. The whole afternoon was just an absolute waste."

They laughed again, and we drifted off into a new round of war stories. I was glad we'd gotten off the subject. I was still a little ashamed of myself.

It took us a good hour to get to Sloane's house out in Ruston. The sun had gone down, and the streets were filled with the pale twilight. People were still out in their yards, guys cutting their lawns and kids playing on the fresh-cut grass and the like. Suddenly, for no particular reason, it turned into a very special kind of evening for me.

Ruston perches up on the side of the hill that rises steeply up from both sides of Point Defiance. The plush part, where Sloane lived, overlooks the Narrows, a long neck of salt water that runs down another thirty miles to Olympia. The Narrows Bridge lies off to the south, the towers spearing into the sky and the bridge itself arching in one long step across the mile or so of open water. The ridge that rises sharply from the beach over on the peninsula is thick with dark fir trees, and the evening sky is almost always spectacular. It may just be one of the most beautiful places in the whole damned world. At least I've always thought so.

Sloane's house was one of the older places on the hill—easily distinguishable from the newer places because the shrubs and trees were full grown.

We pulled up behind McKlearey's car in the deepening twilight and got out. Jack's Plymouth and McKlearey's beat-up old Chevy looked badly out of place—sort of like a mobile poverty area.

"Pretty plush, huh?" Jack said, his voice a little louder than necessary. The automatic impulse up here was to lower your voice. Jack resisted it.

"I smell money," I answered.

"It's all over the neighborhood," Mike said. "They gotta have guys come in with special rakes to keep it from littering the streets."

"Unsightly stuff," I agreed as we went up Sloane's brick front walkway.

Jack rang the doorbell, and I could hear it chime way back in the house.

A small woman in a dark suit opened the door. "Hello, Jack—Mike," she said. She had the deepest voice I've ever heard come out of a woman. "And you must be Dan," she said. "I've heard so much about you." She held her hand out to me with a grace that you've got to be born with. I'm just enough of a slob myself to appreciate good breeding. I straightened up and took her hand.

"It's a pleasure to meet you, Mrs. Sloane," I said.

"Claudia," she said, smiling. "Please call me Claudia."

"Claudia," I said, smiling back at her.

We went on into the house. The layout was a bit odd, but I could see the reason for it. The house faced the street with its back to the view—at least that's how it looked from outside. Actually, the front door simply opened onto a long hallway that ran on through to the back where the living room, dining room, and kitchen were. The carpets were deep, and the paneling was rich.

"You have a lovely home," I said. I guess that's what you're supposed to say.

"Why, thank you, Dan," she said. She seemed genuinely pleased.

The living room was huge, and the west wall was all glass. Over beyond the dark upswell of the peninsula, the sky was slowly darkening. Down on the water, a small boat that looked like a lighted toy from up there bucked the tide, moving very slowly and kicking up a lot of wake.

"How on earth do you ever get anything done?" I asked. "I'd never be able to get away from the window."

She laughed, her deep voice making the sound musical. "I pull the drapes," she said. She looked up at me. She couldn't have been much over five feet tall. Her dark hair was very smooth—almost sleek. I quickly looked back out the window to cover my confusion. This was one helluva lot of woman.

There was a patio out back, and I could see Sloane manhandling a beer keg across the flagstones. McKlearey sprawled in a lawn chair, and it didn't look as if he was planning to offer any help. Sloane glanced, red-faced, up at the window.

"Hey, you drunks, get the hell on out here!" he bellowed.

"We're set up on the patio," Claudia said.

"Thinkin' ahead, eh, Claude?" Jack said boisterously. "If somebody gets sick, you don't have to get the rug cleaned."

I cringed.

"Well," she said, laughing, "it's cooler out there."

"Which one of you bastards can tap a keg?" Sloane screamed. "I'm afraid to touch the goddamn thing."

"Help is on the way," Mike called. We went on through the dining room and the kitchen and on out to the patio through the sliding French doors.

"I'm sure you fellows can manage now," Claudia said, picking up a pair of black gloves from the kitchen table and coming over to stand in the open doorway. "I have to run, so just make yourselves at home." She raised her voice slightly, obviously talking to Sloane. "Just remember to keep the screens closed on the French doors. I don't want a house full of bugs."

"Yes, ma'am," Sloane yelped, coming to attention and throwing her a mock salute.

"Clown," she said, smiling. She started to pull on the gloves, smoothing each finger carefully. "Oh, Calvin, I finished with the books for the car lot and the pawnshop. Be sure to put them where you can find them Monday morning—*before* you swandive into that beer keg."

"Have we got any money?" Cal asked.

"We'll get by," she said. "Be sure and remind Charlie and Mel out at the Hideout that I'll be by to check their books on Tuesday."

"Right," he said. He turned to us. "My wife, the IBM machine."

"Somebody has to do the books," she said placidly, still working on the gloves, "and after I watched this great financier add two and two and get five about nine times out of ten, I decided that it was going to be up to me to keep us out of bankruptcy court." She smiled sweetly at him, and he made a face.

"I'm so glad to have met you, Dan," she said, holding her hand out to me again. Her deep musical voice sent a shiver up my back. "I'm sure I'll be seeing you again."

"I'd hate to think we were driving you out of your own house," I said sincerely.

"No, no. I have a meeting downtown, and then I'm running over to Yakima to visit an aunt. I'd just be in the way here anyway. You boys have fun." She raised her voice again. "I'll see you Monday evening, Calvin."

He waved a brusque farewell and turned his attention back to the beer keg.

She looked at him for a moment, sighed, and went smoothly on back into the house. I suddenly wanted very much to go down to the patio and give Sloane a good solid shot to the mouth. A kiss on the cheek by way of good-bye wouldn't have inconvenienced him all that much, and it would have spared her the humiliation of that public brush-off.

I went slowly down the three steps to the patio, staring out over the Narrows and the dark timber on the other side.

There was a sudden burst of spray from the keg and a solid "klunk" as Mike set the tap home. "There you go, men," he said. "The beer-drinking lamp is lit."

"Well, ahoy there, matey," Jack said, putting it on a bit too much.

The first pitcher was foam, and Sloane dumped it in the fishpond. "Drink, you little bastards." He giggled.

Somebody, Claudia probably, had set a trayful of beer mugs up on a permanently anchored picnic table under one of the trees. I got one of them and filled it at the keg and drifted over to the edge of the patio where the hill broke sharply away, running down to the tangled Scotch-broom and madrona thicket below.

I could hear the others horsing around back at the keg, but I ignored them for the moment, concentrating on the fading line of daylight along the top of the hills across the Narrows.

"Pretty, huh?"

It was Sloane. He stood with a mug of beer, looking out over the water. "I used to come up here when I was a kid and just look at it. Weren't many houses or anything up here then."

Somehow I couldn't picture Sloane as a kid.

"I made up my mind then that someday I was gonna live up here," he went on. "Took me a long time, but I made it."

"Was it worth it?" I couldn't resist asking him. I didn't like him much right then.

"Every lousy, scratching, money-grubbing, fuckin' minute of it," he said with a strange intensity. "Sometimes I sit up here lookin' out at it, and I just break out laughing at all the shit I had to crawl through to get here."

"We all do funny things," I said. Now he had me confused.

"I'd have never made it without Claudia," he said. "She's really something, isn't she?"

"She's a real lady," I said.

"She was hoppin' tables in a beer bar when I met her," he said. "She had it even then. I can meet guys and swing deals and all, but she's the one who puts it all together and makes it go. She's one in a million, Dan."

"I can tell that," I said. How the hell do you figure a guy like Sloane?

"Hey, you bastards," Jack called to us, "this is a *party*, not a private little confab. Come on back here."

"Just showin' off my scenery," Cal said. The two of us went back to the keg.

Sloane went over and pawed around under one of the shrubs. "As soon as you guys get all squared away," he said, "I've got a little goodie here for you." He pulled out a half-gallon jug of clear liquid.

"Oh, shit!" Jack said. "Auburn tanglefoot. Goddamn Sloane and his pop-skull moonshine."

"Guaranteed to have been aged at least two hours." Sloane giggled.

"I thought the government men had busted up all those stills years ago," Mike said.

"No way," Jack said. "Auburn'd blow away if it wasn't anchored down by all those pot stills."

McKlearey got up and took the jug from Sloane. He opened it and sniffed suspiciously. "You sure this stuff is all right?"

"Pure, one-hundred-per-cent rotgut," Sloane said.

"I mean, they don't spike it with wood alcohol, do they?" There was a note of worry in Lou's voice. "Sometimes they do that. Makes a guy go blind. His eyes fall out."

"What's the sense of poisoning your customers?" Sloane asked. "You ain't gonna get much repeat business that way."

"I've heard that they do it sometimes, is all," McKlearey said. "They spike it with wood alcohol, or they use an old car radiator instead of that copper coil—then the booze gets tainted with all that gunk off the solder. Either way it makes a guy go blind. Fuckin' eyes fall right out."

"Bounce around on the floor like marbles, huh, Lou?" Jack said. "I can see it now. McKlearey's eyes bouncin' off across the patio with him chasin' 'em." He laughed harshly. He knew about Lou and Margaret, all right. There was no question about that now.

"I don't think I want any," McKlearey said, handing the jug back to Sloane.

"Old Lou's worried about his baby-blue eyeballs," Jack said, rubbing it in.

"I just don't want any. OK, Alders?"

"Well, I'm gonna have some," Mike said, reaching for the jug. "I cut my teeth on Auburn moonshine. My eyes might get a little loose now and then, but they sure as hell don't fall out." He rolled the jug back over his arm professionally and took a long belt.

"Now, there's an old moonshine drinker," Jack said. "Notice the way he handles that jug."

We passed the jug around, and each of us tried to emulate Mike's technique. Frankly, the stuff wasn't much good—I've gotten a better taste siphoning gas. But we all smacked our lips appreciatively, said some silly-ass thing like "damn good whiskey," and had a quick beer to flush out the taste.

McKlearey still refused to touch the stuff. He went back to his lawn chair, scowling.

"Hey, man," Jack said, "I think my eyes are gettin' loose." He pressed his fingers to his eyelids.

"Fuck you, Alders," Lou said.

"Yeah," Jack said. "They're definitely gettin' loose—oops! There goes one now." He squinted one eye shut and started pawing around on the flagstones. "Come back here, you little bastard!"

"Aw, go fuck yourself, Alders!" Lou snapped. "You're so goddamn fuckin' funny!"

"Oh, Mother," Jack cried, "help me find my fuckin' eyeball." He was grinding Lou for all he was worth.

Lou was starting to get pretty hot, and I figured another crack or two from my brother ought to do it. I knew I should say something to cool it down, but I figured that Jack knew what he was doing. If he wanted a piece of McKlearey, that was his business.

"Hey, you guys," Mike said, inspecting Sloane's substantial outside fireplace, "let's build a fire." It was a smooth way to handle the situation.

"Why?" Sloane demanded. "You cold or something, for Chrissake?"

"No, but a fire's kinda nice, isn't it? I mean, what the hell?"

"Shit, I don't care," Cal said. "Come on. There's a woodpile over behind the garage."

The four of us left McKlearey sulking in his lawn chair and trooped on over to the wood pile.

It took us a while to get the fire going. We wound up going through the usual business of squatting down and blowing on it to make it catch. Finally, it took hold, and we stood around looking at it with a beery sense of having really done something worthwhile.

Then we all hauled up lawn chairs and moved the keg over handy. Even Lou pulled himself in to join the group. By then it was getting pretty dark.

Sloane had a stereo in his living room, and outside speakers as well. He was piping out a sort of standard, light music, so it was pleasant. I discovered that a shot of that rotten homemade whiskey in a glass of beer made a pretty acceptable drink, and I sat with the others drinking and telling lies.

I guess it was Jack who raised the whole damned thing. He was talking about some broad he'd laid while he was on his way down to Willapa Bay to hunt geese.

". . . anyhow," he was saying, "I went on down to Willapa—got there about four thirty or five—and put out my dekes. Colder'n a bastard, and me still about half blind with alcohol. About five thirty the geese came in—only by then my drunk had worn off, and my head felt like a goddamn balloon. Man, you want to see an act of raw courage? Just watch some poor bastard with a screamin' hangover touch off a 12 gauge with three-inch magnum shells at a high-flyin' goose. Man, I still hurt when I think about it."

"Get any geese?" I asked.

"Filled out before seven," he said. "Even filled on mallards before I started back—a real carnage. I picked up my dekes, chucked all the birds in the trunk, and headed on back up the pike. I hauled off the road in Chehalis again and went into the same bar to get well. Damned if she wasn't right there on the first stool again."

And that started the hunting stories. Have you ever noticed how when a bunch of guys are sitting around, the stories kind of run in cycles? First the drinking stories—"Boy did we get plastered"—then the war stories—"Funny thing happened when I was in the Army"— and then the hunting stories, or the dog stories, or the snake stories. It's almost like a ritual, but very relaxed. Nobody's trying to outdo anybody else. It's just sort of easy and enjoyable. Even McKlearey and Jack called a truce on the eyeball business.

I guess maybe the fire had something to do with it. You get a bunch of guys around an open fire at night, and nine times out of ten they'll get around to talking about hunting sooner or later. It's almost inevitable. It's funny some anthropologist hasn't noticed it and made a big thing out of it.

We all sifted back through our memories, lifting out the things we'd done or stories we'd heard from others. We hunted pheasant and quail, ducks and geese, rabbits and squirrels, deer and bear, elk and mountain lions. We talked guns and ammunition, equipment, camping techniques—all of it. A kind of excitement—an urge, if you want to call it that—began to build up. The faint, barely remembered smells of the woods and of gun-oil came back with a sharpness that was almost real. Unconsciously, we all pulled our chairs in closer to the fire, tightening the circle. It was a warm night, so it wasn't that we needed the heat of the fire.

"You know," Jack was saying, "it's a damn shame there's no season open right now. We could have a real ball huntin' together—just the bunch of us."

"Too goddamn hot," Lou said, pouring himself another beer.

"Not up in the mountains, it's not," Mike said.

"When does deer season open?" Sloane asked.

"Middle of October," Jack said. "Of course we could go after bear. They're predators on this side of the mountains, and the season's always open."

"Stick that bear hunting in your ear," Mike said. "First you've got to have dogs; and second, you never know when one of those big hairy bastards is gonna come out of the brush at about ten feet. You got time for about one shot before he's chewin' on your head and scatterin' your bowels around like so much confetti."

"Yuk!" Sloane gagged. "There's a graphic picture for you."

"No shit, man," Mike said. "I won't go anywhere near a goddamn bear. I shot one just once. Never again. I had an old .303 British—ten shots, and it took every goddamn one of them. That son of a bitch just kept comin'. Soaked up lead like a blotter. The guys that hunt those babies all carry .44 magnum pistols for close work."

"Hell, man," McKlearey said, "you can stop a *tank* with a .44 mag."

Mike looked at him. "One guy I talked to jumped a bear once and hit him twice in the chest with a .300 Weatherbee and then went to the pistol. Hit him four times at point-blank range with a .44 mag before he went down. Just literally blew him to pieces, and the damned bear was still trying to get at him. I talked to the guy three years later, and his hands were still shakin'. No bears for this little black duck!"

"Would a .45 stop one?" I asked.

"Naw, the military bullet's got a hard jacket," Mike said. "Just goes right through."

"No, I mean the long Colt. It's a 250-grain soft lead bullet."

"That oughta do it," Jack said. "Just carryin' the weight would slow him down enough for a guy to make a run for it."

"I've got an old Colt frontier-style stored with my clothes and books in Seattle," I said, leaning over and refiling my beer mug.

"No kiddin'?" Jack said. "What the hell did you get a cannon like that for?"

"Guy I knew needed money. I lent him twenty, and he gave me the gun as security—never saw him again. The gun may be hot for all I know."

"Ah-ha!" Sloane said. "Pawnbroking without a license!" He giggled.

"It's got a holster and belt—the whole bit," I said. "I'm going to have to pick up all that junk anyway. I'll bring it on down."

"I'd like to see it," Jack said, "and Sloane here knows about guns—he takes in a lot of them in pawn—he ought to be able to tell you what it's worth."

"Sure," Sloane said, "bring it in. Maybe we can dicker."

"Hey!" Mike shouted suddenly. "Shut up, you guys. I just thought of something." He leaned forward, his slightly round face suddenly excited. "How about the High Hunt?"

"Are you kiddin'?" Jack demanded. "You really want to try the 'Great White Hunter' bit?"

"What the goddamn hell is the High Hunt?" McKlearey demanded harshly.

"Early high Cascade Mountains deer season," Mike said, his eyes gleaming in the firelight.

"—In some of the roughest, emptiest, steepest, highest country in the whole fuckin' world," Jack finished for him.

"It's not *that* bad," Mike said.

"Aw, bullshit!" Jack snorted. "The damned boundaries start right where the roads all end. And do you know why the roads end there? Because there's not a fuckin' thing back up in there, that's why. Man, most of that country's above the timberline."

"All alpine meadow," Mike said almost dreamily. "It gets snowed in so early that nobody ever got a chance to hunt it before they opened this special season. Some of the biggest deer in the state are up there. One guy got a nine-pointer that weighed four hundred pounds."

"Eastern count, I'll bet," Jack said.

"Eastern count my ass. Full Western count—the number of points on the smallest side not counting brow tines. Eastern count would have gone twenty—maybe twenty-one points. That was one helluva big deer."

"And the guy got a hernia gettin' it out of the woods." Sloane giggled.

"No—hell, they had horses."

". . . and guides," Sloane went on, "and a wrangler, and a camp cook, and a bartender. Probably didn't cost more than a thousand a week for two guys."

"It's not all *that* much," Mike said tentatively. "I know a guy—a rancher—who'll take out a fair-sized party real reasonable. You could get by for fifty bucks apiece for a week—ten days. Food extra, of course. He's tryin' to get into the business, so he's keepin' his rates down for the first couple years." Mike's voice was serious; he wasn't just talking. He was actually proposing it to us as a real possibility. His face had a kind of hunger on it that you don't see very often. Mike wanted this to go, and he wanted it badly.

"Who the fuck wants to pay to go up in the boonies for ten days?" McKlearey demanded harshly, putting it down.

It hung there, almost like it was balanced on something. I knew that if I left it alone, McKlearey's raspy vote for inertia would tip it. At that moment I wasn't really sure if I wanted to go up into the high country, but I *was* sure of one thing; I didn't much like McKlearey, and I did like Mike Carter.

"It's what we've been talking about for the last hour," I said, lighting a cigarette. "All you guys were so hot to trot, and now Mike comes up with something solid—a real chance to do some real hunting, not just a little Sunday-morning poaching with a twenty-two out of a car window—and everybody gets tongue-tied all of a sudden."

"Didn't you get enough of maneuvers and bivouac and shit like that in the Army?" McKlearey demanded, his eyes narrowing. I remembered what Jack had told me about crossing him.

"I did my share of field-soldiering," I told him, "but this is hunting, and that's different."

"Are *you* gonna pay to go out and run around in the brush?" He was getting hot again. God, he was a touchy bastard.

"If the price is like Mike said it was, and if we can work out the details, you're goddamn right I will." A guy will make up his mind to do something for the damnedest reasons sometimes.

"You're outa your fuckin' skull," McKlearey said, his voice angry and his face getting kind of pinched in.

"Nobody's twistin' your arm, Lou," Jack said. "You don't have to go no place."

"I suppose *you'd* go along, too, huh, Alders?" For some reason, McKlearey was getting madder by the minute. He was twisting around in his chair like a worm on a hot rock.

"You damn betcha," Jack said. "Just give me ten minutes to pack up my gear, and I'll be gone, buddy—long gone."

"Shit!" McKlearey said. "You guys are just blowin' smoke outa your fuckin' ears. You ain't even got a rifle, Alders. You sure as shit can't go deer huntin' with a fuckin' shotgun."

"I could lend you guys rifles from the pawnshop," Sloane said very quietly. He was leaning back, and I couldn't see his face.

Mike swallowed. I think the hope that it would go had been a very faint one for him. Now, a strange combination of things had laid it right in his lap. "I'd better get a piece of paper and figure out a few things," he said.

"The bugs are about to get me anyway," Sloane said. "Let's take the keg into the kitchen."

We carted it inside and sat down around the table in the breakfast nook to watch Mike write down a long list with figures opposite each item.

McKlearey straddled a chair over in the corner, scowling at us.

Mike finally leaned back and took a long drink of beer. "I think that's it," he said. "Figure fifty for the horses and the guide—that's for a week or ten days. Food—probably twenty-five. License, ammunition, stuff like that—another twenty-five. Most of us probably already have the right kind of clothes and a guy can always borrow a sleeping bag if he don't already have one. I figure a guy can get by for a hundred."

We sat in the brightly lighted kitchen with the layer of cigarette smoke hovering over our heads and stared at the sheet of paper in front of Mike.

I glanced out the window at the rusty glow of the dying fire. The hills over on the peninsula loomed up against the stars.

"I'm in," I said shortly.

Mike scratched his cheek and nodded. "A man owes himself one good hunt in his life," he said. "It may start a small war in the Carter house, but what the hell?" He wrote his name and mine on the bottom of the paper. "Jack?" he asked my brother.

"Why not?" Jack said. "I'll probably have to come along to keep you guys from shooting yourself in the foot."

Mike put Jack's name down on the list.

"God damn!" Cal said regretfully. "If I didn't have the shop and the lot and—" He paused. "Bullshit!" he said angrily. "I own *them*; they don't own *me*. Put my name down. I'm goin' huntin'. Piss on it!" He giggled suddenly.

Mike squinted at the list. "I'm not sure if Miller—that's this guy I know—will go along with only four guys. We might have to scrounge up a few more bodies, but that shouldn't be too tough. You guys might think about it a little though. I'll call Miller on Monday and see if we can't get together on the price of the horses and the guide."

"Guide?" Jack yelped. "Who the hell needs a goddamn baby-sitter? If you can't find your own damn game, you're not much of a hunter."

"It's a package deal, shithead," Mike said. "No guy is just gonna rent you a horse and then point you off into the big lonely. He may not give two hoots in hell about you, but he wants that horse back."

Jack grumbled a bit, but there wasn't much he could do about it. It was going to go; it was really going to go.

Mike called a guy he knew and found out that the season opened on September 11, just about a month away. "At least that'll give us time to get our affairs in order." Mike laughed. "You know, quit our jobs, divorce our wives, and the like."

We all laughed.

Suddenly McKlearey stood up. He'd been sitting in the corner, nursing his beer. "Where's that fuckin' paper?" he demanded.

Mike blinked and pulled it out of his shirt pocket.

McKlearey jerked it out of his hand, picked up the pencil Mike had been using, and laboriously wrote along the bottom.

"Louis R. McKlearey," he wrote.

"What the hell—" Jack said, stunned.

"Fuck ya!" Lou snapped. Then he leaned back his head and began to laugh. The laugh went on and on, and pretty soon the rest of us were doing it too.

"Why you sneaky son of a bitch!" Jack howled. "You bad-mouthed the whole idea just to get us all hooked. You sneaky, connivin' bastard!"

Lou laughed even harder. Maybe the others accepted Jack's easy answer, but I wasn't buying it. Not by a damn sight, I wasn't.

After that, things got noisy. We all got to hitting the keg pretty hard, and it turned out to be a pretty good party after all.

I guess it was almost three in the morning by the time we got Mike home.

"I was gonna take you by to see Sandy," Jack said as we drove back to the trailer court, "but it's pretty late now." His voice was a little slurred.

"Sandy? Who's that?"

"Little something I've got on the side. She's a real fine-lookin' head. Tends bar at one of the joints. You'll get a chance to meet her later."

I grunted and settled down in the seat. I realized that I didn't know this brother of mine at all. I couldn't understand him. A certain amount of casual infidelity was to be expected, I guess, but it seemed to him to be a way of life. Like his jobs and his wives, he just seemed to drift from woman to woman, always landing on his feet, always making out, always on the lookout for something new. Maybe that's why he wasn't so worked up about Lou and Margaret. I guess the word I was looking for was "temporary." Everything about him and his life seemed temporary, almost like he wasn't real, like nothing really touched him.

I drifted off to thinking about the hunt. Maybe I was kind of temporary myself. I didn't have a family, I didn't have a girl, and I didn't have a job. I guess maybe the only difference between Jack and me was that he liked it that way, and I didn't. To him the hunt was just another thing to do. To me it already seemed more important. Maybe I could find out something about myself out in the brush, something I'd sure as hell never find out on a sidewalk. So I sat musing as the headlights bored on into the dark ahead of us.

 6

It wasn't until Thursday that we finished up the deal on the car I was buying from Sloane's lot. I guess I got a pretty good deal on it. It was a ten-year-old Dodge, and I got it for a hundred and fifty. One of the fenders was a little wrinkled, and the paint wasn't too pure, but otherwise it seemed OK. Jack assured me that I wouldn't have been able to touch it for under three hundred anywhere else on the Avenue.

It was cloudy that day, one of those days when the weather just seems to be turned off—not hot, not cold, not raining, not sunny—just "off." I kind of wandered around the car lot, kicking tires and so forth while McKlearey finished up the paper work in the cluttered little shack that served as an office. I hate waiting around like that, I get to the point where I want to run amok or something. It wasn't that I had anything to do really. I just hated the standing around.

Finally Lou finished up and I took the paper and the keys from him.

"Be sure to keep an eye on the oil," he told me.

"Right."

"And watch the pressure in the right rear tire."

"Sure thing." I climbed in and fired it up. Lou waved as I drove off the lot. I didn't wave back.

There's something about having your own car—even if it's only four wheels and a set of pedals. You aren't tied down any more. You're not always in the position of asking people for a lift or waiting for buses.

I drove around for an hour or so through the shadowless light, getting the feel of the car. It was still fairly early—maybe ten thirty or eleven in the morning—and finally it dawned on me that I didn't have anyplace to go really. Jack was busy at the trailer lot, and I hate to stand around and watch somebody else work.

I thought about taking a run up to Seattle, but I really didn't want to do that. None of the people I'd known would still be around. Maxwell had taken off and Larkin, too, probably. I sure as hell didn't want to look up my old girlfriend; that was one thing I knew for sure.

Larkin. I hadn't really been thinking at all. Last time I'd heard from him, he'd been teaching high school here in Tacoma someplace. I guess I'd just associated Tacoma with guys like my brother and McKlearey and Carter—beer-drinking, broad-chasing types. Stan Larkin just didn't fit in with that kind of picture.

Stan and I had roomed together for a year at the university. We didn't really have much in common, but I kind of liked him. There are two ways a guy can go if he's a liberal arts major—provided, of course, that he doesn't freak out altogether. He can assume the pose of the cultured man, polished, urbane, with good taste and all that goes with it. Or he can play the role of the "diamond in the rough," coarse, even vulgar, but supposedly intelligent in spite of it all—the Hemingway tactic, more or less. Larkin was the first type—I obviously wasn't.

I think liberal arts majors are all automatically defensive about it, probably because we're oversensitive. The dum-dums in PE with their brains in their jockstraps, the goof-offs in Business Administration, the weird types in the hard sciences, and the campus politicians in the social sciences, have all seen fit at one time or another to question the masculinity of any guy in liberal arts. So we get defensive. We rise above them, like Stan does, or we compensate, like I do. It kind of goes with the territory.

Anyway, Stan had spent a year picking up my dirty sox and dusting my books, and then he'd given up and moved back to the dorm. Even our literary interests hadn't coincided. He was involved with Dickens, Tennyson, Wordsworth, and Pope, while I was hung up on Blake, Donne, Faulkner, and Hardy. It's a wonder we didn't wind up killing each other.

I'd dropped him an occasional postcard from Europe, and he'd responded with the beautifully written letters that seemed, to me at least, almost like my picture of Stan himself—neat, florid, and somehow totally empty of any meaning.

At least he'd be somebody to talk to.

I wheeled into a tavern parking lot, went in and ordered a beer. I borrowed a phone book from the bartender and leafed through the *L*'s. He was there all right: *Larkin, Stanley*, and right above it was *Larkin, Monica*. Same address, same number. I remembered that he'd mentioned a girl named Monica something or other in a couple of his letters, but I hadn't paid much attention. Now it looked like he was married. I don't know why, but he'd never seemed to be the type. I jotted down the number and the address and pushed the phone book back to the bartender.

I finished my beer and had another, still debating with myself, kind of working myself up to calling him. I have to do that sometimes.

"Hey, buddy, you got a pay phone?" I finally asked the bartender. He pointed back toward the can. I saw it hanging on the wall.

"Thanks," I said and went on back. I thumbed in a dime and dialed the number.

"Hello?" It still sounded like him.

"Stan? I didn't really think I'd catch you at home. This is Dan—Dan Alders."

"Dan? I thought you were in the Army."

"Just got out last weekend. I'm staying here in town, and I thought I'd better look you up."

"I guess *so*. It's good to hear your voice again. Where are you?" His enthusiasm seemed well-tempered.

"Close as I can figure, about eighty-seven blocks from your place."

"That's about a fifteen-minute drive. You have a car?"

"Just got one. I think it'll make it that far."

"Well then, come on over."

"You sure I won't be interrupting anything?"

"Oh, of course not. Come on, Dan, we know each other better than that."

"OK, Stan." I laughed. "I'll see you in about fifteen minutes then."

"I'll be waiting for you."

I went back to the bar and had another beer. I wasn't sure this was going to work out. I wouldn't mind seeing Stan again, but we hadn't really had a helluva lot in common to begin with, and now he was married, and that along with a couple of years can change a guy quite a bit.

The more I thought about it, the less I liked it. I went out and climbed in my car. I pulled out of the lot and headed off toward his house, dodging dogs and kids on bicycles, and swearing all the way. It had all the makings of a real bust.

Oddly enough, it wasn't. Stan had aged a little. He was a bit heavier, and his forehead was getting higher. He was combing his hair differently to cover it. He was still neat to the point of fussiness. His slacks and sport shirt were flawlessly pressed, and even his shoe-soles were clean. But he seemed genuinely glad to see me, and I relaxed a bit. He showed me around a house that was like a little glass case in a museum, making frequent references to Monica, his wife. The house was small, but everything in it was perfect. I could almost feel the oppressive presence of his bride. The place was so neat that it made me wonder where I could dump my cigarette butt. Stan gracefully provided me with an ashtray—an oversized one, I noticed. He obviously hadn't forgotten my slobby habits. He had changed in more ways than just his appearance. He seemed to be nervous—even jumpy. He acted like somebody who's got a body in the cellar or a naked girl in the bedroom. I couldn't quite put my finger on it.

We sat down in the living room.

"How's Susan?" he asked me.

My stomach rolled over. "I wouldn't know really," I answered in as neutral a tone as possible.

"But I thought you and she—"

"So did I, Stan. But apparently she shopped around a bit while I was in Germany. She must have found somebody more acceptable to her mother—you know, some guy who thought that the Old Lady was a cross between the Virgin Mary, Joan of Arc, and Eleanor Roosevelt."

"I'm sorry, Dan. I really am." He meant it.

"Those are the breaks, old buddy," I said. "It's probably all for the best anyway. Her Old Lady and I probably would have been at each other's throats most of the time anyway. About the first time I told her to stick those chest pains in her ear, the proverbial shit would have hit the proverbial fan."

"Did she have a bad heart?"

"She had a *useful* heart. It may have been rotten to the core, but it was as sound as the Chase Manhattan Bank—how's that for mixing metaphors?"

"Scrambling them might be a little more precise."

"Anyway, the old bag would get this pained look on her face, and the old hand would start clutching at the maternal bosom anytime Sue and I were about to leave the house. One of the great weapons of motherhood, the fluttery ticker. My Old Lady never tried it. I don't think she was ever sober enough."

"You still haven't much use for motherhood, have you, Dan?" he asked me, an amused look on his face.

"As an institution, it ranks just downstream of San Quentin," I said sourly.

Stan laughed. I think that's one of the reasons he and I had gotten along. With him I could be as outrageous as I liked, and he was always amused. I'd never really offended him.

"Could you drink a glass of wine?" he asked suddenly. The perfect host.

"I can always drink—anything," I told him.

"Alders, you're a boozer, you know that?"

"It's part of my charm." I grinned at him.

He went out to the kitchen and came back a minute later with two glasses of pink wine. "This is a fairly good little domestic rosé," he said handing me one of the glasses.

"Thank you," I said. "Your manners, charm, and impeccable good taste are exceeded only by your unspeakable good looks."

"Steady on," he said. He glanced at his watch. I seemed to catch that edginess again. Maybe I was imagining things.

"How's your gun eye?" I asked him. Oddly enough—or maybe not, when you think about it—Stan was a spectacular shotgunner. He'd started out on skeet and trap—gentlemanly, but not very nourishing in terms of meat in the pot—and had moved on up to birds. I'd actually seen him triple on ducks once—one mallard coming in high, another on a low pass right out in front of the blind, and a widgeon going away like a bat out of hell. He'd just raised up and very methodically dumped all three of them, one after another.

"Probably a little rusty," he said. "I've only been out to the range a few times this summer."

"You'd better get on it, old buddy," I told him. "The season's coming on, you know."

"I don't know if I'll get the chance to go out much this year," he said regretfully. "Monica and I are pretty busy."

I got another flash of that nervousness from him. Something was definitely wrong. I decided to let it drop. I didn't want to be grinding on any open sores.

"Say," I said suddenly, "do you ever hear from Maxwell?"

"He was in California last I heard," Stan said. Maxwell had been a sometime visitor when we had roomed together. He was a nut, but we'd both liked him.

"Did he really burn his draft card that time?" I asked.

"Of course not," Stan snorted. "He was just trying to make a big impression on a girl who had an acute case of politics. He told me later that he just pulled out one of those printed ID cards—you know, the kind that comes with the wallet—and set fire to it before anyone could see what it was. The real joke was that he was really 4-F or whatever they call it."

"You're kidding. A hulk like that?"

"He had a kidney removed when he was eleven. The military wouldn't touch him."

"Man"—I laughed—"what a con artist. Did he ever make it with the girl?"

"I suppose," Stan said. "He usually did, didn't he?"

"That's why he flunked out of school. If he'd spent half as much time on his classes as he did on those elaborate campaigns of seduction, he'd have chewed up the department." I took a belt of his wine.

"Alders, you know, you're a beer drinker at heart. You drink a fine rosé like you would a glass of draft beer in a tavern two minutes before closing time."

"Baby, I've had the best. Liebfraumilch, Lacrima Christi, Piper Heidsieck—you name it, I've swilled it."

He winced. "What a word—swilled. All right, now that we've gotten past the amenities, tell me, how was Paris?" I should have known that was coming. Paris is always the favorite city of anybody who hasn't been to Europe.

"It's a dirty town, Stan," I said sadly, telling him the truth. "I think that all my life I've wanted it to be great, but it's just another dirty town with a lot of dirty people trying to stick their hands in your pockets.

Berlin was wild, very sad; Florence was lovely—but the flood—'' I shrugged. ''Venice is a crumbling slum in the middle of a sewer; Naples is still in rubble; Rome is—well, it's Rome—a monument. If you can get clear of the tourist traps, it's fine. London is dignified, honorably scarred, and—where the action is supposed to be at—cheap. The plays are good, but the eating and drinking are rotten. You want my vote, try Vienna—or Heidelberg—or Zürich. And that completes the Cook's toe-nail tour.''

''Germanophile,'' he snorted.

''No,'' I said seriously. ''The others are out to make a buck, any way they can. Most of them would sell you their little brother if their little sister or their mother wasn't to your taste. The Germans don't give a shit if you like them or not, and God knows they don't need your money. Benson—this guy I knew—and I used to ride bicycles across a small mountain to a little farming village—the kind of no-name sort of place with only a church, a *Gasthaus*, a few other shops, and a dozen or two houses, maybe two-three hundred people all together. We were the only Americans in the whole damned town. We rode through one afternoon and stopped for a beer. We just kept going back. The people there really got to like us, and we liked them. They had a big party for the oldest guy in town—everybody knocked off work for the whole day. The old boy was about ninety-seven or so. Benson and I were the only two outsiders invited to that blast. Not just the only two Americans—the only *outsiders*. It was absolutely great.''

''Ah, the pleasures of rural life,'' he said. ''Swains and maidens in the first flower of youth.''

''Larkin,'' I said, ''you're a phony bastard, you know that?''

''I know,'' he said, and I think he was serious. He had a habit of going into those ''I'm not really real'' depressions. As I recall, that's one of the reasons we parted company. Too much of that stuff can get on a guy's nerves.

Then Monica came in. I vaguely remembered seeing her around school when I'd still been there. She was a sleek brunette; and, I don't know—polished is the word, I guess—or maybe brittle. I'd seen a couple of girls like her in Germany—the hundred-marks-a-night sort of girl. At first she treated me like a piece of garbage on the floor, but when she learned that I'd been to *Europe*, her attitude changed. She started poking the usual bright questions at me, trying to make sure I'd really been there—though how in hell she'd know is beyond me. She wanted to talk about Paris, naturally, and mentioned a lot of names I remembered only as the tourist-trappy kind of places to stay away from. About the only thing we agreed on was the Rodin Museum, but I think it was for different reasons. It began to sound as if she'd been there and I hadn't. I think she was a little peeved that I didn't fake it for her as others I knew did so often, gushing about places they really couldn't stand, simply because it was the ''thing to do.'' I listened to her chatter politely. There was something sort of odd here, but I couldn't quite get hold of it.

"Stanley," she said, turning to him. "Did you run those things through the washer that I asked you to this morning?" There was a threat in her tone, a kind of "You'd better have, if you know what's good for you" sort of thing.

"Yes, dear," he said meekly.

That was it then. The whole thing fell into place. She had the big stick, and he knew it—and he'd been ashamed to let me find out. Married not more than a couple of years on the very outside, and he was pussy-whipped already. Poor Stan.

"Good," she said. She turned back to me and smiled briefly—like switching on a light in an empty room and then switching it off again. Click-click. "I'd *love* to stay and talk with you, Dan, but I've really *got* to run. We're trying to set up a little drama group, and there are a *million* details. You know how it is." Click-click went the smile again. That room was still empty.

"Oh, Stanley," she said, "don't forget that we're going over to the Jamisons' for dinner this evening." That was obviously for my benefit. She didn't want me hanging around the house. "Wear the blue suit. You know how conservatively Mr. Jamison dresses, and we do need their support if this little theater group is going to go anywhere."

He nodded. Stan needed instructions on how to dress like I needed instructions on opening beer bottles. It was just a little dig to keep him in line.

"I'll be back about fourish," she went on, "and I'll be in the mood for a Manhattan by then. You *will* be a good boy and mix up a small pitcher, won't you?"

Click-click went the smile again. What a phony bitch!

"Of course," he said. She was humiliating him, and she damned well knew it. I guess he wasn't allowed to have any friends that she hadn't passed on first.

"I've really *got* to run," she said. "It's been *lovely* meeting you, Dan."

We all stood up, and she left. We sat down again.

"Well, Dan," Stan said, rather quickly, I thought, "what are you going to do now that you're a civilian again?"

"Graduate school, I guess," I said.

"Up at the U?"

I nodded.

"Going into Education?"

I shook my head. "Straight English. Education courses are a waste of time."

"Oh, I don't know. I went on and took *my* MS."

"Hey, Stan, that's really fine," I said, ignoring the defensive tone in his voice. "I didn't know whether you'd finished or not."

"Oh, yes," he said, "about a year ago. I'm teaching high school now, but after I get a little more experience, I'm going to apply at several colleges. Monica's working on her master's, too, and we'll be in excellent shape as soon as she finishes."

"That's fine, buddy," I said. "I'm glad to hear it."

"We should get together a few times before you go back up to Seattle," he said.

"We'll do that, Stan. I'm a little tied up right now. We're getting ready to go hunting in early September."

"Hunting?" Stan said with sudden interest. "I didn't know there were any seasons open this early."

"We're going up on the High Hunt—high Cascade deer season— way to hell and gone back up in the mountains. We've got a guide and horses all lined up. We're going up to the Methow River into the country on the back side of Glacier Peak. We'll be in there for about ten days."

"God," he said, "I'd really love to do something like that." He meant it. I must have hit a nerve. "It must be pretty expensive though."

"Not bad—fifty skins apiece for the whole deal—food extra. There are five of us going altogether."

"That would be just great," he said longingly. "I'd been hoping to get a chance to get away this year, but it doesn't look like I'll be able to make it even for birds. Monica's going to be pretty tied up during the regular season this year—her drama group and all—so I'll have to manage the house." He hesitated a moment. "I imagine your plans and arrangements are all made."

"No. We're pretty fluid."

"You know, I've been working pretty hard for the last few years— getting my degree and then getting the house here and setting everything up just the way Monica and I want it. I haven't had much of a chance to really take a look at myself—you know, stop and really see where I am."

"That happens to all of us now and then, Stan," I said.

"Something like this, you know—getting away for a while, going way back up into the mountains away from all the rush and pressure. It would give a man a chance to really think things through."

"That's why I'm going," I said seriously. I lit another cigarette. "I'm at loose ends—kind of in between the Army and school. It's a good time to do some thinking."

"That's it exactly," he said. "And the hunting is something just thrown in extra really. It's the getting away from things that counts— oh, not Monica, of course—but the other things, the pressure and all."

"You ever been out for deer?" I asked him, trying to cover it over a little so I wouldn't have to see the naked trapped look in his eyes.

"Just once," he said, "a few years ago. It was just absolutely great, even though I didn't even see any. I certainly envy you, Dan."

"You could probably come along, if you feel like it," I said. I think I really threw it out to see if he'd bite at it. I didn't really expect him to go for it.

"Oh, I couldn't do that," he said. "I'm sure the others wouldn't want a stranger horning in." But he was hooked. Suddenly I wanted to do him a favor. Stan and I might not have agreed about much, but I figured he deserved a better break than he'd gotten. Maybe if he got away from her for a while he could get his balance again.

"I doubt if these guys would give a damn about that. It's just a bunch my brother knows, and we just decided to take off and go."

"I'm sure I couldn't get away at the school!"—he paused thoughtfully—"although I *have* got some sick leave accumulated, and in a way it would be for health reasons, wouldn't you say?"

"You're doing the talking." I laughed.

He sat back, smiling sheepishly. "I guess I do sound like I'm trying to talk myself into something," he said.

"I don't think the deal with our guide is really very firm yet," I told him, "and it could just be that another guy would help swing it. I'll talk with the others and see what they say, if you want me to."

"Well," he started, "don't make it too definite. I'll have to give it some thought and talk it over with Monica—not that I have to—" He left it hanging, but I understood. He went on quickly. "Well, we *do* kind of like to talk things over. We make better decisions as a team. We feel that marriages work better that way, don't you agree?"

"Makes sense," I said. "I'll sound out the other guys and let you know."

"I'd appreciate it," he said. "But mind, nothing definite yet."

"Sure, Stan," I said. "I understand."

We kicked it around for another hour or so before I finally made an excuse to get away. Stan was all right, but the house was so damned neat it gave me the creeps. I guess I'm just a natural-born slob.

7

On Friday morning I went up to Seattle and picked up my stuff from the place where I'd had it stored. I kind of putzed around a little but I couldn't find anybody I knew, so I drove on back to Tacoma.

I spent most of the afternoon unpacking the stuff. I wound up with books all over the place. After I got it all squared away, it dawned on me that I was just going to have to pack it all up again anyway in a little while, but what the hell? I like having my books and things out where I can lay my hands on them. It was a little crowded though. My stereo alone took up a sizable chunk of the living room.

That evening I went across town to the "art movie" theater to catch an Italian flick I'd been wanting to see for three or four years.

"I don't see why you want to see that silly thing anyway," Jack said when I asked him if he wanted to go along. "I know a guy who seen it Tuesday. He said it was a real loser. Nothin' happens at all."

"Maybe he just looked too fast," I said. "You want to come along or not?"

"Naw, I don't think so, Dan," he said. "I really don't get much out of foreign movies."

"Just thought I'd ask," I told him. It kind of bugs me when somebody puts something down that I'm really enthusiastic about. Probably everybody's the same way really.

The "art theater" was like all the others I've been to—a grubby, rattletrappy, converted neighborhood showhouse with maybe a hundred and fifty uncomfortable seats. The lobby was painted a nauseating shade—something like a cross between pea-soup green and antique egg-yolk yellow—and the walls were cluttered with poster art and smeary abstracts. The popcorn counter had been replaced by card tables covered with paper cups full of synthetic espresso.

The movie itself was preceded by a couple of incomprehensible short subjects, an artsy cartoon, and about two years' worth of coming attractions. Then there was the intermission, and everybody went out to gag down some of that rotten coffee and stand around making polite conversation.

I choked on a mouthful of the lukewarm ink and drifted over to lean against the wall and watch the animals.

Across the lobby I spotted Stan Larkin and Monica, she looking very bright and very chic and he hovering over her like a man with a brand-new car he's afraid someone's going to scratch. They chatted back and forth with bright, cultured expressions on their faces, drawing a fairly obvious wall around themselves, keeping the college kids and the freaks who thought all foreign movies were dirty at arm's length. With that attitude, it was pretty unlikely that either of them would notice me, but I turned my head away from them anyway. A little bit of Monica went a long way.

When I turned my head, I caught a familiar face. Where in hell had I seen that little girl before? I was sure I didn't know any of the local college kids, and with the straight hair, bare feet, granny glasses, jeans, and sweatshirt, she had to be a college girl.

Then Joan came out of the women's john, and I snapped to it. It was Clydine, the little Pacific Avenue pamphleteer I'd met on my first night back in Tacoma. It was an impulse, but I needed some protective covering in case Stan spotted me. I pushed my way through toward them.

"Clydine!" I said in simulated surprise. "Joan! How *are* you girls anyway?"

They looked at me blankly for an instant, not having the faintest notion who I was. "Uh—just fine," Clydine said, covering up beautifully. "We haven't seen you in—" She left it hanging, hoping I'd give her a clue. Joan was still looking at me doubtfully, her eyes flickering to my haircut. While it wasn't exactly GI, it was still too short to put me in their crowd.

"Let's see," I said, "it must have been just before I got sent to Leavenworth."

Their eyes bulged slightly.

"I'll bet you didn't even recognize me with this haircut and without my beard," I said, "but they keep you clipped pretty short in the Big House." It was a little thick, but they bought it.

"How long have you been—out?" Joan asked sympathetically, the suspicion fading from her face.

"About a week now."

"Was it—I mean—well—" Clydine's eyes were brimming, and her hand had moved to touch my arm comfortingly. I was a martyr to the cause. She wasn't sure exactly what cause yet, but whatever it was, she was with me all the way. Some girls are like that.

I carefully arranged my face into what I hoped was an expression of suffering nobility. "Anything," I said in a voice thick with emotion, "anything is better than participating in an immoral war." That ought to narrow it down for them.

Clydine embraced me impulsively. For a moment I thought she was going to plant ceremonial kisses on each of my cheeks. As soon as Clydine let go, Joan gave me a quick squeeze. I began to feel a little shitty about it. The kids were pretty obviously sincere about the whole thing.

"Come on, girls," I said, trying to cool it a little. In about a minute one of them would have made a speech. "It wasn't really that bad. It's gonna take a whole lot more than a year and a half in a federal joint to get old Dan down." I thought I'd better give them a name to hang on me.

The lobby lights blinked twice, letting us know that the projectionist was ready if we were. I was about to ease away gracefully.

"We'd better go find our seats," Clydine said, glomming onto my arm like grim death. Joan caught the other one, and I was led down the aisle like a reluctant bridegroom.

I'd overplayed it, and now I was stuck with them. All I'd really wanted was someone to hold Stan off with, but they weren't about to let a bona fide hero of the revolution get away. I was hauled bodily into the midst of a gaggle of college types and plunked down into a seat between Joan and Clydine. I could hear a ripple of whispers circling out from where I sat, and I slouched lower in my seat, wishing the floor would open under me.

The movie was good—not as good as I'd expected, but then they never really are—and I enjoyed it despite the need to keep up my little masquerade.

After it was over, one hairy young cat suggested we all go up to his pad and blow some grass. I saw an easy out for myself. I took Clydine aside out in the lobby.

"Uh—look, Clydine," I said in a slightly embarrassed undertone, "I don't want to crimp the party, but my parole officer and the local office of the FBI are staying awfully close to me. They're just waiting for the chance to bust me back into the big joint, and if they caught me at a pot party, well—I'll just split out and—"

Her eyes flashed indignantly. She had gorgeous eyes, very large. "Stay right here," she ordered me. "Don't you dare move." She circled off through the crowd with her long dark hair streaming out behind her, and her little fanny twitching interestingly in her tight jeans. She was back in about a minute and a half.

"It's all fixed, Danny," she told me. "We're all going to the Blue Goose for beer instead." She grabbed my arm again. I felt Joan move in on the other side. Trapped.

The Blue Goose was a beer joint near the campus, and by the time we got there the place was packed to the rafters. Word had leaked out.

Clydine and Joan brought me in like the head of John the Baptist. All they needed was a plate—and maybe an ax.

"Danny," Clydine said in an undertone, "I hate to say this, but I've forgotten your last name, and if I'm going to introduce you—"

"No last names," I muttered to her quickly. "The FBI—" I left it hanging again.

Her eyes narrowed, and she nodded conspiratorially. "I understand," she said, "leave everything to me."

"I won't be able to stay long," I said. "I think I've shaken off my tail but—"

The rest of the evening was like something out of a very bad spy movie or one of those Russian novels of the late nineteenth century. I said as little as possible, concentrating on drinking the beer that everybody in the place seemed intent on buying for me.

A number of girls insisted on kissing me soundly, if indiscriminately, about the head. Even one guy with a beard slipped up behind me and planted one on my cheek. He called it the "kiss of brotherhood," but if he carries on like that with his brothers, his family has serious problems. Still, it *was* the first time I'd ever been kissed by anybody with a beard. I can't really say that I recommend it, all things considered.

After a couple of hours I was getting a little bent out of shape from all the beer. Most of the time the place was deadly quiet. Everybody just sat there, waching me guzzle down the suds. Now I know how the girl feels who provides the entertainment at stag parties.

Most of the conversation consisted of half-spoken questions and cryptic answers, followed by long intervals of silence while they digested the information. "Was it—?" one young guy with a mustache asked.

"Yeah," I said, "pretty much."

They thought about that.

"Is there any kind of—well, you know—among the resisters, I mean?" another one asked.

"I don't think I should—well—the guys still inside—you know."

They kicked that around for a while.

"Do the other inmates—?"

"Some do. Some don't."

That shook them.

"Do you think a guy really ought to—? Instead of—well, you know."

"That's something everybody's got to decide for himself," I said. I could say that with a straight face, because I really believed it. "When the time comes, *you're* the one with your head in the meat grinder. After all the speeches and slogans—from all possible sides—you're still the one who has to decide which button you're going to push because it's *your* head that's going to get turned into hamburger."

That really got to them.

"I'd better split now," I said, lurching to my feet. I walked heavily toward the door, feeling just a little like James Bond—or maybe Lenin—or just possibly like Baron Munchausen. I turned at the doorway and gave them the peace sign—they'd earned it. Look at all the beer they'd bought me.

"Keep the faith," I said in a choked-up voice. Then I went on out.

The patter of little bare feet behind me told me that I hadn't really escaped after all.

"You'd better go on back to your friends, Clydine," I said, not bothering to look around.

Glom! She had me by the arm again. She pulled me to a halt beside my car.

"Danny," she said, looking up at me. "I think you're just the most—well—" She climbed up my arm hand over hand and pulled my face down to hers.

Despite some bad experiences, I'm not a woman-hater. On the whole, I think the idea of two sexes is way out front of any possible alternatives. I responded to Clydine's kiss with a certain enthusiasm.

After a while she pulled her face clear and looked at me, her big eyes two pools of compassion behind those gogglelike granny glasses.

"How long has it been, Danny?" she whispered.

As a matter of fact it *had* been a little better than a month.

"Too long," I said brokenly, "too long."

She let go of me, opened the door of my car, and got in.

"Will there be any problem at the place where you live?" she asked matter-of-factly.

"No," I told her, starting the car.

We drove across town to the trailer park in silence. Clydine nestled against my shoulder. In spite of the shabby clothes which she wore as a sort of uniform, she smelled clean. That's a pretty common misconception about girls like Clydine. I've never met one yet who wasn't pretty clean most of the time.

As a matter of fact, the first thing she did when we got to my trailer was go to into the bathroom and wash her bare feet.

"I wouldn't want to get your sheets all filthy," she said. She stopped suddenly, her hand flying to her mouth. Silently she mouthed the words "Is this place bugged?" at me. Too many movies.

Motioning her to silence, I picked up my FM transistor from the coffee table and stuffed the earplug into the side of my head. I turned it on, picking up a fairly good Beethoven piano sonata—which she, of course, couldn't hear. I made a pretense of checking out the trailer.

"It's clean," I told her, switching it off.

"How does that—"

"It's a little modification," I said. "An old con in the joint showed me how. You get anywhere near a microphone with it and you pick up a feedback—you know, a high-pitched whistle." I jerked the plug and switched the piano sonata back on. "And that'll blank out any directional mike from outside." I moved carefully to all the windows, looking out and then pulling the drapes. Then I locked the door. I go to movies, too.

"We're all secure now," I said.

"Do you want to talk about it?" she asked.

I shook my head.

"I understand, Danny. Maybe after."

I wished to hell she wouldn't be so cold-blooded about it.

"You want a drink?" I asked. I always get nervous. I always have.

"Well, maybe a little one."

I mixed us a couple, hitting hers a little hard with bourbon. I didn't want her to get away.

We sat on the couch drinking silently. I just sipped at mine. I didn't want to booze myself out of action.

She took off the granny glasses and laid them on the table. Without the damned things, she had a cute little face. She was one of those short, perky little girls who used to get elected cheerleaders before all this other stuff came along. Then, without so much as turning a hair, she shucked off the sweatshirt. She wasn't wearing a bra.

My faint worry about the booze turned out to be pretty irrelevant.

She stood up, her frontage coming to attention like two pink little soldiers. "Let's go to bed now, shall we?" she said and walked on back down the narrow hallway to the bedroom.

I put down my drink and turned out the lamp in the living room.

"Don't forget to bring in the transistor," she reminded me.

I picked it up and went on back.

She had finished undressing, and she was lying on the bed. My hands began to shake. She had a crazy build on her—real wall-to-wall girl. I started to take off my shirt.

"Do you have to leave it on that station?" she asked, pointing at the transistor. "I mean is that the only frequency that—"

"That's the one," I said. "I'd have to take it all apart to—"

"It's OK," she said. "It's just that I've never done it with that kind of music on before. Groups most of the time or folk rock—never Beethoven."

At least she recognized it.

I was having a helluva time with my shirt.

"Here," she said, sitting up, "let me." She pushed my hands out of the way and finished unbuttoning my shirt. "Do you like having the light on?"

"It's a little bright, isn't it?" I asked, squinting at it.

"Some men do, that's all—that's why I asked."

"Oh."

"Do you like to be on top, or do you want me to—"

I reached down and gently lifted her chin. "Clydine, love, it's not just exactly as if we were about to run a quarterback sneak off-tackle. We don't have to get it all planned out in the huddle, do we? Let's just improvise, make it up as we go along."

She smiled up at me, almost shyly. "I just want it to be good for you, is all," she said softly.

"Quit worrying about it," I told her. I sat down on the bed and reached for her. "One thing though," I said, cupping one of the little pink soldiers.

"What's that?" she asked, nuzzling my neck.

"How in the hell did you ever get a name like Clydine?"

She told me, but I promised never to tell anybody else.

8

"What's this doing here?" Clydine was standing over me the next morning, stark naked, with my Army blouse clutched in her little fist. She shook it at me. "What's this doing here?" she demanded again.

"You're wrinkling it," I said. "Don't wrinkle it."

"You're a GI, aren't you?" she said, her voice shaking with fury. "A no-good, lousy, son-of-a-bitching, mother-fucking GI!"

"Clydine!" I was actually shocked. I'd never heard a girl use that kind of language before.

"You bastard!"

"Calm down," I told her, sitting up in bed.

"Motherfucker!"

"Clydine, please don't use that kind of language. It sounds very ugly coming from a girl your age."

"Motherfucker, motherfucker, motherfucker!" she yelled,

stamping her foot. Then she threw the blouse on the floor and collapsed on the bed, sobbing bitterly.

I got up, hung the blouse back up in the closet, and padded barefoot on out to the kitchen. I got myself a beer. I had a bit of a headache. Then I went on back to the bedroom. She was still crying.

"Are you about through?" I asked her.

"Son-of-a-bitching motherfucker!" she said, her voice muffled.

"I'm getting a little tired of that," I told her.

"Bite my ass!"

I reached over and got a good grip on her arm so she couldn't get a swing at me, then I leaned down and bit her on the fanny, hard.

"Dan! Stop that! Ouch, goddammit! Stop that!"

I let go. I'd left a pretty good set of teethmarks on her can. "Any more suggestions?" I asked her.

"Of all the—" She rubbed at her bottom tenderly. "Goddammit, that *hurt*!"

"It was *your* idea," I said, taking a pull at the beer bottle.

"Can I have some?" she asked me after a minute or so. She sounded like a little girl.

"If you promise not to throw it at me."

"I'll be good."

I gave her the bottle, and she took a drink. "Oh, Danny, how *could* you? All that beautiful story about letting them put you in prison for a principle. It was all a *lie*, wasn't it?"

"Are you ready to listen now?"

"I *believed* in you, Danny."

"You want to hear this?"

"I really *believed* in you."

I got up and walked on out to the living room.

After a minute she came padding out, still rubbing at her bare fanny. Her little soldiers were still at attention. She was just as cute as hell.

"All right. Let's hear it," she said.

"First off," I said, plunking myself on the couch. "I'm not a GI—not anymore anyway."

"You've *deserted*!" she squealed, sitting down beside me.

"No, dear. I was discharged—honorably."

"You mean you didn't even—"

"Hush," I said, "I was drafted. I thought it all over, and I went ahead and went in. I spent eighteen months in Germany."

"*Germany!*"

I kissed her—hard. Our teeth clacked together. "Now I'm going to do that every time you interrupt me," I told her.

"But—"

I did it again. It was kind of fun.

"I did *not* run off to Canada. I did *not* go to Leavenworth. I did *not* go to Nam. I didn't kill anybody. I didn't help anybody kill anybody. I drank a lot of German beer. I looked at a lot of castles and museums. Then I came home.''

"But how—''

I kissed her again.

"Not so hard—'' she said, her fingertips touching her mouth tenderly.

"All right. Now, on my first night back from the land of Wiener schnitzels, you and Joan braced me down on Pacific Avenue with a fistful of pamphlets—we chatted a minute or two. That's how I came to know your names.''

She looked at me, her eyes widening suddenly.

"At the theater last night,'' I went on, "there were some people I didn't want to talk to, so when I saw you and Joan, I just moved in on you with the first silly-ass story that came into my head. After that, things just got out of hand. I *did* try to get away several times. You'll have to admit that.''

"Can I talk?'' she asked.

"Go ahead,'' I told her. "End of explanation.''

"Once we got away from the others—I mean, once we got here, why didn't you tell me?''

"Because, little one, you are an extremely good-looking, well-constructed, female-type person. You are also, and I hope you'll forgive my saying this, just a wee bit hooked on things political. I wasn't about to take a chance on losing the old ballgame just for the sake of clearing up a few minor misconceptions. I'm probably as honest as the next guy, but I'm not a nut about it.''

"Danny?''

"Yes?''

"Do you really think I'm—what you said—good-looking?''

I laughed and gathered her into my arms. I kissed her vigorously about the head and neck. "You're a doll,'' I told her.

Later, back in bed, she nudged me with her elbow.

"Hmmm?''

"Danny, if you ever tell Joan that you haven't been in prison, I'll *kill* you. I'll just *kill* you.''

"Watch that, my little nasturtium of nonviolence. That kind of talk could get you chucked out of the Peace Movement right on your pretty, pink patootie.''

"Piss on the Peace Movement!'' she said bluntly. "This is serious. Don't ever *dare* tell Joan. I'd be the laughingstock of the whole campus. Do you know that I turned down a date with the *captain* of the football team because I thought he was politically immature? I've got a reputation to maintain on campus, so you keep your goddamn mouth shut!''

I howled with laughter. "We've got to do something about your vocabulary,'' I told her.

"To hell with my vocabulary! Now I want you to promise."

"All right, all right. Put the gun away. My lips are sealed. Whenever I'm around Joan I'll be an ex-con. I'll flout my prison record in everybody's face. But it's gonna cost you, kid."

"Well, it's the *only* way I'll be able to hold up my head," she explained.

After I drove her back to the campus and made a date for that night, I went on downtown to buy myself some clothes. A lot of my old things that I'd picked up the day before were too tight now—and probably a little out of date, though I really didn't much give a damn about that. I didn't want to go overboard on clothes, but I did need a few things.

I had a fair amount of cash, the four hundred from the poker game, three hundred in mustering-out pay, and I'd religiously saved twenty-five a month while I was in the Army—about six hundred dollars there when I got out. I had maybe thirteen hundred altogether. The car and the rent and my share of the hunt and some walking-around money took me down to under a grand, but I figured I was still OK.

It was kind of nice to go into the stores and try on the new-smelling clothes. I got a couple pair of slacks and a sport jacket, some shirts and ties and a couple pair of shoes—nothing really fancy.

About one o'clock, I bagged on back out to the Avenue and dropped into Sloane's pawnshop. Sloane had a lot of new stuff in it as well as the usual sad, secondhand junk. I thought I could see the influence of Claudia there. I kind of halfway hoped she'd be there so I could see her again.

"Hey, Dan," Sloane said, "be right with you." He turned back to the skinny, horse-faced guy he'd been talking to. "I'm sure sorry, friend," he said, "but five dollars is as high as I can go. You saw the window—I've got wristwatches coming out my ears."

"But I ain't tryin' to *sell* it," the man objected with a distinct, whining Southern drawl. "I'd be in here first thing on payday to get it back. I jus' gotta have ten anyway. Y'see, m'car broke down and I had a feller fix it fer me, and now he won't give it back to me 'lessen I give 'im at least part of the money. That's why I just *gotta* have ten for the watch anyway."

"I'm just as sorry as I can be, friend, but I just can't do a thing for you on that watch."

"I noticed the prices you got on them watches in the window," the man said accusingly. "I didn't see no five-dollar watches out there."

Suddenly I remembered another five-dollar watch not too long ago.

"I'm really sorry, friend," Sloane said, "But I just don't think you and I can do business today."

"That there's a semdy-fi'-dollar watch," the man said holding it out at Sloane and shaking it vigorously, "an' all I want is for you to borrow me ten fuckin' dollars on it for about ten measly little ol' days. Now I think that's mighty damn reasonable."

"It could very well be, friend, but I just can't do 'er."

"Well, mister, I'm agonna tell you som'thin'. They's just a whole lotta these here pawnshops in this here little ol' town. I think I'll jus' go out and find me one where they don't try to screw a feller right into the damn ground."

"It's a free country, friend," Sloane said calmly.

"You just ain't about to get no semdy-fi'-dollar watch off'n *me* for no five measly fuckin' dollars. I'll tell you that right now. And I can shore tell you one thing—you ain't gonna get no more o' *my* business. And I'm shore gonna tell all the fellers in my outfit not to give you none o' their business neither. It'll be a cold day in hell when anybody from the Hunnerd-and-Semdy-First Ree-con Platoon comes into *this* stingy little ol' place!"

"I'm sorry you feel that way, friend."

"Sonnabitch!" the man growled and stomped out of the shop.

Sloane looked at me and giggled. "I get sonofabitched and mother-fuckered more than any eight other businessmen on the block," he said. "Stupid damned rebels! If that shit kicker paid more than fifteen for that piece of junk, then he *really* got screwed right into the ground."

"Why didn't you tell him?"

"Doesn't do any good. They'd a helluva lot rather believe that I'm trying to cheat them than that somebody else already has. That way *they're* smart, and *I'm* the one who's stupid."

"That's a GI for you."

"Yeah. He's got all the makings of a thirty-year man. Chip on his shoulder instead of a head. What can I do for you?"

"I thought I'd look over your guns."

"Sure—right over there in the rack behind the counter. Gonna decide which one to take on the hunt, huh?"

"No, I thought I might buy one, if we can get together."

"Well, now. A real cash customer." He hustled on ahead of me to the rack. "Here's a good-looking .270," he said, handing me a well-polished, scope-mounted job.

"Little rich," I said, looking at the price tag.

"I can knock fifteen off that," he said.

"No. Thanks all the same, Cal, but what I've really got in mind is an old Springfield .30-06 military. That's a good cartridge, and I've got a little time to do some backyard gunsmithing."

"Just a minute," he said, scratching his chin. "I think I might have just the thing." He led me back into the storage room and pulled a beat-up-looking rifle down off the top shelf. He looked at the tag attached to the trigger guard and then ripped it off. "I thought so," he said. "It's two weeks past due. That bastard won't be back." He handed me the gun. "I'll let you have that one for thirty-five dollars. It's a real pig the way it sits, but if you want to take a little time to fix it up, you'll have a good weapon."

I took it out into the shop where the light was better and checked the bore. It looked clean, no corrosion. The stock was a mess. Some guy had cut down the military stock and then had painted it with brown enamel. The barrel still had the lathe marks on it. I glanced at the receiver and saw that it had been tapped and drilled for a scope. The bolt and safety had been modified.

"All right," I said, "I'll take it."

Sloane had been following my eyes, and his smile was a little sick. He hadn't noticed the modifications before he'd quoted me the price. I wrote him a check and tucked the gun under my arm. "Pleasure doing business with you, Calvin," I said.

"I think I just got screwed," he said ruefully.

"Win a few, lose a few, Cal baby," I said, patting his cheek. "See you around. Don't take any semdy-fi'-dollar watches."

A man creates a certain amount of stir walking up the street with a rifle under his arm, but I kind of enjoyed it. I put the gun on the floor in the back seat of my car and went on down a couple blocks to the gunsmith's shop. I bought a walnut stock blank, scope mounts, sling-swivels, a sling, a used four-power scope, some do-it-yourself bluing, and a jar of stock finish. Altogether, it cost me another forty dollars. I figured I'd done a good day's business, so I went into a tavern and had a beer.

About an hour or so later the phone rang and the bartender answered it. He looked up and down the bar. "I don't know him," he said, "just a minute." He raised his voice. "Is Dan Alders here?"

It always gives me a cold chill to be paged in a public place—I don't know why. It took me a moment to answer. "Yeah," I said, "that's me."

It was Jack. "You gonna be there a while?" he asked.

"I suppose."

"Sit tight then. I'll be there in about twenty minutes. I got somebody I want you to meet, OK?"

"Sure," I said. "How'd you find me?"

"I called Sloane. He said he could see your car, so I figured you might be at a water hole. I just called all the joints on the Avenue."

"Figures," I said.

"Say," he said, his voice sounding guarded, "didn't you have a tomato over at your pad last night?"

"Yeah."

"Pick her up at that foreign flick?"

"Sure," I said. I thought I'd rub him a little. "There was one there for you, too—a blonde, about five eight, thirty-six, twenty-four, thirty-six, I'd say. I threw her back."

"You son of a bitch!" he moaned. "Don't *waste* 'em, for Chrissake."

"You're the one who doesn't like foreign flicks," I told him.

"Not a word about any other women when I get there with this girl, OK?"

"Sure."

About half an hour later, Jack came in with a tall, very attractive brunette. He waved me over to a booth and ordered a pitcher and three glasses.

"Dan," he said, "this is Sandy. You remember—I told you about her. Sandy, this is my long-lost brother, Dan."

"Hello, Dan," she said quietly, not really looking at me. She seemed frozen, somehow indifferent to everything around her. She concentrated on her cigarette.

"Hey," Jack said, "I hear you broke it off in Sloane."

"He quoted the price," I said a little smugly, "I didn't."

"He claims he could have got fifty bucks for that gun."

"I doubt it," I said. "It's a pretty butchered-up piece."

"What do you want it for if it's such a junker?"

"I'm going to rework it. New stock, dress down the barrel, and so forth, and it should be a pretty fair-looking rifle."

"Sounds like a lot of work to me," he said dubiously.

"I've got lots of time." I shrugged.

We went on talking about guns and the hunt. Sandy didn't say much. I glanced at her from time to time. She seemed withdrawn and seldom looked up. She was quite a nice-looking girl. I wondered how she'd gotten tangled up with a son of a bitch like my brother. Her hair was very dark and quite long—almost as long as Clydine's, but neater. She had long lashes which made her eyes seem huge. She seemed to smoke a helluva lot, I noticed. Other than lighting cigarettes, she hardly moved. There was an odd quality of frozen motion about her—as if she had just stopped. She bugged me. When I looked at her, it was like looking into an empty closet. There wasn't anything there. It was like she was already dead.

"Hey," Jack said, "did you pick up that pistol the other day in Seattle?"

"Yeah, it's over at the trailer."

"You know," he said, "I've been thinking maybe I ought to take along a handgun, too. There *are* bears up there, and you know what Mike was saying."

So we kicked that idea around for a while. We had another pitcher of beer.

Sandy kept smoking, but she still didn't say much.

⚡ 9

I worked—off and on—at the gun all the next week, and by Saturday it was beginning to take shape. I did most of the work over at Mike's since he had a vise and a workbench in his garage. Also, it was a good place to get away from Clydine's three-hour-long telephone calls. I began to wish that classes would start so she'd have something to keep her busy.

I had the shape of the rifle stock pretty well roughed in, and I was working on the metal. I'd filed off the front sight, and now I was taking the lathe marks off the barrel with emery cloth—a very long and tedious job.

Betty was feeling punk, and I was checking in on her now and then to see if she was OK. She had a recurrent kidney problem that had Mike pretty worried. She'd had to spend a week in the hospital with it that spring, and he was afraid it might crop up again.

I was about ready to start polishing on the barrel with fine-grade emery cloth when Betty called me from the back door. I made it in about two seconds flat.

"Are you OK?" I demanded breathlessly.

"Oh, it's not me"—she laughed—"I'm fine."

"Please," I said, "don't do that anymore. I like to had a coronary."

"You've got a phone call."

"Oh, for God's sake! How did she find the number?" I grabbed up the phone. "Now look, you little clothhead, I'm busy. I can't spend all day—"

"Hey." It was Jack. "What's got you so frazzled?"

"Oh. Sorry, Jack, I thought it was that dizzy little broad again. I swear she spends at least six hours a day on the horn. I'm starting to get a cauliflower ear just listening to her."

"Why don't you do something about it?"

"I am," I said, "I'm hiding."

He laughed. "Could you do me a favor?"

"I suppose. What?"

"I'm over here at Sloane's pawnshop sittin' in for him. He said he was going to be back, but he just called and said he was tied up. I've got some stuff at the cleaners on Thirty-eighth Street—you know the place. They close at noon today, and if I don't get that stuff outta there, I'll be shit out of luck until Monday. You think you could make it over there before they close?"

"Yeah, I think so. I'm about due to take a beer break anyway. Will you be at the shop?"

"Yeah, I'll stick around till you get here. Sloane ought to be back before then, but you can't depend on him."

"OK," I said, "I'll crank up and bag on over there—on Thirty-eighth Street?"

"Yeah—you know the place. Right across from that beer joint with the shuffleboard."

"Oh. OK."

"Thanks a lot, buddy. You saved my bacon."

"Sure. See you in a bit."

I made sure that Betty was feeling OK and then took off. My hands were getting a little sore anyway.

The weather had begun to break, and it was one of those cloudy, windy days we get so often in Tacoma. It's the kind of day I really like—cool, dry, windy, with a kind of pale light and no shadows. I made it to the cleaners in plenty of time and then swung over onto South Tacoma Way.

Sloane still hadn't shown up, and Jack was puttering around in the shop. "Thanks a million, Dan," he said when I came in with his cleaning. "How much was it?"

I told him and he paid me.

"How you comin' with that gun?" he asked me.

"I'm about down to the polishing stage on the barrel," I told him. "I've still got to dress off the receiver and trigger guard. A couple more days and I can blue it. Then I'll finish up the stock."

"You get a kick out of that stuff, don't you?"

"It's kind of fun," I said. "Gives me something to do besides drink beer."

"Let me show you the gun I'm takin'," he said.

We went on into the back of the shop. He took a converted military weapon out of one of the cubbyholes.

"Eight-mm German Mauser," he said.

"Good cartridge," I told him. I looked the piece over. Somebody'd done a half-assed job of conversion on it, but it had all the essentials. "It'll do the job for you, Jack."

"Oh, hey, look at this." He reached back into another bin and came out with his hand full of .45 automatic. The damned thing looked like a cannon. He stood there grinning, pointing that monster right at my belly. I don't like having people point guns at me—even as a joke. The goddamn things weren't made to play with. I was still holding the Mauser, but I was being careful with the muzzle.

"Let's see it," I said, holding out my left hand.

He pulled back the hammer with the muzzle still pointed at me. His face got a little funny.

Slowly, with just my right hand, I raised the Mauser until it was pointing at him. I thumbed off the safety. It was like being in a dream.

"All right, Jack," I said softly, "let's count to three and then find out which one of these bastards Sloane forgot to unload."

"Christ, Danny," he said, quickly turning the .45 away from me. "I never thought of that."

I lowered the Mauser and slipped the safety back on. Jack hadn't called me Danny since we were very little kids.

"You ain't mad, are you?" he asked, sounding embarrassed.

"Hell, no." I laughed. Even to me it sounded a little hollow.

We checked both guns. They were empty. Still, I think it all took some of the fun out of Jack's day. We put the guns away and went back out into the pawnshop.

"Where the hell *is* that damned Sloane anyway?" he said to cover the moment.

"Probably visiting Helen What's-her-name," I said. I'd run into Sloane and Helen a few times, and I didn't like her. Maybe it was because of Claudia.

"I wouldn't doubt it a goddamn bit. Say, that reminds me, you want to go on a party?"

"I'm almost *always* available for a party," I said with more enthusiasm than I really felt. I wanted to get past that moment in the back room as badly as he did.

"It's Sloane's idea really. That's why I kind of wanted to wait for him to show up, but piss on him. He owns this house out in Milton that he rents out—furnished. The people who were livin' there just moved out, and the new people aren't due in until the first of the month—Wednesday."

"What's all this real estate business got to do with a party?" I asked.

"I'm gettin' to it. Anyway, the place needs cleanin'—you know, sweep, mop, vacuum, mow the lawn—that sort of shit."

"*That's* your idea of a party?"

"Keep your pants on. Now, Sloane'll provide the beer and the booze and some steaks and other stuff."

"And brooms, and mops, and lawnmowers, too, I hope," I said.

"All right, smart ass. Here's where the party comes in. We each bring a tomato—Sloane'll bring Helen, I'll bring Sandy, and you can bring What's-her-name. We'll bag on over there tomorrow afternoon about four, hit the place a lick or two—the girls can get the inside, and we'll do the outside—and then it's party-time. Give me and Sloane a perfect excuse to get away from the wives."

I shrugged. "I'm not sure Clydine would go for the domestic scene," I said. "That's not exactly her bag."

"Ask her," Jack said. "I bet she goes for it. Where else can you stir up a party on Sunday afternoon?"

"I'll ask her," I said. It was easier than arguing with him. "But I'm not making any promises."

"I'll bet she goes for it," he said.

"We'll see."

We batted it around for about half an hour, and then Sloane called. He was still tied up. Jack grumbled a bit but promised to hang on. I wanted to swing on by the trailer court to check my mail, and he asked me to drop the cleaning off at his trailer so Marg could hang it up before it got wrinkled. I took his clothes on out to my car again and drove on up the Avenue toward the court.

That whole business with the guns had been just spooky as hell. *"Maybe someday I'll just decide that you're no good, and I'll take my gun and shoot you. Bang! just like that, and you'll be dead, and I'll betcha you wouldn't like that at all."* When had I said that to Jack? Somewhere back in the long, shabby morning of our childhood. The words came echoing down to me, along with a picture of a dog rolling over and over in the snow. I tried to shrug it off.

I saw McKlearey's car in the lot at the Green Lantern Tavern about two blocks from the court, and I decided that if he was still there when I came back, I'd haul in and buy him a beer. If we were going to go hunting together, I was going to have to make some kind of effort to get along with him. I still didn't much like him though.

When I drove past Jack's trailer, I saw the two little girls out in their play-yard, and I waved at them. I parked at my place and checked the mail—nothing, as usual. Then I slung Jack's cleaning over my shoulder and hiked on up to his trailer. Maybe I could promote some lunch out of Marg if she didn't have a whole trailerful of gossiping neighbors the way she usually did.

As I came up to the trailer, I glanced through the front window. I saw that mirror back in the hallway I'd noticed the first time I'd visited. I'd meant to tell Jack about it, but I'd forgotten. The angle from where I was standing gave me a view of part of the bedroom. I had visions of Margaret unveiling her monumental breasts to the scrutiny of casual passersby. I straightened up and craned my neck to see just how much of the bedroom you could really see.

Margaret was on the bed with McKlearey. They were both bare-ass naked, and their hands were awfully busy.

I have my faults, God knows, but being a Peeping Tom is not one of them. I think I was actually frozen to the spot. You hear about that, and I've always thought it was pure nonsense, but I honestly couldn't move. Even as I watched, Lou raised up over her and came down between her widely spread thighs. Her huge, dark nippled breasts began to bob rhythmically in a kind of counterpoint to Lou's bouncing, hairy buttocks. Her head rolled back and forth, her face contorted into that expression that is not beautiful unless you are the one who is causing it. I don't think I'd ever fully realized how ugly the mating of humans can look to someone who isn't involved in it. Even dogs manage to bring it off with more dignity.

I turned around and walked on back to my trailer, suppressing a strong urge to vomit. I went inside and closed the door. I laid Jack's clothes carefully on the couch, went to the kitchen and poured myself a stiff blast of whiskey. Then, holding the glass in my hand, I took a good belt out of the bottle. I put the bottle down and drank from the glass. It didn't even burn going down.

The phone rang. It was Clydine.

"I've been trying to get you all morning," she said accusingly. "Where have you been?"

"I was busy," I said shortly.

She started to tell me about some article she'd just read in some New Left journal she was always talking about. I grunted in appropriate places, leaning over the sink to watch Jack's trailer out of the kitchen window. Even from here, I could see the whole damn thing rocking. I'll bet you could walk through any trailer court in town and tell who was going at it at any given moment. Old Lou had staying power though—I had to admit that.

"Are you listening to me?" Clydine demanded.

"Sure, kid," I said. "I was just thinking."

"About what?"

"We've been invited to a party."

"What kind of a party?"

"Probably a sex orgy," I told her bluntly. "My brother and another guy and their girlfriends—it's in a house."

"I thought your brother was married."

"So's the other guy," I said. I told her the details.

"No swapping?" It sounded like a question—or maybe an ultimatum, I don't know.

"I doubt it. I've met the girls—one of them would probably dig that sort of stuff, but I'm pretty sure the other one wouldn't. You want to go?"

"Why not? I've never been to an orgy."

"Come on, Clydine," I said. "It's like being spit on. They're not inviting you to meet their *wives*—just their mistresses."

"So? I'm *your* mistress, aren't I? Temporarily at least."

"It's different. I'm not married."

"Danny, honestly. Sometimes you can be the squarest guy in the world. I think I might get a kick out of it. Maybe I can catch some of the vibrations from their sneaky, guilty, sordid, little affairs."

"You're a nut, do you know that? This thing tomorrow has all the makings of a sight-seeing trip through a sewer."

"Boy, you're sure in a foul humor," she said. "What's got you bum-tripped now?"

"My brother pulled a gun on me."

"He *what*?"

"Just a bad joke. Forget it. Are you sure you want to go on this thing tomorrow?"

"Why not?"

"That may just be the world's *stupidest* reason for doing anything," I told her. "Hey, let's go to a drive-in movie tonight."

"What the hell for?"

"I want to neck," I said. "No hanky-panky. I just want to sit in the car and eat popcorn and drink root beer and neck—like we were both maybe sixteen or something."

"*That's* a switch. Well, why not?—I mean, sure." She paused, then said rather tentatively, "you want me to get all gussied up—like it was a real—well—*date* or something?" She sounded embarrassed to say the word.

"Yeah, why don't you do that? Wear a dress. I'll even put on a tie."

"Far out," she said.

"And wear your contacts. Leave those hideous goggles at home."

"Are you sure we aren't going to—well—I mean, I wouldn't want to lose my contacts." I'd asked her before why she didn't wear contact lenses. She told me she had them but didn't wear them because they popped out when she made love. "I don't know why," she'd said, "they just pop out." I'd laughed for ten minutes, and she'd gotten mad at me.

"They're perfectly safe," I said. "Hang up now so I can call my brother and tell him you want to go to his little clambake tomorrow."

"Bye now." She hung up, then she called right back.

"What time tonight?"

I told her.

I opened myself a beer and sat down at the kitchen table. What in the hell was I mixed up in anyhow? This whole damned situation had all the makings of a real messy blow-up. Christ Almighty, you needed a damned scoreboard just to keep track of who was screwing who— whom. When they all caught up with each other, it could wind up like World War III with bells on it, and I was going out in the woods with these guys—every one of them armed to the teeth. Shit O'Deare!

I didn't belong in this crowd. But then I didn't belong with a guy like Stan either, with the chic little gatherings and the little drama groups. Nor probably with my little Bolshevik sweetheart with her posters and pamphlets and free love. Nor with the phony artsy crowd with the paste-on beards and the Latvian folk-music records. Maybe for guys like me there just aren't any people to really be with. Maybe if they were really honest, everybody would admit the same—that all this buddy-buddy crap or "interaction" shit was just a dodge to cover up the fact that they're all absolutely alone. Maybe nobody's got anybody, and maybe that's what we're all trying to hide from. Now there's an ugly little possibility to face up to in the middle of a cool day in August.

Finally Lou left. I waited a while longer and then took the cleaning up to Jack's trailer. Marg pulled a real bland face. She'd be a tiger in a poker game. We talked a few minutes, and then I drove back over to Mike's place and went back to work on the rifle. At least that was something I could get my hands on.

10

I picked up Clydine about three thirty the next afternoon, and we drove on out to Milton for the combination GI-party-sex-orgy Sloane had cooked up. I was still a little soured on the whole thing, but Clydine seemed to think it would be a kind of campy gas to watch a couple of Establishment types and what she persisted in calling "their sordid little affairs."

"You're beginning to sound like T. S. Eliot," I told her.

She ignored that.

"What kind of a cat is your brother?" she asked me. "Is he anything like you?"

"Jack? Hell no," I snorted. "He's a couple years older than I am. He was in trouble a lot when he was a kid. Then six years in the Navy right after high school. Married three times. Works in a trailer lot—part-time sales and general flunky. Drinks beer most of the time because he can't afford whiskey. Chases women. Screws a lot. He can charm the birds right out of the trees when he wants to. Something of an egomaniac. I guess that covers it."

"Typical Hard Hat, huh?" she said grimly.

"Look, my little daffodil of the downtrodden, one of the things you'll learn as you grow older is that group labels don't work. You say Hard Hat, and you get a certain picture. Then you close your mind. But you scream bloody murder when some fortyish guy in a suit looks at you and says 'Hippie' and then closes *his* mind. These goddamn labels and slogans are just a cop-out for people who are too lazy to think or don't have the equipment. Your labels won't work on my brother. He's completely nonpolitical."

"You know," she said quietly, "I wouldn't take that from anybody but you. I think it's because I know you don't care. Sometimes it gives me goose bumps all over—how much you don't care."

"Come on," I said, "don't get dramatic about it. I'm just at loose ends right now, that's all."

"You'd make a terrific revolutionary," she said. "With that attitude of yours, you could do anything. But that's inconsistent, isn't it? To be a revolutionary, you'd have to care about something. Oh, dear." She sighed mightily.

I laughed at her. Sometimes she could be almost adorable.

"I'm *serious,*" she said. "What about the other guys?"

"Sloane? A hustler, *Petit-bourgeois* type."

"That's a label, too, isn't it?" she demanded.

"Now you're learning. Calvin Sloane is a very complex person. He was probably fat, unloved, and poor as a child. He went right to the root of things—money. He's a pawnbroker, a used-car dealer, a part-owner of several taverns, and God knows what else. Anything that'll turn a buck. He's got it made. He uses his money the way a pretty girl uses her body. As long as Sloane's buying, everything's OK. Maybe he's accepted the fact that nobody's really going to like him unless he pays them for it. He can't accept honest, free friendship or affection—not even from his wife. That's why he takes up with these floozies. They're bought and paid for. He understands them. He can't really accept any other kind of relationship. Don't ever tell him this, but I like him anyway—in spite of his money."

"You sure make it hard to hate the enemy," she said.

"Walt Kelly once said, 'We have met the enemy, and he is us.' "

"Who's Walt Kelly?"

"The guy who draws *Pogo*."

"Oh, I prefer *Peanuts*."

"That's because you're politically immature," I told her.

She socked me on the shoulder. I think our popcorn-root-beer-drive-in-movie date the night before had caused us both to revert to adolescence. She'd been almost breathtaking in a skirt, sweater, and ponytail, and without those damned glasses but I'd stuck to my guns—we'd only necked. Both of us had gone home so worked-up we'd been about ready to climb the walls. She'd made some pretty pointed threats about what she was going to do to me at the orgy.

"What about the women?" she asked. "The concubines?"

"Helen—that Sloane's trollop—is a pig. She's got a mind like a sewer and a mouth to match. Even in the circles she moves in, she's considered stupid since she does all of her thinking, I'm told, between her legs. Her husband's in the Air Force, and he's maniacally jealous, but she cheats on him anyway. I think she cheats just for the sake of cheating. I've about halfway got a hunch that this little blowout today was her idea. She likes her sex down and dirty, and probably she's been thrilled by orgies in some of the pornography she's always reading—undoubtedly moving her lips while she does—and she figures diddling in groups has just got to be dirtier than doing it in pairs. Maybe she figures to get a bunch-punch out of the deal."

"Bunch-punch?"

"Multiple intercourse—gang-bang."

"Oh. What about the other one?"

"Sandy? You got me, kid. She's good-looking, but she never says anything. You think *I'm* cool? She's so cool, she's just barely alive—or just recently dead, I haven't decided which. If you can figure her out, let me know."

We drove on across the Puyallup River bridge and on out toward Fife and Milton.

The house Sloane had out in Milton was a little surprising. I'd half-expected one of those run-down rabbit hutches that are described euphemistically as "rental properties"—not good enough to live in yourself, but good enough to house former sharecroppers or ex-galley-slaves—always provided that they can come up with the hundred and a quarter a month.

Sloane's house, on the other hand, was damned nice. It was an older frame place with one of those deep porches all across the front, and it nestled up to its eaves in big, old shrubbery. There was about a half acre of lawn in front and probably more in back. A long driveway went up to the house and along one side of it to the garage behind the house. On the other side of the driveway was a garden plot that had pretty much gone to weeds.

I ran my car on up the driveway and pulled up just behind Sloane's Cadillac.

"Nice place," Clydine said, looking out at the white-picket-fence-enclosed backyard.

"Well, well, well," Jack said, bustling out of the house with a bottle of beer in his hand. "What have we here?"

Clydine and I got out of the car.

"My"—Jack grinned, coming through the gate—"she's a *little* one, isn't she?" He was giving her the full benefit of the dazzling Jack Alders' smile, guaranteed to melt glaciers and peel paint at a hundred yards.

"Jack," I said, "this is Clydine."

"*Clydine*? How the hell'd you ever get a name like that, sweetie?"

"I won it in a raffle," she said with a perfectly straight face.

"She won it in a raffle!" Jack chortled with a forced glee. "That's pretty sharp, pretty sharp. Come on in the house, kids. Fuel up." He waved the beer bottle at us and led the way toward the house.

"Far out," Clydine murmured to me.

"Hey, gang," Jack announced as we went in the back door, "you all know my brother Dan, and this is his current steady, *Clydine*. Isn't that a handle for you?" He pointed to each of the others standing around in the kitchen and repeated their names. "Tell you what, sweetie," he said to Clydine, "I'm never gonna be able to manage that name of yours, so I'm just gonna call you *Clyde*." He winked broadly at the rest of us.

She smiled sweetly at him, and then said very pleasantly but very distinctly, "If you do, I'll kick you right square in the balls."

Sloane shrieked with laughter, almost collapsing on the floor. Jack looked stunned but covered it well, laughing a little hollowly with the rest of us. His jaws tightened up some though.

We had a couple of beers, got the girls organized, and then Jack, Sloane, and I went outside to tackle the yardwork.

I fell heir to a scythe and the chore of leveling the jungle that had been a garden. Once I got into it, I discovered that in spite of the weeds, there was a pretty fair amount of salvageable produce there. By the time I got through, I'd laid a couple bushels of assorted vegetables over on the grass strip between the garden and the driveway—radishes, carrots, lettuce, onions, cucumbers, and so forth. I hauled great armloads of weeds and junk back to a brush pile behind the garage. The place looked a lot better when I was done.

I washed off my produce at an outside faucet and put it on the back porch. Then I grabbed another beer and went to see how Jack and Cal were doing. I found them sitting on the front porch, staring down at the half-mowed lawn.

"Takin' a beer break, hey, Dan?" Sloane said.

"No. I finished up."

"No shit?"

They had to come out and inspect the job. Then they looked at my haul on the back porch, and then we went back to the front porch to sit and stare at the lawnmower some more.

Sloane sighed. "Well," he said, "I guess it's my turn in the barrel." He walked heavily down the front stairs and cranked up the mower.

"That tomato of yours has got kind of a smart mouth, hasn't she?" Jack said sourly, lighting a cigarette.

"She just says what she thinks," I told him.

"If she was with me, I'd slap a few manners into her." He was still stinging from the put-down.

"You'd get your balls kicked off, too," I told him. "She meant what she said about that."

"A tough one, huh?" he said. "Where'd you latch onto her anyway?"

"She's the one I met at that Italian movie, remember?"

"Oh, *that* one. You sure got a weird taste in women, is all I can say."

"She's a human being," I said, "not just a stray piece of tail. As long as you treat her like a human being, fine. It's when you come on like she was a cocker spaniel that you run into trouble." I knew there wasn't much point in talking to him about it. He wasn't likely to change.

"I'd still slap some manners into her if it was me," he said.

"I don't hit women much," I said, looking out toward the sunset.

He grunted and went down to spell Sloane on the mower.

Sloane came back up the steps, puffing and sweating like a pig. "Man," he gasped, "am I ever out of shape. I'm gonna have to start jogging or something before we go up into the high country."

"You said a mouthful there, buddy," I said. "We probably all should. Otherwise one of us is going to blow a coronary."

"Hey"—he giggled—"I like that little girl of yours. She's cute as a button, isn't she?"

"She's a boot in the butt," I agreed.

"Boy, did she ever get the drop on old Jack. I thought he was gonna fall right on his ear when she threatened to bust his balls for him."

"I think he's still a little sore about it."

"He isn't used to havin' women react that way to his line."

"She just doesn't buy the glad-hand routine," I said, "and Jack doesn't know any other approach."

"How'd you manage to latch onto her?"

"You'd never believe it," I said.

"Try me."

I told him about it.

"No kidding?" he said, laughing. Then a thought flickered across his face. "Say, she isn't a user, is she? I mean, a lot of those kids are. She hasn't got any stuff with her, has she? I can square the beef if the cops come in here because we're makin' too much noise or something, but if they come in and find her stoned out of her mind on something, that could get a little sticky."

"No," I told him. "No sweat—oh, she blows a little grass now and then, but I've told her that I don't particularly care for the stuff, and I don't get much kick out of talking to people when they're stoned. It's like talking into a wet mop. She stays away from it when she's with me. We've got a deal; I tell all her friends I'm an ex-con, and she stays off the grass when I'm around. What she does on her own time is her business."

"Sounds like you two have quite an arrangement going."

"For the most part, we don't try to tell each other what to do, that's all. We get along pretty good that way."

"There, you lazy bastards!" Jack yelled, killing the lawnmower. "It's all done."

"You do nice work," Sloane said. "Let's go get cleaned up. I brought towels and soap and stuff. I get firsties on the shower."

The girls had finished the inside cleanup and had already bathed and changed clothes. Sloane, Jack, and I all showered and changed while they cooked up the steaks and whipped up a salad out of some of my produce. We all had mixed drinks with dinner and a couple more afterward. Along about sundown things started to loosen up a bit.

"Hey," Helen said, her hard, plastered-on face brightening, "let's play strip poker."

"I didn't bring any cards," Sloane said.

"Oh, darn," she pouted. "How about you, Jack? Dan? Haven't one of you guys maybe got a deck of cards in your car?"

We both shook our heads.

"Maybe the people who lived here—" She jumped to her feet and ran into the kitchen to start rummaging through the various drawers.

"Je-sus *Christ*!" Clydine said, "if she wants to take her clothes off so goddamn bad, why doesn't she just go ahead and take her clothes off?"

Sandy smiled slightly. It was the first time I'd ever seen her do it.

"Come on, you guys," Helen called, "help me look."

"We cleaned out all those drawers this afternoon," Sandy said, her voice seeming very far away.

"Damn it all, anyway," Helen complained, coming back into the living room. She plunked herself back down on the couch beside Sloane, sulking.

The orgy wasn't getting off the ground too well.

"Jeeze," Helen said, "you'd think somebody'd have a deck of cards. Myron *always* has a deck of cards with him. All the sergeants do. They play cards all the time."

"At least when they're playing cards, they're not dropping napalm on little kids," Clydine said acidly.

Helen's eyes narrowed. "I don't know about some people, but I think we ought to back up our servicemen all the way."

"So do I," Clydine said. I blinked at her. What the hell? "I think we ought to back them up as far as Hawaii, at least," she finished.

It took Helen a minute or two to figure that one out.

"I'm *proud* to be the wife of a serviceman," she said finally, not realizing how that remark sounded under the circumstances.

"Let it lay," I muttered to Clydine.

"But—"

"Don't stomp a cripple. It's not sporting."

"Hey," Jack said, moving in quickly to avert a brawl, "I meant to ask you, Cal, are we gonna take pistols with us, too? On the hunt, I mean?"

"Sure," Sloane said. "Why not? If we don't get any deer, we can always sit around and plink beer cans." He giggled.

"You got anything definite out of that other guy yet, Dan?" Jack was pretty obviously dragging things in by the heels to keep Helen and Clydine away from each other's throats. A beef between the women could queer the whole party.

"Carter says the whole deal could hang on him goin'. You better nudge him a little."

"He's gotta make up his own mind," I said. "I can't do it for him."

We kicked that around for a while. We had another drink. I imagine we were all starting to feel them a little, even though we'd been pretty carefully spacing them out. Even Sandy started to get loosened up a bit.

Then we started telling jokes, and they began to get raunchier and raunchier—which isn't unusual, considering what this party was supposed to be. In all of her jokes, Helen kept referring to the male organ as a wiener, which, for some reason, just irritated the hell out of me.

I went on out to the kitchen to get a beer, figuring to back off on the whiskey a little to keep from getting completely pie-eyed. I heard the padding of bare feet behind me. Clydine had her shoes off again.

She caught me at the refrigerator. "*This* is an *orgy*?" she said. "I don't think these people know *how*. They're like a bunch of kids sitting around trying to get up nerve enough to play spin the bottle."

"You want some action?" I leered at her.

"Well, after that popcorn and purity routine last night, I'm pretty well primed. When does something happen?"

"Hey, in there," Helen called, "no sneaking off into dark corners. If you're gonna do something, you gotta do it out here where we can all watch." She giggled coarsely.

"That does it!" Clydine said. She grabbed my arm. "Let's go screw—right in the middle of the goddamn rug!"

"Cool it," I said, "I'll get things moving."

"Well, somebody's going to have to. This is worse than a goddamn Girl Scout camp."

I rummaged around until I found a large glass. Then I got a couple more bottles of beer and went back to the living room.

"I'll bet he was copping a feel." Helen snickered. "How was it, honey?"

I ignored that, but Clydine glowered at her.

"I just remembered a game," I announced. "The Germans play it in the beer halls."

"What kinda game?" Helen demanded a little blearily.

"It's a kind of drinking game," I said, pouring beer into the large glass.

"A *drinking* game," she objected. "That's no goddamn fun. How about a *sex* game?"

"Just hang tough," I said. "The point of this game is that the person who takes the *next* to the last drink out of his glass—not the last one, but the *next* to the last one—has to pay a penalty of some kind."

"What kind of penalty?" Sloane asked.

"Any penalty we decide. Everybody gets to kick him in the butt, or he has to go outside and bay at the moon, or he—or she—has to take off one piece of clothing or—"

"Hey," Helen said, "I like that last one." Somehow I *knew* she would. "That sounds like a swell game."

"That's a pretty big glass," Jack objected.

"That's the point," I explained. "Nobody can just chug-a-lug it down. You can take a big drink or a little one, but remember if the next player finishes it off, you gotta peel off one item of clothing—a sock, your pants, a bra, or whatever."

We haggled a bit about the rules, but finally everybody agreed to them. We all discarded our shoes to get that out of the way. I caught a glimpse of Sandy's face. It seemed completely indifferent. We pulled our seats into a kind of circle and began passing the glass around.

Sloane, of course, polished off the first glass, and Helen, with a great deal of giggling and ostentatious display of leg, peeled off a stocking. I think that mentally she was still at the "You show me yours, and I'll show me mine" stage of development. Then Jack caught Sandy, and she mutely followed Helen's example.

It went several rounds, with Sloane, Jack, and me pretty well able to control it—simply because we could take bigger drinks. I hadn't dropped it on Clydine yet.

"Come on, crumb," she hissed at me. "I'm beginning to feel like a virgin." Helen was down to her panties and bra, and Sandy was in her slip. I'd lost one sock and both Jack and Sloane were down to their slacks and shorts. I was trying not to look at Jack's tattoos.

"How much have you got on under that?" I asked Clydine. She had on a dark jersey and a pair of slacks. No sox.

"Just panties," she said. "I want to beat that dim-witted exhibitionist down to skin." Her competitive spirit was up. It was a silly game, but we were all drunk enough to start taking it a little seriously.

So the next time around, I emptied the glass, Clydine stood up and slowly pulled off the jersey. Her little soldiers snapped to attention. I heard a sharp intake of breath from Jack. Clydine took a deep breath, and Sloane choked a little.

"Come on, come on," Helen snapped, "let's get on with the game. That's not the only set of boobs in the room." What a pig!

Sandy lost her slip, and then Helen's bra went. She thrust her breasts out as far as she could, but they were pretty sorry-looking in comparison to my two little friends. It's a funny thing about nudity. Helen looked vulgar, but Clydine didn't. My little Bolshevik was completely natural about the whole thing. After the first shock wore off, her nude breasts were almost an extension of her face—pretty but not vulgar. Helen's face stopped at her neck with the sharp line where her makeup left off. Below that she was obscene.

I lost my other sock, Jack lost his pants, and Sandy's bra went. There was a sort of simplicity, almost a purity in the way she numbly exposed herself.

"Break-time," Sloane giggled. "My kidneys are awash." He hustled on back to the can with Jack right behind him. Clydine wandered around a little, looking at the furniture, and Helen sat sulking. She was obviously outclassed; Sandy had a great shape, and Clydine, of course, was out of sight.

"It's not much of a game really," I said apologetically to Sandy.

She lit a cigarette, seemingly oblivious of her own nakedness. "It doesn't matter," she said. "It's only for a little while, so it doesn't make any difference." I was suddenly disgusted with myself for having come up with the whole silly idea. Why does a guy do things like that?

"I'm not being nosey," I said, lying in my teeth, "but why do you hang around with Jack anyway? You know there's no future in it for you."

"Oh, Jack's all right," she said. "If it wasn't him, it would just be somebody else. It's only for a little while anyway."

She kept on saying that. Nobody was *that* cool. Maybe it was just a way of keeping things from getting to her.

"I like your little friend," she said, suddenly flashing a quick smile toward Clydine. The smile made her face suddenly come alive, and there was something just under the surface that made me look away.

Sloane and Jack came back, and the rest of us trekked back one at a time to use the facilities.

The game continued in a fairly predictable way, with all the girls winding up totally nude, and Sloane, Jack, and me in just our shorts. Despite some fairly obvious suggestions from Helen about where the final penalty should be paid, each couple retired to a separate bedroom for the last stages of the party.

As I said before, Clydine and I had both gotten pretty well worked-up the preceding night, and we went at each other pretty hot and heavy the first time. The booze, however, took its well-known and pretty obvious toll. I wasn't really making much headway the second time around, just sort of trying to entertain a friend, so to speak.

"It's not working, Danny," she said softly. "We're both too tipsy. Let's talk."

I started to roll over.

"No," she said, locking her legs around me, "just stay there. It's kind of nice, and this way I'm sure I've got your attention."

"Oh, *gosh*, yes," I said, mimicking Carter. "This may add an entirely new dimension to the art of conversation."

"Just relax," she told me. She pulled me down.

"We're not for keeps, Danny," she said after a moment. "You know that, don't you? I'm saying this because I keep having this awful impulse to tell you that I love you."

I started to say something, but she squeezed me sharply with her legs.

"Let me finish," she said, "while I've still got the courage. I know you think it's silly, all this—well—political stuff I'm involved in, but it's awfully important to me. I believe in it. I wish you did, too. Sometimes I just wish you'd believe in *something—anything*, but you don't."

I started to say something again, and she gave her pelvis a vicious little twist that damned near emasculated me.

"I'm going to do that every time you interrupt me," she said. She had a long memory. I don't think I've ever been so completely helpless before or since. She had me—as they say—at her mercy.

"In about a month," she went on, "you're going back up to the U, and I'll be starting to go to class here in a couple of weeks. You're going to be gone for ten days on this hunting expedition of yours. Between now and the first of October—less than ten days—is all we've really got. Am I getting maudlin?"

I didn't dare answer.

"If you've gone to sleep, damn you, I'll cripple you."

"I'm here," I said, "don't get carried away."

"Have I made any sense?" she asked.

"I'm tempted to argue," I said, "but I think you're probably right. If we try to keep it going after I get to Seattle, it'll just die on us anyway, and we'd both feel guilty about it. It's easy to say that it's only thirty miles, but the distance between Seattle and Tacoma is a lot more than that really."

"It's a damned shame," she said. She rocked her hips a few times under me, gently. "When it comes to this, you're just clear out of sight, but that's not really enough, is it?"

"Not in the end, it isn't," I said sadly. "At first it is."

"Let's give it another try," she said. "I want to say something silly, and I want you to be too distracted to hear me."

This time we made it, and just as we did she said, "I love you," very softly in my ear.

I whispered it back to her, and then she cried.

I held her for a long while, and then we got up and got dressed.

Sandy was standing at the kitchen sink with a cigarette and a glass of whiskey, still nude, looking out the window at the moonlight.

"We have to run, Sandy," I told her softly. "Tell Jack, OK?"

She nodded to me and smiled vaguely at Clydine. "He's asleep now," she said. "He always goes to sleep. Sometimes I'd like to talk, but he always goes to sleep. They all do." She took a drink of whiskey.

"It'll be all right," I said inanely.

"Of course," she said, her voice slurring a bit. "In just a little while."

Clydine and I went on out and got in the car. I backed on out to the road and drove on down toward Fife.

"She kept saying that all night," I said. " 'It's only for a little while.' What the hell is that supposed to mean?"

"You're not as smart as I thought you were," Clydine said to me. "It's as plain as the nose on your face."

"What?"

"She's going to kill herself."

"Oh, come on," I said.

"She'll be dead before Christmas."

I thought about it. Somehow it fit. "I'd better tell Jack," I said.

"Mind your own business," she told me. "It hasn't got anything to do with him."

"But—"

"Just stay out of it. You couldn't stop it anyway. It's something that happened to her a long time ago. She's just waiting for the right time. Leave her alone."

Women!

"Let's go back to your place," she said. "I want us both to take a good hot bath, and then I want to sleep with you—just sleep. OK?"

"Why not?" I said.

"Seems to me you said that was the worst reason in the world for doing anything."

"I'm always saying things like that," I told her.

⊰⊱ 11

The following Wednesday, the first of September, we were all going to get together out at Carter's to make sure we had everything all set for the hunt. We were going to be leaving on the ninth, and so we were kind of moving up on it.

Stan had finally committed himself to going along, which surprised me since I figured Monica would just flat veto the idea. I guess maybe she figured that that would be too obvious—or maybe she'd tried all the tricks in her bag, first the nagging, then crossing her legs, and none of them had worked. Stan was pretty easygoing most of the time, but he could get his back up if the occasion came along. I'd gotten a vague hint or two about the kind of pressure she was putting on him, but he was hanging in there. Then, quite suddenly, she seemed to give in. She got real nice to everybody, and that *really* worried me.

The other guys had decided to bring their wives on out to Carter's to kind of quiet down the rumblings of discontent which were beginning to crop up as a result of our frequent all-male gatherings and planning sessions. I'd asked Clydine, but there was a meeting of some kind she wanted to attend. Besides which, she told me, she'd about *had* the establishment types and their antics. I'd wanted her to meet Claudia; but, all things considered, it was probably for the best that she didn't come. Jack and Cal would have been as jumpy as cats with her around after the little orgy on Sunday. I knew she could keep her mouth shut, but they wouldn't have been so sure.

Anyhow I was over at Mike's that afternoon finishing up the rifle. Maybe it was just luck, but the thing was coming out beautifully. I hadn't really taken pride in anything for a long time, and I was really getting a kick out of it. Mike came out when he got home from work and sat on the edge of the workbench with a quart of beer while I put the last coat of stock-finish on the wood. I'd finished bluing the action the day before. All that was left was a last rubdown on the wood, mounting the sling swivels and assembling the gun.

"Man," he said admiringly, "that's gonna be one fine-looking weapon. How much you say you've got into it?"

"About seventy-five bucks altogether," I said, "and about thirty-four hours of work."

"Beautiful job," he said, handing me the quart. I took a guzzle and gave it back.

"Now I just hope the son of a bitch shoots straight," I said. "I never fired it before I started on this."

"Oh, I wouldn't worry," he said. "That old Springfield was always a pretty dependable piece of machinery. As long as you can poke one up the spout, she'll shoot."

"I sure hope you're right," I said, carefully leaning the stock against the garage wall to dry. I scoured my hands off with turpentine and began working at them with some paste hand-cleaner.

"Betty says you're staying to dinner." He finished the quart and pitched it into a box in the corner.

"Yeah," I said. "I'll have to start paying board here pretty quick." I *had* been eating with them pretty often.

"Glad to have you," he said, grinning. "It gives me somebody to swap war stories with." Mike and I got along well.

"Hey," he said. "I hear that was quite a party Sunday."

"It was an orgy," I said. "You ever met Helen—that pig of Sloane's?"

"Once or twice."

"Then you've probably got a pretty good idea of how things went."

"Oh, *gosh*, yes." He chuckled. "Jack was telling me that little girl you brought has got quite a shape on her."

"You can tell that she's a girl."

"He said he didn't much care for her though."

I laughed about that, and then I told Mike about the little confrontation.

"No kidding?" He laughed. "I'd sure love to have been able to see the expression on his face."

"What face?" I laughed. "It fell right off."

"Was Sandy What's-her-name there with Jack?" he asked.

"Yeah. Quiet as ever."

"She's a strange one, isn't she?"

"Clydine—that's my little girl-chum—says that Sandy's gonna kill herself pretty quick." I probably shouldn't have said anything, but I knew Mike had sense enough to keep his mouth shut.

"What makes her think so?"

"I don't know for sure—maybe they talked or maybe my little agitator is relying on the well-known, but seldom reliable, intuition women are supposed to have."

"Maybe so," Mike said thoughtfully, "but I've heard that girl say awfully weird things sometimes. If that's what she's got in mind, it would sure explain a helluva lot. You tell Jack?"

I shook my head. "He wouldn't believe it in the first place, and what could he do about it?"

"That's true," Mike admitted. He slid down off the bench and looked ruefully at his belly. "Sure is gonna get tiresome carryin' this thing up and down mountains. God damn, a man can get out of shape in a hurry." I think we both wanted to get off the subject of Sandy.

"Beer and home cookin'," I said. "Do it to you every time." I washed my hands at the outside faucet, dried them on my pants, and got my clean clothes out of my car. We went inside, and I changed clothes in the bathroom. After we ate, Mike and I had a couple beers and watched TV while Betty cleaned up in the kitchen. She sang while she was working, and her voice was clear and high, and she hit the notes right on. There's nothing so nice as a woman singing in the kitchen.

Jack and Marg showed up about seven with a case of beer, and we all sat around talking. Marg looked like she'd gotten a head start on the drinking. She was a little glassy-eyed.

"How'd you get tangled up with this Larkin guy, Dan?" Jack asked me. "He seemed a little standoffish when I met him the other day."

"Oh, Stan's OK," I said. "He's just a little formal till he gets to know you. He'll loosen up."

"I sure hope so."

"We shared an apartment for a while when I was up at the U," I said. "We got along pretty well."

"He done much hunting?" Mike asked.

"Birds, mostly," I said. "I've been duck hunting with him a few times. He's awfully damned good with a shotgun." I told them about Stan's triple on ducks.

"That's pretty good, but I'll bet I could still teach him a thing or two about shotgun shootin'," Jack boasted.

"Here we go," Margaret said disgustedly, "the mighty hunter bit." Her words were a little slurred.

"I'm good, sweetie," Jack said. "Why should I lie about it? I am probably one of the world's finest wing shots. Every time I go out, you can count on pure carnage."

"You know what's so damned disgusting about it?" Mike said. "The big-mouth son of a bitch can probably make it stick. I saw him bust four out of five thrown beer bottles one time with a twenty-two rifle."

"Never could figure out how I missed that last one," Jack said. "Must have been a defective cartridge."

"You're impossible." Betty laughed. Nothing bothered Betty.

"Just good," he said, "that's all. Class will tell." Jack smirked at us all.

"When you guys get him out in the woods," Margaret said dryly, "why don't you do the world a favor and shoot him?"

We drank some more beer and sopped up dip with potato chips. Mike and Betty had a comfortable little house with furniture that was nice but not so new as to make you afraid to relax. It was a pleasant place to talk.

Sloane and Claudia drifted in about eight with some more beer and Sloane's ever-present jug of whiskey.

"Hey"—he giggled—"is this where the action is?" He bulked large in the doorway, the case of beer under one arm and his hat shoved onto the back of his head. Claudia pushed him on into the room. They looked odd together. She was so tiny, and he was so goddamn gross. It dawned on me that she was even smaller than my little radical cutie. I wondered how in the hell she'd ever gotten tangled up with Sloane.

With him at the party, of course, any hope of quiet conversation went down the drain. He was a good-natured bastard though.

"Wait till you see what Dan's done with the rifle you unloaded on him," Mike said.

"Get it done, old buddy?" Sloane asked me.

"Not quite," I said.

"Bring it around when you get done with it," he said. "I might just buy it back."

"I believe I'll hang onto this one," I told him.

Stan and Monica came a little later, and I could see the icicles on her face. She clicked that smile on and off rapidly as I introduced them to everybody. Stan seemed ill at ease, and I knew she'd been at him pretty hard again.

"I thought Stanley said there were going to be *six* of you on this little expedition," she said brightly. "Somebody must be missing."

"McKlearey," Jack said. "He's pretty undependable. Likely he's in jail, drunk, or in bed with somebody's wife—maybe all three."

"Really?" she said with a slightly raised eyebrow. She looked around the room. "What a charming *little* house," she said, and I saw Betty's eyes narrow slightly at the tone in the voice.

So *that* was her new gimmick. She was going to put us down as a bunch of slum-type slobs and make Stan feel shitty for having anything to do with us.

"It's a lot more comfortable than the trailer the 'great provider' here has me cooped up in," Marg said, playing right into her hands.

"Oh, do you live in one of *those*?" Monica asked. "That must be nice—so *convenient* and everything."

I ground my teeth together. There was nothing I could do to stop her.

"Sometimes I wish *we* lived in one," Claudia's low voice purred. "When your husband needs a living room the size of a basketball court to keep from knocking things over, you get a bit tired just keeping the clutter picked up."

I knew damned well Claudia wouldn't be caught dead in a trailer, but she wasn't about to let this bitch badmouth Betty and Marg.

"Oh," Monica said, "you have a *large* house?"

"Like a barn." Sloane giggled.

"I just adore big, *old* houses," Monica said. "It's such a shame that the neighborhoods where you find them deteriorate so fast."

Jack laughed. "Sloane's neighborhood up in Ruston isn't likely to deteriorate much. He's got two bank presidents, a mill owner, and a retired admiral on his block. The whole street just reeks of money."

Monica faltered. Certain parts of Ruston were about as high class as you were going to get around Tacoma.

Sloane giggled again. "Costs a fortune to live there. They *inhale* me every year just for taxes."

"Oh, Calvin," Claudia said suavely, "it's not that bad, and the neighbors are nice. They don't feel they have to 'keep up' or put each other down. They don't have this 'status' thing."

Monica's face froze, but that put an end to it. Claudia had real class, the one thing Monica couldn't compete with. The little exchange had backfired, and *she* was the one who came out looking like a slob. She hadn't figured on Claudia.

Then Lou showed up. He was a little drunk but seemed to be in a good humor. "Hide your women and your liquor," he announced in that raspy voice of his. "I'm here at last." A kind of tension came into the room very suddenly. McKlearey still seemed to carry that air of suppressed violence with him. Maybe it was that stiff Gyrene brace he stood in all the time.

Why in hell couldn't he relax? I still hadn't really bought that quick changeover of his on the night when we'd first started talking about the High Hunt. I'd figured it was a grandstand play and he'd back out, but so far he hadn't. One thing I knew for sure—I'd have sure felt a lot better if he and Jack weren't going up into the woods together. Both of them could get pretty irrational, and there were going to be a lot of guns around.

"Where in hell have you been McKlearey?" Jack demanded. "You're an hour late."

"I got tied up," Lou said.

"Yeah? What's her name?"

"Who bothers with names?" McKlearey jeered.

I saw Margaret glance sharply at Lou, but his face was blank. She was actually jealous of that creepy son of a bitch, for Chrissake!

"Let's all have a belt," Sloane suggested. He hustled into the kitchen and began mixing drinks.

I sat back, relaxing a bit now that all the little interpersonal crises were over for the moment. I think that's why I've always been kind of a loner. When people get at each other and the little tensions start to build, I get just uncomfortable as hell. It's like having your finger in a light socket knowing some guy behind you has his hand on the switch. You're pretty sure he won't really turn it on, but it still makes you jumpy.

I glanced over at Claudia. I liked her more and more. I wished to hell I didn't know about Sloane and his outside hobbies.

Stan caught my eye with a look of strained apology. He, of course, had been on to Monica's little performance even more than I had. I shrugged to him slightly. Hell, it wasn't *his* fault.

Sloane distributed the drinks and then stood in the archway leading to Mike's dining room. "And now," he announced, "if you ladies will excuse us; we'll adjourn to the dining room here and discuss the forth-coming slaughter." He giggled.

"Right," Jack said, getting up. "We got plans to make." He was a little unsteady on his feet, but I didn't pay much attention just then.

The rest of us got up, and we trooped into the dining room. I saw Monica's face tighten as Stan got up. She didn't want him out of sight, not even for a minute.

"Now," Mike said after we'd pulled up the chairs and sat around the table, "I've made the deal with this guy named Miller in Twisp, so that's all settled."

"Where in hell is Twisp, for Chrissake?" Lou demanded.

Mike got a map, and we located Twisp, a small town in the Methow Valley.

"How'd you get to know a guy way to hell and gone up there?" Sloane asked.

"I've got a cousin who lives up there," Mike said. "He introduced me to Miller when I was up there a year ago."

"What kind of guy is he?" Jack asked.

"Rough, man. He tells you to do something, you damn well better do it."

"He better not try givin' *me* a bad time," Lou said belligerently.

"He'd have *you* for breakfast, Lou," Mike said. "I've seen him, and you can take it from me, he's *bad.*"

"Yeah?" Lou said, his jaw tightening.

"Knock it off, McKlearey," Sloane said; he wasn't smiling. Lou grumbled a bit, but he shut up.

"Anyway, this is the deal," Mike went on. "It's fifty bucks each for ten days. He'll buy the food, and we'll pay him for it when we get there. He figures about thirty bucks a man. It would usually be a helluva lot more, but, like I told you, he's just getting into the business, and so he doesn't want to charge full price yet."

"How the hell is he gonna feed us on three bucks a day each?" Jack demanded, taking a straight belt of whiskey from Sloane's bottle.

"We'll eat beans mostly, I expect," Mike said. "I told him we weren't exactly rolling in money, and not to get fancy on the chow. He said we could get by with a little camp meat to tide us over."

"Camp meat? What the hell's that?" Lou asked. He was being deliberately dense.

"He'll knock over a doe once we get up into the high country," Mike explained. "We'll eat that up before we come out. All the guides up there do it. I guess the game wardens don't much care as long as you don't bring any of the meat out—or if they do, there's not a helluva lot they can do about it."

"Good deal," I said, lighting a cigarette.

"Now," Mike went on, "he said we'll each need a rifle, one box of shells, a pair of good boots, a good warm coat, several pair of heavy sox, a couple changes of clothes, and a good sleeping bag. Oh, one other thing—he wants us to put our clothes and stuff in some kind of sack so we can hang them here and there on the packhorses."

"Hell," Lou said, "why don't we just roll 'em up in our sleeping bags?"

"Then what do you do with them at night, you dumb shit?" Jack demanded.

"Hang 'em on a fuckin' tree," Lou said.

"They'd be soaking wet by morning," I told him.

"Can everybody get all the stuff I just read off together?" Mike asked.

"Shouldn't be much trick to that," Jack said. "The clothes shouldn't be any problem, and Cal's bringin' most of the guns. Sleeping bag's about the only big thing, if a guy can't borrow one." He took another drink of whiskey.

"Miller says it's colder'n hell up there in the high country," Mike said, "and we damn well better be ready for it. He says he's got the tents and cookware, so we won't have to worry about that."

"Oh, hey," I said, "I was down at the surplus store downtown. I got a pretty good bag—army job—for about ten bucks. Some of you guys might want to check them out."

"That sure beats the twenty or thirty they cost at the department stores," Jack said. His voice sounded a little thick. He'd been hitting the jug pretty hard.

"I'd have to take a look at them," Lou said, his voice surly. By God! He was *still* fighting this thing, even now. If he didn't want to go, why the hell didn't he just say so and quit bugging the rest of us?

"I guess that's about everything then," Mike said, looking at the list. "We get together at Sloane's on the evening of the eighth for a final check-through on all the gear, and then we leave at midnight on the ninth."

"One thing," Jack said. "Are we gonna take pistols or not?"

"What did Miller say about it?" I asked Mike. I hoped to hell that he'd vetoed the idea. A guy might stop and think with a rifle, but a damned pistol is just too easy to use.

"He didn't say, one way or the other," Mike said.

"Well," Jack persisted, "are we gonna take 'em or not?" He'd been pushing the handgun business from the very start, but he'd never told me why.

"All right," Sloane said, "let's take 'em." There went my last hope. Most of the guns that were going were Sloane's, from the pawnshop. If he'd said no, that would have been it.

"I'll take that .45 automatic," Jack said. The gun he'd pulled on me that day. That just brightened hell out of my whole evening.

"Say," Stan said, coming into the conversation for the first time, "while you're all here maybe I can get a question answered. I've shot a lot of birds, but I've never shot at a big animal. This may sound a little silly, but where exactly are you supposed to aim for?" Stan was trying to be one of the guys, but he still seemed a little stiff.

"Right through the neck," Lou said, poking at Stan's windpipe with his finger. It was supposed to look like a demonstration, but like always, Lou poked a little harder than necessary.

"Depends on how far away you are," I said. "I wouldn't try for a neck shot at two hundred and fifty yards. Best bet all around is right behind the front shoulder."

"Right through the boiler factory," Jack agreed. "I'll go along with Dan on that. You've got heart, lungs, and liver all in the same place. You're bound to hit something fatal." He sounded drunk.

"And you don't spoil much meat," I said. "A few spareribs is about all."

"But for God's sake, don't gut-shoot," Mike said. "A gut-shot deer can run five miles back into the brush. You've got to track for hours to find him."

Stan shook his head. "I don't know," he said. "When it gets right down to it, I wonder if I could really pull the trigger. I went out once after deer, but I didn't see anything. I thought about it that time, too. A bird is one thing, but a deer is—well, a lot more like we are. It might be a little hard to shoot if you think about it too much." Oh, God, I thought, the Bambi syndrome.

"Shit!" McKlearey exploded. "You make more fuss about a damn deer than I ever did about shootin' *people*!" It's the same thing—just point and pull and down they go." McKlearey had taken an instant dislike to Stan—just like I had to *him*.

Stan looked at him. "I guess it's what you're used to," he said. These two were about as far apart as two guys are likely to get.

"If you feel that way about it, why are you comin' along?" Lou said belligerently.

"Lou, why don't you shut up?" Mike said. "You're getting obnoxious."

"Well, he gives me a pain."

Stan stood up. His face was set. He looked like he was getting ready to paste McKlearey in the mouth. I was a little surprised to see him take offense so easily—maybe Monica's chipping was putting him on edge.

"Sit down, Stan," I said. "He's drunk."

"What if I am?" Lou said. "What if I am?"

"That's enough, Lou," Sloane said. His voice was rather quiet, but you could tell he meant what he said. Sloane could surprise you. He was such a clown most of the time that you forgot sometimes just how much weight he could swing. Not only was he big enough to dismantle Lou with one hand, but he could fire him when he got done.

Lou sat back and shut up.

We talked about it a little more, and then went back into the living room with the girls. I had a couple more beers and sat back on the couch, watching. Margaret seemed to be pretty well loaded. Her voice was loud, and she seemed to be hanging around McKlearey. I thought that she'd have had better sense. I hadn't been counting drinks on her, but she was flying high.

Claudia came over and sat beside me. "You boys get everything all squared away in there?" she asked, her deep, soft voice sending the usual shiver up my back.

I nodded. "I think everything's all lined up."

"Sounded like there might have been a bit of an argument."

"McKlearey," I said. "I wish to hell he'd show up someplace sober some time."

"He's rotten when he's drunk," she agreed, "but he's not much better sober."

"He's a real creep," I said.

"I wish Calvin would get rid of him," she said. "I just hate to have him around." She paused for a moment. "Dan," she said finally, "what's the problem with Mrs. Larkin? She had no reason to talk to Margaret and Betty the way she did."

"I don't know, Claudia. I think what it boils down to is that she doesn't want Stan to go on this trip, and she's doing her level best to make things miserable for him."

"Oh, that's sad," she said. "Is she that unsure of herself with him?"

"I thought it was the other way around," I said. "She seems to have him on a pretty short leash."

"That's what I mean," she said. "A woman doesn't do that unless she's not sure of herself."

"Never thought of it that way," I said. Suddenly it all clicked into place. Claudia knew about her husband and his affairs, and it wasn't that she didn't care—as Jack had said that first night. She probably cared a great deal, but she knew Cal and the squirming insecurity that kept driving him back to the gutter for reassurance. She could live with it—maybe not accept it entirely—but live with it. But why Sloane, for God's sake?

"Oh-oh," Claudia said, "trouble." She nodded her head toward the dining room. I saw Jack and Margaret standing in there talking to each other intensely. Margaret's face was flushed, and she looked mad as hell. They were both drunk.

Her voice rose a little higher. "I'll drink as much as I damn well please, *Mister* Alders," she said.

"You're gettin' bombed, stupid," Jack said. Loaded with charm, my brother.

"So what?" she demanded.

"You're makin' a damn fool of yourself," he said, his voice mushy. "You been crawlin' all over Lou like a bitch in heat."

"What if I have?" she said. "What's it to you?"

"Grow up," Jack said.

"He doesn't seem to mind," she said.

"He's just bein' polite."

"That's all you know, Mister Big Shot!" Margaret said, her voice getting shrill.

"Shut up," he told her.

"Don't tell me to shut up, Big Mouth," she said loudly. "There's a few things you don't know, and maybe it's time I wised you up."

"Oh, boy," I muttered, "here we go." I glanced over at Lou and saw him easing toward the door. I shifted, getting ready to move. If anybody was going to get a piece of McKlearey, it was going to be me. If this blew, I'd stack him up in a corner if I could possibly manage it.

"Will you shut your goddamn stupid mouth?" Jack demanded.

"No, I won't," she said. "I'm gonna tell you something, and you're gonna—"

Then he hit her. It was an open-handed slap across the face but a good solid shot, not just a pat. She rocked back, her eyes a little glazed. I came up moving fast and got hold of him. Claudia and Betty got Margaret and led her off toward the bathroom. She seemed a little wobbly, and she hadn't started hollering yet.

"Let's get some air, buddy," I said to Jack and took him on out through the kitchen door into the backyard.

"That stupid big-mouth bitch!" he said when I got him outside. "She was gonna blab it all over the whole damn room about her and Mc-Klearey. I shoulda had my head examined when I married her."

He knew about it. He'd known about it all along.

"That was a pretty hefty clout you gave her, wasn't it?" I said.

"Only way to get her attention," he said, trying to focus his eyes on me. "Got to hit her hard enough to shut her up."

"Maybe," I said. There's no point in arguing with a drunk.

"Sure. Only way to handle 'em. Couldn't let her shoot her mouth off like that in front of everybody, could I?"

I could sure see why he didn't stay married for very long at a time. I took his car keys out of his pocket and sat with him on Mike's lawn couch. I didn't want him getting any wild ideas about trying to drive anyplace.

"Why don't you cool off a bit?" I suggested.

"Good idea," he said, leaning back. "It was gettin' pretty hot in there."

"Yeah."

"God damn, I'm sure glad you came back home, little brother," he said. "You're OK, you know that?" He patted my arm clumsily. "Never knew how good it'd be to have you around." His eyes weren't focusing at all now.

I stood there for a few minutes, and then I heard a snore. I decided it was warm enough. I'd pour him in the back seat of my car later. I went back inside.

"Really? That sounds *terribly* exciting," Monica was saying. She was sitting on the couch with Lou, and he was telling her war stories. She was up to something else now, and I thought I knew what. Lou, of course, was just stupid enough to go along with her. Somebody was going to have to shoot that son of a bitch yet.

I glanced at Stan, and his face made me want to hide. "Or maybe her," I said to myself. Her little tactic was pretty obvious.

Mike came over to me. "Jack OK?" he asked quietly.

"He's asleep on that couch thing in the backyard," I said. "We'll have to wring him out to get him home."

"Yeah," Mike said, "he gets drunk pretty easy sometimes." He stopped a minute. "Come on out in the kitchen," he said, jerking his head. I followed him. "Dan," he said hesitantly, "is something going on between Margaret and Lou?" I looked quickly at him. I'd thought that he was about half in the bag. He was a shrewd bastard and no more drunk than I was.

"Yeah," I said shortly. Again I knew I could trust him. "Jack knows about it, too," I added.

He whistled. "Son of a bitch! This could get a little intense. And the way that Larkin broad is throwin' her ass at him, Lou's likely to get a piece of her before too long, too. You know, Dan, this has the makings of a real fun trip."

"You know it, buddy," I said. "We may have to haul that Jarhead son of a bitch out of the woods in a sack."

"He's pure trouble. I wish to hell he was out of this little hunt."

"You and me both," I agreed. "Mike, you're not screwing anybody's wife, are you? I don't think my nerves could take any more of this crap."

He laughed. "Betty would castrate me," he said. "You got no more worries."

"God"—I chuckled—"what a relief." I looked on into the living room. Monica was really snuggling up to old Lou, and he was lapping it up. "We'd better get McKlearey away from her before he throws the blocks to her right there on the couch," I said. "She doesn't know what she's messing with, I don't think. Or maybe she does—anyway, she can diddle with King Kong for all of me, but I'd rather not have Stan watching."

"Right," he said. "I'll get him to help me with Jack. You want us to put him in your car?"

"Yeah," I said, "you'd better. Here are the keys. Why don't you drive him on over and take McKlearey and Sloane with you? I'll bring Marg along in Jack's car when the girls get her straightened out. Then I can run you guys back here. That ought to break up the action a little."

"We can hope," Mike said and went to get McKlearey and Cal.

This whole damned thing was getting wormier and wormier. We'd be damn lucky if *any* of us got out of the woods alive. I went on back to the bedroom to see how the girls were doing with Margaret.

~~~~ **12**

By the next Saturday we were all getting things pretty well in shape. I had decided that I could find enough clothing in my duffle bag to keep me warm and dry in the woods. All I needed was a good warm jacket and a red hat. There was no trick to locating those.

It took a little more scrounging, but I found a guy—a GI out at the Fort, I think—who sold me a whole bucketful of .30-06 military ammunition at five cents a round. I suspect that he'd stolen it, but I didn't ask.

That morning, I took my guns to the police range and began the tedious business of sighting in the rifle. It was cool and cloudy, with no wind—a perfect day for shooting. I finally got it honed into a good tight group about an inch high at two hundred yards and decided that would do it. Then I went over to the pistol range and pumped a few through that old single action .45. I came to the conclusion that if I ever had to shoot anything with it, I'd better be pretty damn close.

I was supposed to pick up Clydine about three thirty, but I still had plenty of time, so I swung on by Stan's place on the way back from the range. I knew he was having a real bad time, and he needed all the support he could get. Monica was making life miserable for him, if her behavior at the party was any indication. For some reason this hunt had become a major issue between them. I figured that if he could just win this one, it might change the whole picture.

"How's it going, old buddy?" I asked with false cheerfulness when he answered the door. The place was still uncomfortably neat.

"Not too well," he said with a gloomy face. "Sometimes I think this was all a mistake."

"Oh, come on now," I said. "You've just got the pre-season jitters."

"No. Monica isn't really very happy about my going. She said some pretty nasty things about you and the others when we got home Wednesday."

"I'll bet," I said. "Wednesday night was kind of a bummer anyway. Don't let it shake you—her being against it, I mean."

"Still," he said dubiously, "it's the first really serious disagreement we've ever had. I don't know if it's worth it." She just about had him on the ropes. I was goddamned if I'd let her win now.

"Look, Stan," I said, "no woman has ever been that excited about her man's wanting to hunt and fish. It's in the blood—you know, basic functions, cave-keeping and bringing home the meat. Modern women have got us cave-broken, and they hate to see us reverting. But a man needs to bust out now and then. Give him a chance to get dirty and smelly and unhousebroke. It's good for the soul. Deep down, women really don't mind all that much. Oh, they put up a fight, but they don't really mind. It puts things back in perspective for them." It was crack-pot anthropology, but he bought it. I kind of thought he would. He wanted to win this one, too.

"Are you sure?" he asked, wanting to believe.

"Of course," I told him, "you're dealing with primitive instincts, Stan. Monica doesn't even know why she's fighting it. You can be damn sure, though, that she really wants you to stand up to her. She's *testing* you, that's all." *That* ought to throw some reverse English on the ball.

"Maybe you're right," he said.

"Sure," I told him, "that's what hunting is really all about. God knows we don't need the meat. You can buy better meat a helluva lot cheaper at the supermarket. Deer meat is going to average about five dollars a pound—that's for something that tastes like rancid mutton." I was laying it on pretty thick, and he was buying every bit of it. He really wanted to go, and convincing him wasn't all that hard.

"You get that rifle you were going to borrow?" I asked him, wanting to change the subject before he caught me up a tree. I'd planted enough, though, I thought. At least he wouldn't roll over and play dead for her.

"Yes," he said, "I picked it up this morning. It belongs to a fellow at the school, but he had a heart attack and can't hunt anymore. He said that if I like the way it shoots on this trip, he'll sell it to me."

He fetched the gun, and I looked it over. It was one of those Remington pumps in .30-06 caliber, scope-mounted and with a sissy-pad on the butt. I felt my shoulder gingerly. Maybe a recoil pad *would* be a good investment if a man planned to do a lot of shooting.

"Good-looking piece," I said. "You sighted it in yet?"

"The fellow said that it was right on at two hundred yards."

"Probably wouldn't hurt to poke a few through it just to make sure," I told him. "Sometimes they get knocked around a little and won't hit where you're aiming. I'll give you a fistful of military rounds so you can make sure." I told him where the police range was, but he already knew. So I showed him how to adjust the sights, gave him about fifteen rounds and took off. I didn't want to be around if Monica came back. He'd told me she'd been gone since early that morning on some kind of errand, and he didn't expect her back until evening, but I didn't want to take any chances. I might just have trouble being civil to her.

I wanted to swing on by Sloane's pawnshop to see how things were shaping up with the other guys, so I buzzed right on over there. My ears were still ringing and I could have used a beer, but I figured that could wait.

Sloane was in the place alone when I got there.

"Hey, Dan," he said, "how'd it shoot?"

"Dead on at two hundred," I said.

"Good deal. Say, you hear about Betty?"

"What? No. What's up?"

"That damned kidney of hers went sour again. Mike had to put her in the hospital again last night."

"Oh, no," I said, "that's a damned shame."

"Yeah. I'm afraid Mike won't be able to go with us, poor bastard. He wouldn't dare leave now."

"Christ, Cal," I said, "that'll wash out the whole deal then, won't it?" I felt sick.

"No, I don't think so," Sloane said. "I called Miller this morning as soon as I heard about it. He wasn't any too happy, but he'll still take us. It's too late for him to get another party."

"It's still a damn shame," I said. "Poor Betty was just getting back on her feet from last spring, and Mike's really been counting on this trip. I was looking forward to getting out with him."

"It's a lousy break," Sloane said. "It's a good thing we included Larkin in. Miller wouldn't have held still for just four guys."

"I had to give Stan a shot of high life just a little while ago," I said. "His wife's giving him a whole bunch of crap about the trip."

"She's a real bitch, isn't she?"

"They'd have been ahead to have drowned her and raised a puppy," I agreed.

"She was really out to raise hell last Wednesday," Sloane said. "Hey, could you use a blast? I've got a jug in the back, and it's about time for my early afternoon vitamin shot."

"Oh, I guess I could choke some down," I said. "Might take some of the sting out of my shoulder."

"That old aught-six steps back pretty hard, doesn't it?" he said, leading me into the back room.

"You know she's there when you touch 'er off," I agreed.

He took a fifth of good bourbon down from one of the shelves. "I stick it up high," he said, "so Claudia doesn't find it. She's sudden death on drinking on the job. I wouldn't want to get fired." He giggled.

"Hadn't you better sit where you can keep an eye out front?" I asked.

"What the hell for? On the fourth of the month the GI's are fat city—rollin' in money. Everybody's already redeemed last month's pawns, and nobody looks for pawnshop bargains on Saturday afternoon. Their neighbors might see them and think they were hurting for money. Here." He passed me the jug.

I took a long pull. "Good whiskey," I said as soon as I got my breath.

"Fair," he agreed, taking a drink. "Oh, hey. I wanted to show you the pistol I'm taking along." He rummaged around and came up with a .357 Ruger, frontier style.

"Christ, Sloane," I said, "isn't that a little beefy?"

"It shoots .38 special as well," he said. "I'll probably take those."

"It's got a good heft to it," I said, holding the pistol.

"Got a holster too," he said, pulling a fancy Western-type cartridge belt and holster out of one of his bins.

"Man," I said, "Pancho Villa rides again. We're going to go into the woods with more armament than a light infantry platoon."

"Jack's got that Army .45 auto, and McKlearey's taking a Smith and Wesson .38 Military and Police," he said.

"I don't know if Stan's got a handgun," I said. "When you get right down to it, they're not really necessary." I wanted to say something more about that, but I figured it was too late now.

"It just kind of goes with the trip," Sloane said, almost apologetically. "If it's the kind of thing you only do once, you might as well go all the way."

"Sure, Cal," I said, looking at my watch. "Say, I've got to run."

"O.K. Here, have one for the road." He handed me the jug again. I took another belt, and we walked on back out into the shop again.

"Keep in touch," he said.

"Right." I waved and went on out to the street. Goddamn Sloane was just a big kid. I began to understand Claudia even a little better now. God knows he needed somebody to take care of him.

I dropped the guns and clothes off at the trailer and buzzed on out to the Patio for a few beers. I still had a couple hours before I was supposed to pick up Clydine. It was still cloudy, but no rain. It was the kind of day that's always made me feel good. Even the news about Betty hadn't been able to change that. I parked the car and went inside whistling.

McKlearey was there at the pinball machine—as usual—still standing at attention. He saw me before I could back out.

"Hey, Danny," he said, "come have a beer." I hate having people I don't like call me Danny. My day went sour right about then.

"Sure," I said. I followed him to the bar and ordered a draft.

"Hey, old buddy," he said, slapping me on the shoulder with a false joviality that stuck out like a sore thumb. "How you fixed for cash money?"

"Oh," I said cautiously, "I've still got a couple bucks."

"Can you see your way clear to loan me five till payday?"

I couldn't think up an excuse in a hurry. I reached for my wallet before I even stopped to think. You get that reflex in the Army, I don't know why.

"I get paid on Wednesday," he said, watching me, "and I'll get it right back to you then."

I pulled out a five and handed it to him.

"Got to pick up some stuff, Lou," I said. "I don't think I'd better cut it any tighter."

"Sure," he said, "that's OK. This'll get me by. I'll be sure to get it right back to you on Wednesday."

"No sweat, Lou," I said.

"No," he said, "a guy ought to stay on top of his obligations."

There was five bucks down the tube.

"You hear about Carter's wife?" he asked, settling back down at the bar.

"Yeah," I said, "I just stopped by the pawnshop. Sloane told me."

"Damn shame," he said indifferently. "Oh, well, there's enough of us to make the trip OK." He seemed almost glad that Mike wasn't going. He was a rotten son of a bitch.

"Sure," I said, "we'll be able to swing it."

"I just got here a few minutes ago," he said. "You was lucky to catch me. I just had a real high-class broad in the sack at my place."

"Oh?" I had a picture of what he'd call a "high-class broad."

"Yeah. I only met her a few days ago, but it don't take a guy long to make out if he knows the score. You know her, but I ain't gonna tell you who she is. Nice set of jugs on her and a real wild ass."

McKlearey was about as subtle as a brick. What in hell was Monica up to? If she wanted a little strange stuff, she sure as hell could have done better than this creep.

McKlearey chuckled obscenely. "You should have seen it, Danny boy. She comes to my fuckin' pad about ten this morning, see. Some dumb routine about something she'd 'misplaced' at a party we was both at, and had I seen it. At first I thought she was trying to say I'd stole it, see, so I was a little hot about it—you know, cut her right off. Well, she hung around and hung around, smilin' and givin' me the glad eye and stickin' her tits out at me, see, so I ask her if she wants a beer, see. She says she don't mind, and we have a beer and start to get friendly."

I could just picture Monica gagging down a beer at ten in the morning.

"Well, I make my move, see," he went on, "and all of a sudden she gets cold feet, see. Comes on with this 'I don't know what you *think* I came here for, but it certainly wasn't *that*!' " He mimicked her voice fairly well. "But I know women, see, and she was just pantin' for it. I figure she wanted it rough, see—them high-class broads always like it like that—so I says, 'Come here, you bitch,' and I yanks off her clothes and throws her on the bed, and I poke it to her, right up to the hilt. At first she kind of half-ass tries to fight me off, but pretty soon she gets with it, see. Wild piece of tail, man!" He chuckled again and ordered another beer.

I began to hope he'd get hit by a truck before we ever went into the woods. This was going to be a bum trip, and now I was out five bucks. I told him I had to run, and I took off. The whole business with Monica had me a little confused though. Why McKlearey, for Chrissake?

I asked Clydine about it that evening at my place, explaining the situation and describing the people and what had happened.

"Now, why in God's name would she want to have anything to do with that creepy Jarhead?" I asked her.

Clydine sighed and shook her head. "Oh, Danny," she said in a long-suffering tone. "You're so smart about some things and so hopeless when it comes to women."

"I manage to get by," I said, slipping my hand up under her sweatshirt and grinning at her.

"Do you want to play or do you want to listen?" she asked tartly. "Somehow I've never been able to believe a man's seriously listening to what I'm saying if he's fondling me at the same time."

I pulled my hand out. "OK," I said, "all serious now. No fondling. Shoot."

"All right. One: Wifey doesn't want Hubby to go out and shoot Bambi—right?"

"No—Wifey doesn't want Hubby to get off the leash."

"Whatever. Two: Hubby is jealous of Wifey's good-looking round bottom, right?"

"OK," I said.

"Three: Wifey knows there's bad blood between Hubby and Creepy Jarhead, right?"

"Go on."

"Four: Wifey figures that if Creepy Jarhead makes big pass at Wifey's good-looking round bottom, Hubby will blow his cool, punch Creepy Jarhead in the snot-locker and stay home and hold Wifey's hand instead of going out with the bad old hairy-chested types to dry-gulch poor little Bambi, right?"

"Wrong," I said. "Creepy Jarhead did *not* just make a pass. Creepy Jarhead threw the blocks to Wifey's little round bottom. It shoots your theory all to hell."

She shook her head stubbornly. "Not at all," she said. "Wifey moves in those circles where when a lady says no, the men are polite enough to stop. Poor little Wifey underestimated the Creepy Jarhead, and that's why she got blocks in her bottom."

I blinked. By God, she had it! "You are an absolute doll," I told her. "Now tell me, since this went gunnysack on her, what position is Wifey in now?"

"Little Wifey's got her tit in the wringer," Clydine said sweetly. "She can't scream rape—it's too late for that, and besides, Hubby might go to the Fuzz and then the Creepy Jarhead would spill his guts about her being the one who made the first move. She is, if she's a normal Establishment woman, feeling guilty as hell about now for having committed adultery with a man she doesn't even like. I'd say she screwed herself right out of action—literally. Hubby can go out and exterminate the whole deer population and she won't be able to raise a finger. End of analysis. Satisfied?"

"It all fits together perfectly," I said. "You know, my little pansy of the proletariat, you are absolutely beautiful."

"I'm glad you noticed," she said, snuggling up to me. "Now you may fondle, if you like."

━━━ 13

On Tuesday night we gathered at Sloane's with all our gear. Jack and I got there a little late, and the others were already sitting around the kitchen waiting for us. Stan's face looked grim, and McKlearey was already a little drunk. Sloane seemed relieved to see us, so I imagine things had been getting a bit strained.

"There they are," Sloane said as we walked in. "Where in hell have you guys been?"

"I had to get cleaned up," Jack said. "I've been crawlin' around under a fuckin' trailer down at the lot all day."

"Have a beer, men," Sloane said, diving into the refrigerator. He came up with a fistful of beer cans and began popping tops. "You guys bring your gear?"

"Yeah," I said, "it's out in the car."

"Why don't you go ahead and bring it on in," he said. "I've got the list of all the stuff we'll each need, so I'll check everybody off." It was sort of funny really. Sloane was such a clown most of the time that you hardly took him seriously, but when Mike had dropped out, he'd taken charge, and nobody questioned him about it.

"What we'll do," he went on, "is get everything all packed up, and then we'll store it all here. That way nobody forgets anything, OK?"

We all agreed to that.

"Then tomorrow night, we all take off from here. Stan is going to ride with me, right Stan?"

Stan nodded.

"We can swap off driving that way," Sloane said. "Dan, you and Jack are going in his car, right?"

"Yeah."

"And Lou wants to take his own car, I guess. Damned if I know why, Lou. There'd be plenty of room in either of the other cars."

"I just want to take my own car," Lou said. "Does anybody have any objections to me takin' my own fuckin' car?" He was sitting off by himself like he had that first night, and his eyes looked a little odd. I thought maybe he was drunker than I'd figured at first.

"It just seems a little unnecessary, that's all," Sloane said placatingly.

"Does anybody have any objections to me takin' my own fuckin' car?" Lou repeated. He really had a bag on.

"Take the motherfucker," Jack said. "Nobody gives a shit."

"All right, then," Lou said. "All right, then." His voice was a little shrill.

"All right, calm down, you guys," Sloane said. "If we start chipping at each other, we'll never get done here." Everybody seemed to be in a foul humor.

Jack and I went back out to the car to pick up our gear. "That fuckin' McKlearey is gettin' to be a big pain in the ass," Jack said as he hauled out his sack. "I wish to Christ we'd included him out."

"We needed the extra guy to make the deal with Miller," I said.

"We could have found a dozen guys that would have been better."

"He's a first-class shitheel, all right," I agreed, lifting out my rifle. "He tapped me for five bucks the other day."

"Oh, no shit?" Jack said. "Didn't I warn you about that? Well, you can kiss that five good-bye."

We went on inside with the gear.

"Let's take it all into the living room," Sloane said. "We've got room to spread out in there, but for Chrissake don't spill any beer on

Claudia's carpet! She'll hang all our scalps to the lodge-pole if some-body messes up.''

"We're all housebroke," Jack said. "Quit worryin' about the god-damn carpeting." He was in a particularly lousy mood tonight for some reason.

"OK, you guys, spread out and dump out your gear," Sloane said. For some reason he reminded me of a scoutmaster with a bunch of city kids.

"Sleeping bag," Sloane said.

Each of us pushed his sleeping bag forward.

"Gear-bag—or clothes bag, or whatever the hell you want to call it." He looked around. We each held up a sack of some kind. Looky, gang, Daddy's going to take me camping. "OK, now as we check off the items of clothing and what-not, stow them in your sack, OK?"

He went down through the list of items—clothing, soap, towels, ev-erything.

"OK," he said, "that takes care of all that shit. You'll each be wearing your jackets and boots and all that crap, so we're all set there. Now, have you all got your licenses and deer-tags?"

"I'll pick up mine tomorrow," Lou said.

"McKlearey," Jack said angrily, "can't you do one fuckin' thing right? We were all supposed to have that taken care of by now."

"Don't worry about me," Lou said. "Just don't worry about me, Alders. I'll have the fuckin' license and tag."

"But why in hell didn't you take care of it before now, you dumb shit?" Jack shouted. "You've had as much time as the rest of us."

"All right," I said. "It's no big deal. So he forgot. Let's not make a federal case out of it."

"Dan's right," Sloane said. "You guys are touchy as hell tonight. If we start off this way, the whole thing's gonna be a bust." He could feel it, too.

"Let's get on with this," Stan said. "I've got to get home before too late."

"Keepin' tabs on that high-class wife of yours, huh?" Lou snickered.

"I don't really see where that's any of your business," Stan said with surprising heat. I guess that McKlearey had been at him before Jack and I got there.

"McKlearey," I said, trying to keep my cool and keep the whole thing from blowing up, "you're about half in the bag. You'd be way out in front to back off a little, don't you think?"

"You countin' my fuckin' drinks?" he demanded. "First your shit-head brother, and now you, huh? Well, I can get my own fuckin' li-cense, and I sure as hell don't need nobody to count my fuckin' drinks for me."

"That's enough," Sloane said sharply, and he wasn't smiling. "You guys all got your rifles with you?"

We hauled out the hardware. Sloane had the .270 he'd tried to sell me, Stan had the Remington, Jack had that Mauser, Lou had a converted Springfield, and I had the gun I'd been working on. All the rifles had scopes.

"Two boxes of ammunition?" Sloane asked. We each piled up the boxes beside our rifles.

"Hunting knives?"

We waved our cutlery at him.

"I guess that's about it then."

"Say," Jack said, "how about the handguns?"

"God damn"—Sloane giggled—"I almost forgot. I've got them in the closet. Let's see. Dan, you and Stan each have your own, don't you?"

Stan nodded. "I have," he said quietly. He reached into one end of his rolled sleeping bag and after some effort took out a snub-nosed revolver. He fished in again and came out with a belt holster and a box of shells. Somehow the gun seemed completely out of character. I could see Stan with a target pistol maybe, but not a people-eater like that. And he handled it like he knew what he was doing.

"Christ," I said, "that's an ugly-looking little bastard."

"We had a burglar scare last year," he said, seeming a little embarrassed.

"What the hell can you hit with that fuckin' little popgun?" Lou sneered.

"It's a .38 special," Stan said levelly. "That's hardly a popgun. And I've had it out to the range a few times, and I can hit what I shoot at." He gave Lou a hard look that was even more out of character.

Lou grunted, but he looked at Stan with an odd expression. Maybe the son of a bitch was thinking about how close he'd come to getting a gutful of soft lead bullets for playing silly games with Monica. I hoped he'd get a few nervous minutes out of it.

"You got yours, haven't you, Dan?" Sloane asked.

I nodded. I'd rolled up the gun belt, holster, and pistol and brought them over in a paper sack. I pulled the rig out and laid it across the sleeping bag. The curve of the butt and the flare of the hammer protruding from the black leather holster looked a little dramatic, but what the hell?

"Jesus," Sloane said, almost reverently, "look at that big bastard."

Nothing would do but to pass the guns around and let everybody fondle them.

"You got ours here, Cal?" Jack asked. He sure seemed jumpy about it—like he wasn't going to relax until he got his hands on that pistol.

Sloane got up and went out of the room for a minute. He came back with three belts and holsters. The .357 Ruger of his was almost a carbon copy of my old .45, a little heavier in the frame maybe. His holster and belt were fancier, but the leather was new and squeaked a lot. McKlearey's .38 M & P had a fairly conventional police holster and belt, but Jack's .45 auto was in a real odd lash-up. It looked like somebody had rigged up a quick-draw outfit for that pig. I don't know how anyone could figure to get an Army .45 into operation in under five minutes, but there it was.

We sat around in a circle, passing the guns back and forth. My .30-06 got a lot of attention. Sloane particularly seemed quite taken with it.

"I'll give you a hundred and a half for it," he said suddenly.

"Come on, Cal," I said. "You can get a brand-new gun, scope and all, for that. You couldn't get more than a hundred and a quarter for that piece of mine, even if you were selling it to a halfwit."

"I don't want to sell it," he said. "I just like the gun." He swung the piece to his shoulder a couple more times. "Damn, that's a sweet gun," he said.

Stan took the gun from him. "You did a nice job, Dan," he said.

"Poor Calvin figures he got royally screwed on that deal," Jack said, laughing.

"No," Sloane said, "it was my business to look at the merchandise before I set the price. I screwed myself, so I've got no bitch coming."

Lou went out and got another beer.

Jack held up his rifle. "This thing's a pig, but it shoots where you aim it, so what the hell?"

"That's all that counts," Stan said.

McKlearey came back.

"We're all pretty well set up," I said. "I was about half afraid somebody'd show up with a .30-30. That beast's got the ballistic pattern of a tossed brick. About all it's good for is heavy brush. Out past a hundred yards, you might as well throw rocks."

"And we're not likely to be in brush," Jack said. "You get up around the timberline and it opens up to where you're gettin' two- and three-hundred-yard shots."

"Miller says we'll be camping just below the timberline," Sloane said, "and we'll be riding on up to where we'll hunt, so it'll likely be pretty soon."

"Good deal," Lou grunted. "I've about had a gutful of fuckin' jungle."

"Air gets pretty skimpy up there, doesn't it?" Jack asked.

"At six to eight thousand feet?" Sloane giggled. "You damn betcha. Some of you flatlanders'll probably turn pretty blue for the first couple days."

We carried the gear into Sloane's utility room and piled it all in a corner and then went back into the breakfast room just off the kitchen. Sloane opened another round of beers, and we sat looking at a map, tracing out our route.

"We'll go on up to Everett and then across Stevens Pass," Sloane said. "Then, just this side of Wenatchee, we'll swing north on up past Lake Chelan and up into the Methow Valley to Twisp."

"I thought that was *Mee-thow*," Lou said.

"No," Sloane answered. "Miller calls it *Met*-how."

Lou shrugged.

"Anyhow," Cal went on, "if we leave here at midnight, we ought to be able to get over there by eight thirty or nine. Some of those roads ain't too pure, so we'll have to take it easy."

"We'll be leaving for camp as soon as we get to Miller's?" Stan asked.

"Right. He said he'd feed us breakfast and then we'd hit the trail."

"Gonna be a little thin on sleep," I said.

"I'm gonna sack out for a few hours after work," Jack said.

"Probably wouldn't be a bad idea for all of us," Sloane agreed.

We had a few more beers and began to feel pretty good. The grouchy snapping at each other eased off. It even seemed like the hunt might turn out OK after all. We sat in the brightly lighted kitchen in a clutter of beer cans and maps with a fog of cigarette smoke around us and talked about it.

"Hey, Danny," Lou said suddenly, "you pretty fast with that old .45?"

"Oh, I played with it some when I first got it," I said. "I guess everybody wants to be Wyatt Earp once in his life."

"How fast are you?" he insisted.

"God, Lou, I don't know. I never had any way to time it. I could beat that guy on *Gunsmoke*—Matt Dillon—you know how he used to draw at the start of the program? I'd let him reach first, and then I'd beat him."

"Pretty fast," he said, "pretty fast. Let's see you draw." He wasn't going to let it go.

"Aw, hell, Lou, I haven't handled that thing for two years. I probably couldn't even find the gun butt."

"Go ahead, Dan," Jack said. "Show us how it's done. You a gun-fanner?"

I shook my head. "I tried fanning just once—out at the range—and I splattered lead all over the country. That might be all right across a card table, but at any kind of range, forget it."

"Let's see you draw," Lou said again, prodding me with his elbow. Once again it was a little harder than necessary.

"Sure, Dan," Sloane said, "let's see the old pro in action."

Now don't ask me, for Chrissake, why I gave in. I don't know why. The whole idea of having pistols along had spooked me right from the start, and the more that things had built up between these guys, the less I liked it. In the second place, I don't like to see a bunch of guys messing around with guns. It's too easy for somebody to get hurt. What makes it even worse is that this quick-draw shit starts too many people's minds working in the wrong direction. All things considered, the whole damned business may just have been one of the stupidest things I've ever done in my life. I suppose when you get right down to it, it was because that goddamn McKlearey rubbed me the wrong way. He acted like he didn't believe I knew how to handle the damned gun. The fact that I didn't like McKlearey was pushing me into a whole lot of decisions lately, it occurred to me.

Anyway, I got up and went back into the utility room and got my gun belt. I pulled the wide belt around my waist and buckled it. I was a notch bigger around the belly than I'd been before I went in the Army. Too much beer. I tied the rawhide thong at the bottom of the holster around my thigh and checked the position of the holster. I made a couple of quick passes to be sure I could still find the hammer with my thumb. It seemed to be where I'd left it. I took the gun out of the holster and went back out to the kitchen.

"Hey," Jack said, "there's the gunfighter. God damn, that gun belt sure looks evil strapped on like that." Jack was getting a little high again.

"If you start with the gun already out of the holster," Lou said, "I can see how you could beat Matt Dillon."

"You want to take a chance on my having forgotten to unload this thing?" I asked him flatly.

"God, no," Sloane yelped. "For Chrissake don't shoot out my French doors."

I opened the loading gate, slipped the hammer and rolled the cylinder along my arm at eye level, checking it carefully. I figured I might as well give them the whole show. I snapped the gate shut and spun the gun experimentally a couple times to get the feel of the weight again. Frankly, I felt a little silly.

"Fancy," Sloane said.

"Just limbering up," I told him.

"Let's see how it's done," Lou insisted.

I slipped the pistol into the holster and positioned my hand on the belt buckle.

"Draw!" Lou barked suddenly.

As luck would have it, I was ready, and I found the hammer with my thumb on the first grab. The gun cleared smoothly, and I snapped it about waist high and a little out. It was a fair draw.

"Jesus!" Sloane said blinking.

"God damn!" Jack said. "Just like a strikin' snake." He was getting a kick out of it.

"Lucky," I said.

Even Lou looked impressed. Stan grinned. He'd seen this before. God knows how many hours he'd watched me practice when we'd been roommates.

"Do that again," Jack demanded.

"Why don't I quit while I'm ahead," I said. "Next time I might not even be able to find the damn thing."

"No," he insisted, "I mean do it slow, so we can see how it's done."

I holstered. "Look," I said. "You spread out your hand and come back, see? You catch the curve of the hammer on the neck of your thumb, like this. As soon as you hit it, you close in your hand—you cock the gun and grab onto the butt at the same time. Then you pull up and out, putting your trigger finger inside the guard as the gun comes out. You're ready to shoot when it comes up on line. The idea is to make it all one motion." Silly as it sounds, I was getting a kick out of it. The sullen scowl on McKlearey's face made it all worthwhile.

"You did all *that* just now?" Jack said incredulously. "Shit, if a man was to blink, he'd miss the whole thing."

"It took a few hours to get it down pat," I said, doing the tie-down. I'd grabbed a little hard, and my thumb was stinging like hell. I could feel it clear to the elbow. I'd done it OK though, so I figured it was a good time to quit. No point in making a *complete* ass of myself.

"Here," Sloane said, getting up, "give me some lessons." He went into the utility room and came out with the Ruger and the new belt and holster. He cinched the belt around his middle.

"Lower," I said, sitting back down.

He pushed down on the belt. "Won't go no lower," he complained.

"Loosen it."

He backed it off a couple of notches. "That's the last hole," he said.

"It'll do."

"He looks like a sack of potatoes tied in the middle." Jack laughed.

"Just keep mouthin' off, Alders," Sloane threatened, "and I'll drill you before you can blink." He took on a menacing stance, his hand over the gun butt.

"OK," I said, "tie it down."

He grunted as he bent over and lashed the thong around his leg.

"Let's see the gun," I said. He handed it to me and I opened the loading gate. The pale twinkle of brass stared back at me. I felt a sudden cold hand twist in the pit of my stomach. He must have reloaded it when he put it back in the utility room after we'd been looking them over out in the living room. I should have known this was a mistake. I tipped up the gun, slipped the hammer, and dropped the shells out of the cylinder onto the table, one by one, slowly. They sounded very loud as they hit the table and bounced.

"Shit, man!" Lou said in a strangled whisper.

I picked up one of the shells and looked at the base, ".357 magnum," I observed in a voice as calm and mild as I could make it. "You could blow the refrigerator right through the wall with one of these."

Sloane blushed, I swear he did. "I forgot," he mumbled.

"Or you could knock McKlearey's head halfway down to the bay—beer can and all."

"All right, I forgot. Don't make a federal case out of it." Sloane was getting pissed off.

"Well, that's lesson number one," I said, handing him back the gun. He holstered it.

"Lesson number two. Don't trust anybody when he says a gun is empty. Always check it yourself." I palmed the shell I was holding.

"But I saw you unload it," he protested.

"How many bullets on the table?"

He counted and his eyes bulged. He snatched out the gun and checked the cylinder. I dropped the last one on the table.

"Smart ass!" He snorted.

"Never hurts to be sure. Guns are made to kill with. If you're going to play with them, you damn well better be sure they understand. A gun's got a real limited mentality, so *you've* got to do most of the thinking." Maybe if I could shake them up a little, they'd stop and give the whole business a little thought.

"All right, don't rub it in. What do I do now?"

"Hold your hand about waist high and spread out your fingers."

"You started from over here," he objected putting his hand on his belly.

"You can get fancy once you get the hang of it," I told him. I talked him through the draw a couple of times. Then he tried it fast and naturally he dropped it on his foot.

"God damn!" he bellowed, hopping around holding the foot.

"Heavy, aren't they?" I asked him pleasantly. "And somehow they always seem to land on your foot."

He gingerly put his weight on his foot and limped heavily around the room.

"That's called gunfighter's gimp," I told the others. "Next to the Dodge City Complaint, that's the most common ailment in the business."

"What's the Dodge City Complaint, for God's sake?" Sloane demanded.

"That's when you start practicing with a loaded gun and blow off your own kneecap."

"Bull*shit*, too!" He winced. "Not this little black duck." He started unstrapping the belt. "I'll stick to Indian wrestling. These goddamn things are just as dangerous from the back as from the front." That's what I'd been trying to tell them.

"Let's see that fuckin' thing," Lou demanded, getting up. He strapped it on. It hung a little low, but it looked a lot more businesslike on him than it had on Sloane. He went through it slowly a couple times and then began to pick up speed. He was pretty good and not quite as drunk as I'd thought.

"Come on, Alders," he said to Jack, "I'll take you." He snapped the gun at Jack's head.

God *damn* it, I hate to see somebody do that!

"Come on, shithead," Jack told him, waving his hand. "Don't point that fuckin' thing at me."

"Strap on your iron, hen-shit," Lou said.

"Give me your gun, Dan," Jack said suddenly. He was about half-drunk, too.

I saw that there was no point in trying to talk them out of it. I stood up, stripped off the belt and handed it to Jack. He strapped it on and tied it down.

"You've got to give me a couple minutes to practice," he said.

"Sure," Lou said. "Take as long as you want."

Jack hooked and drew a few times. He picked it up fairly fast, but I knew he was no match for McKlearey. As I watched him, I noticed for the first time how small my brother's hands were. That .45 looked like a cannon when he pulled it.

"All right, you big-mouth son of a bitch," he said to Lou. "Somebody call it."

They squared off about ten feet apart.

"On three," I said. It might as well be me. I was hoping Jack would win by some fluke. That might quiet things down.

I counted it off, and Lou won by a considerable margin.

"Now I guess we know who's the best man." He laughed.

"Big deal," Jack said disgustedly.

Lou snapped the gun at him again. "Back in the old days, you'd be buzzard-bait right now, Alders," he said. "Well, who's next? Who wants to take on the fastest fuckin' gun in Tacoma?" He stood at a stiff brace, his face fixed in a belligerent leer.

Jack dropped the gun belt back on the table. He was grinding his teeth together. He was really pissed. I knew I should have just let it die, but I couldn't let that bastard get away with it. Goddamn McKlearey rubbed me the wrong way, and I didn't like the way he'd put down my brother. I figured it was time he learned that he wasn't King Shit. I stood up and strapped on the gun.

"Well, well," he said, "the last of the Alders. I beat you and I'm top gun, huh?"

"That'll be the day," Stan said quietly.

"You don't think I can?" Lou demanded.

I finished tying down the gun.

"Who's gonna count?" Lou said.

"Never mind the count," I said. "Just go ahead when you're ready." I wanted to rub his face in it, and I'd noticed that Lou always squinted when he started to draw. I figured that was about all the edge I'd need.

It was. I had him cold before he got the gun clear. I didn't snap the trigger but just held the gun leveled at his face. He froze and gawked at the awful hole in the muzzle of that .45. I guess Lou'd had enough guns pointed at him for real to know what it was all about. I waited about ten seconds and then slowly squeezed the trigger. The snap of the hammer was very loud.

I spun the gun back into the holster, grinding him a little more. He was still standing there, frozen in the same place. He was actually sweating, and his eyes had a weird look in them.

(

"And that about takes care of the fastest gun in Tacoma," I said, and I took off my gun belt.

Lou tried to get Sloane or Stan to draw with him, but they weren't having any. Sloane and I put our guns away, and I figured we'd gotten past *that* little shit-pile. These guys weren't kidding, empty guns or no. I think we were *all* starting to slip a few gears.

"I can still outhunt you bastards," Lou said, his voice getting shrill again.

"You'll have to prove that, too," Jack said.

"Don't worry, I'll prove it," Lou said. "Any bet you want. First deer, biggest deer, longest shot. You name it, and I'll beat you at it." He was pissed off now. He'd been put down, and no Marine can ever take that. What was worse, he knew I could do it again, any time I felt like it. Even that might help keep things under control. If he knew I'd be there and I could take him if I had to, it might just keep his mind off the goddamn guns.

"Hey, there's an idea," Sloane said. "Best deer—using *Boone and Crockett* points—the other guys pitch in and buy him a fifth of his favorite booze."

"Why not a jug from each guy?" Lou said. "I can drink one jug in an afternoon."

"All right," Jack said. "One jug of Black Label from each guy, OK?"

"Why not?" Stan said.

"Sure," I agreed.

Sloane shrugged. Money didn't mean that much to him.

"And a little side bet, too," Jack said. "Just between you and me, Lou. Ten bucks says I get a better deer than you do." I don't think he'd have made the bet if he'd been sober.

"You got it," Lou said. "Anybody else want a piece of the action?" He looked around.

"I'll cover you," Stan said. I looked at him quickly. His face was expressionless. "Ten dollars. Same bet." What the hell was this? I suddenly didn't like the smell of it. Stan didn't make bets—ever. How much did he know anyhow?

"You got it," Lou said. "Anybody else." He looked at me. I looked back at him and didn't say anything. I didn't have anything to prove—I didn't have a wife.

Sloane opened another round of beer, and we drifted off into talking about the trip and hunting in general.

"I think I'd better go," Stan said. "I've got classes tomorrow, and it's going to be a long night tomorrow night."

"You got a point, Stan," Jack said.

"Don't forget our fuckin' bet, Larkin," Lou said. He went into the utility room and came back with that M & P .38 strapped on. He stood in the kitchen, snatching the gun out of the holster and putting it back. "Take that, you motherfucker," he muttered, jerking out the pistol and snapping it. I had a vague feeling it was me he was talking to.

Sloane, Jack, and I went with Stan to the front door.

"That McKlearey and I don't get along too well," he said as he went out.

"Don't feel like the Lone Ranger, Stan," Jack said. "I got a gutful of that bastard already, and we ain't even left yet."

"Maybe we can push him off a cliff," I said.

"*After* he's paid his share of our guide fee." Sloane giggled.

Stan went on out to his car, and the rest of us went back into the house.

"Son of a *bitch*!" Lou's voice came from the kitchen. We trooped in, and he stood there with blood dripping onto the tiles from a gash in his left hand. The stupid bastard had been trying to *fan* that double-action .38.

Hot-diggety-damn, this was going to be a fun trip!

14

It rained all the next day. The sky sagged and dripped, and the trailer court was gloomy and sad. I tried sleeping, but after about eleven or so it was useless. I visited with Margaret, but she was drying clothes on a rack in the living room, and the place was steamy and smelled of wet clothes so badly that it made me even more miserable. Then a couple of her coffee-drinking friends came in and started the usual woman talk. There was nothing after that but to go to a tavern and drink beer. Clydine was busy registering for classes until about three or so.

The inside of my car felt damp and clammy as I fired it up, and the windshield fogged over immediately. I drove up the street to the Patio, listening to the hiss of my tires on the wet pavement. The parking lot was sodden and full of puddles. I ran inside to get out of the rain as quickly as possible, and sat down on a stool at the bar and ordered a beer. There were four other guys in the place, all about as dispirited as I was.

I sat at the bar, hunched over, watching the cars whoosh by with the spray flying and the windshield wipers slapping back and forth. By three I was so goddamn depressed I couldn't stand myself. I called Mike from the bar and found out that Betty was better. He sounded pretty bitter about not being able to go with us as well as half-sick with worry over Betty, so I cut it pretty short.

I was still depressed when I got to Clydine's place. She lived in a shabby little second-floor apartment with Joan—the usual stuff—old sofa cushions on the floor to sit on, posters on the wall, bricks and boards for bookcases. Joan had gone home right after she'd finished registering, probably to keep on the good side of her folks, so Clydine and I had the place to ourselves.

She'd been standing around in the rain, and her hair was soaked. She looked very young, sitting cross-legged on a sofa cushion as she dried her hair with a big towel—very young and very vulnerable.

"What's the matter, Danny?" she asked me, looking up. I was slouched in their ruptured armchair with a sour look on my face, looking out the steamy window.

"The rain, I guess," I said shortly.

"You're living in the wrong part of the country if the rain bothers you that much," she said.

"I don't know, Clydine," I said, "maybe it's not really the rain."

"You're worried about this trip, aren't you?" she said.

"I suppose that's it," I said. "Things got a little hairy last night." I told her about it.

"Wow!" she said. "It sounds like a bad Western."

"Maybe that's the point," I said glumly. "The only way a bad Western can end is with a big shoot-out. You ever seen a Western yet that didn't have a shoot-out?"

"Why don't you just back out?" she asked.

I shook my head. "It's too late for that. Besides, I really want to go; I really do."

She shivered.

"Are you cold?" I asked her.

"I'll warm up in a little," she said.

"You little clobberhead," I said. I went over, knelt down beside her, and felt her bare foot. It was like a dead fish. I ran my hand up her leg. Her Levis were soaked.

"Watch it," she murmured.

I ignored that and slid my hand up under her sweatshirt. The little soldiers were clammy. "You knucklehead," I said angrily. "You're going to get pneumonia."

"I'll be all right," she said, shivering again. "You're just a worrier."

I stood up and went into her dinky little bathroom. I dumped all the dirty clothes out of the bathtub and started to fill it with hot water. I went back into the living room and snapped my fingers at her. "Up," I said.

"What?"

"Up. Up. On your feet." I wasn't about to take any crap from her about it. She grumbled a bit but she got up. "Now march," I ordered, pointing at the bathroom.

"This is silly," she said.

I swatted her on the fanny. Not too hard.

"But the bathroom is such a mess," she wailed.

I pushed her on inside. The tub was almost full. I turned it off and checked it out. It was hot but not scalding.

"Strip," I said.

"What?"

"*Strip*! Peel. Take it off."

"*Danny!*" She sounded horribly shocked.

"Oh, for Christ's sake! Look, Rosebud, you've been running around my place wearing nothing but your sunny smile for weeks now. This is no time to come down with a case of false modesty."

"But not in the *bathroom*!" she objected, still in that shocked tone of voice.

Women! I reached out and very firmly pulled off her sweatshirt.

"Danny," she said plaintively, "please." She crossed her arms in front of her breasts. She was blushing furiously. I sat down on the toilet seat and hauled off her soggy Levis.

"Danny." Her complaining voice was very small.

Then I took off her panties. They were wet, too. She went into the "September Morn" crouch.

"All right," I said, "in the tub."

"But—"

"In the tub!"

"Turn your head," she insisted.

"Oh, for God's sake!" I turned my head.

"Well," she said defensively, "it's in the *bathroom*. Ouch! That's *hot*!"

I looked at her quickly.

"You turn your goddamn head back where it was, you goddamn Peeping Tom!"

I looked away again.

"All right," she said finally in that small voice, "I'm in now." She was all scrunched up in the tub, hiding all her vital areas.

"Sit tight," I told her. "I'll be back in a minute."

"Where are you going?" she yelled after me as I hurried out. I didn't answer. I clumped on down the steps and went out in the rain to my car. I had a pint of whiskey in the glove compartment, and it was about half full. I got it and went on back up to her apartment.

"Is that you?" she called.

"No, it's me," I said. Let her figure that one out. It'd give her something to do. "Not in the *bathroom*"—for Chrissake! I heard a lot of splashing.

"Stay in the damn tub!" I yelled in to her.

"I *am*," she yelled back. "I don't know why you got so bossy all of a sudden."

I mixed her a good stiff hot toddy. As an afterthought, I mixed myself one as well. I carried them into the bathroom.

She'd poured about a quart of bubble bath in the water and had stirred it all up. She was in suds up to her chin.

"Well," she said in that same defensive tone, "if you're going to insist on this 'Big Brother is washing you' business, at least I'm going to be *decent*." She sounded outraged.

"Drink this," I said, handing her one of the cups.

"What is it?"

"Medicine. Drink it." I sat back down on the john.

"Boy, are *you* ever a bear," she said, sipping at the toddy. "Hey, I like this. What is it?"

I told her.

Somehow in the interim she'd tied her hair up into a damp tumble on top of her head. She looked so damn appealing that I got a sudden sharp ache in the pit of my stomach just looking at her.

We sat in silence, drinking our toddies.

"Oooo," she finally said with a long, shuddering sigh, "I *was* cold."

"I don't know why you gave me so much static about it," I said.

"But, Danny," she said, "it's the *bathroom*. Don't you understand?"

"Never in a million years." I laughed. "And don't try to explain it to me. It would just give me a headache."

We sat in silence again.

"Danny," she said tentatively, studying the sudsy toe she'd thrust up out of the water.

"Yes, Blossom?"

"What we were talking about before—this hunting thing. You said you really wanted to go."

"Yeah," I said, "I really do.

"It just doesn't fit," she said. "You aren't the type. I mean, you're not some fat forty out to assert his manhood by killing things." She'd never talked about it before, but I guess it had been bothering her.

"You're labeling again," I said. "Oh sure, I've seen the type you're talking about—probably more of them than you have, but that's not the only kind of guy who hunts. For one thing, I eat everything I kill. That kind either gives it away or throws it in the garbage can. I don't give game away either. If I don't like the taste of an animal, I won't hunt it—I won't butcher for somebody else. And I don't collect trophies—not even horns. People who do that are disgusting. They have contempt for the animal they kill. They want a stuffed head around to prove to their friends that they're smarter than the deer was. Well, big goddamn deal!" Suddenly I was pretty hot about it.

"Well, don't get mad at *me*," she said.

"I'm not mad at you, kid," I said. "It's just that it burns me to think about it. The beery blowhard with the broad ass and the big mouth is the picture everybody's got of the guy who hunts—probably because he's so obnoxious. He's the shithead who litters the woods with beer cans and poaches a big buck before shooting time, and wastes game, and hangs mounted heads all over his wall, and pays his dues to the NRA, and calls himself a 'sportsman,' for God's sake—like hunting was some kind of far-out football game."

"And he probably belongs to the John Birch Society, too," she added.

I let that go by.

"Well, I *know* why he's trying to be a mighty hunter," she said, splashing her feet under the slowly dissolving suds, "but you still haven't told me why *you* are."

I shrugged. "I have to," I said. "It's something I have to do. That's the thing the Bambi-lovers can't understand. They simper about 'immaturity,' and 'man doesn't need violence toward his fellow creatures,' and 'let's have a reverence for life and keep our forests and wild life just to look at—as nature intended.' I get so goddamn sick of the intentional fallacy. Whatever the hell some half wit decides is right is automatically what nature or God intended. Bullshit! Preserve the pheasant from the bad old hunter so that the fox can tear him to pieces with his teeth. Preserve the cute little bunny so the hawk can fly him up about a thousand feet and drop him screaming to the ground. You ever hear a rabbit scream? He sounds just like a baby. Preserve the pretty deer—Bambi—so he can overmultiply, overgraze, and then starve to death—or get so weak that the coyotes can run him down and start eating on his guts while he's still alive and bleating.

"Nature isn't some well-trimmed little park, Flower Child. It's very savage. These idiots get all mushy and sentimental about our little furry friends, and they get upset when a grizzly in the Yellowstone chews up a couple kids."

"You sound like you hate animals," she said. "Is that it?"

"I love animals," I said. "Nobody who hates animals hunts. But I respect the animal for what he is—wild. I don't try to make a pet out of him. When I go into the woods, I'm going into his territory. I respect his rights. Am I making any sense?"

"I'm not sure," she said. "But you still haven't told me why you like to go out and kill things."

I shrugged again. "It's something I have to do—every so often I have to go out. It's not the killing—that's really a very small part of it. It's the woods, and being alone, and—well—the hunting. That word gets misused. Actually, it's going out, finding the animal you want in his own territory, and then getting close enough to him to do a clean job. He deserves that much from you. Call it respect, if you like. Anybody who gets all his kicks out of the killing has got some loose marbles."

"I don't understand," she objected, "I don't understand it at all."

"You're not a hunter," I said. "Very few people really are."

"Of course not," she said sarcastically, "after *all*, I'm a *woman*."

"I've met women who were hunters," I said, "and damn good ones, too."

"Is it—well—now don't get mad—sexual?"

"You've been reading too much Hemingway." I laughed. "People use sexual terms to describe it because that's about as close as you can get to it in everyday language that nonhunters would understand. Hemingway knew the difference, and he knew other hunters would, too, and he knew they'd excuse him."

"You make it sound awfully exotic," she said doubtfully.

"It's not," I said, "actually, it's very simple. You just can't explain it to people, that's all."

"Are you a good hunter?" she asked.

"I try," I said, "and I keep on learning. I guess that's about all any guy can do."

"You know," she said, looking straight at me. "I don't think this conversation is really happening. It's surrealistic—me in the bathtub and you sitting on the john trying to eff the ineffable to me."

"What makes it even more psychedelic"—I grinned at her—"is the fact that you're convinced that you're concealed up to the neck when in reality your suds melted about five mintues ago."

She blinked and looked down at herself. Then she squealed, suddenly contorting herself into a knot. She glared at me, her face flaming. "You get out of here!" she said. "You get out of my bathroom, right now!"

I laughed and went on out to the living room. I could hear her perking and grumbling like a small pot behind me. I mixed myself another drink. I felt better. She made me feel good just being around her. I sat down in the chair and looked out at the soggy tail end of the afternoon in a much better humor.

"Hey, *you*!" She was standing in the doorway. Her hair was still tucked on top of her head. Except for the hair ribbon she was stark naked. She pitched her damp towel back through the bathroom door and snapped her fingers at me. "Up!" she said. "On your feet, Buster!"

I got up. "Now, what—"

"March," she said, pointing imperiously at the bedroom.

"I don't think you ought to get too overheated," I started. "I mean, you got a bad chill and—"

"Bullshit! Nobody—and I mean *nobody*—is going to yank my panties off like you did just now and then tip his hat and walk away. Now you get into that bedroom!"

I went into the bedroom.

After she finished her revenge, or whatever you want to call it, we talked some more. About ten o'clock that evening I kissed her goodbye and went out to my car. "Not in the *bathroom*!" For Christ's own private sake! I laughed all the way back across town.

I took a shower, dressed in my hunting clothes, and then clumped on up to Jack's trailer, wincing as the rain spotted my Army boots. I'd spent a lot of hours polishing them.

Jack was a little groggy from his nap, but he dressed quickly, and we drove on over to Sloane's house through the rain-swept streets. We didn't say much except to complain about the weather.

"Sure as hell hope it isn't rainin' on the other side of the mountains," Jack said. I grunted agreement. We stopped by a liquor store and each bought a fifth of bourbon.

"God knows if we'd be able to find a store open later on," Jack said.

We got to Sloane's place about a quarter to twelve and sat down and had a beer with Calvin after we'd stowed our gear in the car. Stan and Lou both showed up about five to twelve, and they loaded up. All of us had a good stiff belt of Cal's whiskey, and we took off.

We stopped at a roadhouse tavern just before we got to Seattle and laid in a supply of beer, about a case in each car. It was one of those overchromed joints, all fancy and new. The only guy in there besides the bartender was a drunk in the back booth, snoring for all he was worth. The bartender had a solitaire game laid out on the bar. Real swinging joint. We bought our beer, pried Lou away from the pinball machine, and took off again, blasting along in the wake of Sloane's Cadillac. We didn't get to Everett until almost two, and we stopped for gas. Once we got past Snohomish, we were about the only cars on the road. The flat farmland of the Snohomish River Valley stretched on back into the mist and darkness on either side of us, and the fences with the bottom strand of wire snarled in weeds sprayed out on either hand as we passed. Now and then we'd see a house and barn—all dark—near the road. Once in a while a car would pass, going the other way like a bat out of hell and spraying muddy water on the windshield.

Jack and I switched off, and I drove for a while. There's something about driving late at night in the rain. It's almost as if the world has stopped. The rain sheets down in tatters, and the road unrolls out in front of your headlights. We went up through the small silent, mountain towns, always climbing. Each town seemed emptier than the last, with the rain washing the fronts of the dark old buildings, and the streetlights swinging in the wind. We kept the radio going, and neither one of us said much until we got on past Gold Bar, the last town before we really started to climb. Once we got up into the mountains, the radio faded, and after about ten miles of static, I switched it off.

"Bust me open another beer, Jack," I said, breaking the silence.

"Sure." He cracked one and handed it to me.

"Damn. I hope this weather breaks at the summit," I said.

"Didn't you hear that last weather report?" he asked. "It's pretty much all on this side."

"That's a break."

"Yeah." We lapsed into silence again, watching the headlights spear on out in front of the car and the windshield wipers flopping back and forth. I turned up the heater.

"God damn," he said suddenly, "I wish to hell Mike could have made it. It's a damn shame, you know that? He's been tryin' to get away for the High Hunt for the last four years now, and some damn thing always comes up so he can't make it."

"Yeah," I said, "and Mike's a good head. He'd have been fun to have along."

Jack nodded gloomily. "You want a belt?" he said suddenly.

I wasn't really sure I did, but I saw that he needed one. "Why not?"

He fished his bottle out from under the seat and cracked the seal. He took a long pull and handed it to me. I took a short blast and handed it back.

"I guess we'd better go easy on this stuff," he said. "We show up drunk and Miller's liable to send us back down the mountain." He put the jug away.

"Right."

"You know, Dan," he said after a while. "I'm damn glad we got the chance to do this together. We never got to know each other much when we were kids, what with one damn thing and another—the Old Lady and all. Maybe it's time we got acquainted."

"I've had a pretty good time the last few weeks," I said. "I'm not sorry I got in touch with you." It was more or less true.

"It'd all be great if it wasn't for that son-of-a-bitchin' McKlearey," he said bitterly.

"Yeah. What the hell's got him off on the prod so bad, anyway?"

"Aw shit! He was the big-ass gunnery sergeant in the Corps—you know, a hundred guys jumped every time he farted. He was a big shot. Now he's low man on the totem pole at Sloane's used-car lot—a big plate of fried ratshit. He's not in charge anymore. Some guys just can't hack that."

"Institutional mentality," I said.

"What the hell's that?"

"It's like the ex-con who gets busted for sticking up a police station two days after he gets out of the pen. He really wants to go back. They take care of him, do his thinking for him. He's safe inside. Guys in the military get the same way."

"Maybe that's it," Jack said. "When I knew him in the service, he was a different guy. Now he's drunk all the time and shacked-up with a half dozen women and a real first-class prick. I wouldn't be surprised if he's been throwin' the wood to Marg every time my back's turned."

I was suddenly very wide awake. Christ, had he been so drunk that night he couldn't remember what he'd said? "Oh?" I said carefully.

"It wouldn't be the first time she's played around. Maybe I've given her reason enough. She was pretty young and simple when I married her, and I'm not one to pass up some occasional strange stuff. Maybe she figures she's entitled. I don't give a shit. Me and her are about ready to split the sheets anyway." He slumped lower in the seat and lit a cigarette.

"Sorry to hear that," I said. I meant it.

"I've been through it a couple of times already. I know the signs. I don't really give a rat's ass; I'm about ready to go the single route myself anyway. Marriage is fine for a while—steady ass and home cookin'—but it gets to be a drag."

"I'm still sorry to hear it."

"But no matter what, I'm a blue-balls son of a bitch if I want to get cut out by that fuckin' McKlearey while I'm still payin' the bills. That's one of the reasons I'm gonna outhunt that motherfucker if it kills me. Maybe if I rub his nose in it hard enough, he'll get the idea and move on." Jack's voice was harsh.

"I don't know," I said. "As stupid as he is, getting an idea through his head might take some doing."

"I suppose I could always shoot the bastard."

"Not worth it." I was about half-afraid he meant it.

"I suppose not, but he could sure use shootin'."

"You know it, buddy."

"Another beer?"

"Sure."

The moon was slipping in and out of the clouds as we climbed higher, and the drops that hit the windshield were getting smaller. The rain was slacking off. The big fir trees at the side of the road caught briefly in our headlights had their trunks wreathed in tendrils of mist. I leaned forward and looked up through the windshield at the slowly emerging stars.

"Looks like it's going to quit," I said.

"That's what I told you," he said.

THE HIGH HUNT

15

Sₗₒₐₙₑ's Cₐᴅɪʟʟᴀᴄ wₐₛ ₛₜɪʟʟ ʟₑₐᴅɪₙg, and at the summit he signaled for a left.

"Where the hell's he going?" I asked. "Off into the timber?"

"Naw. He probably wants to use the can. McKlearey's been droppin' back for the last ten miles anyway, so we better let the son of a bitch catch up."

I turned Jack's car into the lot at the summit behind Sloane, stopping beside his car and switching off the engine.

Sloane stuck his head out the window on the driver's side and yelled, "Piss call!" The echoes bounced off down the gorge we'd just come up.

"Christ, Sloane," Jack hissed, "keep it down. There's people livin' over in the lodge there."

"Oooops," Sloane said. He and Jack hotfooted it over to the rest room while Stan and I stood out in the sprinkling rain waiting to flag down McKlearey. It was so quiet you could hear the pattering drops back in the timber.

"Pretty chilly up here," Stan said. His voice was hushed, and his breath steamed. He had his hands jammed down into the pockets of his new bright-orange hunting jacket. The jacket clashed horribly with his old red duck-hunting cap.

"It's damned high," I said.

"What time is it?"

"About three thirty," I said.

"You think Lou's car has broken down?"

"About right now I wouldn't give a damn if that bastard had driven off into the gorge somewhere. I've had a gutful of him, and a steering post through the belly might civilize him some."

"I've met people I've liked a lot more," Stan agreed. That's Stan for you. Never say what you mean.

"How are you and Sloane getting along?"

"Just fine. He's a strange one, you know? He plays the fool, but he's really very serious. He was telling me that he hates that pawnshop and all the sad little people who come in wanting just a couple of dollars for a piece of worthless trash—they know it's not worth anything, but it's all they have—but he can't get his money back out of the place right now, so he has to stay there."

"Yeah," I said. "Sloane's a really odd duck."

"And he's really very intelligent—well-read, aware of what's going on in the world—all of this foolishness is just an act."

"I wouldn't want to try to outsmart him," I agreed.

Cal and Jack came back. "Hasn't that shithead made it yet?" Jack demanded. "Oh, hell, yes," he imitated McKlearey's voice, "I'm gonna drive *my* car. It's a real goin' machine. Cost me sixty-five bucks. I'd feel perfectly safe drivin' from here to the end of the block in that car."

"I think that's his car now," Stan said. He pointed far off down the mountain we'd just climbed. We saw a flash of headlights sweeping out across the gorge, flaring out in a sudden bright swipe through the mist.

Stan and I went to the rest room, came back, and joined the others watching Lou's old car labor up the highway.

"Is this the fuckin' top?" he demanded as he pulled up alongside, his radiator hissing ominously.

"This is her," Sloane said. "Car heat up on you?"

"Aw, this cripple," Lou said in disgust. "Is there any water here?"

"Over by the latrine," I said, pointing.

He pulled over to the side of the rest-room building and popped the hood. He got out and threw a beer bottle off into the trees. The bandage on his left hand gleamed whitely in the darkness. He eased off the radiator cap, and the steam boiled out, drifting pale and low downwind. He poured water into the radiator, and pretty soon it stopped steaming. Then he fished out a can of oil from the trunk and punched holes in the top with an old beer opener. He dumped the oil into the engine and then threw the can after the beer bottle. He slammed the hood, unzipped his pants, and pissed on the front tire.

"Christ, McKlearey!" Jack said, "there's the latrine right there."

"Fuck it!" Lou said. "What time is it?"

"Nearly four," I told him.

"Let's go huntin', men," he said and climbed back in his car. The rest of us went to our cars, and we started down the other side.

Jack was driving again, and I slumped down in the seat. The sky was clear on this side, and the stars were very bright. I picked one out and watched it as we drifted down the mountain.

What in the goddamn hell was I doing here anyway? I was running off into the high mountains with a bunch of guys I didn't really know, to do something I didn't really know all that much about, despite what I'd told Clydine. Maybe I was still running and this was just someplace else to run to. But I had a strange feeling that whatever I'd been running after—or away from—was going to be up there. Maybe Stan was right. When you strip it all away, and it's just you and the big lonely out there, you can get down to what counts.

Maybe it was more than that, too. Up until Dad died, I'd heard hunting stories—about him and Uncle Charles, about Granddad and Great-Uncle Beale—all of them. And I'd started going out as soon as I was old enough—alone most of the time. It was something where you couldn't work the angles or unload a quick snow job or any of the crap I'd somehow gotten so good at in the last few years. There was no way to fake it; it had to be real. If you didn't kill the damned deer, he wouldn't fall down. You couldn't talk to him and tell him that he was statistically dead and convince him to take a dive. He had too much integrity. He knew what it was all about, and if you didn't really nail him down, he'd go over the nearest mountain before you could get off a second shot. He knew he was real. It was up to you to find out if you were.

"Hey, Jack," I said.

"Yeah?"

"You remember Dad?"

"Sure."

"He liked to hunt, didn't he?"

"Whenever he could. The Old Lady was pretty much down on it. About all he could do by the time you were growin' up was to go out for ducks now and then. He used to sneak out of the house in the morning before she woke up. She wouldn't let him go out for deer anymore."

"Whatever happened to that old .45-70 Granddad left him?"

"She sold it. Spent the money on booze."

"Shit! You know, I've got a hunch we'd have been raised better by a bitch wolf."

"You're just bitter," he said.

"You're goddamn right I am," I said. "I wouldn't walk across the street for her if she was dying."

"She calls once in a while," he said. "I try to keep her away from the kids. You never know when she's gonna show up drunk."

"How's she paying her way?"

"Who knows? Workin' in a whorehouse for all I know."

"I wonder why the Old Man didn't kick her ass out into the street."

"You and me, that's why," my brother said.

"Yeah, there's that, too, I suppose."

We passed through Cashmere about five and swung north toward Lake Chelan. The sky began to get pale off to the east.

"God damn, that's nice, isn't it?" Jack said, pointing at the sky.

"Dawn the rosy-fingered," I said, misquoting Homer, "caressing the hair of night."

"Say, that's pretty good. You make it up?"

I shook my head.

"You read too goddamn much, you know that? When I say something, you can be pretty goddamn sure it's right out of my own head." He belched.

We drove on, watching the sky grow lighter and lighter. As the light grew stronger, the poplar leaves began to emerge in all their brilliant yellow along the river bottoms. The pines swelled black behind them.

"Pretty country," Jack said.

"Hey," I said, "look at that."

A doe with twin fawns was standing hock-deep in a clear stream, drinking, the ripples sliding downstream from where she stood. She raised her head, her ears flicking nervously as we passed.

"Pretty, isn't she?" he said.

We got to Twisp about eight and hauled into a gas station. Sloane went in and called Miller while we got our gas tanks filled.

"He's got everything all ready," he said when he came back out. "He told me how to get there."

"How far is it?" Lou asked. "This bucket is gettin' pretty fuckin' tuckered." He slapped the fender of his car with his bandaged hand.

"About fifteen miles," Sloane said. "Road's good all the way."

We paid for the gas and drove on out of town. Twisp is one of those places with one paved street and the rest dirt. It squats in the valley with the mountains hulking over it threateningly, green-black rising to blue-black, and then the looming white summits.

The road out to Miller's wasn't the best, but we managed. The sun was up now, and the poplar leaves gleamed pure gold. The morning air was so clear that every rock and limb and leaf stood out. The fences were straight lines along the road and on out across the mowed hayfields. The mountains swelled up out of the poplar-gold bottoms. It was so pretty it made your throat ache. I felt good, really good, maybe for the first time in years.

Sloane slowed up, then went on, then slowed again. He was reading mailboxes. Finally he signaled, the blinker on his Caddy looking very ostentatious out here.

We wheeled into a long driveway and drove on up toward a group of white painted buildings and log fences. A young colt galloped along beside us as we drove to the house. He was all sleek, and his muscles rolled under his skin as he ran. He acted like he was running just for the fun of it.

"Little bastard's going to outrun us," Jack said, laughing.

We pulled up in the yard in front of the barn and parked where a stumpy little old guy with white hair and a two-week stubble directed us to. He was wearing cowboy boots and a beat-up old cowboy hat, and he walked like his legs had been broken a half dozen times. If that was Miller, I was damn sure going to be disappointed.

It wasn't.

Miller came out of the house, and I swear he had a face like a hunk of rock. With that big, old-fashioned white mustache, he looked just a little bit like God himself. He wore cowboy boots and had a big hat like the little white-haired man, and neither of them looked out of place in that kind of gear. Some guides dress up for the customers, but you could tell that these two were for real. I took a good look at Miller and decided that I'd go way out of my way to keep from crossing him. He was far and away the meanest-looking man I've ever seen in my life. I understood what Mike had meant about him.

We turned off the motors, and the silence seemed suddenly very solid. We got out, and he looked at us—hard—sizing each one of us up.

"Men," he said. It was a sort of greeting, I guess—or maybe a question. His voice was deep and very quiet—no louder than it absolutely had to be.

Even Sloane's exuberance was a little dampened. He stepped forward. "Mr. Miller," he said, "I'm Cal Sloane." They shook hands.

"I'll get to know the rest of you in good time," he said. "Right now breakfast's ready. Give Clint there your personal gear and sleepin' bags, and we'll go in and eat." I never learned Clint's last name or Miller's first one.

We unloaded the cars and then followed Miller on up to the house. He led us through a linoleumed kitchen with small windows and an old-fashioned sink and wood stove, and on into the dining room, where we sat down at the table. The room had dark wood paneling and the china was very old, white with a fine-line blue Japanese print on it. The room smelled musty, and I suspected it wasn't used much. There was a wood-burning heating stove in the corner that popped now and then. Miller came back out of the kitchen with a huge enameled coffee pot and filled all our cups.

The coffee was hot and black and strong enough to eat the fillings out of your teeth. The stumpy little guy came in and started carting food out of the kitchen. First he brought out a platter of steaks.

"Venison," Miller said. "Figured we'd better clean up what's left over from last winter."

Then there were biscuits and honey, then eggs and fried potatoes. There were several pitchers of milk on the table. We all ate everything Miller ate; I think we were afraid not to.

But when the little guy hauled out a couple of pies, I had to call a halt.

"Sorry," I said. "I'll have to admit that you guys can outeat me." I pushed myself back from the table.

"The Kid just can't keep up." Jack laughed.

"Well, you don't have to eat it all," Miller said. "We just figured you might be a little hungry."

"Hungry, yes," I said, grinning, "but I couldn't eat all that if I was starving."

"Better eat," the man Miller had called Clint growled. "Be four hours in the saddle before you feed again."

"I think I'm good for twelve," I said. I lit a cigarette and poured myself another cup of coffee.

"After a few hours in the high country," Clint warned, "your belly's gonna think your th'oat's been cut." He sounded like he meant it.

The others finished eating, and Clint poured more coffee all around. Miller fished out a sheet of paper from one of his shirt pockets and a pair of gold-rimmed glasses out of another.

"Guess we might as well get all this settled right now," he said, putting on the glasses. "That way we won't have it hangin' fire."

We all took out our wallets. Clint went out and came back with a beat-up old green metal box. Miller opened it and took out a receipt book.

"Ten days," Miller said, "fifty dollars a man." We all started counting money out on the table. He looked around and nodded in approval. He started filling out receipts laboriously, licking the stub of the pencil now and then. He asked each of us our names and filled them in on the receipts. Clint took our money and put it away in the tin box.

"Now," Miller said, squinting at the paper, "the grub come to a hundred and fifty dollars. I got a list here and the price of ever-thing if you want to check it. I already took off for me and Clint. Your share come to a hundred and fifty and a few odd dollars, but call it a hundred and fifty. I figured it out, and it's thirty dollars a man. You can check my figures if you want. I kept it down as much as I could. We won't eat fancy, but it'll stick with us." He looked around, offering the paper. We all shook our heads.

"I'll give you the hundred and a half," Sloane said. "The others can settle up with me." The receipt-writing had obviously bugged him.

"Thanks anyway," Miller said, "but if it's all the same to you men, I'd a whole lot rather get it from each man myself. Then I know it's right, and there's no arguments later."

Sloane shrugged, and we each counted out another thirty dollars. Miller struggled through another five receipts and then took off his glasses. I noticed the sweat running down the outer edges of his mustache.

"There," he said with obvious relief. "Well, men, this ain't gettin' us up into the high country. Let's go pick out some horses and get 'em loaded up in the truck. We got a ways to drive before we get to the horse trail."

We all got up and followed him on out of the house. Clint began picking up the dishes as we left. It was still chilly outside, and the morning sun was very bright. Miller stopped out in the yard and waited for us all to gather around. He looked up into the mountains and cleared his throat.

"Just a few more things I want to get straight before we leave, men," he said, and I could see that he'd have preferred not to say it. "I've been known to take a drink now and then myself, but you men are goin' to be up there with loaded guns, and it's damn high where you'll be huntin'. You might be able to drink like a fish down here, but two drinks up there and you'll be fallin' over your own feet. I know you've got liquor with you, and I'll probably take a bottle along myself, but I don't want any of us takin' a drink before the sun goes down and the guns are all hung up. I sure don't want nobody shootin' hisself—or me. OK?''

We all nodded again. He wasn't the kind of man you argued with.

"And if any of you got any quarrels with each other, leave 'em down here. Any trouble up there, and we'll all come out, and no refunds. We all straight on that?'' He looked around at us, and his face was stern.

We all nodded again.

"Good,'' he said, and he looked relieved. "Last thing. I know that country up there and you men don't. If I tell you to do somethin', you'd better do 'er. I ain't gonna be tellin' you 'cause I like bossin' men around. I'll have a damn good reason, so don't give me no hard times about it. OK, now I've said my piece, all right?''

We nodded again. What else could we do?

"Well then, I guess that takes care of all the unpleasantness. Let's go down to the corral and pick out some horses. Sooner we get that done, the sooner we can go hunt deer.'' He started off, and we fell in behind him. He took damn big steps.

I began to feel better about this. Miller knew his business, and there wouldn't be any horseshit nonsense with him around. I looked up at the mountains, blue in the morning light.

God damn, it might just be a good trip after all.

16

It took us the better part of an hour to cut out horses from the herd in the corral down by the big log barn. Miller and Clint leaned across the top rail, pointing out this horse, then that one, calling them by name and telling us their good points—almost like they were selling them. I picked a big gray they called Ned. He looked pretty good at first, but then I caught a glimpse of his other eye and wasn't so sure. We herded them up into the back of a big stock-truck along with some packhorses and then began hauling saddles out to a battered pickup.

"Some of you men'll have to ride in the back of the pickup,'' Miller said, squinting into the tangle of saddles, straps, and ropes we'd piled in there. "Might be a bit uncomfortable, but it ain't too far.''

"I'll take my car,'' Lou said shortly.

"Here we go again,'' Jack muttered to me disgustedly, yanking his red baseball cap down over his forehead.

"Road's pretty rough,'' Clint warned.

Miller shrugged, "Suit yourself,'' he said. "Couple of you can go with me in the pickup, then, and one of you with Clint in the stock-truck, and one other man in the car with this man here, all right?''

We all nodded and started pitching the sleeping bags and clothing sacks that Clint had hauled down here earlier into the back of the pickup.

"I'll go with McKlearey," Sloane told the rest of us, "and we can pile the guns in his back seat." Sloane was thinking ahead. He was probably the only one of us who could ride five miles with Lou without getting into a fight.

"Good idea," Miller said. "Guns could get banged around some in the pickup." He turned to Clint. "You lock up?" he asked.

"Right, Cap," Clint said, "and I got it all squared away with Matthews. His oldest boy's comin' by to feed the stock while we're gone."

"Good," Miller said. "Well, men, let's get goin'." He led the way over to the trucks. I hung back a little, letting Jack and Stan go ahead. They both got into the pickup with Miller, so I climbed up into the cab of the stock-truck with Clint. Sloane and McKlearey rode along with us, hanging onto the outside of the cab as far as the main yard where our cars were parked. Then we all got out, put our guns in the back seat of McKlearey's car, and climbed back in.

We drove on out of the yard and on down the long driveway, the pickup leading, then McKlearey's weary Chevy, and Clint and I bringing up the rear in the stock-truck. The colt ran along beside us again as we drove on down to the highway.

"Little fella sure likes to run, doesn't he?" I ventured to Clint.

"Young horse ain't got much damn sense," Clint growled. "Just like a damn kid. About all he wants to do is run and play. Older horse rests ever' chance he gets."

"Looks like he's going to be pretty fast," I said.

"Sure as hell ought to be," Clint said, "considerin' what ol' Cap paid for stud fee. We got this quarter-horse mare—that's her standin' over there in the shade. Got good blood-lines, so he goes all out on gettin' her bred." He cranked the wheel around, swinging wide out onto the highway. I could hear a thump or two from the back as the horses stumbled around with the sudden shift in direction.

"Sure as hell hope that fella can keep up with ol' Cap's pickup," Clint said, thrusting his stubbled chin toward the blue fog coming out of the tailpipe of McKlearey's car.

"I wouldn't bet on it," I said sourly. "He's been lagging behind all night. That car of his is a cripple. We have any big hills to climb?"

"Nothin' too bad," Clint said, "and we got good gravel all the way after we turn off the tar."

"That's a break," I said.

"What'd he do to his hand?" he asked. I'd seen both him and Miller eyeing McKlearey's bandage.

"He cut it. It isn't bad."

"That's good."

We drove on up the highway for a few miles.

"I didn't catch your name," he said finally.

"Dan," I said, "Dan Alders."

He stuck out a knobby hand without looking away from the road, and we shook. "Just call me Clint," he said. "Ever'body else does."

"Right, Clint," I said.

We wound along the paved road that hugged the bottom of the valley, crossing the narrow bridges that stepped back and forth across the twisting little stream that sparkled in the mid-morning sun. I suddenly wished that Clydine were along so that she could see this.

"Many fish in here, Clint?" I asked, looking down into the water.

"I can usually pick up a few," he said. "I got a hole I work pretty often. Some pretty nice cutthroat in there."

I glanced down at the water as we crossed the stream again. "Looks pretty shallow," I said, watching the clear water slide over the smooth brown pebbles.

"It backs up behind rocks and downed trees," he told me. "Fish'll hole up in there. Hit 'em with a small spoon or bait, and they'll go for it ever' time."

"Any size?" I asked.

"Lifted a three-pounder this spring," he said.

"That could get pretty wild and woolly in that fast water," I said.

"It was sorta fun." He grinned. "You fish much?"

"When I get the chance," I said.

He grunted approvingly, and we drove on a ways in silence.

I slid a little lower in the seat, sliding my tail to the edge of the cushion. "Getting a little butt-sprung," I said, explaining.

"Wait'll later," he said, grinning again. "That car seat's soft compared to a saddle."

"I don't suppose anybody's ever figured out a way to ride standing up."

"Not so's you'd notice it."

"Oh, well," I said.

"You done much ridin'?" he asked me tentatively after a long pause.

"I know which end of the horse is which is about all."

He scratched his stubbled chin. "I'd kinda watch old Ned then if I was you." He squinted into the morning sunlight as we swung off the pavement onto a graveled road. "He ain't been rode for a few weeks, and he's had time to build up a good head of steam. He could be pretty green, so you might have to iron a few of the kinks out of him."

My stomach lurched. "You figure he'll buck?" I asked nervously.

"Oh, nothin' fancy. He'll probably rear a couple times and maybe hump up a little. Just be ready for him. Keep kinda loose, is all, and haul him up tight. That's the main thing—don't let him get his head down between his front legs. If he gets too persnickety, just slap him across the ears with the end of the reins. That'll bring him around."

"I'd hate to start off the trip getting dumped on my butt in the gravel," I said.

He chuckled. "I didn't mean to spook you none. You'll be OK if you're ready for him."

"I sure hope so," I said doubtfully.

We had begun to climb up out of the valley. The white trunks and golden leaves of the poplar trees that had bordered the little stream gave way to dark pines. The gravel road was splotched with alternate patches of shadow and bright sunlight. It looked cool and damp back in under the trees. Every so often a red squirrel scampered across the road in front of us, his tail flirting arrogantly.

"Pushy little guys, aren't they?" I said to Clint.

"I think they do that just for the fun of it," he agreed.

We came around a corner, and I could suddenly see all the way up to the summit of the surrounding mountains. The sun sparkled on the snowfields outlined against the deep blue of the sky.

"God damn!" I said, almost reverently.

"Pretty, ain't it?" Clint agreed.

"Are we going up there?" I asked, pointing up toward the snow.

"Not quite," he said. "Pretty close, though."

We drove on, twisting up along the gravel road. There's a kind of bluish color to the woods in the morning that makes things look unreal. An eagle or hawk of some kind turned big wide circles way up, hunting, or just flying for the hell of it.

"Where 'bouts is it you work?" Clint asked after another mile or so.

"I just got out of the service," I told him. "I'll be going back to school pretty soon."

"Which branch you in?" he asked.

"Army."

"Me and Cap was in the Horse-Marines when we was younger."

"Oh? Lou up there—guy who's driving his own car—was a Marine."

"I kinda figured he mighta been. Tell by the way he walks."

We drove on up the gravel road for about an hour, climbing gradually but steadily. The road grew narrower and narrower but was still in pretty good shape. It was close to ten thirty when Miller pulled out into a wide place beside the road. The rest of us pulled off and stopped.

"This is where we saddle up," Clint said, pulling on the hand brake. "Road goes on about another hundred yards and then gives up."

We climbed down from the truck and went over to where the others had gathered at the back of the pickup. It was quite a bit colder up here than it had been in the valley. Lou's radiator was steaming again.

"We'll unload the horses one at a time," Miller said. "They stay calmer that way."

Clint and I went to the back of the stock-truck and pulled out the unloading ramp.

"Packhorses first, Clint," Miller said.

Clint grunted and went up the ramp. He unhooked the gate and swung it back. There was a thumping and several snorts as he disappeared inside the truck. He came to the door leading a somewhat discouraged-looking horse by the halter. Miller passed him up the snap-end of a lead-rope, and he fastened it to the halter. Then Miller pulled, and Clint slapped the horse sharply on the rump. The horse laid back his ears and carefully stepped down the ramp. Clint hopped out and closed the gate again.

They led the horse over to the pickup and put a cumbersome-looking packsaddle on him. Then they tied him to a sapling and went back to the stock-truck. They unloaded three more packhorses, one by one.

"We could get by with just a couple," Miller explained, "but we'll need this many to bring out the deer."

Then they began bringing out the saddle horses. Jack's horse came out first. After he'd been saddled and bridled, Miller told Jack to mount and walk him up and down the road a ways to loosen him up. I could see that Jack was getting a kick out of it. That baseball cap of his made him look like a kid.

McKlearey's horse was next, and Lou took off at a gallop.

"Hey!" Miller said sharply as Lou came back up the road. "I said to walk him! That horse plays out on you, and you're gonna be afoot." Lou reined in and did as he was told. I thought that was a good sign. I began to have hopes that Miller might just be able to keep McKlearey in line.

They brought out Ned next, and my stomach tightened up. He looked meaner than ever. I particularly didn't like the way he kind of set himself when Clint threw the saddle on him. I walked up to the horse slowly. He laid his ears back and watched me. I pulled off my quilted red jacket and red felt hat. No point in messing up my hunting gear. Skin heals. Clothes don't.

Clint held the stirrup for me while Miller held the horse's head. They hadn't done that for anybody else, and that sure didn't help my nerves any. I got up into the saddle and got my feet arranged in the stirrups.

"You all set?" Miller asked, with the faintest hint of a smile under his mustache.

"I guess."

Miller nodded sharply, and both he and Clint jumped back out of the way. Now, that *really* makes you feel good. Ned stood perfectly still for a minute. I could feel him wound up like a spring under me.

"Give 'im a boot in the ribs," Miller said. I nudged the horse gently with my heels. Nothing happened. I looked around for a soft place to land.

"Kick 'im," Miller said, grinning openly now.

I gritted my teeth and really socked the horse in the ribs. His front feet came up off the ground. If old Clint hadn't warned me, I think I'd have been dumped right then. That big gray horse pranced around on his hind feet for a minute, fighting to get some slack in the reins so he could get his head down. Then he dropped down again, still fighting. I was hanging onto the reins with one hand and the saddle horn with the other. He jumped a couple times and spun around.

"Kick 'im again, Dan!" Clint shouted, laughing. "Stay with 'im, boy!" I kicked the horse in the ribs again, and he reared just as he had the first time. This time I wasn't so surprised, so I let go of the saddle horn and swung the reins at his ears the way Clint had told me to. Then he twisted around and tried to bite my leg. I whacked him in the nose with the reins, and that seemed to settle him a little. He humped a couple more times, shivered, and took off down the road at a trot.

"Better run that horse a little," Miller called. "Others don't need it, but Old Ned's a bit frisky."

"Right," I said, and nudged the horse into a lope. I kicked him a little harder. "The man says run," I explained to the horse.

McKlearey scowled at me as I barreled on past him.

The wind whistled by my ears, and I could feel the easy roll of Ned's muscles as he ran. I slowed him up and turned him about a half mile down the road. Then I opened him up to a dead run. I was laughing out loud when I pulled up by the trucks. I couldn't help it. I hadn't had so much fun in years. Ned pranced around a little, blowing and tossing his head. I think he was getting a kick out of it, too.

"Hey, cowboy," Jack yelled, "where'd you learn to ride like that?"

"Beginner's luck," I said. I looked over to where Miller and Clint were saddling Stan's horse. "OK to walk him now?" I asked.

"Yeah, he looks to be settled a bit," Miller said, still grinning.

I pulled Ned in beside Jack's horse, and the two of us rode on back down the road.

"You looked pretty fancy there, little brother," he said.

"I picked the wrong horse," I told him. "That little exhibition back there was all his idea."

"How the hell'd you manage to stay on?"

"Clint warned me about this knothead in the truck on the way up. I was ready for him. You might not have noticed, but I had a pretty firm grip on this saddlehorn."

Jack laughed. "You two didn't slow down long enough for me to see that part of it."

I gingerly felt my rump. "I sure hope he doesn't feel he has to go through this every time we start out."

Jack laughed again, and we plodded down the road.

"How's this Miller strike *you*?" I asked him.

"I don't think I'd want to cross him."

"Amen to that, buddy," I agreed.

"He sure as hell acts like he knows what he's doin'," my brother said.

"He's an old-time Marine," I said. "Him and Clint both."

"McKlearey'll cash in on that," Jack said, unbuttoning his quilted hunting vest.

"Wouldn't doubt it."

"How's Clint? He seemed pretty grouchy back at the house."

"That's mostly bark," I said. "We talked quite a bit on the way up. Like I told you, he was the one that warned me about this horse and his little habits."

"Yeah," Jack said. "I noticed that he was callin' you by name when you guys got down from the truck."

We turned around and rode back on up to the others. Stan and Sloane were mounted now and were starting off down the road. Sloane seemed to be puffing pretty hard. Maybe his horse had him a little spooked, or maybe his down-filled parka was a little too warm.

Jack and I got down and helped Miller and Clint load up the pack-horses. Then Miller called in the others.

"Now here's how we'll go," he said after they had dismounted. "I'll lead out and Clint'll bring up the rear with the packhorses. Don't try nothin' fancy along the trail. Let the horse do all the work and most of the thinkin'. Just set easy and watch the scenery go by. The horses know what they're doin', so trust 'em."

He showed us how to tie our rifles to the saddle where they'd be out of the way. His own gun case was lashed to the back of one of the packhorses, and Clint's .30-30 was tucked in beside it.

I think we all saw the quick glance that passed between Miller and Clint when we hauled our pistol belts out of McKlearey's car.

"Bears," Sloane explained, almost apologetically.

"Bears!" Clint snorted. "Ain't no damn bears up that high."

"Oh," Sloane said meekly. "We thought there might be."

Miller scratched his mustache dubiously. "Can't leave 'em here," he said finally. "Somebody might come along and steal 'em. I guess you'll have to bring the damn things along. They might be some good for signalin' and the like." He shook his head and walked off a ways by himself, his fists jammed down into the pockets of his sheepskin coat and that big hat pulled down low over his eyes.

We all looked at each other shamefacedly and slowly strapped on our hardware.

"Looks like the goddamn Tijuana National Guard," Clint muttered in disgust.

We stood around like a bunch of kids who'd been caught stealing apples until Miller came back.

"All right," he said shortly, "get on your horses and let's get goin'."

We climbed on our horses—Ned didn't even twitch this time—and followed Miller on up to the end of the road and onto the saddle trail that took off from there. The trail moved up along the side of a ridge. Once we got up a ways, the pines thinned out and we could see out for miles across the heavily timbered foothills. The horizon ahead of us was a ragged line of snow-covered peaks; to the east, behind us, it faded off into blue, hazy distance. The grass up here was yellow and knee-high, waving gently in the slight wind that followed us up the ridge. I could see little swirls and patterns on top of the grass as gusts brushed here and there.

It was absolutely quiet, except for the horses and the sound of the wind. I felt good—I felt damned good.

At the top of the ridge we stopped.

"Better let the horses blow a bit," Miller said. "Always a good idea to let 'em settle into it easy." He seemed to have gotten his temper back.

"Do we have quite a bit farther to go?" Sloane asked, breathing deeply. He looked pretty rough. I guessed that he was feeling the lack of sleep.

"We're just gettin' started," Miller said. "We'll cut on up across that saddleback there and then down into the next valley. We stay to the valley a piece and then go up to the top of the other ridge. Then on into the next hollow." 'Bout another twelve miles or so."

Sloane shook his head and took another deep breath. "I think I've got this damned belt too tight," he said. He opened the parka, undid his gun belt, looped it a couple times around the saddle horn and buckled it. He eased off on his pants belt a couple notches. "That's better," he said.

"I told you your beer-drinkin' habit would catch up to you someday, Calvin," Jack said laughing.

"Doe!" Miller said suddenly, pointing up the ridge at a deer that had stopped about a quarter of a mile away and was watching us nervously.

Sloane pulled a pair of small binoculars out of his coat pocket and glassed the ridge. "Where?" he demanded.

"See that big pine off to the left of that patch of gray rock?"

"Back in the shade a bit," I said.

"I don't—oh, yeah, now I see her."

We watched the doe step delicately on over the ridge and go down into the brush on the other side.

"There's a big game trail up there," Miller said. "I followed it down last winter during the big snow. It was the only place I could be sure of the footing."

"On horseback?" Stan asked.

"I was leadin' 'im," Miller said. "He'd gone lame on me up the ridge a ways. I had to hunker down under a ledge for two days till the snow eased up."

Stan shook his head. "That would scare me into convulsions," he admitted. "Did you ever think you weren't going to make it?"

"Oh, it give me a few nervous moments," Miller said. A stray gust of wind ruffled that white mustache of his. He squinted up the ridge, his face more like a rock than ever.

McKlearey came up. He'd been hanging back, riding about halfway between the rest of us and Clint, who was a ways back with the packhorses. Maybe he was ashamed of himself because Miller'd had to speak to him about running the horse. He reined in a little way from the rest of us and sat waiting, watching us and rubbing at his bandaged hand.

"It's good country up here," Miller was saying. "Ain't nobody around, and things are nice and simple. Air's clean, and a man can see a ways. Good country."

I reached out and scratched Ned's ears. He seemed to like it. My eyes were a little sandy from lack of sleep, but Miller was right—you could see a ways up here—a long ways.

➤➤ **17**

About three thirty that afternoon we crossed the second ridge and dropped down into a little basin on the far side. There were several small springs in the bottom, all feeding into a little creek that had been dammed a couple times by beavers. There were several old corrals down there—poles lashed to trees with baling wire—and a half dozen or so tent frames back under the trees. You wouldn't have expected to find a place like this up on the mountainside.

"Old sheep camp," Miller said as we rode down into the basin. "Herders are all down now, so I figured it'd be about right."

"Looks good," Jack said.

"Got water, shelter, and firewood—and the corrals, of course," Miller said. "And the deer huntin' up on that ridge is about as good as any you'll find." He nodded to a ridge that swelled on up out of the scrubby timber into the open meadows between us and the rockfalls just below the snow line.

We reined up in the camp area and climbed down off the horses. My legs ached, and I was a little unsteady on my feet. We tied our horses to the top rail on one of the corrals and walked around a bit, looking it over.

The six tent frames were in a kind of semicircle at the edge of the trees, facing a large stone fire pit and looking out over the grassy floor of the basin and the largest of the beaver ponds out in the middle. Out beyond the pond, the draw rose sharply in a series of steeply slanted meadows. Directly overhead, almost as if it were leaning over the little basin, the bulky white mass of Glacier Peak rose ponderously, so huge as to be almost unbelievable.

There was a rocked-up spring behind the last tent frame, a sandy-bottomed pocket of icy water about two feet deep and perhaps three feet across. The outflow trickled off along the edge of the trees toward the horse corrals at the lower end of the camp.

None of the trees in the little grove were much more than fifteen feet tall, and they were brushy—spruce mostly. We were within a quarter of a mile of the timberline. There were a lot of low shrubs—heather,

Miller said—lying in under the trees, and moss in the open spaces. I noticed a lot of sticks and downed trees lying around.

"Beaver," Miller said. "Greatest firewood collectors around."

McKlearey rode on in and climbed down off his horse. He still kept off to himself.

"Clint'll be along in a few minutes," Miller said. "Let's get a fire goin' so we can have some coffee."

We all moved around picking up firewood, and Miller scraped the debris out of the fire pit. The wood was bone dry, and it only took a few minutes for a good blaze to get started.

Then Clint came in with the pack-string, and we started to unpack. The two-gallon coffee pot and a big iron grill that looked like a chunk of sidewalk grating were the first things to come off. Clint filled the pot from the spring behind the tent frames while Miller piled several big rocks in close to the fire to set the grill on.

"A man can cook with just a fire if he's of a mind," he said, "but this makes things a whole lot simpler." He set the grill in place while Clint dumped several fistfuls of grounds into the water in the pot.

"Don't you use the basket?" Stan asked.

"Lost it a couple years ago," Clint said. "Don't do no good up this high anyway. Water boils at about a hundred and seventy up here. You gotta get the grounds down close to the fire and kinda fry the juice out. Gives you somethin' to chew on in your coffee with them grounds floatin' loose, but that never hurt nobody."

He rummaged around in one of the packs and came up with a sack of salt and dumped a couple pinches in. Then he did something that still makes my hair stand on end. He fished out a dozen eggs, took one and cracked it neatly on a rock. Then he drank it, right out of the shell. I heard Sloane gag slightly. Clint paid no attention to us but crumbled the shell in his fist and dropped it in the pot. Then he clamped on the lid and put the pot down on the grill over the fire.

"I've heard of the salt before, Clint," I said when my stomach settled back down, "but why the eggshell?"

"Damn if I know," he said. "Only thing is, I never tasted coffee fit to drink without it had some eggshell in it."

I didn't ask him why he'd drunk the raw egg. I was pretty sure I didn't want to know.

"We'll have some jerky and cold biscuits with our coffee," Miller said. "That'll tide us till we get camp set up and Clint can fix a real meal."

We all sat around the fire on logs and stumps waiting for the coffee to boil. It boiled over, hissing into the fire with a pungent smell, three times. Each time Clint doused cold water into the pot and let it boil again. Then, the fourth time, he decided it was ready to drink. I'll have to admit that it was damned good coffee. The strips of beef-jerky chewed a bit like old harness leather, but they were good, too, and the cold biscuits with honey set things off just right. I don't think I'd realized just how hungry I was.

Miller brushed the crumbs out of his mustache and filled his coffee mug again. "First thing is to check out the corrals," he said. "We'll need two good ones anyway—that way we won't be stirrin' up the pack animals ever'time we want a saddle horse. Way we'll do it is this: Go around those nearest two corrals and yank real hard on ever' place that's wired. Any place that comes loose, we'll rewire. Balin' wire is looped around that dead tree by the spring. Soon as we get that done, we can unsaddle the stock and turn 'em loose in the corrals. We brought some oats for 'em, but we'll have to picket 'em out to graze in the daytime while you men are up on the ridge. After we get the horses tended to, we'll set up the tents."

"Couldn't some of us start on the tents while the others work on the corrals?" Sloane asked, puffing slightly again.

"I suppose we could," Miller said, "but we'll do 'er the way I said before. Me'n old Clint there was in the Horse-Marines when we was pups, and the first thing we learned was to see to the stock first. Up here a man without a horse is in real trouble. She's a long damn walk back down."

"I see what you mean," Cal said, breathing heavily. He was used to making the decisions, but Miller was in charge, and now we all knew it.

It only took us about fifteen minutes to check out the corrals. Most of the lashings were still tight. Then we unsaddled the horses and turned them into the corrals, laying the saddles over the top rail of a corral we weren't using. Miller dumped oats from a burlap sack into a manger that opened onto both corrals. The horses nuzzled at him and he moved among them. He spoke to them, his voice curiously gentle as he did.

Then we all went up to the fire and had another cup of coffee. The sun was sliding down toward the tops of the peaks above us, and the air was taking on a decided chill. We stood looking at the welter of packs, sleeping bags, and rolled-up tenting that lay in a heap under the tent frames.

"Take a week to get all that squared away," Jack said.

"Hour on the outside," Clint disagreed.

First we put up the tents. They were little six-by-eight jobs that fit neatly over the frames. Miller and Clint showed us how to set them up and pull them tight. We set up five tents and then piled all the packs in the end one.

"Leave the front of that one open and tied back so's I can get in and out easy," Clint said. He showed us where to put the packs to make sure he knew where everything was. Then Miller sent us out to gather moss to pile into the rectangular log bed frames on the ground inside the tents.

"Next to feathers, that's about the softest bed you're gonna find."

"Right now, I could sleep on rocks," I told him.

"No point in that unless you have to." He grinned.

It really took a surprisingly short period of time to set up camp. Miller and Clint had it all down pat, and McKlearey was a damned good field soldier. He seemed to be everywhere, checking tent ropes, ditching around the tents, cleaning dead leaves out of the spring. His cut hand didn't seem to bother him, but the bandage was getting pretty used-looking. Miller took to calling him "Sarge," and Lou responded with "Cap," something the rest of us didn't have guts enough to try yet. Maybe it was that they'd both been in the Marines. Lou seemed to be coming around. He even gave Stan some friendly advice about his bedding, pointing out that the sticks Stan had gathered with the moss he put in his bed frame might be just a touch lumpy.

Sloane grinned at us all as we hauled in our third load of moss and began to blow up an air mattress.

"You goddamn candy-ass," Jack said.

"Brains," Sloane said, tapping his forehead. "This ol' massa ain't *about* to sleep on no col' groun'." He went on blowing into the mattress. He was sitting on the ground near the fire, and his face kept getting redder and redder. He really didn't seem to be making much headway with the mattress. Then he got a funny look on his face and sort of sagged over sideways until he was lying facedown in the dirt.

"Christ, Sloane!" Jack said sharply. We all jumped to get him up again.

"Leave 'im be!" Miller barked. He stepped in and rolled Sloane over onto his back. He felt Sloane's pulse in his throat and then pulled over a chunk of log to put the big man's feet up on.

"Altitude," he said shortly. He looked around at us. "His heart OK?"

"He's never had any trouble I know of," Jack said, "and I've known him for years."

"That's a break. Get some whiskey."

We all dove for our sacks, but Lou beat all of us. He was already out. Miller nodded approvingly. He and McKlearey began working on Sloane, and soon they had him awake.

"Son of a bitch!" Cal said thickly. "That's the first time *that's* ever happened."

"Better take 'er easy for a bit," Miller said. "Takes some men a while to get adjusted to it. You come from sea level to better'n eight thousand feet in less'n a day."

"I just couldn't seem to get my breath," Cal said.

I picked up his air mattress and blew it up for him. Toward the end I got a little woozy, too.

"Easy, boy," Clint growled. "We don't need two down."

"Sloane, you dumb shit," Jack said, "why didn't you bring a bicycle pump? You like to scared the piss outa me."

Sloane grinned weakly. "I figured as windy as this bunch is, I wouldn't have any trouble gettin' enough hot air to pump up one little old air mattress."

"Are you sure you're all right?" Stan asked.

"I'll be OK," Cal said. "Just a little soft is all."

"If I was carryin' as much beer as you are," Jack said, "I'd be pooped, too."

"For God's sake, don't die on us," Lou said. "You still owe me three days' pay."

"You're all heart, McKlearey," I said.

He grinned at me. It suddenly occurred to me that he could be a likable son of a bitch when he wanted to be.

We eased Cal onto his air mattress and then stood around watching him breathe.

"We better get to work on the firewood, men," Miller said. "Ol' Sarge here can watch the Big Man." He gathered up the lead-ropes we'd taken off the packhorses. "Slim," he said to Jack, "you and the Professor and the Kid there take these two axes and that bucksaw and go down into that grove of spruce below the corrals. Bust the stuff up into four-or-five-foot lengths and bundle it up with these. Then haul 'em out in the open. We'll drag 'em in with a saddle horse." I guess that was his way. Miller seldom used our names. It was "Sarge" or "Slim" or "Big Man" or "Professor" or "the Kid." I suppose I should have resented that last one, but I didn't.

The three of us grabbed up the tools and headed off down into the spruce grove.

"You think Cal's going to be OK?" I asked Jack.

"Oh, he'll snap out of it." Jack said. "Sloane's a tough bastard."

"I didn't much like the way his eyes rolled back when he passed out," Stan said.

"Did look a little spooky, didn't it?" Jack said. "But don't worry. Soon as he gets his wind back, Sloane'll run the ass off the whole bunch of us."

We spread out, knocking off dead limbs and dragging downed timber out into the open. We started to bundle the stuff up, tying it with the lead-ropes.

"Say, Dan," Stan said after a while, "give me a hand here with that ax."

I went over to where he was working on a pile of dead limbs.

"It'll take me all night with this saw," he said.

I grunted and started knocking limbs off. I could hear Jack chopping away back in the brush.

"It's beautiful up here, isn't it?" Stan said when I stopped to take a breather. I looked around. The sun had just slid down behind the peaks, and deep blue shadows seemed to be rising out of the ground.

"Good country," I said, echoing Miller.

"I wish Monica could see it," he said, zipping up that bright orange jacket. "Maybe she'd understand then."

I sat down and lit a cigarette. "She gave you a pretty rough time about it, didn't she?"

"It wasn't pleasant," he said. "You have to understand Monica though. She's an only child, and her parents were in their forties when she was born. I guess they spoiled her—you know how that could happen under the circumstances. She's always been a strong-willed girl, and nobody's ever done anything she didn't want them to before."

"She's got to learn sometime," I said.

"I've tried to protect her," he went on. "I know she's not much of a wife really. She's spoiled and willful and sometimes spiteful—but that's not her fault, really, is it? When you consider how she was raised?"

"I can see how it could happen," I said.

"But this trip got to be such an issue," he said, "that I just *had* to do it. I couldn't let it go any longer."

"You've got to draw the line someplace, Stan."

"Exactly," he said. "She just had to realize that I was important, too." He was rubbing his hands together, staring at the ground. "I know she'd do anything to get her own way, and I'm just afraid she might have done something stupid."

"Oh?" I got very careful again. Damn it, I hate this walking on egg-shells all the time!

"Some of the things McKlearey's been saying the last few days—I don't know."

"I wouldn't pay too much attention to McKlearey," I said.

"If I thought there was anything—I'd kill him—I swear it. So help me God, I'd kill him." He meant it. I knew he meant it. Stan didn't say things like that. His hands were clenched tightly into fists, and he was still staring down at the ground. I knew that one wrong word here would blow the whole thing.

"McKlearey and Monica? Get serious. She wouldn't touch that crude bastard with a ten-foot pole. McKlearey?" I laughed as hard as I could. It may have sounded a little forced, but I had to get him backed off it. It wouldn't take too much for his mind to start ticking off the little series of items as Clydine had done in her little breakdown of the "Hubby-Wifey-Creepy-Jarhead" caper. Once he did, somebody was liable to get killed.

Stan looked off into the distance, not saying anything. I don't think I'd been very convincing. Then Jack came up, dragging a big bundle of limbs.

"Hey, you guys," he said, puffing hard, "I hit a bonanza back in there. I got enough wood to last a month, but I'm gonna need help gettin' it out."

"Sure, buddy," I said with a false heartiness. "Come on, Stan, let's give him a hand." I hoped to get Stan's mind off what he was thinking.

We spent the next half hour dragging piles of wood out from under the trees. The light faded more and more, and it was almost dark when Miller rode down to where we were working.

"I got them other piles you left farther up the line," he said. "Looks like you got into a pretty good batch here."

"There's plenty more back in there," Jack said, "but it's gettin' too goddamn dark to be climbin' over all that stuff."

"We can haul out some more tomorrow," Miller said. "This'll last a while."

He had a rope knotted around his saddle horn with a long end trailing on each side of the horse. We lashed several bundles of the limbs to each end of the rope and followed his horse back toward the campfire and the greenish glow of the Coleman lantern hanging from a tree limb in front of the storage tent. The grass and moss felt springy underfoot, the air was sharp, and the stars had started to come out.

I think we'd all figured that we'd be able to just sit around the fire now that it was dark, but Miller kept us busy. McKlearey was just finishing up a table. It was the damnedest thing I'd ever seen—crossed legs, like a picnic table and a top of five-foot poles laid side by side. The whole thing was lashed together with baling wire. At first glance it looked rickety as hell, but Lou had buried about two feet of the bottom of each leg in the ground. It was solid as a rock.

"Hey, Professor," Lou said to Stan as we came into camp, "you want to bring that bucksaw over here and square off the ends of this thing?" Lou had immediately picked up Miller's nicknames. Stan gritted his teeth a little, but he did as Lou asked.

"Damn!" Clint said, grinning, "this'll make things as easy as workin' in the kitchen back at the ranch." He had pots and pans spread out on the table even before Stan had finished sawing the ends square.

Miller put Jack and me to work chopping the limbs we'd hauled in into foot-and-a-half lengths and piling them up along one side of the storage tent.

"Latrine's over there, men," Lou said importantly, coming up to us and pointing to a trail leading off into the trees. "I dug a slit-trench and put up a kind of a stool." He was getting a kick out of all this.

"How's Sloane?" Jack asked him.

"Better, better," McKlearey said. "He'll be fine by morning. It was just blowin' up that goddamn air mattress that laid him out."

Jack grunted and went back to chopping wood. We kept at it for about another half hour, and my stomach was starting to talk to me pretty loud.

"Chow," Clint hollered, and we all homed in on the fire and the food.

"Plates and silverware there on the table," Clint said. "Grab 'em and line up."

We had venison steaks from Miller's freezer at the ranch, pork and beans and corn on the cob.

"Better enjoy that corn, men," Clint said."That's all I brought. I figured we could spread out a little, first night out."

We took our plates back to the logs and stumps on the far side of the fire and began to eat. Sloane was up and about now and seemed to be a little better.

"Damn good," Jack said with his mouth full.

"Yeah, man," Lou said, shoveling food into his mouth.

It took me a while to get the hang of holding the plate on my knees, but as soon as I got the idea that there was nothing wrong with picking up a steak in my fingers, I had it whipped.

After we finished eating and had cleaned up the dishes, we finally got a chance to sit down and relax. We all had a drink—whiskey and that icy-cold springwater—and sat, staring into the fire.

"Sure is quiet up here," Jack said finally. He'd be the one to notice that.

"Long ways from the roads," Miller said.

We sat quietly again.

Then we heard the horses snort and start to stir around, and a few minutes later a kind of grumbling, muttering chatter and a funny sort of dragging noise came from the woods.

"What's that?" Stan demanded nervously.

"Damn porkypine," Clint said. "Probably comin' over to see what we're up to."

McKlearey stood up, his eyes and teeth glowing sort of red in the reflected light of the fire. He pulled out his pistol.

"What you figgerin' on Sarge?" Miller asked, his voice a little sharp.

"I'll go kill 'im," McKlearey said. "Don't want 'im gettin' into the goddamn chow, do we?"

"No need to do that," Miller said. "He ain't gonna come in here while we're around. Long as we don't figure on eatin' 'im, there's no point in killin' 'im. I'm pretty sure the woods is big enough for us and one porky, more or less." He looked steadily at McKlearey until Lou began to get a little embarrassed.

"Anything you say, Cap," he said finally, holstering the pistol and sitting back down.

"Knew a feller sat on a porky once—" Clint chuckled suddenly.

"No kiddin'?" Jack laughed.

"Never did it again," Clint said. "Matter of fact, he didn't sit on *nothin'* for about three weeks afterward."

"How did he manage to sit on a porcupine?" Stan asked, amused.

"Well sir, me'n him'd been huntin', see," Clint started, "just kinda pokin' through the woods, havin' a little look over the top of the next ridge, like a feller will, and along about ten or so we got tuckered. We found what looked to be a couple old mossy stumps and just set down on 'em. Now the one *I* set on was a real stump, but *his* stump wasn't no stump—it was a big ol' boar porky—''

The story went on, and then there were others. The fire burned lower, popping once in a while as it settled into bright red coals.

McKlearey had several more drinks; but the rest of us had hung it up after the first one.

"I'd go a little easy on that, if it was me, Sarge," Miller said finally, after McKlearey had made his fourth trip back to the spring for cold water. "It'll have to last you the whole time. It's a pretty fair hike back to the liquor store."

We all laughed at that.

"Sure thing, Cap," McKlearey said agreeably and put his bottle away.

"Well," Sloane said finally, "I don't know about the rest of you mighty hunters, but I'm about ready to tap out. Last night was a little shallow on sleep." He was looking a lot better now but tired. I think we all were.

"Might not be a bad idea if we was all to turn in," Miller said. "Not really a whole lot to do in camp after dark, and we might as well get used to rollin' out before daybreak."

We got up, feeling the stiffness already settling in our overworked muscles. We all said good night and went off to our tents. Miller and Clint were in the one right by the storage tent, Sloane and Stan in the next one, then Jack and I, and finally, in the farthest one up the line, McKlearey in one by himself—it just worked out that way.

Jack and I stripped down to our underwear and hurriedly crawled into our sleeping bags. It was damned chilly in the tent. I fumbled around and got out my flashlight and put it on the ground beside the gun belt near the top of my bed.

"You suppose we oughta close the flap?" he asked after a few minutes.

"Let's see how it works out leaving it open," I said. I was looking out the front of the tent at the dying fire.

"Well"—he chuckled—"I sure wouldn't want to roll over on that porky."

"I don't think that tent-flap would really stop him," I said.

"Probably not," he agreed. "Man, I'm tired. I feel like I've been up for a week."

"You and me both, buddy," I said.

"It's great up here, huh?"

"The greatest."

There was a long silence. The fire popped once.

"Good night, Danny," he said drowsily.

"Night, Jack," I said.

I lay awake staring at the fire, thinking the long thoughts a man can think alone at night when there are no noises to distract him. Once again I wished that somehow my little Bolshevik could be here to see all of this. Maybe then she'd understand. For some reason it was important to me that she did.

I guess I must have drifted off to sleep, because the fire was completely out when the first scream brought me up fighting.

"What the goddamn hell?" Jack said.

There was another scream. It was a man—right in camp.

I grabbed up the flashlight in one hand and the .45 in the other. I was out the front of the tent when the next scream came. I stubbed my toe on a rock and swore. I could see heads popping out of all the other tents except one. The screams were coming from McKlearey's tent.

I whipped open the front flap of his tent and put the beam of the flash full on him. "Lou! What the hell is it?"

He rolled over quickly and came up, that damned .38 in his right hand. *Son of a bitch*, he moved fast! "Who's there?" he barked.

"Easy, man," I said. "It's me—Dan."

"Danny? What's up?"

"That's what I just asked *you*. You were yelling like somebody was castrating you with a dull knife."

"Oh," he said, rubbing at his face and lowering his gun, "musta been a nightmare."

"What's wrong?" I heard Miller's voice call.

I pulled my head out of the tent. "It's OK," I called back. "Lou just had a nightmare, that's all. He's OK." I stuck my head back in the tent. "You *are* OK, aren't you, Lou?"

His face looked awful. He rubbed his bandaged hand across it again, and his hand was shaking badly. He tucked the gun back under his rolled-up clothes. "Keep the light here a minute, OK?" he said. He rummaged around in his sack and came out with a bottle. He took a long pull at it. I suddenly realized that I was standing there with that silly .45 pointed right at him. It had just kind of automatically followed the light. I lowered it carefully.

"Want one?" he asked, holding out the bottle toward me.

"No thanks. You OK now?"

"Yeah," he said, "just a nightmare. Happens to a lot of guys."

"Sure."

"All the time. Lotsa guys have 'em."

"Sure, Lou."

"That's true, isn't it, Danny?" he said, his voice jittery as if he were shivering. "A lot of guys have nightmares don't they?"

"Hell," I said, "I even have some myself." That seemed to help him.

"Hey, man," I said, "I'm about to freeze my ass off. If you're OK, I'm going back to my nice warm sack."

"Sure, man," he said. "I'm fine now. 'Night, Danny."

"Good night, Lou."

"Oh, hey, man?"

"Yeah?"

"Thanks for comin' in with the light."

"Sure, Lou."

I closed up his tent and hustled back to my sleeping bag. Damn, it was cold out there!

⚡ 18

When the gun went off I think we all came up in panic. After the screaming in the middle of the night, I for one thought McKlearey had been having another nightmare and had unloaded on whatever it was that was haunting him. It was morning or at least starting to get light outside. I could see Miller standing calmly by the fire with a coffee cup in his hand. He didn't look particularly excited.

"What's up?" I heard Sloane call. "Who's shootin'?"

"Clint," Miller said. "He took a little poke out this mornin' to see if he couldn't scare up some camp-meat. Sounds like he found what he wanted."

"Jesus!" Jack exclaimed. "Sounded like he was right in camp."

"No, he's back down the trail about a quarter mile or so," Miller said.

I jerked on my pants and boots, wincing slightly at their clamminess, grabbed up the rest of my clothes, and hustled on out to the warmth of the fire. I stood shivering in my T-shirt for a few minutes, staring back along the trail that poked back into the still-dark woods.

"Hey, Cap," Clint's voice called in from out there.

"Yeah?" Miller didn't raise his voice too much.

"I got one. Send somebody out with a packhorse and a knife. I clean forgot mine."

"Right, Clint," Miller looked across the fire at me. "You want to go?" he asked.

"Sure." I said. "Let me finish getting dressed." I hauled on my shirt and sat down to lace up the boots.

"No big rush." He grinned at me. "That deer ain't goin' noplace. Ol' Clint don't miss very often. Have yourself a cup of coffee whilst I go throw a packsaddle on one of the horses." He raised his voice again. "Be a few minutes, Clint."

"OK, Cap," Clint's voice came back. "Better send along a shovel, too."

"Right." Miller went off toward the corral, and I poured myself a cup of coffee and finished lacing up the boots. I went back into the tent and picked up my gun belt.

Jack was struggling into his plaid shirt, trying to stay in the sleeping bag as much as possible at the same time. "You goin' out there?" he asked me.

Al nodded, buckling on the belt. "Clint wants a horse and a knife," I said. I pulled the smaller of the pair of German knives from the double sheath that hung on the left side of the gun belt and tested the edge with my thumb. It seemed OK. I grabbed my jacket and hat and went on back through the pale light to the fire.

"I'll be along in a little bit," Jack called after me.

There was a bucket of water on the table, and I scooped some out with my hands and doused it in my face. The shock was sharp, and I came up gasping. I raked the hair back out of my face with my fingers and stuffed my hat on. Still shivering, I drank the cup of coffee.

There was a kind of mist or cloud hanging up on the side of the mountain, blotting out the top. I waded down toward the corral through the gray-wet grass. I could see Miller's dark track through it and Clint's angling off toward the woods.

"You bring a knife?" Miller asked, handing me the lead-rope to the sleepy-looking packhorse he'd saddled.

I nodded. Somehow, it didn't seem right to talk too much.

"He's prob'ly 'bout four-five hundred yards down that trail," he said, pointing. "When you get out there a ways, sing out, and he'll talk you in."

"Right."

I led the horse on into the woods. It was still pretty dark back in there, the silvery light filtering down through the thick spruce limbs. The horse walked very close to me—maybe they get nervous about things, too.

"Clint?" I called after about five minutes.

"Over here," his voice came. "That you, Dan?"

"Yeah." I followed his voice.

"I kinda figured it might be you," he said. "You bring a knife and a shovel?"

"Yeah," I said. Then I saw him sitting on a log, smoking a cigarette. His .30-30 was leaning against the tree behind him.

"She's right over there," he said, pointing. He got up, and we walked back farther into the dim woods.

The deer, a young mule doe, had fallen on its side in a clump of heather, its sticklike legs protruding awkwardly. A dead deer always looks tiny somehow, not much bigger than a dog. They look big when they're up and moving, but after you shoot them, they seem to kind of shrink in on themselves. A doe looks even smaller, maybe because there aren't any horns.

"This one ought to last us," Clint said. "Give me a hand and we'll drag 'er out in the open."

We each grabbed a hind leg and pulled the deer out of the heather-bed. Her front legs flopped limply and her large-eared head wobbled back and forth as it slid over the branches of the low-lying shrub. I didn't see any blood.

"Ever gutted many deer?" he asked me.

"One," I said. "I didn't do a very good job of it."

"Well, now," he said, "I'll show you how it's done. Hold that leg up and gimme your knife."

I handed him the smaller knife and held the hind leg up for him.

"Now, you start here—" He made a slit through the deer's white belly-fur and continued it back toward the tail, just cutting through the skin.

"Idea is to keep as much hair out of the meat as you can," he told me.

I watched as he sliced the skin from chin to tail.

"You going to cut her throat?" I asked him. "I thought you were supposed to do that."

"Not much point," he said. "We'll have the head off in about five minutes. Carcass'll bleed out good enough from that, I expect." He pushed the point of the knife through the belly-muscles with a hollow, ripping sound, and started to saw up through the ribs.

"Here," I said, handing him the big knife, "use this one."

He grunted, laying the smaller knife aside. He hefted the big one. "Quite a frog-sticker," he said, looking at the ten-inch blade. He bent back over the deer.

I tried not to look too closely at the way the sliced muscles twitched and quivered.

"Hey, where are you guys?" Jack called from back at the trail.

"Over here," I said.

Clint took the big knife and chopped through the pelvis bone, making a sound a lot like somebody chopping wet wood.

"Ooops," Jack said as he came up on us. "I'll just wait till you guys finish up there."

"Squeamish?" Clint asked, his arm sunk up to the elbow inside the deer's body cavity.

"Not really," Jack said, "but—" He shrugged and went back to where McKlearey was coming through the trees. The two of them stood back there, watching.

"Now then," Clint told me, "you just grab hold of the windpipe here and kind of use it as a handle to pull everything right out." He grabbed the severed windpipe and slowly pulled out and down, spilling out the deer's steaming internal organs. Once they were clear of the carcass, he dragged them several feet away and dumped them in a heap. He came back and chopped away the lower half of each leg, the big blade grating sickeningly in the joints.

"No sense haulin' anything back we can't use," he said. Then he turned to the head.

"Where'd you hit her?" I asked, looking into the body cavity. "I don't see any hole."

"Right here," he said, probing a finger into the fur just under the base of the skull.

"Good shot," I said. "What was the range?"

" 'Bout forty—maybe fifty yards. If you're quiet you can get pretty close."

He made a slice around the neck with the big knife about where he'd had his finger and then cut the head away. Bone fragments and small gleaming pieces of copper from his bullet were very bright against the dark meat.

"Let's dump 'er out," he said.

We picked up the surprisingly heavy carcass and turned it over to drain.

"Hey, Slim," Clint called to Jack, "why don't you and the Sarge there get that shovel off the packhorse and dig a hole so's we can bury the guts?"

"Sure," Jack said, going over to the drowsing horse.

"Ordinarily, I'd leave 'em for the coyotes and bobcats," Clint said, "but then I got to thinkin' that maybe we wouldn't want 'em comin' in this close to camp." He went to the steaming gut-pile and cut the liver free of the other organs. "Breakfast," he said shortly. He fished a plastic bag out of his coat pocket and slid the dripping liver inside.

"This deep enough?" McKlearey asked, pointing at their hole. I noticed that he had on a fresh bandage.

"Yeah, that'll do it," Clint answered. "Just kick them guts and hooves and the head in and cover 'em up. We'll pile rocks on top when you're done."

I looked away. It hadn't bothered me so far, but the deer's eyes were still open, and I didn't want to see them kicking dirt in them.

"That's got it," Jack said.

Clint gave me back my knives. "Pretty good set," he said. "Where'd you come by it?"

"In Germany," I said. "Got it when I was in the Army."

"Damn good steel," he said. "Holds the edge real good."

"They're a bitch to sharpen." I grinned at him. Actually, Clydine had sharpened them for me. I don't know where she'd learned how, but she sure could put an edge on a knife.

We piled rocks on the buried remains of the deer, and then the three of us lifted the carcass onto the pack-frame saddle while Clint held the horse's head to keep him from shying at the blood-smell.

Clint picked up his rifle, and we went back to camp.

"Dry doe," Clint told Miller when we got back to the corral. "Picked 'er up on that little game trail back in there a ways."

"Looks like she'll last us," Miller said.

"Should. I'll skin 'er out after breakfast when you fellers go up on the ridge."

They put a short, heavy stick through the hocks of the hind legs and hung the carcass to a tree limb a ways behind camp.

After they'd unsaddled the packhorse, we all walked back on up to the fire. Clint washed up and started hustling around the cook table McKlearey'd built for him.

"First blood," Sloane said in the kind of gaspy voice he'd developed since we'd gotten up into the high country.

"This one don't really count." Miller chuckled.

"At least there are deer around," Stan said.

"Oh, there's plenty of deer up here, all right," Miller said.

I got the enameled washbasin and filled it with warm water from the big pot on the fire and did a little better job of washing up than I'd managed earlier. Then Clint ran us all away from the fire because we were in his way.

I walked on down to the edge of the beaver pond and looked out over the clear water. It was about four or five feet deep out in the middle, and the bottom was thinly sprinkled with matchstick-sized white twigs. I saw a flicker under the surface about ten feet out and saw a good-sized trout swim slowly past, his angry-looking eye glaring at me with cold suspicion.

"Hey, man, fish in there, huh?" It was McKlearey. I could smell the whiskey on him. Christ Almighty! The sun wasn't even up yet!

"Yeah," I said. "Wonder if anybody thought to bring any gear."

"Doubt it like hell," he said, jamming his hands deeper into his field-jacket pockets.

I squatted down by the water and washed off my knives. The edges were still OK, but I thought I'd touch them up a little that afternoon.

"Sun's comin' up," Lou said.

I looked up. The very tip of the looming, blue-white peak above us was turning bright pink. As I watched, the pink line crept slowly down, more and more of the mountain catching fire. The blue-white was darkly shadowed now by comparison.

"Nice, huh?" Lou said. His face was ruddy from the reflected glow off the snow above us, kind of etched out sharply against the dark trees behind him. "I can think of times when I'd have give my left nut for just one look at snow. It never melts up there. Did you know that? It's always there—summer and winter—always up there. I used to think about that a lot when I was on the Delta. It's always up there. Kinda gives a guy somethin' to hang on to." He snorted with laughter. "Bet it's colder'n a bitch up there," he said.

"If it got too cold you could always think about the Delta, I guess," I said.

"No," he said, still staring at the mountain. "I never think about the Delta. Other places, yeah, but never the Delta."

I nodded. "How's the hand?" I pointed at the bandage.

"Little sore," he said. "It'll be OK."

"Chow!" Clint hollered from camp.

Lou and I walked on back up toward the tents. Maybe there was more to him than I'd realized.

Clint had fried up a bunch of bacon and then had simmered onion slices in the hot grease and had fried up thin strips of fresh deer liver. There were hot biscuits and more coffee. The little old fart could sure whip up a helluva meal on short notice. We fell on the food like a pack of wolves, and for about ten minutes all you could hear was the sound of eating. The altitude does that to you.

After we'd eaten and were lazing over a last cup of coffee, watching the edge of the sunlight creep down the mountain toward us, Miller cleared his throat.

"Soon as you men get your breakfast settled, we'll saddle up and take a little ride on up the ridge there. I want to show you the stands you'll be usin'. You'll need to see 'em in the daylight 'cause it'll still be dark yet when you get up there tomorrow. Then, too, it'll give us a chance to scout around some."

"You think we'll see any deer?" Stan asked.

"We sure should," Miller said. "I've seen five cross that ridge since we set down to breakfast."

We all turned and looked sharply up at the ridge.

"None up there right now though," he said. "Your bucks'll all be up there. Now some of you men may've hunted mule deer before, and some of you've hunted white-tail. These are all mulies up here. They're bigger'n white-tail and they look and act a whole lot different. A mulie's got big ears—that's how he gets his name—and he can hear a pin drop at a half a mile. He's easy to hunt 'cause you can count on him to do two things—run uphill and stop just before he goes over the ridge. He'll always run uphill when he's been spooked—unless, of course, he's just been shot. Then he'll go downhill.

"A white-tail runs kind of flat out, like a horse or a dog, and if you're a fair shot you can hit him on the run. Your mulie, on the other hand, bounces like a damn jackrabbit, and you can't tell from one jump to the next which way he's goin'. Looks funnier'n hell, but it makes him damn hard to hit on the run. You shoot over 'im or under 'im ever' time.

"That's why it's good to know that he's gonna stop. As soon as he gets a ways away from you—and above you—he'll stop and look back to see what you're doin'. Some people say they're curious, and some say they're dumb, but it's just somethin' he'll always do. Wait for it, and you're likely to get a clear, standin' shot."

"What's the range likely to be?" Sloane gasped.

"Anywhere from one hundred to three hundred yards," Miller said, looking closely at Cal. "Much out past that and I wouldn't shoot, if it was me. Too much chance of a gut shot or havin' the deer drop into one of these ravines. He does that and he'll likely bounce and roll for about a mile. Won't be much left when he stops."

He stopped and looked around. It was the longest speech I ever heard him make.

"Let's go get the horses," he said, almost as if he were ashamed of himself for talking so much.

We trooped on down to the corral, and he made each man saddle his own horse. "Might as well learn how to do it now as later," he said.

I approached that knotheaded gray horse of mine with a great deal of caution. He didn't seem particularly tense this morning, but I wasn't going to take any chances with him. I got him saddled and bridled and led him out of the corral. The others all stopped to watch.

"Well, buddy," I said to him as firmly as I could, "how do you want to play it this morning?"

He turned his head and looked inquiringly at me, his long gray face a mask of equine innocence.

"You lyin' son of a bitch," I muttered. I braced myself and climbed on his back. His ears flicked.

"All right," I said grimly, "let's get it over with." I nudged him with my heels and he moved out at a gentle walk with not so much as an instant's hesitation. I walked him out into the bottom, turned him and trotted him back to the corral.

"How about that?" I called to the others. "Just like a pussycat."

"You got him all straightened out yesterday," Miller said. "He won't give you no more trouble."

The others mounted, and we rode off down to the lower end of the basin, crossed the creek, and started up the ridge. Clint's horse, alone in the saddle-horse corral, whinnied after us a couple times and then went over to the fence nearest the pack-horses.

I was a little stiff and sore, but it didn't take too long for that to iron itself out.

The ridge moved up in a series of steps with low brush breaking off each side. A little way out we rode into the sunlight.

About a half mile up from camp, Miller stopped.

"This'll be the first stand," he said. "The Big Man'll be here." It made sense. This was the lowest post, and Sloane was having trouble with the altitude.

"You want me to wait here now?" Cal asked, disappointment evident in his voice.

"No need of that," Miller said, "but we'd better look around a mite so's you can get it all set in your mind. I'll be droppin' you off by this white rock here." He pointed at a big pale boulder. "Best place to set is right over there."

We all got off and walked on over. A natural rock platform jutted out over the deep ravine that ran down the right-hand side of the ridge. The other, shallower, ravine with its meadows ran down into the basin where we were camped.

"You see that notch over on the other side?" Miller said, pointing it out to Sloane.

"Yeah."

"That's a main game trail. They'll be comin' across that from the next ravine. Then they'll turn and go on down to the bottom. They'll be in sight all the way."

"How far is it to that notch?" Sloane gasped.

" 'Bout a hundred and fifty yards. It's best to let 'em get all the way to the bottom before you shoot. That way they won't fall so far and you'll have plenty of time to look 'em over."

"OK," Sloane said.

"Don't get so interested in this trail that you ignore this draw here that runs on down to camp though. They'll be crossin' there, too—lots of 'em. And they'll be grazin' in those meadows."

Sloane looked it all over. "I think I've got it located," he said, taking a deep breath.

Jack's post was on the next step up the ridge. There was a bit more brush there, but another big game trail cut into the ravine from the far side.

"Watch your shots over there, Slim," Miller said. "It breaks off pretty sharp, and a deer'd get busted up pretty bad if it was to go over that edge."

"Yeah," Jack replied, his eyes narrowing, "I can see that."

Stan was next up the hill, his post much like the two below.

McKlearey's post was down in a notch.

"You'll have to watch yourself in here, Sarge," Miller told him. "You're right in the middle of a trail here, and you might get yourself stampeded over if they start to runnin'."

"Stomp your ass right into the ground, McKlearey," Jack laughed. "Wouldn't that be a bitch?"

"I'll hold 'em off till you guys get here." Lou grinned. "We'll ambush the little bastards."

My post was the highest on the ridge. The horses scrambled up the rocky trail from McKlearey's notch, their iron-shod hooves sliding and clattering.

"I'm puttin' the Kid up here," Miller explained, " 'cause that horse he's ridin' is the biggest and strongest one in the string. This little stretch of trail can be a bitch-kitty in the dark."

"Anybody wanna trade horses?" I asked, not meaning it.

We came out on the rounded knob at the top of the trail and looked around.

"At least you'll have scenery," Jack said. He was right about that. You could literally see for a hundred miles in every direction except where the peak whitely blotted out a quarter of the sky.

We all got down and walked around, looking out at the surrounding mountains.

"Buck!" Miller said, his voice not loud but carrying to us with a sharp urgency.

The deer was above us. I counted him at five points, but that could have been off. He was a hundred and fifty yards away, but he still looked as big as a horse. He watched us, his rack flaring arrogantly above his head like a vast crown. It was probably my imagination, but his face seemed to have an expression of unspeakable contempt on it, an almost royal hauteur that made me feel about two feet tall. None of us moved or made a sound.

Slowly he turned the white patch of his rump to us, flicked his tail twice, then laid his ears back and bounded up the mountainside as if he had springs on his feet. He soared with each jump as though the grip of earth upon him was very light and he could just as easily fly, if he really wanted to.

Far up the rockslide he slowed, stopped, and looked back at us again. Then he walked off around the ridge, picking his way delicately over the rocks, his head up and his antlers carried proudly.

I still felt very small.

━━ 19

Miller split us up then and sent us on back down the ridge by several different trails. He told us to ride slowly and keep a good sharp eye out for any really big bucks.

"Come on, Cal," I said to Sloane, "let's ease on down this way."

Miller glanced at me and nodded once. One of us was going to have to stick pretty close to Calvin from here on out.

"Sure thing," Sloane said with a heartiness that sounded hollow as all hell. He was looking pretty tough again.

We rode off slowly, and I concentrated pretty much on picking as easy a trail as I could find. The sun was well up by now, and the air up there was very clear. Every limb and rock stood out sharply, and the shadows under the bushes were very dark. I could hear the others clattering over rocks now and then above us. After about five minutes Cal called weakly to me.

"Better hold up a minute, Dan." He jumped down off his horse and lurched unsteadily off to the side of the trail. I rolled out of the saddle and caught his bridle before his horse could wander off. I tied both horses to a low bush.

He was vomiting when I got to him, kneeling beside a rock and retching like a man at the end of a three-day drunk.

"You OK?" I asked. A guy always asks such damned stupid questions at a time like that.

He nodded jerkily and then vomited again. He was at it for quite a long time. Finally he got weakly to his feet and stumbled back toward the horses.

"Jesus, Cal," I said, trying to help him.

"Don't tell the others about this," he said hoarsely, waving off my hand.

"Christ, man, you're really sick, aren't you?"

"I'll be OK," he said, hanging onto his saddle horn. "Just don't tell the others, OK?"

"If you say so," I said. "Let's sit down a bit."

"Sure," he agreed.

I led him over to a clear place and went back to get the water bag hanging on my saddle horn. When I brought it back, he drank some and washed off his face. He looked a little better, but his breathing was still very bad, and his face was pale inside the framing fur of his parka hood.

"I just can't seem to get used to it." He gasped. "God damn, I can't. It's like there was a wet blanket over my face all the time."

"You ever have trouble at high altitudes before?" I asked him.

"No more than anybody else, I don't think. Oh sure, I'd get a little woozy and I'd get winded easy, but nothing like this. Of course, I haven't been up in the mountains for five or six years now."

"It'll settle down," I said—not really believing it. "Hell, we've only been up here for a day or so."

"I sure hope so," he said. "I don't know how much more of this I can cut."

"Cal," I said after a minute or so, "if it gets bad—I mean really bad—you'll let me know, won't you? I mean, shit, none of this is worth blowing a coronary over."

"Hell," he said, "my heart's in good shape—it's my fuckin' *lungs*."

"Yeah, I know, but tell me, huh? I mean it."

He looked at me for a moment. "OK, Dan," he said finally, "if it really gets bad."

That was a helluva relief.

"Like you said, though, it'll settle down." His face had a longing on it that was awfully damned exposed.

"I've just *got* to make this one, you know?" he said. "If I don't make it this time, I don't think I ever will."

"I'm not sure I follow you," I said.

"Look, Dan," he said, "let's not kid each other. I know what I am—I'm a big fuckin' kid—that's what I am."

"Hey, man—"

"No, let's not shit each other. I wouldn't say this to any of the others. Hell, they wouldn't understand it. But you're different." He lit a cigarette and then immediately mashed it out. "I sure as shit don't need *those* things."

"I've cut way down, too," I said, wanting to change the subject.

"This whole damn trip," he went on, "it's a kid thing—for me anyhow. At least it was when it started. It was just another of the things I do with your brother and Carter and McKlearey and a whole bunch of other guys—parties, booze, broads, the whole bit—all kid stuff. I gotta do it though. You see, my old man was fifty-five when I was born. My old lady was his second wife. I can't ever remember him when he wasn't an old man. I get this awful feeling when I get around old people—like I want to crawl off and hide someplace."

"You're not alone there," I told him. "I ever tell you about the Dan Alders' curse? With me it's old ladies on buses. Drives me right up the wall every time."

He grinned at me briefly. He almost looked like the old Cal again.

"So I hang around with young guys," he went on, "and I do the stuff they do. Shit, man, I'm forty-two years old, for Chrissake! Don't you think it's time I grew up? I own four businesses outright, and I'm a partner in about six more. Let's face it, I'm what they'd call a man of substance, and here I am, boozin' and partyin' and shackin' up with cheap floozies like that goddamn Helen. Jesus H. Christ! Claudia's ten times the woman and about a million times the lady that pig was on the best day she ever saw." He shook his head. "I've gotta be outa my goddamn rabbit-ass mind!"

"We all do funny things now and then," I said, wishing he'd change the subject.

"I don't know why the hell Claudia puts up with me," he said. "She knows all about it, of course."

"Oh?"

"Shit yes! Do you think for one minute I could hide anything from *her*? But she never gives me hell about it, never complains. Hell, she never even mentions it. The goddamn woman's a saint, you know that?"

"She's pretty special," I agreed.

Sloane looked out over what Mike used to call the Big Lonely.

"God, it's great up here," he said, "if only I could get my goddamn *wind*!" He pounded his fist on his leg as if angry with his gross body for having failed him.

"Anyway"—he picked it up again—"like I was sayin', this started out as just another kid thing—something I was gonna do with Jack and Carter and some of the guys, right?"

"If you say so," I said. He had me baffled now.

"Only it isn't that anymore. This is *it*, baby. This is where little Calvin grows up. This time I make it over the hump. By God, it's about time, wouldn't you say? Claudia deserves a real husband, and by God I'm gonna see that she's got one when I get back." He looked up at the sky again. "This time I'm gonna make it, I really am." Then he started coughing again, and I started worrying.

After he got straightened around with his breathing apparatus again, we got up and went back to the horses.

"You think I can make it, Dan?" he asked after I'd helped him back on his horse.

I looked at him for a minute. "You already have, Cal," I said. "That was it back there. Anything else is just going to be a souvenir to remember it by." I went over and climbed up on Ned. A guy can say some goddamn foolish things sometimes. But Cal needed it, so I said it—even though we both knew "growing up" doesn't happen like that. It takes a long time—most of your life usually.

Then we heard the other guys yelling farther up the slope. We nudged the horses over to where we could get a clear view of the ravine. We both looked up and down the opposite ridge for a minute and then we saw what they were yelling about.

It was a white deer.

He was a buck, maybe about a seven-pointer, but he wasn't as big as the five-point we'd seen earlier. His coat was a sort of cream-colored, but his antlers were very dark. He stood about a quarter of a mile away on the other ridge, his ears flickering nervously at all the shouting the others were doing. I suppose like most albinos, his eyes weren't really too good.

"Look at that!" Sloane said reverently. "Isn't that the most beautiful goddamn thing you ever saw?" He handed me his binoculars. They brought the thing up pretty close; they were damn good glasses.

The deer's eyes were a deep red, so he was a true albino. You could actually see the pink skin in places where the wind ruffled his fur back. He looked more completely defenseless than any animal I've ever seen. For some reason, when I looked at him, I thought of Clydine.

I gave the glasses back to Sloane and sat on the horse watching until the deer's nerves finally got wound too tight and he bounded off across the other ridge and out of sight.

"Isn't that something?" Cal gasped.

"Never seen one before," I said. "I've seen a lot of deer, but that's the first white one I've ever seen."

"The son of a bitch looked like a ghost, didn't he?"

"Or like Moby Dick," I said, and then I wished I hadn't said it. It was so goddamn obvious.

"Yeah. Moby Dick," Sloane said. "They got him at the end of the book, didn't they?"

"No," I said. "He got *them*—the whole damn bunch. All but Ishmael, of course."

"I never read it," Sloane admitted. "I saw the movie though—first half of it anyway. I was with this girl—"

"I'd rather you didn't mention that name to the others," I said, forgetting Stan for a moment.

"What name?"

"Moby Dick."

"Why not?"

"It's a real bad scene, man. Just say it's a superstition or something, but don't get Jack and McKlearey started on something like that. Somebody's liable to wind up dead."

"You *are* jumpy," Sloane said. "What's got you all keyed up?"

"Man, I'll tell you, this whole damn trip is like settting up house-keeping on top of a bomb. McKlearey's been playing McKlearey-type games with a couple women we both know. If we don't keep a lid on things, Jack and Stan are going to go off in a corner and start to odd-man to see who gets to shoot the son of a bitch."

"Jesus!" Sloane said.

"Amen, brother, amen. This whole trip could turn to shit right in our faces, so let's not buy trouble by starting any Moby Dick stuff. That son of a bitch sank the whole goddamn boat, and I left my water wings at home."

"Hell," he squawked, "I can't even swim."

Of course the first thing Stan said to me when Sloane and I came trailing into camp was "Call me Ishmael," in a properly dramatic voice.

"I *only* am escaped to tell thee," I grated back at him just as hard and as sharp-pointed as I could make it, hoping to hell he'd get the point.

"What the hell are you two babblin' about?" Jack demanded.

Stan, of course, had to tell him.

We unsaddled the horses, turned them loose in the corral, and then all went on up to the fire where Clint was working on lunch.

"Man"—Jack was still carrying on about the white deer—"wasn't that the damnedest thing you ever saw?"

"Pretty damn rare," Miller said. "Most likely a stag though."

"Stag?" Sloane asked. "I thought any buck-deer was a stag."

"Well, not really," Miller said. "A stag is kinda like a steer with cows. Either he's been castrated or had an accident or he just ain't got the equipment. Most of them freaks are like that—I don't know why."

They talked about it all the way through lunch. I kept trying to pour cold water on it, but I could see all the others visualizing that white head over their mantelpieces or what-not. I began right about then to hate that damned deer. I wished to hell he'd fall off a cliff or something.

After lunch we hauled in more firewood and cleaned our rifles. McKlearey lashed together a kind of rifle rack and put it in the back of the supply tent. "Keep the scopes from gettin' knocked around that way," he rasped. His bandage was dirty again.

The sun went down early—it always would here, right up against the backside of that peak like we were. The twilight lasted a long time though. We had venison steak for dinner and settled down around the fire to watch the last of the daylight fade out of the sky.

They went back to talking about that damned white deer again.

I'd been kind of half-assed watching McKlearey. He'd been making a lot of trips to his tent for one reason or another, and his eyes were getting a little unfocused. I figured he was hitting his jug pretty hard again.

I caught Miller's eye, and I knew he'd been counting McKlearey's trips, too. He didn't look too happy about it.

"Well, I'll sure tell you one thing," Jack was saying, "if that big white bastard crosses *my* stand, I'll dump 'im right in his tracks."

"You said it, buddy," McKlearey said, his voice slurring a little. "How about you, Danny Boy?"

"I came up here to hunt," I said. "I'm not declaring war on one single deer."

"There's lots of deer up on that mountain," Miller said. "Lots are bigger'n that one."

"Just like the girls in Hong Kong, huh, Danny?" McKlearey said, trying to focus his eyes on me.

"I wouldn't know, Lou," I said. "I've never been there, remember?"

"Sure you have, Danny. Me'n you made an R and R there once."

"Not me, Lou. You must have me mixed up with somebody else."

He squinted at me very closely. "Yeah," he said finaly, "maybe so. I guess maybe it *was* another guy."

What the hell was *that* all about?

We kept on talking until it got completely dark, and Miller suggested that we all get to bed. I walked on down to McKlearey's slit-trench to unload some coffee. On the way back I met Clint.

"Say, Dan," he said, his voice hushed, "What's the score on old Sarge anyway? Does it seem to you he's actin' a little funny?"

"Lou? I don't know, Clint. I don't really know him all that well. Seems to me he's been acting a little funny ever since I first met him."

"Well," he said, "I know one thing for sure. He hits that bottle about as hard as any man I've ever seen. That ain't good up this high."

"He's used to it," I said.

"Maybe so, but Cap's a little worried about it. He wants this trip to go smooth, and already he's got a sick man and one that's actin' kinda funny. Don't take too much to spoil a trip for ever'body."

"I think it'll work out, Clint. Once we get to hunting, we'll be OK."

"I sure hope so," he said.

"Sure, Clint, it'll all settle down, don't worry." I wished that I could be as sure as I sounded. I walked on back up to the tent.

Jack was already in bed and about half-asleep, so I just undressed and crawled in my sleeping bag.

I lay in my sack, staring out at the fire and remembering the other deer—not the white one—and how he'd soared and bounced up the mountainside. Almost as if he could fly, if he really wanted to. For me, at least, it was going to be a good hunt.

━━ **20**

"Time to roll out." Clint's head blotted out the looming white mountain in the doorway of the tent. I was immediately awake. It's funny, in town or anyplace else, I always have a helluva time waking up. When I'm hunting though, I snap awake just like I was a different guy.

I was dressed and out to the fire while Jack was still mumbling around looking for his pants. I washed up and hunkered down by the fire waiting for the coffee to finish boiling. Slowly one by one the others joined me.

"Darker'n hell," Jack said. "What time is it, anyway?"

"Four," I said. We both spoke quietly, our voices hushed by the deep silence around us. Lou came out rubbing down the tape on a fresh bandage. I wondered why he didn't wear a glove or try to keep that hand out of the dirt.

Miller came up from the corral about the same time Stan and then Sloane came out of their tent.

"Cold," Stan said shortly, zipping up his new jacket and getting up close to the fire.

"Mornin', men," Miller said. "Coffee ready?"

"In just a minute or so, Cap," Clint said. He looked around, his battered old cowboy hat pushed back from his face. "You fellers are gonna have to step back from the fire if you want any breakfast."

We all moved obediently back away and he began slapping his pans down on the grill. "Coffee's ready," he said. "Take it over to the table there."

I carried the heavy pot to the table and started pouring coffee into the cups. Then we all stood back in the bunch in front of the tents watching Clint make breakfast.

"We'll get up there well before first light, men," Miller said. "I'll ride all the way up to the top with the Kid here, and then I'll come on back down with the horses. They'd just get restless on you and move around and spook the deer. Besides, they might run off if you happen to get off a shot today."

"It's ready," Clint said. "Come and get your plates."

We lined up, and he filled our plates for us. We sat down to eat. Miller continued with his instructions. "I'll bring the horses down and put 'em out to graze in this meadow out here. I'll be back up to get you about ten or so. Isn't likely there'll be much movin' after that. We'll go out again about three thirty or four this afternoon." He bent his face to his plate and scooped in three or four mouthfuls of scrambled eggs. He stared off into the dark while he chewed, his white mustache twitching with each bite.

"I don't know as I'd shoot today," he said. "Just kinda get an idea of the size of the deer. Lots of men bust the first one they see with horns. There's a lot of deer on this mountain. A lot of big ones, so take your time."

He ate some more. By then the rest of us had finished. He looked at his watch. "I guess we'd better saddle up," he said, rising.

The rest of us followed him on down to the corral. The moon was still high over the shoulder of the peak, and it was very bright out from under the shadow of the spruces. I'd had visions of fumbling around with flashlights and lanterns while we saddled the horses, but the moonlight was bright enough to make it almost as easy as doing it in broad daylight.

After we'd saddled the horses, we led them back up to the tents and picked up our rifles.

"How about the signals?" Sloane gasped, patting the butt of his Ruger.

"Oh, yeah," Miller said. He didn't sound very enthusiastic. "How 'bout this? One shot means a down deer. Two shots for one wounded and running. Three shots if you're in trouble—hurt or sick or hangin' off a cliff by one hand. OK?"

"Sure," Sloane said. "Anything'll work as long as we all know what it is."

"You fellers better get movin' if Cap's gonna get them horses back down by shootin' time," Clint said.

We tied our rifles to the saddles and climbed on. Miller led the way, and we strung out behind him single file.

By the time we got to his stand, Cal was breathing hard. Even though the horse was doing all the work, he was puffing as if he'd climbed the hill by himself.

"You OK?" Miller asked him.

"Fine," Sloane gasped. "You gonna take the horse with you now?"

"No. Just tie him to that bush there. I'll be back down in about half an hour or so—before shootin' time anyway. You might as well go on over and get settled now though."

"Right," Cal said, grunting as he slipped off his horse.

"Good luck, Sloane," Jack said. "Try not to bust anything bigger'n a twelve-point."

"Sure," Cal grinned. Then he giggled, and I think that made us all feel better. We waved and moved on up the mountainside.

Jack tied down his horse and faded back into the shadowy bushes with a backward wave.

Stan dismounted stiffly and stood by his horse, watching us as Miller, McKlearey, and I rode on up the ridge.

It was darker than hell in McKlearey's notch. His face was nothing more than a pale blur as he reined in his horse.

"This is as far as I go," he said.

"I'll be back down in a few minutes, Sarge," Miller said.

"I'll be here, Cap. Good luck, Danny boy."

"Same to you, Lou," I answered.

Then Miller and I went slowly on up the steep trail to my post.

The moon was just slipping behind the shoulder of the mountain as we came out on the knob at the top of the ridge.

"Better let my eyes settle into the dark a bit before I start back," Miller said. "Give the horse a rest, too." We both climbed down.

I offered him a cigarette and we squatted down in the darkness, smoking.

"Clint tells me you went to college," Miller said after a while.

"Yeah," I said. "Before I went in the Army."

"Always wished I'd had the chance to go," he said. "Maybe then I wouldn't be finishin' up on a broke-down horse-ranch, scratchin' to make a livin'."

"From the way I see it," I said, "you're one of the lucky ones. You're doing something you like."

"There's that, too," he admitted. "I don't know as it all adds up to all that much though. The work's hard and the pay's pretty slim. A man always wonders if maybe he coulda done better."

"I know a lot of people who'd trade even across with you, Cap," I said.

He chuckled. "I guess there ain't much point worryin' about it at this stage."

I untied my rifle and the water bag from my saddle.

"You got ever'thing, son? All your gear, I mean?"

"Yeah," I said, "I'm all set."

He stood up. Then he scuffed his boot in the thin dirt a couple times. Finally he blurted it out. "What's eatin' on old Sarge, anyway?"

"God, Cap, I don't know. Maybe he's just having trouble reconverting to civilian life. I met him about a month ago, and he's been jumpy as hell all that time. I've about halfway got a hunch he had a pretty rough time in Vietnam—he's out on a medical. Malaria, I think."

"Mean stuff," he said. "Clint gets a touch of it now and then."

"Oh?"

"Puts him flat on his back."

"Yeah. I've heard it's no joke."

"I sure wish ol' Sarge would go a little easier on the liquor though. I can sure tell you that."

"At the rate he's going," I said, "that bottle of his won't last much longer."

"He's got more'n one," Miller said gloomily. "That sack of his clinks and gurgles like a liquor store. I wonder he had room for spare sox."

"Oh, brother," I said.

"Did you talk with the Big Man on the way down yesterday?" he asked, changing the subject.

"Yeah," I said. "He's going to let me know if he gets really bad."

"That's a real good idea. Clint can take him back on down if he gets too sick. Most men start to get their wind before this."

"I think he'll be all right now," I said.

"I sure hope so." He looked around. "Well, I guess I better be gettin' on down."

"Yeah," I said. I glanced at my watch. "About half an hour till shooting time."

"Ought to work out about right, then," he said. "Well, son, good luck."

"Thanks, Cap."

I watched him ride on off down the trail with Ned trailing behind him. Then I slung my rifle and walked on up to the top of the knob. I sat down and lit another cigarette. I'd meant to ask him if the smoke would spook off the deer, but I'd forgotten.

I unslung my rifle and started pulling cartridges for it out of my gun belt and pushing them one by one into the magazine. I eased the last one up the tube with the bolt and then pushed the bolt-handle down. I snapped on the safety and carefully laid the rifle down on a flat rock. Then I loaded the pistol and put it back in the holster. Now what the hell was I supposed to do for the next twenty-five minutes?

I sat down on the rock beside the rifle again and looked off toward the east. I could just make out the faintest hint of light along toward the horizon out there.

I remembered a time in Germany when I'd pulled the four-to-six shift on guard duty and had watched the sun slowly rise over one of those tiny little farming villages with the stone-walled, red-tile-roofed houses huddled together under a church spire. It's a good time for getting things sorted out in your mind. I wonder how many times other guys have thought the same thing—probably every guy from along about the year one.

One thing was sure—I was a helluva long way from Germany now. I started to try to figure out what time it would be in Wertheim about now, but I lost track somewhere off the east coast. I wondered what Heidi was doing right now. I still felt bad about that. If only she hadn't been so damn trusting. No matter what I'd told her, she'd gone on hoping and believing. It was a bad deal all the way around. She'd gotten hurt, and I'd picked up big fat guilt feelings out of it.

And naturally that got me to thinking about Sue. Oddly enough, it didn't bother me to think about her anymore. For a long time I'd deliberately forced my mind away from it. About the only time I'd thought about her was when I was in the last stages of getting crocked—and that usually wound up getting maudlin. At first, of course, I'd been pretty bitter about it. Now I could see the whole thing in a little better perspective. I'd told a lot of people that it wouldn't have worked out between Sue and me, but that had been a cover-up really. Now I began to see that it was really true—it *wouldn't* have worked out. It wasn't just her old lady either. Sue and I had looked at the world altogether differently. She'd have probably turned into a Monica on me within the first six months.

That made me a little less certain about graduate school. Maybe I'd just gone ahead and made those plans to go back to the campus in Seattle with some vague idea in the back of my mind about possibly getting back together with her again. Or maybe I was just looking for a place to hide—or to postpone things. I was awfully good at postponing things.

The streak of light off along the eastern horizon was spreading now, and the stars were fading. A steel-gray luminosity was beginning to show in the rocks around me. It was still about fifteen minutes until it would be legal to shoot. Once again I found myself wishing my little Bolshevik could see this. Talk about an ambivalent situation, that was really it. I guess I knew she'd been right that night at Sloane's orgy—she and I weren't for keeps. There was no way we could be, but lately I couldn't see anything nice or hear anything or come up with an idea without wanting to share it with her. She was a complete and absolute nut, but I couldn't think of anybody that was more fun to be around.

A deer crossed the brow of the ridge on the far side of the ravine. I think I looked at it for about thirty seconds before I actually realized it was a deer. It was still too dark to tell if it was a buck or a doe. I began to get that tight excitement I get when I'm hunting—a sort of a double aliveness I only get then. I picked up my rifle and tried to see if I could catch the deer in the scope, but by that time it was down in the brush at the bottom of the ravine. Then I started paying attention to what I was doing. I began scoping the ravine and the ridge carefully.

It was getting lighter by the minute. I counted three more deer crossing the ridge—three does and a small buck.

I checked my watch. It was legal to shoot now.

In the next hour, thirty or forty deer crossed the ridge and another dozen or so drifted across the meadow behind me. Most of them were does, of course, and the bucks were all pretty small. I put the scope on each one and watched them carefully. Deer are funny animals, and I got a kick out of watching them. Some would come out of the brush very cautiously, looking around as if the whole world was out to get them. Others just blundered on out as if they owned the woods.

The pink sunlight was slipping down the peak above again, and it was broad daylight by now.

The white deer crossed the ridge above me from the meadow at my back just before the sun got down to the rockfall.

I caught the flicker of his movement out of the corner of my eye and swung the scope on him. He crossed about seventy yards above me, and he completely filled the scope. I think he looked right straight at me several times. I could see his pale eyelashes fluttering as he blinked nearsightedly in my direction.

It never occurred to me to shoot. Maybe if I had, I could have headed off a whole potful of trouble, but it just didn't occur to me—I'm not even sure I *could* have shot. I just wasn't so hungry that I had to kill something unique.

➤➤ 21

"You see any with any size?" Miller asked when he came back up about ten thirty.

"One pretty good three-point was all," I told him. I'd decided the less I said about the albino, the better.

"There'll be bigger ones," he said. "The others already went on down." He was looking at me kind of funny.

"I haven't seen anything in the last hour or so," I told him, walking over to Ned. The damn fool horse reached out and nuzzled at me, almost like a puppy. I scratched his ears for him.

"You two sure seem to be gettin' along good." Miller chuckled.

"I think he's all bluff," I said, tying the rifle to the saddle and hooking the water bag over the horn. I climbed on, and we started down the ridge.

"The Big Man don't seem much better," he said when we got out past McKlearey's notch.

"He'll hold on," I said. "This is awfully important to him."
Miller grunted.

It was close to eleven when we got back down to camp.

"What the hell's the matter with your eyes Dan?" Jack demanded as I climbed down at the corral. "That big white bastard damn near walked over the top of you up there—couldn't 'a been more'n thirty yards from you."

"Oh?" I said. I saw Miller watching me closely. "I must have been watching another deer."

"Hell, man, that's the one that counts."

I unsaddled Ned and ran him into the corral.

Jack shook his head disgustedly and stalked back up to the fire. I followed him.

"I'm not shittin' you," he told the others. "Just goddamn near ran right over him. I was watchin' the whole time through my scope."

"Why didn't you shoot?" McKlearey demanded.

"Christ, Lou, he was almost a mile away, and Stan, you, and Dan were all between me and him. I ain't about to get trigger-happy."

"Are you sure it was the same deer?" Stan asked.

"Ain't very likely there's more than one like that on the whole mountain," Jack said. "I still can't see how you missed spottin' him, Dan."

"Coulda been brush or a rise of ground between the Kid and that deer," Miller said, pouring himself a cup of coffee. "That ground can be damn tricky when you get at a different angle."

"Now that's sure the truth," Clint said. "I seen a nine-pointer walk no more'n ten yards in front of ol' Cap here one time. From where I was sittin' it looked like they were right in each other's laps, but when I got down there I seen that deer had been in a kind of shallow draw."

Miller chuckled. "Biggest deer we seen all that year, too."

"I guess that explains it then," Jack said dubiously.

"Where's Sloane?" I asked.

"He's lying down in the tent," Stan said. "He's still not feeling too well."

"Is he asleep?"

"I think he was going to try to sleep a little."

"I won't pester him then," I said. "Any of you guys see any good ones?"

"I seen a four-point," McKlearey said, "but I figure it's early yet."

"That's playin' it smart, Sarge," Miller said. "We got plenty of time left."

"What time you think we oughta go back up?" Jack asked him.

"Oh, 'bout three thirty or so," Miller said. "Evenin' huntin' ain't all that productive this time of year. Deer'll move in the evening, but not near as much as in the mornin'."

We loafed around until lunchtime and then ate some more venison and beans. We tried to get Sloane to eat, but he said he didn't feel much like it, so we left him alone.

The rest of the guys sacked out after we'd eaten, but I wasn't really sleepy. I was feeling kind of sticky and grimy and thought a bit about maybe trying to swim in the beaver pond, but one hand stuck in there convinced me that it would be an awful mistake. I think that water came right out of a glacier somewhere. I settled for a stand-up bath out of the washbasin and called it good. Then I washed out my shirt and underwear and hung them on limbs to dry. I felt better in clean clothes and with at least the top layer of dirt off.

At three thirty we went down to the corral. Sloane was still feeling pretty rough, and Miller suggested that maybe he ought to just stay in bed so he'd be better tomorrow. Cal didn't give him much of an argument.

"Horses'll be OK to stay with you men," Miller said. "They're a whole lot quieter come evenin'. I'll just ride on up to the top with the Kid here, and we'll come on down end of shootin' time."

We all got on our horses and started up the ridge. It felt a little funny not having Cal along. Each of the others peeled off at their regular stands, and Miller and I scrambled on up to my knob at the top.

We got down and tied the horses securely and went on up to the rock where I'd sat that morning.

Miller lit a cigarette. "Sun's still pretty warm, ain't it?" he said.

"Yeah," I agreed. I could see that something was bothering him.

After a long while he said it. "How come you didn't shoot this mornin'?"

"I didn't see anything I wanted to shoot," I said.

"I was down below watchin' you with my field glasses," he said. "I saw you follow that freak deer with your scope all the way across the ridge. I don't think your brother saw you."

"I don't know, Cap," I said. "I just didn't feel like shooting him."

He nodded. "Maybe I'd feel the same way," he said. "I've seen a few of 'em and I've never shot one."

"I just watched him," I said. "I don't think I even considered pulling the trigger on him."

"In a way I almost wish you had. It would put an end to it. Your brother and ol' Sarge are startin' to get at each other about it."

"I know," I said. "I wish the damn deer would get the hell off this side of the mountain."

"Ain't very likely."

I had a cigarette.

"Doe," Miller said, nodding at the other ridge.

We watched her step daintily down into the ravine. Then something spooked her. She snorted and bounded up the side of the ravine and on over the ridge.

"Picked up somebody's scent," Miller said. "Breeze gets a little tricky this time of evenin'."

We sat in silence, watching several does and a couple of small bucks pick their way on down the ravine. The sun crept slowly down toward the shoulder of the peak, and the shadows of the rocks and bushes grew longer. It was very quiet up there.

The sun slid behind the mountain, and the lucid shadowless twilight settled in. After a while Miller checked his watch.

"I guess that's about it," he said.

We got up and went back to the horses.

"Evenings *are* a little slower, aren't they?" I said.

"Yeah," he agreed, "like I said."

We mounted up and started down. McKlearey was already on his horse waiting for us, but we had to whistle for Stan and Jack. It was almost dark by the time we got down to the corral. We unsaddled and went back up to camp.

"Boy," Jack said, "you weren't kiddin' when you said pickin's were lean at night. I don't think I seen more'n half a dozen."

"You saw more than I did then," Stan said.

"I seen eight or ten," McKlearey said.

"I know some fellers don't even go out in the afternoon," Clint said, "but a man never knows when that big one'll come easin' by. Besides"—he grinned—"it gives me a chance to get supper goin' without havin' all you men under foot."

We got the point and backed away from the fire to give him a little more room.

"I don't mind goin' out," McKlearey said. "That's what we came up here for. I wouldn't want old Whitey gettin' past me."

"Don't be gettin' no wild ideas about *my* deer," Jack said.

"He ain't yours till you get your tag on 'im, Alders."

"I'll tag 'im," Jack said, "don't worry about that."

"Not if I see 'im first, you won't," McKlearey snapped.

"I told you men yesterday," Miller said, "that there's a whole lot of deer up on that mountain. You get your mind all set on just that one, and you're liable to come up empty."

"One of us is bound to get 'im," Jack said.

"Not necessarily," Miller said. "There's a hundred or more trails on that ridge. He could be crossin' on any one of 'em."

"I'm still gonna wait a few days before I fill my tag," Jack said.

I went over to see how Sloane was doing. I'm afraid that about two or three more smart remarks from my brother, and I'd have had to get in on it. Jack could be awfully knot-headed stubborn when he got his back up.

"Hey, Cal," I said, poking my head into his tent. "How's it going?"

"A little better now, Dan," he said from his bed. "I think it's startin' to settle down finally."

"Good deal, Cal. I'm glad to hear it."

"Come on in," he said, "have a blast." He giggled. That made me feel better right there.

"Now there's an idea," I said. I went on into his tent. He fished out his bottle and we each had a small snort.

"I'll tell you, buddy," he said, "it just damn near had me whipped there for a while. About ten this morning it was all I could do to climb up on that horse."

"You been sleeping straight through?" I asked him.

"Dozing," he said. "I feel pretty good now. Except I'm hungrier'n hell."

"Wouldn't be surprised," I said. "We couldn't interest you in lunch."

"I couldn't have eaten lunch if you guys had all held guns on me."

"You about ready to make an appearance?" I asked him.

"Sure thing. Chow about ready?" He sat up, carefully.

"Should be."

"Good." He pulled on his boots and got slowly to his feet. "I ain't about to rush it this time," he said.

"Good thinking."

We went out to join the others, and there were the usual wisecracks about Sloane loafing around camp. He laughed and giggled as if nothing were wrong. I could see the relief in Miller's face. We all felt a helluva lot better. Having a man sick like Cal had been is just like having a heavy weight on top of everybody's head.

"You're lookin' a helluva lot better there, Sullivan," McKlearey said.

"Who?" I asked him.

"Sullivan there." He pointed at Cal with his bandaged hand.

I shrugged. Maybe it was some kind of goof-off nickname.

"Come and get it," Clint said, "or I'll feed it to the porky."

"Where is that little bastard anyway?" Jack said as we walked toward the fire.

"Oh, he's still around," Miller said. "Just watch where you set."

We lined up and Clint filled our plates. Then we went over and sat around the fire to eat.

"Hell," McKlearey said suddenly, staring at Cal. "You ain't Sullivan."

"I never said I was." Sloane giggled through a mouthful of beans.

"Hey, Danny?" McKlearey said, "where the hell is Sullivan?"

"Sullivan who?" I asked.

"Oh, shit, you know Sullivan as well as I do."

"Sorry, Lou. It doesn't ring a bell."

He looked at me closely. "Oh," he said. "No, I guess it wouldn't. I guess I was thinkin' about somebody else."

"McKlearey," Jack said, "what the hell are you smokin' anyway?"

"Well," Lou said, grinning broadly at him, "I tried a pinecone this morning."

"How was it?" Sloane giggled. "Did it blow your mind?"

"Aw, hell no," Lou said. "Turned it inside-out a couple times, but it didn't even come close to blowin' it."

Who the hell was Sullivan, for Chrissake?

We finished eating and cleaned up our dishes. Then we all sat down around the fire with a drink.

"Same layout for tomorrow as this morning?" Sloane asked.

"Seems to work out pretty well," Miller said, "and you men all got them posts you're on pretty well located by now."

"God, yes," Jack said. "Let's not switch around now. I'd get lost sure as hell."

"Well, then," Sloane said, polishing off his drink, "if there aren't gonna be any changes, I think I'll hit the sack."

"Christ, Sloane," Jack said, "you been sleepin' all day."

"Man, I need my beauty sleep." Cal giggled.

"Somehow," I said, grinning, "I think it's a little late for that."

"Never hurts to give it a try," he said, getting up.

"I'll call it a day, too," Stan said.

"What a buncha candy asses," McKlearey rasped.

"Four o'clock still comes damned early," Clint growled at the rest of us. It occurred to me that the little old guy had to be up at least a half hour before the rest of us, and he might feel it was bad manners to go to bed before we did.

"Why don't we all hang it up?" I suggested. "Maybe then you mighty hunters won't be so damn rum-dum in the morning."

"I suppose a good night's sleep wouldn't kill me," Jack said. We all got up.

"Man," Lou said, "this is worse than basic training."

"But this is fun, Lou," I said.

"Oh, sure"—he grinned at me—"I'd rather do a little sack-time with some high-class broad." He winked knowingly at Stan.

Christ! Was he *trying* to get killed?

Stan's face tightened up, and he went off to his tent without saying anything.

The rest of us said good night and scattered toward our sacks.

"Sloane seems a lot better," Jack said after we'd gotten settled.

"Yeah," I agreed. "That's a helluva relief."

"God, it must be awful—gettin' old like that," he said suddenly.

"What the hell are you talking about?" I asked him. "Sloane isn't old."

"You know what I mean," Jack said."When your lungs or your legs give out like that."

"Oh, hell. Sloane's got a lot of miles left in him," I said. "He's just a little winded."

"It gives me the creeps, that's all."

"That's a helluva thing to say."

"I know, but I can't help it."

"What's eating at you, Jack?" I asked him, sitting up.

"I'm not gettin' anyplace. It's like I'm standin' still."

"What the hell brought this on?"

"God damn it, I've known Sloane since I was a kid. He's always been able to handle himself and anything that came along. He's always been the roughest, toughest guy around."

"Jesus, Jack, it's not his fault he gets winded up here. It could happen to anybody."

"That's just it. A couple more years, and it's damn likely to happen to *me*."

"Oh, bullshit! You're not carrying the gut Sloane is."

"It's not only that," he said, and his voice had an edge of desperation. "It's what I was sayin' before—I'm not gettin' anyplace. Hell, I'm not any further ahead right now than I was five goddamn years ago. I've got a marriage goin' sour. I've got a pissy-ass, two-bit job—hell, I had a better job year before last. Man, I'm just goin' downhill."

What the hell could I say? As far as I could see, he was calling it pretty close.

"It's been just too much booze, too many women, too many different jobs," he went on. "I've just *got* to dig in, goddammit, I've got to!"

"All you have to do is make your mind up, they say." What an asinine thing to say!

"Christ! I wish I could be like you, Dan, you know that? You know where you're goin', what you're gonna be. Me, I'm just floppin' around like a fish outa water. I just can't seem to settle down."

"Man, it's not just exactly as if you were over the hill or anything."

"You know what I mean. I keep hopin' something will click—you know—make it all snap into place so I can get settled down and get started on something. Maybe this trip will do it." He stared gloomily at the fire.

He was *afraid*! Jack had been talking for so long about how he wasn't afraid of anything that I guess I'd almost come to believe it. Now it came as a kind of shock to me. Jack was afraid. I didn't know what to say to him.

"You want a belt?" I asked him.

"Yeah. Maybe it'll help me sleep."

I fished out my bottle and we each had a quick drink. Then we both sat staring out at the dying fire.

We were still awake when McKlearey started screaming again.

"Sullivan," he screamed, "look out!" Then there was a lot more I couldn't understand.

By the time I got untangled from my sleeping bag and got outside the tent, Lou was standing outside, still hollering and waving that god-damn .38 around. I wasn't just exactly sure how to handle it.

"McKlearey!" It was Sloane. He had his head out of his tent, and there was a bark to his voice that I hadn't heard him use very often.

"Huh?" McKlearey blinked and looked around, confused. "What's up, Cal?"

"You're havin' another bad dream," Sloane said. "Settle down and put that goddamn gun away."

"What?" Lou looked down and saw the pistol in his hand. "Jeez!" he said. "Sorry, you guys. I musta had another damn nightmare." He lowered the gun and went back into his tent holding his left hand carefully in front of him to keep from bumping it.

After a minute or so I heard the clink of a bottle in there. What the hell? As long as it kept him quiet.

━━━ 22

I woke up the next morning before Clint came around to shake us out. I could see the little old guy and Miller standing over by the fire and hear the low murmur of their voices. I got up and went on out of the tent.

"Mornin', Dan," Clint said.

"Clint. Cap," I said.

"Coffee'll be done in just a bit," Clint said.

"Ol' Sarge seems to have got settled down," Miller said, his low voice rumbling. "At least I didn't hear him no more last night."

"I think he's only good for about one of those a night," I said.

"Well," Clint growled, "I don't know about him, but it's about all I'm good for."

"Amen," I agreed.

"I better go check the horses," Miller said and went off down toward the corrals.

I finished dressing and asked Clint if I could give him a hand with breakfast.

"Naw, Dan, thanks all the same, but I got 'er just about ready to go on the fire."

"OK," I said and got cleaned up.

"Coffee's done," he said as Miller came back up.

"Thanks, Clint," I said. "It's a little chilly this morning."

"Some," Miller agreed, shaking out his cup.

"I sure hope we don't get any snow," I said.

Miller grinned at me. "You got a thing about snow, son?"

"I went on maneuvers two winters in a row in Germany," I said. "I got a little used up on it."

"We *could* get some," he said, "but it's not very likely. I wouldn't lose no sleep over it."

The three of us had coffee. It was kind of sleepy and quiet—a private sort of time of day. None of us said much. The moon over the top of the peak was very sharp and bright.

"I better roust out the others," Clint said finally.

"I'll get 'em," I said.

"OK. I'll get breakfast on."

I woke up the others and then went back down to the fire. The smell of bacon and frying potatoes was very strong, and I realized I was hungry.

Jack came straggling down to the fire, his unlaced boots flopping loosely on his feet and his baseball cap stuffed down on his scrambled hair. "Son of a bitch!" he said, "it's colder'n a witch's tit."

"You keep company with some mighty strange women," I said, just to be saying something.

Clint doubled over with a wheezy, cackling kind of laugh. Even Miller grinned. I didn't really think it as all that funny myself.

"Always a smart-ass in the crowd," Jack growled. He finished dressing and washed up. By then the others had come out.

Sloane looked a lot better, and we all felt relieved about that.

"This cold'll hold the deer back a little," Miller said as we started to eat. "They're liable to be dribblin' across them ridges most of the mornin', so I won't be back up to get you men till 'bout noon or so." We all nodded. "Clint'll fix you up with some sandwiches to kinda tide you over."

"That's a good idea," Jack said. "I got a little gaunt yesterday."

We finished eating and went down to the corral and saddled up by moonlight again. Then we led the horses back up to camp, got our rifles and sandwiches and started up the ridge.

None of us said very much until after we'd dropped Sloane off. Then Stan dropped back to where I was riding and pulled in beside me.

"Did you hear him last night?" he said, his face tight in the moonlight.

"Who?"

"McKlearey."

"You mean all that screaming? Hell, how could I help it?"

"No," he said. "I mean before we went to bed. That clever little remark he made—about a 'high-class woman.'"

"It didn't mean anything, Stan," I said. "He was just talking."

"Maybe, but I don't think so."

"Oh, come on, Stan. He talks like that all the time. It doesn't mean a thing."

"I wish I could believe that," he said, "but somehow I just can't. I'm about to go out of my mind over this thing."

"You're imagining things." God, he acted so positive!

"Your post, Professor," Miller said from up in front of us.

Stan nudged his horse away before I could say anymore.

"He was daydreamin'." McKlearey chuckled raspingly. "He's got a young wife with a wild body on her." He laughed again. Stan didn't turn around, but his back stiffened.

We rode on up the ridge and dropped off McKlearey.

At the top Miller wished me luck and went on back down. He seemed to have something on his mind—probably the same thing the rest of us did.

I sat on my rock waiting for it to get light and trying not to think about it. I didn't want it to spoil the hunting for me.

Once again the sky paled and the stars faded and the deer started to move. I saw one pretty nice four-point about seven or so, but I held off. I still thought I might be able to do a little better. The rest were all either does or smaller bucks.

The sun came up.

By eight thirty I began to feel as if that rock was beginning to grow to my tailbone. I'd swung my scope up and down the ravine so many times I think I knew every branch and leaf on the scrubby, waist-high brush, and there must have been trails out in the meadow behind me from my eyeballs. Nothing had gone by for about fifteen minutes, and frankly I was bored. Sometimes that happens when you're hunting—particularly stand-hunting. Maybe I just don't have the patience for it.

I stood up and walked down the knob a ways. I wondered if I could see any of the others. I made damn sure the safety was on and then ran the scope on down the ridge. I could see the camp a mile and a half or so away. It looked like a toy carelessly dropped at the edge of the spruces. The beaver pond looked like a small bright dime in the middle of the yellow-green meadow.

I was sure I could make out Clint moving around the fire, and I thought I saw Miller among the horses grazing in the lower meadow. I swung the scope up the ridge a ways.

I could see the white boulder that marked Sloane's post, but Cal himself was under the upswelling brow of the next hump. I spotted Jack rather quickly. He was standing up, tracking a doe over in the ravine with his rifle.

I searched the next post for a long time but couldn't locate Stan—which was odd, since his post was all out in plain sight with no obstructions in my line of sight. I thought maybe he was lying under some brush, but that orange jacket of his should have stood out pretty vividly against or even under the yellowing leaves of the sparse brush.

I moved the scope on up to the notch. A lazily rising puff of cigarette smoke pinpointed Lou for me—even though he was the only one of us who wasn't wearing any kind of bright clothing. He'd rigged up a kind of half-assed blind of limbs and brush and was sprawled out behind it, his rifle lying against a limb. He was only about a hundred and fifty yards down the hill. He raised his arm to his face with a glint and a flicker of that white bandage. He had a bottle with him. Maybe that's what had Miller so worried. McKlearey sure didn't seem to be hunting very hard.

I was about ready to go on back up to my rock-roost when I caught a flash of color in the thick brush between Stan's post and McKlearey's notch. I put the scope on it.

It was Stan. He was crawling through the bushes on his hands and knees. His face looked sweaty and very pale. He seemed to be trembling, but I couldn't be sure.

"What the hell is he up to?" I muttered under my breath. I watched him inch forward for about five minutes. When he got to the edge of the notch, he stopped and lay facedown on the ground for several minutes. He was about fifty yards above and behind McKlearey.

I didn't like the looks of it at all, but there wasn't a helluva lot I could do at that point.

Then Stan raised his face, and it was all shiny and very flushed now. He slowly pulled his rifle forward and poked it out over the edge of the bank.

I suddenly was very cold.

Stan got himself squared away. There wasn't any question about what he was aiming at.

"No, Stan!" It came out a croak. I don't think anybody could have heard it more than five feet away from me. Helplessly I put my scope on McKlearey.

Stan's shot kicked up dirt about two feet above Lou's head. McKlearey dove for cover. Instinct, I guess.

I didn't really consciously think about it. I just snapped off the safety, pointed my rifle in the general direction of the other side of the ravine and squeezed the trigger. The sound of my shot mingled and blurred in with the echo of Stan's.

I saw the white blur of his face suddenly turned up toward me for a moment, and then he scrambled back into the brush.

McKlearey was burrowing down under his pile of limbs like a man trying to dig a foxhole with his teeth.

There was something moving on the other side of the ravine. It flickered palely through the bushes, headed down the ridge.

It was the white deer. Apparently the double echo was confusing hell out of it. It ran down past McKlearey and on down the ravine. A couple minutes later I heard several shots from the stands below. Jack and Cal were shooting.

I hoped that they'd missed. The poor white bastard was just an innocent bystander really. He had no business being on that other side just then.

I looked down and saw that my hands were shaking so badly that I could barely hold my rifle. I took several deep breaths and then slowly pulled back the bolt, flipping out the empty in a long, twinkling brass arc. It clinked on a rock and fell in the dirt. I closed the bolt, put the safety back on, and picked up the empty. Then I went back up to my rock and sat down.

23

"Man!" Jack said when I got back down to camp, "the son of a bitch ran right through the whole damn bunch of us!"

"I shot at him five times!" Sloane gasped, his face red. "Five goddamn times and never touched a hair. I think the son of a bitch is a ghost, and we all shot right through 'im." He tried to giggle but wound up coughing and choking.

"You OK?" I asked him.

He tried to nod, still choking and gasping. It took him a minute or so to get settled down.

"Did you shoot, Dan?" Jack asked me.

"Once," I said, taking out the empty cartridge case, "and I think Stan did too, didn't you, Stan?"

He nodded, his face very pale.

"I got off three," Jack said. He turned to Miller. "I thought you said they always ran uphill, Cap."

"Ninety-nine times out of a hundred," Miller said.

"Maybe one of us hit him," Sloane gasped.

Miller shook his head. "He cut back on up over that far ridge when he got past you men. I expect all the shootin' just kept pushin' him on down. I don't imagine he can see too good in broad daylight with them pink eyes of his."

Lou didn't say anything, but his eyes looked a little wild.

We ate lunch and then all of us kind of poked around looking for something to do until time to go back up again.

I wound up wandering down to the pond again. I stood watching the fish swim by and trying not to think about what had happened that morning.

"Why don't you watch where the hell you're shootin'?" It was Mc-Klearey.

I looked at him for a moment. "I know where I was shooting, Lou," I told him.

"Well, one of them damn shots just barely missed me," he said. His hands were shaking.

"Must have been a ricochet," I said.

"I ain't all that sure," he said. He squatted down by the water and began stripping off his bandage.

"I've got no reason to shoot you, Lou. I don't have a wife." I just let it hang there.

He looked at me for a long time, but he didn't answer. Then he finished unwinding his hand. The gash in his palm was red and inflamed-looking, and the whole hand looked a little puffy.

"That's getting infected," I told him. "Clint's got a first-aid kit. You'd better put something on it."

"It's OK," he said. "I been pourin' whiskey in it."

"Iodine's cheaper," I said, "and a helluva lot more dependable."

He stuck the hand into the water, wincing at the chill.

"That's not a good idea either," I said.

"I know what I'm doin'," he said shortly.

I shrugged. It was his hand, after all.

"Danny," he said finally.

"Yeah?"

"You didn't see who shot at me, did you?"

I didn't really want to lie to him, but I was pretty sure Stan wouldn't try it again. He'd looked too sick when we'd gotten back down. "Look, Lou," I said, "with the scopes on all the rifles in camp, if somebody was trying to shoot you, he'd have nailed you to the cross with the first shot. If one came anywhere near you, it was more than likely just what I said—a ricochet."

"Maybe—" he said doubtfully.

"You're just jumpy," I said. "All keyed up. Shit, look at the nightmares you've been having. Maybe you ought to go a little easy on the booze."

"That's why I drink it," he said, staring out across the beaver pond. "If I drink enough, I don't dream at all. I'm OK then."

I was about to ask him what was bothering him, but I was pretty sure he wouldn't tell me. Besides, it was none of my business.

We went back up to camp, and he went into his tent.

We went out at three thirty again, the same as we had the day before.

"I thought you wasn't gonna shoot at that deer," Miller said when we got up to the top.

I couldn't very well tell him why I'd shot, and I didn't want to lie to him. "I was just firing a warning shot," I said. In a way it had been just that.

He looked at me for a minute but didn't say anything. I'm not sure if he believed me.

None of us saw anything worth shooting that evening either, and we were all pretty quiet when we got back down.

"Come on, men," Miller said, trying to cheer us up. "No point in gettin' down in the mouth. It's only a matter of time till you start gettin' the big ones."

"I *know* which one I'm gonna get," Jack said. "I'm gonna bust that white bastard."

"Not if I see 'im first," McKlearey said belligerently, nursing his hand.

They glared at each other.

"All right," Jack said finally, "you remember that bet we got?"

"I remember," Lou said.

"*That* deer is the one then."

"That's fine with me."

"That wasn't the bet," I said flatly.

They both scowled at me.

"Dan's right," Sloane said, gasping heavily. "The original bet was best deer—Boone and Crockett points." His voice sounded pretty wheezy again, but his tone was pretty firm.

"There's still the side bet," Stan said very quietly. I'd forgotten about that one.

McKlearey stared back and forth between the two of them. He looked like he was narrowing down his list of enemies. "All right," he said very softly. It didn't sound at all like him.

"I don't want you men shootin' at that deer when he's up on top of no cliff or somethin'," Miller said. "I seen a couple men after the same deer once—both of 'em so afraid the other was gonna get it that they weren't even thinkin' no more. One of 'em finally shot the deer right off the top of a four-hundred-foot bluff. Wasn't enough left to make a ten-cent hamburger out of it by the time that deer quit bouncin'."

"We'll watch it," Jack said, still staring at McKlearey.

Lou edged around until he had his back to a stump and could keep an eye on both Jack and Stan. His eyes had gone kind of flat and dead. He was sort of holding his bandaged hand up in the air so he wouldn't bump it, and his right hand was in his lap, about six inches from the butt of that .38. He looked like he was wound pretty tight.

We tried talking, but things were pretty nervous.

After a while Stan got up and went back to the latrine. I waited a couple minutes then followed him. He was leaning against a tree when I found him.

"Stan," I said.

"Yes." He didn't look at me. He knew what I was going to say.

"Be real careful about where you place your shots from now on, OK?"

He took a quick breath but didn't say anything. I waited a minute and then went on down the trail.

When the others got up to go to bed, Miller jerked his head very slightly to me, and he and I sat by the fire until they had all gone into their tents.

"I've got to go check the stock," he said. "You want to come along, son?"

"Sure, Cap," I said. "Stretch some of the kinks out of my legs."

We stood up and walked on down toward the corrals. Once we got away from the fire, the stars were very bright, casting even a faint light on the looming snowfields above us.

Miller leaned his elbows across the top rail of the corral, his mustache silvery in the reflected starlight, and his big cowboy hat shading his eyes. "Them boys seem to be missin' the whole point of what this is all about," he said finally.

"I'm not very proud of any of them myself, about now," I said. "They're acting like a bunch of damn-fool kids."

"I've seen this kinda stuff before, son. It always leads to hard feelin's."

"Maybe I *should* have shot that deer."

"Not if you didn't want to," he said.

"I wouldn't have felt right about it, but it'd sure be better than what's going on right now."

"Oh, a friendly bet's OK. Men do it all the time, but them boys are takin' it a little too serious."

"Well, most of that's just talk," I told him. "They go at each other like that all the time. I wouldn't worry too much about it. I just don't like the idea of it, that's all."

"I don't neither," he said, "and I'll tell you somethin' else I don't much like."

"What's that?"

"The feelin' I keep gettin' that we ain't all gonna finish up this hunt. I've had it from the first day."

I couldn't say much to that.

"I sure wouldn't want one of my hunters gettin' shot on my first trip out." He looked at me and grinned suddenly. "Wouldn't be much of an advertisement, now would it?"

━━ 24

Sloane was much worse the next morning. Much as he tried, he couldn't even get out of the sack. Both Stan and I offered to stay with him, but he insisted that we go ahead on up.

Breakfast was kind of quiet, and none of us talked very much on the way up the ridge.

Miller looked down at me from his saddle after I'd dismounted at the top. "If the Big Man don't get no better," he said, "Clint's gonna have to take him on down. This is the fourth day up here. He just ain't comin' around the way he should.''

"I know," I said.

"I like the Big Man," Miller said. "I don't know when I've ever met a better-natured man, but I ain't gonna be doin' him no favors by lettin' him die up here."

I nodded. "I'll talk with him when we get back down to camp," I said.

"I'd sure appreciate it, son," he said. "Good huntin'." He took Ned's reins and went on back down.

It was chilly up there in the darkness, and the stars were still out. I sat hunched up against the cold and tried not to think too much about things. Every now and then the breeze would gust up the ravine, and I could pick up the faint smell of the pine forest far down below the spruces.

The sky began to pale off to the east and the stars got dimmer.

I kind of let my mind drift back to the time before my father died. Once he and I had gone on out to fish on a rainy Sunday morning. The fish had been biting, and we were both catching them as fast as we could bait up. We both got soaked to the skin, and I think we both caught cold from it, but it was still one of the best times I could remember. Neither one of us had said very much, but it had been great. I suddenly felt something I hadn't felt for quite a few years—a sharp, almost unbearable pang of grief for my father.

It was lighter, and that strange, cold, colorless light of early morning began to flow down the side of the mountain.

I quite suddenly remembered a guy I hadn't thought about for years. It had been when I was knocking up and down the coast that year after I'd gotten out of high school. I'd been working on a truck farm in the Salinas Valley in California, mostly cultivating between the mile-long lettuce rows. About ten or so one cloudy morning, I'd seen a train go by. About as far as I was going to go that day was eight or ten rows over in the same field. I walked the cultivator back to the farmhouse and picked up my time. That afternoon I'd jumped into an empty boxcar as the train was pulling out of the yard headed north.

There was an old guy in the car. He wasn't too clean, and he smelled kind of bad, but he was somebody to talk to. We sat in the open doorway looking at the open fields and the woods and the grubby houses and garbage dumps—did you know that people live in garbage dumps? Anyway, we'd talked about this and that, and I'd found out that he had a little pension of some kind, and he just moved up and down the coast, working the crops and riding trains, with those pension checks trailing him from post office to post office. He said that he guessed he could go into almost any post office of any size on the coast, and there'd be at least one of his checks there.

He'd said that he was sixty-eight and his heart and lungs were bad.

Then he'd kind of looked off toward the sunset. "One of these days," he'd said, "I'll miss a jump on one of these boxcars and go under the wheels. Or my heart'll give out, or I'll take the pneumonia. They'll find me after I been picked over by a half-dozen other bums. Not much chance there'd be anything left so they could identify me. But I got that all took care of. Look—"

He'd unbuttoned his shirt and showed me his pale, flabby, old man's chest. He had a tattoo.

"My name was Wilmer O. Dugger," it said. "I was born in Wichita, Kansas, on October 4, 1893. I was a Methodist." It was like a tombstone, right on his chest.

He'd buttoned his shirt back up. "I got the same thing on both arms and both legs," he'd said. "No matter what happens, one of them tattoos is bound to come through it. I used to worry about it—them not bein' able to identify me, I mean. Now I don't worry no more. It's a damn fine thing, you know, not havin' nothin' to worry about."

I think it had been about then that I'd decided to go to college. I'd caught a quick glimpse of myself fifty years later, riding up and down the coast and waiting to miss my jump on a boxcar or for my heart to quit. About the only difference would have been that I don't think I'd have bothered with the tattoos.

The breeze dropped, and it got very still. I straightened up suddenly and picked up my rifle. It felt very smooth and comfortable. Something was going to happen. I eased the bolt back very gently and checked to make sure there was one in the tube. I closed it and slipped the safety back on. I could feel an excitement growing, a kind of quivering tension in the pit of my stomach and down my arms and legs, but my hands were steady. I wasn't shaking or anything.

A doe came out on the far side of the ravine. Very slowly, so as not to startle her, I sprawled out across the rock and got my elbows settled in so I could be absolutely sure of my shot.

The doe sniffed a time or two, looked back once, and then went on down into the ravine.

Another doe came out of the same place. After a minute or so she went on down, too.

Then another doe.

It was absolutely quiet. I could hear the faint *toc-toc-toc* of their hooves moving slowly on down the rocky bottom of the ravine.

I waited. I knew he was there. A minute went by. Then another.

Then there was a very faint movement in the brush, and he stepped softly out into the open.

I didn't really count him until later. I just saw the flaring rack and the calm, almost arrogant look on his face, and I knew that he was the one I wanted. He was big and heavily muscled. He was wary but not frightened or timid. It was his mountain.

He stood broadside to me and seemed to be looking straight across at me, though I don't really think he saw me. Maybe he just knew that I was there, as I had known that he would be.

I put the cross hairs of the scope just behind his front shoulder and slipped off the safety. His ears flicked.

I slowly squeezed the trigger.

I didn't hear the shot or feel the recoil of the rifle. The deer jerked and fell awkwardly. Then he stumbled to his feet and fell again. He got up again slowly and kind of walked on back over the other side of the ridge, his head down. It didn't occur to me to shoot again. I knew it wasn't necessary.

I stood up, listening now to the echo of the shot rolling off down the side of the mountain. I jacked out the empty shell, slipped the safety back on and slung the rifle. Then I started down into the ravine. I could hear the three does scrambling up through the brush on the far side.

The going was pretty rough, and it took me about ten minutes to get to where he'd been standing. I looked around on the ground until I found a blood spot. Then another. I followed them down the other side.

He'd gone about a hundred yards down the easy slope of the far side of the ridge and was lying on his side in a little clump of brush. His head was still raised but wobbling, as I walked carefully up to him. His eyes were not panicky or anything. I stepped behind him, out of range of his hooves, and took out my pistol. I thumbed back the hammer and put the muzzle to the side of his head between his eye and ear. His eye watched me calmly.

"Sorry I took so long to get here, buddy," I said.

Then I pulled the trigger.

The gun made a muffled kind of pop—without any echo to it, and the deer's head dropped heavily, and the life went out of his eye. I knelt beside him and ran my hand over his heavy shoulder. The fur felt coarse but very slick, and it was a kind of dark gray with little white tips shot through it. He smelled musky but not rank or anything.

I stood up, pointed the pistol up toward the top of the mountain, and fired it again. Then I began to wonder if maybe I'd given the wrong signal. I put the pistol back in the holster and slipped the hammer-thong back on. Then I leaned my rifle against a large rock and hauled the deer out in the open. I walked back on up to the ridge and hung my jacket over a bush to mark the spot for whoever came up with a horse.

I went back to the deer and started gutting him out. I wasn't nearly as fast as Clint was, but I managed to get the job done finally. I did seem to get a helluva lot of blood on my clothes though, but that didn't really matter.

I was trying to get him rolled over to drain out when Clint came riding down the ridge, leading Ned and a packhorse.

"Damn nice deer," he said, grinning. "Six-pointer, huh?"

"I didn't count him," I said. I checked the deer. "Yeah, it's six points, all right."

"Have any trouble?" He climbed down.

"No. He came out on the ridge, I shot him, and he kind of staggered down here and fell down. I'm afraid I busted up the liver pretty bad though." I pointed at the shredded organ lying on top of the steaming gut-pile.

"Where'd you take him?" he asked.

"Right behind the shoulder."

"That's dependable," he said. "Here, lemme help you dump 'im out."

We rolled the deer over.

"Heavy bugger, ain't he?" Clint chuckled.

"We're gonna get a rupture getting him on the horse," I said. "Say, how'd you get above me anyway?"

"I come up through the meadows and then across the upper end of the ravine at the foot of the rockslide. Gimme your knife a minute."

I handed it to him.

"Better get these offa here." He cut away two dark, oily-looking patches on the inside of the deer's hind legs, just about the knees. "Musk-glands," he said. "Some fellers say they taint the meat—I don't know about that for sure, but I always cut 'em off on a buck, just to be safe." Then he reached inside the cut I'd made in the deer's throat and sliced one on each side. "Let's turn him so's his head's downhill," he said.

We turned the deer and blood slowly drained out, running in long trickles down over the rocks. There really wasn't very much.

Clint held out his hand. I wiped mine off on my pants, and we shook hands.

"Damn good job, Dan. I figure that you'll do."

It was a little embarrassing. "Hey," I said. "I damn near forgot my coat." I went on up to the ridge-top and got it. The sun was coming up. I felt good, damned good. I ran back down to where Clint was standing.

"Easy, boy,"—he laughed—"you stumble over somethin' and you'll bounce all the way to Twisp."

"OK," I said, "now, how do we get him on the horse?"

"I got a little trick I'll show you," he said, winking. He took a coil of rope off his saddle and dropped a loop over the deer's horns. We rolled him over onto his back, and Clint towed him over to a huge flat boulder with his horse. The uphill side of the boulder was level with the rest of the hill and the downhill side was about six feet above the slope. Then he led the packhorse over and positioned him below the rock. I held the packhorse's head, and Clint slowly pulled the deer out over the edge.

"Get his front feet on out past the saddle, if you can, Dan," Clint said.

I reached on out and pulled the legs over. When the deer reached the point where he was just balanced, Clint got off his horse and came back up.

"You're taller'n me," he said. "I'll hold the horse, and you just ease the carcass down onto the saddle."

I went around onto the top of the rock and carefully pushed the deer off, holding him back so he wouldn't fall on over. It was really very simple. Once the deer was in place we tied him down and it was all done.

"Pretty clever," I said.

"I don't lift no more'n I absolutely have to." He grinned. "Fastest way I know to get old in a hurry is to start liftin' stuff."

"I'll buy that," I said. "Which way we going back down?"

"Same way I come up," he said. "That way we don't spook the deer for the others. You 'bout ready?"

"Soon as I tie on my rifle," I said. I went back and got it and tied it to the saddle. Ned shied from me a little—the blood-smell, probably.

"Steady, there, knothead," I said. He gave me a hurt look. I climbed on and we rode on up to the top of the ridge. We cut on across the foot of the rockfall and out into the meadows.

"Cap was gonna come up," Clint said, "but somebody oughta stay with the Big Man, and I know these packhorses better'n he does."

I nodded.

We rode on slowly down through the meadows toward camp. I could see the others over on the ridge, standing and watching. I waved a couple times.

"God damn, boy," Miller said, "you got yourself a good one." He was chuckling, his brown face creased with a big grin.

"Had it all gutted out and ever-thin'," Clint told him.

Sloane came out of his tent. He was still breathing hard, but he looked a little better.

"Hot damn!" he coughed. "That's a beauty."

I climbed down off Ned.

"I fixed up a crossbar," Miller said. "Let's get 'im up to drain out good."

Clint slit the hocks and we slipped a heavy stick through. Then we led the packhorse over to the crossbeam stretched between two trees behind the cook-tent. Miller had hooked up a pulley on the beam. We pulled the deer up by his hind legs and fastened him in place with baling wire.

"Damn," Miller said, "that's one helluva heavy deer. Three hundred pounds or better. Somebody in the bunch might get more horns, but I pretty much doubt if anybody'll get more meat."

We stood around and looked at the deer for a while.

"How 'bout some coffee?" Clint said.

"How 'bout some whiskey?" Cal giggled and then coughed.

"How 'bout some of both?" Miller chuckled. "I think this calls for a little bendin' of the rules, don't you?"

"Soon as I see to my horse." I grinned at them. I walked over toward Ned, and my feet felt like they weren't even touching the ground, I felt so good.

25

I got up at the usual time the next morning and had breakfast with the others. I felt a little left out now. The night before had been fine, with everyone going back to look at the deer and all. Even with the skin off and the carcass in a large mesh game bag to keep the bugs off, it looked pretty impressive. Clint and I had salted the hide and rolled it into a bundle with the head on top. I wasn't sure what I'd do with it, but this way I'd be able to make the decision later. After the big spiel I'd given Clydine the day I'd left about not being a trophy hunter, I was about half-ashamed to keep the head and all, but I knew I'd have to have it in case of a game check. I thought maybe I could have the hide tanned and made into a vest or gloves or something—maybe a purse for her.

At breakfast I watched Cal carefully. He was coughing pretty badly, but he insisted on going down. I noticed that he didn't eat much breakfast.

We all walked on down to the corral, and I watched the others saddle up. Ned came over and nuzzled at me. I guess he couldn't quite figure out why we weren't going along. I patted him a few times and told him to go back to sleep—that's what I more or less had in mind.

"Go ahead and loaf, you lazy bastard," Jack said.

Miller chuckled. "Don't begrudge him the rest—he's earned it."

"Right," I said, rubbing it in a little bit. "If you guys would get off the dime, you could lay around camp and loaf a little bit, too."

"Of course, all the fun's over for you, Dan," Sloane gasped.

I'd thought of that, too. We went back up to the tents so they could pick up their rifles.

I stood with my back to the campfire watching them ride off into the darkness. The sound of splashing came back as they crossed the little creek down below the beaver dam.

"More coffee, boy?" Clint asked me.

"Yeah, Clint. I think I could stand another cup."

We hunkered down by the fire with our coffee cups.

"Now that you've shown them fellers how, I expect we'll be gettin' a few more deer in camp."

"Yeah," I agreed. "If they'll just get off that damn nonsense about that white deer."

"Oh, I expect they will. I got about half a hunch that all you fellers shootin' at 'im the other day spooked 'im clear outa the territory."

"I sure as hell hope so," I said.

"Knew a feller killed one once," he said. "He gave me some steaks off it. I dunno, but to me they just didn't taste right. The feller give up huntin' a couple years later. I always wondered if maybe that didn't have somethin' to do with it—'course he was gettin' along in years."

I wasn't really sure how much Clint knew about what had happened that day, so I didn't say much.

"What you plannin' on doin' today?" he asked me.

"Oh, I thought I'd give you a hand around camp after a bit," I said.

"You'd just be under foot," he said bluntly.

"We can always use more firewood." He grinned.

"Then I might ride old Ned around a little, too. I wouldn't want him to be getting so much rest that he's got the time to be inventing new tricks."

"Oh, I wouldn't worry none about that. I think you and him got things about all straightened out."

"But the first thing I'm gonna do is go back to bed for a while," I said, grinning at him. "This getting up while it's still dark is plain unhealthy."

"It's good for you." He chuckled. "Kinda gets you back in tune with the sun."

The more I thought about that, the more sense it made. Whatever the reason, when I went back to bed, I rolled and tossed in my sleeping bag for about an hour and a half and then gave it up as a bad job. I got up, had another cup of coffee, and watched the sunrise creep down the side of the mountain.

I finally wound up down by the beaver pond, watching the trout swim by.

"You wanna give 'em a try?" Clint hollered from camp.

"You got any gear?" I yelled back.

"Has a duck got feathers? Come up here, boy."

Miller was sitting by the fire mending a torn place on the skirt of one of the saddles. "Old Clint never goes no place without his fishpole," he said. "He'd pack it along on a trip into a desert—probably come back with fish, too."

The little guy came back out of his tent putting together a jointed, fiber-glass rod. He tossed me a leather reel case. I opened it and took out a beautiful Garcia spinning reel.

"Man," I said, "that's a fine piece of equipment."

"Should be," he growled, "after what I paid for it."

Somehow I'd pictured him as the willow-stick, bent-pin-and-worm kind of fisherman.

"How you wanna fish 'em?" he asked me.

"What do you think'll work best? You know a helluva lot more about this kind of water than I do."

He squinted at the sky. "Wait till about ten or so," he said. "Sun gets on the water good, you might try a real small spoon—Meppes or Colorado spinner."

"What bait?"

"Single eggs. Or you might try corn."

"Corn?"

"Whole kernel. I'll give you a can of it."

"I've never used it before," I admitted.

"Knocks 'em dead sometimes. Give it a try."

We got the pole rigged up, and I carted it and the gear down to the pond. I'd never used corn before, and it took me a while to figure out how to get it threaded on the hook, but I finally got it down pat. After about ten minutes or so I hooked into a pretty nice one. He tailwalked across the pond and threw the hook. I figured that would spook the others, so I moved on down to the lower pond, down by the corrals.

The lower pond was smaller, deeper, and had more limbs and junk in it. It was trickier fishing.

On about the fourth or fifth cast, a lunker about sixteen inches or so flashed out from under a half-buried limb and grabbed the corn before it even got a chance to sink all the way to the bottom. I set the hook and felt the solid jolt clear to my shoulder. He came up out of the water like an explosion.

I held the rod-tip up and worked him away from the brush. It was tricky playing a fish in there, and it took me a good five minutes to work him over to the edge.

"Does nice work, don't he?" Clint said from right behind me. I damn near jumped across the pond. I hadn't known he was there. When I turned around, they were both there, grinning.

"He'll do," Miller said.

I lifted out the fish and unhooked him.

"Want to try one?" I asked, offering the pole to Clint.

I saw his hands twitch a few times, but he firmly shook his head. "I get started on that," he said, "and nobody'd get no dinner."

"Shall I throw him back?" I asked, holding out the flopping fish.

"Hell, *no!*" Clint said. "Don't *never* do that! If you don't want 'em, don't pester 'em. Put 'im on a stringer and keep 'im in the water. Catch some more like 'im and we'll have fresh trout for lunch—make up for that liver you blew all to hell yesterday."

"Yes, *sir!*" I laughed, throwing him a mock salute.

"Don't *never* pay to waste any kind of food around Clint here," Miller said.

"I went hungry a time or two when I was a kid," Clint said. "I didn't like it much, and I don't figger on doin' it again, if I can help it."

The hollow roar of a rifle shot echoed bouncingly down the ridge.

"Meat in the pot," Clint said.

There were three more shots, raggedly spaced.

"Not so sure," Miller said, squinting up the ridge.

"We going up?" I asked, gathering up the fishing gear.

"Let's see what kind of signal we get," Miller said.

We waited.

There finally came a flat crack of a pistol. After a minute or so there was a second.

"Cripple," Clint said disgustedly.

"It happens," Miller said. "I'll go. This might take some time and—"

"I know," Clint said. "I gotta fix dinner."

"I'll come along," I said.

Miller nodded. "Might not be a bad idea. We might need some help if the deer run off very far."

I took the gear back to camp and then went on down to the corral. "Any idea who it was?" I asked Miller, who was scanning the ridge with his glasses.

"Not yet," he said. "Yesterday we could see you goin' on over the other ridge."

"I got a hunch it was Stan," I said. "That pistol of his has a short barrel."

"Ain't the Big Man or your brother," he said. "I can see both of them, and they ain't movin'."

I waited.

"Yeah, it's the Professor, all right. He's just comin' up out of the gully."

We saddled our horses as well as Stan's horse and the pack-horse.

"We'll cut along the bottom here and go up on the other side," he said.

"All right."

We rode on up to the head of the basin and crossed the ravine just above the tree line. We could see Stan's fluorescent jacket in the brush about a mile up above. We started up.

We found him standing over the deer about a half mile from the ravine. The deer was bleating and struggling weakly, several loops of intestine protruding from a ragged hole in his belly.

"Why didn't you finish him off?" I demanded, swinging down from the saddle.

"I—I couldn't," he stammered, his face gray. "I tried but I couldn't pull the trigger." He was standing there holding his pistol in a trembling hand.

I pulled out the .45, thumbed the hammer, and shot the deer in the side of the head. He stiffened briefly and then went limp.

I heard Stan gag and saw him hurry unsteadily away into the bushes. We heard him vomiting.

"His first deer?" Miller asked me very softly.

I nodded, putting the .45 away.

"Better go help 'im get settled down. I'll gut it out. Looks a little messed up."

I nodded again. The deer was a three-point. I think we'd all passed up bigger ones.

"Come on, now, Stan," I said, walking over to him. "It's all done now."

"I didn't know they made any noise," he said, gagging again. "I didn't think they *could*."

"It doesn't happen very often," I said. "It's all over now. Don't worry about it."

"I made a mess of it, didn't I?" he asked, looking up at me. His face was slick and kind of yellow.

"It's all right," I said.

"I just wanted to get it over with," he said. "I tried to aim where you said, but my hands were shaking so badly."

"It's OK," I said. "Anybody can get buck-fever."

"No," he said, "it wasn't that at all. It was what happened the other day—when you saw me."

I didn't say anything. I couldn't think of anything to say.

"I know you saw me," he said. "I really wasn't trying to kill him, Dan. You have to believe that. I just had to make him quit talking the way he was—about Monica."

"Sure, Stan. I know."

"But I just had to get it over with. I've got to get away from him. Next time—" He left it.

I glanced over at Miller. He was almost done. He was even faster than Clint. I was sure he couldn't hear us.

"You all right now?" I asked Stan.

"You're pretty disgusted with me, aren't you, Dan?" he asked.

"No," I said. "It's not really your fault. Things just got out of hand for you, that's all. You OK now?"

He nodded.

"Let's go give Miller a hand with the deer," I said.

He stood up and wiped his face with his handkerchief.

"I'm awfully sorry, Mr. Miller," he said when we got back. "I guess I just froze up."

"It happens," Miller said shortly, cleaning off his knife. "Bring that packhorse over here."

I got the horse.

We loaded the deer onto the horse and lashed him down.

"Did you leave any of your gear over on the other side?" Miller asked him.

"No," Stan said, "I brought everything along."

"Well, let's go on down then."

We climbed on the horses and rode on down to the bottom and across the ravine.

"What's the matter with Cal?" Stan said, pointing up the ridge.

I looked, up, Sloane was standing up, weakly waving both hands above his head at us.

I looked at Miller quickly.

"Somebody better go see," he said.

I nodded and turned Ned's nose up the hill.

Above me, Sloane fumbled at his belt briefly and then came out with his Ruger. He pointed it at the sky and fired slowly three times, then he sagged back down onto the ground.

I booted Ned into a fast lope, my stomach all tied up in knots.

26

"Dan," Sloane gasped when I got up to him, "I'm sick. I've got to go down." He looked awful.

"Your chest again?" I asked, sliding down out of the saddle. Ned was panting from the run uphill.

Sloane nodded weakly. "It's all I can do to breathe," he said.

"Here," I said, "you get on the horse."

"I can't handle that horse," he said.

"I'll lead him," I said. I tied his rifle and canteen to the saddle and helped him up. Ned didn't much care for being led, but I didn't worry about that.

"How is he?" Miller asked when I got him down.

"Bad," I said, "worse than ever."

"Let's get 'im off the horse."

We got him down and over to the fire.

"Do you want a drink, Cal?" I asked him.

He shook his head. "My goddamn heart's beatin' so fast now it feels like it's gonna jump out of my goddamn chest."

Miller squatted down in front of him and looked him over carefully. "I hate to say this," he told Cal, "but I'm afraid you're gonna have to go on back down. You're gettin' worse instead of better."

Cal nodded.

"I'll refund part of what you paid."

"No," Cal said. "It's not your fault. You took us on in good faith. You don't owe me a dime."

Miller shrugged. "I wish to hell it hadn't happened," he said.

"I was doin' OK there for a while," Cal said, "but it came back this morning worse than ever."

"Well, let's get you laid down for now. That way you can get rested up for the ride."

We got Sloane over to his tent and came back to the fire.

"Somebody's gonna have to go out with him," Miller said. "He ain't gonna be able to drive the way he is."

I felt a sudden pang—almost a panic. I didn't want to leave yet. Then I was ashamed of myself for it.

"I'll go," Stan said very quietly. "I rode with him coming over, and besides, I'm all finished up now anyway."

Miller nodded, not saying anything.

"I could just as easily go, Stan," I said, not meaning it.

"There are other reasons, too," he said.

I looked at him. He really wanted to go. "All right, Stan," I said.

Miller looked at me. "You want to go fetch the others down for dinner, son?" he said. "I'll help Clint get things together for the trip down."

"Sure," I said. I went on down to get the horses.

Neither Jack nor McKlearey seemed particularly upset when I told them that Cal and Stan were leaving.

"I didn't figure Sloane would be able to hold out much longer," Jack said. "I've been sayin' all along that he wouldn't get it under control."

That wasn't how I remembered it.

McKlearey had merely grunted.

When we got back down though, the camp was pretty quiet. Stan had packed his and Sloane's gear and had it all laid out by the corral.

After we ate, we all pitched in and helped get things ready.

Clint skinned out Stan's deer and got it in a game bag. "I'll take yours down, too," he told me. "I'll hang it in the icehouse at the place."

"Have you got an icehouse?" I asked him. "I didn't think there were any of those left in the world."

"Well, it ain't really an icehouse. We got a big refrigeration unit in it. We don't keep it set too cold. Works about the same way."

McKlearey came over and looked Stan's deer over. "Ain't very big, is it?" he said.

"I don't see yours hangin' up there yet," Clint said.

McKlearey grunted and walked off.

"I'm gettin' to where I don't much care for ol' Sarge," Clint said.

"You're not the only one," I told him.

"Still," Clint said, squinting at the skinned carcass, "it really ain't much of a deer."

"Better than nothing," I said.

Clint, Stan, and Sloane left about two that afternoon. The rest of us stood around and watched them ride out. We'd tried to joke with Cal a little before he left, but he'd been too sick. His face was very pale, framed in the dark fur of his parka hood. The day seemed pretty warm to me, but I guess he felt cold. Just before they left, he gave Miller his tag.

"If you get a chance"—he gasped—"you might have somebody fill it for me."

"Sure," Miller said, "we'll get one for you."

"I think I'll go on up a little early," McKlearey said after they'd disappeared down the trail.

Jack looked at him narrowly. "Maybe I will, too," he said.

"Not much point," Miller said.

"We can find our way up there," Jack said.

Miller looked at them. Finally he shrugged. "Just don't stay too late," he said.

"We both got watches," McKlearey said, nursing his bandaged hand.

Miller walked away.

I felt like there'd been a funeral in camp. Jack and Lou went on up the hill, and I sat around watching Miller get things squared away for dinner. I offered to help but he said no.

"You take care of that fish?" he asked me.

"Oh, hell." I'd completely forgotten the fish.

"Why don't you see if you can get a few more?" he said.

"Sure." I got Clint's pole and went on down to the pond. It was a little slow, but I managed to get three more before the sun went down. I cleaned them and took them back up to camp.

"Enough to go around." Miller grinned at me. He seemed to be in a better humor now.

"I guess if I was fishing to eat, I wouldn't starve," I said, "but I don't think I'd gain too much weight."

"Not many would," he said. "Clint, maybe, but I sure wouldn't. Maybe I just ain't got the patience."

"Maybe you just can't think like a fish," I told him.

He didn't answer. He was looking on off toward the mountains.

"Weather comin' in," he said.

I looked up. A heavy cloudbank was building up along the tops of the peaks.

"Bad?" I asked him.

"Hard to tell. Rain, most likely."

Lou and Jack came on down about dark, and we ate supper. There weren't enough trout to make a meal of, so we just ate them as a kind of side dish.

With Clint, Stan, and Sloane gone, the group around the fire seemed very small, and it was a whole lot quieter.

"I think I seen 'im today," Lou said finally.

"Where?" Jack asked quickly.

"Up above me. I think I'll move on up to Danny's spot tomorrow."

"You'll have to walk that last bit," Miller said. "That horse of yours ain't that good."

"I can do that, too," Lou told him.

After that, nobody said much.

"Clint coming back tonight?" I asked Miller finally.

"More'n likely," he said. "He'll probably try to beat the weather."

"Think we'll get snow?" Jack asked him.

"Could. Rain more likely."

"What'll that do to the deer?"

"Hold 'em back at first. They'll have to come out eventually though."

I sat staring at the fire. I didn't much like the way Lou and Jack were beginning to push on Miller. The whole situation had changed now. With the others out of camp, things were getting pretty tight. Before, Cal and Stan had been around to kind of serve as a buffer between these two, and, of course, Clint's stories had helped, too. It was a lot grimmer now. I almost began to wish I'd gone down with the others. That would have left Miller right in the middle though, and that wouldn't have been any good. He didn't know what was going on.

"I suppose we might as well bed down," Miller said finally. "I imagine we'll get woke up when Clint comes in."

We all stood up and went off to our tents.

"I wish to hell you and McKlearey would get off this damn thing about that stupid deer," I told Jack after we'd crawled in our sacks.

"You know what's goin' on," he said shortly. "I ain't gonna back away from him like Larkin did."

"Stan didn't back away," I said. "Stan finally got smart."

"How do you figure?"

"Day before yesterday he took a shot at Lou. Sprayed dirt all over him."

"No shit?" Jack sounded surprised.

"Scared the piss out of him."

Jack laughed. "I wish I coulda seen it."

"It's not really that funny," I said. "That's why Stan left camp. He wasn't sure he could make himself miss next time."

"I sure wouldn'ta missed. So Lou was playin' around with Stan's wife, too, huh? I didn't think he was her type."

"He isn't. She got stupid, is all."

"Well, don't get shook. I ain't gonna shoot 'im. I'm just gonna out-hunt 'im. I'm gonna get that deer."

I grunted and rolled over to go to sleep.

McKlearey had another nightmare that night, screaming for Sullivan and for some guy named Danny—I knew that it wasn't me. It took us quite a while to get him calmed down this time.

Then about two thirty or so Clint came in, and we all got up again to help him get the horses unsaddled. It had started to drizzle by then, so we had to move all the saddles into the now-empty tent where Stan and Cal had slept.

All in all it was a pretty hectic night.

⟶➤⟶ 27

It drizzled rain all the next day. Miller had told Jack and Lou that there was no point in going out in the morning if it were raining, so we all slept late.

Camping out in the rain is perhaps one of the more disagreeable experiences a man can go through. Even with a good tent, everything gets wet and clammy.

Ragged clouds hung in low over the basin, and the ground turned sodden. Clint and Miller moved around slowly in rain-shiny ponchos, their cowboy hats turning darker and darker as they got wetter and wetter. The rest of us sat in our tents staring out glumly.

The fire smoked and smoldered, and what wind there was always seemed to blow the smoke right up into the tents.

"Christ, isn't it *ever* gonna let up?" Jack said about ten o'clock. It was the fourth time he'd said it. I was pretty sure that if he said it again I was going to punch him right in the mouth.

"Piss on it," I said. "I'm going fishing."

"You're outa your tree. You'll get your ass soakin' wet out there."

I shrugged. "I've got plenty of dry clothes," I said and went on out. "Can I use your pole, Clint?" I asked.

"Sure. See if you can get enough for supper."

"I'll give it a try." I picked up the pole and went on down to the ponds again. I'd kind of halfway thought I'd alternate between the two ponds, giving the fish time to calm down between catches, but I didn't get the chance. The larger, upper pond was so hot I never got away from it. The top of the water was a leaden gray, roughened up with the rain and the little gusts of wind. Maybe it was just obscured enough that the fish couldn't see me, I don't know for sure, but they were biting so fast I couldn't keep my hook baited. I caught seven the first hour.

It slowed down a little after lunch, about the time the rain slackened off, so I hung it up for a while and went on back up to camp. Jack and Lou took off for the ridge, and Clint, Miller, and I hunched up around the fire.

"Should clear off tonight," Clint said. "Weather forecast I caught last night down at the place said so anyway."

"I sure hope so," I said. "With the other two gone down and the rain, it's so damned gloomy around here you can carve it with a knife."

"How many fish you get?" he asked me.

"Nine or ten so far," I said. "I'll go get some more after I dry out a bit."

"There's no rush, son," Miller said. "You're right about missin' the other two though—I mean like you said. When a bunch of men start out on somethin' together, it always kinda upsets things if some of 'em don't make it all the way through." He turned to Clint. "'Member that time the bunch of us went out to log that stretch up by Omak and old Clark got hurt?"

"Yeah," Clint said.

"I don't think old Clark had said more'n about eight words in two months," Miller went on, "and he always went to bed early and stayed off by himself, but it just wasn't the same without him there."

"Yeah, that's right," Clint said.

They started reminiscing about some of the things they'd done and some of the places they'd gone. They'd covered a helluva lot of ground together, one way or the other—particularly after Miller's wife had died about twenty years or so ago.

I listened for a while, but I kind of felt as if I were intruding on something pretty private. I guess they were willing to share it, or they wouldn't have talked about it, but I've never much enjoyed that kind of thing. I'd a whole lot rather take people as I find them and not know too much about their past lives.

"Well," I said, standing up, "I guess I'd better get back to work if we're going to have trout for supper."

"Work?" Clint chuckled. "Who are you tryin' to kid?"

I laughed and went on down to the lower pond.

It was a lot slower now, and the fish seemed sluggish. I let my mind drift. I don't think I intended to. Usually I kept a pretty tight grip on it.

It had been on a day like this that I'd taken off from the Old Lady that time. I could still remember it. I'd gotten a job at one of the canned goods plants when I'd gotten out of high school, and when I came home from work that day, I'd found her in bed with some big slob. I'd yelled at him to get the hell out of the house, but he'd just laughed at me. Then I'd tried to hit him, and he'd beaten the crap out of me.

"Hit the little snot a time or two for me, Fred," my mother had yelled drunkenly.

After he'd finished with me and gone back into the bedroom, I had packed up a few clothes and taken off. I'd only stopped long enough to paint the word "whore" on the side of the house in green letters about five feet high and swipe the distributor cap off Fred's car. Both of my little revenges had been pretty damn petty, but what the hell else can you be at seventeen?

There was a shot up on the ridge. Then another. Then three more from a different rifle. The echoes bounced around a lot, muffled a little by the still lightly falling rain.

I stood waiting for the pistol-shot signal, but one never came. "Trigger-happy bastards," I said and went back to fishing.

I caught three more pretty good-sized ones just before the sun went down, and I cleaned the whole bunch and carted them up to the fire. By then the rain had stopped, and the sky was starting to clear.

"Got a mess, huh?" Miller said.

"Best I could do," I said.

When Lou and Jack came back, they were both soaked and bad-tempered.

"Keep your goddamn shots off my end of the hill, McKlearey," Jack snarled as soon as Lou came in.

"Fuck ya!" McKlearey snapped back.

"That's about enough of that, men," Miller said sternly. "Any more of that kinda talk, and we'll break camp and go down right now."

They both glared at him for a minute, but they shut up.

Clint fried up the trout, and we had venison and beans to go along with them. I was starting to get just a little tired of beans.

McKlearey had taken to sitting off by himself again, and after supper he sat with his back to a stump a ways off from the fire, holding his bandaged hand with the other one and muttering to himself. He hadn't changed the bandage for a couple of days, and it was pretty filthy. Every now and then I'd catch the names "Sullivan" and "Danny," but I wasn't really listening to him.

We all went to bed fairly early.

"Goddammit, Jack," I said, "Miller's not kidding. He and Clint have just about had a gutful of you and McKlearey yapping at each other about that damned white deer. Now I know a helluva lot more about what's happening than they do, and I'm starting to get a little sick of it myself. If you're going to hunt, hunt right. If you're not, let's pack it up and go down the hill."

"Butt out," he said. "This is between that shithead and me."

"That's just the point," I said. "You two are slopping it all over everybody else."

"If you don't like it, why don't you just pack up and go on down? You're all finished anyway."

"Then who the goddamn hell would be around to keep you and McKlearey from killing each other?"

"Who asked you to?"

"I invited myself," I said. "In a lot of ways I don't think much of you, but you're my brother, and I'm a son of a bitch if I want to see you get all shot up or doing about thirty years in the pen for shooting somebody as worthless as McKlearey." Maybe I came down a little hard. Jack's ego was pretty damned tender.

"As soon as they get those saddles out of there," he said, "I'll move over to Sloane's old tent."

"Don't do me any favors," I said. "I'll be all moved out by noon."

"Whichever way you want it," he said.

We both rolled over so our backs were to each other.

28

After he got back from taking Jack and Lou up the hill next morning, Miller came up to where I was sitting by the fire. "Feel like doin' a little huntin', son?" he asked me.

I looked up at him, not understanding what he was talking about.

"Somebody ought to fill the Big Man's tag for him," he said. I'd forgotten that.

"Sure," I said, "I'll get my rifle."

"We'll poke on down the trail a ways and hunt in the timber. That way we won't bother them two up on the hill."

The sky had lightened, and the pale light was beginning to slide back in under the tree trunks.

"Try not to shoot up the liver this time," Clint said, faking a grouchy look.

"OK, Clint." I laughed.

Miller and I got our rifles and went on down to the corral. I saddled Ned and we started on out.

"We'll go on down into the next valley and picket the horses," he said after a while. "Do us a little Indian huntin'."

"You'd better field-strip that for me," I said.

"Put our noses into the wind and walk along kinda slow. See what we can scare up."

"Good," I said. "That's my kind of hunting."

"Get restless sittin' still, is that it, son?"

"I suppose," I said.

"If I'm not bein' nosy, just how old are you?"

"Twenty-five last April," I said.

He nodded. " 'Bout what I figured. 'Bout the same age as my boy woulda been."

I didn't push it. He and Clint had said a few things about "the accident" the day before. I hadn't known he'd had any kids.

"Lost him the same time I lost my wife," he said quietly. Then he didn't say any more for quite a while.

We rode on down into the valley and got into the pine trees.

"Creek there," he said. "Wind'll be comin' up the draw this time of day."

"Good little clearing right there for the horses," I said pointing.

"Should work out about right," he said.

We went on, dismounted, and hooked Ned and Miller's big Morgan to a couple of long picket-ropes. We unhooked our rifles and went on down into the creek-bottom. Miller's rifle was an old, well-used bolt-action of some kind with a scope that had been worn shiny in a couple places from being slid in and out of the case so many times. It had obviously been well taken care of.

"I see you brought that hog-leg along," he said, nodding at my pistol belt.

"Starting to be a habit," I said. "Besides, I keep extra rifle cartridges on one side, and my knives are on it," I said. I still felt a little apologetic about the damned thing.

"Can you hit anything with it?" he asked me.

"Not at any kind of range."

"You shootin' high or low?"

"Low."

"You're pushin' into the recoil just before you shoot," he said. "Clint always used to do the same thing."

"How do you mean?"

"Just before you fire. You push your hand forward to brace your arm for the kick." He held out his right forefinger pistol-fashion and showed me.

"Maybe you're right," I said, trying to remember the last time I'd fired it at a target.

"Get somebody to load it for you and leave a couple empty. Then shoot it. You'll be able to spot it right off. Barrel dips like you was tryin' to dig a well with it when you click down on an empty chamber."

"How does a guy get over it?"

"Just knowin' what you're doin' oughta take care of most of it."

I nodded.

"Well, son," he said, grinning at me, "let's you and me go huntin', shall we?"

"Right, Cap," I said.

"You take the left side of the creek, and I'll take the right. We'll just take our time."

I jumped the creek, and we started off down the draw, moving very slowly and looking around.

Miller stopped suddenly, and I froze. Slowly he pointed up the side of the draw and then passed the flat of his hand over the top of his big hat. No horns. Doe.

She stepped out from behind a tree, and I could see her. Miller and I both stood very still until she walked on up out of the draw. Then he motioned, and we went on.

The trees were fairly far apart, and there wasn't much underbrush even this close to the creek. The floor of the forest was thickly covered with pine needles, softened and very quiet after the rain from the day before.

A faint pink glow of sunlight reflected off the snow-fields above began to filter down between the tree trunks. The air was very clean and sharp, cold and pine-scented. I felt good. This was my kind of hunting.

We walked on down the creek-bed for about a half hour or so, spotting seven or eight more deer—all does or small bucks.

We went around a bend, and Miller froze. He poked his chin straight ahead.

I couldn't see the deer. Apparently Cap couldn't either, at least not clearly. He kept moving his head back and forth as if trying to get a clear view between the trees. He lifted his rifle once and then lowered it again. He held out his hand toward me, the fingers fanned out. Five-point.

Then he pointed at me and made a shooting motion with his hand, his forefinger extended and his thumb flipping up and down twice. He wanted me to shoot. Shoot what, for God's sake?

I put my scope on the woods ahead, but I couldn't see a damn thing. Then the buck stepped out into an open spot about a hundred yards away and stood facing me, his ears up and his rack held up proudly. I started doing some quick computations. I leaned the rifle barrel against a tree to be sure it would be steady and drew a very careful aim on a point low in the deer's chest, just between his front legs. I sure didn't want to mess up this shot with Cap watching me.

I slowly squeezed the trigger. When a shot is good and right on, you get a kind of feeling of connection between you and the animal—almost as if you were reaching out and touching him, very gently, kind of pushing on him with your finger. I don't want to get mystic about it, but it's a sort of three-way union—you, the gun, and the deer, all joined in a frozen instant. It's so perfect that I've always kind of regretted the fact that the deer gets killed in the process. Does that make any sense?

The deer went back on his haunches and his front feet went up in the air. Then he fell heavily on one side, his head downhill. The echoes bounced off among the trees.

"Hot damn!" Cap yelled, his face almost chopped in two with his grin. "Damn good shot, son. Damn good!"

I felt about fifteen feet tall.

I jumped the creek again, and the two of us went on up toward the deer.

"Where'd you aim, son?"

"Low in the chest—between the legs."

He frowned slightly.

"I'm sighted an inch high at two hundred," I explained. "I figured it at a hundred yards, so I should have been four to six inches above where I aimed. I wanted to get into the neck above the shoulder line so I wouldn't spoil any meat."

"Or the liver." He chuckled.

"Amen to that. I'd get yelled at something awful if I shot out another liver."

"Old Clint can get just like an old woman about some things." He laughed.

The deer was lying on his side with blood pumping out of his throat. His eyes blinked slowly. I reached for my pistol.

"You cut the big artery," Cap said. "You could just as easy let 'im bleed out."

"I'd rather not," I said.

"Suit yourself," he said.

I shot the deer through the head. The blood stopped pumping like someone had turned off a faucet.

"You always do that, don't you, son?" he said.

I nodded, holstering the pistol. "I figure I owe it to them."

"Maybe you're right," he said thoughtfully.

We stood looking at the deer. He had a perfectly symmetrical five-point rack, and his body was heavy and well-fed.

"Beautiful deer," he said, grinning again. "Let's see how close you figured it. Where'd you aim?"

"About here," I said, pointing.

"Looks like you were about eight inches high," he said. "You took him just under the chin."

"I must have miscalculated," I said. "I'd figured to go about six high."

He nodded. "You was shootin' uphill," he said. "You forgot to allow for that. It was a hundred yards measured flat along the ground—only about seventy yards trajectory though."

"I never thought of that."

He laughed and slapped my shoulder. "I don't think we'll revoke your license over two inches," he said.

"Tell me, Cap," I said, "why didn't *you* shoot 'im?"

"Couldn't get a clear shot," he lied with a perfectly straight face.

"Oh," I said.

"Well, son, let's gut 'im."

"Right."

With two of us working on it, it took only a few minutes to do the job.

"Why don't you go get the horses while I rig up a drag?" Cap said.

"Sure." I leaned my rifle against a tree and took off. We were only a short distance from the horses really, and it took me less than ten minutes to get them. I rode on back, leading Miller's big walnut-colored Morgan.

"You move right out, don't you, son?" Cap said as I rode up.

"Long legs," I said.

"I'm just about done here," he said. He was sawing at a huckleberry bush with his hunting knife. I got off and handed him the big knife. He chopped the bush off close to the ground.

"That's sure a handy thing," he said. "Almost like an ax."

"That's what I figured when I got the set," I said.

He'd rigged up a kind of sled of six or eight of the bushes packed close, side by side, and lashed to a big dead limb across the butts and another holding them together about three feet or so up the trunks. He doubled over a lead-rope and tied it to the limb across the butts. Then we lifted the deer carcass onto the platform and tied it securely with another lead-rope. He tied a long rope to the doubled lead-rope at the front of the drag and fastened it to his saddle horn.

"You want me to hook on, too, Cap?" I asked him.

"Naw," he said. "Trail's too narrow, and old Sam here's big enough to pull the bottom out of a well if you want 'im to."

We stood for a moment beside the place where the deer had fallen.

"Good hunt," he said finally, patting me on the shoulder once. "We'll have to do 'er again some time."

I nodded. "This is the way it ought to be," I said.

"Well," he said, "let's get on back, shall we?"

We mounted and cut across up to the trail.

"Damn nice deer." Clint grinned when we got back to camp.

"Look at that shot," Miller said. "Right under the chin at about seventy or eighty yards uphill. The Kid there could drive nails all day with that rifle of his at about two hundred yards. Made the gun himself, too. Restocked one of them old Springfields."

"He fishes OK, too," Clint said, "and it don't seem to me he snores too loud. Reckon we oughta let 'im stay in camp?"

Miller looked at me for a minute. "He'll do," he said. We all grinned at each other.

"How 'bout us all havin' a drink?" Miller said. "I'll buy." He went into his tent and came out with a fifth of Old Granddad. He poured liberally into three cups and we stood around sipping at the whiskey.

"I ain't had so much fun in years," Cap said. "It was a real fine hunt."

"I ain't too much for all that walkin' you're partial to," Clint said, slapping one of his crooked legs.

Cap chuckled. "I told you that rodeoin' would catch up to you someday. Any action up there on the hill this mornin'?"

"Heard a couple shots earlier," Clint said. "No signals though."

"Probably missed," Cap said sourly. "Them two are each so worried that the other one's gonna get that damn freak that they can't even shoot anymore."

Just thinking about Jack and Lou almost spoiled the whole thing for me. I tried not to think about them. The morning had been too good for me to let that happen.

━━━ 29

At lunchtime I rode up the ridge to pick up Jack and Lou. Jack just grunted when I brought him his horse, and McKlearey took off down the hill ahead of me. They'd both moved uphill a ways, McKlearey onto my old post, and Jack up to Stan's.

I came up to the corral about the time Lou was getting off his horse. Jack was waiting for him.

"Now look, you son of a bitch," he started. "I told you to do your goddamn shootin' in your own territory."

"Fuck ya!"

"I mean it, goddammit! That goddamn deer came out right in front of me, and you were at least five hundred yards away. You didn't have a fuckin' chance of hittin' 'im. You shot just to run 'im off so I couldn't get a clear shot."

"Tough titty, Alders. Don't tell me how to hunt."

"All right, motherfucker, I can see the whole hillside, too, remember. I can play the same game. And even if you dumb-luck out and hit 'im, I'll shoot the son of a bitch to pieces before you can get to 'im. You won't have enough left to be worth bringin' out."

McKlearey glared at Jack, his face white. They were standing about ten feet apart and they were both holding their rifles. Jack's hand was inching toward the butt of his automatic.

"That's just damn well enough of that kinda talk," Miller's voice cracked from behind them.

"This is between him and me," Jack said.

"Not up here, it ain't," Miller said. "Now I don't know what kinda trouble you two got goin' between yourselves back in town, but I told you the first day to leave all that stuff down there. I meant what I said, too."

"We paid you to bring us up here," McKlearey said, "not to wet-nurse us." His eyes were kind of wild, and he was holding his rifle with the muzzle pointed about halfway between Jack and Cap.

I'm still not sure why I did it, but I slipped the hammer-thong off my pistol. I think Lou saw me do it because he slowly shifted his rifle until it was tucked up under his right arm so there was no way he could use either of his guns.

Miller had thought over what Lou had said. "I guess maybe we better just pack up and go on back down," he said. He turned his back on them and walked back up to the fire.

"We paid for ten goddamn days!" McKlearey yelled after him.

I hawked and spit on the ground, right between them.

"He can't do that," Jack said.

"Don't make any bets," I said flatly. "You guys made a verbal contract with him that first day. He told you that if there was any trouble in camp, we'd all come out. You agreed to it."

"That wouldn't stand up in court, would it?" Lou asked.

I nodded. "You bet it would. Particularly around here. If you were going to take him to court, it'd be in this county, and the jury'd all be his neighbors." I wasn't that sure, but it sounded pretty good.

"Well, what the hell do we do now?" Jack demanded.

"You might as well go pack your gear," I said. "He meant it about going back down."

"Who needs 'im?" Lou said. "Let 'im go."

"It's twelve miles back to the road, McKlearey," I said, "and he'll take the horses, the tents, and all the cooking equipment with him. Even if you got that damned freak deer, how would you get him out of the woods?"

He hadn't thought of that.

"You sound like you're on his side," Jack accused me.

"How 'bout that?" I said. I walked off down toward the pond. It was a helluva goddamn way to wind up the trip.

I guess both Jack and Lou did a lot of crawfishing, but Miller finally relented. I suppose he really didn't want his first trip as a guide to wind up that way. Anyway, they managed to talk him out of it.

Much as I wanted to stay up there, I still thought Miller was making a mistake. I went back to camp and moved all my gear into the empty tent.

"You don't have to do that, Dan," Jack said quietly as I started to roll up my sleeping bag.

"We'll both have more room this way," I said.

"Christ, Dan, you know how McKlearey can rub a guy raw."

"Yeah," I said, "but you're grown-up now, Jack. You're not some runny-nosed kid playing cowboys and Indians." I stopped in the doorway of the tent. "One other thing, old buddy," I said, "keep your goddamn hand away from that pistol from now on. There's not gonna be any of that shit up here." I went on out of the tent. McKlearey was standing outside. I guess he'd been listening.

"That goes for you, too, shithead," I told him.

Christ! I was right in the middle again. How the hell do I always get myself in that spot?

It took me about fifteen minutes to get settled in, and then we ate lunch. Nobody talked much. Both Jack and Lou went back to their tents after we finished.

"I probably shouldn't have changed my mind," Cap said quietly. "I got a feelin' it was a mistake."

"They've quieted down a bit," I said. "I'll go on up with my brother from now on—maybe I can keep him from getting so hot about things."

"What's got them two at each other that way?" Clint asked me.

"They just don't get along," I said. I knew that if I told them the real story, it would blow the whole trip. "This has been building for quite a while now. I thought they could forget about it while they were up here, but I guess I was wrong."

"Sure makes things jumpy in camp," Miller said shortly.

"It sure does," I agreed.

Jack wasn't too happy about my going up the hill with him, but I don't think he dared to say much about it in front of Miller.

When we got up there, he wouldn't talk to me, so I just let it go.

A good-looking five-point came out just about sunset, but he ignored it. No matter what he might have told Miller, he was still after that freak. After shooting time, we rode back to camp without waiting for Lou.

"That was a nice deer you got for Sloane," Jack said finally. I guess he wanted to make peace.

"Fair." I said. "It was a lot of fun hunting that way."

"How'd you do it?"

"Miller and I just pussyfooted through the woods until we spotted him."

"Sloane'll be pretty tickled with him."

That seemed to exhaust that topic of conversation pretty much.

Supper was lugubrious. Nobody talked to anybody else. Jack stared fixedly into the fire, and McKlearey sat with his back to a stump, watching everybody and holding that filthy bandage out in front of him so he wouldn't bump his hand. I wondered how bad the cut was by now.

I fixed myself a drink and settled back down by the fire.

"Watch yourself, Danny," Lou said suddenly, his eyes very bright. "Same thing might happen to you as happened to Sullivan."

It didn't make any sense, so I didn't answer him. I noticed, though, that after that he concentrated on me. He seemed to flinch just a little bit every time I moved. Did the silly bastard actually think I was going to shoot him?

"Bedtime," he finally said. He got up and went to his tent. Jack waited a few minutes, and then he went to his tent, too.

I talked quietly with Cap and Clint for a while, trying to stir up the good feeling we'd had going that morning, but it didn't quite come off. I think we were all too worried.

I went on back to the latrine. On my way back to my tent I heard a funny slapping kind of noise over in the woods. I stopped and waited for my eyes to adjust to the dark a little more. Then I saw a movement.

It was McKlearey. I guess he'd rolled out under the back of his tent or something, and he was back in the trees practicing his draw.

He was getting pretty good at it.

30

Clint woke me the next morning, and I rolled out of the sack quickly. It was chilly, and for some reason it seemed darker that morning than usual. Then it dawned on me. The moon had already set. It had been going down earlier and earlier every morning, and now it was setting before we even got up.

Breakfast was as quiet as supper the night before, and we had to take the lantern down to the corral with us when we went to saddle the horses. Miller seemed particularly grim. We mounted up and rode on up the ridge. It was a damned good thing the horses knew the way by now because it was blacker than hell out there.

Miller had insisted that Jack take Sloane's old spot, the lowest on the hill, and that Lou take the very top one. I guess he wanted to get as much distance between the two of them as possible.

As soon as Cap dropped us off, Jack went over to the edge of the ravine. I stayed with the horses until Cap came back from dropping off Lou.

"I sure hope they both fill today," he said. "All the fun's gone out of it now."

"Yeah," I said. "I'll remind Jack that there's only three more days. Maybe that'll bring him to his senses."

"Somethin' is gonna have to. See you about noon, son."

"Right, Cap."

He rode off down into the darkness, and I went over to find Jack.

"See anything?" I asked.

"Still too goddamn dark," he said, and then, "I don't know why I had to get stuck with the bottom of the hill like this."

"Man," I told him, "I got a five-point yesterday four miles below here. They're all over the side of the mountain."

"Not the one *I* want," he said.

"Are you still hung up on that damn thing?"

"I said I was gonna get that white one, and I meant it."

"Goddamn it, Jack, there are only three days left after today. You're going to wind up going down empty."

"Don't worry about it," he said, "I know what I'm doin'."

We sat waiting for it to get light.

The sky paled and the shadowy forms of the rocks and bushes began to appear around us. Several does and a couple small bucks went down the ravine below our post.

"They're starting to move," I said.

"Yeah."

I looked at the thin, dark man beside me with the wiry stubble smudging his cheeks and chin. Jack's eyes were hollow, with dark circles under them. The red baseball cap he was wearing was pulled low over his eyebrows, and he was staring fixedly up the gorge. I tried to make out the shadow of the boy I'd grown up with in his face, but it wasn't there anymore. Jack was a stranger to me. I guess I'd been kidding myself all along. He always had been a stranger. The whole business when I'd gotten back to Tacoma had been a fake. I suppose we both knew it, but neither one of us had had the guts or the honesty to admit it.

When the white deer came out, he was on top of that bluff that was opposite Jack's old post. The rock face dropped about forty or fifty feet onto a jumble of rocks and gravel and then fell again into the wash at the bottom of the hill. Maybe Jack wouldn't see him.

"There he is!" Jack hissed.

Damn it!

"What is it?" he demanded, his hands trembling violently. "Two hundred yards?"

"It's pretty far," I said, "and he's right on top of that cliff."

The deer looked around uncertainly, as if he were lost. Somehow he looked more helpless than ever.

Jack was getting squared away for a shot.

"Wait, for Chrissake!" I said. "Let him get away from that goddamn cliff."

"I can't wait. McKlearey'll spot him." His hands were shaking so badly that the end of his gun-barrel looked like the tip of a fishing rod.

"Calm down," I snapped. "You'll never get off a shot that way."

"Shut up!" he snapped and yanked the trigger.

His Mauser barked hollowly. The deer looked around, startled. "Run, you son of a bitch," I muttered under my breath.

Jack was feverishly trying to work the bolt of his gun, his shaking hands unable to handle the simple operation.

"Calm down," I said again.

"He'll get away," Jack said. "Oh, Jesus, he'll get away!" He rammed another shell up the tube. He fired again, not even bothering to aim.

McKlearey's gun barked from up the ridge. He must have been at least six hundred yards from the deer.

"Oh, Jesus!" Jack said, fighting with the bolt again. He stumbled to his feet.

"Jack, for Christ's sake, calm down! You'll never hit anything this way!" I put my hand on his arm.

"Get away from me, you bastard!" he screamed. He spun on me, pointing the rifle at me and still fighting with the bolt.

It was happening—it wasn't exactly the way it had been that day in the pawnshop, but it was close enough.

I thumbed off the hammer-thong and left my hand hanging over my pistol-butt. "Don't close that bolt with that thing pointed at me, Jack," I told him.

Maybe some day you'll be no good, and then I'll shoot you. There it was again.

"I mean it, Jack," I said. "Point that gun-muzzle away from me." I felt very cold inside. I knew he could never close that bolt and get his finger onto the trigger before I got one off. I was only about five feet away from him. There was no way I could miss. I was going to kill my brother. It hung there, an absolute certainty—no fuss, no dramatics, nothing but a mechanical reflex action. I felt disconnected from myself, as if I were standing back, watching something I had no control over. I even began to mourn for my dead brother.

Then his face kind of sank in on itself. He knew it, too.

Then McKlearey fired again.

Jack spun back around and fired at the deer three times in a row from a standing position, his hand very smooth on the bolt now.

The deer had frozen up. I thought I could see him flinch with the sound of each shot.

McKlearey fired.

Jack fired his last round. His hand dove into his jacket pocket and came out jerkily with a handful of shells. He started feverishly shoving them down into the magazine.

McKlearey fired again.

The deer lurched and fell on his side, his sticklike legs scrabbling at the rocks and bushes.

"Aw, no!" Jack said in an agonized voice.

The deer stumbled to his feet, staggered a step or two and, with what looked almost like a deliberate lunge, fell off the cliff.

"Aw, God damn it!" Jack said, his voice breaking oddly.

The deer hit the rock-pile below and bounced high in the air. I could hear his antlers snap off when he hit. His white body plunged into the brush like a leaping trout reentering the water. I heard him bounce again and tumble on down the ravine.

"Aw, goddamn son of a bitch!" Jack sobbed, slamming his rifle down on the ground. He sat down heavily and buried his face in his hands. He was crying.

Up the ridge McKlearey gave a wild yell of triumph followed by a barrage of shots from his pistol. He must have emptied the thing. Maybe, with any kind of luck, one of them would drop back in on him.

 **31**

I went straight on down into the ravine, leaving Jack on the ridge to get himself straightened out. The brush was a little tough at first, but I got the hang of it in a couple minutes. I just bulled on through, hanging onto the limbs to keep from falling—kind of like going down hand over hand.

I could still hear McKlearey screaming and yelling up on the knob at the top of the ridge.

I'd marked the last place where I'd seen the deer, and I hit the bottom a good ways below where that had been. I was pretty sure I was below the carcass.

The wash at the bottom of the ravine was about fifteen feet wide and six to ten feet deep. I imagined that when the snow melted, it was probably a boiling river, but it was bone-dry right now. Most of the sides were steep gravel banks with large rocks jutting out here and there.

I finally found a place where I could get down into the wash. I seemed to remember hearing some gravel sliding after the deer had stopped bouncing. I started up the ravine.

The deer was about a hundred yards from where I'd come down. He was lying huddled at the foot of a gravel bank in a place where the wash made a sharp turn. He was dead, of course.

Only one of his legs was sticking out; the others were all kind of tucked up under him. The protruding leg was at an odd angle.

His head was twisted around as if he were staring back over his shoulder, and a couple of his ribs were poked out through his skin. His fur wasn't really white but rather a cream color. It had smudges and grass stains on it—either from his normal activity or from the fall through the brush.

His antlers were shattered off close to his head, and the one red eye I could see was about half open. There was dirt in it.

A thin dribble of gravel slithered down the steep bank and spilled down across his shoulder. A heavy stick protruded from the bank just above him.

"You poor bastard," I said softly. I nudged at his side with my toe, and I could hear broken bones grating together inside. He was like a sack full of marbles.

"Probably broke every bone in his body," I muttered. I took hold of the leg. It was loose and flopping. I tucked it back up beside the rest of him. Folded up the way he was, he didn't take up much more room than a sack of potatoes. I squatted down beside him.

"Well," I said, "you did it. God knows we ran you off this hill often enough. You just *had* to keep coming back, didn't you?" I reached over and brushed some of the dirt off his face. The eye with the dirt in it looked at me calmly.

"I sure wish I knew what the hell to do now, old buddy," I said. "You're Lou's deer, and I suppose I ought to make him keep you, no matter what shape you're in. Christ only knows, though, what that'll lead to."

How did I always get into these boxes? All I wanted to do was just look out for myself. I had enough trouble doing that without taking on responsibilities for other people as well. I had to try to figure out, very fast, what would be the consequences of about three different courses of action open to me right now, and no matter what I decided to do, I had no guarantees that the whole damn mess wouldn't blow up in my face. I sure wished that Miller were here.

I could hear McKlearey yelling, but he sounded like he was coming down the hill now. Whatever I was going to do, I was going to have to make up my mind in a hurry.

I put my hand on the deer's shoulder. He was still warm. A kind of muscle spasm or reflex made his eyelid flutter at me.

"You're a lot of help," I said to the deer. I stood up.

I could hear McKlearey crashing around in the brush several hundred yards up the ravine.

"Well, piss on it!" I said and pulled on the limb sticking out of the gravel bank. The whole bank gave way, and I had to jump back out of the way to keep from getting half-buried myself. The slide completely covered the carcass. I stood holding the stick for a moment, then I pitched it off into the brush. I turned around and went on back downstream.

Lou crossed the wash and came down over the rock-pile at the foot of the cliff. He stopped yelling when he started finding pieces of antler. He was there for quite awhile, gathering up all the chunks and fragments he could find. Then he came on down. I had climbed up out of the wash and was standing up on the bank when he got to where I was.

"You find 'im, Danny?" he asked me from down in the wash. His face was shiny with sweat, and his eyes were feverish.

"I came up from down that way," I said. "He must be above here somewhere." It wasn't exactly a lie.

"No, I came down this creek-bed. He ain't up there."

I shrugged. "Maybe in the brush somewhere—"

"The bastard busted his horns," he said, holding out both hands full of dark fragments.

"Damn shame," I said.

He began stuffing the pieces into various pockets. "A good taxidermist oughta be able to glue 'em all back together, don't you think?"

"I don't know, Lou. I've never heard of anybody doing it before."

"Sure they can," he said. "But where the hell is the goddamn deer?"

"It's got to be up above," I said. "Did you get any kind of blood-trail?"

"Shit! The way that fucker was bouncin'?"

"Maybe if we find one of the places where he hit—"

He'd finally finished stuffing chunks of horn in his pockets, and suddenly his eyes narrowed and he squinted up at me. His face was very cold and hard looking.

"Oh, *now* I get it," he said. "You and your *brother*, huh? You two are tryin' to keep *my* deer."

"You couldn't *give* me that deer after you knocked it off that cliff," I told him flatly.

"That's *my* goddamn deer," he said angrily.

"I never said it wasn't."

"Where the hell is it? Where the hell have you got my deer?" His voice was getting shrill.

"Come on, Lou, get serious."

"Don't do this to me, Danny." His eyes were bulging now.

"Settle down, Lou. Let's go back up and check out the brush."

"Danny? Is that you, Danny?" His face was twitching, and his voice was kind of crooning.

"Come on, Lou," I said, "let's go back up to where he hit."

"You know what I did to Sullivan, don't you, Danny?"

"Come on, Lou," I said.

Now what the hell was going on?

"It wasn't my fault, Danny. It was so fuckin' dark, and Charlie was all around us."

"Lou, snap out of it!"

"It wasn't my fault, Danny. He come sneakin' up on me. He didn't give me no password or nothin'."

"Lou!"

"Nobody knows where he is, Danny. I hid 'im real good. Nobody'll ever know."

I suddenly felt sick to my stomach.

"Don't tell the lieutenant, Danny. Everything will be OK if you just keep your mouth shut about it." His eyes were wild now.

"Come on, Lou, snap out of it. That's all over now." I was starting to get a little jumpy about this. It could get bad in a minute. And I still wasn't over the little session with Jack up on the ridge.

"I'll pay you, Danny. I got five hundred or so saved up for a big R and R. It's all yours. Just for Chrissake, don't say nothin'."

Very slowly I eased off the hammer-thong again. How many times was this going to happen in one day?

"Please, Danny, I'm beggin' ya. They'll *hang* me for God's sake." His rifle was slung over his left shoulder, and his right hand was on his belt, real close to that damned .38. I wondered if he'd remembered to reload it. Knowing McKlearey, he probably had.

"OK, Kid," he said, "if that's the way you want it." The pleading note had gone out of his voice, and his face was pale and very set.

"McKlearey," I said as calmly as I could, "if you make one twitch toward that goddamn pistol, I'll shoot you down in your tracks and you damn well know I can do it. You know I can take you any time I feel like it. Now straighten up and let's go find that deer." I sure hoped that I sounded more convincing than I felt. Frankly, I was scared to death.

"I been practicin'," he said, his face crafty.

"Not enough to make that much difference, Lou," I said.

He stood there looking up at me. I guess it got through to him—even through what had happened on the Delta—that I had him cold. At least I had him cold enough to make the whole thing a bad gamble for him. Finally he shook his head as though coming out of a bad dream.

"You say you came up the creek-bed?" he asked as if nothing had happened.

"Yeah," I said. "The deer's gotta be above us somewhere—maybe off in the brush."

"Maybe if we each took one side," he said. "It sure as hell ain't down in here." He turned and clambered up out of the wash on the other side.

"Danny?" he said from the other side of the wash.

"Yeah?"

"Sullivan and the other Danny are both dead, did you know that? Charlie got 'em. They been dead a long time now."

"Sorry to hear that, Lou."

"Yeah. It was a bad deal. They was my buddies—but Charlie got 'em."

I didn't want to get started on that again. "Work your way up to where you found those pieces of horn, Lou," I said. "I'll go up this side."

"Sure. Fuckin' deer had gotta be here someplace."

I let him lead out. I wasn't about to let him get behind me.

"You find 'im?" Miller called from the ridge.

"Not yet, Cap," I called back.

"Any sign?"

"Lou found some pieces of horn," I said.

"And some fur," Lou called to me. "Tell 'im I found some white fur, too."

"He got some fur, too," I relayed.

"He's gotta be down there then."

"Yeah. I know."

"Did he go off that bluff?"

"Yeah. I saw him fall."

Cap shook his head disgustedly and started to come down into the ravine.

The three of us combed the bottom for about an hour and a half. We passed the collapsed gravel bank about a half dozen times, but neither of them seemed to notice anything peculiar about it.

"It's no good," Miller said finally.

"But he's down here," Lou said. "We all seen 'im fall. I got 'im. I got 'im from way up there." He pointed wildly.

"I ain't doubtin' you shot him," Cap said, "but we ain't gonna find 'im."

"He's *gotta* be here," Lou said frenziedly. "Let's go back just one more time. He's here. He's *gotta* be here."

Miller shook his head. "Face it, Sarge," he said. "He's under a rockslide." He nudged the bank of the wash with the toe of his cowboy boot. A small avalanche resulted. "This whole gully is like this. One little bump brings it right down. There's two dozen places in this stretch we been workin' where the bank has give way just recently. He could be under any one of 'em. Only way you're gonna find that deer is with a shovel—and even then you wouldn't get him till the snow came."

"Maybe he's under a bush," Lou said. "Did we look over there?" He pointed desperately toward a place we'd all checked a half dozen times.

"We ain't gonna find 'im," Miller said.

"I *gotta* find 'im!" Lou screamed. "I gotta!" Then his face fell apart, and he started to cry like a little kid.

Miller stepped up to him and slapped him sharply in the face.

"Come out of that, now, Sergeant!" he barked. "That's an order."

Lou's eyes snapped open. "Sorry," he said. "Sorry, sir. I—I guess I lost my head."

"Let's get on up to the ridge," Miller commanded.

We started climbing. McKlearey coughed now and then—or maybe he was sobbing, I'm not sure.

I still didn't let him get behind me.

32

I don't think either Jack or Lou said more than ten words the rest of that day. Miller, Clint, and I were so busy watching them that we didn't say much either, so it was awfully quiet in camp. Neither one of them went out that evening, and we all sat around staring at each other. At least McKlearey had quit talking to himself.

The next morning they were still pretty quiet, and I got the idea that they both wanted to finish up and get on back down the mountain.

I went up the ridge with Jack again, and almost as soon as it was legal shooting time, we heard McKlearey's gun bang off once, and then a minute or so later the flat, single crack of his pistol.

"Lou got one," I said to Jack. It was pretty obvious, but the silence was beginning to bug me.

"Yeah," Jack answered indifferently.

We saw Miller going on up, trailing Lou's horse and a pack animal. About twenty minutes later he went on back down with Lou and what looked like a pretty damn small deer.

"Shit!" Jack snorted. "The great hunter! I've seen bigger cats." Maybe he was coming out of it a little—maybe not. I couldn't tell for sure.

It was almost lunchtime when a fair-sized buck came down the draw.

"Four-point," I whispered to Jack, who hadn't even been watching, I don't think.

"Where?"

"Coming down the bottom of the gully."

"Yeah, I see 'im now," he said. His voice was very flat. "I'll take 'im." He squared himself around into a sitting position, aimed, and fired. The buck dropped without a twitch.

"Good shot!" I said.

He shrugged and cranked out the empty. It clinked against a rock and rolled on down the hill.

"You going to signal?" I asked him.

"Miller'll be up in a few minutes anyway," he said.

"Yeah, but we'll need a packhorse."

"Maybe you're right," he said. He wearily pulled out the automatic, thumbed it, and touched it off in the general direction of the mountain above us. "Let's go gut 'im," he said.

We went down and field-dressed the deer. By the time we were done, Miller was there with the horses and a rope. He tossed us one end, and with a horse pulling from up above and the two of us guiding the carcass, getting the deer up was no trick at all.

"Damn nice deer," Miller said rather unconvincingly.

"It's worth the price of the tag, I guess," Jack said. He seemed pretty uninterested.

We got everything loaded up and went on back down to camp.

Clint and McKlearey had already gone on down. Miller told us that Lou had been all hot to leave, and there weren't really enough pack-horses to haul out all of our gear and the deer as well, so Clint had loaded up and they'd gone on down.

"How big a one did he get?" Jack inquired.

"Two-point," Miller said. "Nice enough deer, but I think old Sarge musta made a mistake. He probably shoulda waited till he had a little more light."

Jack didn't say anything.

"Clint won't be back till late again," Miller said, "so we'll go on out tomorrow mornin'. We oughta skin your deer out and let it cool anyway. I tried to tell that to Sarge, too, but he seemed to be in a helluva rush for some reason."

"Probably got a hot date back in Tacoma," Jack said sourly.

Miller let that one go by.

We ate lunch and skinned out Jack's deer, and then Jack went into his tent to lie down for a while. I wandered around a bit and then went on down to the pond to molest the fish. The sun was hot and bright on the water, and the fish weren't moving.

Miller came on down after about a half hour and stood watching me as I fished. "Any action?" he said finally.

"Pretty slow, Cap," I said.

"Usually is this time of day."

"Maybe if I pester 'em enough, they'll bite just to get rid of me."

He chuckled at that.

I made another cast.

"Trip sure turned out funny," he said finally.

"Yeah," I agreed.

"I got a hunch Ol' Sarge oughta see a doctor of some kind. He sure went all to pieces yesterday."

I nodded. "I guess something pretty bad happened to him over in Vietnam," I said. I didn't want to go into too many details. I'd pushed the whole business about Sullivan and Danny—the other one—into the back of my mind, and I was doing my level best not to think about it.

"I kinda thought that might have somethin' to do with it," Cap said. "It's all kinda soured me on this guidin' business though."

"Don't judge everybody by us, Cap," I said. "You run a damn fine camp, and you know this country as well as any man could. None of what happened up here was your fault. This was all going on before we ever got up here."

"I keep thinkin' I shoulda done somethin' to head it all off before it went as far as it did though," he said, squinting up at the mountain. He still looked a lot like God.

"I don't think anybody could have done anything any differently," I told him. "You just got a bad bunch to work with, that's all. Nobody could have known that Cal was going to get sick or that McKlearey was going off the deep end the way he did. It was just the luck of the draw, that's all."

"Maybe," he said doubtfully. "Then, maybe too, I just ain't cut out for it. I can tell you right now that you're the only one of the whole bunch I'd care to go out with again. Maybe if a man's goin' into the business, he can't afford to have them kinda likes and dislikes."

I couldn't say much to that really.

Finally he cleared his throat. "I'm gonna ask you somethin' that ain't really none of my business, so if you don't want to answer, you can just tell me to keep my nose where it belongs, OK?"

"Shoot," I said. I knew what he was going to ask.

"You found that freak deer yesterday, didn't you, son?"

I nodded.

"Thought maybe you had. You're too good a hunter not to have, and you was the closest one to the place where he dropped into that gully."

"He was down in the wash," I said quietly, not looking at him, "all busted up. I dumped one of those gravel banks over on him. I just didn't think he was worth somebody getting killed over."

"Was it really that bad between your brother and the Sarge?" he asked.

"Yeah," I said, looking out over the pond. "It was getting real close. I figured that if neither one of them got the damn thing, it'd cool things down."

"You think pretty fast when you have to, don't you?"

"I was right in the middle," I said. "It was the only thing I could come up with in a hurry to keep the roof from falling in on me. I'm not very proud of it really." That was the truth, too.

"I don't know," he said after a minute, "from where I sit, it makes you look pretty tall."

I didn't understand that at all.

"A man's more important than a deer," he said, hunkering down and dipping his fingers in the water. "Sometimes a man'll forget that when he gets to huntin'. You're just like me, son. You wouldn't never try to take another man's deer or keep 'im from findin' it. It's just somethin' a man don't do. So you figure that what you done was wrong—particularly since it was the Sarge who shot the damn thing, and you don't like him very much. But you'd have done the same thing if it'd been your brother shot 'im. A lot of men wouldn't, but *you* would. Takes a pretty big man to do the right thing in a spot like that."

I felt better. I'd been worrying about it a lot.

"You gonna reel that fish in, or let 'im run around on the end of your line all day?" he said to me.

"What?" I looked at the pole I'd laid down across a log. The tip was whipping wildly. I grabbed the rod before the fish could drag it into the water. I brought him in close to shore, reached down into the water and carefully unhooked him. "Don't tell Clint," I said, shooing the exhausted trout back out into deeper water.

"Wild horses wouldn't get it out of me." He laughed. We went on back up to camp.

After that, things were OK again. Jack kept pretty much to his tent except for supper, and Cap and I spent the rest of the afternoon getting things squared away so we could break camp the next morning. I moved my gear back into Jack's tent so we could strike the one I'd been sleeping in as well as McKlearey's.

After supper, Jack had a couple of drinks and went back to his tent. Cap and I sat up telling stories and waiting for Clint to get back.

The little guy came in about ten thirty, madder than hell.

"That damn burrhead run off on me, Cap," he growled as he rode up.

"Run off? What do you mean, run off?"

"We got about a half mile from the bottom, and he kicks ol' Red in the slats and took off like a scared rabbit. When I got to the bottom, ol' Red was all lathered up and blowed and wanderin' around not tied to anything, and that burrhead and that pile of nuts and bolts he called a car was gone."

"Didn't he take his deer?" Cap asked.

"He didn't take nothin'! He even left his rifle tied to the saddle."

"He say anything at all?"

"Not a word—not a good-bye, go to hell, kiss my ass, or a damn thing. I figured maybe he'd gone on down to the place. I was gonna have some words with him about runnin' off and leavin' me with all the work, but there wasn't a sign of 'im there neither. He just clean, flat took off. I left all his stuff in the barn. I don't know how the hell we'll get it all back to 'im."

"We'll take it back," I said. "I'll see that he gets it all."

Clint grunted, still pretty steamed.

Cap shook his head. "I sure misjudged *that* one," he said.

"Somebody oughta take a length of two-by-four to 'im," Clint said. "That was a damn-fool kid stunt, runnin' off like that."

"Well," Cap said, "we can't do anything about it tonight. Let's unsaddle the stock and get to bed. And you better cool down a mite. You know what the doctor told you about not losin' your temper so much."

"Hell," Clint said, "I'm all calm and peaceful *now*. 'Bout time I started up the hill, I was mad enough to bite nails and spit rust."

We finally got things squared away and got to bed.

The next morning I was up before the others, so I got the fire started and got coffee going and then wandered around a bit, kind of getting the last feel of things. I like to do that with the good things. The others I kind of just let slide away.

It had been a good hunt—in spite of everything—and I'd worked out whatever it was that I'd needed to work out. Some people seem to think that things like that have to be all put down in a set of neatly stated propositions, but it isn't really that way at all. A lot of times it's better not to get too specific. If you feel all right about yourself and the world in general where you didn't before, then you've solved your problem—whatever it was. If you don't, you haven't. Verbalizing it isn't going to change anything. One thing I could verbalize, though, was the fact that I had made a couple of friends I hadn't had before. Just that by itself made the whole trip worth everything it had cost.

"Who's the damn early bird?" Clint growled, coming out of the tent all rumpled and grouchy-looking.

"Me." I grinned at him.

"Mighta known," he said. "You been bustin' your butt to get your hands on the cookware ever since we got up here."

"I figured I could ruin a pot of coffee just as well as you could," I said.

"Oh-ho! Pretty smart-alecky for so damn early in the mornin'," he said. "All right, boy, since you went and started it, we'll just see how much of a camp cook you are. *You* fix breakfast this mornin'. Anythin' you wanna fix. There's the cook tent."

"I think I've been had," I said.

"I guess they don't teach you not to volunteer in the Army no more," he said. "Well, I'm goin' back to bed. You just call us when you got ever-thin' ready." He chuckled and went on back into his tent.

"You're a dirty old man," I called after him.

He stuck his head back out, thumbed his nose at me, and disappeared again.

I rummaged around in the cook-tent and dragged out everything I could think of. I'd fix a breakfast like they'd never seen before.

Actually, I went a little off the deep end. A prepared biscuit-flour made biscuits and pancakes pretty easy, but I kind of bogged down in a mixture of chopped-up venison, grated potatoes and onions, and a few other odds and ends of vegetables. I wound up adding a can of corned-beef hash to give the whole mess consistency. I didn't think I could manage a pie or anything, so I settled for canned peaches.

"All right, dammit!" I yelled. "Come and get it or I'll feed it to porky."

They stumbled out and we dug into it. I'd fried up a bunch of eggs and bacon to go with it all, and they ate without too many complaints—except Clint, of course.

"Biscuits are a little underdone," he said first, mildly.

"Can't win 'em all," I told him.

"Bacon could be a mite crisper, too," he said then.

Cap ducked his head over his plate to keep from laughing out loud. Even Jack grinned.

"Flapjacks seem a little chewy, wouldn't you say?" he asked me.

I was waiting for him to get to that hash. He tried a forkful and chewed meditatively.

"Now *this*," he said, pointing at it with the fork, "is the best whatever-it-is I've ever had." He looked up with a perfectly straight face. "Of course, I ain't never *had* none of this whatever-it-is before, so that might account for it."

I didn't say anything.

"I ain't gonna ask you what's in it," he said, " 'cause I don't really wanna know till I'm done eatin', but right after breakfast, I *am* gonna go count the packhorses."

Miller suddenly roared with laughter, and pretty soon we were all doing it.

After breakfast we struck the rest of the tents and began to pack up. It didn't really take very long to get everything all squared away.

A camp you've lived in for a while always looks so empty when you start to tear it down. We even buried McKlearey's slit-trench and covered over Clint's garbage pit.

"Well," Cap said, looking around. "What with that table and all, I guess we're leavin' the place better'n we found it."

"You bet," Jack said. He seemed to be getting over it all.

We loaded up the packhorses, saddled up, and rode on down the trail. I looked back once, just before we went into the trees. I didn't do it again.

"Down there is where Cap and I got the deer for Sloane," I told Jack as we passed the place.

"That was a nice deer," Jack said. "You wound up shootin' the best two deer we got, you know that?"

"I hadn't thought of it," I said.

"That's because you were concentratin' on huntin' instead of all that other shit like the rest of us." Coming from Jack, that was a hell of an admission really.

We didn't say much the rest of the way down.

It was a little after noon when we got back down to where the trucks were. It took us a while to get the gear all off the horses and into the stock-truck and the pickup, but by about one we were on our way back to Miller's ranch. Jack got me off to one side and told me he wanted to ride on down with Cap, if I didn't mind.

"I've got a few things I ought to explain to him," my brother said. "I think I screwed up pretty bad a few times up there, and I'd kinda like a chance to square things, if I can."

"Sure, Jack," I said. I went over and climbed up into the stock-truck with Clint.

Maybe there was some hope for Jack after all.

33

"I don't know how the hell we're gonna get all that stuff in that car of mine," Jack said when we got to Miller's.

"We'll have to put a couple of those deer in the back seat," I said. "If we put them all in the trunk, it's going to overbalance so bad it'll pull the front wheels right up off the ground."

It took some juggling, but we finally managed it all.

"I'm gonna have to go on into Twisp and pick up a few things," Miller said, coming back from turning the horses out to pasture. "I'll call the game warden. He'll give you a note explainin' why you got so many deer. That way you won't have no trouble with any game checks on down the line."

"We'd appreciate it, Cap," I said. I walked with him back up toward the house.

"Your brother told me a few things on the way down," he said.

"Yeah," I said, "he told me he planned to."

"I can see where he had a lot workin' on him," Cap said, dumping his clothes bag on the back porch.

"He's not as bad as he seemed to be up there," I said.

"He's a lot younger'n you," Cap said.

"No. He's two years older."

"That's not what I meant."

"Oh. Maybe—in some ways anyhow."

"In a lotta ways. I got a feelin' that in a lotta ways your brother ain't never gonna grow up. I started off callin' the wrong man Kid. He's likable enough; he just ain't grown-up."

"Who really ever grows up all the way, Cap?" I asked him.

He grinned at me. "If I ever make it, I'll let you know."

I laughed. "Right," I said.

"You got my address here?" he asked me.

"Yeah," I said.

"Drop me a line once in a while, son. Let me know how you're makin' out."

"I will, Cap. I really will." I meant it, too.

He slapped my shoulder. "We stand here talkin' all afternoon, and you two'll never get home."

We went on back out to the cars. Miller and Clint climbed in the pickup and led out with Jack and me laboring along behind in the overloaded Plymouth.

I saw Ned rolling out in the pasture where the colt had run when we'd first come here. The old boy was acting pretty frisky. Maybe he wasn't really grown-up either.

The game warden met us in Twisp and put all the necessary information down on a piece of paper for us.

"Nice bunch of deer," he said. He shook hands around and left.

"Well, men," Cap said, "I don't want to keep you. I know you got a long trip ahead of you."

"Cap, Clint," Jack said, "maybe I didn't show it much, but I enjoyed the trip, and I appreciate all you did for us up there." He shook hands with them both and got back in his car.

I shook hands with Cap and then with Clint.

"Thanks for everything," I said.

"You come back, son," Miller said, "you hear me? Even if it's only to borrow money."

"And don't make yourself obnoxious by not writin' neither," Clint growled, punching my shoulder.

We were all getting a little watery-eyed.

"I'd better go," I said quickly. "I'll keep in touch." I got quickly into the car.

Jack backed out from the curb, we all waved, and then we drove off.

We stopped for a case of beer and then got out onto the highway. The sun was bright and warm, and we drove with the windows rolled down, drinking beer.

"You get all squared away with Cap?" I asked my brother after a few miles.

"I told him a little about what was goin' on," Jack said. "I don't know how much it squared away."

"He probably understood," I said.

"Ilcy," he said suddenly, "what day is today anyway?"

"Sunday."

"Man, I lost track up there."

I laughed.

We traded off at Cashmere, and I drove on over the pass. The sun went down before we got to the top, and I switched on the headlights.

"Let's make a piss-call at the summit," he said.

"Sure."

We stopped and used the rest rooms and then drove down into the fir trees on the west side.

"Dan," he said after a while.

"Yeah?"

"I'm sorry I threw down on you up there."

"You didn't mean it, Jack. I knew that."

"You'd have shot though, wouldn't you?"

"I only said that to try to jar some sense into you," I told him.

"Bullshit," he said quietly. "You were all squared off and so was I. It came about that close." He held up his thumb and forefinger about an eighth of an inch apart. "You had me cold, too."

I didn't say anything.

"What the hell was goin' on up there anyway?" he said suddenly. "I'd cut off my leg before I'd do anything to hurt you, and I think you feel the same way. What in hell got into us?"

"McKlearey and that goddamned leper of a deer," I said.

"Maybe it's best nobody found the thing," he said. "God only knows what might have happened."

"I *did* find it," I told him bluntly.

"What?"

"You heard me. I found the son of a bitch and buried it before Mc-Klearey got down there."

"No shit?"

"No shit. I wasn't about to get caught in the middle of a pitched gun battle."

"You did that just to keep him from puttin' me down?"

"You weren't listening," I said. "That's not why I did it. I'd have probably buried the damned thing even if *you'd* shot it. All I wanted to do was keep somebody from getting killed—probably me. You two were wound so damned tight you were ready to start shooting at anybody who came near you up there. Do you know that I had to back *both* of you off in the space of less than fifteen minutes?"

"McKlearey, too?"

"Hell, he was all squared away like Billy the Kid. I had to remind him loud and clear that I could take him if I had to. I got so many guns pointed at me that day I thought somebody had opened season on me.

"Jesus, Kid, I'm sorry as hell."

"Let's forget it," I said. "Everybody was all keyed-up."

"Man, McKlearey sure fell apart at the end, didn't he?"

"His hand was pretty badly infected," I said. "He might have been picking up some fever or something from that, I don't know."

"Yeah, he was holdin' it pretty careful all the time. You want another beer?"

"Yeah. I'm a little tired of whiskey for a while."

We had another beer and bored on down through the darkness, following our headlights.

We grabbed a hamburger and switched off again at Snohomish, and Jack drove on the rest of the way to Tacoma. We pulled into the trailer court about ten thirty.

Jack called Clem and got an OK to hang the deer in a garage at the end of the court. Then we unloaded all our gear, said good night, and went to our own trailers. I sat on the couch in my filthy hunting clothes with my feet up and a bottle of beer in my hand. I was bone-tired, and I damn near fell asleep a couple times.

"You look like the wrath of God," she said, coming in. She was still as cute as ever.

"How did you get over here, Clydine?" I asked.

"Joan's folks bought her a car. I've been borrowing it. I've been past here a dozen or so times since Wednesday." She came over and kissed me. "Did you lose your razor?" she asked. Then she sniffed. "*And* your soap?"

"I've been busy."

"All right," she ordered. "Strip and get into that bathroom."

"The *bathroom*?" I laughed. "Not in the *bathroom*!"

"Move it!" she barked.

I grunted, sat up, and started to unlace my boots.

"What a mess," she said, glaring at the pile of gear on the floor. "Are those things loaded?"

"The rifle isn't," I said. "The pistol is, I guess."

She shook her head disgustedly. "What were you doing with a pistol anyway?"

"Trying to stay alive," I said, a little more grimly than necessary.

"*Men!*" she said.

By the time I'd finished showering and shaving, she had everything but the guns put away. She wouldn't touch them. She had fixed me up a big platter of bacon and eggs and toast.

It felt awfully good just having her around.

"Well," she said when I'd finished eating and we'd moved back to the living room, "did you bushwhack Bambi?"

"Two Bambis," I told her.

"Do you feel better now?"

"I feel better, but not because I shot the deer," I said.

"Something happened up there, didn't it?" she asked me. I don't know how, but she saw right through me.

"A lot of things happened," I told her, "some good, some bad."

"Tell me."

"Do you have to get back home tonight?"

"Not really," she said, "but don't get any ideas—it's the wrong time of the month."

"No idea, my little wisteria of the workers," I said. "I'm too tired anyway." I really was.

"I've missed the botanical nick names," she said, wrinkling her nose at me.

"I've missed *you*, Rosebud."

"Really?"

"Really."

She leaned over and kissed me. "Did you unload that damned frog leg?" she asked me.

"The *what*?"

"The frog leg. The pistol—isn't that what they call it?"

"That's *hog*leg, love."

"Hog-frog, whatever. Get it empty. I'm not going to sleep in a house with a loaded gun."

I reached over and took it out. She watched it the way some people watch snakes. I slipped the hammer and dropped the shells out one by one.

"It's a hideous thing." She shuddered.

"It saved my life a couple times up there," I told her. I was overdramatizing it, I knew that.

"That's the second time you've made noises like John Wayne," she said. "Are you going to tell me what happened or not?"

"I'll tell you in bed," I said. "It's a very long, very involved story, and we're both liable to tap out before I get halfway through it."

"Did it turn out like a bad Western, after all?" she asked.

"Pretty close," I said.

We went to bed, and I held her very tightly and told her what had happened—all of it.

I wasn't sure she was really awake when I finished the story. ". . . and that's it," I said, winding it up.

"Was he really white?" she asked drowsily.

"Kind of cream-colored."

"He must have been beautiful."

"At first he was," I said. "After a while, though, I got to hate him."

"It wasn't *his* fault."

"No, but I hated him anyway."

"You don't make sense."

"I never pretended to make sense."

"Danny?"

"Yes, love?"

"Do you think Cap and Clint would like me?"

"I think they'd love you, Blossom."

She nuzzled my neck. "You say the nicest things sometimes," she said, her voice blurry and on the edge of dropping off.

"Go to sleep, Little Flower," I said.

She nestled down obediently and went to sleep quickly, like a child.

I lay staring into the darkness, and when I did go to sleep, I dreamed of the white deer. It got all mixed up with a dream about a dog until none of it made too much sense, but I guess dreams never really do, do they?

THE PARTING

34

Aᴛᴇʀ she left for class the next morning I called Mike at work to see how Betty was.

"She seems to be coming out of it OK," he said. "She's home now, but she's got to take it pretty damned easy."

"I'm glad to hear she's better," I said.

"Sloane and Larkin both called me after they came down—say, how sick was Cal anyway? He says one thing, and Stan says another."

"He was pretty damn sick," I said.

"Yeah, I kind of thought he might have been. How was the hunt?" His voice sounded wistful.

"The *hunt* was pretty good," I said. "Things got a little hairy a time or two though."

"McKlearey?"

"Yeah."

"I figured Miller'd be able to keep him in line."

"He did OK, but things still got a little woolly a time or two."

"Did anybody get that white deer Sloane told me about?"

"McKlearey shot him and he fell off a cliff. We never found him."

"Too bad—say, Dan, I gotta get back to work. Gimme a buzz tonight, OK?"

"Sure, Mike. After supper, OK?"

"Right. Bye now."

I guess his boss had been standing over him. I called the pawnshop. Sloane answered. His voice sounded a little puny, but otherwise he seemed OK.

"How are you feeling, Cal?" I asked him.

"Hell," he said, "I'm OK now. I was startin' to come out of it by the time we got back down the hill."

"You see a doctor?"

"Yeah." He giggled. "Claudia was on me about it as soon as I got back. He says it happens to guys my age some times. He's got me takin' it kinda easy for a couple of weeks."

459

"Good idea," I said. "Oh, we got your deer for you."

"Hey, great, man—how big?"

"Five-point. He's in prime condition."

"Thanks a lot, Dan. Who shot 'im?"

"I did. Miller and I went out and found him."

"Shoot out the liver?" He giggled.

"Not a chance," I said. "Old Clint was threatening to burn me at the stake if I did."

He told me he'd call a processing plant to take care of the deer, and I said I'd drop the hide and horns by later that morning after I'd cleaned my guns.

After I hung up I sorted out all my hunting clothes and took them over to the washhouse. Then I went back and cleaned my guns and McKlearey's rifle. Then I bundled up Lou's gear and the two deer hides and drove on over to the shop.

"Come on in, Dan," Cal called as I pushed my way on in with a big armload of gear.

"I brought Lou's stuff on over," I said.

Cal wanted to know where Lou was. He hadn't shown up for work that morning. I told him that I didn't know and filled him in on the way Lou'd taken off from Clint.

"God," Sloane said, "that doesn't sound like Lou. He's pretty irresponsible sometimes, but he's never gone *that* far before."

"He was pretty badly shook up," I said. "I don't think he was thinking straight toward the end." I told him about McKlearey's shooting the white deer and then not being able to find it.

"God damn," Cal said, "you say he took that .38 along with him?"

"That's what Clint said."

"Christ," he said, his face darkening, "that damn gun's on the record as being here in the shop. If he's gone off the deep end or something and does something stupid with it, it could get my ass in a helluva lotta trouble."

"Shit," I said, "I hadn't thought of that."

"Now what the hell do I do? I don't want to report the gun stolen— that'd get him in all kinds of trouble. I wish I knew where the hell he was."

"Beats me, Cal. He didn't even say good-bye when he left."

Sloane shook his head. "I'll figure something out," he said. "You want a drink?"

"Sure."

"Come on back." He jerked his head, and we went on into the back room. I dumped Lou's gear in a corner and Cal reached down the bottle and handed it to me.

I took a belt and handed it back to him. He capped it up and put it away.

"Doctor said I oughta back off for a while," he said. "I'm cuttin' way down on my smoking, too—and I'm on a diet."

"Jesus, Sloane, you're going whole hog, aren't you?"

"Let me tell you, man," he said seriously, "I could feel the buzzards snappin' at my ass up there. The doctor told me I came about that close to havin' a coronary." He measured off a fraction of an inch with his fingers. "Goddamn heart was workin' doubletime to make up for the lack of oxygen. About one more day and I wouldn't of made it back down. He says I gotta quit smokin', cut way back on the booze, lose fifty pounds, and get ten hours sleep a night. Christ, I feel just like a goddamn invalid."

"Jesus," I said, "you were sicker'n any of us figured then."

"I was sicker'n *I* figured even," he said. "That damned doctor like to scared the piss outa me."

"You're going to be OK, aren't you?"

"Oh, I'll come out of it OK. He said there wasn't any permanent damage, but little Calvin's gonna walk the straight and narrow for a while."

"Not a bad idea," I said, lighting a cigarette. I saw the hungry look in his eyes and mashed it out quickly. "Sorry, Cal," I said.

"It's a little tough, right at first," he said.

We went on back out to the shop.

"You know," he said, "it's funny."

"What?"

"You remember that day up there when I told you I was gonna buckle down after the trip—maybe grow up a little?"

"Yeah," I said, "I remember."

"Looks like I'm gonna have to do just exactly that." He giggled, suddenly sounding like the Cal I'd always known. "This ain't exactly what I had in mind though."

"Somebody once said that a guy shouldn't make promises to himself," I told him. "He winds up having to keep them."

"Boy, that's sure as hell the truth," he said.

He gave me the address of the packing plant where they'd process the deer for him, and I told him that Jack and I would get it over there for him that afternoon.

About noon, Claudia came in.

"Hello, Dan," she said in her deep voice.

"Claudia," I said. She still gave me goose bumps.

"How many cigarettes, Calvin?" She wasn't badgering; she was just asking.

He mutely held up three fingers.

"Truth?" she asked.

"Ask Dan," he said.

"He's only had one since I got here about ten thirty," I said. "Cross my heart and hope to turn green all over."

She laughed, and her hand touched my arm affectionately.

"And how many nips from your hide-out bottle?" she asked him.

"What bottle?"

"The one on the top shelf in the storeroom."

"How'd you find out about *that*?"

"I've always known about it," she said.

He stared at her for a minute and then started laughing. "I give up," he said. "What the hell's the use anyway?"

"How many?" she repeated.

"Not one. I gave Dan a belt, but I haven't touched a drop."

"Good," she said. "I'm not nagging you, Calvin. This is for your own good."

"I know, dear," he said. It was the first time I'd ever heard him use any term of endearment to her.

"You'd better run on along home now," she said. "I put a big bowl of salad in the refrigerator for you."

"I'm startin' to feel like a damn rabbit," he complained. "I got lettuce comin' out of my ears."

"But you've lost weight, haven't you?" she said.

"Yeah, I guess so," he said grudgingly.

"And take your nap this time," she commanded.

"Yes, ma'am."

I said good-bye to him, and he went on out. I'd been ready to leave, too, but Claudia had given me a quick signal to stick around. After he left she turned to me, her face serious.

"Just how bad was he up there, Dan?" she asked me.

"He was pretty sick," I told her. "He couldn't seem to get his breath, and there were a couple times when he couldn't keep anything down. We all figured he'd snap out of it, but he just couldn't seem to get adjusted."

"Why didn't you send him down earlier?" she asked.

"I don't think any of us really knew how sick he really was," I told her. "A couple times it seemed like he was getting better. He'd go out hunting and things seemed to be coming along fine, but then he'd conk out again. We were all watching him pretty closely, but he kept telling us that he'd be all right in just a little bit."

She shook her head. "Men!" she said. "You're all just a bunch of overgrown children."

"I've been finding that out," I told her.

"I'd die if I lost him, Dan."

Sloane?

I guess it must have shown on my face.

"You don't understand, do you, Dan?"

"It's none of my business really," I told her.

"I know," she said, "but I want to tell you anyway."

Why me, for God's sake? Why always me?

"I think I'm as happy now as I've ever been in my life," she said, looking out the window. "For the first time, Calvin needs *me*—not just the fact that I can keep his books or pick out furniture or any of that. He needs *me*. When he came home, he was frightened—terribly frightened. He came to me for the first time without making it some kind of deal—you know, 'I'll do this for you if you'll do that for me.' It was the first time he didn't try to buy me. You have no idea what that means to a woman."

"I think I do," I said quietly.

"I suppose maybe you would," she said. "You seem to see a lot of things that other people don't." She looked steadily up at me for a minute. "You see, Dan," she said finally, "I can't have any children. I did something pretty stupid when I was about seventeen, and I had an abortion. It wasn't even a doctor who did it, and of course I went septic. I wound up losing everything." She passed her hand across her lower abdomen. "Calvin and I decided not to adopt children—I suppose we could have, but we just decided not to. So *Calvin* is my baby. That's the way it's always been."

I nodded.

"But this is the first time he's ever turned to me this way. Maybe it really isn't much of a basis for a good marriage but—" she shrugged.

"It's probably as good as any," I said, "and better than a lot of them."

She smiled at me. "Thank you," she said, "I thought you'd understand."

We talked a while longer, and then I took off. She was one helluva woman.

I picked up Clydine after her last class, and we went on back to my place. She'd told me quite emphatically that morning that she was going to spend every spare minute with me until I left for Seattle. I wasn't really about to argue with her.

⚡ 35

I didn't see Stan until the next weekend. I'm not sure why, but I think I was avoiding him. When I called to make sure he was home, I got the distinct impression that he'd have preferred to keep it that way, but it was too late then.

He was growing a mustache, and it made his face look dirty. Stan didn't have the kind of face you'd want to put a mustache on. And instead of one of the usual sober-colored, conservative sport shirts I'd always seen him in, he was wearing a loud checkered wool shirt—outdoorsy as hell, and on him about as phony as a nine-dollar bill.

"Well, Dan," he said with a nervous joviality, "how the hell have you been?" As if he hadn't seen me in ten years, for God's sake.

"Fair, Stan. Just fair."

We went into his tidy little living room.

"How's old Cal?"

"He's coming along. His doctor's got him on a short schedule and cut him off booze and cigarettes."

"He gave me a damn bad scare up there, the poor bastard."

What the hell was all this?

He fidgeted around a little, and our conversation was pretty sketchy. I wasn't sure what this he-man role he was playing was all about, but I desperately wanted to tell him that it wasn't coming off very well.

"Oh," he said, "I've been fixing up the den. I wanted you to see it." He led me back to the room he'd identified as the study the last time I'd been there.

He'd redone the place in early musket ball. The rifle and his shotgun were hanging on the wall where they could collect dust, and there were hunting prints hanging all over the place. I could see copies of *Field and Stream* and *The American Rifleman* scattered around with a studied carelessness. The place looked like a goddamn movie set.

"I'm having that buck's head mounted," he said. "How do you think it would look right there?" He pointed to a place that had obviously been left empty for the trophy.

"Ought to be OK, Stan," I told him.

We went back into the living room and I listened to him come on like the reincarnation of Ernest Hemingway for about a half hour or so.

Then Monica came in and suddenly it all fell into place.

"Did you pick up the beer like I asked you to?" he said to her, his voice cocked like a gun.

"Yes, Stan," she said—rather meekly, I thought.

"Why don't you open a couple for Dan and me?"

"Of course," she said and went on back out to the kitchen.

I watched Stan, who had never smoked, light a cigar. I wanted to tell him that he was overplaying it, but I wasn't sure how to go about it.

I sat around for another half hour or so, listening to him swear and give Monica orders, and then I'd had a gutful of the whole thing. I made an excuse and got away from them.

I suppose that what made the whole thing so pathetic was the fact that it was all so completely unnecessary. After her little misjudgment with McKlearey, Monica would have been pretty docile even without his big hairy-chested routine. Stan was saddling himself with the necessity of playing a role for the rest of his life. He'd get better at it as time went on. In a few years he might even get to the point where he believed it himself, but I don't think he'd ever really be comfortable with it.

I picked up Clydine and told her about it as we drove back on across town to my place.

"What are you going to do about it?"

"I can't do a damn thing," I said. "I sure as hell can't tell him that McKlearey got to Monica, and that's the only way I could convince him that this act of his isn't the thing that put him in the driver's seat."

"But if this is so unnatural for him," she objected, "he's really no better off than he was before, is he?"

"No," I said, "he isn't. He's still in a box—it's just a different box, that's all."

"But you ought to be able to do something," she said.

"Hell, Rosebud," I said, "I didn't hire on as God. Last time I tried to walk on water, I got wetter than hell."

She crossed her arms and glowered straight ahead. "I still think there's *something* you could do," she said. "It's just awful to think about what they'll have to go through for all the rest of their lives."

"Well," I said in my best Hemingway manner, "don't think about it then."

She didn't catch the allusion, and so she was angry with me for being an insensitive clod. You can't win.

When we got to my place, she was still steamed, so we sat around listening to records and not talking to each other. She sure could be stubborn when she wanted to be.

Then Cal called. "Dan," he said, "I just got a call from one of the bartenders on the Avenue, and he said he just saw McKlearey."

"No shit? I thought he'd blown town."

"I really don't much give a damn what he does," Cal said, "but I sure as hell want to get that goddamn pistol back from him. I could write it off on the three days' pay I owe him from the car lot, but the paper has got to be straightened out."

"Yeah," I said, "I see what you mean."

"Are you busy right now? I tried to get hold of Jack, but he's out delivering a camper trailer."

"What do you need?" I asked him, glancing at Clydine. She still wasn't looking at me.

"Somebody's gonna have to run him down—somebody who knows the score. I can't get away until later, and I'm afraid he'll go back in his hole before then."

"You want me to find him?"

"Right. Just tell him to come by the shop. I want him to pick up all this shit of his anyway—and tell me what he wants done with his goddamn deer."

"Which way was he going?"

"God, I really don't know."

"I'll just have to hunt him down then, I guess," I said.

"Thanks a lot, Dan."

"Sure, Cal."

I hung up and went back to the dinky little living room.

"Do you want to play private detective?" I asked her.

She brooded for a minute or so, probably trying to decide whether it would be more fun to keep sulking or to find out what I was talking about. I couldn't quite make up my mind whether I wanted to give her a good solid spanking or a big kiss right on the end of her little snoot.

"What do you have in mind?" she finally asked, not really wanting to give up the good pout she had going.

"We've got to go find McKlearey," I told her.

"Old Creepy-Jarhead himself?"

"That's our man," I told her. "He's got a hot gun, and we've gotta get to him before the fuzz do or before he pulls a caper with it. Our client would find that pretty embarrassing." I lit a cigarette and squinted at her through the smoke.

"Have you been watching television?" She laughed, unable to help it.

"It's a big case, baby," I said, putting the Bogart accent on even more thickly. "Every shamus in town would give his eyeteeth to get a piece of the action."

"OK, Knuckles," she said toughly, standing up and hitching up her blue jeans. "Let's go run down the subject. We gonna rub 'im out when we find 'im?"

"Not unless we have to," I said. "You got your .38 handy?"

She took a deep breath, cocked one eyebrow at me, and gave me a long stare over her upthrusting frontage. "I've always got *my* 38 handy," she said.

"You nut," I laughed. "Let's go."

We went out to my car and began bar hopping back down the Avenue toward town. Some of the bartenders knew McKlearey and some didn't, so it was pretty hit and miss. I still wasn't sure which way Lou was going, and I couldn't be sure if he was still on the Avenue or if he'd cut on over toward Parkland or what.

"We'll try the Patio, and then I'll do what I should have done in the first place," I said.

"What's that, Knucks?" she said.

"Go back to my place and use the phone and the yellow pages."

"Clever," she said. "I can see how you got your rep as the best private nose in the business."

"Eye, baby. It's private eye—not nose."

"Whatever," she said and then laughed. I guess she'd gotten over her mad.

Lou was at the Patio. He was sitting in a booth alone, with a pitcher of beer in front of him. His left arm was in a sling, and his hand had a professional-looking bandage on it.

"Hey, there, Lou," I said with a heartiness I didn't really feel. "How the hell have you been?"

He looked up at me, his eyes kind of flat, as always.

I introduced him to Clydine, and he invited us to join him. He had that gun on him. I didn't see it, but I could almost smell it on him. I wished to hell I hadn't brought my little Bolshevik along.

"Where in hell have you been, Lou?" I asked him after the

bartender brought the pitcher I'd ordered. "Nobody's seen you since the hunt."

Something happened back behind his flat, empty eyes. Suddenly he was all buddy-buddy, friendly as a pup.

"Christ, man," he said, "I been in the goddamn *hospital*." He waved his bandaged hand at me. "I picked up a damn good case of blood poisoning in this thing."

"No shit?" I said. "I knew it was giving you some trouble, but I never even thought about blood poisoning."

"Hell," he said, "I had a red streak an inch wide goin' up my arm all the way to the armpit. Man, I was flat outa my head by the time I got to that VA hospital up in Seattle."

"So *that's* why you took off so fast," I said, helping him along.

"Shit, yes, man," he said. "I was about halfway outa my skull even up there—with the fever and all. I knew damn well I was gonna have to get to a doctor in a hurry."

"Christ, Lou," I said, "you should have said something."

"I didn't think it was that bad at first."

Clydine was watching him closely, not saying anything. I think she was trying to fit Lou into all the things I'd told her about him.

I passed Sloane's message on to him, and he said he'd take care of it.

"Hell," he said, "as far as that deer goes, you guys can just go ahead and split it up. I don't care that much about venison myself."

"I suppose we could give it to Carter," I said. "After all, he didn't get to go."

"Hey, there's a good idea. Why don't you just give it to Carter?"

"Tell Sloane when you drop by the shop," I told him, nailing down that point again. I wasn't sure how much it was going to take to separate Lou from that gun. "Oh, Cal says to tell you he'll let you have the pistol for what he owes you from the lot, but he's gotta get the paper on it straightened out."

That seemed to make Lou feel even better. He got positively expansive.

After about a half hour Clydine had to make a run to the ladies' room.

"I bet I acted pretty fuckin' funny up there, huh?" Lou said while she was gone.

"You weren't raving or anything," I said carefully, "but sometimes you didn't make too much sense."

"It was the fuckin' fever," he said. "You know, from the blood poisoning. I can only remember about half of what went on up there."

"Hell," I said, "it's lucky you were even able to walk, as sick as you were."

"Yeah," he agreed. "I was pretty far gone, all right. I bet I *said* a lotta wild stuff, too, huh?"

"Most of it was pretty garbled," I said. I was walking right on the edge and about all I had to defend myself with was a ballpoint pen.

"Guy'll say fuckin' near *anything* when he's out of his head like that, won't he?"

"Hell, man," I said, "you were having screaming nightmares, and you were talking to yourself and everything. I'm not kidding, old buddy, we thought you were cracking up."

He laughed. "I'll bet it scared the piss outa you guys, huh?"

"Shit! We were waiting for you to start frothing at the mouth and biting trees."

"Yeah, I was really gone," he said. "Did I ever say anything about the Delta?" He asked it very casually—too casually.

"Nothing that made any sense," I said. "You said something about how you used to think about snow when you were out there."

"Yeah," he said. "I remember that—not too well, of course, but I remember it. Did I mention any names while I was out my head?"

"I think so," I said, "but I didn't really catch them."

Clydine came back.

"I'm gonna blow this town," Lou said. "Winter's comin' and the rain bugs me."

"Yeah," I said, "it can get pretty gloomy around here."

"And I gotta work outside, too. I can't cut bein' penned up inside. I think I'll cut out for Texas or Florida or someplace. I just came back today to get my gear together."

"Be nice down South this time of year," I agreed. "Make sure you see Sloane before you go though, huh? He's pretty worried about it."

"Sure," he said, emptying his glass. "Hey, tell Jack I'm sorry about givin' 'im such a hard time up there, huh? Chances are I won't get a chance to see 'im before I take off."

"Sure, Lou."

"I probably won't ever be comin' back up here again," he said. "That probably ain't gonna hurt some guys' feelin's."

"Oh," I lied, "you haven't been all *that* bad, Lou."

He laughed, the same harsh raspy laugh as always. "Look," he said, "I'm gonna have to take off—if I'm gonna see Sloane and all. Just forget anything I said up there, huh—about the Delta or anything, OK?"

"What Delta?" I said.

He grinned at me. "You're OK, Danny—too bad we didn't get to know each other better." He stood up quickly. I could see the bulge of the gun under his jacket. "I gotta run. You take care now, huh?"

"So long, Lou," I said.

He waved, winked at Clydine, and started out. Then he stopped and came back, his face flat again.

"Hey," he said. "I owe you five, don't I?"

I'd forgotten about it.

"Here." He pulled out his billfold and fumbled awkwardly in it. He was carrying quite a wad of cash. He dropped a five on the table. "We're all square now, right?"

"Good enough, Lou," I said.

He poked a finger at me pistol-fashion by way of farewell, turned, and went out.

"Wow," Clydine said in a shuddery voice, "I don't want to play cops and robbers anymore."

"I shouldn't have brought you along," I said.

"I wouldn't have missed it for the world," she said. "He's a real starker, isn't he?"

"He's got all the makings," I said, picking up the five-dollar bill. I looked it over carefully.

"What's the matter?" she said. "You think it may be counterfeit?"

"Nobody counterfeits fives," I said.

"What are you looking for then? Blood?"

"I don't know," I told her. "I think he was pretty close to broke when he came out of the woods, though."

"Maybe he went to the bank."

"That's what worries me," I said, still looking at the bill.

"OK, Knucks," she said, "I told you I didn't want to play cops and robbers anymore. What's on for the afternoon?"

"Let's go to Seattle."

"Why?"

"I'm going to have to go house hunting."

"Oh," she said. I don't think either of us liked the reminder that I'd be leaving soon.

━━➤ 36

On the first of October I moved to Seattle and began the tedious process of getting enrolled for classes and so forth. I'd found a little place the landlord referred to as a cottage but for which the word "shack" might have been more appropriate. Even when compared to the shabby little trailer I'd been living in, the place was tiny. The fold-down couch that made into a bed was perhaps the most uncomfortable thing I've ever slept in, but the place was close enough to the university to compensate for its other drawbacks.

Even though Clydine and I had both been convinced that my move to Seattle would more or less terminate what some people chose to call our relationship, it didn't work out that way. I kept coming across reasons why I just *had* to make a quick trip to Tacoma, and I think she made seven shopping jaunts to Seattle during my first month up there.

I guess when you get right down to it, I got out of Tacoma just in time to miss the big messy bust-up between Jack and Marg—or maybe Jack just held off until I left town, though that was a kind of delicacy you just didn't expect from my brother.

About ten o'clock on a drizzly Saturday morning I came down the steps of the library with a whole dreary weekend staring me in the face. The bibliographical study for Introduction to Graduate Studies that I'd assumed would take from twelve to fourteen hours had, in fact, been polished off in just a shade under forty-five minutes. I spent another half hour trying to figure out what I'd done wrong. As far as I could see, the job was complete, so I left the library feeling definitely let down and vaguely cheated somehow.

I had absolutely nothing to do with myself, so I decided, naturally, to bag on down to Tacoma. At least down there I should be able to find somebody I knew to drink with.

The highway was dreary, but it didn't really bother me. Without even thinking, I swung on over to Clydine's place. Who the hell was I trying to kid? There was only one reason I'd come down to Tacoma, and it sure wasn't to find somebody to drink with.

I went up the stairs two at a time and knocked at the door.

Her folks were there.

"Danny," she said in surprise when she opened the door, "I thought you had to work this weekend." She was wearing a dress and her hair was done up.

"I finished up sooner than I thought," I said.

"Well, come on in," she said. "Meet my folks." She gave me one of those smark-alecky grimaces that conveyed a world of condescension, sophomoric superiority, and juvenile intolerance. It irritated the piss out of me for some reason, and I made a special effort to be polite to them.

Her father was a little bald-headed guy with a nervous laugh. I think he was in the plumbing supply business, or maybe hardware. Her mother was short and plump and kind of bubbly. I think they liked me because of my haircut. Some of Clydine's friends must have looked pretty shaggy to them.

I could see my little leftist smoldering in the corner as I talked about fishing with her father and Europe with her mother. I knew that about all I was doing was mildewing the sheets between the little nut and me and breeding a helluva family squabble which would probably start as soon as I left. I told them I had to run across town and see my brother and then left as gracefully as I could.

I snooped around the Avenue a bit, but I really didn't feel like seeing Jack yet, and the pawnshop had a whole platoon of guys lined up inside, so I took a chance and drove on over to Parkland to see Mike. Surprisingly, he was home, and the two of us went into his living room and sprawled out in a couple of chairs and drank beer and watched it rain.

"Damn shame about Jack and Marg," he said.

"Yeah, but it was bound to happen, Mike. It was just a question of time really."

"I've never been able to figure out what it is about Jack," he said thoughtfully. "I *like* him—hell, everybody *likes* the son of a bitch, but he just can't seem to hang in there the way most guys do."

"I think maybe Cap Miller came closer to Jack's problem than anybody else really," I said.

"Oh?"

"He said that the way he saw it Jack isn't ever really going to grow up. Maybe that's it."

"Not much gets by old Miller," Mike commented.

"It's funny, too," I said. "It's the one thing Jack's been obsessed with ever since I can remember—growing up. He used to think about that more than anybody I ever knew."

"Maybe he tried too hard."

"I think he tried too soon, Mike. Have you ever seen one of these girls who start going out on dates when they're eleven—lipstick, high heels, the whole bit?"

"Yeah, but what's the connection?"

"Have you ever known one of them that ever really grew up? I mean one who wasn't still pretty damned juvenile even when she got to be twenty-three or twenty-four?"

"I always thought that kind of girl was just stupid."

"Maybe that enters into it," I said, "but there's a kind of immaturity there, too."

He shrugged. "I still don't get the connection."

"Well," I said, "I've got a hunch that the patterns we set up when we first start doing something are usually going to be the patterns we're going to follow for the rest of our lives. Now, if you start out trying to be grown-up—or adult, if you prefer that term—while you're still physically and mentally a child, you're going to start the whole business all wrong. You'll start a pattern of *playing* grown-up. You'll contaminate all of your adulthood with that juvenile pattern. I think that's what happens to the little girl with her gunked-on makeup and wobbly high heels. She spends the rest of her life *playing* grown-up. I sort of think that the same thing happened to Jack."

"You mean he's just playing?"

"The worst part of it is that he doesn't know he's playing," I said. "He just doesn't know the difference. He's impatient, he's flighty, he's self-centered, he's intolerant—he's got all the classic traits of immaturity."

"Shit, man"—Mike laughed—"you've just described about three-quarters of the people in the whole damn country."

"Including you and me, probably," I said. "That's another thing Old Cap said. I asked him when *anybody* really grows up, and he told me that if he ever made it, he'd let me know."

"Sounds like you and old Cap got along pretty well," he said.

"I don't think I've ever met a man I liked or respected more," I said, "except maybe my old man."

"He kinda hits a guy that way, doesn't he?"

I nodded. "Say, how's Sloane doing? I was going to stop by the shop, but the place was mobbed."

"Christ"—Mike laughed—"you wouldn't recognize the old fart. He's lost thirty pounds and gone teetotaler on us. He doesn't even drink beer anymore."

"He got a pretty good scare up there, I guess."

"It musta been pretty hairy."

"You know it, buddy. Between him and McKlearey it was a real nervous trip."

"Lou took off, you know."

"Yeah. He told me he was going to."

"That damned trip sure changed a lot of things around here," Mike said.

"I guess it was sort of a watershed. Maybe we were all due for a change of some kind, and the trip just brought it all to a head."

"I sure wish I could have gone along," he said wistfully.

"So do I, Mike."

We talked for another hour or so, and then Betty wanted Mike to take her to the grocery store, so I took off.

I went on by the trailer court, but Jack's trailer was gone. That's always kind of a jolt. The damn things look sort of permanent when they're set down on a lot with fences and grass around them, so you forget that they've got wheels on them. I dropped down to the trailer sales lot and Jack was sitting in the grubby, cigarette-stinking office with his muddy feet up on the desk.

"Yeah," he said, grinning tightly at me. "I moved Sandy in with me, and I didn't want Marg to pick up on that with the divorce comin' on and all."

"Oh?"

"Yeah," he said, lighting a cigarette. "We got things all kinda hammered out to where I don't get nicked too bad for support money, and I don't want her gettin' the idea that she's the aggrieviated party in this little clambake. I'm not about to get screwed into the wall with alimony payments."

"Where'd you move to?"

"I'm in a court out toward Madrona."

"Where'd Marg go?" I asked.

"She got an apartment out in Lakewood. Not a bad place. I found it for her."

"Sounds pretty civilized," I said.

He shrugged. "I didn't want her gettin' the idea she had any kinda claim on my trailer. I guess her lawyer was pissed-off as hell about it. I got her all moved out before he got the chance to tell her to stay put.

Now that *she* abandoned *me*, it kinda cuts down on her share of the community property."

"You figure all the angles, don't you, Jack?"

"I been though it all before," he said. "If a guy uses his head, he don't have to get skinned alive in divorce court. Hey, you want a drink?"

"Sure." I didn't care much for that particular conversation anyway.

"Come on." He got up, hauled on a coat and led me across the soggy lot to a fairly new trailer. "Try to look like a customer," he said, leading the way inside. The trailer was clammy, but it was a little more private than the office. Jack went into the little utility room and pulled a fifth of cheap vodka out of one of the heating ducts.

"The boss can't smell this on me," he explained. "I have a coke afterward, and I'm pure as the driven snow." He laughed flatly.

We each had a couple of pulls from the bottle and then sat around in the chilly living room talking.

"Did McKlearey get that business with the gun straightened out with Sloane before he took off?"

"Yeah," Jack said, "he and Sloane dummied up the paper work and got it all squared away with the police department."

"Did you see him before he took off?"

"Naw, I got a gutful of that motherfucker up in the woods."

"The silly bastard had blood poisoning in that hand," I said. "He claims he was out of his head with the fever and the damned infection."

"I wouldn't bet on that. I think he just plain flipped out."

"It's possible," I said. "He was carrying that .38 when I saw him. Had it tucked under his belt."

"That silly bastard! He's just stupid enough to try to use it, too. He'll get about half in the bag some night and try to knock over a liquor store or a tavern. I hope somebody shoots him."

"At least he's out of *our* hair," I said.

"Yeah."

Somehow Jack and I didn't really seem to have much to talk about. I guess we never had really. I got the feeling that splitting up with Marg had hit him a lot harder than he was willing to admit to me.

"Hey," he said suddenly, "you wanna do me a favor?"

"Sure."

"When I moved the trailer, I found a bunch of stuff that belongs to the kids. I got it all in a box in the trunk of my car. You think you could run it on over to Marg's place for me? I think it's better if I stay away from there for a while."

"Sure, Jack."

"I'll give her a call and let her know you're comin'."

We went over to his car and transferred the box from his trunk to mine.

"Hey, Dan, look at this." He popped open his glove compartment. That stupid .45 automatic was in there.

"Shit, Jack," I said, "you'll get your ass in a sling if they catch you carrying that thing in your car that way without a permit."

He shrugged. "I got kinda stuck on it up in the brush, you know? Shit, a man oughta own himself a pistol—home protection and all that bullshit."

"Maybe so," I said, "but you sure as hell shouldn't be carting it around in your glove box."

"Maybe," he said. We went back in the office and he called Marg.

"She'll be there," he said after he hung up. He gave me the address and I took off again.

It took me a while to find the place. It was one of those older houses that had had the second floor remodeled into a self-contained apartment that you reached by way of an outside staircase. I went on up and knocked.

"Hi, Dan," she said, smiling blearily at me. She smelled pretty strongly of whiskey. "Come on in."

"I can only stay a minute," I said, carting in the box.

"Just set that down," she told me. "The girls are asleep. How about a drink?" She didn't wait for any answer but whipped me up a whiskey and Seven-Up almost before I got the box put down. "Come on in the living room," she said.

I pulled off my wet jacket, and we went on in and I sat on the couch. She sat in the armchair just opposite me and crossed her legs, flashing an unnecessary amount of thigh at me. "How's school?" she asked.

I shrugged. "Takes a while to get back into it," I said. "I think I'm doing OK."

"That's swell."

"I wish I'd gotten here sooner," I said. "I'd have liked to get a chance to see the kids."

"They'll be up in an hour or so," she said, leaning back to stretch her arms. She was wearing a sleeveless blouse, cotton, I think, and when she pulled it tight like that, her nipples stood out pretty obviously. Margaret was too big a girl to run around without a bra.

"Sure has been lonesome around here lately," she said.

"You have any plans—I mean for after—" I left it up there. Under the circumstances it was kind of a touchy subject really.

"Oh," she said, polishing off her drink in two gulps, "nothing definite yet. I'm not worried." She got up, went into the kitchen and came out with a fresh drink.

"You got any special plans for the rest of the day?" she asked, sitting on the couch beside me.

"I've got to get back across town before too long," I lied, ostentatiously checking my watch.

She didn't even bother with subtlety. Maybe she was too drunk or maybe the years with my brother had eroded any subtlety out of her. She simply reached out, grabbed my head and kissed me. Her tongue started probing immediately. I felt her hand fumbling at the front of her blouse and then the warm mashing of her bare breasts against me.

"You wouldn't run off and leave a girl all alone like this, would you?" she murmured in my ear.

"Margaret," I said, trying to untangle her arms from around my neck, "this is no good."

"Oh, come on, Danny," she coaxed. "What difference does it make?"

"I'm sorry, Margaret," I said.

She sat back, not bothering to cover herself. Her nipples were very large and darkly pigmented and not very pretty. "What's the matter?" she demanded. "Has Jack been telling you stories about me?"

"No," I said, "that's not it at all. I just don't think that under the circumstances it would be a good idea." I stood up quickly and gulped down the drink. "I've really got to run anyway."

"Boy," she said bitterly, "you're just not with it at all, are you?"

"I've got to run, Marg," I said. "Tell the kids I said hello."

"I sure never figured you for a square," she said.

"I'm sorry, Margaret," I said. I went out very quickly. Hell let's be honest, I ran like a scared rabbit.

I stopped at the Patio and had a beer to give myself a chance to calm down.

Clydine's folks had left when I got back to her place, and she tore into me for being nice to them.

All in all, I got the feeling that I'd have been away to hell and gone out in front to have just spent the whole day in bed.

 37

Dear Cap and Clint,

   I've been so busy I kind of got behind in my letter writing. I guess I'm doing OK in school—at least they haven't kicked me out yet.

   I was down to Tacoma a couple weeks ago and saw most of the others. Sloane has gone off his diet a little, but he hasn't started putting any weight back on yet. At least he'll have a beer with the rest of us once in a while, if we all get together and twist his arm. His doctor is sure now that there wasn't any permanent damage, so you can quit worrying about that.

   My brother's divorce should be final about the end of Feb., and I think he'll be making himself kind of scarce around here for a while after that. He'll probably want to go someplace else for a while to get himself straightened out.

   Nobody has had any word about McKlearey. We don't even know where he went. *It's probably just as well, I suppose. He wasn't just the most popular guy around here anyway. I can't really say that any of us miss him.*

I haven't seen Stan Larkin for a couple months now, but the last time he was still playing that same silly game I told you about before. It's kind of sad, really, because it's all so unnatural for him.

I guess we were a pretty odd bunch, weren't we? I'm glad you changed your mind about giving up guiding. You just happened to get a bunch of screwballs the first time out.

My girlfriend and I made up again. I think that's about the fourth or fifth time since school started. She's a 24-karat nut, but I think you'd like her.

Well, you fellows have a merry Christmas now, and don't let the snow pile up so deep that it won't melt off in time for me to get through when fishing season starts.

> *Well, Merry Christmas again.*
> *So long for now,*
>
> *Dan*

I write a lousy letter. I always have. I knew that if I read it over, I'd tear it up and then write another one just damn near like it, so I stuck it in an envelope and sealed it up in a hurry.

It was Wednesday night, and my seminar paper on Faulkner's *The Sound and the Fury* was due on Friday, but I just couldn't seem to get it to all fit together. I went back and tried to plow my way through the Benjy section again. I knew that what I needed was buried in there someplace, but I was damned if I could dig it out.

I kept losing track of the time sequence and finally wound up heaving the book across the room in frustration.

I wondered what the hell Clydine was up to. Lately I'd taken to listening to the news and buying newspapers to check on any demonstrations or the like in Tacoma. I think my most recurrent nightmare was of some big cop belting her in the head with a nightstick—not that she might not have deserved it now and then.

Maybe that was why I couldn't really concentrate. I was spending about half my time worrying about her. God damn it, as harebrained as she was about some things, she needed a fulltime keeper just to keep her out of trouble.

I leaned back and thought about that for a while. I thought about some of the creeps she hung around with and decided that most of them needed keepers a whole lot worse than she did.

I guess it really took me quite a while to come to the realization that I really didn't want just anybody looking out for her. As a matter of fact, I didn't want it to be anybody but me, when I got right down to it. I knew finally what that meant. Of all the stupid, inappropriate, completely out of the question things to get involved in at this particular

time! I was still running down the long list of reasons why the whole
idea was crazy as I reached for the telephone.

"Hello?"

"Hi, Joan. Is Rosebud there?"

"Yeah, Danny. Just a minute—Clydine!" I wished to hell she
wouldn't yell across the open mouthpiece like that.

"Hello." Damn, it was good to hear her voice.

"I want you to listen to me very carefully, Flower Child. I don't want
to have to repeat myself."

"My, aren't we authoritarian tonight."

"Don't get smart. This is serious."

"OK. Shoot."

"I want you to transfer up here next quarter."

"Are you drunk?"

"No, I'm stone sober."

"Why the hell would I want to do a dumb thing like that? This isn't
much of a school, I'll admit, but it's sure a lot better than that processing plant up there."

"Education is what you make of it," I said inanely. "I want you up
here."

"All my friends are down here."

"Not *all* of them, Clydine."

"Well, it's terribly sweet, but it's just completely out of the question."

"Dear," I said pointedly, "I didn't *ask* you."

"Oh, now we're giving orders, huh?"

"Goddammit! I can't get any work done. I'm spending every damn
minute worrying about you."

"I can take care of myself very nicely, thank you," she said hotly.

"Bullshit! You haven't got sense enough to come in out of the rain."

"Now you look here, Danny Alders. I'm getting just damned sick
and tired of everybody just automatically assuming that I'm a child
because I'm not eight feet tall."

"That has nothing to do with it."

"I'm going to hang up," she said.

"Good," I said. "I'm going to be down there in an hour anyway."

"Don't bother. I won't let you in."

"Don't be funny. I'll kick your goddamn door down if you try that."

"I'll call the police if you do," she yelled at me.

"The *fuzz*? *You*? Oh, get serious! I'll be there in an hour." I slammed
down the receiver.

As a matter of fact, I made it in less than an hour. I saw Joan scuttling
down the steps as I climbed out of my car.

"Good luck," she called. "I'm heading for the nearest bomb shelter."

"She pretty steamed?" I asked.

"Don't forget to duck."

"Thanks a lot, Joan. You're all heart."

I went on up the stairs. She didn't have the door locked, but she did try to hold it shut against me. I pushed my way on through and we got down to business.

It was a glorious fight—the whole bit. We yelled and screamed at each other, and she slammed doors and threw books at me. I insulted her intelligence and her maturity, and she screamed like a fishwife.

Then she tried to hit me, and I held her arms so she couldn't, so she kicked my shins for a while—barefoot of course.

I'm sure we both knew we were behaving like a couple of twelve-year-olds, but we were having such a good time with the whole thing that we just went ahead and let it all hang out.

Finally she ran crying into the bedroom, slamming the door behind her. I went right on in after her. She was lying across the bed, sobbing as if her heart were about to break.

"Come on, Blossom," I said soothingly, sitting down beside her.

"You—you said such aw—*awful things,*" she sobbed.

"Come on, now. You know damn well I didn't mean any of it."

"No, I *don't,*" she wailed. "First that awful phone call and now you come down here yelling, and calling me names, and ordering me around, and grabbing me, and—oh, Danny, why?"

"Because I'm in love with you, you little knothead," I said. I hadn't really meant to say it, but it was pretty damned obvious by then.

She rolled over very quickly and looked up at me, her face shocked. "What?" she demanded.

"You heard me."

"Say it again."

I did, and then she was all over me like a fur coat. She tasted pretty salty from all the crying, but I didn't mind. I kissed her soundly about the head and shoulders for ten minutes or so—as I said before, it was a glorious kind of fight.

"You're going to transfer up to the U next quarter," I said firmly.

"All right, Danny," she said meekly. "I know it's stupid, but I can't fight you and me both."

"You knew damn well you were going to do it anyway," I said kissing her again. "Why did we have to go through all of this?"

"I just wanted you to say it, that's all," she said, nestling down in my arms.

"You knew that was what it was all about, for God's sake. You're not dense."

"A girl likes to be told," she said stubbornly.

Women!

38

And so, after the holidays, Clydine Stewart, the terror of Pacific Avenue, transferred to the University of Washington. I'm not exactly sure what she'd threatened her parents with to get them to go along with the switch like that in the middle of her junior year, when the loss of credits probably set her back almost two full semesters, but somehow she managed to pull it off.

She rented a sleeping room down the block from my shack—primarily for the sake of appearances and to have a place to store her spare clothes and her empty luggage. She slept there on an average of about once a month.

I suppose that if a man lives with a woman long enough, he gets used to the damp hand-laundry hanging in the bathroom and the bristly hair-curler that he steps on barefoot in the middle of the night, but I wouldn't bet on it.

"You don't put your hair up," I said one morning, as calmly as I could, "so why in the name of God do I keep stepping on these damned things?" I held out a well-mashed curler.

"A girl never knows when she might want to," she said, as if explaining to a child.

We were horribly crowded, and our books and records got hopelessly jumbled, and we were always stumbling over each other. We argued continually about who was going to use the desk and who got firsties on the bathroom in the morning. All in all, it was a pretty normal sort of arrangement. We even wound up sharing the same toothbrush after she lost hers and always kept forgetting to buy a new one.

She even read my mail, which bugged me a little at first, but I couldn't see much point in making an issue out of it since we read all our letters to each other anyway.

"Hey," she said one afternoon as I came in, "you got a letter from Cap Miller."

"Where are you?"

"In the bathtub."

I went on in. She'd gotten over *that* little hang-up.

"Where is it?"

"On the desk."

I bent over and kissed her and then dabbled foam on the end of her nose.

"Rat," she said.

"Are we going to have to go to the store this afternoon?" I asked her, going on back out to the living room-bedroom-study-reception hall-gymnasium.

"We'd better, if you want any supper tonight. Why?"

"Just wondering, that's all."

"Did you get any word on that fellowship yet?"

I picked up Cap's letter.

"Yeah," I said. "I got it." I tried to sound casual about it.

She squealed and came charging, suds and all, out of the bathroom. I got very wetly kissed, and then she saw that the shades were up and scampered back to the tub. What a nut!

I unfolded the letter. It was in pencil.

Dear Dan,

I have been meaning to write a letter to you ever since we got your fine letter just before X-mas. I was real glad to hear about the big man. I have been awful worried about him ever since the trip last fall.

I was awful sorry to hear that your brother and his Mrs. broke up. That's always a real shame.

The snow here is pretty deep this time of year, but you don't need to worry about being able to get through come spring. Clint says he'll carry you piggyback from Twisp if need be. Ha-ha.

We are all wintering pretty well considering our ages. Clint has a little trouble with his legs that he broke so many times when the weather turns cold. And I have a little trouble getting started out of a morning myself, but otherwise we don't have no complaints to speak of.

Well, Dan, it's about time I went down and fed the stock. Old Ned is resting up so he'll be all full of p—— & vinegar when you come up. I knew you'd like to know that. Ha-ha. I have been going on here about long enough. Next thing you know I'll be turning into one of them book writers your learning about at college. So long till next time.

Your friend,

Cap

Oh. Clint says to say hello for him, too.

I could see him laboring over the letter with that stub-pencil of his, the sweat trickling down the outer edges of his white mustache.

"He isn't very well educated, is he?" she called from the bathroom.

"He's one of the smartest men I know," I said.

"That's not the same thing."

"I know."

"You can see how hard he worked on that letter," she said. "I kept trying to see through all that stiffness to the real man."

"You have to meet him to see that," I said.

"I hope I get the chance," she said.

"You will," I promised her.

Somebody knocked at the door, and I put Cap's letter down, swung the bathroom door shut and answered it.

It was my mother.

"Danny, baby," she said, her mouth kind of loose and her tongue a little thick.

I couldn't say anything. Just seeing her was like having somebody grab me by the stomach with an ice-cold hand. I know that sounds literary, but that's the only way to describe it. I held the door open and let her in. My hands started to shake.

The years on booze had not been very kind to my mother. Her hair was ratty and gray, and not very clean, and her hat was kind of squashed down on top of it. She'd tried to put on some makeup and had done a rotten job of it. Her coat was shabby, and she had a large hole in one of her stockings.

She stood uncertainly in the middle of the room, waiting for me to say something.

"Sit down, Mother," I said, pointing at the couch.

"Thank you, Danny," she said and perched uneasily on the edge of the couch.

"How have you been, Mother?" I asked her.

"Oh," she said tremulously, "not too bad, Danny. I've got a pretty good job down in Portland. I'm in maintenance." She pronounced it "maintain-ance." "It is with the company that owns this big office building. I work nights."

I nodded. It was about what I'd expected.

"I got a week off," she said. "I heard about poor Jackie's marriage going on the rocks. You heard about that, didn't you?"

"Yes, Mother."

"Well, quick as a shot I went to my boss and I told him I was going to have to have a few days off so I could come up to Tacoma and see if I couldn't help him maybe patch things up. Poor Jackie. He's had such bad luck with his marriages."

"Yeah," I said.

"But he told me it was too late for that, and I was just so awful sorry. Then he told me you'd gone back to school up here, so I just had to come up here and see you. I mean, you *are* my baby and all, and we haven't seen each other in just years and years, have we?"

"It's been a long time, Mother," I agreed.

She was nervously trying to light a cigarette, and finally I fired up my lighter for her. Her hands were shaking as badly as mine were.

"Would you like a drink, Mother?" I asked her.

She raised her face quickly, and the sudden look of anguish cut right through me. She thought I was being snotty.

"No games, Mother," I said. "I'm going to have one, and I just thought you might like one too, that's all."

"Well," she said hesitantly, "maybe just a little one. I've been cutting way down, you know."

"Mixer? Water? It's bourbon."

"Just a little ice, Danny, if you got any."

I fixed us a couple, and I could see by the way her hands were shaking that she needed one pretty badly.

We both drank them off, and I refilled the glasses without saying anything. I think we both felt better then.

"I'm so proud of you Danny, baby," she said. "I mean your college and all. I never told you that, did I? There's so many things I never got the chance to tell you. You and Jackie both seemed to grow up so fast. It just seems like I no more than turned around and you were both gone. First Jackie in the Navy, and then your father passing away, and then you leaving like you did. It just all happened so fast."

"It's like that sometimes, Mother," I said. "Nothing ever stays the same."

"I can still remember you two when you were little," she said. "Jackie always so lively and full of fun, and you always so quiet and serious. Just like day and night, you two. And now poor Jackie getting divorced again." She dug out a handkerchief and held it to her face. She wasn't crying; she was just getting ready.

"He's a big boy now, Mother," I said.

"It's just all so rotten," she said. "You're the smart one. Don't ever get married, Danny. Women are just no good. We're all bitches."

"Now, Mother."

"No, it's true." The tears were running down her face now, smearing her makeup. "Your father was a good man—a fine man, and look what I did to him. He didn't understand me, but that didn't give me the right to hound him the way I did. I tried to be a good wife, but I just couldn't help myself."

"It's all right now, Mother. Just try not to let it get you down."

She finished her drink and mutely held out the glass. I doubt if she was even aware that she was doing it. I filled it again. She was making a good-sized dent in my bourbon, but what the hell?

"I'm pretty much a failure, do you know that, Danny? I failed your father, and I failed you boys." She was crying openly now, the wet, slobbering, let-it-all-go kind of crying you see once in a while in an old wino.

"I'm so sorry, Danny. I'm so sorry."

"It's all right, Mother. It was all a long time ago." How could I get her off it?

"Please forgive me, Danny, baby."

"Come on, Mother." That was too much.

"You've got to forgive me," she said. She looked at me, her eyes pleading and her face a ruin.

"Mother."

"I'm begging you to forgive me, Danny," she said. "I'll get down on my knees to you." She moved before I could stop her. She slid off the edge of the couch and dropped heavily to her knees on the floor.

"Come on, Mother," I said, trying to lift her back to the couch, "get up."

"Not until you forgive me, Danny."

This was silly. "All right, Mother, I forgive you. It wasn't your fault."

"Really, Danny? Really?"

"Yes, Mother. Come on now. Get up."

She let me haul her to her feet, and then she insisted on giving me a kiss. Then she kind of halfway repaired her face. She seemed a little calmer after that. She talked for a few minutes and then got ready to leave.

"I've got just enough time to make connections for the Portland bus," she said.

"Have you got your ticket?" I asked her.

"Oh, yes," she said brightly. "I'm just fine."

"Do you need any money—for a bite to eat or anything?"

"No, Danny, I'm just fine, really." She stood up. "I've really got to go now." She went over to the door. "I feel so much better now that we've had the chance to get things straightened out like this. I've worried about it for the longest time."

"It was good to see you, Mother."

"I'm so proud of you, baby." She patted my cheek and went out quickly. I watched through the window as she carefully made her way around the house in front. Her hat was on lop-sided, and her dark coat had a large dusty path on one shoulder where she'd stumbled against something. She went on out of sight.

"Oh, Danny," Clydine said. "Oh, Danny, I'm so sorry." She was standing behind me, wrapped in a bath towel, huge tears bright in her eyes.

"Oh, it's all right, Blossom. She's been like this for as long as I can remember. You get used to it after a while."

"It must have been *awful*."

"I don't even hold any grudges anymore," I said. "I thought I did, but I really don't. I really forgave her, do you know that? I didn't think I ever could, but I did. I wasn't just saying it." It surprised me, but I meant it. "I just wish she could quit drinking, is all," I added.

39

It was a Thursday morning several weeks after Mother's visit and Clydine had just got up. I was still lying in bed. She stood nude in front of the full-length mirror that was bolted to the bathroom door. She cupped her hands under her breasts.

"Danny," she said thoughtfully, hefting them a couple times.

"Yes, love?"

"Do you think I ought to start wearing a bra? I'm pretty chesty, and I wouldn't want to start to droop."

I howled with laughter.

"Well," she said, "I *wouldn't*! I don't see what's so goddamn funny."

She was absolutely adorable. Sometimes I'd catch myself laughing for no reason, just being around her. I loved her, not with that grand, aching, tragic passion that I'd pretty well burned out on Susan, but rather with a continual delight in her, a joy just in her presence. Believe me, there's a lot to be said for joy as opposed to tragic passion. For one thing, it's a helluva lot less exhausting in the long run.

Anyhow, nothing would do but our cutting classes and my taking her out immediately so she could buy herself some new bras.

We got back about eleven, and she modeled them for me.

"What do you think?" she said doubtfully.

"It's different," I said.

"You don't like it."

"I didn't say that. I just said it's different. How does it feel?"

"Like a darn straitjacket," she admitted. Then she sighed deeply. "Oh, well, I guess it's just another one of the curses of being a woman."

"Poor Blossom." I laughed.

She stuck her tongue out at me. I'd noticed, but hadn't mentioned, the fact that she'd backed way off on the truck-driver vocabulary and hadn't really gotten much involved with the militants up here. She'd told me that she disagreed ideologically with the main thrust of the university militants, but I suspected that she'd just plain outgrown them. At least I didn't have to worry about her getting her cute little fanny chucked into jail every weekend. That was something anyway.

After lunch she had a couple of classes, so I had a chance to get some concentrated work done. I was tackling the possibility that Melville's *Billy Budd* was not a simple hymn of praise to the natural man, but rather a much more complex parable of the struggle of good and evil— represented by Billy and Claggart—for the soul of Captain Vere. I'd landed on it by way of the chance discovery that Melville had practically camped on the New York Public Library copy of Milton's *Paradise Regained* all during the time he was writing *Billy Budd*.

I was deep in the mystic mumblings of the Old Dansker when Jack showed up.

He looked awful. He hadn't shaved for several days, and his eyes looked like the proverbial two burned holes in a blanket.

"Jesus, man," I said, holding the door open for him, "what the hell happened to you?"

"I just got out of jail," he said.

"*Jail?*"

He nodded grimly and collapsed into the armchair by the door. "You got anything to drink?"

I got him a water glass and poured it half-full of whiskey. His hands were shaking so badly that it was all he could do to get a good solid slug of bourbon down.

"What the hell happened, Jack?" I demanded.

"You know that .45 I bought from Sloane?"

"Yeah."

"Well, Sandy stuck the damn thing in her mouth and blew her brains all over the ceiling of my bathroom."

"Oh, Jesus!"

"The cops held me on suspicion of murder for three days in the Tacoma jail until they finally decided that she did it herself. They had the inquest this morning."

"Christ, man, why didn't you get in touch with me?"

"I thought you knew. It's been in all the newspapers and on the radio and TV."

"We've been pretty busy, and I just haven't paid any attention to the news for a while. God, Jack, I'm sorry as hell. I should have been there."

"Nothin' you coulda done." He shrugged. "They were just playin' games is all. Who the hell ever murders anybody by stickin' a gun in their mouth?"

"When did it happen?"

"Monday night. I'd been out—just kinda pokin' up and down the Avenue, you know. Anyhow, when I got back, there she was all sprawled out over the toilet stool with blood and hair and all that other gunk splattered all over the ceiling. Christ, Dan, I can still see it." He covered his eyes with one trembling hand.

"Finish your drink," I said, holding out the bottle to refill his glass.

He nodded and drank off the whiskey, shuddering as it went down. I filled his glass again.

"Look at that," he said, holding out his hands. They were trembling violently. "I can't stop *shakin'*. I been shakin' ever since I found her. My hands shake all the time."

"Come on, Jack, settle down," I said. He was in tough shape. I should have warned him about it. God damn it, I should have warned him!

"Christ, Dan, I can't. My nerves are all shot. I feel like somebody just kicked all my guts out."

"Was she acting funny or anything before it happened? I mean, did she give you any kind of warning at all?"

"Hell, no," he said. "She always was kinda strange—you know, kinda quiet—but she wasn't any different at all. Christ, the last thing she said when I left was, 'See you when you get back.' God, Dan, that sure as hell don't sound like somebody who's gonna kill theirself, does it?"

"No way," I said.

"We was gettin' along just fine. Hell, no beefs, no trouble, nothin'. And then she just ups and kills herself."

"Did she leave a note or anything?"

"Nothin'. I think that's why the cops put the arm on me. She even cleaned the place all up before she did it."

"They got it all straightened out at the inquest, didn't they? I mean, they didn't leave the case open or anything?"

"No. It's settled. They had a lotta medical experts in and all. Angle of the bullet and all that shit. I was there because I found the body and called the cops. I got to hear the whole thing. Couple guys she'd gone with before I met her got called in, and they both said she'd talked about it when they knew her. Anyway, they finally ruled it 'death by suicide,' and the cops had to let me go. The bastards sure as hell didn't *want* to, I'll tell you that. Once those motherfuckers get their hands on you, they hate like hell to have to turn you loose."

"Yeah," I agreed.

"God," he said, "I couldn't even go back inside my trailer."

"What'd they do, padlock it all up?"

"No, nothin' like that. I just couldn't make myself do it. I went on out there, but I just couldn't go inside. Ain't that a helluva note?"

"You want to bunk in here for a few days?" It wouldn't set too well with the Little Flower, but this was an emergency.

"No, Dan, thanks anyway, but I gotta get outa the area for a while. I'm goin' down to Portland. Maybe stay with the Old Lady or something."

"You're welcome to stay here," I said.

"It's too close, man. I gotta get away. I was just wonderin' if you could maybe come back down with me and get some of my clothes and stuff out of the trailer for me. I can't make myself go back in there. I just can't do it." He sat hunched over, holding both hands around his glass.

"Sure, Jack," I said, "I'll leave a note for my roommate."

"How is she?" he asked.

"She's fine," I said. I scribbled a quick note to her and we took off. I followed his Plymouth on down to Tacoma and on out toward Madrona. It was cloudy and calm that day, and the trailer court seemed kind of shadowy, tucked back in under a bunch of big old pine trees.

I got out and went over to where he'd parked his car. "What do you need, Jack?" I asked him.

"Grab my clothes and some shoes and stuff," he said, not looking at the trailer. "Oh, get my transistor radio, too, huh? It's in the bedroom."

"Sure, Jack."

"Don't go in the bathroom, man. It's awful."

"I'll have to," I said. "You'll need your razor and all."

"Oh," he said.

"It'll be OK," I told him. I went on into the trailer. It took me about twenty minutes to pack up all his clothes. I didn't go into the bathroom until I'd got everything else squared away.

Actually, it wasn't as bad as I'd expected. Most of the mess was in a dried pool between the toilet and the tub. I gathered up Jack's stuff and took it on out to the living room. I tucked it all in various places in his suitcases and then hauled them on out to his car. On my last trip I carried out his radio and his shotgun.

"No, man," he said, his face turning a kind of pasty color, "leave that fuckin' gun here!"

"You can't leave it here," I told him. "Somebody might swipe it."

"*You* keep it then. I can't stand to look at the goddamn thing. I told you, Danny, my nerves are all shot."

I took the gun over and put it in my car.

"Did you lock up?" he asked me.

I shook my head. "I'll slip the latch when I leave. I'll clean up that mess in there."

"You don't have to do that."

I shrugged. "Somebody has to."

"Thanks, Danny," he said in a shaking voice. "I don't think I'm ever gonna be able to go in there again."

"You probably ought to sell it," I told him.

He nodded. "Hey," he said suddenly, "I think there's some beer in the refrig. Why don't we sit out here and have a couple? I need something."

"Sure, Jack." I went on back in and carted out the six-pack.

"I'll make arrangements with Clem to pick up the trailer," he said as I got into the front seat with him. He started the car.

"Where we going?" I asked him.

"Just down the road a ways. I can't stand to look at that damn trailer is all."

"OK."

We drove on out to the highway and then pulled off into a little roadside park.

"God, man," he said, opening a can of beer. "I'm just completely wiped out. It was all I could do to keep from tossin' my cookies when you hauled out my shotgun."

"It'll probably take you a while to get over this," I told him, popping open a can for myself.

"I don't know if I *ever* will," he said. "Danny, my *hands* shake all the time. I'm *afraid,* and I don't know what the hell it is I'm afraid of— maybe everything. Shit, I'm afraid of guns, the trailer, bathrooms, blood—Christ, anything at all, and I just come all apart."

"You'll be all right, Jack. It's just going to take you some time, that's all."

He sat at the wheel, staring moodily out at the murky day. "I don't know if you remember or not, but I had an argument with the Old Man once when I was a kid. I said that when a guy grew up, he wasn't afraid of anything anymore."

"I remember," I said.

"He tried to tell me I was all wet, but I wouldn't listen to him. I know what he meant now."

We sat drinking beer and not saying much.

"You fixed OK for money?" I asked him.

"Christ, I don't know. I don't think Old Clem'll spring loose with my check until Saturday. I hadn't thought about that."

"I can give you twenty," I said.

"Hell," he said, "I could always tap Sloane."

"I'd rather give it to you myself," I said.

"Shit," he said, "you already done more than enough."

I shrugged. "You're my brother, Jack. That's what it's all about." I gave him a twenty.

"Thanks, Kid," he said. "I'll get it back to you."

"No rush," I said.

"I suppose I ought to get goin'," he said. "I'd like to make it to Portland before too late."

"Sure, Jack. Just drop me at the gate of the trailer court, OK?"

"Right."

We drove on back and stopped outside the court.

He held out his hand and we shook.

"I probably won't see you for a while," he said, "but I'll keep in touch."

"Sure, Jack."

"It's been a wild six months or so, hasn't it?"

"Far out," I said.

"At least we got to go huntin' together," he said. "That's somethin' anyway."

"It was the best of it," I told him.

He nodded and I opened my door.

"You know somethin', Danny? What I was sayin' about a guy bein' afraid of things—that argument me and the Old Man had?"

"Yeah?"

"He was right, you know that?"

"He usually was, Jack."

"Yeah. Well, I'll tell you somethin', and this is the straight stuff. Maybe I hide it pretty good, but to tell you the honest-to-God truth, I been afraid all my life. It just took somethin' like this to make me realize it."

"Everybody's afraid, Jack, not just you. That's what Dad was trying to tell you. You've just got to learn to live with it."

He nodded. "Well," he said, "take care now."

"You too, Jack."

We shook hands again, and I got out.

I stood at the side of the road watching his battered Plymouth until it disappeared around a corner about a half mile down the highway.

That evening I told Clydine about it.

"I told you a long time ago that it was going to happen," she said.

"Yeah," I said. "How did you know, anyhow?"

"I just knew, that's all."

"That sure isn't much help," I said. "I mean, if I were to suddenly go into the business of suicide prevention, it wouldn't give me much to go on, would it?"

"I don't know," she said thoughtfully, "the girl just seemed to think of herself in the past tense somehow. Even that creepy Helen talked about what she planned to do next week or next year. Sandy just never did. She didn't have any future. A woman *always* thinks about the future—always. When you find one who doesn't, watch out."

"As simple as that?"

She nodded. "Along with a good healthy gut-feel for it. Being around her was like being at a funeral. It wasn't anything recent, because she had gotten pretty well used to it by then. She was just waiting for the right time."

"I should have warned Jack," I said.

"He couldn't have stopped her."

"That's not what I meant. He got tangled up in it, and it's tearing him all up inside."

"He'll come out of it," she said. "He's too much of an ego-maniac not to."

"Why, you heartless little witch!" I said.

"Oo, poo," she said.

"*Poo?*"

"All right then, *shit!*" she snapped. "Your brother's got all the sensitivity of a telephone pole, and about as much compassion as a meat grinder. He'll make out."

There was no point pushing the issue. She didn't like Jack, and she wasn't about to waste any sympathy on him.

That night I had the dream again. I caught flashes of a sad-eyed old dog rolling over and over in the snow and of the white deer lying huddled at the foot of that gravel bank, the masculinity of his antlers sheared off by his fall and his deep red eye gazing reproachfully at me through the film of dust that powdered it. And Sandy was there, too, standing nude by the sink in that house out in Milton, her nudity sexless—even meaningless, and her voice echoing back to me:

"It doesn't matter. It's only for a little while, just a little while."

EPILOGUE

I didn't get the chance to get back up to the Methow Valley that spring. The money ran short on me. I wrote to Cap, of course, telling him how sorry I was, and through the stiff formality of his letters, I could sense his disappointment as well.

I guess I had talked up the high country to my little Bolshevik to the point that she finally got a bellyful of hearing about it because she finally put her foot down.

"This is it," she said in early July, delivering her nonnegotiable demands. "We are both going to take two weeks off and go up there. I'm going to meet the great Cap Miller and his crotchety but lovable sidekick Clint. I am also going up to look at that damned Valhalla of yours."

"We can't afford it."

"Chicken-pucky we can't. We've both got a steady income during the school year and good steady jobs this summer. The office I work in shuts down for the first two weeks in August so that all the regular people can take their vacations, and that crazy Swede boat builder you work for is so convinced that you're the greatest thing since sliced bread that he'll probably give you the two weeks with pay."

"Chicken-pucky?"

"Oh, shut up!"

We argued about it for a week or so, but my heart wasn't really in it.

When I approached Norstrom, my boss, he screamed for twenty minutes about how he couldn't possibly spare me and wound up trying to convince me that I ought to go fishing up the inside passage instead.

I had to lie a little in my letter to Cap, and I didn't like that at all. Though I knew he wouldn't have said anything, I also knew that he probably wouldn't have approved of the irregularity of Clydine and myself going off into the hill without benefit of clergy, as it were. I told him we were going to elope, and that this was going to be our honeymoon. It was a big mistake because he insisted on furnishing everything for our trip at no charge. I felt like a real shitheel about it.

Anyway, on the third of August, Blossom and I were batting along on the highway north to Lake Chelan, headed for Twisp. It was about eight o'clock in the morning and we were both a little sleepy.

"I don't see why we couldn't have slept a little later," she complained. We'd spent the night at a motel in Cashmere.

"It takes a good long while to get up there," I said. "It's not exactly a roadside campground, Tulip."

"Couldn't we at least stop someplace? I'm starved."

"We'll be there in another hour," I told her. "You'll need all the appetite you can muster to get even partway around the kind of breakfast Clint cooks up."

She grunted and curled back up in the seat.

I woke her when we got to Twisp, and she insisted on stopping at a gas station. I fidgeted around for the twenty or so minutes that she was in the rest room with her overnight bag, wondering what she was up to.

When she came out, she looked like a different girl. She'd put in her contact lenses, caught her hair in a loose coil at the back of her neck, and she was wearing a white blouse and tailored slacks. She'd even put on lipstick, for God's sake!

"Wow," I said.

"Oh, be quiet."

"You're gorgeous, Rosebud. I mean it."

She looked at me to see if I were kidding her, and when she saw that I wasn't, she actually blushed.

"All right," she said, "let's go meet your family."

What she'd said didn't really register on me until we were a ways out of town.

"Why did you say that?" I asked her.

"Say what?"

"About meeting my family?"

"Just a bad joke," she said. "Forget it."

We drove along the twisting, narrow road out toward Miller's place. The road looked different with the poplar leaves all green instead of the gold I'd remembered from the preceding autumn, but the whole stretch of road was still breathtaking.

"It's really beautiful, isn't it?" she said finally, touching nervously at her hair.

"Wait till we get up higher," I said. "It gets even better."

I slowed the car and turned into Miller's driveway. The colt was a yearling now, but he still loved to run. He galloped alongside us, tossing his head.

"I didn't know horses chased cars, too," she said.

I laughed. I hadn't thought of it that way.

"Oh, dear," she said, her voice faltering.

Cap was waiting for us out in the yard, and he looked even more rugged than I remembered him. Then he grinned and it was like the sun coming up.

The two of them almost fell all over themselves charming each other, and I got a helluva big lump in my throat watching the two people in the world I cared most about getting along so well. Then Clint came out, and the party really got started.

Finally we went on into the big, musty old dining room and sat down to breakfast. Miller bowed his head and said grace, probably in Clydine's honor, just a few simple words, but it moved me pretty profoundly.

"My wife always used to like havin' grace before a meal," he said. "Me and Clint kinda got out of the habit since we take a lot of our meals standin' up."

"Let's eat it before it gets cold," Clint said gruffly. He'd outdone himself on the whole meal. I knew damned well he'd been at it since about four that morning. He'd even shaved in her honor.

"I'm real sorry, Dan," he said with his eyes sparkling at me, "but I just couldn't manage to whip up a big mess of that whatever-it-was you fixed for us that time. I just never got around to gettin' the recipe from you."

"All right, smart-aleck," I said.

"Besides," he said, "we're runnin' a little short of packhorses."

"What's this?" Clydine asked.

They told her.

"What was in it?" she asked me.

I explained how I'd made it.

"No wonder it tasted like stewed packhorse," she commented blandly.

I thought Cap and Clint were going to fall off their chairs laughing.

After breakfast we went on back outside.

"I figured Old Dusty would be about the best horse for the little lady," Cap said. "That's the one the Professor rode up there. He's pretty easygoin', and he's good and dependable."

I nodded.

"We knew you'd want Old Ned again." He grinned.

"You're all heart, Cap."

He laughed and slapped me on the shoulder.

We loaded the horses in the stock-truck and the camping gear and saddles in the pickup and drove on down the driveway again, Cap in front in the pickup, then Clydine and me in my car and Clint bringing up the rear in the stock-truck.

"Oh, Danny," she said, nestling up beside me, "I just love them both. They're wonderful."

I nodded happily.

"Do you think they liked me at all?"

"They loved you, dear."

"That's just because of you," she said.

"No," I said. "They can't do that. Not either one of them. They don't know how."

"I guess they couldn't, could they?"

"No way."

"You love them two old men, too, don't you?" she said suddenly.

I nodded. I probably wouldn't have put it exactly that way, but that's what it boiled down to.

The sun was very bright and the sky very blue. The whole world seemed as if it had been washed clean just that morning.

We turned off the highway and started up the long gravel road toward the beginning of the trail. When we came around that corner and caught the first full glimpse of Glacier Park looming white above us, she gasped.

"Pretty impressive, huh?" I said.

"Wow!" was all she could say.

We all stopped when we got to the road-end and went through the ritual of unloading the packhorses first again.

"Boy, did *you* get lucky," Clint said as we climbed up into the truck after Dusty.

"How's that?"

"That wife of yours. Now, I just *know* you ain't been good enough to deserve somebody like her. You ain't got it in you."

I laughed and the little old guy grinned at me.

We led Dusty out and saddled him.

"Just ride 'im up and down the road kinda easy like, honey," Cap told Clydine after he'd helped her get aboard.

The three of us watched her amble the patient old horse on down the road.

"She sets a saddle well, too," Cap said approvingly. "I think you got yourself a good one, son."

"She'll do," I agreed happily.

Then Clint and I got Ned out.

The big gray glared at me with suspicion and then sniffed at me a couple times. I scratched his ears.

"I think the damned old fool remembers you," Clint said.

"We'll find out in a minute or so," I said, swinging the saddle up on Ned's back. I cinched it good and tight and then climbed on.

"Just how big a head of steam have you two let him build up?" I asked them.

Then they really started to laugh.

"Hell, boy," Cap said, still laughing, "we worked him every day this week. We weren't about to let him break one of your legs for you on your honeymoon."

"Everybody's a comedian these days," I said dryly and rode off down the road to catch up with Clydine.

"Did you see his face?" I heard Clint howl from behind me.

Just before we left, she jumped down off her horse and kissed the two surprised old men and then hopped back up into the saddle. We rode off on up the trail towing a pair of packhorses, leaving the two of them blushing and scuffing their boots in the dust like a pair of schoolboys.

When we stopped at the top of the first ridge to let the horses blow a little, we could see their tiny figures still standing down by the parked vehicles. We all waved back and forth for a while, and then Clydine and I rode on down into the next valley.

It was about three thirty in the afternoon when we came on down into the little basin. In spite of Cap's assurances, I'd been about halfway worried that we might find about a thousand sheep and a couple herders up there, but the camp was empty.

She sat in her saddle, looking around, not saying anything.

"Well?" I said.

She nodded slowly. "I see what you meant," she said simply.

"Let's get to work," I said. "We've got a lot to do before the sun goes down."

We got down from our horses and checked the corrals. They were still sound. I unsaddled the horses and turned them loose in the corrals and then we went on up to the tent frames. It took us a while to get the two tents up, but we finally got them squared away. The moss we'd all gathered the year before was gone—deer or something, I suppose—so we got to work and hauled in fresh stuff.

Miller or Clint—one or the other—had substituted, with some delicacy, a pair of sleeping bags that zipped together into a double for the mismatched pair that we'd brought, so I modified the log bunk frames in our tent to accommodate the double bag.

The beaver had scattered our firewood, but it didn't take long to get together enough for the night at least.

"I don't know about you, Bwana," she said finally, "but I'm starved again."

I kissed her nose for her. "I'll get right on it," I said. I dug out the big iron grill and got a fire started.

"Clint said he had supper all packed up for us," she said.

"Yeah," I told her, "it's that big sack right at the top of the food pack."

She fished around in the cook tent and came out with the big sack. She carried it over to McKlearey's table and opened it.

"Oh, wow!" she said. "Look at this." She ripped down the side of the sack. "There's a banquet in here. How am I supposed to cook all of this over an open fire? They even put in a bottle of champagne, for cryin' out loud."

"Oh, for Christ's sake," I said.

"What a pair of old sweeties," she said.

Clint had included a note, the first of a dozen or so we found tucked away in various places among the packs. It gave very specific instructions on how to fix supper.

"Well," she said, pulling up the sleeves of the sweatshirt she'd changed into as soon as we'd gotten into camp, "now we find out if I know how to cook out in the woods."

"I'll drop the booze in the spring," I said.

"Then see what you can do in the way of some chairs," she said.

"Chairs?"

"*You* may plan to eat standing up or all squatted down like a savage of some kind, but *I* sure don't."

Women!

I examined the construction of Lou's table and managed to fix up a kind of rickety bench. It was a lot more solid when I dug it into the ground.

"There's a tablecloth in that bag over there," she told me.

"A *tablecloth*?"

"Of course."

The sun had gone down and I built up the fire and cranked up the Coleman lantern to give us light enough to eat by.

We had steak and baked potatoes and all kinds of other little surprises.

"Well?" she said, after I'd taken several bites. "Do I pass?"

"You'll do, Blossom, you'll do."

"Is *that* all?"

"That's enough, kid." I kissed her noisily.

"Tomorrow night you get a big plate of whatever-it-was."

"Oh, God," I said, "anything but that."

We saved the champagne until it was good and cold. Then we sat by the fire and drank it from tin cups. We both got a little fuzzy from it—maybe it was the altitude.

"Danny," she said drowsily after we'd finished the bottle.

"Yes, Rosebud?"

"Let's go to bed and make love."

"What brought that on?"

"Well, damn it, it *is* my honeymoon, isn't it?"

And so we did that.

The days drifted along goldenly. The biting chill of autumn had not yet moved onto the high meadows and, though the nights were cool, by ten in the morning the sun was very warm. As soon as she found out that there wasn't a soul for ten miles or more in any direction, my flower child turned nudist on me. Her skin soaked in the high sunlight, and she started to tan deliciously. All I managed was a sunburn.

She even tried swimming in the beaver pond, but only once. She was almost blue when she came out. I was just as happy about that, all things considered, since I had designs on the trout.

We hiked around a bit and went horseback riding and laid around in the sun and made love at odd intervals. It was strange, seeing her walking around in her pink, innocent nudity in the places where so many other things had happened.

One night, in our cozy double sleeping bag, it got down to confession time.

"Danny?" she said tentatively.

"Yes?"

"You remember that first night—the time when you picked up Joan and me at the theater?"

"Of course I do."

"I knew," she said in a small voice.

"You knew what, dear?"

"I knew you'd never been to prison."

"Oh? How was that?"

"You don't have any tattoos," she said, tracing designs on my chest with her finger. "Everybody who's ever been to prison has tattoos— even if it's only a few spots or something."

I hadn't thought about that. "Why didn't you just blow the whistle on me then?"

"I wasn't really sure until I got your clothes off," she said.

"You sure could have brought it all to a halt at that point," I said.

"I know," she said, her voice even tinier.

"Why didn't you?"

She buried her face in her arms. "I didn't want to," she said.

I kissed her on the ear. "I won't tell anybody if you won't," I said.

"There's something else," she said, her face still buried in her arms.

"Oh? I'm not sure how much truth I can take in one day."

"You remember how I used to talk—about orgies and all that kind of thing?"

"Yes."

"Well," she said, "I was kind of exaggerating. There was only one other boy really."

I didn't say anything. I'd more or less figured that out for myself.

"Are you mad at me?"

"For not being promiscuous?"

"No, dum-dum, for lying to you."

"Well," I said, "it's pretty awful."

She looked up, stricken, until she saw that I was grinning at her.

"You rat!" she said suddenly, pounding on my chest as I laughed at her. "You absolute, unspeakable rat."

I folded her up in my arms and kissed her soundly. It was one of the better nights.

I suppose I'd been putting it off, but I knew that sooner or later I was going to have to go up there. I'd brought the damned pistol belt along— I'd told myself it was for coyotes or something, but I knew that wasn't really it. I had to duplicate as closely as possible what it had been like, so the gun had to go along.

"I've got to go up on the ridge today," I told her as I came out of the tent that morning.

"Oh? I'll go along," she said.

"I don't think you should really," I said.

"Why not?"

"I'm going to see if I can find that deer," I told her.

"Whatever for? Won't it be all—well—"

"Probably."

"Then why on earth do you want to mess around with it?"

"It's not that I want to," I told her.

"I don't suppose there's any point trying to talk you out of it?"

"Not really."

"Well," she said, "have fun."

"That's not why I'm doing it."

"*Men!*" she snorted. We'd both taken to doing that a lot lately.

After breakfast I saddled Ned and came back up to camp. I went in and strapped on the pistol.

"Wow," she said, "if it isn't Pancho Villa himself."

"Lay off," I said. "I shouldn't be too long."

"Take your time," she said, stretching. "I'm going back to bed myself." She went on back to the tent.

I nudged Ned on around and on down to the lower end of the basin and across the creek. "Come on, buddy," I told him. "You know the way as well as I do."

He flicked his ears, and we started up the ridge. Even after this short a period of time, the ridge looked different. I couldn't be really sure if it was the fact that the leaves hadn't started to turn or what, but it took me quite a while to find Stan's old post. I figured that would be about the best place to go down. I tied Ned to a bush and climbed on down to the wash at the bottom of the draw.

I covered the wash from the place where I'd entered it that day the year before to the cliff where the deer had fallen. Apparently, there'd been a helluva run-off that spring, because the whole shape of the thing was different. I'd have sworn that I could have gone straight to the spot, but once I got down there, I couldn't find any recognizable landmarks.

I finally settled on a place that had to have been pretty close, but the shape of the banks was all wrong.

It was gone. There was no way I'd ever be able to verify for myself whether it had ever really been there or not. I suppose I'd dreamed about the damned thing so often that I'd begun to almost doubt my own memory of it.

Now, with the wash so changed from the way I remembered it, I was less sure than ever. And so the pale flicker in the brush that I remembered would always be a doubtful phantom for me. There in the shadows at the bottom of the wash, I felt a sudden chill. I climbed back up to the ridge and untied Ned.

"Struck out, old buddy," I said, climbing up into the saddle.

He flickered his ears at me, and we went on back down.

That evening, as the sun was going down, Clydine and I were sitting on a log near the edge of the beaver pond.

"It's just lovely up here, Danny," she said. "I think it's the most beautiful place in the whole world."

I nodded. I don't think I'd said more than three words to her since I'd come back down the ridge.

I suppose I'd been building up to the question for several months. I knew that it was inevitable that sooner or later I should ask it despite all its obvious banality under the circumstances. Even so, it surprised me when I heard myself say it—for one thing, it was badly phrased. You kind of halfway expect something a little more polished from somebody with my background.

"Don't you think it's about time we got married?" I asked her.

Just as I had known I was going to ask her, so she had known she was going to be asked. I guess every girl knows that even before the man has actually made up his mind. And so it was that she'd had plenty of time to devise an answer that would let me know how she felt and at the same time assert her independence.

She looked up at me, smiled, and squeezed my arm.

"Why not?" she said.

About the Author

DAVID EDDINGS was born in Spokane, Washington, in 1931 and was raised in the Puget Sound area north of Seattle. He received a Bachelor of Arts degree from Reed College in Portland, Oregon, in 1954 and a Master of Arts degree from the University of Washington in 1961. He has served in the United States Army, worked as a buyer for the Boeing Company, has been a grocery clerk, and has taught English. He has lived in many parts of the United States.

His first novel, *High Hunt* (published by Putnam in 1973), was a contemporary adventure story. The field of fantasy has always been of interest to him, however, and he turned to *The Belgariad* in an effort to develop certain technical and philosophical ideas concerning that genre.